CW01390595

In A Moment...

Book One of The Ley Of The Land.

Russell K. Lewis

Hence, in a season of calm weather,
Though inland far we be,
Our souls have sight of that immortal sea
Which brought us hither,
Can in a moment travel thither,
And see the children sport upon the shore,
And hear the mighty waters rolling evermore.

Ode. Intimations of Immortality (1807) st. 9

William Wordsworth

AuthorHouse™ UK Ltd.
500 Avebury Boulevard
Central Milton Keynes, MK9 2BE
www.authorhouse.co.uk
Phone: 08001974150

First published by AuthorHouse 6/25/2007

ISBN: 978-1-4343-2014-8 (sc)

Printed in the United States of America
Bloomington, Indiana

This book is printed on acid-free paper.

Our story ends

Suddenly where there had been darkness, black as ink, there was absolute darkness. An absence of light. An absence of dark.

Nothing.

The heat that had been building steadily during his long journey now reached an almost intolerable level.

The voices in his head that had kept him company for so many years, so many miles, were gone.

He drifted alone… alone, but strangely unafraid. He should have been frightened, his heart should have thundered, but he felt nothing.

No fear… no elation… nothing.

No, not nothing, but *Nothing*.

Having come so far, what was there to find?

Where was he?

When was he?

Who was he?

He tried to speak, but made no sound.

He tried to see, but was blind.

He tried to touch, but felt nothing.

When all external senses are removed, what is left?

Is there anything?

Are you anyone in such barren darkness?

He may have drifted, but had no way of knowing.

Very quietly a voice did manage to tickle its way through, a strangely alien sensation, in this place of no sensation.

'Are you alright? Can you hear me? Are you there?'

It was soft and gentle, not an interrogation, more an offer of comfort if it were needed. The voice appeared to enter his head from the inside. There was after all, nowhere for it to come from. There was nowhere for anything to come from.

Every nerve strained to hear and he was sure his heart must be pounding, his breath coming in gasps, his hands suddenly curled into fists.

He replied silently.

He spoke to the voice inside his head, but received no reply.

He was alone.

Forever.

Only his thoughts remained.

How long is forever?
How is eternity measured?
Is there an end?
Is there a beginning?

And what happens when you reach one of them?

Can you journey back?
Or forward?

And then, for the briefest of moments, he knew that the lips he no longer felt were probably smiling - and even his thoughts left him.

He finally had his answer.

But what had been the question?

Now Fin (1)

The nightmare had come again that night, but this time so powerfully that he had ended up perched on the toilet in the dark and in tears for fear of what might happen next. He was *very* scared; indeed even his bowels were in agreement with the aptness of a fairly obvious but also fairly tasteless phrase which sprang to his mind. He might had laughed, had he not been so terrified.

His sobbing had awoken his father who knocked tentatively on the bathroom door.

'Fin, are you okay in there?'

'Fine Dad.'

Sniff…

'You sure?'

'No.'

Sniff…

'Oh. Anything I can help you with?' This time said with a degree of foreboding. What could be going on behind the bathroom door that he could possibly lend a hand with?

'I've had The Nightmare again.'

Sniff…

His father noted, not for the first time that it was *The Nightmare*. This was more than just a bad dream, to his son at least.

Jarmon LeMott pushed the door open to be met by the image of his dear and only son, his eyes reddened and cheeks still wet with tears, and a smell to take your breathe away. Whoa there, this was a bad one! This wasn't the first time; indeed he'd lost count of the number of times that Fin had cried out in the middle of the night for someone to help him escape from the visions. They came without warning, as all the best nightmares do, and left a lingering afterimage that sleep would find hard to banish. From the age of five, for the last eight years, Fin had been having his sleep disturbed by an horrendous feeling of the world moving faster than he was, of everything speeding away from him in the dark of night, but sometimes also during the bright light of early morning as well. They'd tried everything; milk (warm and cold), Camomile tea, hot chocolate, water, even one or two homeopathic remedies, but nothing seemed to help. Eventually they'd had to simply hope that he'd grow out of it.

At first Jarmon and his wife Lidine had put it down to Fin's progressively worsening eyesight, but that had settled down now, to a slightly better than appalling myopia. Then they had considered stress; too much cheese for supper; too much loud music; the wrong sort of video games, but nothing, nothing could prevent the return of *The*

Nightmare. It was strange even to give it that name, since it wasn't a nightmare as such, just an unsettling sensation of being out of tune with his surroundings.

Jarmon moved to put his hand on the shoulder of his frightened little boy.

'When you've finished we'll have another chat about it. Give me a nudge before you go back to bed.'

Even his son's weak grin failed to make him feel better about another night of broken sleep.

Good grief, how many times had they been through this? How long would it be before he could tell his son that everything would be all right with any conviction? The odd thing was that Jarmon could remember having exactly the same problem at his son's age, but it had been very infrequent and the feeling passed without the fear that had such a dire - no pun intended - affect on the boy. He had always put it down to the mental equivalent of growing pains, but with Fin it seemed to be something more.

Jarmon settled into the small nursing chair that sat at the far end of the landing, and waited for his son to leave the bathroom, it could be minutes or hours away.

As it happened, this time it was only about five minutes later that Fin emerged, looking very small and cold, and somehow lost. He had that faraway look that came from not being able to see much more than a blur where the world should be – his glasses were on his bedside table, and he was virtually blind without them. His father could also see that he was still upset. His gold flecked, green eyes held a haunted look under the wreck of his dishevelled dark hair. Tall for his age and filling out into his adult frame, he still managed to look small and vulnerable when frightened into wakefulness in the middle of the night.

'It's still happening Dad, but not as bad.'

The two hugged, as they often did in the course of a day. Theirs was very much an extrovert and loving family, their frequent physical contact making them all feel secure. Both Fin and Jarmon held the embrace, one to give, and one to receive, the comfort implicit in the touch.

'Come on down to the kitchen, we'll have a quick drink and see how you feel then.'

Jarmon went into his son's bedroom to pick up his spectacles.

Father and son walked down the stairs together, Jarmon with his arm protectively around Fin's trembling shoulders, and into the large kitchen at the back of the house. The night showed itself in the large black windows when Jarmon switched on the light and he pulled down the blinds before making them both a cup of tea. The clock on the wall read one thirty. Lidine was sleeping with their daughter Lillibet, since their little girl always wanted company at night, usually at about twelve o'clock - only fitting, since Lilli had been born on the last day of October and in fun they had always all called her a little witch, so she appeared to feel the need to awake at the witching hour and call for her mother even at the age of ten. Both Jarmon and Lidine were hoping that all the night-time disturbances would have ended by this age but it seemed only a distant dream these days.

Although only thirteen, Fin was already as tall as many of his adult friends, and it seemed strange that such a large boy, with his larger than life personality should suffer from night frights. Simply telling him to grow out of it would never work and seemed rather unfair given the effect the experience had on him.

Jarmon sat over his tea, his hands wrapped around his cup.

'So was it the same as always?'

'Yes, only worse than usual. Even with the lights on everything keeps rushing around faster than I can keep up. I'm frightened Dad.' Fin sniffed, as though he was about to cry again.

'What can I do? It's awful. Even when I just look down at my feet they seem so far away, like that film *Vertigo*. Everything keeps moving away from me and I can't stop it.' This time his eyes did fill up as he spoke and a large tear rolled slowly down each cheek. Fin looked wretched and miserable, and Jarmon had to try to find a way to pull Fin back from the despair that was in danger of engulfing him.

'Part of the problem is that you never try to go to sleep when you're in bed. The only time your poor old body gets any rest is when you're totally exhausted. You need to get some shut-eye instead of always reading.' said Jarmon.

Fin got the hump, as ever. His head dropped down, his shoulders rose and he refused to meet his father's gaze.

'I sleep when I'm tired' he said.

'Yes, but only when you're physically tired. What about giving your brain a break once in a while and sleeping when everyone else does, like sometime before midnight?'

Fin's shoulders rose even higher and Jarmon could see this was heading nowhere, so he changed the subject slightly.

'So what are you reading that's so interesting anyway?'

'Ley lines and stuff. It's all in a book from the library. It's dead interesting Dad. You can read it after me if you want.'

'Well, maybe if I have time, Fin. Maybe.' But probably not. It didn't sound like a subject that would keep his father awake until the wee small hours. Ley lines. What next? Fairy rings? Those weird UFO books that entranced so many in the early 70s? Fin would read anything and everything and rarely seemed to get bored with a book around, which was often a blessing, but also caused major problems since he had to be up and about at six forty every morning to be able to get to school on time.

'Feeling any better?'

'Yeah, thanks Dad.'

'Okay. Come on, back up to bed with you. Let's try and get a couple of hours undisturbed sleep at least.'

They both returned to the landing as the clock chimed two.

'Night-night Fin. See you in the morning.'

'Night Dad. Sleep tight.'

'Don't let the bed bugs bite.' Jarmon could never resist that final line, although no-one else ever seemed to find it even remotely funny.

Back in his own bed, Fin settled down and was soon sleeping again, and remained happily undisturbed for the rest of the night.

Jarmon however had to explain the reason for his early morning tea with Fin to Lidine, who had been woken by that sixth sense that only mothers seem to possess when children can't sleep at night.

'I hope he'll be okay Jar.' said Lidine anxiously.

'He'll be fine now. Don't worry Liddy. In the morning he probably won't remember any of it. You'll see.'

The two settled down, accompanied by the not-quite-snoring-but-still-very-audible breathing of Lilli lying between them, blissfully unaware of anything, deserving a first class honours award from the Lets-Play-At-Being-Comatose Order of Sleepers.

God, she can be so annoying. was Jarmon's last thought, before sleep finally claimed him.

The following morning Fin appeared to have forgotten all about the previous night's disturbances, or maybe he was just pushing it to one of the far corners of his mind. An uneventful early morning rush around the house was followed by the thirty-five minute drive to school.

Jarmon however, was now in the mood to try, and not for the first time, to get to the root of the problem.

'So, everything alright at school Fin?' said Jarmon squinting against the just rising sun.

'Yeah sure Dad.'

'No problems with bullying?' prompted Jarmon as he put on his sunglasses. They were flashy-looking silver ones, and he was under the sad misapprehension that they made him look roguish and unbelievably attractive to the schoolgirls they were driving past.

'Nah. Honest.' replied Fin as he groped for the big wrap-around glasses with virtually black lenses that covered his specs and did, in fact, make him look like someone who was at least acquainted with fashion and style.

Both could remember the problems from a previous school where being short-sighted, taller, slower in football and athletics and more intelligent than his classmates had marked Fin out for special attention from two particular boys who took delight in tormenting him...

For several years...

Until the point where Fin had broken down in front of his father while on the way to school. Having had his son pour out his young and tortured heart to him, Jarmon had tried to make the school take action, but had singularly failed. Fin was a big lad and he should have been able to take care of himself - that appeared to be the school's take on the matter, ignoring the boy's gentle nature. When all else failed he and Lidine had decided to move Fin to another school, several miles away, and the change had proved a turning point for him and his confidence had soared.

It sounded as though the problem, whatever it was, wasn't anything to do with school. Jarmon was certain that at this point in his life Fin would always let him know of school related worries if asked directly, though he may not always reveal his feelings without prompting. Fin was, after all, a young man now, with all the conflicting emotions that entailed. He wanted to be adult about things, but still inhabited the world of children - for a little while longer at least.

Jarmon pondered. So, if it wasn't school, where else could tensions lie?

'Getting on all right with Nell and Simeon and Tam?' he queried. Fin didn't have many friends but these three were as close and loyal as anyone could hope for.

'Of course Dad. Look, I know you think my Nightmare is because of some problem or other in my life, but really Dad, just at the moment there isn't one. I haven't seen Simeon for a couple of days, but that's okay, we'll catch up when he gets back to school. And Eleanor came round a couple of days ago. Everything's fine. Cross my heart and hope to die, terrapins tickle me if I lie.'

'Bloody hell! The Goodies are coming back haunt me now.' cried Jarmon in mock horror.

'And there's plenty more where that came from young fella me lad!' said Fin in his favourite upper-class twit voice. 'You just mark my words - Graham, Bill and Tam are all still alive and well and twitching. Eckie Thump!'

'Okay. Now I'm beginning to worry. You've just regressed me thirty years, when you were aged about minus twenty. How do you remember all this crap, Fin?

'Dunno Dad, but it's good innit?

'Yeah, sure.'

So that was that. Jarmon still had no idea what might be behind the nocturnal upsets, and Fin didn't appear to know either, or wasn't prepared to share.

The two sat in companionable silence for the rest of the trip to school. A tape of Rick Wakeman's Six Wives Of Henry VIII played in the background. Jarmon still played a lot of his old favourites, and Fin had grown up to enjoy them as much as his father. He turned the music up. Loud.

When they arrived, Fin gave his father a kiss on the lips, reminding Jarmon of himself as a small boy with his Dad, and went happily into school. Jarmon knew that very few other fathers at the school would be privy to such a show of affection by their thirteen year-old sons, especially where they might be seen by other boys.

It's a shame for them, both boys and dads. He thought, as he turned the car and headed back home, driving one-handed as he smoked a cigarette, held languidly out of the window. As the car moved through the gathering young women walking to the nearby girls school Jarmon tapped out the beat of the James Taylor track now playing on the CD and happily contemplated all the broken hearts he must be leaving in his wake.

Now Mike (2)

Michael Nutter settled down with a cocoa and crumpet to listen to Philip Glass on his music centre. He smiled at the thought. Hi-fi it wasn't, being almost thirty years old, but it still did the job, and 'Northstar' was as good on LP as CD, as far as he was concerned.

He knew the boys at school thought his name was good for a joke. For his style of teaching though, it was quite apt, since Mister Nutter was convinced that boys would learn more if they had a bit of fun with their lessons. Certainly in the eighteen years of teaching at the Boys Grammar he had achieved far more than most teachers, with a one hundred percent pass rate at 'O' and 'A' level. He was proud that no one ever failed in his class and that for the past seven years he had been voted 'Best Teacher In School' by the boys he taught.

Michael thought of the Second Year English class from the afternoon, he had one or two very bright lads in that group and expected them to produce something well worth reading, since he was allowing them to interpret his latest homework request in any way they liked: fictional, factual, humorous – whatever.

Tomorrow should be interesting.

Now Fin (3)

Fin never particularly enjoyed homework, and he wasn't normally keen on essay writing, although it was one of the things he excelled at in school. He didn't even have to try, he had an innate ability. Maybe it was because it took so little effort that he never seemed to enjoy it. Tonight was an exception.

'Give me a two page essay on 'A Mysterious English Landscape' boys', Mister Nutter had said.

Since Mister Nutter had intentionally been very vague about exactly what he wanted from the boys, they could give full rein to their imaginations. Fin had immediately decided on Ley Lines, since it was his pet subject at the moment. The beauty of it was that the subject was as fuzzy as Mister Nutter's request. As far as Fin could tell no one knew whether Ley Lines really existed or what they were if they did. Oh, sure, a fair amount had been written about them, but none of it was scientific or verifiable. So this essay should be easy peasy lemon squeezy.

He knew the definition by heart since he had read it only a couple of days before, and his almost photographic memory could hold the image of a printed page for far longer.

Ley Lines: Straight lines linking hilltops, tumuli, church sites, and other traditional places of sanctity in the British Isles. They often appear to correspond with prehistoric tracks. From Ley, variant of Lea (grassland): the lines are supposed to have demarcated ancient meadows.

He'd had to check tumuli, it turned out they were ancient hills or mounds, but apart from that the dictionary entry had been short and self-explanatory. So, now to cherry pick the best of the rest he'd read.

The book he used as his main source, indeed his only source bar a couple of short pieces downloaded from the Internet, was made up of a series of articles printed during the twentieth century. He carefully changed the language used but maintained the general idea behind the articles he had read. Some said the lines were simply tracks between places of power and sanctity, others that they marked lines of power around the earth, still others that they were streams of magic. Many quoted Line Seekers explaining how they could find the lines in much the same way as water diviner, and indeed there were even right and left handed lines. Oh yeah! Soooo likely.

Fin agreed with the final contributor to his piece, who stated quite categorically that they were nothing more than artificial markings that could be made on any map with a reasonable amount of detail on it. He'd tried it earlier in the week and had managed to construct a line of power between half a dozen pubs and another magical connection between three sets of public lavatories. Hmmm, what would the streams between those consist of eh?

Eventually, after about half an hour he had completed the essay and packed his bag ready for the following school day.

Jarmon sat with Lillibet and Lidine watching an old Norman Wisdom film on TV. The lights were turned down to allow Lilli to pretend that they were on a visit to the cinema, and Fin arrived with the biscuit jar and a drink for himself and his little sister.

He snuggled into the couch between Jar and Liddy so that all four were squashed together. After a short time spent adjusting their positions and realigning cushions they settled back to enjoy the remains of the film.

'All done Fin?' asked his mother.

'Sure Mum.' he answered without looking up.

'Fin, are you sure? It's only an hour since we finished tea.'

'Mum, it's all done, honest. The essay was easy and the Latin and Maths only took about ten minutes each. It's done, and my bag's packed.'

'Well, all right, but don't you start rushing it again, we had enough of that last year.'

'All right Mum!' Fin protested, his anger rising. Everyone knew he had a short fuse when it came to homework and it was obviously smouldering along quite nicely now.

'Just as long as it is Fin. Oooooh, and look at that face.' Lidine, pinching Fin's chin between thumb and forefinger, tried to joke Fin out of his approaching mood. If anything he scowled even more.

'All red and hot like the fire!' laughed Lilli holding out her hands as though to warm them on the flames.

Fin was ready to go ballistic, intercontinental even.

'More like a slapped arse!' guffawed Jarmon.

'Jarmon!' gasped Lidine.

'Oooh Daddy, what you said.' giggled Lilli.

But it had done the trick and they all laughed, Fin a little ruefully. He knew he had a foul temper at times and did try to hold himself in check.

They settled down and watched the film in a warm comfortable silence, apart from the laughter at the antics of the black and white clown on the screen.

That night *The Nightmare* returned with a vengeance...

It was dark and cold and very, very quiet. Shadowy objects that looked very like his bedroom and its furniture were all around him. Like that clever camera thing they did in the beach scene in Jaws, everything seemed to be rushing past Fin without actually getting any further away. He looked down. Even his feet seemed to be dropping away into the blackness. The sensation of falling, but at the same time being stationary, engulfed Fin and filled his very being with terror.

Because he knew, beyond all doubt, that he wasn't asleep!

This was happening now and it was real and he didn't know why or how it could be possible.

He was lying on his back, in his bed, but at the same time he wasn't. He was falling but he was still, the air rushing by while he lay silently on his back, panic stricken.

Suddenly there was sound.

Not loud as he might have expected, but a soft whisper, like the wind in the leaves of the trees in the garden. The sound grew slowly louder, and the darkness began to fade. His bedroom came more clearly into focus, and the feeling of movement grew stronger as familiar objects continued their strange non-rush past.

Actually being able to see things clearly made it worse.

Fin became aware of other things in his room and these really were moving and were undeniably flying by. His ears were assailed by the booming of massive objects moving past at extreme speeds, displacing the air around him as they went. Huge rocks planted in a grassy landscape, and trees in sunlit woods rapidly expanded in his field of vision and hurtled around him in all directions, some even seeming to pass through him as he lay paralysed.

The wind howled in his ears now and the sweat running freely down his face began to sting his eyes. His body began to shake and his ears to ring.

There was a voice in there somewhere, and he was sure it wasn't his, but he couldn't make out words, or even what language it was, but it was unquestionably a voice. Probably.

Then, as suddenly as it had all begun, the chaos vanished.

Not a gentle return to normality.

Not fading away.

Just here one second - and entirely gone the next.

The clock above Fin's window showed twelve forty-five. Darkness filled the room and all was hushed once again. Fin's heart was pounding and he still couldn't move. The clock read one o'clock before Fin had finally managed to regain control. He desperately wanted to see his mum and dad and curl up in their protecting presence, but resisted the urge. He was thirteen years old for God's sake and would not go running like a frightened baby to mumsy and daddums just because of a bad dream.

He'd done that too often before.

Nor was he going to give in to the desire to rush to the loo. He was not a child. Well, yes, technically he was, at thirteen, but he had a Mensa sized IQ and it was about time he used it. Tonight was the last straw – he would not cry, he would be adult and figure this out – it was getting worse and he had to put a stop to it somehow.

The more he thought about the dream the more obvious it became that it was more, much more than just too much cheese and biscuits for supper.

He hadn't been asleep for a start. He was absolutely certain of that.

So what the Hell was going on?

'Shitshitshitshitshitshitshit……..'

Like a rapid-fire mantra he kept it up until he just felt stupid saying it.

'Oh Jeez, I am going mad.' he said to himself. Then he remembered that daft Catch-22 thing his father had told him about.

'Mad people don't think they're mad, so if you do, you're not.'

Strange but true, apparently.

At least according to Dad, who knew a lot of daft things, most of which proved to be true, although sometimes he'd been found out telling the most enormous porkies with a completely straight face.

Fin began to settle down a little more in his bed.

'But if I'm not mad, what's going on?'

He knew his parents would put it down to getting older, just like growing pains. In fact Jarmon had said he remembered similar sensations when he was about Fin's age, both during the day and at night. Fin fancied they had never been as bad as this though, or his Dad would have been able to discuss it more with him.

No. Fin was definitely experiencing something outside of anything his family could help with.

He fell asleep around three thirty still trying to decide on what his best course of action would be.

Now Leon (4)

Leon Messenger always seemed to be on the verge of being on the wrong side of the law. He had never, as far as he was aware, broken it and had no intention of doing so. However, the police always seemed to take an inordinate interest in his activities whenever he was out and about, which was a rare occurrence these days.

Leon was a strikingly good-looking Englishman from Cheshire. He was born and lived in an area known as Vale Royal, where kings of old had hunted stag in lush forests stretching as far as the eye could see. Most, but not all, of the forests had disappeared now of course, but the image of a king and his court riding around his home town always appealed to Leon.

With his six foot four frame, dark hair and startlingly icy blue eyes he was often the centre of attention when he was out with friends, or even when he just walked down the street. At thirty-two his pheromones were at the height of their powers, attracting the admiration of women and the envy of men. It also helped that he was black as the ace of spades, with a skin that had the appearance of blotting paper. He almost seemed to suck light into his frame, and his apparent looming menace is what caused his problems.

Wherever Leon was, if trouble raised its ugly head, it was he who was the obvious fall-guy. He wore large wraparound sunglasses and a full-length black leather coat because he knew he looked good in them, not to frighten people. Well maybe to intimidate them a little, but no more than that. But frighten them he did, even those who couldn't take their envious eyes off him.

The police always made straight for 'the big black bloke' at the back of the crowd. Security always asked him – often with a degree of burly trepidation – to leave 'wivvaht nah twouble mate, okay?'

In a lesser man it would have all been very tiresome.

But Leon didn't mind, because Leon had a secret.

Leon had a secret that no one, absolutely no one, knew about, or even vaguely suspected. If they had he would probably be in far more trouble than he was at this moment, sitting quietly in the back of the police van.

'Alright Leon, what happened?' asked one of the uniforms in front of him as Leon relaxed back against the seat.

'Nothing Dick, I was just watching that's all.'

The voice sounded as intimidating as the man looked. So deep it almost rumbled up from his boots, with no accent at all, and no sign of the nerves that usually became apparent when questioned by the police. Nor was there the 'don't touch me copper or I'll have you' attitude that often came to the fore when alcohol or stupidity were involved. And yet the big black guy didn't give the impression of being a hardened thug either, his voice was calm and even a little deferential, a throwback to his mum drilling into him a respect for the law, even if it wasn't always right.

Leon smiled and PC Richard Hedd (and Oh! how he had suffered at school with that name, his parents either had an evil sense of humour, or none at all) smiled back, but the second man jerked back, almost as though Leon had pushed him. The smile was so bright and so wide that it gave the appearance of the Cheshire Cat, with headlights, at night. Leon had used that smile a lot in his life. He had learned at an early age that when you look big and tough, almost any sort of trouble can be avoided by a big friendly smile, and he had a very big, very dazzling and hugely friendly smile.

'So how did it all start then?' asked Dick offering Leon a cigarette, which was accepted with a nod. PC Hedd was never quite convinced of the innocence of his big friend, though in truth he had singled him out for no other reason than that he wanted someone to chat to – it was going to be a long boring night, especially when on duty with Magnull Flint, the most stupid and unpleasant of the men operating out of the local station. He settled back in his seat as though preparing for a long interview.

Leon looked over to his friend from childhood and the smile flashed again. He'd never understood why Dick, at five-eleven, with well trimmed brown hair (never out of place), a well toned physique, boundless energy and handsome hazel-eyed countenance, had joined the local constabulary. He could have walked into almost any job available and probably have received a Golden Hello by way of thanks. Academically brilliant, and able to charm the birds out of the trees (and - Leon had seen with his own amused eyes - out of any of the local nightclubs, if he so desired) with his ready smile and wit, he had settled for the work-a-day life of a local beat bobby, insofar as that particular position still existed in the modern force. It had always puzzled Leon, when there were so many opportunities open to Dick, but each to his own, he thought.

'Look Dick, a couple of guys had a little too much to drink and decided to take their argument – and no, I don't know what it was about – outside. One thing led to another and before you know it there was a fight. I do not know the men involved, but I most definitely was not – I was about to leave when you two arrived and I was picked on – sorry, I mean up.'

The second officer, who still hadn't introduced himself to Leon looked uncomfortable, as though expecting the shadowy figure in front of him to erupt, and squared his shoulders.

'Oi, yer keep a civil tongue in yer gob mate, or I'll learn yer a lesson. Okay?'

Dick and Leon ignored him totally, and smoked their cigarettes in companionable silence, neither even deigning to look over at him.

'Yer lissenin' pal?' prompted Flint a little more angrily.

Leon glanced over at Dick and they both grinned as he continued.

'I have nothing to do with the affray outside, which is still ongoing by the sounds of it, so I would be grateful if you would open the door, let me out and exercise your power over the common man, to end the fracas and bring peace and harmony back to lower Daneham.

Now, if you don't mind.'

Dick grinned along with his friend, knowing that Flint had no idea that he and Leon had spent virtually their entire lives living in each other's pockets. That was why he had a healthy distrust of his friend – they'd been in too many scrapes together. And there had always been something else about Leon, but he'd never been able to put his finger on what it was.

Dick also knew that his fellow officer was probably struggling with 'fracas'.

PC Flint, none too bright at the best of times simply stared at Leon, then at Dick.

Dick shrugged and ground out his fag end.

Well, that seemed to be that.

The door to the van opened and Leon stepped out, followed by a slightly flustered Flint and PC Hedd exhaling the last of his cigarette smoke.

Somewhere in the back of Flint's mind he was sure that he hadn't been trained to question big, sinister West Indians in that way. Where was his truncheon when he needed it?

As he looked at the large leather coated figure leaving the vicinity of the disturbance with hardly a glance at the crowd and combatants, now being dispersed by Constable Dick, he gave a little shudder. On second thoughts it was probably just as well that the truncheon was nowhere to be seen. He suddenly had a panic-inducing image of Leon taking it off him, and teaching him a lesson in tolerance and inter-racial harmony. He was becoming sure that he had missed something when namby-pamby Dick 'ead had been questioning the man now leaving the car park. And yet the man, whose surname he had omitted to ask for, had been friendly and quietly spoken, until that final '*Now*', which had brooked no argument. Yes, the copper was very definitely relieved to see the back of him, but couldn't have told anyone why.

Weird effect to have on someone.

'Buggerit. Once more into the fray.' thought Flint, with a literary reference totally wasted on himself.

And with that Leon was forgotten, and the policeman turned to the ludicrous sight of two mightily drunken men attempting to commit actually bodily harm to each other with damp bar towels, whilst his fellow officer struggled hard not to laugh as he held them apart like Samson at the temple. Even the surrounding crowd were losing interest and re-entering the pub. Eventually the whole thing fizzled out with a warning to the two protagonists, and only Leon suffering any form of inconvenience. But he'd had little else to do and Dick was the best friend he had ever had, and probably would ever have.

It was still a little annoying that the good people of the village would have seen Leon being loaded into the police van, and after what was presumably a short lecture, being let out again, just because his friend was at a loose end.

But such is life.

Dick watched his friend leave over the tops of the now diminishing crowd. Leon was still, even after all these years, an enigma. In the early days at school he was just like all the other local lads, apart from being the only coloured boy in the school. The two had become fast friends almost immediately, but at the age of fourteen, following the death of his parents, Leon had closed in on himself somehow. Not surprising really. He still gave the appearance of easy-going camaraderie, but something inside him had changed, and Dick had never managed to find out what it was. He would trust Leon with his life, but no longer knew the man as he had the boy.

And Dick wanted to know.

He wanted to return to the innocence of their youth.

He wanted to know his best friend as he had at school.

He wanted to know what Leon did with his time, and how he always seemed to have money without even his best friend, and Dick knew he was it, having the faintest idea where it came from.

He also wanted to get out of the police and live a different life – without quite knowing what the difference would be. For the time being, however, this was the only job he felt suited for. He was respected by friends and colleagues alike and was an able officer, but still felt that he was heading nowhere. He also knew that in many ways he was wasting his life. Even at school he'd wanted to help people, and the police had seemed the most immediate way of making a difference. The presence of such as Flint had soon disillusioned him to some extent about his fellow man, but his belief in the essential good in everyone - well almost everyone - had kept him plodding away over the years.

At a snails pace.

In a world that was racing ever faster.

But such is life.

Leon opened the door to his isolated home and deactivated the burglar alarm. It was a very expensive alarm, which used iris recognition scanning equipment to verify Leon's identity. It was expensive because you couldn't actually buy it anywhere, and was still undergoing trials at a number of banks and airports where it was hoped it could fast-track selected customers through the rigors of ATM and check-in. For Leon it meant his little castle was totally secure from outside interference. Which was just as well, because his home housed the evidence, on every available surface, of his secret.

The house was more like a minor manor house, situated in a small wooded dell and surrounded by a moat. Each of the half-timbered upper floors extended beyond the one below, giving the whole structure a top-heavy appearance. Yet somehow it all looked right. And the gatehouse, although fairly small, added the finishing touch to Leon's castle.

There was only one road in and out and the sides of the glade were steep enough to prevent anyone strolling by. He rarely had visitors, and those he did were generally at night, the only exception being PC Dick. The gardens were landscaped in keeping with the site, and gave an overall impression of a medieval idyll somehow transported into modern day Cheshire. The idea appealed to Leon, especially given the means by which most of his possessions had been amassed. He smiled his easy smile and strolled through his domain.

Now Fin (5)

Mister Nutter seemed very perky in class today. Fin had noticed as soon as he entered the room and so had Tamburlaine Riggleby who sat alongside him.

'He seems very perky today.' whispered Tamburlaine, 'wonder what's going on.'

'Dunno. Shhhh.' hissed Fin, and sat down along with the rest of the class once Michael Nutter was seated.

The whole class awaited the teacher's first utterances, except Tam.

'Thought you must be having the day off, when you weren't on the train.' he whispered. Fin gave his friend a sidelong glance.

'Got a lift off Dad. He's going in late today, writing reports or something.' he replied through the side of his mouth. 'When he's got no meetings, he's got time to drop me off.'

Mister Nutter glanced up from the pile of exercise books on his desk.

'Well Matey-boys, you've excelled yourselves this time. Most of the homework you gave me last week was absolutely…' the pause caused more than one boy to wince (they knew the type of comment he prefixed with a pause) '…ordinary.'

'Oh-oh.' muttered Tam.

He was never keen on the return of English homework. This was partly due to the total lack of grammatical ability he demonstrated, along with woefully inadequate handwriting for a thirteen year old, but was mainly because he could never think up an original story. It was just one of those things. If you needed a quick joke or a humorous story Tam was your man, but the only time Tam ever achieved a grade higher than B minus was when he plagiarized. He knew Fin did the same, though not very often, but Fin had the skills to make whatever he wrote his own. Such ability was beyond Tam.

Mister Nutter handed the books back.

Tam had a C for his efforts, Fin had been given an A. Mister Nutter threw a quick comment at Tam along the lines of "less time strumming and humming – more time thinking and writing."

The voice of Bishop came from the back of the class - whispered, but intentionally loud enough for everyone to here.

'Riggleby's been playing his instrument too much. He'll go blind!'

Several boys laughed even though Mister Nutter aimed a laser-like glare at Bishop and his cronies. Paulie Wright giggled irritatingly for several seconds after the rest of the boys quietened.

'Mister Wright! That will be enough!' said the teacher. Accepting of banter, he knew that Tam and his group suffered at the hands of some of the others in the class. And not just through the odd comment like Bishop's.

'Oh that's okay sir.' said Tam. 'You know what they say.'

Mister Nutter raised an eyebrow.

'He who laughs last…' he left it hanging, waiting for the teacher to respond.

'Go on Tam.' said Mister Nutter. 'Put me out of my misery.'

'Well sir, he who laughs last, thinks slowest.' said Tam straight faced.

And his teacher had to turn back to his desk to hide his smile. Maybe Tam and Co. managed okay on their own, he thought.

Grinning at the guffaws from those around him, but noticeably not from the back of the class, Tam looked over to Fin and rolled his eyes heavenwards when he saw Fin's usual excellent score.

'Never mind,' he muttered, 'I can beat you anytime at music.'

Fin grinned too. Tamburlaine Riggleby was more than a head shorter, even when they were seated, with brilliant green eyes (the girls loved those, even at this early age) that always sparked with mischief. With his small stature and unruly mop of dark hair that matched his sunny character - totally uncontrollable, but in an oddly attractive way - he looked like a pre-pubescent Bill Oddie and had the wicked sense of humour to match. He also giggled; a high pitched laugh that often forced those around him to join in. Infectious was the word, "Like a nasty rash", their friend Simeon often pointed out in his heavy Lancashire brogue, "you can itch it, but it won't bleedin' go away an', in th'end, you jus' tav t'accept it an' make the best o' things. One day certain bits of 'is anatomy will fall inta place an' mebbe then we'll be able t' live wiv 'im. But I'm not holdin' me breath." (Curiously Fin and Tam seemed to tune out the accent when they were with Sim, friendship cuts through such inconsequential things.) This was one of Simeon's favourite quips, since he and Fin had fast developing baritone voices, while Tam was still a high treble. "Eunuch" was also a word he liked to use when winding up his friend, but it was all in fun and the three of them were inseparable, both inside and outside of school.

Sim was sitting just in front of them now, his close cut blonde hair doing nothing to disguise the fact that he was attempting to make himself very small with his head hunched down between his shoulders. As in most lessons, all three boys knew that Sim wouldn't be collecting any commendations for his work, unless Shakespeare or Marlowe was involved. Tam reckoned Sim was a savant, "thick as a brick except for long-dead writers", and the comment was only half-mocking, because, for some strange reason, Sim's academic ability only showed itself when it came to the drama club. The accent vanished along with the self-conscious stoop, and the bard lived for the brief moments that Sim could be persuaded to act out snippets of iambic pentameter.

'So boys, who do we think did better than appallingly average?' prompted Mister Nutter.

'Willis and Fin, sir.' came the reply, in that odd sing-song monotone that only groups of school children seem to master.

'Teachers pet.' hissed Ian Bishop from behind Fin.

'Nancy boy Finbar kisses arse again.' That was Paul Wright.

An ink sodden scrap of paper hit Fin just below the ear and fell onto his desk beside his essay.

Tam gave Fin a sidelong look.

'Ignore them Fin. Bloody morons.'

The two boys behind guffawed quietly to each other.

Fin stared stoically ahead., but Tam could see the red flush of embarrassment rising from his shirt collar.

'Congratulations boys. Yes, these two at least have a semblance of talent in their mother tongue. Indeed, I've decided to give them the chance to enter a regional competition to find the best young writers in the county, so we shall vet their contributions and you can decide whether their work warrants such high regard.'

Fin grinned along with the rest of the class except for Willis Masseer, a quiet and withdrawn boy and the only other Grade A student in the class. He always seemed so… what was the best word to describe it?... sad, yes that was it. Not sullen or morose or unfriendly, just unaccountably sad. Having said that, the poor boy had lost his parents at the age of seven and by all accounts the aunt and uncle with whom he lived were not best suited to parenthood. Poor lad.

Michael Nutter sat down and surveyed his audience. This was what teaching was about, it had nothing to do with targets and tests, it was about bringing out the best in the boys and helping them enjoy their all too-brief childhood. He recognised with a sigh all the signs of adolescence now appearing in his young charges, the petty arguments that somehow evolved into something far more serious unless nipped in the bud.

Life would be difficult enough later on and he was damned if it was going to invade his sphere of authority so soon. The boys of his class would all be friends. He would make it so.

'Right boyos, grab your scrawl and come to the front, so we can all hear.'

Fin was on his feet instantly.

Willis was more reluctant.

Fin arrived home with a bound through the back door, closely followed by Tam. Both of them gave Lidine a kiss and a hug. Tam was like a second son and was treated accordingly, just as Mrs Riggleby, Sue - Tam's mum, treated Fin.

'Had a good day boys?' asked Lidine.

'Yeah, great mum. What's for tea?' asked Fin.

Tam giggled 'I dunno Fin, you and your stomach.'

'But I'm a growing boy. I've got to keep my strength up. And I don't remember ever seeing you refuse second helpings.'

'Ah, but that's good manners, that is. It's got nothing to do with being a pig like you.'

And Tam finished with a grunt that made up for its lack of realism with quite staggering volume.

'Good Lord Tam, you'll do yourself a mischief.' Lidine grinned at the pair, 'Drinks?'

Both nodded and found glasses for their Dandelion and Burdock.

As Lidine poured the drinks two more bodies bundled through the door.

The first was Sim, who had called in at home and, finding it empty, had hurried along to Fin's house. He lived just down the road and spent as many of his waking hours in the LeMott household as he did in his own. He caught the train to Appleton along with Tam and Fin and they all returned the same way, but Sim always went home straight after school to drop off his books and check whether his dad was home early.

His mother had run out on his father not long after his birth, leaving Silas to look after his son without the guiding hand of a woman. Silas though, was determined that single-parenthood would not mean that Sim missed out on any of life's possibilities. This meant that he worked long hours as a car mechanic, but in return the two of them had great fun when they shared their 'quality time'. A good man, but there were times when Simeon thought he would have been happier just to have his dad home more. 'Quality time' really only counted if it lasted more than a few minutes each night. Weekends were terrific, but the working week was a real sod, as far as Simeon was concerned.

The second new arrival was a girl, again of about thirteen years, with glossy long auburn hair and a face that boys and men would gladly die for in a few years time. Eleanor DePuiz was tall for her age and called 'willowy' by Lidine. She was the only female friend that Fin had, and despite her looks, was as much 'one of the lads' as any of the boys. Nell lived next door and often popped around after school.

The four children, having said their hellos and made the usual noncommittal references to their school-day all retired to the biggest room at the rear of the house. Fin put Greenday on the micro system and the four settled down to spend the next half hour or so together, doing nothing in particular, but simply enjoying each other's company.

Sim had had a better day than usual, having managed to play himself into the school rugby team as fullback during PE – his final lesson of the day. The following Sunday would see him make his debut and he couldn't stop explaining in minute detail how he had played such a blindingly brilliant game that afternoon that he wouldn't be surprised if he was discovered for the National side before long and would soon be trotting out with the rest of the guys at Twickers. His enthusiasm and excitement wasn't dented in the least by the guffaws of his audience.

Nell had not had such a good day.

Being bullied at school seemed to be the norm for so many kids these days that she accepted it as just another part of the school day, but that didn't mean she had to like it. She was bright and good-looking and was an obvious target, not least because she hung around with the three boys she now sat with. The girls at school couldn't understand why she wasn't interested in mobile phones, boy bands and the latest heartthrob footballer.

They wouldn't believe that Nell simply found her friends more interesting.

So she had suffered the hair pulling, the tripping and the nasty remarks with her usual equanimity. The three boys nodded sagely and offered their commiserations, they all knew what it was like to be an outsider, but the four of them together would face any foe and still come out smiling.

Each was bullied, on an ongoing basis and each for different reasons; Fin was bright and wore glasses and was crap at sport; Tam was small and had long fingernails because he played guitar – very well as it happened, but long fingernails on a young man brought all the obvious remarks from the testosterone pumped lads that seemed to make up the bulk of the country's young male population; Simeon was tall, good looking, good at sport and not the brightest boy in the school and so was bullied for exactly the opposite reasons as Fin; Nell was just not a girlie type girl and so never quite fitted in.

All had their own unique qualities that made them who they were. Compassion, intelligence, a willingness to stand outside the sheep mentality of the "yoof culcha" propagated by TV and radio (by those who purported to know what was best for "kids") and a over-arching friendship that would last them for the rest of their lives – though they had no way of knowing that.

But we digress...

Tam was eager to let Sim and Nell hear about the result of Fin's masterpiece in English.

'You'll never guess what,' he gushed 'Fin's going to have a piece of English entered into a national essay competition. It's well cool.'

'You what?' said Fin 'what kind of talk is 'well cool'?'

'You tryin to be hip and trendy, man?' asked Sim and Nell giggled loudly.

'Hey dude, I've got my bag together.' droned Nell, in her worst mid-Atlantic accent, whilst making the love-not-war V sign with both hands.

'Oh, sod off you lot. I forgot meself for a minute, that's all.' Tam reddened as the others laughed.

They had always agreed that they would set themselves apart from their contemporaries by not using the current jargon and buzzwords. They felt themselves to be outsiders and comforted themselves in being their own little four-man (and woman) clique.

They didn't text...

They rarely emailed...

They liked to talk, and laugh, together.

The four believed that you couldn't do that successfully without being in the same room.

'So what happens now?' asked Sim.

'Well Mister Nutter...' began Tam.

'Who?!!' squealed Nell.

'Mister Nutter.' repeated Tam.

'You've got to be joking. Nutter?' Nell had started laughing, and she'd set Sim off as well - he was always the first to crack when faced with someone else's merriment.

'No, Mister Nutter. Teaches us English. He's been one of our teachers since the First Year.' said Fin, in support of his friend.

'What's so funny?' asked Tam, straining hard. But he couldn't hold out and suddenly all four were laughing uproariously, with Simeon approaching hyena country.

'Oh, no! Tell me it's not true, you've got to be making that up...' Nell managed to gasp out as the tears rolled down her cheeks. Sim was nearing Bladder Control Hell as he rolled around the floor curled up in a ball. No one could speak for the moment, since every attempt to open their mouths resulted in a fresh wave of wild laughter. Sim knew all about Mister Nutter, but Nell's guffaws were still too infectious for him to ignore.

Lillibet came into the room to see what all the noise was about and for several seconds could only smile indulgently as her brother and his friends tried to control their mirth. She was about to become very upset that they weren't sharing the joke with her until she realized that it was just the four fools being foolish, and went back to the kitchen to help Lidine with tea. Even Lilli was too mature for her older brother and his friends when they were in that sort of mood.

Slowly calm returned and Tam continued.

'Mister Nutter....' he began, and then had to wait a further minute whilst Nell tried to recover her composure following another fit of giggles. She finally achieved this by stuffing her hanky in to her mouth - which almost set Sim off again.

Tam made another attempt to explain.

'Mister Nutter...' he said firmly, ignoring Nell and Sim when they groaned as their eyes rolled back in their heads and the tears threatened to start again. '...will send Fin's essay into Manchester where a panel of experts will decide whether it should be entered into the regional finals, and from there maybe on to the nationals.'

'And from there who knows. The sky's the limit. Only don't forget your old pals, when your rich and famous and all hoity-toity.' joked Nell.

The four sat and daydreamed and chatted about nothing in particular for another half an hour, until Sim had to go home to begin getting tea ready for his dad. Nell and Tam left with him to saunter slowly back to their parents and the early evening meal.

Fin sat down to eat with his family and explained about his essay being entered into the competition.

'Mister Nutter decided that in the end Willis and I should be put forward. I was quite excited but Willis didn't seem to care much. He never seems that bothered about anything'

'Well it's not that surprising poor lad. No mum or dad and living with the Blades in that place out on The Moss.' Lidine sounded as though Fin's attitude needed a bit more thought.

'You know he's had a rough couple of years, maybe you should all take a little more interest in him. You know. Bring him out of himself. You never know, he might be a fun lad if you knew him better.'

Fin didn't look convinced.

'He's a miserable devil, I know that.' said Fin.

'Oh Fin, give the lad a chance.' urged Jarmon. 'So tell me again what was the essay about.'

'Mister Nutter says we're both in with a good chance of winning the regional contests. I wrote about Ley Lines and Willis did something all about The Moss.'

Jarmon nodded as he remembered Fin working on the tale the previous week.

'And though I hate to admit it' said Fin 'I think Willis' was a better piece of work than mine.'

'I wouldn't worry' commented Lidine 'I know you'll win, and you know I'm never wrong.'

Her stare dared anyone to disagree. No one did, because they all knew that, daft as it sounded, Lidine was usually right in her predictions.

'I wonder why Willis chose The Moss. You know they're going to turn it into a big retail park, with cinemas and goodness knows what else. All we need around here, another flaming retail park.' Jarmon was clearly astride a hobbyhorse and building up to a full gallop. 'The town won't be able to cope with all the new housing and shops. Where are they going to put all the cars for a start?'

'Yes, we know Jarmon dear. Eat your tea before it gets cold.'

'And what's it all for, eh? Just so that someone at the top of a huge executive pile can make an extra few thousand on top of the obscene salary he receives anyway.'

Jarmon was waving his knife and fork around now, to emphasize his disgust.

Lidine leaned over and whispered not very quietly in his ear 'So do something about it. Join the council, join Friends of the Earth, Greenpeace... someone. Only do it soon before we all decide you're all talk and no action. Go on, do it.'

The kitchen went very quiet as everyone waited for the reply. Dad had well and truly painted himself into a corner, and was obviously looking at the dripping brush and wondering where it had come from and how it had come to be in his hand.

'All right, I bloody-well will!' announced Jarmon, and with a rueful smile continued, 'Got no damned option, have I, after that.' His voice softened and he looked wistful for a moment, which wasn't like him at all. 'But honestly it would be nice to do something to stop it all; it's getting out of hand; the shops, the houses, the roads that can't cope with the traffic. So, yes, I will start to try to do something about it.'

They all smiled indulgently. It wasn't the first time they'd listened to him go on like this, but this time he might actually have taken the first steps towards trying to do something about the injustice and stupidity he believed was all around him.

Well you never know what some people are capable of until they're given a gentle push in the right direction.

You never know...

As promised earlier in the week, the names of both Fin and Willis were in the local paper that Wednesday. It was just a short article to let everyone know that the two boys had made it to the regional finals for their essays, with the titles of both pieces mentioned – 'Secret Cheshire' from Willis and 'Ley Lines – fact or fiction' from Fin. The article was hidden away in the middle of lost cats and new planning permission applications, but Fin was still excited to see his name in print.

With a self-satisfied smile, Fin tossed the paper onto the table and settled down to more Latin translation.

Now Leon (6)

Leon had been on one of his trips.

He'd picked up some useful tips to help him with some DIY he was carrying out on the house. He no longer needed to use nails to hold the timbers of the new extension in place – a chap called Lucian Task had ably demonstrated the cutting and use of wooden pegs to hold the whole frame together. Leon was certain that there were people all over the world who knew about this, but it was new to him. It made his building all the more satisfying, since it was being done the right way, as the joiners and carpenters of Old England had done it, even down to using original tools for the job.

And he wasn't guessing, he knew this was how they did it.

The manor was coming along nicely. He'd used only original timbers he found in various places, original tools and, to a very large extent, original materials for the walls and roof. His friend Lucian would approve, he was sure.

After spending the morning on the extension, he settled down to lunch. Bacon and eggs with haggis and bread and butter. As far as Leon was concerned you could keep your 'healthy diet'. He used a lot of energy on his trips and subsequent building, and salads weren't going to bridge that yawning hunger he always felt when he got home. He used his gym, housed in the gatehouse for an hour every day and his work kept his body hard and lean no matter what he ate. He was built like a weight lifter, but was always light on his feet like a dancer, and almost feline in his movements. He looked good in any clothing and took pride in it. His friend Dick had always said he should have been in films, but Leon enjoyed his present lifestyle too much to ever consider changing it.

Lunch over, he glanced out of the window and across the courtyard smiling contentedly at his morning's work

The new addition to the house was for storage. Every year he accumulated more and more clutter, which he had been storing in his barn, but rust had recently become a problem and he needed somewhere with humidity and temperature controls. The two-storey wing would be purpose built and large enough to house his entire collection and far more besides.

Tonight he had finally decided to show Dick around the entire house. Normally visitors only saw the outside of the buildings and a few carefully selected rooms. Today though, Leon had come to a fairly momentous decision.

He was going to let his closest friend in on his secret.

Although Dick was a policeman, Leon was confident that he would be fascinated enough to keep all that he was told to himself. In many ways the two men were alike and Leon was gambling everything that his friend would prefer the life he was about to be offered to that of PC Plod.

That evening Dick drove his car towards the setting sun. The approach to what he always thought of as "Castle Leon" was through a large wood bordering the main Chester road, the house being over a small hill and totally invisible to anyone who didn't know it was there. He doubted that anyone who hadn't been invited had ever seen it. Leon purposely kept the undergrowth very thick indeed and walking to the glade surrounded by trees was virtually impossible, especially given the ten-foot high rough wooden wall that stretched for four miles around the property. This too was hidden from inquisitive eyes by the woods. Oh, there was a six-foot wide, six-foot deep moat on the outside of the wooden barricade too, just in case.

The evening air was filled by the smell of wild flowers and freshly mown lawns as Dick climbed out of the car and surveyed Leon's demesne.

He marvelled, as he always did, at what delights Leon had wrought here. The lawns swept down from the trees, with peacocks strolling between small islands of flowerbeds, mainly Old English roses, but also abundant perennials for the arrangements Leon always seemed to have time to create within the house. He even seemed to be able to coax Fritillaries up from the South to bask in his garden.

The fading sun cast dappled shadows on the grass and the last birdsongs of the day were coming to an end, as the lazy buzz of insects faded. He thought he had a sudden glimpse of someone in the trees, but the changing light made it impossible to be certain, and when he tried to find the spot again there was nothing to be seen.

The sun was setting behind the house and once again Dick was struck by the fact that all this was owned by his old school friend, who never seemed to have gainful employment. He was aware that Leon went on trips abroad several times a year, but had no idea where or to what purpose. He had a nagging suspicion that they may have had nefarious intent behind them.

Maybe tonight he would broach the subject again. Though he had small hope of being given an answer to his understandable worries about his friend.

Leon met him in the courtyard formed by the three wings of the house that formed a three storey U shape opening to the drive. The large arched oak entrance door stood ajar behind him.

'Hello Dick. Come in.' he said with his ever present smile. He clapped his friend on the back and led him into the twilight of the Great Hall.

'Wotcha Leon.' grinned Dick as he strolled through the doorway and onto the stone paved floor.

'Thanks for coming, I've had a long day. Fancied a bit of company' said Leon, 'and when it comes to company, you're the only man I'd want to see'.

Dick suddenly felt a rush of affection for his host.

'Thanks, Leon, it's always a pleasure, though I thought I saw someone else in the garden over by the rose beds as I drove up. Must have been a trick of the light.'

Leon's habitual grin grew wider, if that were possible, and he showed a total lack of concern.

'Unlikely to find anyone else here Dick, don't you think? So how's life treating you then? Still got you're nose to the constabulary grindstone?'

'Yeah, same as ever. Paperwork mostly and not enough good old fashioned beat bobbying.' replied Dick glumly.

'I had a feeling that was the case old friend. Last time we met you seemed a bit down.'

'Oh, that was bloody Flint wasn't it? I've never met another copper with so little brain. He drives me mad. I honestly don't know how he ever made it through training, he's always been an idiot as far as I can tell. But there it is. There's not a hell of a lot I can do about it. And yes, I am a bit low, but I can't seem to find a way around the fact that life is just so damn dreary.'

'Oh come on. That's not the Dickhead I know.' joked Leon. 'You were the one who always kept me going. Especially after Mum and Dad died. You were always there for me. I don't know how I would have managed without you. So don't start telling me you can't handle modern life with all it's excitement'

'Come off it Leon. You never really needed me - not deep down. You always seemed so secure in yourself, even as an orphan. Far more self-assured than I ever was. I've always just stumbled through life, but you always seemed to know what you wanted. And your Nan must have helped. I loved going round to her house when you lived there. What a strange old girl she was, with all her weird dolls and stuff. Used to give me the willies sometimes, but God she was entertaining.'

'That's true. Nan taught me a lot. More than you ever knew Dick.'

There was something in the way Leon said that that made his friend look up.

'Jeez you can be a mysterious beggar at times Leon. Anyway since we've started in on the deep philosophical stuff, I think modern life stinks. I know we've got all the mod cons and that, but don't you ever dream of a life without mobile phones, housing estates and endless sodding traffic jams. 'Cos I know I do. We spend all our time rushing around to have an extra few spare minutes for new experiences and 'quality time' but we end up rushing through that too. Or sitting in the car waiting for the end of the world. At least that's how it seems when you can't get where you want to go in the sliver of time you've given yourself to get there. I find myself thinking 'What's the flaming point?' more and more often. It's all so depressing.'

He stared gloomily at his plate and pushed the food around without attempting to eat any of it.

'Sorry Leon. Not having a good week, or year for that matter. So cheer me up you rum bugger. Come on, why the invitation tonight. We both know you always have a reason.'

Leon looked him straight in the eye, in a way that he found a little disconcerting.

'What's happened Leon? Your not in some kind of trouble are you?' asked Dick worriedly.

'No Dick, not at all. Sorry to be so daft. It's just there's something I want to tell you. But you have to swear not to tell a soul. On your honour as a copper, and on our friendship.'

'Bloody hell, Leon. What are you on about?'

'Swear it Dick. Or we revert back to just two mates having supper and you can forget this conversation ever started.'

Leon was in deadly earnest about something and Dick had never, in twenty odd years, seen him like this. Where was the easy-going giant with the big smile? There was no evidence of him at this dining table.

'Okay, okay. I swear on my life as a policeman and on our friendship never to reveal to a soul what you are about to tell me. Unless it's illegal.'

'Don't worry. It's not.' answered Leon with the briefest of smiles.

And so he told Dick everything.

Their food forgotten, the two friends talked late into the night. Or rather it began as a chat, which became just a little bit heated at an early stage, and then continued as Leon talked and Dick listened first in disbelief and then with very real fear.

Leon didn't rant or rave.

But everything he said was just too insane for words.

Now Fin (7)

Fin had packed his bag himself for the three night school trip to the Lake District. They would be staying at a Youth Hostel near Boot in Eskdale and needed clothes to allow for the vagaries of the British summer. Lidine was in the process of repacking since she knew from long experience that there was no way he'd think to take what was needed. Even Jarmon couldn't manage to pack sensibly for holidays. It was A Man Thing.

As expected, all the necessities, from the point of view of her son, were packed. His CD player and two CDs packed with an eclectic mix of MP3 files were buried in amongst his clothes, along with three books; Dean Koontz, Dick Francis and a new one from Pterry Pratchett. (Yes, she prided herself on knowing about the 'P'.)

He had at least remembered his walking boots and several thick pairs of socks, specially bought for the trip. Hopefully Fin had got the size right, so at least blisters and sore feet shouldn't be a problem. She popped some fabric plasters in just in case though.

Having found the essentials Fin appeared to have lost interest in the rest, even though Mister Nutter had sent every boy home with a list of requirements several weeks in advance of the trip. Me Laddo had forgotten incidentals like fresh underwear and socks and his spare specs, more of an essential given his propensity for breaking his glasses in the rough and tumble of school life. Lidine sighed and found herself smiling, despite having to hunt around for the missing items, as she packed them into the rucksack. A mother's work is never done, especially where the male members of the family were concerned. A lightweight waterproof and thick sweater finished the job and she attached a note to the top of the bag urging the inclusion, following their use this morning, of toothbrush, paste and a comb. She sat back on the floor and wondered how Simeon was managing without a mother to keep an eye on his packing.

The trip was organised to coincide with an outdoor play being staged at the youth hostel. 'Much Ado About Nothing' was a favourite of Fin and his friends and the trip included every boy in the class. It was the first outing for Year 8 and it would be interesting to see how everyone managed with six to a room in bunk beds. Fin would be sharing with Simeon and Tam, so he should enjoy himself. Mister Nutter had also made room for Willis Masseer with them and Lidine suspected a bit of social engineering on the part of the teacher, who knew his wards better than some of their parents, she was sure.

'Right Fin, come and check all this out with me." She called. She could picture the effect the appeal would have had on her son downstairs. The deep sigh of indulgence from the study below could be heard even from his bedroom. Almost immediately the slow methodical stamp of his climb up the stairs came to her and she heard the mumbling as he came nearer.

'Oh, for heavens sake Fin, hurry it up a bit. I'm not going to torture you. Get in here.' she said, as he finally arrived.

As expected Fin looked as though he'd been torn away from far more important things, but Lidine knew that if she didn't show him her additions, he would probably never think to wear them.

She pointed to the bag.

'Socks and pants, you scruffy 'erbert.' she admonished.

'Oops. Sorry Mum, but it's only a couple of nights and I bet I won't need them.' He tried a woefully inadequate high defensive lob.

'What? You were planning to fester for four days in the same socks! You're sharing a room, or at least you would for the first night, then the others would hang you out of the window overnight, in the hope that you might be a bit less whiffy the next day.' Her overhead smash obliterated any further discussion.

Fin tried to keep the glower going, but knew she was right. She always was.

'Well pick it up then! Make sure it's not too heavy for you.'

'Oh Mum!' he whined. 'I am thirteen. I can manage. I'm a big boy now remember.'

'Yes, and one who nearly went away without socks and undies.' she grinned 'Big boy my foot. Pick it up.'

He bent and lifted the bag with no trouble.

'See, told you so.' he smiled smugly.

'Better safe than sorry my lad. Anyway, what's with all the books, I hope you don't hide yourself away and read all the time. You're supposed to be sociable on trips like this you know.'

Lidine smiled, knowing that although Fin was sociable enough, he was never happier than when his face was buried in a book. She looked up, and it was always up now - he was growing so fast, and the smile broadened. Her son was becoming a young man and she was pleased that he had few of the faults she heard of so often these days. She was proud of both her children but often wondered what the future held in store for them. Fin, always so worried about other people and their problems, would go through life as a friend to all with rarely a harsh word for anyone, except those who ignored his attempts at empathy. Hence his current dislike of Willis. Lillibet on the other hand sailed through life without a care in the world, just as long as she had one or two trusted friends about her. Everyone loved Lilli, and she accepted their affection as her due. She was a pretty young thing and on first meeting everyone was captivated. Yes, family life probably couldn't get much better than this.

Lidine was content with life, and Life seemed to be content to leave her to drift, at her own pace, through motherhood.

Fin carried the bag downstairs followed by his mother, who still fretted about the possibility of him falling over his own feet on the way down. She'd probably never get over that – it's what mothers do, no matter how old their children.

Lilli kissed Fin goodbye at the front door and Lidine followed him to the car. Jarmon stuffed the bag in the boot and gave her a peck on the cheek that somehow transformed into a full-on snog.

'Oh, good grief, get a room for Heaven's sake.' Lilli shouted as the two laughed at her discomfort. To their daughter's mind there was a time and a place for that sort of thing and seven-thirty in the morning on the drive was neither. But she grinned anyway.

The sun was already beating down in preparation for the heat of the day ahead and all was as it should be in their little cocoon of a family.

'Bye bye Fin.' called Lilli as Lidine said her farewells to Fin and he climbed into the car with his father.

'Have fun Fin. See you on Thursday' said Lidine, and the car drew away into the warm summer day. She turned back to the house and her daughter.

'Come on then madam, let's get you ready for school.'

As they pulled out onto the main road Jarmon looked at his son.

'Okay Fin?'

'Yes fine Dad. I've been looking forward to this all term.'

'Good-oh. I know you'll enjoy the trip.' He paused. 'By the way, how's things on the sleep front. Still having nightmares? Only you haven't been waking up so much recently.'

Fin stared ahead as he replied.

'No, I'm fine, honest. They seem to have gone away. For good with a bit of luck.' And he grinned. Jarmon relaxed and thanked God that his son may well have outgrown the problem that had dogged his sleep for so long.

As they arrived at the station for the train to take Fin to school they both got out and walked around to get the bag from the car. Jarmon bent (he was still the tallest in the family, but not for much longer, he thought) and kissed his son.

'See you in three days mate.' he said, ruffling the boy's hair. 'Give us a ring if there are any problems'.

'Honestly Dad! There won't be. I'm going to have a great time, don't worry.'

'Oh I won't. Well maybe just a bit, but I'm your dad. It's allowed. Anyway here's the train, so get going.'

Fin scuttled off through the platform gate.

'See ya dad.'

And he was gone.

Jarmon turned and drove off to work with Billy Joel for company. He turned the CD up far louder than was necessary and rampaged through the quiet Cheshire countryside to the office in Chester.

All was right with the world, and the day looked set to be the first real day of the, so far, elusive English summer.

Fin settled back in his seat for the thirty-minute journey to Appleton. He felt a little bit guilty about lying to his Dad, but there was no point in worrying him about The

Nightmare anymore. He had decided that it was something he had to cope with. After all there wasn't much anyone could do was there? And he had begun to overcome the fear that he had always felt when the world decided to rush past him. It wasn't that the dreams were any better, just that he was finally getting used to them after so much time. They no longer made him whimper or cry out in his sleep and that was a huge relief. It was only in the last few weeks that he had managed to cope so well with his disturbed nights - maybe it was all part of his growing-up. If that was the case maybe adolescence wasn't going to be as bad as the social skills and slightly embarrassing sex education classes made out. If his Mum didn't wake in the night then he must be suffering in silence, because, like all Mums, she always knew if either of her children made the slightest sound whilst abed. So at least he wouldn't be waking any of his roommates during the trip. Anyway, Tam's snoring could drown out a jet engine at full throttle once he got started. His close friends were the only people outside of the family who knew about the problem and they wouldn't let on to anyone else. Tam and Simeon were the sort of friends you could trust with your life, probably through you whole life. That was a comforting thought. He liked the idea of always having these same friends around him, along with Nell, forever.

'Won't happen, mind, but it's a nice idea.' he said, and then looked around sheepishly. Eek! He thought, blushing, maybe I am a nutcase after all, talking to myself. What a dickhead!

He passed the rest of the journey staring out at the villages and landscape as they sped by and contemplating the fun to be had with your mates on a three-day sojourn away from prying parental eyes.

In the event it took almost five hours by coach to get to Eskdale, including a one and a half hour wait in traffic on the M6. Tam, Simeon and Fin passed the time playing cards, chatting about nothing in particular and reading. Tam read Clive Barker, which was always a little too dark for the other two; Sim had just discovered Bernard Cornwell's modern-day seafaring yarns and Fin was engrossed in Koontz at the moment. For them the long journey flew by. It must have passed even faster for Willis. He slept the whole way and no-one felt inclined to wake him. Like it or not, he was always a loaner.

On arrival they were all shown their allocated rooms and made their own decisions regarding beds. The three friends were sharing with Charlie Robinson and Mark Antrobus as well as the ever-morose Willis. Charlie and Mark did everything together, and while not part of the Fin-Tam-Sim triumvirate, were pleasant enough company and well liked by their roommates.

After a very brief and cursory unpacking, the five headed down to the main reception to join the other boys and find out what immediate plans Mister Nutter had for them. His first words were a surprise to them all.

'For the duration of the trip call me Mike. I know it's not normally done, but we're out of school now and it will make life a lot easier for us all if you don't have to keep calling me Mister Nutter all the time. Okay?'

All the boys were in agreement. This was brilliant! Not only were they out and about without so many of the restrictions of school, but also Mister Nutter wanted to be on first name terms with them. He was more like a surrogate uncle than their English teacher. Things were just getting better and better.

'Right then, off you go lads. Have a look around, but don't do anything stupid and don't wander off. Back here for six o'clock on the dot for din-dins. Go on then. Shoo!'

And off they went, heading for the lake that bordered the land surrounding the hostel.

As they left, Michael Nutter considered the effects of letting the boys drop the formality of the school rule regarding the 'Mister' appellation. On the whole it was probably going to help things along during the holiday. He just hoped that it wouldn't cause ructions when they returned to the classroom environment. Probably not, in his opinion. The lads were all pretty sensible and would hopefully appreciate the less formal atmosphere he was trying to adopt for these three days. He had discussed the matter with the only other adult along on the trip, Mister Lightfoot, and it was Herbert who had suggested they let the boys call him Bert. As the classics teacher he always enjoyed role-playing in the classroom to get his points across and knew that the boys liked the relaxed attitude he always tried to foster.

Herbert Lightfoot entered reception as the boys were leaving.

'Enjoy yourselves boys, but not too much messin' about.' he called as they rushed passed.

'Okey-dokey Bertie, me ol' mate!' called one of the crowd. Raucous laughter dwindled into the distance as the boys raced down to the lake-edge.

Hmm. Not too sure about the Bertie. That was that young devil Antrobus, if he wasn't very much mistaken. Still the masters had both agreed, so he was going to have to put up with a bit of leg pulling until the lads became used to the first name terms.

The two masters sat at one of the tables in the café that would serve as their main meeting place during the stay. One in his early thirties, fit and at the peek of his physical and intellectual powers, capable of turning more than a few feminine heads and opposite him a man now in bespectacled late middle-age and beginning to run to fat, but still displaying all the signs of an active life spent doing exactly what he had always wanted to: keeping fit and healthy and teaching the boys in his care how to be men.

The two grinned across at each other.

From the day Michael had joined the staff at Appleton as a young and inexperienced novice, Bert had noticed that he had that spark that led all the boys to like him. Not just as a very good master, but as a friend, that favourite uncle who always knew the right thing to say whatever the situation. That was not to say he wasn't strict. All the boys knew how far they could push him and that exceeding the bounds he set on class discipline would bring down his very considerable wrath. Bert also knew that Mike still looked up to him as a mentor and it was gratifying to know that even after thirty-five years at the same school, he could engender such friendship and approbation in the younger teachers. Good Lord! Was it really that long he'd been there? It seemed like no time at all. The two were ever the best of friends, despite the age difference, but unlike Joe and Pip they had never had a cross word, not in the thirteen years they had worked together. Coming from different generations occasionally gave them slightly different outlooks on life, but never enough to cause them any real grief.

'Well, hopefully it will help to make the trip a bit more fun for them.' said Michael.

'Jolly well hope so, there has to be an upside to having to put up with being called Bertie. I don't suppose there's any chance they might revert to Bert is there?'

'I wouldn't get you hopes up Herbert.'

Well, yes, I suppose it could be worse, couldn't it?' replied Mister Lightfoot, 'Oh, well, down to business. What's on the agenda for tonight then?'

Michael glanced down at his notes.

'So far as tonight's concerned, there's nothing on. We can do as we please. But as we said when we first arranged the trip, they've had a long drive up, so let's get them out for the evening. After tea we can walk for a couple of hours to blow the cobwebs away, and then get them bedded down.'

'Even so, I think we're in for a late night Mike. You know what they'll be like on the first night. Probably all three nights. God help us.'

'We've handled it okay before Bert, and this lot are far better than last year's bunch.'

'Aye, true enough. So that's this evening sorted. We've got the play on Tuesday evening and the trip on to the bobbin mill on Wednesday afternoon. That still leaves plenty of time for mischief doesn't it? Surely we aren't going to hike all the rest of the time? I'm not sure I'm up to it any more.' said Bert with a self-deprecating smile.

'Rubbish man! You may be retiring in a couple of year's time, but you'll still out do us all. I've had to take a few of your famous strolls before, remember? We'll be fine. And a lot of these lads never walk further than the tuck shop. As long as we don't push it too much we'll all be okay and I'm sure they will have been forewarned by some of the older lads.'

'You're right, of course. So it's up to me to plan the route?'

'Of course. You have done some forward planning I trust?'

'You trust correctly.' smirked Bert. 'Used to come here as a lad. We'll start easy and then floor them on the last day. Mumsy and Daddy will wonder what the Hell they've been up to when they get home. I guarantee their little treasures will want an early night and sleep the sleep of the just on Thursday. I'm going to shatter the little beggars on Thursday morning. Up at six-thirty, out at seven-thirty and walking for six hours. That should do the job.'

'Bloody-hell Bert! This is an English trip with a bit of hiking thrown in, not The Strongman. Remember, I said some of them aren't used to exercise.' Mister Nutter seemed genuinely worried.

'Now who's worried about the walks? Surely not Mister Superfit Adonis, the pinup of the Girls School. No, I can't believe that.' laughed Bert. 'Don't you bother your little head young sir, we'll have a great time.'

Now Dick (8)

Richard Hedd sat alone in his flat wondering what he should do about Leon. They had been friends for a long time and he was having trouble equating the man he knew with the one he'd met last night. Previously he had considered Leon as a little mysterious, even secretive, but never in his wildest dreams, or worst nightmares, had he thought that Leon could be even remotely unbalanced. Now he had no option but to consider the possibility that he was a complete nutter and he'd met plenty of them during his time at work. By the end of the meal last night he had left under a cloud as Leon had told him to 'at least think about it' and 'come back when his mind was clearer'. Well his mind was clear, as it had been all day and he couldn't get away from the absolute belief that Leon had lost it, big time. Having said that, the big black man had spoken very matter-of-factly about his 'gift', with no sign of having any sort of psychotic episode that might have explained his story away as purest fantasy. What's more, Leon had offered to give him a demonstration of his abilities, but only if he returned alone the following night and adhered to his commitment not to tell a soul. Dick took that to mean without a straitjacket and white-coated officials in attendance. He'd left the manor shaken to his core and had been trembling uncontrollably for most of the journey back to the flat, where he drank a large gin and tonic as he sat alone in front of blank TV. Eventually sleep had claimed him and he'd woken feeling distinctly rough but a little more able to think straight about the strange conversation of the night before and, as the day had progressed he had to admit that it did tend to explain a lot about his friend. His equilibrium returned as the day wore on – the night before he'd had trouble driving home such was his state of mind.

Luckily it was one of his days off, so at least he didn't have to think about anything else today, but maybe it would have been better if he could have taken his mind off the previous night's proceedings.

Having spent all day going over and over what had been said he still couldn't see how Leon could be serious, but there had been no hilarity in anything that his friend had said. Leon had been in deadly earnest and wanted, well Dick was unsure about exactly what Leon did want. He said that a partner would help in the work to be done and he wouldn't trust another soul with the information he was offering to his friend. Dick could understand that – who else would have even stayed until the end of his descriptions of what he'd seen and done?

The whole thing was preposterous, but still he was trying hard not to believe that his closest friend was a lunatic. Eventually he made up his mind to return that night and try to find out what could have caused such a change in the man's character. Maybe that was it. Maybe Leon had always had these fantasies and it was just that no one had the slightest inkling of what lay beneath his benevolent façade.

'Please God, don't let my only good friend be a loony. Please no, not Leon.' He almost wept with frustration and had absolutely no idea how best to approach the problem, mainly because he couldn't quite decide what the problem was.

In a strange way though it would explain all the things that had always puzzled Dick. Where did Leon go on his often prolonged trips away? Where did he get the money from for his exuberant home life? The house and gardens alone must have cost a fortune. Then there were the ornaments, the armour, the paintings and the endless antiques. Even though he was a copper Dick found himself wishing that Leon were some sort of master criminal rather than the outlandish reason his mate had given him.

'Oh, stuff it. I'll go off *my* head too if I don't start thinking about something else.' And with that he went to find his bike. As he set off for a quick ride to his local woods he considered how much more he would have enjoyed being a bobby a generation ago. A time when he would have known all the locals and could stop off for a chat as he toured his patch in the open air. Oh sure, in the bad weather it would have been a bit of a drag compared to driving, but on the whole he felt that the pros far outweighed the cons. On duty he only ever met people when things went wrong and knew that to most of them he was about as much use a chocolate fireguard, the damage had been done and he was just another symbol of the lack of comfort to be found in modern society.

Oh great, now he was feeling even worse than before he set off. He wondered whether anyone else felt the same way and found himself studying the few pedestrians and car drivers he passed. Were they as confused by the world as he was? Well no, to be honest it wasn't confusion, it was a sort of desperate longing for something that didn't seem to exist in modern Western Life, and maybe it didn't exist anywhere. He couldn't even put it into words, it wasn't adventure exactly, it was….. something! Did the people passing by also long for a different life, a return to 'the good old days'? Had there ever really been such a thing, or would he have been just as disillusioned if he'd been born fifty years ago? Well there was a question that he knew would never be answered. He was a modern police constable, he was good at it and usually enjoyed his life. The last twenty-four had been odd in that he'd become morose in a way he'd never been before. He realized that the problem was that Leon had opened the door to other possibilities, no matter how outlandish they appeared to be.

He knew without making a conscious decision that he would have to go back to see Leon. The worst that could happen was that all his fears about his friend were proven, at best it would be life changing to say the least. Satisfied that, even with certain misgivings, he was going back to the manse that evening, he turned his bike around and began the journey home. He even whistled and sang as he went, and he hadn't done that for years. 'Oh What A Beautiful Morning' may have seemed incongruous to anyone listening that afternoon, but even Howard Keel couldn't have done it better. Not while dodging potholes on a bike anyway.

Now Fin (9)

The boys had been fed and watered and now gathered for their after-dinner treat – a four-mile hike.

Bertie, as the boys had inevitably continued to call him, had explained the route and timing of the walk.

'A good stretch of the legs, to get you used to the country air.' he had informed them. 'We'll be out the best part of two hours, so I want you all to come armed with a bottle, preferably of water Antrobus.' This to Neil Antrobus, who had begun to smirk even before the sentence was finished. Whilst one of the quieter boys in school, he was obviously a bit of a rogue outside of it. One to watch when they were out and about.

'On our return there'll be time for a bit of supper before bed. Both Mike and I would like you all to remember that we are still the masters here and you will do as you're asked when you are asked. Is that clear to you all?

When the response was more muted than he'd hoped for he repeated the question.

'Is that clear to everyone?'

'Yes, sir!'

This time they all but shouted. Michael noted however that Antrobus had called 'Spot on Bertie!' Yes, definitely one to keep an eye on.

Mike led the way out of the hostel precincts with Bert bringing up the rear.

'Like an old mother hen' whispered Tam.

'Careful Riggleby.' came the teacher's voice from the back.

'Bloody hell, talk about AWAC ears.' mumbled Tam to Simeon and Fin as they walked on over the sheep-shorn grass.

'I heard that too sonny boy.'

Now all the lads were grinning at Tam's discomfort.

'I'd give up while you're behind, Tam.' shouted Charlie Robinson as they began to laugh en-masse at Tam's beetroot blush.

They walked steadily behind the leading teacher. Through Boot itself, over the pack bridge, past the old mill and off the road onto a sheep track to the right. Although the sun had been shining all the time they were in the hostel, and even now it was pleasantly warm, the track was like a miniature river. Several boys now realised why they had been advised to wear waterproof walking boots, and why they should have heeded the advice and not worn their rather fetching logo-strewn trainers.

'Too late now fellas' admonished Bertie, 'you've just got to make the best of it. On our other walks I'll try to avoid too much water, but it's inevitable we're going to get wet while we're here. Isn't that so Mike?'

'Fraid so lads, but you'll be able to dry out tonight. Don't worry. For now though, as my colleague has already said, you're stuffed. Sorry.'

Michael made a point of not sounding very sorry though. They had been warned about the possibility, indeed the probability, of rain, after all. 'Come on, get a move on, only another four miles to go.'

A light drizzle began to fall and, apart from those boys who chose to speak to the teachers, they became a muted and somewhat bedraggled little band. Mike noticed that Willis walked apart from the others and appeared to be quite happy to do so. In fact he noticed that, of all the lads, only Willis and Fin seemed to be enjoying themselves, though a few others were trying to make the best of things. Fin kept up an almost continuous stream of chatter about the scenery, the weather and the other boys.

Bert was surprised at the way Willis was reacting to the hike. He was obviously taking great pleasure in inspecting every new vista that presented itself to them and was even asking the occasional question. He seemed especially interested in a disused bobbin mill they came across which had been built alongside Wilham Beck. The millrun had collapsed and the massive wheel sat forlornly in the water alongside the building. There was an air of desolation about the mill but both Fin and Willis were eager to explore, though not together Mike noticed.

He called them back from the wheel.

'Careful Fin, Willis. Come on, we'd better keep going or we're still going to be out when it starts getting dark. Let's get a shift on Bert.'

'Right Oh, Mike. Follow me lads.'

'But it's great sir. Look at the roof. It's all still there. I bet it's nice and dry inside. Pity we can't get in out of the rain.' called Fin.

'Rain boy! This is just a bit of a mist. I'll warrant we'll see worse than this before the end of the trip.' answered Bert. His shout was greeted by mumblings of dismay by all but Fin and Willis. Even Mark Antrobus and Tam Riggleby had become more subdued as they walked, so they really must have been fed up. Mike smiled. Maybe Bert had been right and they were going to get a quiet night after this. Certainly the boys gave every indication of being very tired indeed, bar Fin and Willis who seemed to be growing more energetic as the walk progressed.

By the time they reached the warmth of the hostel most of the boys were ready for bed and all but half a dozen headed straight off to their rooms. After a cup of warming hot chocolate all but two retired. To the surprise of neither of the masters, it was Fin and Willis who were still wide-awake and apparently eager to keep their discussions going. They had sat with the teachers in the smoky lounge. The furniture had all seen better days and the mustard coloured walls were hung with faded prints of the surrounding country. The four lone occupants were seated around a battered old card table, the teachers with a cup of tea, the boys with cocoa. The boys, while sitting close together, were still not talking to each other, but more to, and through, the teachers.

'Good Lord lads, what's got into you? Aren't you even a little bit tired?' asked Mike.

'Well maybe a bit sir,' answered Willis, 'but I really liked the walk, and the mill'

'Yeah, definitely the mill.' put in Fin, as Mike held up his hand.

'It's Mike and Bert remember Will.' he reminded the boy.

'Sorry sir.... I mean Mike. It's just that I'm not used to it yet. Even my guardians like to be called sir and ma'm. It seems a bit odd, that's all.'

'Okay son, but try to remember.' Mike urged. 'This is supposed to be a break from the formality of school.' He smiled. 'We're glad you enjoyed it lads. Before we go back home, we'll visit another operational bobbin mill, well it's a museum really, a few miles away, but it was still turning out stuff up until the nineteen sixties, so you'll be able to see what they were like to work in. Hopefully some of the others will find it a bit more to their liking than this evening's outing.'

'And it appears that you two were the only ones with any sort of interest in what we were looking at. So are you finally getting on?' asked Bert.

Mike almost cringed at the lack of subtlety demonstrated by his colleague. The boys also seemed a little taken aback by the question.

Fin looked over at Willis, unsure as to how to answer.

'Well, it's not that we never got on. We've just never really spoken.' he smiled uncertainly at Willis.

'We never seemed to have a reason to get to know each other before.' said Willis. 'I don't know any of the class that well really. They always seemed to have their mates and I never managed to get a look in, even though there were times when I wanted to. I just felt a bit left out. I've never felt like I belonged.'

'And we always thought you were a bit of a stuck-up misery guts who never wanted to get to know us. We're a nice lot really. Honest.' said Fin with a hurt expression whose pretence was dispelled by a smile.

'Yeah, I know that Fin. It's just that I struggle to make friends.' Willis hurried on. 'I always want to, but never seem to make the right impression. Since Mum and Dad died I've not really had much to smile about and I know that doesn't help. The Blades – my Aunt and Uncle, like me to call them Mister and Mrs or Sir and Ma'am, and that's an indication of how wonderful life is at home. So I know I've become a bit quiet and everything, but no-one's helped me much either, since the crash.'

This was the first time Fin had heard Willis talk about the car crash that killed his parents and he shuddered at the thought of life without his own Mum and Dad.

'What exactly happened Will?' asked Fin in a faint and sympathetic voice. 'No-one knows and there were all sorts of stories.' He stopped as though shocked that he'd asked the question and saw the disapproving look that passed between his teachers. 'Sorry Will, I didn't mean to pry, but maybe if you tell me..' he glanced at the masters, 'I mean us, about it, you might feel better. You know it's not always true what they say about A Friend In Need...'

The other three looked non-plussed.

'...Is A Pain In The Arse.' he explained.

The adults looked scandalised, but Willis laughed.

'*That* was always the problem. I always thought you'd think I was just a moaning minnie, and I'm not, not really. But if I go on about my parents I get upset and then I'd be a cry baby too. So I can't win you see. It's not fair, but that's how other kids are.

Even at my old school my friends didn't understand. It was almost a relief to be move to Appleton Hall after the Blades took me in.'

'The Blades?' asked Fin.

'Yeah' said Willis, who was beginning to look upset.

'Don't feel you have to talk about it lad,' put in Bert, 'after all, it must still be a bit difficult for you.'

'No that's okay sir. I haven't really told anyone about it. My Aunt and Uncle have heard everything from the police and the hospital, but they don't ever talk to me about Mum and Dad.' Willis smiled weakly. 'I was told what happened by the policeman who went to tell them about it. He took me to one side to let me know. I'd been staying with them for a couple of days while my Mum and Dad had a weekend break for their wedding anniversary.'

'They were driving home on the Sunday night last Summer when a couple of idiots decided to have a race down the road they were on. It happens a lot the policeman said. They reckon the car that hit Dad's was doing over a hundred when it smashed into them. They never stood a chance and the pillock driving the other car got away with a broken leg. That's all, just a broken leg'

There were tears in his eyes now and an air of deep melancholy had descended on the little group. The teachers both sat silently, but Fin looked about ready to burst into tears himself.

'The worst thing was, the policeman they sent to talk to me... he was really nice... and he told me that the guy who killed Mum and Dad had a son of his own, only two years old at the time. Apparently he'd told everyone who'd listen that he'd be devastated if anything happened to his little boy, but didn't seem to care about me and my family. Said it was worth the risk for the adrenaline rush. Bastard!'

'Now then Will, calm down' said Bert trying to settle the boy a little. Oh yes, he thought, and how am I supposed to do that in a situation like this? He settled for patting the boy sympathetically on the shoulder.

Probably best to let him get it out of his system, since by all accounts, this was his first chance since the crash to talk to someone about the whole tragic incident.

'Oh Willis, I'm so sorry. I didn't know. I just thought you were standoffish and awkward. I never really thought about it before, but the idea of never seeing Mum and Dad again – it's just awful.' And with that he put his arm around his new-found friend and tried to offer some anguished comfort as Willis cried silently for a few seconds, big bitter tears rolling down his face.

'Don't worry Fin, I'll be okay.' Willis sniffed and wiped his nose on the sleeve of his jumper, looking a little sheepish. 'If I can dig myself out of being so depressed I'll be fine. I've got to be adult about it says Uncle Ralph.' (Willis pronounced it Rafe) 'Thanks for listening. I think it's helped just taking to someone. I hadn't realised what the other lads thought of me, I just couldn't get myself into any of the little gangs at school. I've been so fed up...(sniff) and...(sniff) so...(sniff) so lonely.'

A silent message passed between the two adults.

'Okay, lads.' said Mike putting his hand on Willis' shoulder. 'Time for bed, hey? Come on. Try to get some sleep and then have some fun tomorrow. At least you know your not all alone anymore Will, and maybe Fin will think a bit more about your situation, eh Fin?' But it wasn't an admonishment, merely a comforting comment.

All four were subdued as they left the lounge, but Willis wiped his eyes on his sleeve and grinned sheepishly at Fin, who was still looking pale at the thought of the other boy's miserable home life, as they walked up the stone stairs and the mood began to lift.

'Don't forget mine's the top bunk.' whispered Fin as they left the teachers at the turn of the dimly lit corridor.

'Oh yeah? Race you for it.' challenged Willis as he began to run down the tiled passage.

'Oi, not fair!' called Fin as he began to give chase.

Their feet echoed loudly as they ran laughing towards bed.

'Quietly boys!' thundered Bert behind them, with various gestures and 'shushing' motions.

Their headlong rush slowed as they approached the door to the room they shared with the other four boys, and Fin, who had arrived first, pushed it open with a flourish and an elegant bow.

'After you sire.' he said as he swept his hand towards the darkened room. The two of them tiptoed in and, after silently undressing, they climbed into bed, with Willis taking the lower bunk.

'Night, night Will, sleep tight.' whispered Fin.

'You too Fin.' came the already sleepy reply. 'Thanks.'

Neither boy really knew what the gratitude was for, but both went to sleep content that something had passed between them that had a deeper meaning than a simple word.

Neither of them had even the slightest idea of the horrors that lay in store in the days and weeks ahead.

Now Dick (10)

Dick set out early for the hall in the woods – he could think of no good reason to delay the visit. This was either going to be a complete disaster with goodness knows what consequences, or the start of something quite extraordinary. He tried to keep his mind on other things as he cycled over the moat and onwards up the drive towards the house. Leon was sitting in the garden as he approached, and appeared to have no doubts about how the evening was going to progress. The big smile was there as ever, but Dick felt wary - in a way he never had before - with his big friend.

'Dick, great to see you again. Glad you decided to give it a go.' When Dick did no more than give an uncertain smile, the grin widened. 'Come on man, what's the worst that can happen?'

'I end up having you committed, you daft sod' grated back Dick, 'and who would blame me? Certainly not anyone with an ounce of sense. Hells Teeth Leon, I seem to have checked all my common sense at the door.'

'Ah yes Dick, but where we're going good sense is not always a requirement.' laughed Leon as he ushered his friend into the house and over to a pair of huge Victorian armchairs which sat in front of a small fire in the large stone fireplace. 'From an abbey in Yorkshire a few years ago' Leon informed him

'Sit down, sit down and I'll explain my plans for this night's entertainment.' He passed Dick a cup of coffee, 'No alcohol I'm afraid. We both need clear heads for this.'

He settled into a chair opposite Dick and steepled his fingers under his chin. He looked hard at his friend and then began to reiterate some of the points he had made during the last visit.

'Okay Dick, I daresay you've had plenty of time to think over the things I told you last night and I fully appreciate your scepticism. Indeed I'd have been disappointed if you hadn't been a little… no, on the contrary, very… yes, very, disturbed by some of what I revealed.'

'Leon, I'm still not convinced you aren't mental. That's why I had to come again, to give you a sort of second chance.' Dick broke in.

'Yes, yes. I understand. Honestly I do. So I've decided to give you more detail, in fact all the details of what we're about to do. There's no point to any of this unless I can convince you, and I'm convinced that I can. No equivocation. Otherwise, I might as well have just kept my mouth shut and we could have gone on as before. It's just that I've felt the need to share it for a while. I have this sort of mounting tension in me that I'm sure is coming from elsewhere. *Or elsewhen.*'

'Oh damn-it-all Leon, just get on with it.' barked Dick.

'Alright, alright, calm down. But we will return to this later on, I promise.' said Leon, a little more seriously than he had been a moment before.

'This evening and tonight Dick, cos it's going to take longer than just a few hours, I proposed to demonstrate to your complete satisfaction, that everything I've told you is true. However, throughout your time here tonight you must do exactly what I tell you, when I tell you, or we could both end up in a world of hurt. This is not a game, and it is all true. Get it wrong and it can also be very painful, both physically and, probably more importantly for both of us, mentally. Before we go any further I'm going to give you a very small idea of what I'm talking about. Then we can decide how to proceed further and I'll answer any questions'

Dick was beginning to look worried again as Leon went on, but before he could interrupt, Leon held a placating hand in front of him and continued.

'Please Dick wait just a little longer, you won't be disappointed.'

He gave a shrug as though deciding what to do next, though Dick suspected his friend knew precisely what was coming.

'We're going to start off indoors, until you have a better idea of where we're going with this and we can repeat anything you're unsure of. We may as well begin now okay? And here's as good a place as any.'

Leon dimmed the lights as he made his way to the large oak table in the centre of The Hall. A large pile of newspapers along with scraps ripped out of them covered the far end. A couple of folders were also stuffed with the clippings.

'A bit of a daft hobby.' Leon explained, as he swept the papers onto the floor and kicked them away. 'Always looking for signs…'

The sentence hung enigmatically between them.

He beckoned Dick to sit on the other side of the huge slab of wood and once they were both seated he edged in towards the table. Perched on the edge of his chair, he placed his hands before him on the table. He beckoned Dick closer and seemed to lose a modicum of patience when his friend seemed reluctant to begin, now that the moment was at hand.

'Come on man, there's no point in holding back now. Don't worry, I'll take it nice and slow. Ask if there's anything you're uncomfortable with.'

He proffered his hands, palm up, to Dick, and taking his hands placed them in what appeared a very specific position on the table.

'What's this for Leon, we're not at a séance for God's sake.' said Dick. He was aware that his hands were beginning to sweat, even in the cool of the Great hall.

'It's to stop you fidgeting, you old woman! Now close your eyes and try to relax.'

Leon released the other man's hands and sat back a little in his seat, hands still resting lightly on the table. The subdued lighting helped a little, but Dick was too keyed up to be able to relax properly.

'Come on Dick, it'll be okay. Just try to clear your mind.' Leon could see the perspiration on his friend's forehead, 'Everything will be fine.'

Leon's voice had the desired effect, although Dick still found himself in the uncomfortable position of sitting in a darkened room with a man whose mental stability was highly suspect. He had to keep reminding himself that this was Leon, a man he knew better than anyone else in the world. However, the nagging thought kept creeping around his mind that he had already discovered that he didn't know him half as well as he'd thought.

'Bloody Hell Leon, what am I doing here?' he murmured involuntarily.

'You're going to have the time of your life my friend' whispered his long-ago schoolfriend, 'now sit back, this will take a while. Just relax.' And oddly he did. After all, if he couldn't trust Leon, even in this strange situation, who would he ever be able to trust?

Leon rose and switched on an unseen hi-fi with a small remote control. Vivaldi's Four Seasons started up quietly in the background, and Dick found himself floating into a twilight of half-wakefulness. His mind wandered and although not sleeping, he wasn't fully conscious either. He was vaguely aware of the other man moving slowly, silently around the room, dimming the lights a little more, turning the music up a little loader.

Leon rejoined his friend at the table and Dick opened his eyes. The Four Seasons continued their procession through the year.

'Right Dick, lets get to it.' said Leon softly, 'close your eyes again and try to empty your mind. I'm going to take you on a journey. Not a long one, but this will blow your mind.'

Dick sat in the darkness of his eyelids and waited. Leon took his hands again and raised them slightly off the tabletop. He could hear Leon breathing slowly opposite him and felt a slight draft across the back of his hands, as though a door had suddenly been opened to the garden. He gave a small involuntary shudder and Leon released his grip.

'Take a look Dick' he murmured.

Dick opened his eyes and blinked in surprise.

'Soddin' 'ell Leon.' he breathed and Leon grinned.

The room had remained exactly as it had been, but now the table and chairs and he and Leon were ten feet closer to the fireplace. Oh, and the chairs on which they sat were now on top of the table, on which there was laid a beautifully embroidered tablecloth, beneath their feet.

'*Taa Raa!*' breathed Leon sotto voce, as he climbed down and placed the chair back on the wooden floor.

'How the bloody hell did you do that? How much does this table weigh? How did you manage to move me without me feeling it? Leon! It's just incredible. Oh God. I'm feeling just a little faint.' Dick sat for a moment, still unsure of exactly what had just happened. Then he gingerly stood and lowered himself down to the floor, replacing his chair as well, but rather more slowly than Leon had done.

'Leon this is more than a little scary.' he said - and he meant it. His mind was in a whirl, quite literally. His heart was threatening to punch a hole in his chest and he was now sweating profusely. This was too weird for words. He was dumb struck. His old mate could move things without doing anything. And big things! The table must have weighed a fairly large fraction of a ton and he himself was no feather to be lifted onto a table so effortlessly. And where had the tablecloth come from?

'Told you so, me old mate.' smiled Leon as he stood opposite.

'But Leon. I'm just staggered. I know you told me all sorts last night, but how did you do it? Oh, sit down you grinning loon and talk to me. This is just breathtaking.'

His mind was still racing, this was so far beyond anything he had ever encountered before. He was a copper of the first water and had seen allsorts, but nothing, not even the odd conversation the night before had prepared him for the actuality he was now experiencing. This was totally beyond him - so much more than a parlour trick or sleight of hand and certainly not the result of a mere lunatic mind. All his misgivings about Leon had vanished to be replaced by a somewhat humbling awe of what had just happened. He sat down by the fire again, heavily. Numbed in mind and body by the presence of, for want of a better word, magic. This was too enormous.

'Explain please.' he finally managed.

'Okay Dick, I'll tell all. But be warned, I haven't even started yet, and I'll have to go back over a lot of what I said last night.'

He turned away to brighten the lights and change the music. The room was fully illuminated again and the Baroque was replaced by Tubular Bells.

'Good choice Leon,' chided Dick, 'nothing like The Exorcist to lighten the spirits. What, no more music to match the mood? I assume you need calm for it to work. Whatever it is. Along with dimmed lights to weave your magic.'

'No, that was all for your benefit. I thought it added to the atmosphere - made you feel more like something special was about to go down. It's not magic and I can do it anywhere and anytime. All I need to make it happen... is me.' said Leon with just a hint of impatience. 'I told you all this before. Now maybe you'll be a little more inclined to listen.'

'Oh yes Leon, I'm all ears. So explain it all to me again. Slowly, cos I'm new to this remember, and you've been doing it for... how long?'

'Since as long as I can remember. Nanna Messenger taught me when I was only about four or five. She swore me to secrecy on pain of becoming a zombie.'

'What! She threatened you with zombies.' Dick gave a short laugh.

'Oh yes Dick and I believed her. Remember all that spooky voodoo stuff she used to tease us with. She told me years later that it was the only thing she could think of to make sure such a small child didn't tell a soul. All rubbish of course, but I only discovered that when I was in my teens. I'd been so frightened of annoying her and becoming another member of the undead brethren, but it was all garbage. Done for all the right reasons of course, but I had more than a few sleepless nights, believe me. Even when I could only move small things, it wouldn't have been very sensible to start showing off in school, for example. 'So what would she think of you telling, and showing, me? Asked Dick.

'Oh, I think she'd be fine with it, she always had a soft spot for you. And anyway, I've had this strange feeling for a couple of months. I told you earlier, something's going on and it's my guess that I'll need some help sometime soon. And you're the only one I'd ever trust with any of this.' He smiled again, with no trace of being patronising or any embarrassment at revealing the depth of his feelings of friendship towards Dick.

'But who else can do this? Is it passed down through the family, or is it more generally available, to those In The Know?' prompted Dick.

'You know, I really don't know myself, but I suspect that some make money from it. The odd so-called magician at least. There are some things that can't be done even with smoke and mirrors. Apparently, the way Nanna told it, it's all to do with channelling the energy that's all around us. Shift it the right way and you can do almost anything. Just wait 'til we've had another quick cuppa and I'll show you something even better.'

With that they both retired to the kitchen whilst Mike Oldfield entertained them on a myriad instruments.

'So, go on then Leon. What's next?'

'First Dick, let me emphasize that this really isn't kids' stuff, even though I did start very young. Lots of people can do it and many, particularly children, perform very small amounts of this sort of thing when they sleep. Don't you ever remember waking up after that dream most people have about flying, and feeling as though, at the end of it, you really have been falling? Dick nodded. 'Well that's because you did fall. Oh, probably only a fraction of an inch, but that sort of minor levitation is how Nanna first saw my latent talent. I was already living with her after my mother and father died, and while I was still a toddler she caught me hanging around my bed. Well actually, about a foot over my bed, the way she told me. Fast asleep and floating there.'

Dick grinned.

'Always knew you were a flighty beggar, Leon. Always full of hot air.'

'Oh, hardy har har.' mocked Leon as he passed Dick another coffee. 'I promise to wipe that smile off your face before the hour is up. If you still want to find out more, that is.'

'Yeah, like I'm going to want to leave now.' answered Dick with heavy sarcasm.

The two returned to the Great Hall and settled once again in front of the fire. The room had become warmer, Dick noticed, and the air had a vaguely musty smell to it.

'Getting a bit close in here Leon. What about opening a window?'

'No point. When we get started again the smell will just come back anyway. It's a sort of by-product of using the energy streams and so's the heat. It seems that the larger the object, or the bigger the lateral shift, the more energy builds up. This causes some sort of ionisation that can have some pretty startling effects. But I'll come on to all that a bit later. For now, let's try another demonstration. Come on outside Dick. Where's your bike?'

Dick, feeling slightly nonplussed followed him outside to the courtyard, where his shiny, well tended bicycle stood in a corner. They both walked over to it and Leon took the handlebars and kicked away the stand. Dick had no idea what he could have in mind.

'Not trick cycling as well?' he joked, 'or maybe the wall of death around the quad?'

'Bit difficult, given that there's only three sides to it don't you think? replied Leon. He smirked over at his friend as he wheeled the bike out to the drive. One of the peacocks gave a half-hearted call as they approached. The sun was still hovering above the trees, even though it was now fairly late in the evening. The air was still warm and heady with the scent of flowers. The gardens looked magnificent in the amber light cast through the trees and Dick was struck again by the wonders Leon had wrought with his little piece of heaven in the heart of Cheshire.

'Right. You stay here Dick. I'm just popping round the back with your bike. Back in a mo.' And with that Leon disappeared around the corner.

Dick stood staring after him with a bemused expression. What on earth was he going to do with that? There was a momentary rumble of what sounded like thunder in the distance and his eyes roamed the sky in search of clouds. There were none, just the clear blue sky now beginning to fade as the sun completed its arc. Strange sound, he thought, but almost immediately switched his attention back to Leon who had just returned from the rear of the house, minus the bike.

'Come on. You'll love this. This is A Big One, Dick'.

Dick thought back to the previous night, and the tale that had really decided him that his friend was a sandwich short of a picnic. It was so ridiculous that he still couldn't bring himself to believe it. Even after the events of this evening.

'Yeah, sure Leon.'

If he caught the note of scepticism in Dick's tone, Leon chose to ignore it as he led the way through the trees behind the rose beds.

'Ah, here we are, odd that I never noticed it here before. Come and see Dick.' He parted some large almost prehistoric looking ferns to reveal…

'What in God's name have you done to my bike Leon!' yelled the owner of the now very sorry looking machine. The entire frame was rusted through, almost paper thin in places. The tyres had perished away to almost nothing. Surprisingly the seat seemed to have faired the best, but Dick still wouldn't have relished having to sit on it for the journey home. Huh, journey home! Who was he kidding? This was an ex-bike now. It wasn't going anywhere, except maybe in a skip and there was even a problem there. The bike was enmeshed in the roots of a very large and obviously very ancient oak tree. The tree had grown through the frame of the bike, warping it hopelessly out of shape and now towered some sixty odd feet above the wreckage. The gnarled trunk gave every appearance of being there to stay, and so did the bike.

'I just left it here Dick. Nothing else – honest.' replied Leon in a little-boy-in-trouble voice. 'Didun do nuffink copper and ders nowt you can do abaht it, right!' He gently scuffed the ground with his shoe as he peered at Dick from under his beetled brow, but he was still grinning.

'You bugger. What on God's earth have you done? How could it have got into this state in five minutes?' But already Dick knew the answer to the riddle and once again his heart began to pound. Ye Gods, everything Leon had said was true!

Leon insisted that he check to make sure it was definitely his bike, and sorrowfully he did so. What was the point? There was no other way this strange spectacle could have come about, it had to be his virtually new and recently pristine machine. He'd loved that bike. It had certainly cost enough, what with the computer, the low profile wheels and the stylish Y-frame. Fairly obviously not alloy though, given the quite staggering amount of rust it had acquired in the last ten minutes. But it also had the unmistakable owner's mark of his police number painted under the seat. It was somewhat obscure now but he was sure it was his handiwork. Yes, it was his bike. And Leon could bloody well buy him a new one!

'Okay Dick, leave it there and we'll go back, I haven't finished yet. The best is still to come.'

'Well I hope it's a bit better than knackering my flaming bike!' He accompanied Leon back to the house in glum silence. That had been a damn good bike and his supposed friend had rendered it useless – in a very big way!

'Oh calm down you big girl's blouse, and wait here.'

Leon disappeared around the far corner of the house and again there came an ominous rumble of thunder, even though the sky was stubbornly cloudless. Dick was beginning to put two and two together to get a reasonably certain four and wasn't the least surprised when the sound died down moments before Leon returned. However, when Leon strolled back, Dick did receive yet another shock.

'My bike! And good as new! But how?'

Leon grinned and handed the machine back.

'Check it again please, just to satisfy yourself. I promise it's the same one you just inspected, with that keen policeman's eye of yours.'

'Amazing.' was all Dick could find to say. Then he thought about the implications and everything that he'd experienced in the last hour or so. '*Really amazing.* You really can do it can't you? You really can?'

He sat down heavily on the small wall surrounding the nearby rose bed.

Leon gave an almost Gallic shrug and raised his hands in supplication.

'I've never lied to you Dick and it would seem a bit daft to start now. I may not have always told you everything, but I've never lied.' Leon looked to be in deadly earnest here, but he also had a hint of smug about him.

'You bugger! So you took my bike, hid it in the woods for... for what... a couple of hundred years? And then went back after we had a look at it stuck in the tree and picked it up from *whenever* you left it. Is that what you're saying you just did?'

'Exactly mon amis, exactly.'

And this time he really did look smug as he turned to go back indoors ahead of Dick.

'Well, not exactly...' said the retreating figure.

'It was actually nearer to a four hundred.'

Now Fin and When Fin (11)

Even after the recounting of the circumstances surrounding the death of his parents, Willis felt oddly comforted by the fact that he had finally talked to someone about it. When he'd been forced to change schools and move in with his aunt and uncle, he had left behind what few friends he had. He had been a quiet lad even at the prep school, and knew how withdrawn he'd become since the tragedy and the move to Appleton. Yet for some reason he'd unburdened himself to the two teachers and Fin, and no-one had laughed at his tears, and all three seemed genuinely to want to help. Maybe things were going to get better. He said a short prayer, as he did every night, and finally felt as though someone was listening. Hopefully Mum and Dad, wherever they were, heard it too.

Maybe a prayer would have helped Fin, but he doubted it. Almost as soon as his head touched the pillow *It* began. He was so tired after the hike that he felt himself drifting off to sleep almost immediately.

Only after the cold draught from the direction of the window made him shiver under the bedclothes did he realise that sleep was not the first item on his agenda for tonight. As he looked out from his now chilly bed the dormitory walls faded and the surrounding hills and nearby lake became visible with a whisper of a breeze. The sound of the wind began to intensify in the moonlit gloom of the night. Surrounding trees cast long shadows as though they were trying to lift him from his mattress. After so many years he knew better than to try to resist the insistent tug of the dark vision.

Every night now the strange nightmare journeying took him. The fear, that even a few weeks ago was enough to bring on nausea and require the obligatory loo-run, was but a shadow of its former self though. Yes, he still broke out in a cold sweat that brought about shivers, but he'd come to realise that he was being shown something during the dark shrouded forays. He hadn't managed to work out exactly what was going on, but trusted that sooner or later all would become clear.

The wind began to howl in his ears and blast through his hair as he felt himself involuntarily turn onto his stomach and start to move over the landscape in the same direction that the storm was following, as though chasing the landscape as it raced away from him. His ears were already growing numb with the icy blast of the buffeting storm and his hands and feet felt wet from the stair-rod rain that was accompanying him on his flight. His hair became plastered against his face and the raindrops began to sting from the speed with which he moved. The whole world appeared mired in the tempest that clung around him like a cloak. He had found himself wondering if he was invisible to any late-night travellers – he'd supposed he must be, since the tabloids hadn't featured anything weirder than usual in the last few weeks. Certainly nothing along the lines of 'Birdboy unbound over Northwich' or 'Bat boy sucks neighbours dry' had illuminated any of the national press. The broadsheets worried about the future of the world, the tabloids still concentrated on the more important stuff – football, free CD's and Page 3. Not that Fin was that interested (well not much anyway).

More recently the storms would become so fierce that he found he couldn't see where he was going. That worried him. For all he knew he was being trailed around the world and the thought struck him that maybe one night he wouldn't return to his bed. That would be great, stuck in Outer Mongolia or somewhere in his jim-jams and nothing else. Suddenly the idea of wearing underwear in bed, something he never did, began to appeal. Especially when all he had at the moment was fly front pants held together with nothing more than a tie cord.

His brushed cotton pyjamas were now slicked against his wet body, and the cold was seeping into him more than it ever had before. Maybe this was the night that things were going to go wrong. His anxiety grew when he realised he was coming very close to the trees below him and appeared to be slowing. He'd never stopped during an excursion before.

The topmost branches were beginning to whip against his sodden pants.

Oh Lord, this was not good, it really was not good at all.

He dipped lower between the trees and into a small valley, housing a number of small, very old looking, buildings off to the left, and one much larger mill-like structure.

Now he really did become scared. The wind dropped, and he was left standing in the gloom in front of the mill. The storm swept off, leaving a silence undisturbed by anything other than Fin's sniffing. Great! To cap it all he'd got himself a cold too.

But, despite the quip, he wasn't feeling light-hearted as he quickly scuttled into the small doorway in the centre of the massive wall in front of him. All his old fears came racing back. He'd spent so long coming to terms with *The Nightmare* and now the *feckin'* thing had really stuffed him! (He liked "feckin'" cos it wasn't really swearing but gave you the same satisfaction when you said it loud enough.)

This trip hadn't followed the usual pattern, not at all. Whilst he was never comfortable with the nocturnal flights, he had at least managed to remain calm in the later ones. There was a certain routine that he'd adapted to. When it was all over he would always be returned to his bed, none the worse for the experience, and wake in the morning feeling as though he had at least had a reasonable night's sleep. So maybe that was all it was – a dream during his REM time, since he was always dry in the morning, even though sometimes, as tonight, he was absolutely sodden by the accompanying squall. He'd finally managed to rationalise *The Nightmare*, to a point.

It always followed the same pattern. Always.

Just before he fell asleep he was taken somewhere, sometimes at a leisurely pace and sometimes at a headlong rush. Occasionally he recognised his final destination, often he did not. Sometimes he was quite convinced that he was not even on the same planet, but he couldn't really be sure, and that seemed a little far-fetched even given the very strange circumstances. For many years everything seemed to rush past him and he was terrified of having his skull crushed or his neck broken. As a much younger child the visions alone were enough to make him call out. Then, fairly recently, the tone of the visions changed and he felt more in control, in an oddly...um... uncontrolled way. He couldn't stop what was happening but he could stop it from putting naked fear into him. They might be ultra-realistic dreams, phantasms sent for some unknown reason, he still wasn't completely convinced that he ever left his bed. He no longer spoke to anyone, not even Tam and Co., about what went on at night when he was supposed to be asleep. He was almost an adult now, and he would cope by himself damnit! He would handle it like a man. Just like his Dad would. Well, like Dad probably would.

Maybe it was all some sort of weird hallucination brought about by some chemical in the tap water. He was always dry when he awoke, though there always seemed to be storms and rain during his travels, and he'd never suffered any sort of injury, even when the landscape came shooting past at breakneck speed and at times very close indeed. He had also realised that the last few journeys had ended while he slept. He had no recollection of the return to his bed. Maybe that was another sign that he was getting over the whole thing. The idea had occurred to him that if he could relax to that extent during a supposed nightmare, he was probably well on the way to shedding the dark phantasms that had blotted his nights for so many years. He was growing up, that was the most obvious answer. He was finally outgrowing his childish fantasy horrors. As he reached his teens he had also come to realise that his failing eyesight was not going to result in blindness as he had always feared, and indeed the world of tinted contact lenses and all the fun to be had from eyes of different colours beckoned him. He supposed all these things were tied into *The Nightmare* in some way or other, what with the fading walls and things rushing away from him. He still remembered the strange feeling of looking down at his feet and seeing his whole body stretching off into an abyss so deep he could barely see his feet. As a child all these images had frightened him, to the extent that he became incontinent in the night and only slept peacefully whilst with Mum and Dad in their bed. Now it was clear to him, that as he overcame his normal adolescent day-to-day trials and tribulations, the nights were beginning to settle down too.

But he still received *The Nightmare* on an almost nightly basis and he still wished he didn't.

And it always followed the same pattern.

But not tonight.

Fin slid silently to the floor. His stomach felt so hollow and empty. The bile rose in his throat and he vomited freely, his whole body convulsing as he strained as he was gripped by absolute terror. What on earth was he going to do?

Slumped against a lichen encrusted wall, he wept, great shuddering gasps that wracked his whole being. Never in his life had he felt so alone, so totally alone. Sweat soaked his body and his thin pyjamas clung to his clammy skin. After several minutes he rose to his feet and began to look around him in a daze. He had to do something and soon. He shivered violently and it wasn't all due to the cold. Wiping his mouth on the back of his sodden sleeve he walked to the corner of the building, his whole body trembling at every step.

From the shadows cast by the mill he looked out into the gloom of the yard bordered by what looked to be offices and barns about twenty feet ahead.

The main rectangular block consisted of a large two-storey building with several large lean-to structures attached on the two narrower sides. He stepped around the corner nearest to him, after carefully checking that there was no-one around to see him in his nightwear. Inside the sheds he found himself confronted by huge piles of what looked to be newly hewn wood. Each of the horizontal poles was about ten feet long with the average thickness of a handspan and all had each been neatly arranged according to the type of wood. Small signs were nailed to the end of one pole in each stack, identifying them as alder, ash, birch and willow. The still, damp night air was filled with the scent of newly cut wood. The next shed was also filled from floor to rafters with poles, but this time with very little odour. This wood was obviously much older and drier.

Fingers of sunlight filtered through the surrounding trees and Fin realised that the night was ending. Panic gripped him and his heart began pounding heavily in his chest. He had no idea which way led back to the hostel at Boot, nor how far the journey. He would have difficulty explaining what he was doing here and the state of his clothing to anyone who found him sniffing around the mill. Panic was held in check, but just barely.

He edged around the next wall and into a lean-to with no outer wall, just large columns of wood, possibly oak, holding up the slate roof. A massive circular saw sat gleaming in the increasing light, its wicked teeth oiled and ready for the following day's carving to begin. It showed no sign of rust and looked like a relic from an old Hammer Horror film. All greased and ready to slice up its next sacrificial victim.

'Oh, please help... someone... anyone. Anyone who'll believe me when I tell them I'm lost anyway. I really didn't fly here in a storm, I just got lost that's all'

He was still muttering as he crept around the back of the building, keeping a wary eye over his shoulder for anyone emerging from the houses in the distance. He was so busy checking behind that he literally fell over the small boy dozing under the cover offered by a huge ramp behind the mill. The boy woke with a grumble and a moan as Fin jumped back and began to edge towards the bordering trees, his heart once again hammering against his ribs. By now he was so anxious that his already empty stomach threatened to start convulsing again. He held it in check as his desperate eyes sought some place of retreat. Nowhere obvious presented itself.

The waking lad lumbered his way to his feet, leaving an imprint in the slope that he'd been sleeping against.

Fin stared.

How could that be?

Then he saw the flakes caught up in the hair and clothes of the boy, who was vigorously trying to brush them off.

The slope, some fifteen feet high and twice that around the base, was made entirely from sawdust and shavings. Tons of it.

Fin eyed the boy in front of him warily.

'Alrart, alrart, Ahm ge'in up' the child muttered. 'Ahm cummin'. Carn ye see ahm cummin direc'ly'.

'Sorry.' whispered Fin, making shushing motions with his hand. 'Didn't see you. Please keep the noise down. Please.'

At least he'd managed to keep the edge of panic out of his voice.

'Ya wot?'

'Please keep quiet. I don't want anyone else to see me.' whispered Fin again. 'I'm lost and cold and frightened, and need help.'

'Ya don arf tark odd lad.' came the loud reply.

Great! A whole world to get lost in, and his first meeting was with a child who found it impossible to speak at less than the top of his voice.

'Oh, for Heaven's sake keep it quiet can't you? Look I don't come from around here and I'm lost. Could you point me in the direction of Boot? But quietly please.' Fin hissed.

'Oh aye. Boot. It's o'er yonder.' The boy pointed off into the trees. 'But it'll tak thee all day to wak theer, i's miles!' The reply was at least a little encouraging and the boy had managed to lower his voice to the hoped for whisper. 'Tha carn do it dress'd lak tha, tha pudd'n. Where's tha boots?'

'I lost 'em in the night. And my coat.' Fin lied. What else could he do?

The boy rubbed his arms vigorously to ward off the chill that was still in the air despite the early morning sun now reaching them through the trees.

'Tha poor bugga.' whispered the lad 'Wos tha name?'

'Fin... Finbar Lemott. And I'm glad to meet you.' Fin held out his hand.

'An ahm glad to make tha acquaintance too.' said the boy shaking the proffered hand enthusiastically. 'Ahm William Elms, an tha can call mi Bill, if'n tha' like. An if'n tha' needs a bit o' heat cum wi me. Ah 'ave t'key t'stem rum' he announced proudly retrieving the key from a string around his neck and hanging under his shirt.

This accent was giving Fin a headache. He clutched his stomach and doubled over to try to stem the tide of nausea that was suddenly sweeping over him. What that hell was a stem rum? Some weird alcopop? And why did it require a key?

The last thing Fin needed was alcohol. He wanted a coat and shoes so he could head back as soon as he could, and escape this odd little boy with his weird accent. It wasn't Lancashire and it wasn't Yorkshire. Given that Boot was apparently only a longish walk away, Fin could only assume it was a good old fashioned Lake District burr.

The urge to projectile vomit left him as quickly as it had arrived and Fin straightened up, a sheen of sweat now covering his body. He shivered violently.

'Are you ill, lad? Blimey, come over here and try to dry yourself out.' The concern was obvious in the boy's voice.

Bill turned and hurried over to a door in the back of the mill, just to the left of the massive pile of shavings. The door was opened without a problem and inside Fin could see a large oily steam engine, painted green, with a massive leather belt wrapped around a wheel and disappearing up into the roof.

Fin hurried over to join Bill.

'Don't worry, I just felt a bit sick for a second.' An understatement, thought Fin as he stood in the doorway, but of no consequence.

Bill smiled and beckoned him inside.

'Ah, of course,' thought Fin as he entered, 'a steam room, the rum with the stem engine in it.'

The floor was covered to a depth of almost a foot with wood shavings, and Bill began gathering armfuls and throwing them into the fire beneath the boiler.

'I'll open up the coal 'ole, that should help to warm you an' there's a coat over in the corner, and I think John left some boots o'er there.' Bill pointed to the far corner, past the engine, 'so yer can warm yer feet an' all.'

Fin did a double-take. 'Oi, where's the funny voice gone Bill?'

'What? What funny voice? It's you that's stopped acting like a daft lad. There was no need for it you know. I would have helped anyway. You looked so sorry for yourself out there.'

Looking more closely at Bill, Fin could see that they were probably of an age, though his new friend was a good head shorter, and of a much slighter build. In his dark, possibly brown eyes (it was still too dark to be sure), there was no trace of guile. He smiled as he brushed his mop of dark hair back from his now lively face, and seemed happy to have some company. There was something very strange going on here. For a start what was this boy doing asleep at the back of the huge mill? But Fin pushed such thoughts to the back of his mind, he had enough on his plate already without starting to interrogate strangers. For now he was glad to have met up with someone who didn't ask any awkward questions and seemed friendly enough.

In the corner he found a coat that looked as though it had been used in place of an oily rag, and a very worn pair of boots, minus laces. But Fin knew that in all probability he'd been lucky to find even these out in the Lake District hinterland. At least if it rained he couldn't possibly get wet, the ingrained filth on the coat would make it as waterproof as sealskin.

Bill had busied himself shovelling the wood into the boiler fire and soon Fin could hear it beginning to roar as he worked his way back to the far end of the room.

'That was quick Bill. Used firelighters did you? To get it started.' Fin asked.

'What's one of them when it's at home, eh? The fire was still in. Takes too long if it goes out. That's why I was outside. I came to make sure it had been backed up proper and couldn't be bothered to walk back over to the cottage. We use a bit of coal to keep it going overnight and then just use the scrap wood to keep it going through the day.' He spread his arms wide and grinned. 'We've got plenty o' that. If I'd tried to get back to bed I might have woken up the Bobbin Master anyway, an' he's got a foul temper if he's woken too early.'

Fin was intrigued. 'Who on earth's the Bobbin Master?'

His new friend raised his eyes to the roof. 'Good 'eavens lad, don't you know nuthin? He owns the mill. And the houses. And the shop. We all work for him, and spend his money in his shop'.

'Oh, right.' Fin pondered the situation for moment and smiled apologetically. 'Bill I'm going to have to be off I'm afraid. I've got to be back in the hostel we're staying in ASAP, or I'll be in for the high jump.'

'What are you goin' on about? Where's Ay-Ess-Ay-Pee, I thought it was Boot you were after?' asked Bill, clearly totally flummoxed by Fin. 'There's no hostelry round here, the nearest inn is miles away. Oh, I see. You're staying at the coaching inn in Boot, is that it? Well it's a fair stretch of the legs and that's the truth. It'll take you all morning to get there. As for getting to Ay-Ess-Ay-Pee, you'll have to find that yourself, I've never heard of such a strange name, not around here at any rate.'

Fin checked his watch.

'Oh God. It's five-thirty now. They'll murder me, and I've got to think of an explanation for being out all night.' Fin was really beginning to frighten himself again. 'They'll never believe the truth – I'm not even sure I do! They'll murder me when I get back.'

The Nightmare had really screwed him up. He had a walk of several miles to get through, with minimal directions to follow, and Mister Nutter really would be doing his nut long before he could get back. They'd probably call the police in and allsorts. Then his mum and dad would be called. It truly was a disaster of major proportions. His face crumpled into tears as he realised just how much trouble he was in, and Bill rushed up in shock.

'Come on lad, don't take on so. It can't be that bad, can it? Surely they wouldn't do that, not unless they've got you indentured and you've done a runner. You haven't have you?' Fin shook his head and wondered what Bill was on about. Indentured! No-one of his age was apprenticed in this day and age. Bill put his arms around him, and gave him a hug, concern etched in his face. 'You'll be alright. We'll get you out of the mill and pointed in the right direction and you'll be fine once you've put a couple of miles behind you, you'll see.'

Whilst comforted, Fin was still at a total loss as to what he was going to do. Out in the countryside in his pyjamas, wearing the most disgusting coat and boots imaginable and, to all intents and purposes, lost. He was only thirteen for goodness sake. This wasn't fair!

'Have you got a map around maybe? Just something to help me find Boot. If I can get there I can find the youth hostel okay.' asked Fin, with hope more than any belief that Bill would have one handy.

'Don't be daft, you don't need one Fin.' said Bill as he began to steer Fin around the engine. The room was now a good deal warmer than when they had entered, with the fire roaring at the base of the boiler. Fin was thankful for that at least. And maybe this funny little boy was right. If he could get back at a reasonable time, maybe he could justify his absence with sleep walking, or just a desire to take an early morning stroll. The PJs might take a bit more explaining though.

Bill's hair was now slicked against his forehead with sweat after standing so close to the engine. He wiped his hand across his face and beamed. His pinched little face was transformed and his eyes lit up with a mischievous light.

'Tell you what, you could borrow one of the horses – Elijah's a good un. You'd get there a damn sight faster an' if you loosed him afore Boot he'd find 'is way home. E's a right clever bugger.'

'But won't you get in awful trouble if a horse is missing? Asked Fin, 'and anyway, I've never been on a horse. I'd probably end up killing myself.'

'Sweet Lord, I've never met a lad who was so keen to fail before he's even started.' He pushed Fin back out of the door. 'Come on you puddin', let's get you ready'.

Even Fin was beginning to think this might work, but he was more scared of riding a horse than of trekking over miles of fells alone. What if he fell of and broke something. Like his neck. However speed was now more important and Bill had offered him a way of possibly arriving back without anyone suspecting that he'd been whisked away in the night.

They made their way around the back of the mill towards the furthest barn. Bill checked over his shoulder the whole way.

'Hurry Fin, we have to be quick before anyone else rises. Mister Cooper will be about soon to check the engine and get ready to start the line shafting. An' then everyone else will be about to get the lathes working and I'll have to get to working on the block cutter. Pray I don't lose a thumb or worse will you. It's a right beast when you're small like me. I have to throw all me weight on it to cut the blocks.'

Fin had no idea what Bill was talking about, but was too concerned about the up coming ride to question him. They entered the stable to the trumpeting of the rear of a huge chestnut stallion facing the far wall. The enveloping cloud emanating from the arse-end of Elijah (for it was none other than he) was pungent to say the least.

'You bugger!' swore Bill as he slapped the horse and pushed him away. 'He does it on purpose, I'm bloody sure he does. Every time I come near his bum, he farts. He walked passed waving a hand in front of his face and making gagging sounds. 'I reckon he's trying to kill us all!'

Fin couldn't help smiling along with Bill as the two went in search of the tack for his journey.

'I'm still not sure about this Bill. He's a bit bigger than I expected'

'Oh hush man. Once you're on your way you'll be right as rain. Give me a hand with this.' And between them they picked up a large weather-beaten saddle and began to manoeuvre it towards the high broad back of the beast called Elijah.

Just as the leather settled into place there came a loud unsettling shout from outside.

'Oh no. It's Mister Coward. Stay here and keep quiet. I'll try to lead him away while you get that done up.' He gestured towards the saddle.

Bill left the barn and Fin alone with the horse.

'Great. So how do I do this up, eh?' moaned Fin eyeing the saddle. He knew the cinches buckled together, but not how tight, and he didn't fancy aggravating his stable mate by pinching him while trying to fasten the straps. He settled for loosely fastening them and settled back into the straw in the corner of the barn.

Never having spent any time around horses he was nearly overcome by the sweet, sickly smell of the straw and hay (was there a difference? He certainly didn't know) combined with the noxious fumes being released with gay abandon by Elijah.

Good Lord, had he been having curry for tea, or what?

From outside he could hear raised voices, and then what sounded like a single slap. Bill yelped and Fin moved closer to the door to try to find out what was going on.

'But I wasn't doing nuthin Mister Jeremiah, really I wasn't. Just checkin' that Elijah was alright. That's all I were doin', really it were.'

Fin peered around the half open stable door.

Bill was standing hunched over before a large man in a frock coat and tall top hat. With large lamb chop side whiskers he looked like old photos of Mister Gladstone Fin had seen in his history text book. What on earth was going on? Was this some sort of museum? And if so, what was this guy doing hitting Bill?

Much to his own shame, Fin stayed hidden in the stable. He knew he should find some way of helping Bill out of his predicament, but if he did put in an appearance, it was more likely to cause his new friend more problems.

'Is the fire lit?' bellowed the man. 'And is John around yet? There's work to be done, never mind playing with my horse! Get that door shut and be about your proper business William Elms, or there'll be more than just a cuff in it for you!'

And with that the man turned towards the cottages.

'John Coppel! Get your bones out here! The suns arisen and there's bobbins to make!' he shouted into the cool morning air. Turning to Bill, who still cowered behind him he rasped out 'I said shut that stable door and get about your business boy!' And again raised a hand as if to strike.

Bill hurried over to the stable and closed the lower door. Peering over the top of it he spied Fin in the corner.

'Sorry lad, I've got to shut you in. There'll be The Devil to pay if Mister Coward finds you.' He gestured to the back wall. 'There's a little window there. You can get out that way, but you'll be on your own then, I cannot help you further. Though, on my life, I'd as soon leg it across the hills with you than stay here. Still, can't be helped.'

He closed the top of the door with a whispered 'Good luck an' God's speed.'

Fin sat for a moment. Well, it had been a bit too good to be true. So, no horse. No early arrival back at the hostel. Bill had been right, there was going to be The Devil to pay before this morning was over.

He stood for a moment alongside the horse, relieved, if the truth be told, not to have to ride, before making his way around the beast to the back wall of the stable. A window lay above the hay manger about seven foot up the wall.

Great! Now he had to be Chris Bonnington too!

Now Leon and Then Leon (12)

Dick was still sitting on the low wall when Leon rejoined him with two glasses of Irish whiskey. Dick looked again at his long time friend and realised just how little he did know about him. He had only now begun to understand that all the wild tales Leon had told him over the last couple of days were true.

All of them...

Leon had started with the floating above his bed as a very young child, discovered by Nanna Messenger, who strangely hadn't been the least bit surprised. She had carefully explained to him that he was different, not frighteningly different, but special. There was a twinkle in her eye as she spoke to him, as though she had some inside knowledge. Nanna had always been around to wipe away tears and put a plaster on a grazed knee. She'd helped him past the bullying and prejudice - being black and an orphan was never going to be easy. At primary school it was she who had encouraged his friendship with a young white boy called Richard. Somehow she had seen in him a kindred spirit, though of course he had none of Leon's special talents.

At a very young age she had ingrained in him the need to hide his ability, even from Dick. People would never understand, at least in nineteen sixties Cheshire and probably never. It was at this early stage that her fear for him had driven her to threaten the wrath of the undead if he disobeyed her on this point. She had enough strange artefacts from *the old country* to be able to frighten a three year old into silence with her old tales of zombies and voodoo rituals.

When he reached his teens girlfriends were definitely out. The two of them had discovered right at the beginning that strong emotions tended to bring on intense energy bursts that had unpredictable results, luckily never witnessed by anyone outside the house. The restraints placed upon his social life by Nanna had never caused any problems between the two of them though. To Leon she was the sun that shone in the morning and the moon that watched over him at night, right up until the day she died, leaving Leon alone once more. The difference between her death and that of his parents was that Nanna had been able to prepare him for the road ahead, and left this world with a smile on her lips, passing away quietly in her own bed, holding the hand of her beloved grandson. Leon's parents had disappeared when he was only three, when their car vanished into the murky depths of the Irish sea, plunging off the Eastern coast of Ireland in what was just another tragic holiday accident. Leon had been left with his grandmother for the trip, and had simply never left.

She had always been intensely proud of her grandson and he could still remember her boisterous laughter and bright eyes behind her reading glasses, when he demonstrated his ability to move furniture without having to touch it.

Nanna had begun to tell him stories about the energy of the earth. Of how American Cree indians understood the lines of spiritual power that flowed over the world. How their ancient trails led in straight lines over the trackless plains of the great Midwest of America. Of the Ley Lines of not so ancient Britain rediscovered by Alfred Watkins, along which, it was said, you could trace the paths taken by pilgrims to the holy wells that dotted the landscape. In New Mexico, at the Chaco Canyon, the Anasazi had created long dead straight tracks. In ancient Egypt hilltop cairns marked the caravan trails, and in Central Peru in the middle of the city of Cuzco the Temple of the Sun had forty one radiating lines spreading out into the surrounding countryside. Along all these lines of power sacred hills, holy sites, shrines, temples and even battlefields lie. To many this was merely coincidence, it was only natural for such sites to be created along the lines of travel used by the general populace.

But Nanna believed in the streams of power that cocooned the world, and so too, with much encouragement from his grandmother, did Leon. His talent was for manipulating the power that originated from the earth, he could shape it to his will, bend it with his mind alone. The Messengers had the good fortune to live at a crossroads, purely by coincidence, where several of these streams crossed. This, Nanna had explained, resulted in a pool of power swirling around their local area. It was her belief, and who was he to deny it given his ability, that all children had the innate ability to manipulate the energy revolving around the earth, the tragedy being that as they grew older they were constantly told that it was a myth. Children, who saw the world more vividly than their elders, were constantly reprimanded for having more imagination than adults, constantly told that the world was not a garden of delights, but a place of responsibility and labour.

Many cultures still had shamans and witch doctors, those who knew some of the secrets still guarded jealously by the Earth Mother. Many still saw The Earth as the Gaia, a vast self-regulating organism, but very few knew why they held the belief. All these things Nanna had learned partly from folklore back in the old country and partly from her weekly trips to the local library.

'Never take knowledge for granted Leon. Even the most ridiculous snippet of fact or lore may hold a meaning for you much later in life.'

Leon had never forgotten that and luckily he had a mind like a sponge. He had never lost his thirst for knowledge, or his lust for life. Shortly before her death, Nanna had told him about her father, his great-grandfather, who had been troubled by strange dreams and visions throughout his life. He'd been called over-imaginative, or more often, a bit soft in the head, but she had always believed him when he told her of the lights he could see in the air. He saw bands of glorious colours swirling around everything, when everyone else saw nothing but the plain, ordinary world, no different to that seen by everyone else.

'Remember the way young children use every possible colour when they paint or draw. The trees don't have to be green, the sky isn't always blue, the world truly is a wonderful place to them. Then they conform to the norm, while they're still so young, and lose the God given, or Earth given, capacity to see beyond the humdrum everyday colours and sights. Don't ever forget that you have a gift that we all possessed as children. It's just that you've been lucky to hold onto it into manhood. You're blessed

Leon and I love you even more for it, and so does the very ground beneath your feet. You are one of the very few who have retained an age-old link to the world. So many folk these days feel a yearning for something they feel they've lost, but they never find out what it is. They try to go back to the land, they downsize their lives. Some give up nine to five working and travel the world in search of it. They gain a small hint of what they've lost when they visit Giza or Machu Pichu, but they never regain the magic of their very early childhood. And you Leon, maybe alone amongst all the peoples of the world have somehow retained it.'

Although they often talked long into the night, especially when he was older, they never managed to plumb the depths of the mystery. They both knew he was blessed with his magical skill, but not why he was. Maybe it was something passed down through the family from eons before, but why it had manifested itself in his great-grandfather, and then again, but even more powerfully in him, they could not fathom. Certainly the position of their house, in the centre of Vale Royal, long considered a magical place by its peoples, though not in such a concrete fashion, could have something to do with it.

They had pondered the possibility that it had something to do with the size of Leon's brain. It would have been useful to measure its activity during a furniture moving session, but how could that be explained to someone in a position to help.

'Oh, hello doc. Listen could you give me a hand to see how it is that I can perform telekinetic feats that will blow your mind? I'll move the chairs, or the tables, or tell you what, why don't I transport your car into your office? Yes I know we're on the third floor doc. Oh yes, and could you keep shtum about it, even though it's the most amazing thing you will ever have seen? Thanks doc.'

Umm. They had thought about it, but neither of them could see how it could be done. As a result the root of his gifts were never disturbed. They had no idea how it was done, apart from the fact that an awful lot of energy was involved, and that seemed to just appear out of thin air.

When he moved a household item, the air around him would heat up by several degrees. The heavier the object, the hotter the room became. They had even discovered that he could keep them warm in the winter months by shifting things around the room. The downside was that Leon used to wear himself out when he was showing off to Nanna. He once pushed their old Mercedes home over a distance of five miles, when it broke down on the way back from a shopping trip to Chester. He was sixteen at the time, and had used the talent, along with brute strength, to push the vehicle over a one in seven hill, about half way through the journey home. No-one had any inkling as to what he was doing with his mind, since he was indeed pushing the car physically as well as mentally. He had to be within a few feet of his subject to have any effect, and the magnitude of the effect was magnified ten fold if he could actually touch it. The car was almost too hot to touch by the time they'd reached home and he'd ended up in bed for two days, totally exhausted. He'd also found out something new though. When he'd been labouring away on the car push, he had become aware of swirling colours around him. Only dimly at first, but becoming more vibrant with every passing minute, they streamed all around and seemed to be concentrated around him and the car. Other more distant bands became visible, bending towards him as he approached. Here were the colours of his forefather's visions, now manifesting for him. Although he'd called to Nanna as he pushed, she could see nothing from the passenger seat of the old Merc. Leon almost felt pity for her, she would have loved the patterns weaving through the air, but they were a private show just for him. The world was putting on a display because he was special. He was gifted in a way no-one else was. He felt he was closer to the Gaia than any other person he had ever known of. He suspected, but could never be sure, that he was unique. That thought often worried him. Unique was nice for a while, but would he ever be able to share his gift when Nanna was gone? She was over fifty years his senior after all. She wouldn't be around forever. The thought had often bothered him as they grew older and eventually, at the ages of nineteen and seventy-two, she had taken leave of this world with her usual equanimity and with a slight smile.

By pushing himself right to the limit of his abilities Leon had also discovered something that not even Nanna had suspected, and he'd never told her about it. He didn't know why that was. It was the only secret he ever kept from her, but *boy - what a secret this one was!*

Not long after his eighteenth birthday, he'd been out with Dick for a drink, when they'd witnessed an accident in the village. Or at least Leon had.

A large four wheel drive, complete with monstrous bull-bars, had raced along the main feeder road to the local by-pass and the driver had lost control. With a slight drizzle in the air and a skin of water on the road the young driver had been too busy on the phone...

'Oh, Angela of course I still fancy you. Of course I do. Look I'll be there in a couple of minutes!'

Gerry was driving at speed and steering with his knees as he lit a cigarette and kept the phone perched between his cheek and shoulder. The roads were a little damp, but he knew he was a good driver, so speed and danger were his constant companions. Since passing his test earlier in the year there had been a couple of slight shunts, but that was because there were so many idiots on the road. If everyone could drive with his confidence and skill the roads would be a much safer place. He had a couple of friends who thought they could drive, but he knew they were mere amateurs, whereas he was destined for racing stardom, he was that good. And everyone knew it, they just didn't like to harp on about it since he was modest to a fault. The girlies found it irresistible as well. He was good looking and talented and self-effacing and who couldn't resist such a stud? Come on, be honest, he often told his mates Macca and Gazza, you're so jealous it isn't true, but at least they had the good sense to hang out with him. He would always pass on a few morsels from his abundantly filled table of tasty totty, so they could all chill together. He was, at this very moment, off to meet with one such lass. He treated Angela abominably, but that was his prerogative, with so many young ladies after him. God, life was just so good at the moment!

'Yes, of course I'll take you to the pub! I'm not spending a night in with your parents. No way!'

The car rocketed along the main road through Kingsmead, towards the main Chester road. As he approached the last roundabout before the main junction he saw a flash of colour on the island ahead. A group of girls, no older than nine or ten, were pushing and jostling each other, and out of force of habit Gerry strained to see if there was any likely looking skirt amongst them. He was so preoccupied with his quest for future conquests that he completely failed to see the old woman slowly crossing towards the girls. She had an umbrella up against the rain and was clearly visible directly ahead. But Gerry wasn't looking ahead.

Leon had emerged from The King's Hart with Dick just as old Miss Binster had begun to cross towards them. She was about the same age as Nanna would have been, but still quite spritely for all that, and had lived only a couple of doors down from Leon and his grandmother.

The local primary school girls were gathered, as ever, on the central reservation, where they often met to exchange latest crushes and crazes with shrill chatter and laughter. Miss Binster was less than three steps from safety when the huge black 4x4 began to slow its charge with a scream of brakes. Gerry had sighted the stupid old biddy when she was more than two thirds of the way across the road, and with only twenty feet to go before impact, she had no chance to retreat or advance before the inevitable. The phone fell from Gerry's shoulder as he stood on the brake peddle. With half a ton of steel to arrest, he was onto a loser and he knew it.

'You stupid bitch. What you doin' in the middle of the flamin' road. You cow!' he shrieked as he ploughed onwards.

Miss Binster cowered and awaited her fate. She knew she was too old and too slow to make the required athletic leap out of the path of the now sliding car.

The schoolgirls screamed and fluttered like butterflies on a breeze, panic stricken.

'Oh, Christ.' Dick stood frozen in horror as Leon leapt forward with his hand outstretched.

'No!'

But at twenty five yards there was no way to avert disaster. It was too far for his talent to be put to any use and anyway, he'd never attempted to stop a large object that was actually racing towards him, he couldn't do a damn thing.

The image before him was frozen in time, etched forever on the retina of his memory; the car hurtling towards the old woman, the disgust on the face of the driver, not fear as you might expect, but loathing for the old trout who was responsible for his predicament, the terror reflected back by the soon-to-be accident statistic and the hysteria of the young girls.

Leon saw all this with the clarity of a photograph.

The air had become thick around him and his breathing was laboured now as he waited for the impact – which didn't come. The world was quite literally frozen in time. All around him he was aware of a total silence and stillness, except for the vivid colours of the energy streams which had leapt into focus, so sharp and so bright.

It was as though the whole scene was wrapped in a rainbow which pulsed around everything there, swirling thickly about his body. The world had come to a halt at Leon's command.

He slowly turned to look at Dick, who stood beside him, the agony of helplessness showing clearly on his face as he watched the accident unwind, his mouth half open in a shout of horror. He stood like a statue, with not even a pulse beating at his throat.

Leon was conscious of a rising heat now and he began to sweat profusely. He turned back to the about-to-happen accident in wonder, and began to move towards it. It was like walking through water… without the feeling of buoyancy, the air resisting his forward progress. Leon was amazed at the effort it required just to move his leaden feet, but slowly he advanced past the girls frozen in mid-scream and on to Miss Binster. The old lady stood like an effigy cast to portray the loneliness of old-age, alone and seemingly aloof, but only moments from death.

Leon decided he had the choice of dragging, pushing or lifting the woman to safety. He settled for grasping her under the arms and dragging her to the pavement towards which she had been moving. As he moved behind her and reached beneath her arms he held her gently and prepared to lift her. As soon as he touched her old and rather threadbare camel coloured coat Miss Binster burst back into life, as though the pause button had been released on the video of her life. Her strangled shout brought Leon up short and she gave him a startled look. Shocked, he released his light hold of her and stepped back, almost jumping away from the little figure in the road. Again the silence descended and the old lady stood frozen before him. His mind raced. He felt the sweat trickle down his left cheek and wiped it away as he studied the scene around him. Understanding suddenly dawned and with a smile he took hold of the hand which she held out towards him as though to ward off some unwanted advance. Miss Binster jerked at her hand as time began to flow around her again, but Leon tightened his grip. With a face filled with wonder she looked up at the twinkling, piercingly blue eyes regarding her with mild amusement.

'Don't worry Miss B. Just come along with me, out of harms way.'

He bowed politely, still holding her hand and they processed with stately grace over to the pavement to where they could stand alongside the children who were still in mid scream.

'It's Mrs Messenger's boy isn't it?' she said peering at him with her myopic gaze, as they stepped slowly across the kerb. Her voice was quiet, almost a whisper, and her eyes no longer showed alarm, but a sort of awed surprise.

'I remember.' she breathed. 'Leo isn't it. Yes, I never forget a face, or a name. Always a considerate lad, so Louisa said.'

Leon smiled on hearing Nanna's name spoken for the first time in many years. She was always just Nanna to him.

'It's Leon, Miss B.' he said. 'And we don't have to whisper. I don't think anyone can hear us at the moment.'

They both looked around and despite still being just a little disorientated Miss Binster smiled too, and squeezed Leon's hand.

'But how are we doing this sonny boy? What have you done?' Still a whisper.

'Dunno Miss B. but I'm damn glad we've managed it.' chuckled Leon. 'But it's going to have to be our secret. Okay?'

Ethel Binster smiled up at the handsome black boy holding her hand.

'Who's going to believe me anyway, eh?' she giggled, reminding Leon of the way Nanna used to react when he performed some unexpected feat.

She patted his arm with her other hand.

'Our little secret indeed! You're a strange one aren't you lad? But' she puffed with the exertion of forcing her way through the thick air, 'I'd love to know how you've done whatever it is you've done.'

'So would I Miss . So would I.'

Leon turned towards the old lady, who gave every appearance of enjoying this strange moment immensely, and bowed lavishly again.

'Alas, now we must return to the real world fair maid.' he said.

To be honest he was a little concerned at the effect the strain of movement might have been putting on the heart that had seen more than eighty years. They were both sweating heavily now even though they had walked less than ten yards. Then he remembered what Nanna always said.

'Horses sweat Leon. Men perspire, but women glow.' And looking at Miss Binster he had to agree. The old dear radiated a glow that was only partly caused by the effort of moving. It was almost an envelope of light that joined the two of them in this moment in time that only they occupied. They pushed their way through the thickened air around them, Miss Binster beginning to puff slightly at the unexpected effort.

They finally reached the safety of the pavement and Leon made to release her hand as he stepped away from her.

'Remember. It's our secret.' he said as he raised a finger to his lips, conspiratorially.

'Good night, sweet prince.' she said as she gave a little curtsey and a huge beaming smile, showing surprisingly neat, even teeth, Leon thought, for a woman of her age.

Their hands parted and Miss Binster again became frozen, but now standing just behind the silently screaming girls.

In all, his progress out to road, the walk with Miss Binster and then making his way back to Dick must have taken a good ten minutes and by the time he was finished he was exhausted to the point of collapse. The heat was becoming intense, although the stiffened figures around him all looked as they had when the episode began. Except that there had been some movement. Leon noticed that a group of leaves had made stately progress across the road behind the girls, whose hair had been moving in languid waves like a film running in ultra slow motion.

Time had not been paused, merely slowed down to a fragment of its usual speed. Leon had somehow stepped outside to move in a little pocket of his own time. This was something totally new and uncontrolled. Somehow he had summoned the energy to allow him to save the old lady, but how did he get back into the normal world? As he looked about him in an agony of indecision, he found himself wondering how many other such incidents were happening at this very moment. How many other lives could be saved if only he could reach them *inTime*?

But even as he the thought entered his head he understood that he couldn't be everywhere in order to prevent the inevitable, anymore than he could be every*when*. He might never be able to pull off this particular stunt again. Who knew? Certainly not Leon, as he stood feeling more and more faint, and growing more apprehensive with every passing micro-second. How did he reverse this process?

'Start!' he shouted into the thick hot air.

Nothing happened.

'Go!'

'Proceed! Carry On!'

What was the command?

Was it a verbal command at all?

Then, with a clarity of mind that came from, well - who knew where? - Leon began to understand. In the same way that he could move objects so easily through three dimensions, he could move objects through the fourth – time. All that he had done was move himself through time very quickly. It was all in the mind, he told himself. Just like moving things.

So relax. Calm down. Chill man...

And, with a roll of distant thunder on a cloudless day, the world took him back into The Now that everyone else inhabits.

And a very warm looking Miss Binster, from across the road, standing with the astonished group of near hysterical girls, gave him a sly and mightily exaggerated wink as she turned to continue her walk home, ignoring the needless screeching of tyres behind her.

When Fin (13)

Grasping the side of the metal basket Fin levered himself up to stand with his hand on the small windowsill. Peering out of the cobweb festooned window he could see the trees beyond. He lifted the small metal handle on the frame and opened the window to let in the sweet smells of the early summer morning and hoisted himself through the narrow gap. The opening was only about ten inches and he had to exhale in order to slide himself out.

At this point a slight problem presented itself. He was now balanced precariously half way out, with his weight bearing down on his stomach and with nothing to lean on. Another inch and he would fall seven feet onto the turf below. His eyes roamed along the walls and ground to find some way of easing himself down, but all he saw was the sheer face of the building and the ground at its foot. With no alternative, other than remaining locked in the stable with Elijah, Fin leaning out further, using his hands spread out and down the wall to try to steady himself. What larks, eh Pip? he thought as he felt himself reach the point of no return and begin to slide inexorably downwards. His hands scrambled for purchase where there was none, and with the elegance and aplomb of a block of concrete he plummeted to the ground. He tried to roll as his hands hit the floor, but even so he hit with a bone-crunching impact. He lay, somewhat winded, for a few seconds, sucking in deep breathes and checking for the sort of sharp pains you only came across with bone fractures. Amazingly, he seemed fine, and quickly lurched to his feet to look about him. He was about to dust himself down and had raised his hands to do so, when, after a quick glance down his front, he realised that there was little he could do to make his attire any cleaner, or dirtier for that matter. The coat he wore was ingrained with oil and dirt and there was nothing he was going to be able to do about it. Ugh! He lowered his hands.

So his next plan of action was… what?

Fin still had little idea of where he was headed. Bill had indicated that Boot lay somewhere off to the North, judging by the position of the risen sun. But 'somewhere over there' wasn't the ideal set of directions to follow.

It was no good he was either going to have to set off and hope for the best, or try to have another quick chat with Bill. Undoubtedly his favoured option was to see Bill one last time, but where was he?

Fin moved quickly to the left hand corner of the barn and took a quick look around it. The tree-line followed the walls of the building at a distance of ten feet or so, and in the grassy corridor between the two all was still. He rounded the corner and made for the next one. Again peering around it he had a clear view of the whole of the courtyard between the barn and the mill, with the office to his right.

The yard was empty and there was no sign of Mister Coward, Mister Cooper, Bill or John, whose old coat Fin assumed he was now wearing. However the sounds of industry were issuing from the mill door to his right as he edged out of the shadow of the office. He crept slowly towards the door and risked a quick peep inside. The mill had become a riot of noise now that the Mister Cooper had obviously connected the line shafting. Now Fin knew what Bill had been talking about. The steam engine was now in full flow and could be heard off to the right, in its own room. From there a single loop of leather ran up to a shaft on the floor above, and from there a long shaft of wood ran almost the entire length of the mill. From this shaft numerous smaller leather loops led down to shafts connected to every other machine in the mill, some connecting to other shafts via intermediate loops. The floor of the mill was covered in shavings, in the same way as the steam room, but to an even greater depth, up to about three feet in places, with narrow pathways leading through.

Bill sat just inside the door through which Fin was staring aghast. The air was full of noise and dust, with lathes, drills and saws crying stridently as they shaved wood to the desired shape and size.

Bill appeared to be drilling cylindrical blocks from plates of wood. The plates varied in thickness from less than an inch to over three inches. The machine over which he toiled was obviously The Beast he'd spoken of earlier, the block cutter. From what Fin could see, Bill had to stand heavily on a large peddle which brought a massive tubular saw down onto the block he held under it. Fin cringed on seeing the small boy trying to hold the wood in place whilst also throwing his weight onto the peddle of The Beast. The teeth of the drill were very large and sharp and were going about their business within a hairs-breadth of Bill's fingers.

'Bill.' hissed Fin, beckoning the boy over to him.

'Fin! What are you still doing here?' Bill made no move to leave his machine. 'Get going before Mister Coward sees you. I've got to keep blockin' these cakes or I'll be short on my count for the day'

Fin motioned him over to the door again.

'Come on, Bill. I still need some directions. I don't know which way…' but Fin was interrupted in mid sentence.

'Who the 'ell are you and what do you think you're doing here? shouted a very loud voice only inches from the Fin's ear. The question was accompanied by a heavy hand that propelled him through the doorway and into the mill.

'Come on, out with it. What do you think you're doing, interrupting my men whilst they're at work? If it's a job you want, I don't need you and if all you're doing is being nosy, I don't want you. So bugger off before I give you the back of my hand.'

'But I only wanted a quick word with Bill, Mister Coward, that's all.'

From the corner of his eye he saw Bill raise his eyes towards heaven and shake his head mournfully as he kept on working at cutting out the blocks that now almost filled the basket in front of him.

'Are you arguing with me? I said, are you arguing with me?' bellowed The Bobbin Master as he gave Fin another shove backwards past Bill and towards the main body of the mill, with all its noise and dust.

'I'll take my hand off your face you young ragamuffin. Talking back to your elders eh? Well I'll learn you a damn good lesson. Come here!'

Even Fin could see that he'd made a big mistake this time. Although big for his age he was still a good few hands shorter than his antagonist. He turned and ran, much to the amusement of the circular saw operator sitting opposite Bill, who obviously thought this just good sport, a pleasant diversion from the monotony of the day's work. His face suddenly changed though when he took a closer look at Fin.

'Oi, that's my coat, and them's my old boots!'

'You keep to your saw John Coppel, I'll deal with this!' shouted Coward. 'So, a thief as well eh? Well we'll see how the local constable views this once I've given you a bloody good hiding! Come here, you young scoundrel!'

And with that, the chase was on.

Fin went up the stairs before him two steps at a time. At their bottom the mill owner stood laughing, mocking Fin, as he placed a foot on the first step.

'And now where are you going, my young thief?' he questioned loudly as he drew a long coppiced pole from a basket beside him.

'I think I've got you now, haven't I just?' and he slowly began to ascend the stairs with a gloating look on his heavily bewhiskered face.

Fin swung to the left, to be faced by a blacksmith working at his anvil, hammer poised in surprise above a half made iron strap. He immediately turned back to be faced by two doors, one leading into an office from which there was no escape, the other put into the back wall, leading who knew where.

He wiped the sweat which was streaming down his face with the sleeve of his filthy coat. The noise was becoming unbearable and all the heat from the steam room and smithy was making him feel faint. His chest heaved as he drew breath and began a wracking cough as his throat became laden with the wood dust that hung in the air. His body was shaking with fright and adrenaline as he saw that his pursuer had almost reached the top of the steps. His trembling legs carried him past the head of the stairs again and the grinning man, and he reached the last door to possible escape. As his hand closed on the latch he could hear the man behind him laughing.

'No escape that way my little fox. You're mine now and no mistake. Come here!'

As the words were uttered at his back, he flung the door open and rushed out. Too late he realised that he was at the very back of the mill. True, the door led outside, but unfortunately it led from the first floor and there was no balcony surrounding the building, just the steep pile of shavings running steeply away from the back wall.

'Oh bugger!' Was the last thought to enter his head as he overshot the man made hill and, grasping wildly at the air around him, plummeted towards the ground twenty feet below.

Then Leon (14)

Following the extraordinary happenings during which Miss Binster apparently avoided certain death by an athletic leap belying her ancient frame, Leon had begun to test his new talents in secret. Whilst Nanna had helped him throughout his life, he knew that even she would be unable to give him any advice on this latest manifestation of his earth given powers. Best not to worry her about it. She seemed to be becoming more frail with every passing day, and Leon knew she would soon be leaving him forever. No, in these final weeks he would not burden her with this.

As often as he could he would try to freeze time about him. When alone in his room he could stop the clocks, and carry his own pocket of time around with him. He found he carried his *now* with him and could envelope anything he touched in the same cocoon. He was not travelling in time as such, merely moving a little outside of it, in a slower stream. When doing so he was aware of the streams being far brighter than normal, and could see the way in which the colours massed around all living things - and it was positively kaleidoscopic around Nanna.. He read avidly about astral travel, but quickly dismissed most of it as wishful thinking. Supposedly it was possible to project oneself forward in time, but try as he might he found this goal unattainable. After several weeks he gave up all attempts at forward time travel and firmly believed it was not going to happen. He had formed a hypothesis that time took care of itself. He could bend it slightly, but couldn't move ahead of himself, since time knew where he was and would not let him move away from his current thread of existence. Who knew what the future might bring? And if it was unknown, how could he go to have a look to see what it would contain?

It was on the day that Nanna passed away, in the deepest depression and feeling so alone he could hardly bear it, that he made a breakthrough and found a way to alleviate his pain. She died in the early morning, happy that she was embarking on another adventure to who knew where. She gave Leon her final gift – an unwavering belief in there being somewhere better, with a gentle smile and a squeeze of his hand, held long in her frail grasp. He realised she was gone only when her touch relaxed almost imperceptibly and an aura, that had strangely been slowly growing more and more intense as her failing life leeched away and the end approached, suddenly burst upwards and outwards from her, before disappearing like the sparks from a firework. There was no slow fading here, more an affirmation that her belief was correct. She had moved on, to an existence somewhere far more brilliant, and filled with wonders far greater, than anything the world Leon was left to inhabit alone, had to offer.

Leon let time slow to the extent that its passing became imperceptible. He sat beside her for over an hour, holding her hand, and finally telling her of the only secret they had not shared in life. Silently he cried as he let her know of his deep and abiding love, that he hadn't professed often enough while she was around to hear it. But maybe she could still hear him.

How was he going to cope without her patience and wise counsel? He closed his eyes against the hot tears of grief and his whole frame shook with a wracking anguish he could not control.

He thought back to his childhood as an orphan with a funny old grandmother, who seemed to frighten all the local kids, except Dick Hedd, who thought she was a hoot. He smiled.

And thunder rolled overhead.

When Leon (15)

'Come on my little butterfly. Come to Nanna!' called a voice from downstairs.

'Your friend Richard will be here any minute and you still haven't polished these shoes. Hurry up, little bird. I told you you're going nowhere until you tidy yourself up!'

He opened his eyes and lay frozen on his bed, except for his trembling with fright. He had no memory of leaving Nanna's bedside. And anyway, he had watched her die only an hour ago.

So who was calling him?

He slowly swung his feet off the bed, searching for the floor, and realised with a jolt that the bed seemed very large for his six foot frame. He pushed himself off onto the riotously coloured carpet that Nanna has chosen specially for his tenth birthday – what a day that had been, so many hours spent choosing a pattern that all small boys would have wanted, but few parents would have allowed, with spacemen and rockets, planets and suns strewn haphazardly across a deep blue universe - landing heavily because of the unexpected drop.

He looked up into the mirror and realised that he could do with finding a dog, because he certainly wasn't in Kansas anymore...

Now Fin (16)

Fin awoke with a start.

Willis stood beside him, a look of mild exasperation on his face as he shook his new friend out of the depths of his slumber.

'Fin! Come on Fin! Wake up you lazy beggar! You'll be late for breakfast. How did you manage to sleep through that storm earlier? The thunder woke us all up ages ago, but you were dead to the world – lazy sod. Tam was getting a bit worried that you'd died in your sleep, but then you started snoring so he knew you were all right. And you need a wash!' his nose was wrinkled up in disgust 'What is that pong. Phewee!'

The still drowsy boy occupying the bed gazed around him, rubbing his eyes as Willis began to turn away. Fin groped for his glasses and, not finding them under his pillow called over to Willis.

'Throw my bag over will you. I can't find my glasses, so I need my spares.' Then it occurred to him that he hadn't thought to pack them. Cripes! He was next best thing to a bat without his specs. The bag landed heavily on the bed and as he sat up and prepared to start rummaging inside to find his contact lenses, he threw back the covers and the other boy did a double-take.

'Good grief Fin. What have you been up to? Look at the state of this.' He gestured towards the bedclothes that had draped over the side of the upper bunk and Fin looked down. The sheet below him and the exposed parts of the duvet were filthy, to say the least. Fin came across his old glasses first and fished them out, complete with the duck tape on one hinge, *Thanks Dad*. Putting them on, he surveyed the bed in horror.

'You didn't have a little accident in the night did you? You know, you haven't been intestinally challenged?' Will joked with a smirk, but as he said it they could both see what it was that had caused the mess.

'Oh no! Its oil!' wailed Fin.

'And mud... and sawdust! Where on earth did that come from? Fin what have you been doing? And how did you do it without waking anyone? And what is *that*?' he shouted pointing at the noxious coat Fin was lying on top of, 'And what are you doing with boots on in bed?'

Willis looked completely dumbstruck and Fin could understand why. How was he going to explain this to Will, and keep it secret from everyone else?

Oh yes, the feckin' nightmare really had done him up like a kipper. Just peachy.

Despite the amazement he felt on seeing all the mess, Willis was more concerned that Fin was okay.

'Cover it all up for God's sake, or you'll be in the doghouse forever with Bertie and Mike. How did you get into this state while we were all asleep? What's going on Fin?'

'Look Will, stop bloody asking questions.' snapped Fin as he jumped down from the bunk and hurriedly covered all signs of the disaster it held. 'I'll tell you all about it once I've sorted this lot out. Well, at least I'll try to explain, and you probably won't believe a word, but for now I need to get rid of this lot.' He dropped the coat and boots on the floor.

Fin thought he was handling this pretty well just now. After all, he'd been whisked away in the night, left in the dark and farted on by a horse. He'd fallen through a window, been chased by an evil looking mill owner and then plummeted out of a first floor door. Unfortunately he couldn't remember anything after falling through the door towards the pile of shavings outside the mill.

This was going to take some thought, ideally on his own, so he needed to lose Willis and all his questions somehow, but he was glad of his help for now.

They simply dropped the coat and boots out of the window, so that they landed next to the large red-topped rubbish bins below. There were two of them, each as big as a skip. Now even if they didn't manage to get down there to bin the offending (and offensive) items themselves, someone was bound to stuff them in the garbage at some point during the day.

They decided to leave the bed until later. All the bedding would have to be washed, probably boiled, if they could find the machines and whatever else to do it. Neither of them, they both admitted, had too much of an idea when it came to washing domestic fabrics.

'And if there's nothing you can do about it now, leave it till later and move on to something you can sort out.' said Fin with an air of determination.

'Look, you go down to breakfast while I have a shower. There's no point in both of us missing out on it. I'll see you back in the room when you're a bit fatter and I'm a bit less smelly. Okay?'

Willis had been reining in his curiosity for several minutes and could see that he wasn't going to get much out of Fin now. But just you wait Master Lemott, I will find out what's happened here. I'll hound you till I do, thought Willis as he turned with a shrug and headed breakfastward.

Fin stripped off his grimy pyjamas, recognising that he was going to have to clean them too and with a sigh and a wry grin he entered the shower. Turning the water up to as high a temperature as he could bear, he set about scrubbing away the night's grunge.

After his shower, having spent several minutes just cleaning his hands and neck, which were encrusted with grime, he felt immeasurably better. With his hair combed and his old spectacles in place of his usual ones, which he still couldn't find for some reason, he swept the dirty bedclothes onto the floor and sat on the lower bunk to think.

He wasn't quite sure how to handle this latest development. He had never been on a trip like last night. He had set out as normal, or as normal as these things ever got, but then everything had gone haywire. He'd never been dumped before, he just rushed about and came back, every time... and he never brought stuff home with him.

Something had changed somewhere along the line and he couldn't see why. He'd thought things were getting better, but they obviously weren't. He wasn't growing out of it, if anything he was growing further into it and he had to admit to himself – last night had been more frightening than anything he'd experience before. When he was younger he'd been frightened of the unknown, but this time he'd been awake and fully aware throughout it all. Hell he'd even spoken to that boy in the yard. What was his name? Bill. Yes, Bill, that was it. He'd have to try to find him to see what he thought of it all. He'd like to see that weird museum again too, and that flaming horrible Bobbin Master, who took his role playing *way* too seriously. Fin couldn't help smiling to himself as he tried to picture the look on their faces when he'd been whisked back here. He wondered how that had happened as well. He had absolutely no recollection of his return to the hostel. Had he flown back, or just re-appeared here? Had he even left, or just dreamed it all? No, that made no sense. He'd definitely been at the mill, how else had he ended up wearing the disgusting clothes? He'd been seen and seen things he wouldn't otherwise have known about. Oh well, the only way he'd know about an awful lot of things from last night would be to ask Bill.

At the back of his mind though, was a nagging doubt that now ballooned into one huge clear thought, that he couldn't hide from anymore. Optimism was all well and good, but was it really going to be so easy to explain? How could he tell anyone about it, unless he knew what was going on?

Maybe there was a far more obvious answer that he couldn't keep skirting around.

Maybe Wright, Bishop and Co. had been right all along.

Maybe he was just a nutter.

It was amazing how quickly a thirteen year old could swing from optimistic good humour to pitch black pessimism and horrifying doubt. So often things were black or white. There was no grey in between and Fin had just fallen from the bright sunshine into the darkest shadows in the darkest caverns.

In the twinkling of an eye, he'd plunged into an abyss of self doubt, and fear so strong that it made his whole frame tremble.

The door suddenly flew open and Tam rushed in, followed by Simeon and Willis.

'Wotcha Fin. Why weren't you at brekkers? Asked Tam 'And why's this lot all over the floor?'

Simeon was also staring at the pile of dirty bedding at their feet.

'Whoops, who's been having mud fights in his sleep, eh Fin?' he laughed. 'Too busy tidying up to eat? You dirty old man!' he mimicked Harold Steptoe, quite well as it happened.

'Yeah, something like that.' answered Fin sullenly.

'All right Fin. What's been going on? You're gonna have to tell us what's going on sooner or later, so it might as well be sooner.'

Fin made no response and didn't meet their eyes.

'Sooner being *now*, you wassack!' said Tam through gritted teeth, though light-heartedly.

Fin was desperately trying to think of a reply that didn't sound like he was a complete lunatic, but he couldn't. His mind was racing, but the circuit was very short and the chequered flag was approaching faster than a whippet on speed.

'I don't know what happened, I really don't, honestly' Fin couldn't think of an answer. 'If I could tell you I would, but I can't.'

The faces of the other three boys showed their disbelief.

Simeon was first to speak.

'Come on Fin you can tell us. It can't be that bad.'

'No I can't and yes it can! Don't you understand, you bloody halfwit! I can't tell you. So sod off and leave me alone. Go on. Out! Now! Just go away!'

Fin had lost it, big time.

'Now!' he screamed.

The pressure of the last twelve hours had finally breached the dam of his self control and unfortunately his best friends were all downstream. He began trying to usher them out of the room, none too gently.

Willis tried to face him down. He thrust his face towards Fin and stood his ground.

'Fin you promised to tell me! I'll believe you and so will the others! Won't you?' He turned to Simeon and Tam who made affirmative noises. He spun back to Fin, who was still pushing all three of them towards the corridor at their backs.

'Fin. Stop it! If you don't tell us, who are you going to talk to. We're you best friends – at least I thought we were - especially after last night.'

Willis pushed back.

'So don't push me!' He was shouting too now, as he tried to stop his backwards motion, but Fin was a big lad who was in no mood for resistance. He grew even more determined at Willis' refusal to move, pushing and jostling them out of the door, his face flushed. The others looked shocked and hurt and even Tam began to push back, but when Simeon and Willis gave up the stupidly childish shoving Tam was left fighting a losing battle, so that eventually all three retreated on to the landing, their faces crimson with fury and bewilderment.

'Alright Fin we're going, we're going!'

'Stop shoving! That's our room as well, you know.'

'What on earth's wrong with you?'

All three of them, his very best friends, were looking hurt and upset - understandably. Why should he be doing this to them? Fin could see their disappointment, but they didn't know what he was going through and he could think of no way to explain. It was easier to simply let his anger and frustration pour out to crash upon the shores of their friendship, causing untold damage.

In an almost berserk rage, with tears streaming down his face, he punched Simeon on the shoulder – hard. Tam tried to separate them, as Sim threw a punch back. Tam and Willis bundled Sim along the corridor.

'Just leave me alone!' he roared as he slammed the door in their shocked faces and locked it.

His head was pounding and he felt slightly sick and in a fit of anger he banged his head several times, hard on the stone wall alongside the doorframe. Bloody Hell that hurt! So, still being of fairly sound mind, he stopped doing it. But he couldn't stop crying. Huge quaking sobs poured out and he sank down against the door.

Now that the room was empty but for himself, he once again felt wretched. This wasn't like in the films where the hero always knows how to sort things out. This was real life and he was becoming more and more worried about how to cope with the strange turn it was taking. *It wasn't fair!*

He was definitely losing his grip, and his forehead was sore now too. What a berk, he thought to himself.

He would have run after the boys, but suspected that the damage had been done now. It was going to take a lot of bridge building on his part to get them to become friendly again.

Oh God, what had he done.

As so often happens, his anger had vanished, to be replaced by an overpowering guilt. His friends had only been trying to help and he'd bullied them away. He'd done what he'd always had to spend his life avoiding. He was a big lad for his age, but aggression was rarely the answer, and it certainly wasn't in this case.

He felt wretched as he slumped against the wall, to sit with legs outstretched, staring into an uncertain future.

He knew that his outburst was pointless and had achieved nothing other than alienating his mates, but this was all proving too much. He was miles away from Mum and Dad and had absolutely no-one to confide in. Even his parents would be stretching their love and trust to the limits if he asked them to believe him. He curled up on his bed and tried yet again to make sense of the whole thing. Amazingly, even though his mind was still in a whirl, after a few minutes he began to doze.

Suddenly there was a loud banging on the door and Fin was immediately wide awake listening to the hammering of his heart. Oh no, what now?

'Come on young LeMott! Open this door at once!' boomed the voice of Mister Lightfoot.

'We'll have no stay-a-beds today. Day trip to the local museum – no time to be a slacker. Come on boy! There's lads out here who want to get their kit.' Again came the beating on the door. Fin jumped up and unlocked it, then turned away as he pulled it open.

'Good Lord Fin, this isn't like you. Not like you at all. Let's be about it.' The teacher grinned widely, but the smile faltered as he saw Fin sitting disconsolately on his bed. 'Come on Fin, snap out of it lad.'

When the boy showed no sign of enthusiasm despite his urging, Bertie turned his fervour onto the other boys. Simeon, Tam, Willis were equally subdued, whilst Charlie and Mark looked at each of the other boys in turn, in obvious puzzlement at the cold, brittle atmosphere in the room. As they gathered their hiking gear their teacher noted that only Charlie and Mark looked at Fin. Something had been going on, but *between these four?* It seemed so unlikely that a rift like this could have occurred so quickly. That it was these boys, who were as close as any he'd ever taught, that had fallen foul of something that could do this to them, seemed beyond belief.

Oh, well. Bert Lightfoot to the rescue, hopefully.

Fin could feel the atmosphere in the room and couldn't bring himself to raise his head. It was all so stupid and unnecessary. He knew he'd have to apologise and try to make amends – just not now. No, for now this was his business and no-one else's. If they couldn't help, they had no need to know. His mind seemed numbed by the happenings last night, and he was *so* tired. He just wanted to be left alone. For everyone to just go away and leave him in peace, to sleep, and think. Yes, above all to try to create some order out of the chaos that was his life today.

'We shan't be walking too far boys, so don't bother with your weather-proof gear. This is just a trip down the road to Scott Park, half an hour in the charabanc and straight into the working museum.' boomed the ever jolly master, 'We'll be inside apart from an al fresco lunch. Okay boys, off you go, I'll be down in a mo.'

Mister Lightfoot stood, feet planted firmly apart and arms akimbo, and eyed his sorry looking charge speculatively.

'So Master Finbar, what's to do?' he asked.

Fin didn't even raise his head, and seemed to collapse even further in on himself.

The teacher sat slowly down beside him, having to hunch forwards to prevent his head smacking against the frame of the upper bunk.

'Fin, come on, this isn't like you at all. Say something old son, before I start feeling like a drunk chatting to a lamppost. One-way conversations are super if you don't want to listen to anyone, but I do want to Fin. Give me a try. You never know, you might feel better for it.'

'Thank you sir, and I know you're only trying to help, but this is something I've got to sort out by myself.'

Mister Lightfoot looked sceptical. What had happened to the boy from last night, so full of beans, raring to go, even as it had approached midnight. The air around him suddenly felt very warm and still. He had to say something. This wouldn't do, no, Fin had to come out. Apart from anything else unless he was sick they couldn't justify keeping all the boys in the hostel grounds all morning just because of an argument between Fin and his friends.

'Fin, you can't stay in on your own. Either I or Mister Nutter would have to stay behind to babysit, which would mean half the class couldn't go to the mill. So come on.' He put his hand on Fin's shoulder, 'whatever's happened you'll just have to make the best of it.'

'We're going to a mill?' said Fin, finally looking up. A sign of interest finally stirring him.

'Yes lad. Nothing massively exciting. Just a sawmill over in Gillsthwaite. It used to produce bobbins for the clothing trade around here. You know, spinning, weaving and all that. It should be quite fascinating. It's one of the few in this area that still looks as it did a hundred or so years ago.

Although Mister Lightfoot had no idea why, Fin was at least beginning to look interested. The teacher rose from the bed and smiled.

'On your feet then Fin. Let's be off. Everyone else will be waiting downstairs. Get your shoes on and grab your bag.'

Fin shoved his feet into his shoes and picked up his bag, took a moment to drop a writing pad, pen, pencil and rubber into it and followed the master out. As he trailed after Mister Lightfoot his mind was racing. Maybe he could find out where the mill was from his journey last night. Maybe he could find Bill and try to work out exactly what happened after his hurried exit from the mill. He also wanted to check that the boy was okay after he'd tried to help Fin. At least now he had something to do to try to sort himself out. Though the chances were slight that he would manage to find the site of last night's excursion, it was worth a try.

The journey out on the coach was so depressing for Fin that at one point he almost wept. His friends very pointedly sat across the back seat with no space left to allow their erstwhile comrade to join them. He sat, sunk in gloom one seat behind the two teachers. Never before, even when he'd been afraid of going to sleep, had he felt so isolated. Mum and Dad were always there to help and advise him. None of their advice had actually helped, but at least they'd been there for him. Just to be able to sleep with them had been enough to subdue The Nightmare. Now he had to cope by himself, and he wasn't making a very good job of it. But what could he do? He was certain that he couldn't tell anyone about last night, at least not until he had more of an idea about what had happened. Had Bill seen him fly off in the wind or vanish as he fell? Fin had no idea, but was determined to try to find out. The little boy at the mill was the only person who might be able to give him a clue.

Had he dreamed the whole thing? His parents often tried to tell him it was just an over active imagination and too many computer games and videos. But no, that was definitely a non-starter. He had the coat and boots – they were very real.

So it hadn't been a dream. That meant he'd either transported there, which seemed the most obvious answer, or had somehow managed a feat of astral projection hinted at by several of the spiritual advancement books he'd browsed in the library.

The spirit travelling seemed a bit unlikely, but then again, the alternative was that he had flown on the wind in the middle of a midnight storm. Oh, yes. He could see how that would be the most likely alternative. Yes he'd just tell everyone that that was what had happened. They would all believe that, obviously they would. Then everything could get back to normal.

Oh, yeah. Sooooo likely!

He was interrupted in his ponderings by Mister Nutter.

'Come on then Fin, what's it all about? I don't think I've ever seen you look so fed up. A trouble shared is a trouble halved you know.' While the words were still hanging in the air the teacher was thinking - Oh, God. Did I really just say that out loud?

He glanced sideways to where Bert sat looking over at him with an expression of barely concealed (well, not concealed at all, to be completely truthful) mirth on his face.

Yes, apparently he had.

Fin didn't even look at him, but Michael could see the deepening furrow of the boy's brows. Well that hadn't exactly been a winning opening line, had it?

Bert nodded over at the boy again and mouthed something to his colleague along the lines of 'Get a bloody shift on lad before he becomes so morose that we all decide to slash our wrists.' Somehow the news of Fin's argument with his friends was now known throughout the holiday group and strangely the whole lot of them seemed to have been affected by it. Oh some of the boys were still chatting, but that's all it was. There were no shouted ribald comments about who had a girlfriend and who didn't, or who didn't have one and never would, and exactly why. No one seemed interested much in the football on the TV above the teachers' heads, even though both the competing sides had a number of supporters on the bus.

Bert recognised that, although the lad obviously didn't realise it, he was highly thought of by his peers. He wasn't the sportiest of them by any means, and could be self opinionated at times, but throughout his time at the school he had demonstrated an ability to see both sides of an argument and act as a mediator. Always fair almost to the point of obsession, he had few enemies, yet somehow in the space of only a few hours he'd managed to alienate his best friends and put all the other boys at a distance.

The teacher moved across the aisle of the coach and sat next to Fin. Very quietly and with obvious concern, Mister Nutter leaned close and put a hand on the solemn boy's shoulder.

'Fin, what *is* going on? This isn't like you at all. For goodness sake, you're going to have to talk about it sometime you know.' He smiled and raised a quizzical eyebrow.

Fin finally raised his gaze to his favourite teacher.

'I know this doesn't look too good, sir' Mister Nutter raised a hand and pursed his lips, 'Sorry – Mike. I will try to explain, but I have to sort a few things out first. Please just trust me for a little while and hopefully I'll be able to tell you soon. I'm sorry for the mess I've made of this. Very sorry.'

Mike smiled slightly and gave a small shrug.

'Okay Fin. Just don't take too long over it.' He ruffled Fin's hair, much to the boy's discomfort.

'Aw sir!' he mumbled as he tried to adjust his hair with both hands.

With a pat on the boy's knee, Michael Nutter returned to his seat beside Bert.

'Well that didn't go terribly well' he said.

'But it's difficult to see what else we can do. He's got to try to get through this himself. He's always seemed to have his head screwed on, so we'll just have to see what happens. Remember there are a lot of other lads involved in this as well. They are just as much our responsibility as he is. Let's hope it's better by the end of the day.'

Bert nodded to his friend and the two men switched their attention to their surroundings.

'Almost there.' said the driver nodding to the brown road-sign ahead indicating the mill off to the right. The coach rounded the turn and the old mill came into view.

Michael caught the sudden start Fin gave as his saw the mill for the first time from the corner of his eye, and looked across. The boy's face had lost all its colour and he was staring intently at the building amongst the trees.

The coach came to a halt in the small car park in front of the main building. Across the road was a small group of cottages and to each side were what appeared to be outbuildings. The door opened and Fin was out before either teacher could stop him. Mike was about to call him back, when Bert touched his arm and shook his head.

'Let him go Mike. We can keep an eye on him without chasing. Let him go.'

They turned back to their other charges.

'Right boys, out we go. Wait for us outside the main door.' He gestured ahead and looked about for Fin. Where had the boy gone?

Fin was in the stable but there was no horse. Elijah was gone. So was any sign of a horse ever having been there. No straw, no hay basket, not even the smell of a horse. His eyes went immediately to the back wall. A small window was set about seven feet above the floor. It was covered in cobwebs and coated in dust and grime, the undisturbed accumulation of years of not being touched, never mind cleaned. Fin turned on his heel and strode across the courtyard, totally ignoring the boys and both his teachers, despite their curious stares.

He went through the open door into the mill proper. There in front of him was the bulky machine he had seen Bill using earlier that morning.

Fin's head was spinning. It was all here! Everything was as it was when he'd last seen it, except that everything, absolutely everything, looked so old now. So used! Oh God, *what was going on?*

He began to feel faint and he began to shiver uncontrollably. How could this be? He sat on a nearby stool and looked about him again. He began to realise that it wasn't exactly the same anymore. The floor was clearly visible now, more than six inches of sawdust had been removed and there was a lot less wood about. The smell of newly hewn timber was less pungent than it had been just a few hours earlier and the whole place had a more forlorn look about it. A startling thought entered his head.

'Could it be that...'

A sound behind him made him turn with a jerk. A small man stood framed in the door, blocking out the glare from the bright sunlight outside, kicking odd pieces of wood aside with a booted foot.

'Now then sonny, what're you doin' here, eh?' smiled the man. He moved inside, amongst the shadows. He hooked his thumbs into the broad belt at his waist and leaned back against the long wooden bench under the window. The ever brightening light illuminated the motes in the air all around him, giving the man an eerie backlit glow. Fin fancied he could see the air radiating away from the dark figure.

Fin sat as if mesmerised and the man began to look a trifle discomfited. He shifted his position and Fin clearly saw his face for the first time. Although lined with age,

Fin estimated him to be no older than his late fifties. He laid his hands on the bench behind him and pushed himself forward.

With another smile playing around his lips he said, 'Nothin' to say eh? Well come on lad, let's join the others and we'll start the tour.' Fin rose slowly and the two stepped outside, and the man placed his hand on his neck in a good humoured way.

'Found 'im Mister Lightfoot' he called as he propelled Fin forwards. The teachers' smiles vanished as they saw the boy's face. He looked white as a sheet, as though he'd seen a ghost.

Mike leaned over to Bert.

'We've got to sort this out - and soon.' The concern was obvious now. 'Get the boys inside. I'll have another go with him. See you later.'

Fin saw Mister Nutter approaching, and his stomach turned over again. What was he going to do? This situation was truly appalling. He was only thirteen, how was he supposed to cope?

Then came a flash of brilliance, an insight so astounding he couldn't help grinning like the Cheshire Cat.

Mister Nutter seemed taken aback by this sudden turnaround in the boy's attitude and his puzzlement was evident on his face as he walked up to Fin.

'So Fin, do we finally get an explanation?'

'Yessir! You bet. But you have to promise not to tell anyone. Not just yet anyway. After I explain you'll see why.'

'Now Fin, I don't...'

'Please sir – I mean Mike. Please promise and I'll tell all. It's just that I think I know what your reaction is going to be, so you have to swear not to tell, not even Mister Lightfoot.'

'Fin, I can only do that once I know what the problem is. I may *have* to let other people know. Until you spill the beans I can't promise, but I won't do anything to make matters worse, that I can promise.'

'Well that's going to have to do, I suppose.' said Fin, but he'd already known that he had to tell someone and, in the absence of Mum and Dad, Mister Nutter would have to step in as a surrogate parent. Once he was home he would have to let them know what had been going on, but for now he'd decided that he had to let an adult know what had happened. Apart from anything else he needed some reassurance that he wasn't going off his head.

In a soft voice, almost a whisper Fin said, 'This is going to sound like complete nonsense Mike, but I need your opinion on everything that's going on. I haven't even told Mum and Dad about this, but things have come to a head. Please listen to all of it, then I'll try to explain, and prove, that everything I'm going to tell you is true.'

Michael Nutter stood in shocked silence. What on earth was the boy rambling on about? This was beginning to sound more and more worrying.

With a hand placed gently on the boy's shoulder, he guided Fin over to a nearby bench. They both sat in the now brilliant sunshine. Dark shadows filled the surrounding trees and the birdsong and buzz of insects were the only sounds in the still air of the car park. The school party was now inside the mill. The two sat in their own little world under a clear blue sky with the faint smell of wood and newly cut grass filling the air around them. It would have been idyllic if it wasn't for the earnest features on the young man sitting next to his teacher.

Fin smiled again, this time a little more hesitantly. He took a couple of deep breaths, as though preparing to go diving deep into unknown waters. He turned to look directly at Mike and began.

'All I ask is that you let me get to the end of this before you ask any questions, 'cos once I've started I'm not sure I'll be able to stop.'

Mike nodded and wondered what he'd let himself in for here. Why hadn't he asked Bert to have a word with the lad? But he already knew the answer. He knew more about Fin than any other teacher in the school. He'd been his form tutor in his first year at the grammar school, and had helped him, and his parents, through a couple of sticky periods in those early months. Indeed, he probably knew Fin better than anyone other than Lidine and Jarmon. But Fin had started to tell his tale and Mike leaned closer to make sure he missed nothing.

'I've had nightmares for years. Almost every night and getting steadily worse over time. Mum and Dad used to tell me I'd grow out of it, but I haven't. They started at about the time my eyesight started to deteriorate, and everyone put it down to a fear of going blind, of not knowing what was going on around me.' Mike nodded. Lidine had visited the school prior to Fin's arrival in the First Year from his local primary school. She'd warned him about her son's apparent lack of confidence, partly brought on by the bullying in his younger years but also due, she thought, to his failing sight. She'd also mentioned his disturbed sleep. Mike remembered his first sight of Fin, of how he'd felt so sorry for the gangling eleven year-old who always wanted everyone to be his friend, and took any sort of rejection so very personally. Despite being a bright and personable young lad, he thought everyone disliked him, and as a result, often tried too hard to make friends.

Fin continued, 'Then they decided it was due to the kids who used to use me as their punch bag when I was still only five or six. But they were never about being beaten, or blind, or anything like that. I used to dream that I couldn't see the ground below me. My body seemed to stretch out under me so far that my feet disappeared. I also had a sense of things going on around me at a different rate to what I was doing. My life, at night, seemed to be marching to a different beat to everyone else's. Sometimes things moved very quickly at a great distance. At other times, I seemed to be the one who was racing along faster than the rest of the world. It used to terrify me.'

He paused and Mike nodded in commiseration. Fin's Mum had given him some idea of the things that he suffered at night, but it all came into sharper relief when described by the boy who had lived through the nightmares. But he still didn't see what this had to do with what had happened in the last few hours.

Fin was talking again, his pace accelerating like a runaway train.

'Rather than growing out of it, things just got worse and worse. I rarely seem to get more than about five hours undisturbed sleep, and I still go into Mum and Dad's bed quite a lot.' Fin reddened at this confession, but kept going. 'In the last six months or so the nightmares and visions, or whatever you want to call them, have become far more vivid. I started to have a sensation of flying. Well actually, at the start I seemed to be stationary, and everything used to fly around me. And I don't mean the things in my bedroom. I mean the whole world flew by. Big rocks. Trees. Things like that. And I'd wake up screaming or crying and run to Mum and Dad. The nightmares became *The Nightmare*. But I learned to cope. To an extent I even began to quite enjoy it. I never seemed tired in the mornings, and I never actually felt I was going to come to any harm. Most every night I just used to be taken away from home in an incredibly vivid dream and carried around on the wind at incredible speeds. I always ended up back in bed, no matter where I'd visited on my nocturnal journey.'

Mike said nothing. To him it sounded like a very graphic recurrent nightmare, and he wasn't trained to help kids out of such psychological tangles as this. He suspected that some way of ensuring a good solid eight hours kip might be the answer, but he didn't really know how to help.

'It's only recently that I've come to terms with the whole thing. I think I've even managed to fool Mum and Dad into thinking that *The Nightmare* has all but vanished.'

'But it hasn't?' asked Mike quietly.

Fin shook his head.

'But I was coping, so it didn't matter too much. I'm pretty sure I'm not some loony with a medical problem. I don't think I need a shrink or anything like that. It's just something my brain likes to do. It's as though my mind just goes out to play at night.'

'But then it began to feel even more real, if that's possible. I really did begin to feel the rain in the air. It used to soak me while I was flying. I really did feel the wind, and heard the storms that always came with the dream. It really did seem so real, sir. But I still kept quiet. I used to worry that maybe I'd be locked up, sectioned... that's the term for it isn't it? Everyone would just think I was a complete nutcase and shut me away somewhere.'

His voice had gone very quiet now and Mike had to lean close to catch what he was saying.

'And every time I woke up in the mornings, I'd be bone-dry and feel fine, except for the memories of the night's events. It just seemed that it had to be something going on in my own head, even though it always seemed so real... until last night.'

Fin stopped talking now and looked up at his confidante. He'd gone very pale again and no trace of his earlier smile remained.

'And that was when all this mess started with Tam and the others?'

Fin nodded.

'Last night it really was real.'

He saw the teacher's sceptical look, and went on.

'And I can prove it, I'm sure I can. I even have some clothes that aren't mine back at the hostel. They were given to me by a boy who works here last night and I can prove it to you now. Here. Honest.'

The boy had obviously finished his tale, at least for now, so Mike felt he had to query what he was listening to.

'Now hang on a minute Fin. You're telling me that what started out as a nightmare has become something more?'

'Much more sir.'

Mike was completely flummoxed. He threw up his hands in despair and stood in front of the boy.

'Fin this is totally ludicrous. I'm afraid I can't believe this. You may really think you can zip around in the night, but I simply can't believe it. I don't know what it is you're up to but as an explanation for fighting with your friends it's a bit thin, don't you think?'

Strangely, Fin was looking more excited now that his teacher was discussing it all with him. Even though Mike was telling him he didn't accept a word of it. His smile returned.

'If I can convince you will you promise to keep quiet about it, for a little while at least?'

He was in deadly earnest, which made it all worse from Mike's perspective.

'But Fin, it's just crazy. I don't know how else to put it. And will you please stop bloody smiling. It's beginning to unnerve me just a bit.'

'But don't you think there's a sort of poetic justice in this sir? You think I'm a nutter.'

Despite the weird situation Mike still found himself smiling back. There was something about Fin that made you want to believe him. The sun shone down on the two of them cheerfully grinning at each other like a pair of loons.

'So funny Master LeMott. Okay, you say you have proof, then let's see it. Show me something to make me think you travel the world in your sleep. Show me anything in this mill - and why here of all places? - to make me a believer. Anything, please God anything, to make me change my mind. 'Cos I don't want to think you really are mad as a hatter.'

He held out his hand to the boy, and with an 'Oomph!' of effort, Fin rose to his feet too.

'Come with me Mike and tell me how I could know about this then.'

He strode off towards the back of the mill.

'Whoa there son! Tell me what you're going show me first. Tell me, then show me something to support your story.'

Fin stopped and turned back to Mike.

'Last night I was here - well not exactly here as it is now. Everything seems different today, in the warm light of day, but I know what lies around this corner. I know what's inside the mill - the exact layout of certain rooms - but only as they used to be. I don't know how, but I've seen this when it was newer than this. Some time in the past.'

'Oh Lord Fin. You're throwing in a bit of time travel too now are you? Friends with Doctor Who or Doc Brown? Is that it?'

Even though his manner was light, Mike was becoming more concerned. Was this some odd mental illness? Was it stress being caused by something at home, or school? Had the bullying when he was younger caused some sort of brain damage? He was going to have to bring this to a close soon, before it reached the Outer Limits. The only problem was that at teacher training college they hadn't had a unit that dealt with helping young men who were tipping over the edge.

Fin looked up at the teacher. He still had the somewhat idiotic smile.

'Around the corner, Oh Ye Of Little Faith, is the biggest hill of sawdust you've ever seen. It's piled up against the back wall. It's really quite amazing.' He stared intently at Mike, 'And since I've never been to the Lake District before, I can't possibly know of its existence, but I do. This will be your first lesson in The School Of Bizarre High. Come and be astounded.'

And with that he turned on his heel and made for the corner again. Mike followed, wondering how he was going to explain to Fin's parents that although they had entrusted their high spirited and talented son to his care, he was returning a bone fide fruitcake. Totally boni fodo. Great.

He turned the corner a stride behind the boy and knew, before he looked beyond him, that Fin had made a mistake. The boy's body had stiffened with shock.

In the shadows between the surrounding trees and the thirty foot high wall of the mill lay a swathe of grass about twenty foot wide.

And nothing else.

The patch of turf was totally empty.

When Leon (17)

Leon stared aghast at the mirror. Looking back was a slightly scruffy looking little black kid with wide, incredibly blue eyes and tousled hair radiating out from his head like a halo.

Nanna's voice came again from downstairs.

'Did you hear that thunder Leon? There must be some heavy rain a comin'. Now get your scrawny little body down here before I have to come up there and get you.'

Then Leon did hear the rolling bass of thunder overhead.

And found himself back in Nanna's bedroom holding the now cold hand of the only parent he had ever known. He was still sitting on the bed and glancing at the clock on her bedside table he realised his memory trick had lasted at most a few seconds.

Time had begun to run at the same speed as for everyone else and the second hand swept irrevocably on. He was alone.

Eventually he forced himself to rise from the bed, place Nanna's hands gently across her chest and go downstairs. Not knowing what else to do he rang Richard to let him know the bad, or maybe uplifting depending on your point of view, news.

Nanna was gone, but possibly not forever…

This would require some further investigation.

Now Leon (18)

Dick glanced over at Leon. His friend had kept so many secrets, for so many years. Dick felt just a hint of disappointment that Leon had never felt he could share his secret life with anyone but Nanna. As far has he knew Leon had no other close friends. Dick found himself feeling sorry for the dark figure opposite in the dwindling daylight. Leon had a wistful look on his face, lost in his quiet reverie. He seemed to shake himself out of his mood and glanced over to Dick.

'Sorry about that my man. Let's get back to business'. And again the ready smile emerged.

Let's save a bit of time while we discuss everything. This could take quite some time I think.'

Leon held up a hand to prevent Dick interrupting him and reached across to hold Dick by his sleeve. Leon began to frown in concentration. Dick watched almost mesmerised as the air around his friend began to shimmer and glow. The radiance grew slowly and the air began to grow warmer despite the sinking sun. Everything became very quite. Unnaturally silent to Dick's ears. He glanced around and became very quite himself, almost too amazed to breathe into the solitude Leon was creating. The glow had spread from Leon and now enveloped the two of them.

The wind, little more than a gentle breeze, had dropped. No, not dropped, but stopped. A wood pigeon became still in the very action of bursting out of an oak tree across the lawn from where they sat. It hung frozen in the air, perfectly captured in its flight and all sound, every rustle, every birdsong, every breath, simply stopped.

Leon sat motionless on the wall as the temperature rose, the air all about filled with a rainbow of colours, which swirled slowly around the two men and stretched out beyond and between the trees and buildings.

A leaf falling from another tree was held in its descent. It was as though the whole world was set in multicoloured amber.

Within mere seconds, time had stopped for all but Leon and Dick.

Dick sat patiently waiting for his friend to continue.

'I've learned a lot since Nanna died, some of it seems so obvious now, but quite a lot is still supposition. You remember I told you that others can do this?' Dick nodded but said nothing, 'Of course no-one admits to it and I'm sure there are only a couple of dozen in the entire world who can actually use it to their advantage. Imagine the problems that would be caused if people learned that others, maybe those close to them, could do this sort of thing? I'm sure it's been used for money making schemes at various times through history. Magicians are the most obvious, but I suspect that this ability has been used more often to gain some sort of power – over people. Just think, to be able to go almost anywhere you want in not much more than the blink of an eye. How cool is that, man? To be able to slow down time, and have a think about what's going on before coming to what would appear to an inspired snap decision to everyone around you. To use the time you manufacture for yourself to investigate possibilities, to review results from similar situations and decide exactly how to act, or react. Then you simply re-enter The Now and know how to handle it all.'

Leon gave a lopsided grin.

'I never really had a taste for power, so I used it in a different way. To travel back in time, to almost any time, within reason, and learn so much that has been forgotten. I used my ability to bend time to teach myself virtually anything I wanted to know, because I discovered that when I do this I cease to age in the here and now!'

Dick looked puzzled and set his coffee down before interrupting.

'So when you do what you've just done, you don't grow older? I'm not aging now? How in hell does that work do you think?'

Leon looked pleased, presumably because Dick wasn't arguing with what he was being told. He was obviously totally hooked now and Leon was overjoyed that he'd been right about him. Sure he was still a little confused by it all, but then who wouldn't be? But he was intrigued more than anything and Leon wanted to let him know everything. He needed someone to share his world with and Dick was the only real choice, for a myriad different reasons.

'Well actually, we are still here. We're just a bit *outside*, if that's the right word, so we are getting older, just slower than usual. But if we go back in time to somewhere, we'll stay the same age as we are here. You'd be amazed what you can find out when time no longer limits everything you do. I may be the same age as you, but I've lived for what seems like forever at times. I've been a Moor in medieval Europe, I've seen The Crusades from both sides of the conflict. I met Vikings and Saxons. I've been even further back and seen Stonehenge as it was when first built. I've stood in Xanadu and the Great Pyramid and seen the magnificence of ancient Rome, China and India. I've hunted with the Cree and lived with the Incas. I have stories to tell that would fill a library, Dick. I knew Shakespeare – not intimately, but well enough – and Marlowe. I've lived a dozen lifetimes and I'm not yet forty!'

Leon was standing now and began to pace back and forth. Dick watched him as he walked.

'Er, Leon. Aren't you supposed to have to keep a hold on me when you do this?'

'What?' Leon looked puzzled for s second. 'Oh, no - it's just while we're getting here that I need to pull you along. Once we arrive, you'll stay here till I take you back.'

Dick looked shocked.

'Or you get back yourself, of course!" Leon rushed on, realising how that had sounded. "You aren't stranded. If I left, I'm fairly certain you'd come back by yourself at some stage. Time has a way of sorting things out. It puts everything back where it belongs unless there's something to keep it where it is.'

Dick sat like a statue, his mind feeling numb. He'd assumed Leon knew exactly what he was doing - the "*fairly certain*" was a bit of a shock, but he still couldn't stop his mind racing. If he hadn't seen what he had seen in the last few hours he would have left and never looked back. He would have had Leon committed to an asylum., sectioned as a lunatic and visited him occasionally to check on his unfortunate mental state and munch through a few grapes.

This evening he had seen things to change his whole view of the world, and he knew he would never be the same again, no matter what happened now. Oh God, I'm the sorcerer's apprentice. This is magic, no matter what Leon chooses to call it.

Suddenly his lust for life had returned full throttle with an almost physical jolt. The possibilities were endless. Life had taken a marvellous new turn and he found himself trembling with the extraordinary excitements it now presented to him. He was light-headed, dry-mouthed and almost giddy, like a schoolgirl meeting her idol. This was literally breath-taking.

Leon could sense the effect he was having on his lifelong friend, and found himself wondering whether he should have done this long ago. Instead of forcing himself to hide everything from Dick maybe he should have revealed that time didn't have to restrict his life at a much earlier date. Oh the fun and adventures they could have shared as twentysomethings on the rampage through history. But he also recognised that it was really only now that he knew enough to warn of the dangers too, and they were very real.

'Come on Leon, don't stop now.' urged Dick, as he rose to stand before the man who was changing his life. 'How does this all work, and why you and not me? What caused it all?'

Leon clapped him on the back and steered him out towards the lawns.

As they walked he picked a leaf out of the air and passed it to Dick.

'As far has I can tell, and I've looked into this believe me, it's like this: anyone can do it, but only a few discover they can. It's common knowledge that Man only uses about a third of his brain power. So what's the rest for? It seems a very odd bit of design for Homo Sapiens to have the potential to do who knows what, but not know how to.'

He paused, pondering how best to explain this bit, never having really thought it all through before.

'The shamans of most ancient civilisations used to be able to travel in what they called The Spirit World. To most people that's just a joke, very few people believe in it. No-one has every proved it can be done. It's thought of as just stupid mumbo jumbo on the outer limits of some pseudo religions. So unscientific. So loony tunes.'

They began to walk through the ancient oak woods now, in the shadows that grew no longer as time passed.

'But even modern science is moving into the realms of what used to be written about only in science fiction or fantasy. Several very well respected men at the cutting edge of philosophical and scientific thought are beginning to point to the possibility of parallel universes to explain anomalies recently discovered in the field of quantum physics. Michael Faraday was the man who kick started our thoughts on this and he did try to explain it to me once, but obviously didn't expect me to understand. He was right too, I still don't really know how he, or his modern-day counterparts came to the conclusions he and they reached. But it does seem to fit in with my own ideas.'

Leon paused to make sure Dick was still listening and was pleased to see that his walking companion was hanging on his every word.

'It goes like this, and bear with me, 'cos it's a bit complex, even when simplified: we can't see light, only the effects it has on other objects. The individual 'parts' of a ray of light, the photons, are the smallest particle that make up a light beam. These 'lumps' that make up a whole, like the subatomic particles, quarks, charms etc, are each known as a quantum, plural quanta, from which the whole specialisation takes its name – quantum physics.'

'A stream of single photons shone though a hole should produce a single microscopic point of light on a screen it's fired at. Experimentation has proved this to be the case, with some marginal exceptions, accounted for by the photons striking a glancing blow on the side of the hole as they pass through. This causes a penumbra or slightly less dark ring around the central point. Beyond that is the umbra or complete blackness, the total absence of light. Still following Dick?'

His friend nodded as they continued down the wooded path.

'Okay. So we know that the penumbra is caused by occasional bending of the light by it being bounced off the sides of the hole it's shone through. Now, do you remember those seemingly pointless experiments at school where we shone lights through grids to get interference patterns?' Again a quick nod from Dick, who was concentrating hard and wondering where all this was leading.

'So what happens when a stream of single photons is shone through a grid? Eh?'

Dick assumed this was a rhetorical question and kept quiet, simply looking over to Leon and awaiting his answer.

'Quite unexpectedly you get interference! The obvious question here is: if there is only one photon passing through the grid at a time, how can there be interference on the scale you get with a whole white light beam, made up of millions of interfering photons?'

'The answer is the point of this whole diatribe. There must be additional photons involved, which have been called shadow photons be some people. So we have tangible – *our world* photons, being interfered with by shadow photons – *other worldly* photons. At this time there is no other explanation for the effect that's been seen. In effect we have to admit to the existence of a *multiverse*. The universe holds everything physically here and now. The multiverse is made up of countless universes, which, by their very existence aren't in the here and now. They're part of the there and then.'

Again Leon stopped to see the reaction from his friend. Dick was looking slightly confused.

'So you're saying these parallel universes, whatever they are and where ever they are, can be used to time travel? That somehow we can move back and forth in a place outside of our physical world.? Is that it?'

This time it was Leon's turn to nod, as he turned to resume their walk.

'Close, but no cigar Dick. For reasons I haven't been able to fathom yet, it doesn't quite work like that. When I do what I can do, as far as I can tell, I never leave the world we all know and love. I've never had a feeling of travelling outside of the reality we're all experiencing. I may be wrong, but it just never felt like I was moving in the multiverse as opposed to the universe inhabited by everyone – everything – else.'

Leon paused and gazed around him at the wooded glade they had entered. The light filtered through the green boughs overhead, dappling the ground all around them. The place had an eerie quality, solely caused by the total lack of movement anywhere, apart from the rainbow streams that threaded through the sun's rays in amongst the trees and undergrowth. The colours flowed like water in and around every tree and bush, gathering in some places like pools, but rushing past in others.

'I think that the ribbons of light that you can see, and they always appear when time is slowed, are caused by energies from the multiverse. Where different universes edge across each other they 'rub' together if you like, causing energy to be released as the coloured lights we can see. The lights are always there, but you can only see them if you use time to slow everything else down. When I slow, or stop, time, I can't affect what's going on in the countless other universes, and they make their presence known by radiating energy into our world.'

Dick nodded. It all sounded quite reasonable once you accepted that anything was possible. Once you realised how little you knew about anything outside your normal sphere of experience, why not believe in all the endless possibilities presented to you? If Leon believed this stuff, Dick certainly had no reason to argue. Not yet at least.

Leon began to cross the clearing as he began talking again.

'The earth has its own energy. Every living thing, no matter how small has an aura of light around it. Some people claim to be able to see it, some say they have photographs. And maybe they do. Who knows?'

'Yes, it's the kind of thing you see in those semi-scientific books. You know – 'Was God a spaceman' and all that. My Mum used to read those. Always interesting, but never proven. I always took it all with a pinch of salt.'

Dick was pleased to be able to interject, he was beginning to feel like he was back at school, being taught things he should have been able to see for himself. His new outlook on life was making him question a lot of what he thought he knew.

Leon smiled over at him and headed off along an ever thinning path that marked their exit from the dell. For the first time since they had begun walking the path was too narrow for them to walk abreast, so Dick followed as Leon led the way, looking back over his shoulder as he spoke.

'Well I'm sure a lot of it is just bollocks, but not all of it. The world is made up of billions – trillions – who knows how many little life forces, all generating this energy. Unseen and totally unused. There are those that say the world operates as a single huge organism. Then again there are those who see the entire universe as an organism, living somewhere within an even larger place, so vast it can't be imagined.'

'Whoa there boy! Leon, I think you're heading a bit off the beaten track, in more ways than one.' Dick was looking around at the tangle of ferns and brambles that were plucking at his clothes.

'Lets get back onto a path, and back to the subject at hand. Tell me how you think it works. Okay?'

Leon grinned sheepishly.

'Sorry, got a bit carried away there.'

He led his friend back out of the tangled undergrowth, swatting the branches aside with wide sweeps of his arms.

'Oi Leon! Watch what you're doing! You'll have someone's eye out.'

Dick was busy dodging the resulting return swings from the bushes following Leon's passage.

'There's a joke there somewhere.' laughed Leon, 'Something about King Harold tearing a strip off a young bowman at Hastings, isn't it?'

They both laughed as they stumbled and pushed their way back to the animal track that wound throughout Leon's domain. Once they had both regained their breath, they headed on towards the gardens, off somewhere in the far distance, now on the return half of their stroll.

The path began to open out and the two walked happily side by side as they talked.

'Yes. To get back to the original point.' said Leon. 'The world has all this energy streaming around it that we, for the most part, simply can't see. Because we can't see it we don't know it exists, and as a consequence no-one ever tries to use it. But it is powerful and it is *everywhere*. Even rocks possess a little of it, although they aren't living as we understand it. But they are made up of the same things as we are. Molecules, atoms, charms, quarks and God knows what else. Everything Dick, absolutely everything has power, or spirit, call it what you will. The largest concentration of it as far as we're concerned, is Good Ol' Mother Earth. She's wreathed in this amazing energy that wanders in streams over the surface of the world. In places it pools, and in others it's almost non-existent. It seems to extend everywhere but, and this is the important bit, but it is held in place by living things. So everything has its own little cocoon of power, a personal aura. For micro-organisms it might only be a few microns deep, but for a tree it can radiate out several feet. For a forest the power, as you can see, can cause huge swirls of energy, but basically it's just a lot of individual envelopes clustered together. It still only extends a few feet beyond the limits of the woods.'

Dick interrupted again.

'But it seemed quite brilliantly coloured over by the house, and that's a fair way from the wood, isn't it. So there must be something else involved, mustn't there?

Leon's eyes lit up and he almost jumped in excitement as he became more animated.

'Exactly! Exactly! There must be something else involved. And that's where the multiverse comes in!' Leon spun around to face Dick and walked backwards with such a spring in his step that he was almost hopping. 'I think - and I've no way to prove this mind - that the extra energy is coming from the multiverse. Think about it! If shadow photons can affect light in our universe, then why not have a shadow life force? If all things here have an energy that can be tapped into by people like me, why not have the same from other universes? If they exist, maybe they affect our world in the same way as their shadow photons.'

Dick raised a quizzical eyebrow.

'Let me get this straight Leon. You think, but at this stage you only think, that parallel universes exist. Moreover you've made the great leap into a belief that they can have an effect in this world. Come on Leon, that's a bit far-fetched, even given what I've seen in the last few hours. If you really think it's possible, and I'm sorry but it seems a step too far for me, why don't you use the power you've got to go into the future and check. Surely at some point in the years, maybe only a couple, maybe in hundreds, if not thousands, of years, they'll know for definite if the multiverse really is out there? Why not just nip on ahead of time and see? 'Cos it sounds a little bit "X-Files", don't you think?'

For the first time in a long time Leon looked nonplussed. He stopped walking and faced Dick, hands on hips.

'Dick, there are some things that even with my unusual talent I just can't do, and travelling into the future is one of them. It seems that Time itself somehow manages to keep us in check. I can go back as far as I've ever wanted to, so far up to about four thousand years, but I always come back to here and now. Time won't let me get ahead of myself. So the future is still a closed book to me, and maybe to everyone. I dunno. All I can do is go with my gut feelings about it all. It seems that parallel universes do exist, far more eminent people than me are beginning to believe it, so who am I to disagree? They think it can have physical effects in our world and now so do I. I know beyond all doubt that time can be traversed if you have the ability. I also believe that I can do it because I'm using the power that Mother Earth has given me, and that it's available to anyone.'

'So if all this energy is sloshing about, why are you so convinced that something else, this multiverse, must be involved?' Dick was clearly puzzled by Leon's view. 'Convert me to your way of thinking Leon. Make me a believer too.'

Leon looked less certain than he had only a few seconds before. He took his friend by the elbow and steered him back towards the lawns visible through the low hanging branches ahead.

'Hummm. Well, to be honest Dick, I can't be sure. But when I started reading all this stuff about alternative universes I thought that it all seemed to fit. If, when I slow time, the streams keep going, where are they from? If even time can't stop them, where are they coming from? When time slows down all around me, how can the energy of the world keep going? Come on Dick, help me out here, 'cos I'm getting confused. I thought I was sorting it all out, but maybe I've taken a wrong turn.'

Dick shrugged as he walked.

'Sorry mate. This is all too new for me. Let me think about it for a while – but don't hold your breath. Let's have a damn good drink - of something stronger than coffee, and see if anything springs to mind.'

The two smiled together, both with unanswered questions. As they arrived back at the house they paused and Leon closed his eyes. The air moved gently across their cheeks and birdsong returned. The sound of the rustling leaves in the surrounding trees seemed unnaturally loud as they re-entered the hallways of Chez Leon.

By the time they reached the drinks cabinet Leon and Dick both felt in need of another glass of whiskey, and Leon took the bottle outside as they returned to the gathering gloom of late evening to try to make sense of the strange new world that Dick now found himself inhabiting.

Now Fin (19)

Mister Nutter stood looking at the back of Fin, in the silent shade behind the mill. The boy's agitated prattling about time travel and wood had come to a very sudden end and he was obviously shocked that his wild story had been so easily disproved. Even though he couldn't see the boy's face he could clearly perceive the near collapse of the gloom shrouded form before him.

Fin's shoulders had dropped and he stood rooted to the spot in despair. He struggled to keep himself from crying – his youthful frame trembled and the only sounds came from the rustling of the grass, the leaves in the trees and the nearby undergrowth in the gentle summer breeze. How could he have been such a fool! Things had changed, obviously they had. The last time he'd been here with Bill was only last night to him, but had been months if not years for Bill. If only he could prove what he'd said to the teacher he could sense was standing only a few steps behind him. Oh God, what should he do next? The emptiness in his stomach seemed to spread throughout his body. He felt light headed and nauseous. He staggered to the wall on his right and slumped to the ground.

This wasn't fair. He'd tried for years to cope alone with this, and now just when he thought it was safe to say something to someone else, just when he thought he could prove that he wasn't going mad, he'd blown it. There was no way he would persuade anyone now. He'd had a chance to bring Mister Nutter in on his team, and stuffed himself instead, placing friend and teachers firmly with the opposition. The referee was about to blow for kick-off and LeMott United consisted of only one player, the rest of the world was playing for Who's-the- Loony-In-The-Red-Shirt Town.

Maybe he really was insane. Maybe he'd spent most of his youth trying to convince himself that he was just a normal lad having weird dreams, when if fact he was some sort of lunatic. He didn't know what it would be termed but could imagine the fun a psychiatrist could have with him. Schizophrenic, paranoid, neurotic – he was sure they'd have a name for whatever it was he had. Something of his extrovert confident spirit quietly hid itself away in a secret little place inside him.

He finally gave in to abject despair. Why bother trying to go on with it all? Maybe he'd be happier just locked away with his strange dreams, without having to care about how the rest of the world perceived him. He was sure Mum, Dad and Lillibet would be better off without having to worry about how their lunatic relative would act in the future. His brain tried to force him to think more clearly about what had happened to him, but his heart was past caring anymore. It wasn't fair! Mad little boys shouldn't have to dwell on their insanity, they should just be left alone to go quietly insane.

Fin sat, his empty stare gazing out at the desolate future ahead of him. He was mad, and needed to accept it. It wasn't fair, but then he'd often heard that life wasn't fair. So he might as well just shut up and give in.

He stole a quick glance at the teacher, who still hadn't moved from the corner of the mill.

Michael Nutter had no idea how to handle this. In the last few minutes he had witnessed this boy go from the Fin LeMott they all knew and loved, to a not quite ranting lunatic, and thence to the silent heap slumped against the wall. He'd felt he should go and offer some sort of comfort, but what in God's name could he say? They certainly never trained you for this. How do you approach a boy who's just told you he's a time traveller, and full of the joys of spring, but then whose mood appears to swing to the completely opposite extreme. There was clearly no large pile of wood shavings, or anything else here. Fin had been delusional to say the least, and now seemed to have plunged into a pit of misery.

Maybe the lad was having some sort of breakdown, something to do with the nightmares that Lidine and Jarmon had mentioned. That could also account for his falling out with Tam and Co. earlier in the day, but how should he, as Fin's teacher, handle this?

Buggeration! Where was Bert Lightfoot when you needed him?

Mike appeared to be watching the complete spiritual disintegration of the boy he had known as a fun loving extrovert, and was deeply upset by the events unfolding before him.

Well he had to do something, that was certain, so he strode over to Fin and settled down onto his haunches in front of the silent boy. Fin wiped his sleeve across his red-rimmed eyes and looked into the clear blue eyes before him, but then dropped his chin onto his chest and sat in mute anguish. He looked totally defeated and defenceless, and desperately in need of some reassurance.

'Fin?' he quietly queried, but received no reply. 'Come on Fin, talk to me. Try to help me understand what's going on. I hope I'm a friend as much as your teacher, so tell me what's going on in that head of yours.'

Mike was aware that Bert and the other boys would soon begin to wonder what was delaying the two of them and the last thing he wanted, or Fin needed, was for them all to turn up whilst this crisis was upon them. He lifted the boy's chin with a finger, but Fin snatched his head free and continued to stare at the ground between his feet, with his knees drawn up to his chest, encircled by his arms.

'Fin, for God's sake snap out of it.' he begged in a low voice. 'We've got to sort this out now, before the others find out what's happening. Talk to me.'

He was trying very hard to help somehow, but wasn't meeting with any success, as far as he could tell.

He grasped the small shoulders opposite in both hands. Actually they weren't as small as he'd thought. Fin was now a young man, despite his age, in both intellect and physical build. Could all this simply be the result of an overactive imagination inside a burgeoning body? But thinking about it, no - it couldn't be just that. Something more sinister was going on here. Fin looked as though all the life had gone out of him. It all seemed so ridiculous given his usual ebullient self.

Still holding Fin, he stood and pulled him to his feet, almost having to fight against the boy's obvious reluctance. His young charge refused to utter a word.

Mike steered him back towards the coach waiting in the car park.

'I'm sorry Fin, but I've got to help Mister Lightfoot with the group around the mill.'

He ushered the boy up the steps of the coach, whose door was open to let in the pleasant summer warmth. 'You sit here until you feel you can come and join us. We'll be in the main block somewhere. I'm sure the chap on the information desk will be able to point you in the right direction.'

He patted Fin lightly on the head.

'Don't worry old son, we'll sort this out somehow. Don't give in.'

And doesn't that sound trite, he thought as he turned reluctantly back to the mill. As he walked he wondering how on earth he was going to do what he'd just said, given that he hadn't the faintest notion of what was causing the boy's problem and therefore had no idea how to help him.

He entered the mill through the information-cum-reception area, nodding to the old man behind the desk, who gave him a cheery grin and said 'They'll be up on the first floor by now. Hurry up, or it'll all be over before you get there.' and with a smile, returned to checking the well stocked shelves around the room. Stock that consisted mainly of Olde Worlde tooth-rotters such as gob-stoppers and assorted toffees, tea towels with pictures of old-mills and a multitude of small wooden curios manufactured, presumably, on the premises.

Bert gave Mike a questioning look as he rejoined the group of boys at the head of a massive set of stairs that led up from the second large room, towards the back of the mill. Mike gave back a look of helplessness and turned his attention back to the boys who made up the bulk of their charges.

Surprisingly the whole gathering seemed enthralled by the descriptions of the old work practices being given by the elderly tour leader.

'An' 'ere we 'ave the manager's office and to the right the dryin' room. As yuh can see the floor is made from a number of perforated iron plates, like a big metal grid, to allow th' air from th' stem rum to enter through 'oles in't floor. T' bobbins dried in 'ere once they'd been rough cut on t' lathes downstairs an' before they was finished on t' finishin' lathes downstairs an' then polished in't rum roun' corner 'ere.'

The man pointed around the corner to their right and then paused for effect, before saying 'Tis said that a ghost still 'aunts this 'ere rum. Rattlin' the floor as it moves aroun' at night.' With a conspiratorial lowering of his voice he continued, 'An' if the gentlemen 'ere don' mind I'll recount the tale of where this 'ere ghost is said to come from.' He gave a quizzical glance towards Bert and Mike, both of whom chuckled and smirked like schoolboys themselves.

Bert replied first, with a totally straight face. 'Oh, I'm not sure Mister N. Should we allow such things on what is, after all, a serious historical tour of the area?'

Despite his mood, Mike couldn't help joining in, putting on his own serious schoolmasters face he said. 'I find I must agree with you Mister Lightfoot. You are the senior master here, and I feel you may well be right in this. We mustn't go filling young heads with nonsense about spectres and ghoulies should we?

A collective groan rose from the gathered boys. They knew their teachers well, but were having trouble deciding exactly what was going on here.

Mister Lightfoot gazed around at the sea of expectant faces, every one of them obviously wanting to hear more from the knowledgeable old chap standing quietly in the shadows cast by the shafts of light coming up through the strange floor.

'Oh, well said, my young friend. But just this once I think we should be able to handle the resulting hysteria, don't you think?' He waved a careless hand towards the dimly lit figure ahead. 'Carry on Mister Iveson, if you please'

Over the top of the resulting cheer Mister Nutter finished with 'A capital idea Mister L. Capital.'

The two men smiled and managed to look almost as interested as the rest of the captive audience.

Their guide, Mister Iveson, explained that up until only a few years before, when the mill was still in reasonably full production, the air would be thick with dust caused by the working of the turning lathes in the lathe shop below. The floor would sometimes be almost knee deep in wood shavings, a haven for small wildlife from the woods outside. Whilst this helped to keep the workers warm in the winter it posed an ever present fire and health risk, and made work even more difficult in the summer months. Periodically therefore, all the waste had to be removed. When the steam engine was installed in the late nineteenth century, a lot of the wood could be used in the boiler, prior to the engine, the waste was simply that - waste. Every six months or so, all the excess shavings, turnings and off-cuts were simply shovelled out through the low windows. Much of the ever present dust simply blew out through the higher windows on a draught caused by the line-shafts which transmitted power from the original water wheel and then later the steam engine.

'So what were the obvious outcome o' all this?' asked Mister Iveson, with a raised eyebrow. He surveyed the silent boys, who glanced sideways, waiting for someone to answer.

It was Mister Nutter who said, in a rather hushed and curiously quavering voice 'There was a big pile of wood shavings just the other side of this wall?'

'Precisely sir. Ah can see why yer becum a teacher. But it weren't just big, it were 'uge! It got so big that the manager 'ad this 'ere door put in, so's 'e could get out through back of mill, instead of 'avin t' walk all t'way aroun'. Meant 'e didn' 'ave t' walk through all t' mess downstairs y'see. What with all the rain we gets roun' 'ere, the pile outside were solid enough t' walk on. So it were 'is short cut, so t' speak. 'Course when the mill were closed and then turned into this museum, they got rid of it. Full of mice and such like. So now we 'ave a door that leads straight out to a twenty foot drop t' ground below. It were always steep mind, but now it's lethal boys. So don' go tryin' t'open t'door, a'right?'

'When was it moved Mister Iveson?' asked Mike, still sounding a little breathless.

'Oh, back in '85 or '86 I think. Odd to think it 'ad been aroun' for over a 'undred years by then.'

'What about the ghost?' piped up Tam.

'Oh , Aye. That were a strange tale from late in't last century, the 1880s we think, though we can't be certain. There are a number of stories 'bout deaths and dismemberments.' he said, to the obvious glee of several of the boys.

'These machines, and the belts an' all are very dangerous, especially wit' young lads workin' 'ere. But this one tale is the strangest of 'em all. Tis said that one time one o' the young lads came across a boy, not much older than 'imself, who appeared lost in the night. The followin' day he were still about, an' were chased through t' mill by T' Bobbin Master - the owner - a Mister Coward it were back then, an' he got as far as this very spot, where he were cornered. To get away, he ran through this door, which weren't locked in them days, an' fell. Now as I say, there were a great pile of stuff just outside, but by all accounts he were going so fast that he shot straight out over it all, and' should have been badly 'urt, if not killed by the fall. But strangely - an' several o' the workers said they saw the whole thing, an' swore it were true - he went out like a ferret up a drainpipe, but *'e never hit the ground*. It were like he just vanished into thin air. An' from then on, whenever there were any odd noises in th' night, they reckoned it were the lad who vanished that day, never to be 'eard of again.'

Mister Iveson paused for dramatic effect.

'All bloody nonsense o' course, but makes a good tale, don't yer think? And he gave a great blasting guffaw which startled more than a few of the boys who had slipped into the spirit of the moment – so to speak.

'Anyway, let's get on an' visit the blacksmiths shop, which is just 'ere.' he said as he led the group around into the next room just to the left, as they passed the top of the stairway.

'Anything wrong Mike?' asked Bert with some concern. His colleague looked as though he really had seen a ghost. 'And where's young Finbar?'

Mike shuddered as he visibly tried to shake off his mood. He smiled at Bert, but still with a rather sombre expression.

'He's down in the coach. He's not feeling to well so I said he could sit this one out if he wanted to. I'll tell you about it all later. I certainly need some sage advice on how to handle this.'

'Oh Lord, what's happened now? You always begin to worry me when you talk like that.' Bert knew it must be something serious for Mike to need anyone else's opinion on a teacher/pupil issue.

'No - later Bert. Just need to have a chat about young Mister LeMott, that's all.'

And Bert Lightfoot had to be content with that, for now.

Eventually they finished their inspection of the mill and its surroundings and, following a lightening fast pre-emptive strike to the ice cream cabinet in the reception, the boys and their two masters strolled out into the bright sunlight.

'Right boys, get your packed lunches from the coach. You can eat them out here if you wish, seems a shame to waste such a lovely day.' said Mister Nutter shielding his eyes against the sudden glare.

Simeon's voice drifted out of the crowd ahead. 'Can we explore the woods sir, before we have to leave?'

A small gaggle around him all nodded and made sounds of approval as they looked back to the men.

'Okay, Sim, but don't get lost. And that goes for the rest of you as well!' he had to call this last, since almost all the boys were now rushing towards the coach, the quicker to be off into the surrounding trees. Some wanted merely to race about in the cool shelter offered by the woods, but some at least were trying to find the evidence of the coppicing required to keep a constant flow of timber to the mill. Their shouts and calls from amongst the trees told the teachers that the talk from Mister Iveson had not been wasted on all of them. Mister Lightfoot smiled, pleased with the boys for showing more interest than he might have expected in the manufacturing of bobbins. It was nice to know that they still had the ability to surprise him, even after all these years.

He turned to Mike Nutter as the two of them allowed the sun to warm them from a cloudless sky.

'So Mike, what's to do with Fin?'

Mike glanced over to the coach parked in the shade at the edge of the car park, and Bert was disturbed by his vexed expression.

'I think we've got a problem with Fin.' He paused, trying to marshal his thoughts. Trying to work out how to explain what had happened earlier.

'He seems to be having some sort of breakdown' he flicked a quick look up at Bert on hearing the indrawn breath and the 'No!' of disbelief. 'I haven't got the foggiest why he should have come out with such a strange tale, and then withdraw into himself when it was proved to be no more than that almost immediately. He really is in some sort of trouble – mentally, I mean.'

Bert looked so shocked it was almost comical.

'Good Lord Mike. Tell me more. That doesn't seem possible. Not Fin surely?' he was smiling again, not sure how to take the news. 'Fin's always been such a level-headed lad. It's ridiculous.'

'Oh I know Bert, believe me I do. But the most shocking thing is, I've just heard something that supports his story. Except that it's so daft it hardly bears repeating.'

Mike then told Bert what had occurred whilst he was outside with Fin and Bert was inside the mill. When told in the warm light of a Lake District afternoon the story did sound more like a joke than anything else, except that Bert also picked up on Mister Iveson's anecdote about the disappearing boy and the pile of timber waste.

'Relax Mike. He's obviously read a bit of a guide book or maybe been here before. He's heard the tale and decided to pull your leg. It's just Fin playing about. Don't worry about it. Let's get back to the bus, get our sarnies and see how he is now. I bet he'll be laughing his socks off at you. Just wait and see.'

The two men turned towards the coach, thirty yards away, just in time to see Fin emerge and begin to run towards the mill. On seeing the two, he skidded to a halt and ran to them instead with an expression of delight on his face. Mister Lightfoot gave his friend a smile of triumph.

'Told you so, little devil was just winding you up.'

Mister Nutter's face showed only too clearly his anger as Fin stopped in front of them, chest heaving after his sprint.

'Finbar LeMott…' began Mike, but was interrupted by the beaming boy.

'Give me another chance to prove it sir. I'm not a loony honest, and now I've told you, you have to give me another chance. Please let me have a look around the mill and I need to talk to someone who knows the history of the place. Not that chap who found me earlier, it needs to be someone older, much older.'

Now it was Bert's turn to be taken aback.

'Now look here Fin. Mister Nutter has told me what's going on and, to be rather callous about it, you've got to pull yourself together. For Heaven's sake boy, stop this immediately. Time travel in the night indeed! I took you for brighter than that and I do expect you to behave. Starting now! We will have no more of this nonsense, do you hear.' He grabbed Fin by the arm. 'Apart from upsetting both of us, think of how your friends will react if you keep this up. Think of your family. What on earth are they going to make of this. This stupid joke ends now. Get back onto the coach and stay there until the time comes for us to leave. Do not repeat any of this to any of the other boys, they at least are here to enjoy their holiday, don't spoil it for them.' He relaxed his grip on the boy's arm.

'For goodness sake Fin, there has to be another explanation. The most plausible being that you are just causing mischief. So get back on the bus and consider your actions. We will talk about this later, without the other boys. Then you can try to convince me not to keep you on a very tight rein for the rest of the trip.'

'Get back on the coach now Fin. There's a good lad. Go on.' said Mister Nutter in a quiet, sad voice. He looked across at Bert, hardly believing the outburst he'd just heard. 'Go on lad' he urged turning Fin towards the bus.

'Go!' roared Bert Lightfoot at the boy's back.

Mike touched his colleague lightly on the arm as he watched the boy walk disconsolately back to the coach.

'Little hard on him, don't you think Bert? I don't think he needed that just now.'

Bert turned and said 'I never expected such idiocy from young LeMott, and I'm sure he just needs to be taken in hand. It's arrant nonsense Mike, and humouring him won't help, if indeed he needs humouring. Maybe it's just a stupid prank that got out of hand.'

He suddenly looked very guilty indeed, as he too looked over to the coach.

'Let's hope that's what it is. Otherwise we've got an altogether more serious problem on our hands. We'll discuss it later. Maybe Fin will make more sense then.'

He shrugged and began to walk back to the centre of the car park.

'Come on. Let's get the rest of these lads back and make sure we haven't lost any.'

He made a quick three sixty turn and called 'Okay boys, back to me! It's time to go! Let's be having you!'

The group slowly reassembled, until all were waiting outside the door of the bus. A quick head count ensure they were all present and before they began the mad scramble up the steps and back to their seats, Mike 'Shushed' them to silence.

'As I'm sure most of you are aware, Fin isn't feeling a hundred percent just at the moment.' He saw Tam and Willis exchange solemn looks, and Simeon looked concerned.

'So leave him be, for now. Just get back to your seats and enjoy the ride back. It's the play tonight, so it's back to the hostel for a couple of hours, then tea, change and out to see a bit of Shakespeare.' He smiled at the sea of faces. 'On you go then.'

He ushered them inside and then followed Bert aboard.

Fin was sitting at the front again and refused to acknowledge any of his friends as they fought their way passed him.

The door closed and the mill was left behind.

During the trip back Fin was silent beside the two teachers. At one point Mike was about to talk to him, but as he turned to lean across the aisle Bert put a restraining hand on his arm and said.

'Later Mike. Leave him for now. We'll try to sort this out before we eat – while the boys are outside.'

Fin was alternating between staring at his hands, resting on his knees, and the glorious landscape outside. He said nothing and looked at no-one within the bus.

Mike settled back slowly into his seat. He had the distinct feeling that Bert had handled this all wrong. If anything all they'd done was make matters worse. Now all the boys were curious about what was going on and that was going to make it even more difficult to bring Fin out of himself.

He was aware that, sitting immediately behind them, Tam and Simeon, and Willis seated behind Fin, were looking very subdued. He suspected that they were blaming themselves for Fin's predicament, and that was unfair. If he and Bert were unsure about how to handle this, he couldn't see how three young boys could have helped in any way. Glancing across the way, he could see that Willis looked close to tears, and as the boy looked up, he tried to give an encouraging smile, but was all too aware that it probably came over with more than a little grimace showing.

He began to try to see a way through this.

Fin did seem to be convinced that he had visited the mill the night before. So Mike had a choice: he could discount the boy's story, in which case Fin was either having some sort of breakdown or had already suffered one, or he could try to find a way to believe him, which in turn meant he had some sort of amazing time-travelling power. The latter just seemed so utterly ridiculous that he had to admit that pretty soon he was going to have to break the news to the LeMotts that there son was not a well boy, and probably needed some kind of specialist help. The sudden mood swings, the outlandish story, his rejection of his friends – they would have a clear, clinical explanation. They only had to bring in the necessary medical people and, hopefully, Fin could be restored to his former self. But looking across at the youth, who had until today, been a reasonably happy-go-lucky lad, that seemed a very distant prospect. Mike was gripped by a dreadful feeling of foreboding, that he would have to hide from everyone. He came to the conclusion that he would have to talk to Fin's three closest friends, to see exactly what had happened that morning. Maybe they could cast some light on the whole sorry business.

He also decided to ring his wife Bev, as soon as they got back to the hostel. She might be able to offer some advice. In such a delicate situation it could be that a woman's perspective would offer a helpful insight, and Bev's more than most.

But he wasn't holding his breath.

They arrived at the hostel in mid afternoon and as soon as the door opened the boys began to bundle themselves off.

'Bags back in your rooms.' ordered Bert, as he waved them down the steps. 'Then outside for a game of footie before we eat. Off you go then!'

His usual jovial manner had returned as he shepherded the boys back into the building. Luckily most of them were too busy enjoying their time in the sun, to ponder whatever the problem was with Fin, and Mike could hear Antrobus and several of the others planning a race down to the nearby lake to explore the lay of the land. Wast Water offered some incredibly desolate views, with screes running right down to the water and, on this side of the lake, plenty of small islets to try to cross to. The ground was also full of small hillocks and rocky mounds, ideal for re-enacting battles and great feats of exploration. Mike knew they would spend as long as they were allowed just running about and having fun. Which was more than could be said for the four remaining members of the troupe.

Fin was the last off the bus, and he was surprised to find his three erstwhile friends waiting for him.

Tam was first to speak.

'Fin, we're all sorry for this morning. We don't know exactly what caused it all, but we're sorry if we upset you. We really are.'

'Are you feeling any better?' chipped in Simeon, smiling hesitantly.

Fin shook his head, and looked as though he was going to burst into tears. So too did Willis, who reached out to put a trembling hand on Fin's arm.

'Is there anything we can do to help?' he asked in a quavering voice.

Mike was so touched by the scene that he felt like grabbing the lot of them and giving them a huge group hug. They were good kids, and it filled his heart with a deep sorrow to see them all so affected by the pain of their friend. If anyone could help Fin, it was these three boys, along with Mike himself. He was now more determined than ever to steer Fin through this. None of these young men deserved to be so upset and he was damned if he was going to let one of their number sink into such a sea of melancholy that he drowned.

He gestured towards a nearby tree, a huge oak with an encircling wooden bench in its shade.

'Sit over there boys. I'll be back in a minute, and then we'll have a chat. And Fin, tell them what you told me. They're going to have to find out what's wrong sooner or later, so make it now. Maybe we can help, who knows? But boys, listen to your friend and don't jump to conclusions. Fin is our friend.' Fin looked up quickly at this, with a look of almost pathetic thanks on his face, 'and we will be as supportive as we can. I'll be back in a mo.'

He left the sad little group under the tree, with a dreadful sinking feeling in his stomach. Fine words, but how was he going to help, he wondered, as he went to find a phone in reception.

Inside was considerably cooler than out in the sun, and Mike shivered in the sudden change. He approached a young woman at the desk.

'Excuse me.' he said to the winning smile she flashed at him as he came to a halt before her. 'Is there a phone about? I need to call home fairly urgently.'

She directed him to a payphone in its own small booth around the corner. At least it was private. He didn't want anyone passing to overhear this conversation. The fewer who knew about Fin's situation the better, outside those who were already involved.

He reversed the charges and got through to Bev almost immediately.

'It's me Bev. Be a love and accept the call.'

'Oh,,. if I must.' she giggled to the operator, and Mike smiled despite himself.

He could picture her in his minds eye, standing in the kitchen of their cottage in Mereside village, tea cup in hand, gazing out over the fields through the large picture window.

'How's the view gorgeous?' he asked.

'How do you know I'm looking at the view?' she replied. 'Maybe me and the milkman are having fun while the cat's away.' Again she giggled.

'It's three thirty and the sun is shining. I bet you've just decided to have a cuppa and leave the thesis for a while. So you're in the kitchen and looking for sheep.'

'My God Mike. Am I that predictable? Really?'

'No. You're my wife. We both like the same things, and that's what I'd be doing in your position.' He leaned back in the booth and waited for her to talk again. Most days, he was happy just to listen to her voice, even over a phone line. His blond, blue eyed and thoroughly gorgeous wife made him the envy of almost all of his friends and colleagues. Beauty, with an equally amazing brain, a sense of humour and a heart filled with love just for him. What more could a man ask for? Certainly nothing he could think of.

'Social call, or work?' she asked, still with a smile in her voice.

'Work, I'm afraid love. I need to pick your brains for a second.'

'Oh, about what?' she was intrigued now.

'A bit of a situation has come to light and I'm not sure how to handle it. I couldn't think who else to call, so you're *It* I'm afraid.'

'Oh great! Thanks for that glowing endorsement.' Her voice came down the line with the humour still intact. 'Come on then, ask away, Oh Love Of My Life.'

'Given that you're a budding Mind Mechanic and loose nut tightener, I need to now what to do about one of the lads in my tender care.'

'Oh?' Now she really was listening.

'You know young Fin LeMott, I've mentioned him occasionally?'

'Yeah, sure. I remember.'

'Well, he appears to have gone a bit loopy and I don't know why. Nor do I know how to handle it.'

'Golly. Look I'm sorry, but I'll need a bit more to go on than that Mike. Tell me what's happened and we'll see what I can do.'

Mike gave her a cut down version of the day's events in about two minutes, his narrative interrupted by the occasional shocked interjection.

When he'd finished Bev asked, 'Do you really believe that he believes what he's telling you? There's no way it's joke or something?'

'Definitely not. I know this lad, and there's no way he'd do something as outrageous as this just for a laugh. He really is in a bit of a mess. So what should I be doing to try to stop it getting worse.?'

'Well the obvious thing is to get him home and then come and see Professor Tome. Artie will have a much better idea than me. And don't try to persuade him he's having some sort of delusions, you could just make it worse. He sounds as though he's suffering from some sort of schizophrenia, but Artie would have a better idea. We'll also have to discuss this with his parents, they're going to be devastated – you always made him sound like such a level-headed kid. It will be a hell of a shock for them.' Mike could hear the sympathy even over the intervening miles.

'With luck, and the right treatment he should be okay though. So don't get too worked up. He'll almost certainly be alright after some help.' She sounded quite confident.

'I know, but it's not going to be much fun for any of us. And he's not a kid, love - they're baby goats.'

He heard her laugh. He had always hated the word 'kid'. It was just an unnecessary shorthand. They were boys, lads, youngsters, children, young men - anything but kids.

'Problem is, there's no way of getting him home today. We've only got the coach, and that can't leave without the others. We're not due back until tomorrow afternoon. Is that too long to wait, do you think?'

'Good question. I don't know, is the simple answer. Leave it with me. I'll have a chat with the Doc and call back if he thinks we need to do something faster. I could always drive up. It's not as though I don't have a few spare hours. This thesis is driving *me* nuts, and that's no lie. Maybe a quick drive up to the Lakes would do me good. Anyway, we'll see. Give me the number there and I'll leave a message if necessary. And don't worry' she hurried on, overriding his next comment, 'I'll be discrete. I'll go and see Old Tomesy straight away. You go and look after Fin until I get back to you. Talk to you tomorrow maybe.'

She's a mind reader, thought Mike. He'd been about to ask that she leave as innocuous a message as possible, but she'd known.

'Okay. Thanks a million Bev. Bye gorgeous.'

'Bye Love, and don't worry, we'll sort Fin out between us. Speak to you later.'

He settled the phone back in its cradle.

Well at least Bev had sounded hopeful. In truth, he wasn't sure whether he was over-reacting. He'd had trouble with boys before, but nothing quite as unexpected as this. He smiled to himself. Yes, they would sort this out, funny how talking to Bev always helped him to get his head straight about things. He re-entered the bright, sunny day through the main doors and revelled in the feeling of *completeness* he always felt when he'd had contact with his wife. The fact that they were separated by miles made no difference to the effect they always had on each other. Kindred spirits, soul mates – call it what you will, Mike knew there would never be anyone in the world who could make him feel the way he did about Bev.

As he returned to the small group of boys in the shade of the tree, still hearing Bev's voice in his head, he whistled, a little tunelessly he had to admit. 'Rosalinda's Eyes' had been their song since the first time they'd met, and he still couldn't get the damned harmonies right. Sometimes Billy Joel had a lot to answer for.

Fin and the others were now talking animatedly, but the conversation died as they turned to watch Mister Nutter as he sat next to Simeon.

Tam was first to speak.

'Fin just told us what's going on.'

'I think he's spent too much time playing games on the computer and reading Dean Koontz, meself.' said Simeon with a smile. 'He's flipped his lid.'

Tam gave him a light-hearted shove. 'Button it, Carver. You always did lack imagination. You need to get down to the library more often and get hold of those funny paper things… what are they called... oh yes, books… you cretinous philistine.'

'Oooh, sticks and stones…'

Only Willis was still looking worried. Even Fin had brightened noticeably and grinned at the banter of the other two.

'Sir, even if Fin is a bit cracked, he's still our mate and we've got to help him. That's what we're here for isn't it? To lend a helping hand to a friend in need.' said Tam.

Mike couldn't get over the fact that at least two of Fin's friends seemed to have taken this in their stride. Here they were, discussing his failing mental state as though it was just a joke.

'Tam, I'm not sure you've actually grasped the seriousness of this.' said Mike in earnest tones. 'What Fin is saying is that somehow he can travel through space, and time, in the middle of the night. It's science fiction and lala land. He's got a problem that we have to help him with. And why are you looking so pleased Fin? Half an hour ago you we're verging on suicidal, but suddenly all's well with the world. What have you been deciding while I've been away? Come on, give.'

Fin held his hands up for quite when Tam and Simeon began to answer.

'It's like this Mike. I told them everything I told you. The flying, the old mill when it wasn't so old, the fact that I may well be completely Loony Tunes, but Sim remembers a book he read ages ago.' Here he gave a sidelong look at Tam, who looked uncomfortable, while Simeon grinned and gave Tam an elbow in the ribs that said 'see, I'm not a complete dope.'

'And he says that Norman Mailer quotes a thing they had in the American Army called 'Catch 22'.' He raised his eyebrows in query at Mister Nutter.

'Madmen don't know they are mad... therefore men who think they are mad... can't be. That's it, in a nutshell, isn't it?' said Mike.

'Exactly.' said Sim, butting in. 'Therefore, no matter how barmy it sounds, there must be some truth in what Fin says.'

'Unless 'Catch 22' is all a load of bollocks.' said Tam. Then realising what he'd just said he reddened, 'Er... Um... sorry, Mister Nutter.'

'Don't worry Tam, I've got far more important things to think about than your lack of vocab.' He ruffled Tam's hair. 'Just don't let anyone else know I said so. It is, however, a valid point. You two' he pointed at Tam and Simeon, 'are convinced that Fin is telling at least some truth here, based on a hypothesis that's a bit dodgy to say the least. You're saying that since Fin thought he was tipping over the edge into insanity, he couldn't be. Therefore what he's saying must be true.' He looked at the boys with a sweeping glance. 'Is that right? You think he can time travel while we're all asleep.'

He was aware that this sort of questioning might only make things worse as far as Tam was concerned, and dreaded to think what Bev would say when he told her, but he couldn't see a way around it at the moment. This small group was all that Fin had to hold onto, so they had to come to some kind of consensus about it all, and hopefully move on from there.

'That's right.' said Tam. 'Either Fin is off with the faeries, or he's telling the truth. So what harm can it do for us to believe him, until it's proven that he's doo lally? But just imagine if it is true sir. Wouldn't that be epic!'

'My mate the Time Lord!' gushed Simeon, 'Triffic.'

There was a long pause as the boys looked expectantly at their teacher and, much as he hated to admit it, Mike was swayed by their argument. What was the harm in taking the whole thing on faith until they knew it was all just a load of bunkum. Maybe Fin himself could be persuaded that he was wrong, massively confused in some way, just by having all his best friends trying to help him prove he was right.

Mike smiled and turned to Willis, who was still sat quietly next to Fin, gazing at the grass between his trainers.

'And what about you Willis, what do you think of this master plan?'

Without looking up Will said, 'Oh I believe Fin sir, absolutely, I don't have to be persuaded thanks very much. I think he's telling the truth... no... I know he's telling the truth, about some of it at least.'

The other four looked mystified, so he went on.

'My parents died almost a year ago, but I still see them in my sleep. I can touch them and speak to them. It's only happened a couple of times and it might just be memories, but I want to believe that we can go back and relive the past. If Fin started off with a dream, or nightmare, and now thinks that he can physically go back, I want to believe that it's possible. I want to know that I can go and see Mum and Dad again, if I just try hard enough, or find out how to. So it might just be wishful thinking, but I will trust absolutely in what Fin says until someone proves to me that it can't be done.'

And there was such a look of hope, and loss, and yearning in his young face that Mike found himself saying 'Okay boys, we'll do it your way. But I have to say that I'm coming at this from the opposite direction. I *don't* believe it, at all. I'll do whatever I can to let you try to help Fin' he looked at Willis' pleading expression, 'and Will, but I think Fin has a problem whose resolution lies more in medical ability and psychiatric treatment than in faith, no matter how earnestly felt.'

He looked at each boy in turn. What on earth had he committed himself to now? Maybe he should have just kept his mouth shut and waited for Bev to call back. But from the demeanour of the foursome opposite, he guessed he'd probably made the right choice here. But he couldn't rid himself of the feeling that he could have handled it better, certainly where Willis was concerned. Had he just let Will slide into the same morass as the one he was trying to extricate Fin from? Oh well, only time would tell.

For now there was the question of what this small group should do, without revealing Fin's problem to the wider world, and the boys playing far off in the sun-drenched distance in particular.

'Fin, back at the mill you said you had clothes acquired during your nocturnal excursion last night. Lets start with them shall we?'

Fin and Willis both looked up, and Willis let out a gasp of surprise.

'Of course. That's where they came from. Those bloody awful boots and the coat. Of course. Cripes Fin, we forgot about the sheet and things as well!'

Mike looked over in shock. 'So you've seen them as well? Well why didn't you say so Will? Where are they?'

He stood and began to make for the entrance to the hostel, but Will grabbed his arm. 'No sir, not inside, we threw them out of the window, around by the bins. The mucky sheets and duvet are still in the room, but the coat's out here.'

He steered Mike around the side of the building into the shaded rear yard within which stood the industrial sized metal bins. The area around them was totally clear. At some point during the day someone had tidied up and the dirty clothing was gone.

But this time Mike was prepared.

'Okay boys, let's find this stuff. It must be in one of the bins. So, who's up for a spot of bin diving?'

Simeon jumped forward.

'Okey Dokey, Mister N. Let me at it!'

The other boys laughed at the eagerness he showed in wanting to bury himself in the murky depths.

'Watch out for rats.' called Tam. 'Right clever little buggers they are. No telling where they might be hiding.'

'Yeah. I had a mate who owned one. It kept escaping from anything he used as a cage. Metal, glass, plastic – it was all the same to Roly Poly.' said Sim.

'Roly Poly?' asked Tam.

'Yeah. My mate said he was a Dessert Rat.' answered Tam, and they all laughed.

'Plonker.' shot back Sim as he approached the nearest bin.

'Mind you…' said Fin. 'Can't you just see ol' Roly edging his way up to the door…' he stood with his back to the bins and edged sideways, looking left and right as though on the lookout for guards.

'Then out with the skeleton keys!' said Tam, miming extracting a bunch of keys from his pocket.

'And Bobs your Auntie – your car's been nicked!' laughed Willis.

Even Mike joined in here. It was good to see the boys enjoying themselves. This was more like it!

'Look out sir he's going in!' yelled Tam.

'Dive! Dive! Dive!' shouted Fin through cupped hands.

Willis made a great show of leaping out of the way and cowering against the nearest bin as Simeon threw off his coat and made for the first skip-sized container. Mister Nutter picked up Sim's coat and laid it on the lawn.

'All right Mister Carver, I think we've got the idea. Fin, Tam, give him a hand.' he said pointing to Simeon as the boy tried to scramble up the four foot high side in front of him.

As the two boys began to lift their friend, he hoisted the blue lid above his head and peered inside.

'Ugh! Something's burst in here, and it don't half niff! But I don't see any clothes. It's not in this one. Let me down.'

Fin and Tam moved back to let him drop back to the earth between the first and second bins. He moved to wipe his hands on his jeans and then abruptly changed his mind.

'No, maybe not.' Sim sniffed his hands tentatively, 'Whoar! Definitely not'

That led to another burst of laughter, and again Mike joined in. The sun had emerged round the corner of the hostel, and Michael marvelled at the change in atmosphere from only a few hours ago. But he still had his doubts about what was to come.

'Come on then – onto number two.' he grinned.

The boys went through the same procedure again, with the same result. Michael was now most definitely becoming nervous. What were they going to do if they couldn't find anything? Would Fin be back to rock bottom again?

He needn't have worried. The third, and last bin, came up trumps.

'Oh Yessss! Come to Daddy!' yelled Sim, as he tossed what appeared to be an old oily sack at Willis, who jumped back to let it fall to the ground.

'Incoming!' roared Sim and the coat was quickly joined by a pair of very unimpressive boots that whistled past Willis' head.

'Cheers Sim. I don't think I really want to catch them, or anything that might be living in it at the moment.'

'Dying more like.' laughed Sim.

The boots had the appearance of a couple of bricks, with gaping holes in the toes and soles. The coat was made of what seemed to be a very heavy wool that had been drenched in oil and given a liberal brushing of sawdust.

Sim jumped down for the last time and the boys all stood around their teacher. Mike picked up the coat and looked up at Fin and Willis.

'So this is what came back with you last night Fin?' Mike asked, with a sceptical lift to his eyebrow, 'And you saw this too Willis?'

Willis looked a little subdued now as attention turned to him, he gave a nervous cough.

'Well sir, when I came to wake Fin this morning and he was wearing the coat and still had the boots on. I didn't know what to think , but when I told Tam and Simeon and we came back upstairs after breakfast...'

'And young Finbar threw a wobbler, and the rest we all know.' interrupted Mike with a lopsided grin. He dropped the boots and looked closer at the coat.

'Well I have to say that it's not up to Fin's usual sartorial elegance is it? But how can we find out where it came from?'

Silence greeted him. Each boy seemed to be trying to look anywhere but at Fin or the teacher. Mike realised he was going to have to help them out here somehow.

'Come on lads, chins up. We've got some ratty old boots and a disgusting coat. Fin acquired them last night, and as things stand at the moment we're all going along with his explanation that he went back in time and managed to return with them as a memento. So let's think of how we can prove, or disprove, his story.'

He still got nothing but blank looks.

'I tell you what – you lot get off and waste your time in the sun for a while. Give me a chance to have a think about it and I'll see you all later.'

Fin looked a trifle downhearted.

'Don't worry Fin,' said Mike, 'we'll sort this out before the end of the break – so we've got a couple of days. Okay? Go on enjoy yourselves outside for the rest of the afternoon, and remember we've all got to be ready for five-ish.'

All he got were blank stares from the boys. Then Fin remembered.

'Of course, the play's tonight isn't it.' It was a statement rather than a question, and the other three instantly began to nod and agree that they had a '*Great*' (Fin), '*Ace*' (Sim), '*Mega*' (Tam) and '*Jolly good*' (Willis) evening in store.

Mike gestured out towards the front of the building where the sunlight cast sharp black shadows through the trees.

'Get off then lads. See you later.'

'Yeah, come on Fin, leave Mike to work on it. Let's get down to the lake.' urged Willis.

'Forget about it for now - Mister Nutter's on the case." shouted Tam. 'Race you to the lake!'

Mike couldn't help smiling as the four laughing boys raced off across the lawn, past the huge tree, and onwards into the increasing warmth of the summer afternoon, leaving him in the chill shadow behind the building. Finally, they were acting like the young boys they were. Their anticipation of the play later on was infectious and the trials of the morning now seemed to have been forgotten, for a little while at least. He looked at the coat in his hands.

Now to try to think of what to do next...

He could do with having Bev here, but he'd have to wait until tomorrow. He made his way slowly back into the hostel.

Now and Then Dick (20)

Dick and Leon had shunned bed to prolong their discussion, and Dick had listened to his friend reminisce for far longer than either of them realised. By the time the two had finished off a second bottle of Irish, the night sky was beginning to lighten, and Dick had the distinct feeling that Leon had been holding all this back for a long time. Eventually the rushing stream of Leon's recollections swept away into the cooling air and he refocused his gaze onto Dick. Both were now the worse for drink

Leon gave a small lopsided grin.

'Still awake then?' he said softly, and appeared to Dick to be a little embarrassed, 'Sorry. I had no intention of rambling on for so long, but once I'd started I couldn't stop myself.' He gave a small shake of his head, 'Sorry Dick.'

'Bloody Hell Leon. Don't apologise. You're my best mate… my only really close friend if the truth be known. Thanks for sharing all this with me.' He stood up from the low wall and stood before his companion, thrust his hands into his pockets, and swayed back and forth, from tip-toes to heels and back again.

'Think of what lies ahead of us, now you have someone to join you. What larks, eh?'

Leon straightened up and shook his head to try to clear it of the boozy mist clouding his brain.

'But it's not just that I wanted to tell you mate... something's going on… I had to tell someone, and you're the only someone I trust these days.' He saw Dick's quizzical look and continued, 'Look, we both need a bit of kip and something to clear our heads. Bed, for a couple of hours at least and then I'll tell you about what's happening. We can't discuss it with a bottle of wallop inside us - we need clear heads for this. You take the blue room on the right up the stairs. I'll see you later okay?'

Dick was too far gone to argue, and the two men guided each other, very precariously, up the stairs, parting on the landing to progress in drunken, stately manner around the minstrels gallery to their rooms.

When Dick finally awoke, lying atop his bed and still fully clothed, the sun was lancing into his room through the large picture windows. The clock showed ten-thirty, once he'd managed to focus on it. His normally bright and alert eyes felt like they'd been sanded and, just at the moment, his 20-20 vision was anything but.

Once upright, to the accompaniment of sundry grunts and groans, he felt no better. But a cool shower, a shave and a visit to the loo made him feel a lot more human.

'Good Lord' he thought putting a hand to his forehead, 'just how much did we drink last night?'

He quickly changed into the black flannels and roll neck top laid out on the armchair at the foot of the bed, took his watch and small change from the small ornate table next to it (Chippendale?) and crossed the room and admired himself in the mirror. Well, he might feel like crap, but he still scrubbed up well. He posed, as most slightly out of condition men do when they suddenly discover that if they make just a marginal effort they can look quite respectable. Memories of the old chocolate adverts and the man in black diving from high Maltese cliffs came to mind. James Bond eat your heart out.

He made his way downstairs to the kitchen, from where the sounds of Leon busy making breakfast were issuing, along with a selection of Santana's hits.

Leon apeared little better than Dick felt and looked over at him as he entered.

'Tied one on last night, eh?' He grinned speaking over the Rock-Samba beat. 'But this will see us right.'

He put a plate in front of Dick that was overflowing with eggs (2), bacon (3 rashers), sausages(3), kidneys (2), haggis (2 slices), black pudding (1 slice), white pudding (1 slice), beans (lots), tomatoes (several) and mushrooms (heaps). A huge plate of bread and butter sat in the middle of the table and a mug of tea that must have held at least a pint.

Dick surveyed the biggest breakfast he'd ever set eyes on.

'Well, Leon, they say a hearty break of the fast sets you up for the day!' Dick chuckled as he tucked in, and amazingly he found that as he ate his appetite accommodated the gargantuan meal. Even a pint of tea disappeared as the two wolfed down Leon's fairly basic catering.

When they had both finished, Leon refilled the cups, this time with coffee.

'Right Dick. As soon as we've recovered a little more from last night the fun will begin. I'm going to take you on a trip – just a short one to begin, because this isn't something I've ever done before, apart from the little bit of jiggory-pokery last night. Last night I moved a bit of furniture around you. Today I'm hoping to take you back to where I left your bike… and maybe a few more places, just to let you get used to it all. This will be the first time I've taken someone else with me, but I'm pretty certain we'll be fine. That is, as long as you're willing?'

'You don't even need to ask Leon. I haven't felt like this for years – finally a bit of adventure!'

'Yeah, yeah, but I don't want to give you the impression that this is going to be easy. Remember I've had a lifetime of being weird, but this is new for you and you may find it a bit disorientating. This is not like anything you've experienced before.'

'Too late to try to put me off now mate. When do we get started?'

Leon smiled over his coffee, 'No time like the present is there? So lets get going.'

They both went upstairs and under Leon's direction Dick found some black gauntlets and heavy duty, steel toe-capped boots. Leon left for a few minutes and returned dressed in similar garb.

'So Leon, going empty-handed? No bags, no weapons or anything?' Dick asked, only half joking.

'We don't need to take anything. We're only going to have a quick look around and then come back. I reckon a trip to the sixteenth or seventeenth century will do for now. Let's see how it goes, but remember it's very important that you keep clear head and concentrate on everything I tell you. This is probably not without its dangers, but I think we'll be okay.'

He winked as he turned away and Dick was left struggling to tell if Leon was just pulling his leg or whether there really was some risk involved.

He followed Leon down to the Great Hall, brilliantly lit by the early morning sun. The house was silent now. Dick looked about him at the fabulous home Leon had built for himself. Finally the nagging suspicions about where all this came from had been answered and now it was Dick's turn to see Leon in action, to embark on a journey that, for most people, would only exist in children's stories. The oak panelled hall, harking back to an earlier age, waited expectantly for what was to come.

Leon led Dick to the large dinning table and they sat opposite each other, as they had the previous night. Dick, although excited, was also beginning to feel a little apprehensive.

'Leon, what exactly are we going to do?'

Leon could see that Dick was nervous. He'd begun to sweat and was getting paler by the second. He was also beginning to tremble slightly.

Leon looked over with an earnest expression.

'Dick, I promise I'll take this slowly and explain everything as we go along. Don't worry, I don't want to lose you at this stage. Relax, you'll be fine.'

Dick knew that Leon wouldn't do anything to hurt him on purpose, but by his own admission he hadn't done this before.

'Hell, let's just get on with it. We can't stop now, but I can't pretend I'm not frightened. This is very scary mate.'

'Okay, Dick. What I'm going to do is take us both out of the here and now and put us in a place where we can go somewhere else.'

'Or some*when* else.' Dick joked, but now with a tremor in his voice. He could feel his stomach tightening. God, what a time to need the loo. He tried to ignore his disturbing abdominal churnings and smiled.

Leon smiled encouragingly back and began speaking softly.

'So, once we get there, you tell me how you feel. It's all about sensation, it's all in the mind. You're going to use parts of your brain that have lain dormant since very early childhood and you won't even know how you're doing it. Just believe and let it flow.' At the shocked look from Dick he quickly went on, 'I just want to see how intuitive this whole process is. I've always done this, so I'm not sure how easy it will be for you.' He smiled. 'So let's go; this should be interesting for both of us.'

Leon gave an extravagant shrug to loosen himself up and smiled again.

'Watch, and be amazed my friend.'

Dick stared over at Leon and studied him as he closed his eyes and began to concentrate. He talked as he worked his magic.

'It's going to get a bit warm. This takes quite a lot of energy, but I can do this pretty well instantaneously by myself. I'll go a bit slower this first time. Oh, and ignore the sound effects - they're just a by product of the process, part of the reason we had such a good breakfast.' he chuckled.

As Dick watched he realised that it was getting quite hot in the room, and the air began to shimmer as an aura grew around Leon. The air became filled with coloured ribbons of light, a constantly fluctuating rainbow filling the Great Hall. It was getting really hot!

Still without opening his eyes, Leon smiled on. 'Here we go. Hold on to your hat Dick.'

And with that, the room around them faded away to be replaced with complete darkness.

'Whoa, Leon! Where are we?' whispered Dick.

'Ssshhh. Just watch, and be amazed.' answered his friend.

In the distance there was colour.

The two men were floating in the gloom, with nothing solid anywhere around them and only the rapidly increasing light ahead. Dick began to twist slowly and tried to correct himself as he turned his back on Leon, instantly discovering that without the other man as a point of reference it was difficult not to spin uncontrollably. His arms flailed as he desperately tried to relocate Leon who was now several yards away and behind him. Ribbons of colour raced towards and then passed them, so fast he couldn't see what they were, just streams of bright light in what was otherwise complete blackness. There was no gloom, no partial brightness, everything was either black as a very black thing in a black place, or too bright to look at directly. And there was complete silence apart from his own pounding heartbeat and terrified babble, interspersed with his gasping breath. His panic rose higher.

'Leon where are you? What's going on? Leon!'

A strong hand caught his upper arm in a vice-like grip.

'Dick! Calm down. Relax man. I'm here. You're safe!' With a sudden painful jerk he was pulled around to see Leon floating in front of him, but in his panic he kept on struggling.

'For God's sake Dick, stop it!'

Looking at Leon, so stern and in control, Dick did finally manage to calm himself a little, but still couldn't help himself as he shouted.

'Hell's Teeth Leon, where are we? Is this right?'

In this strange place even their voices seemed to be swallowed up into the nothingness that surrounded them. It had a strange damping effect, so that the silence appeared to be devouring every sound they made.

'Dick, you're a copper. So bloody act like one. Calm down and watch. Observe. Tell me how you feel and what you see! I didn't bring you here just so you could throw a wobbler on me.'

He turned Dick to look at the nearest band of bright colour as it raced passed. With a voice full of awe and wonder Leon pointed.

'Watch them, and tell me.'

Dick tried as hard as he could to see something other than bands of light, but try as he might, that's all he saw. Light hurtling passed at alarming rate.

'It's just lights Leon. Fast moving light. There's nothing else there.' Leon noted with relief that at least Dick was no longer struggling against him and had regained a good deal of his composure.

'Look again Dick. Don't rush, we've got all the time in the world – literally. While we're here, time has ceased to exist for us.' He paused, 'Now, how do you feel?'

Dick concentrated again, trying to ignore the vertigo that still threatened to engulf him. By force of will he made himself calm and consider exactly how he did feel. He became aware of an odd tingling at the front of his skull. Not uncomfortable, but not like anything he recalled feeling before. His eyes lost their focus and his body relaxed. The tingling grew, but with it came a strange feeling of euphoria, almost like being drunk. And there's nothing wrong with being drunk, as long as you aren't a glass of water. He grinned to himself. Where on earth had that come from? He felt his whole body, and mind, ease into a feeling of rightness. He continued to stare ahead, and realised that he was seeing lights, not a continuous band, but distinct blocks of light, separated by bars of blackness.

'It's... uh... like windows looking into a house from the night outside.'

Whilst he sounded bewildered, Leon still grinned back at him, unseen by Dick who couldn't take his eyes off the 'film' flowing passed. Leon was also far more relaxed now. He could see that Dick was going to be okay. He couldn't stop smiling now, his teeth showing unnaturally bright in the darkness.

'What you're looking at is time Dick. Time passing by at its own speed. Uncontrolled by anything, or anyone.' He tapped Dick on the shoulder. 'Come on.'

Gripping Dick's arm he guided them closer to the racing lights. The blocks Dick could see were massive. Each panel was a window hundreds of feet high, and through the window Dick could see landscapes. Some were brightly lit, others more dim. As they approached closer the views went by so quickly that he couldn't focus properly on them, but he knew somehow, that he was looking back at the world, from somewhere outside.

'What you're looking at Dick, is my view of history. I've always found it easier to see it as a movie spread through the infinity of space. But I can view it as a book, or a stream, but this always seems the most appropriate to me. I can step in and out whenever I want to. All we have to do is pick a frame, get it to slow down, or maybe I speed up to keep pace - I don't know which, and then step in.' He tugged Dick even closer. 'Come on, I'll show you.'

As they moved even closer Dick realised that each 'frame' was labelled with a date. Now how could that be? His puzzlement was dispersed when Leon spoke again.

'It's all in the mind, Dick. I label the days, years, centuries, millennia, even eons and then zoom in on the one I want. If you can do this for yourself, you'll be able to use your own methods to map time – I just find this the easiest for me.'

'So I can see this in another way if I choose to?'

'Well, I've never been in this situation before, I mean with someone else along for the ride. But I think that what's happened is that we're getting my view because you haven't had enough time,' he chuckled, 'to practise. Presumably at some point we'll be able to enter this *space*, for want of a better word, and see your favoured rendering of time as an object. That will be interesting; to know how someone else sees time.'

Dick was mesmerised.

'Watch.' said Leon quietly.

The blocks going past were slowing. As the light panels began to dawdle in comparison with their earlier headlong rush so the dates became clearer. Dick could see that each screen was labelled with an exact day. At the frames displaying the days of the year 800 the movement halted and the stream reversed its flow. As they neared the blank band between 1500 and 1400 the ribbon again reversed and slowed even more. Closer still they could see the days for 1492 and 1493. The two men kept approaching until they were looking at Autumn 1492 and the whole display stopped totally with the final frame displaying a vista of a medieval dockside. Below the view was a label reading:

Friday, August 3rd 1492.

In front of Dick a middle-aged man, dressed in understated finery, stood at the ship's rail and waved to a large crowd surrounding a dais on the docks, as the ship began to leave the quayside. On the stage near to the side of the dock sat a regal couple on heavy golden thrones.

The King wore a small circlet of gold and sat grim faced as the crowd waved gaily at the crew of the small ship. The objects of their attention were busying themselves with sheets and sails, stowing barrels and chests about and below the decks, with only a few returning or even acknowledging the cheering throng.

'Sometime soon I'm going to talk to that man,' said Leon. 'See you later, Christopher.' he murmured with his own small wave. He glanced over to his companion.

'Come on Dick, I think that's enough for now, lets have a quick look around and do our own exploring before we go home.' He towed Dick forward and, as the picture zoomed in on a nearby hillside, they entered its frame.

'Welcome to Portugal my friend.'

Now Fin (21)

The play was to be acted out in the grounds of the hostel and the lighting crew were the first to arrive. Fin and his friends had wandered over as they began to unload the gantry to hold several large spotlights that lay nearby, alongside two massive floodlights. Two men stood discussing the arrangement of the frame that was to stand behind the audience to light the stage, although there was, as yet, no stage.

'Look mate, I was told to rig all the lights back there,' one was saying as he gestured behind the boys. 'so that we can light this whole area, highlighting the rocks 'ere and givin' a glimpse of the lake. I was told this was where the doings would be, so we're only getting' out these lights 'ere. '

'But what of the roaming actors who will traverse the ground off to the wings? Are they to stumble about in the darkness, my man? Can you not see the peril into which they may be plunged? To wander abroad in the dark.? No, this simply will not do. Where is Mister Hughes the owner of this lamentable equipment? I must speak with him with the utmost urgency.' whined the smaller of the two, dressed in a smart suit and tie. No, not a tie, but a cravat of all things. 'This simply won't do at all, not at all.'

The taller man, dressed in T shirt and jeans rolled his eyes and then winked as he saw the boys staring.

'Okay, mate. I'll get Kenny on the phone and try to get 'im over 'ere. But 'es a busy man. 'E might not be able to get out to this desolate little spot on the arse end of beyond.'

He grinned as the other began to stamp his foot and tremble with indignation.

'Give me your card sir, and I shall call him myself. We are not some ragamuffin group of strolling players my man. I have worked at the Vic, at the RSC. I sir am an actor, in the truest sense of the word. In the matter of sufficient illumination I shall not be thwarted.'

The rigger smiled in an attempt at placation.

'Right-Oh mate. But I think you'll be wastin' your time.'

He turned to the cab of the truck from which the equipment was being unloaded and climbed in.

The small man turned to the boys.

'I don't know young men. What is the world coming to when great - and I do not use the word lightly – great thespians are forced to work in such disagreeable circumstances. There was a time when a young man of such ignorance would not dare to gainsay me.'

He looked up at the cab and with a snap of his fingers in that direction called 'You are not worth the dust which the rude wind blows in your face.' and turned his attention back to the boys.

'Well, anyone?' he questioned with a forlorn expression. 'Anyone?'

Fin and Tam looked at one another and Willis just looked confused.

'The words of the immortal bard, cast as pearls before swine.' he intoned and just as he was about to continue.

'King Lear, Act 4.' piped up Simeon. He blushed at the open-mouthed expressions of surprise all around him, but kept his eyes on the little man before them.

'Good heavens! Finally, a child with a mind for true culture.' he beamed.

Simeon smiled too and came out with 'Study is like the heaven's glorious sun, that will not be deep-searched with a saucy look.'

The others began to giggle. Where on earth was Sim getting this stuff from?

The small actor practically danced with excitement. He took a step back and spread his arms wide as he adopted the pose of someone addressing an audience.

'But to return to Lear - Is't not the king' he intoned.

'Ay, every inch a king' replied Sim.

The man bowed as if taking his applause at the end of a play and swept his left hand up to his chest.

'Thank you child.' He bowed deeply in the old fashioned way, where one foot is extended forward and the weight taken on the back leg.

Then Simeon spoiled it all by turning to the other three and saying in an exaggerated luvvie voice ' Tis the infirmity of his age; yet he hath ever but slenderly known himself.'

The boys began to laugh again, and the man looked up sharply.

'Ingratitude, thou marble-hearted fiend, more hideous, when thou show'st thee in a child, than the sea-monster.' huffed the little man.

All four boys were laughing now. Slapping each other on the back and howling.

The younger man returned from his cab and passed across a card to the, now discomfited, actor.

'Call 'im, if you think it'll do any good. But I've got my instructions.' he said as he grinned at the boys' merriment.

The actor snatched the card and turned on his heel. He retired from the group stiff backed with indignation. However the effect was ruined when he stumbled slightly on the uneven ground and the hysterics began again behind him.

'What was all that about then?' asked the rigger.

'I think Sim annoyed him a bit, knowing Shakespeare – at least I assume it was Shakespeare.' replied Willis.

They all looked at Simeon, who looked a bit sheepish.

'Yeah, me an' Dad playact at home. We did "King Lear" a couple of months ago. We're into '"Love's Labour's Lost" now.'

'And you remembered it all?' asked Fin, surprised as the others with this, until now, hidden talent.

Sim blushed again.

'It's just one of those things. You lot remember all the stuff from Chemistry and things -the only thing I seem to be any good at is remembering plays and films. But, and I know it sounds daft, Shakespeare just seems to stick. I remember almost all of the stuff we've been through up 'til now. It's like Fin with his Gilbert and Sullivan musicals – he does the same with them.'

The other boys nodded remembering the numerous times Fin had bent their ears explaining the ridiculous plots of the G & S operettas he loved and they had all noticed that Sim seemed to have an affinity with the old playwrights. A bit of a dunce in all subjects except English Lit. and Design and Tech., he could recite ancient soliloquies and build great furniture.

'Still,, I'm amazed you can remember so much. Compared with Shakespeare, G and S is easy. At least the language makes sense.' said Fin.

'But that's the strange thing.' said Sim, 'Old Bill makes perfect sense to me, I've never had a problem with understanding any of it. Must just be a funny connection somewhere in my brain.'

'Yeah, right. I wish I had it. All I ever remember is bits of Monty Python, and let's face it, The Philosopher's Song and The Penis Song aren't going to get me very far.' bemoaned Tam, and everyone laughed again, as much at the memories of late night singalongs led by Tam, as at the truth of his comment.

'Okay lads, I'm afraid I've got to get back to work here, and it would be better if you didn't stop to watch. The last thing I need is to have a Super Trouper bouncing of one of your heads. This can be dangerous stuff y'know. But if you like you can come around later and I'll show you how all this works.'

The boys all nodded and made 'Oh yeah!' and 'Epic!' cries of eagerness. The rigger grinned.

'So give me some names so I can warn the other lads to expect company.' He looked at each boy in turn and they gave him their names.

'Right, and I'm Fred. Fred Hughes. My dad owns this "lamentable equipment" referred to by our esteemed actor friend, Mister Sybbilant, who just left. Anyway, I'll see you later. Now bugger off while we get this lot set up.'

Fred waved them away and returned to the job in hand.

'Well at least luvvie Carver took our minds off our main problem at the moment – is Fin a nutter, or are we standing in the presence of a magician?' said Tam.

'Sod off!' cried Fin.

'Oh, thank you Oscar Wilde' retorted Tam with a laugh.

Sim nudged Tam, the two of them determined to keep making light of Fin's problem and make sure he didn't slip back into his melancholia of earlier in the day.

'This is a slight unmeritable man, Meet to be sent on errands.' he quipped.

'You what?' said Fin.

'Julius Caesar.' said Tam. 'See, I remember odd bits of Billy Shakespeare too. It means you're a plonker, so bugger off and see if Mister Nutter's come up with anything yet. He's had a couple of hours.'

'Yeah, let's all go' said Willis, 'let's see if he's decided what we should do next. Come on!' and he and Sim started off for the hostel.

'The game's afoot!' called Tam, running after them

'What?' cried Fin, chasing.

'Henry the Fifth, you philistine!' shouted Simeon, 'Cry God for Harry! England and Saint James!' He thrust his arm into the air as he ran. 'Come on, let's find Mike'.

'I'm surrounded by nutters!' laughed Fin as he sprinted to keep up.

As they rounded the front of the building the bright sunshine glinted blindingly off the front of a small red MG pulling into the car park. A petite, but nonetheless gorgeous blonde woman was just getting out as they ran passed.

'Pwhoar!' said Sim under his breathe as he tapped Tam on the shoulder and nodded towards her.

'Oh, very poetic I must say. Remind me to ask your advice on love sonnets. In about five years, when you've grown up.'

All four of them stopped just outside the entrance and, despite his words, Tam stared with the others as she approached through the warm late afternoon air. The woman removed her sunglasses to reveal startlingly blue eyes and smiled at the boys.

'Hello, boys. I'm looking for one of the Appleton teachers here. Mister Nutter. You are from Appleton aren't you?'

'Yes Miss' said Willis. The silence that followed was about to become pregnant, as the lads tried, without success, to look anywhere but at the shapely legs before them, when Fin finally found his voice.

'We're looking for him ourselves. Come with us if you like, we'll track him down together.'

'Why thank you kind sir.' she replied with another smile and a little bobbed curtsy. To the four adolescents, hers was no simple smile. Beautifully even teeth seemed to make the sun shine even brighter, and with a move surely designed to make them even more uncomfortable, she linked arms with both Fin and Willis as they passed through the main door and into reception. Several other boys from the school were standing around chatting, waiting for the telephone to become free, when the fivesome walked across the tiled floor and away into the main lounge. The silence that descended at their passing was evidence of the effect their new companion had on all the boys present.

The object of their search was sitting alone in the lounge, a large airy room with massive picture windows revealing the tranquil landscape beyond. Off to one side Fred and his mates were busy with the lighting for the performance that evening.

The five approached him and he glanced up as they crossed the thick rugs strewn across the floor. As soon as he saw the boy's companion he leapt to his feet.

'Bev! What on earth are you doing here? I didn't expect to talk to you until tomorrow – I certainly didn't think you'd be driving all this way.

The woman smiled again and threw her arms around him.

'Give us a kiss then, you great hunk of a man!'

As they kissed Mike was aware of the squirming of the four lads behind her. Well, tough, they could always vacate the room, he thought.

He was more than a little put out when they showed no signs of leaving.

The pair broke off from their embrace and Bev chuckled.

'Sorry about that boys, but you should know I love this man to bits, and I've missed him while you've been monopolising his time.'

Mike had the good grace to blush slightly, but was quite comfortable holding her hand in front of his charges. Fin couldn't help thinking that they looked the perfect couple as they stood, backlit by the bright sunshine through the windows, in a halo of gold.

Or was he just being a bit of a girly?

Fin gave a small shrug to dispel the smear on his burgeoning manhood as the adults sank into two of the armchairs, and Mike waved the boys to the settee opposite.

'Sit down guys. I suspect the reason my beautiful oppo here has spent her afternoon trundling up the M6 West has something to do with Fin.'

Bev looked up sharply at the mention of Fin, and he shifted uncomfortably in his seat.

'Got ants in yer pants Fin?' mocked Tam, and Bev's gaze zeroed in. Oh God, he thought, how many more people were going to get involved in this? Maybe he would have been better just going quietly off his head. But, no. He knew that the only chance he had of sorting this all out was with these friends, or his family. Unfortunately he'd kept his ongoing problem a secret from his parents and Lilli. He had the distinct feeling that that was all going to end with his return home. He wondered what sort of reaction he was going to get when Mister Nutter reported his activities during the break.

Oh well, he'd just have to get on with it and see what happened.

Fin returned the steady gaze of Mister Nutter's wife, or maybe they liked to be called partners. But that seemed a little too businesslike for the pair, who were still holding hands as they sat.

'Yes, there's your man Bev. Finbar William LeMott esquire.' He was glad to see all the lads grin at that. Maybe things weren't nearly so bad as they'd appeared that morning. He almost felt like crossing his fingers.

'A pleasure to meet you Fin.' said Bev. 'And who are these other young gentlemen, Mike?'

Mike introduced them all and ended unnecessarily with, 'And this is my poor unfortunate wife – Beverly Nutter neé Shufflebottom.

'Oh thank you so much for that darling.' said Bev sarcastically. 'I really wanted them to know that.' She glared at all four of them. 'That little titbit of information does not leave this room boys - on pain of a good thrashing from me, alright?'

They all grinned, but nodded.

Sim leaned across to Tam. 'I'm not sure whether that's a threat or not, Tam. Are you?' he whispered, not quite sotto voce enough.

'Simeon Carver, go and wash your mind out with soap!' Mike feigned shock. 'I do apologise Mrs Nutter. I don't know what gets into them sometimes.'

Simeon at least had the good grace to look a little abashed. But already the boys knew that Bev was of much the same make up as Mike. She could take a joke, just so long as they didn't push it too far, and none of them were of a mind to do that with either Mike or his wife.

Sim however still appeared to be having problems keeping his eyes off Bev's legs.

'Simeon, you're going to have to leave the room if you don't lift your gaze above waist level.' joked Bev.

'Better still – look at the ceiling young man. Okay?' joined in Mike seeing where Sim's gaze had inadvertently switched.

Now it was Sim's turn to blush.

'But enough of the childish banter. I'm sorry boys but I need to have a word with my husband.'

All four hunched forward to hear better with expressions of rapt attention.

'Alone!' laughed Bev.

But Mike put a hand on her knee to stop her, and Simeon made a great play of almost fainting as he watched.

'All right Sim, let's calm down now shall we?' admonished the teacher. He turned to Bev.

'This lot know exactly what's going on, Bev. I think we might as well let them hear anything you have to say. I have a feeling we're all in this together now, no matter what. Am I right boys?'

'Too true.' said Tam.

'You betcha.' from Sim.

'We can't stop now.' urged Willis.

And Fin just smiled, knowing that these five people at least were going to have a damn good try at finding a way of straightening out his strange problem.

'Okay.' breathed Bev. She looked at Mike, but was really speaking to all of them.

'I spoke to Artie almost as soon as I got of the phone, and he wants to see Fin – ASAP. I've never seen him get so excited about something he's only just heard about. He's desperate to see him, but asked me to try to find out a bit more about what's going on before we return.'

Mike looked more than a little taken aback.

'Well we can't just pack up and leave. There are a couple of dozen other boys here and Bert can't look after them all. I'm afraid it's going to be Friday at the earliest. And then we've got to check that we're alright to do this with Fin's parents. I don't think they'd take to kindly to us taking Fin off to see one of the most eminent psychiatric professors in the land without consulting them.'

'Oh of course' replied Bev. 'I think he wants at least one of them there anyway. I'll give him a call when we're finished here and let him know. He'll be on tenterhooks waiting, but there's not a lot we can do about that, is there?'

She smiled over at Fin.

'What I really need to know can come from just one person and that's Fin.' Her smile faded to be replaced by a puzzlement, overlaid with mild concern. 'The Prof seems convinced that Fin is telling the absolute truth…' Mike gasped and tried to butt in, but Bev waved his interruption aside. 'I don't know why he's so sure but he is and, for now, that's good enough for me. This is so out of character for him - and I'd love to know why. So, starting from the beginning, wherever you think that is Fin, tell me all about it.'

She sat back and watched Fin.

He looked around at the faces staring back and took a deep breath thinking 'here we go again' with faint resignation.

'Well it all started when I was not much more than a baby, right back as far as I can remember really' and once again he told the story, for the third time that day.

Bev interrupted occasionally, checking times and dates and his exact whereabouts during each nightmare, until he brought her up to date with the awful occurrences of the previous night.

'And you still have the coat and boots?' she asked.

'Yes, they're up in my room.' said Mike. 'I'd go and get them, but I'd rather the other lads didn't see what we're doing. And anyway, it's just an old coat and a pair of boots fit only for the bin, which, incidentally, is where Brave Sir Simeon fished them out of earlier this afternoon.'

Sim grinned like the Cheshire Cat and puffed out his chest, hands on hips as he surveyed the lesser mortals around him.

'Settle down Sim.' said Tam, 'Let's face it - you were the only one barmy enough to go thrashing about in a bin full of God knows what. Mike was joking. You're really just a wazzzock!' and he gave Sim a shove that almost sent him to the floor.

'I suppose Tam's right really, but it's the only concrete evidence, if you can call it that, that corroborates Fin's story.' said Bev.

'That means it's proof.' said Sim slowly to Tam, as though explaining the obvious to a not-too-bright child. That earned him another shove, and this time he did fall off.

'Yes, I don't think I need to see them, but I would like to see the mill you visited today, the one that Fin says he went to last night in his dream, or rather, *not* in his dream, which is the fantastical bit.' said Bev.

Again Mike shook his head. 'No can do, doll. Sorry but we're off to The Bard in about half an hour' he jerked his thumb over his shoulder at the scene through the window, 'and by the time that's over this lot will be ready for bed.'

He was met with a barrage of 'Oh Sir' and 'No chance' from the boys, but he would not be budged.

'Look, tomorrow I'll arrange for the four of you to head back there with Bev. We're all supposed to be going canoeing on Wast Water, but I can let you off with it if I sweet talk Bert later. I'll have to stay here, but you lot could go and see if you can find anything else out. But I have to say, I know I said I'd go along with this, but it still seems too weird for words. You can have a little leeway for now, but I'm still not sure how we're going to come to any conclusion other than that Fin had some sort of grand mal , or just a simply sleep walking excursion. Anything else sounds too much like Stephen King. And I do know that you like Dean Koontz - this would be right up his street.'

He cast a world weary eye over them.

'It just beggars belief I'm afraid, and I am deeply worried for Fin. But a deal's a deal, and I said I'd all go along with it for now. But unless something comes up tomorrow I'm going to have to insist that Fin stays under my watchful eye at all times from then on.' At the series of glum looks and *Harrumphs*, Mike shook his head. 'Sorry, but I have a responsibility to him and his parents, and I wouldn't be much of a teacher or in-loco-parentis if I let it go on without taking some sort of definite action. Fair enough?'

He looked at the boys and over to Bev. She smiled a lopsided smile.

'Not really, but it'll have to do, won't it?' she looked over to Fin. 'Don't worry Fin, we'll either get to the bottom of this while we're here, or Professor Tome will help us out.'

Sim and Tam had another quick shoving match, as the former prevented the latter making what would obviously have been a comic aside regarding her boss's name.

Only Fin and Willis appeared subdued.

'Okay boys?' said Bev softly.

'Yeah, I guess so.' said Fin, and Willis just nodded gravely.

'Come on then, you've still got a little while before we all have to meet up in the car park and stroll over to the play. So get out into what's left of the sun and enjoy it. Off you go.' And Mike practically shooed them out of the room before returning to his wife, who stood gazing out over the sunlit lawn and lake through the massive window.

He put his arms around her and she reached up to hold his hands as they both looked out at the boys playing in on the lawn. They watched as Fin and his friends headed back towards the stage area, where the lighting was completed and some of the actors, in full costume, were strolling languidly around in the warmth.

'So what exactly did Artie say when you told him about Fin's problem?' Mike asked.

Bev continued to watch for boys for a few seconds before replying.

'I didn't like to say too much in front of the boys, but to be honest I don't think I've ever seen him get so worked up about a subject.' She frowned, and the tension she felt was transmitted to Mike through their embrace.

'So he was excited about Fin, but why? He's just some poor kid having problems with nightmares, though I'll admit they are pretty serious problems. It's only in the last day or so, less than twenty-four hours in fact, that I've come to realise just what kind of effect they're having on the lad. Honestly Bev, if you'd seen him this morning behind that mill, you'd have cried. I don't think I've ever seen someone look so confused and helpless. It was heartbreaking.'

He gave his wife a squeeze.

'I really am very afraid for him. He seems to be going bonkers and I don't think that's putting it too strongly, and I haven't got the faintest idea how to help him. That's why I rang you – I was all at sea.'

Bev smiled.

'Now *that* I find hard to believe.' she said quietly.

She turned to face him, gave him a small kiss and returned to the armchair she'd been sitting on earlier. Mike stayed at the window.

'Artie said he'd had a similar case years ago, but had never gotten to the bottom of it. He said something about the boy disappearing, police were involved and everything. Everyone seemed to assume that the boy simply ran away. There was no evidence of foul play. By all accounts it destroyed the parents and they held Artie partly responsible – said he hadn't tried hard enough. The way he talked about it, it obviously affected him deeply. He was visibly upset as he told me the story.'

Mike had twisted around from his position at the window with concern on his face, and Bev smiled to try to lighten the mournful atmosphere she'd created.

'But why should he think of this other boy in connection with Fin?' he asked.

'He said that during their conversations the boy had said he could travel when he was asleep! Just like Fin. He was at his wits end because everyone thought he was insane, but Artie says he was adamant that at night storms carried him off to other places. But the real cruncher was that he said he travelled in time! It sounds so similar it's scary. Artie's desperate to see our Fin, he's hoping it could answer a lot of questions that have been causing Artie sleepless nights for years.'

Mike sat down.

'Such as?'

'Well, for starters, what happened to that boy all that time ago? Did he run away or did he vanish…' she snapped her fingers loudly, 'into thin air. I'm telling you Mike, Artie's in a right state over this.'

'So what are you planning to do?' asked Mike.

'First thing tomorrow I want to take Fin back to that mill and see if we can find anything, anything at all, that will corroborate his ridiculous tale.'

Bev stood and began to pace around the chair.

'I know it makes me sound as odd as all these stories, but I hope I can find something, because otherwise I'll have to face the possibility that a man I've admired for years, my mentor throughout my professional career, is as mad as the patients he tries to help every day.'

Her face crumpled in her anguish.

'Oh Mike, what are we going to do? Either we believe what we're being told, and toss aside our whole view of the world, join the humpa-lumpas in the chocolate factory, follow the yellow brick road, or we stick with things as we know them, in which case we're living and working with crackpots. I don't know which is preferable...'

Mike cut in.

'But Bev, it's just too ludicrous to be true. Time travel in your sleep! Come on, be realistic. You're the one who tries to help people get over things like this. You can't believe it's true!'

She looked down at him and gave a lopsided grin.

'So what are you doing with those lads out there?' she indicated the four boys now watching preparations for the play.

'Are you really just humouring him? Or, in your heart of hearts, are you hoping that there may be something in all this?'

Mike considered.

'To be honest I thought I was humouring him, just trying to keep him on an even keel until someone could find out what's happening, but I'm not sure I could live with the idea that that boy,' he pointed towards Fin and his friends, 'was so unhinged. It's just all so bloody weird. I don't know what to think anymore, especially knowing that Professor Tome seems more than a little convinced that there may be something else entirely to explain it all.'

He stood, looking out of the window and then sat again with a look of confusion.

'I feel like I've suddenly entered Narnia or something. I can't believe that I'm even considering the possibility that there could be some truth in what Fin's saying.'

He stood again, and took Bev's hand.

'I need a drink. Something a little more substantial than tea or coffee. Come on, we've got' he paused to check his watch, 'about half an hour before I have to help Bert get the troops in order, ready to meet Shakespeare.'

He headed for the smart red MG, towing his wife along.

Then Dick (22)

After a brief moment of vertigo Dick found himself standing next to Leon on a grassy hillside overlooking the port where the ship they'd seen earlier was taking its leave of Portugal.

He stumbled slightly and grabbed at Leon's arm before straightening to look about them. The bright sun again seemed at odds with the rumbling thunder that was echoing over the far hills as he smiled at Leon.

'Brought rain with us Leon? A bit of good old English weather?' he joked, already pretty sure he knew the answer to the mysterious weather.

Leon returned the smile, glad to see that Dick didn't seem the least bit disturbed by what was happening to him.

'Yeah, afraid that always happens when I go travelling, no matter when I go to. But I do know that the greater the time span the louder the thunder.' He looked up at the clear blue sky. 'But never any rain.' He smiled and looked oddly smug.

Dick sat on the grass looking out to sea and leaned forward encircling his knees with his arms and clasping his hands.

'So we really are in fifteenth century Portugal, watching one of the greatest explorers setting off to find the new world?'

'Got it in one old son.'

'So explain all the stuff that just happened Leon. Can you really just pick out a date like editing a piece of film? Just zoom in to when you want to go and step in. Or is there more to it?'

Leon sat beside him and then lay back to stare at the sky above. He thought for a few seconds and then closed his eyes.

'To be honest Dick, you can do it any number of ways. I think it's just a case of finding the best approach for yourself. I find the film thing works for me. You may have a better method.'

Dick interrupted, looking sharply at Leon while shading his eyes from the bright sun with a hand.

'So you really do mean you think I can do this too?' he asked incredulously. 'I thought I was just along for the ride.'

'Oh no, Dick. I'm hoping that you're going to be just as able at this as I am. As I said before, there's something going on back in the future. The energy streams that we've seen are getting stronger. The Earth seems to be preparing itself for something fairly momentous. As though it's building itself up to something. I've never seen anything like it before, and I've been around a bit. I don't know what's going on, but I feel the need to have someone - and I'm afraid that's you – on my side when it all kicks off. So think of this as a crash course in time travel, 'cos I don't think we've got long to prepare ourselves for whatever it is.'

Dick was beginning to look just a tad alarmed.

'There must be more to it than that Leon. You've kept all this a secret for years, even longer than we've known each other. So come on, you might as well give me the whole story, what's the point in holding back now, eh? Despite his obvious misgivings he grinned at Leon. But Leon still had his eyes closed and didn't alter his relaxed position.

'Fair enough Dick. There is something else that's different. Over the last couple of years I've *felt* a change back home. Occasionally I've heard the thunder late at night, and I can tell the difference between that and real weather related sounds. It's a feeling that's difficult to put into words, but trust me, there's something going on. There's someone nearby and maybe several people, who are also moving about in the void outside of time. I haven't seen anything, but I can feel it. Forces are gathering that I can't fathom and it's got me spooked.'

Now Dick lay next to Leon and propped himself up on an elbow, resting his head on a hand.

'And you want my help to find out what's going on, is that it?'

'Sort of, you are a member of the constabulary after all. If I can't determine the cause of it, I'm hoping you can, as a trained detective.'

'I'm just a beat copper Leon, not Sherlock Holmes!' protested Dick, but he was smiling just the same.

'But I'm also concerned that I might get caught up in something beyond my control.' continued Leon. 'Even if I find out what's going on, knowing what it is isn't the same as being able to cope with it.'

Finally Leon looked across at Dick.

'Two of us may have more luck at...' Leon was interrupted by a shout from behind them, further up the hill. A group of riders were silhouetted against the sky, and their gaudy riding tack sparkled as they began to gallop down the slope towards the two surprised Englishmen. Another shout sounded out in an unintelligible language.

Dick and Leon both watched a group of armed men, in military regalia coming down the hill on horseback. Even to Dick's untrained eye the horses looked magnificent - and the riders too for that matter. They were being led by a burly man astride a massive piebald horse and it was he who had hailed them, but it was the man riding behind him who gave the appearance of being in charge. There was an arrogance apparent even in the way he rode his splendid black mount.

'What do we do Leon? he asked looking across.

Leon shrugged. 'Might as well just sit and see what happens. Where could we run to anyway?'

'You're very calm considering there's half a dozen armed men coming, at speed, towards us. They don't seem too happy to see us either.' said Dick. He couldn't help looking about them, but the nearest cover was several hundred yards away and the troop was far too close for them to be able to escape.

'But I see your point.' he said with a shrug.

Both of them raised their arms in a sign of surrender, though neither could say what it was they were surrendering for. All they'd been doing was sitting and having a chat in the middle of a field.

Again the leading rider called out angrily, and once again neither Leon nor Dick could make sense of what was shouted.

'Portuguese.' said Leon. 'Just wait a few seconds and we'll be sorted.'

'What? Oh, that's okay then. After all we're both fluent in Portuguese, especially the type they spoke in the fourteen hundreds.' He cast a withering glance at Leon, who lifted his chin and ignored the jibe. He had that bloody smile on his face again, but he did have the decency to look just a little bit nervous.

'Leon, what do we do?'

'Just wait and see.' said Leon, the little smile playing on his lips. 'You'll be surprised what we can do.'

Dick felt a flush of annoyance. Why on earth did Leon have to insist on playing these stupid games with him. He obviously felt sure that this wasn't a dangerous situation, but Dick felt totally helpless in the face of the onrushing group of horsemen. The sound of the drumming hooves across the field was growing ever louder and he could actually feel the ground vibrating under his feet.

As the horses came to a shuddering halt only yards away from them Dick recoiled and was irritated to see the arrogant distain with which he was being regarded from the lofty heights of the black beast before him. However, his irritation was held in check by the fact that he was all at sea here, not just in a foreign land, but a completely alien time as well. He took heart from the fact that Leon looked totally at ease, even returning the look being laser-beamed at him by the commander who towered over him.

The horsemen stared down at them and the man who had shouted leant down against the neck of his steed and stared hard at Leon. With a puzzled expression he spoke to Leon, apparently asking a question. Dick began to sweat and he knew it wasn't due to the pleasant summer warmth. Leon didn't seem to have the faintest idea of what was being asked of him, but still his face looked calm, and he smiled up at his interrogator, almost as though he was privy to a joke that no-one else was aware of.

Now the lead rider was beginning to look exasperated as well as mystified. Here he was at the head of a squad of eight of the best men in the household guard of Alphonso da Gloria, and he, Fortunato da Cruz, was being smugly regarded by a Moor. He cast a quick glance at the man standing alongside the foreigner and immediately put him to the back of his mind. The man had the build of an athlete but gave every indication of wanting to flee. As a consideration in any argument, Dick just vanished into the back of the mind of the Portuguese. The dark stranger however, had an altogether different air about him. And the more he looked the more convinced Fortunato was that he was no Moor. Indeed he had no idea of where a man of such looks could come from. Never had he seen such dark skin, nor such distain for the flower of the local gentry. Why, he had refused to even acknowledge the hail sounded from the top of the hill. And where on earth did they wear such outlandish clothes? Da Cruz was aware that his master would be paying close attention to his handling of these two. His future standing in the household depended on his actions in situations such as this and dealing with peasants of low standing was something he was well used to, though usually they cowered somewhat more than these two. The pseudo-Moor in particular seemed completely uncowed by their presence, but da Cruz was still confident of his ability to control the situation, by force if necessary. His dark eyes narrowed as he inspected the two strangers and assured da Gloria that they posed no threat, but were merely wastrels trespassing on the estate.

Since neither Leon or Dick spoke the language, and the conversation went on around them rather than being directed at them, they were in no position to interpret or interrupt. Finally the leader of the troop spoke directly to Leon again.

'Hold hard sirrah. Art thou some devil cast out from the lower hells, that thou appearest on the lands of da Gloria dressed in Satanic black and refuse to answer the call of his guard? From where hast thou come, and what is your business here? Thou hast the appearance of blackguards and will not be welcomed methinks.'

Leon stood, as though awaiting divine inspiration. He gazed up towards the sky and then slowly back at the waiting men. His look went passed da Cruz to the face of Don Alphonso, and the look was of total indifference.

This was too much for da Cruz

'Speak man, or suffer the consequence of such insolence!' Da Cruz drew his long rapier and pointed it towards Leon, but remained on his horse. He would have been even more forthright in his manner, but the calm countenance before him, along with the strange black garb, made him somewhat more reticent than usual to engage in an argument with this man. Who was to know what such peculiar persons would be capable of? Best to restrain himself, for the moment at least. It went against the grain though, for he and his men were capable of brawling with the very best. Indeed Don Alphonso expected no less, he was a hard master who led only hard men.

Dick was beginning to feel sick, his stomach lurching as though empty, despite their recent breakfast. He was sure that only their unusual appearance was forestalling the imminent violence, that much was obvious from the way the horseman were regarding them, but since neither could understand what was being asked of them there was not much to be done. The men had the same look as the drunken scrappers he had to bang up most Fridays and Saturdays. Not overly bright, or overly bothered with regards to who they manhandled, just so long as they could end the day with skinned knuckles, or blooded swords. Then they could stagger off to bed and sleep the sleep of the contented. It was an outlook on life that Dick had never understood, but he was well acquainted with it. He began to lower his arms, wondering whether to try to use hand signs or something – anything – to ease the tension, until the sword of a second rider appeared not a million miles away from his face and Dick raised his arms again. Another barked phrase rang out into the stillness of the day. Dick had no idea whether it was an order or a question. He felt a sudden adrenalin rush that made him feel light headed and his stomach give another nauseous growl and looked over to see Leon beginning to breathe harder and bunch his fists. Oh, Lord, Leon looked as though he was going to try to take them all on single-handed. Dick prepared himself, but was still struggling to come to terms with the fact that Leon had landed him in such a mess with an apparent disregard for their safety.

The sun seemed to have grown much hotter in the last minute or so, and Dick began to sweat. He and Leon both had their hands in the air and all the riders had now drawn their weapons, all of which looked well cared for and lethal.

The gaudily attired rider behind the man who had led the troop finally spoke. Even in an unknown language his voice sounded languid, but heavy with authority. There was no doubt as to whom the other riders deferred and the manner of his speech marked this man out as one for whom giving orders was a lifelong activity.

'For The Lord's sake da Cruz, I don't have time for this. We are already delayed enough! Be done with them and let us continue down to the shore to join the royal entourage before that bloody sailor and his mangy crew are gone and the king and queen removed to the palace of Don Almeida. I will not be baulked at this stage. Our non-appearance may already have placed me outside of the circle I have worked so long to join.'

The men all looked to da Cruz for a lead. He nodded to the three men closest to his master.

'You three continue on with Don Alphonso. My Lord, we' and here he indicated the man nearest to him, 'shall take these vagabonds back to the house of your father, and see if they remain so quiet once we have introduced them to Jacquinetto the blacksmith and some of his toys.'

The guards all grinned at this, and Don Alphonso nodded his agreement.

'Very well. I leave them in your capable hands and will be interested to see if they remain so obdurate on my return.'

He turned his horse towards the crest of the hill again and shouted over his shoulder as his men made to follow.

'Oh and Fortunato, do not feel you have to be overly careful about their persons on the way back. The dark one in particular has done nothing to endear himself to our favour.'

And with that the four riders rapidly made off in the direction of the city.

Da Cruz returned his gaze to the two men before him. The dark-skinned shaven headed one, with eyes that seemed to say he understood exactly what had just passed, and the other, who had the look of an insipid Englishman, or possibly one of those frog-eating Frenchmen from the North.

Da Cruz was still puzzled by their lack of reaction to their situation. Did they not realise that he and his fellow could as easily kill them now as lead them back to the manor-house of his master?

He looked again at the Englishman and saw something different in him. He had suddenly become very still and had lost the appearance of a frightened rabbit.

'Hey Leon, that's a pretty good trick.' said Dick, watching the backs of the receding horsemen.

'Yeah, works every time brother, just takes a little longer sometimes.'

Both of them grinned at each other.

The man who had taken the lead in the conversation up until now looked startled as Dick spoke and cried out.

'So, you rogues, you *do* understand, but merely choose to ignore, is that it? You play some strange game with us, but now you will regret it.' He turned to his companion, 'Duarte, remember they must needs be alive when we return, but his lordship said naught else regarding their health.'

His dark eyes glittered with malice as he and his comrade put spurs to their mounts and casually closed the few yards between them and their prey. Duarte chuckled, and it wasn't a pleasant sound in the warm afternoon calm. The bridles tinkled as the bells adorning them shifted with the gait of the horses. The air was heavy with malevolence and Dick prepared to evade the horse coming towards him and somehow dislodge the rider. He assumed Leon would be doing the same and was surprised to hear Leon say, very softly, 'Don't worry Dick. You'll discover time is a wonderful healer. Here let me show you.' And he stepped forward and dropped his hands to his hips, standing legs apart and feet firmly planted on the turf, seemingly without a care in the world, to cast his defiant gaze at da Cruz.

His stance surprised both riders, who stared down at him in disbelief, but still with their rapiers aimed at the men before them.

With a cry of exasperation da Cruz urged his steed into a trot, moving closer to the figure in front of him and thrusting forcefully towards his opponent's chest. Leon appeared to reach out for the blade and time slowed. In an almost balletic pirouette he grasped the blade and leaned forward, dragging the sword from the rider's hand. To the Portuguesers the moor, swathed all in black, whirled around so quickly it took their breath away. As the horse and rider swept passed, Leon spun to follow them. The horse passed between Dick and Leon and came to a halt only yards passed them. Da Cruz hauled on the reins in order to force his horse to rear up with a crash of ornamental tack and turn sharply to face the standing man again, confusion showing clearly on his face. How on earth had the Moor managed to disarm him so easily? On completing his spin, Leon turned to face his tormentor… and stood holding the sword over his shoulder, with the hilt aimed back towards the open hillside behind. Leon stood casually, not even out of breath, gripping the blade lightly. With a quick flick of his wrist he loosed the shining steel and caught the hilt, looking practiced and at ease with the weapon.

He closed his eyes, lifted his arms with a sweeping motion, raised himself up on the balls of his feet and then gently lowered his hands as he sank back down all in the same elegant movement, the sword blade tracing a bright arc through the air.

'And relax… and breathe.'

He smiled and Dick couldn't help grinning in response.

'Hell Leon, I hope you don't expect me to do that.' called Dick softly.

Leon looked across.

'Not just yet Dick, but it won't be long, I promise.

He casually dropped the sword behind him and moved closer to Dick. They stood between the two horsemen, with their backs to the second rider. Dick was aware that they were in a vulnerable position and Leon had just thrown away their only weapon.

Leon saw Dick's eyes fall upon the rapier and, as though reading his mind said, 'Good swordsman, are you?' with a mocking laugh. Dick was annoyed until he realised that although the sword would be deadly in the right hands, it would be more of a hindrance to them, unskilled as they were in fencing. He shrugged and gave an answering chuckle.

'So what now Leon?' he asked quietly.

Da Cruz had been visibly jolted by the ease and speed with which he'd been disarmed, but quickly regained his composure.

'Duarte, take the rabbit.' He indicated Dick and snarled. 'This one's mine.'

Again Duarte gave a deep rasping laugh as he kicked hard at his horse's flanks. His mount jumped forward and smashed horribly into Dick, who totally failed to evade the lunge. The horseman made no effort to find the standing man with his sword, he merely tried to ride him down, and very nearly succeeded. The shoulder of the beast caught Dick on his right side and blasted him off his feet to land heavily on the seat of his pants, winded and shocked.

Leon gave a booming laugh and doubled over with his hands on his knees.

'Come on Dick, up and at 'em.' he called, waving his friend to his feet. 'And remember that if you believe you can do it, *you can!*

Dick scrambled to his feet as his opponent spurred his horse into another charge. This time he was ready and as the animal bore down on him, now with the rider aiming his rapier squarely at his chest, he waited and began to calm himself. He had only a few seconds – barely enough – to try to capture the feeling he'd had when Leon had bent time to his will. With a fierce effort of will he made himself close his eyes and try to regain the strange otherworldly sensation.

As the horse thundered across the turf a collision seemed inevitable.

Then, magically, marvellously, delightfully - with the blade barely a handspan from his chest - time suddenly slowed to a crawl and all the base notes of the approaching horse vanished. Dick had managed to block out his fear of injury, and the prickly-in-his-brain itch had kicked in. He opened his eyes and stepped smoothly across the front of the hurtling beast - which was now hardly moving and, leaving the sword sweeping slowly through empty space, he grabbed the booted right foot of the horseman and heaved with all his strength. As he touched the soft leather the whole scene burst back into full speed and it was all he could do to thrust the booted foot upwards as it raced past.

To Duarte on the horse, it seemed that the man before him blurred across his field of view beyond his ability to follow. The horse, hopelessly unbalanced by the shifting rider, staggered to the left and the Portugueser spilled off onto the turf, to lie stunned and defenceless. But Dick felt a searing pain in his right shin as the man went down. Somehow as he fell Duarte's right hand had swung under the horses belly and the flailing epee had stabbed into Dick's leg. Dick cursed himself, he'd been too busy revelling in his new-found talent; he simply hadn't seen the whirling blade. Despite the pain he stepped over to his fallen adversary and gave him a good solid kick in a place that he knew would keep him down for several minutes. It might also cause him to speak a little higher, but Dick felt little sympathy; the whimpering man would have done him untold damage without compunction.

The sword lay at his feet and he picked it up before turning to head over to Leon.

Da Cruz was driving his mount at Leon again, with the obvious intent of riding him down, since he was now without his sword. Dick limped over to his friend and the two stood waiting, Leon still grinning, glanced down at the blood on Dick's boot.

'You okay man?'

Dick nodded. His leg felt fine and he was so pumped up with adrenaline he felt he would burst.

'How do we get out of this Leon?' he gasped, as he looked around to see the fallen rider he'd just left, slowly remount and join his comrade in the charge.

'The most obvious way of course. It gets even better Dick. Drop the sword, we don't need it.'

When Dick showed no inclination, and with the horses only about twenty feet away and converging at a fast trot, he said it again.

'Drop it Dick and grab my hand. It's time we were gone!'

Dick threw the sword down and reached for Leon, with the shouts of their attackers loud in his ears and the thunder of hooves and the blast of the horse's breath growing dangerously close. With only yards to spare there was a deafening sound, like a roll of thunder and Dick suddenly found himself viewing the scene over Leon's shoulder, from the darkness of the void, through the window of a frame of film.

The two horsemen reined in their headlong charge and frantically looked this way and that in obvious alarm and astonishment.

'Just watch Dick. In a moment they'll forget we were ever there.'

And as Dick watched, the two horsemen shook themselves as though to clear their heads, dismounted to reclaim their rapiers and, each giving a puzzled look around, remounted and turned up the hill to ride away without a backwards glance.

'Weird.' said Dick quietly.

Leon chuckled.

And, behind Dick, in the all enveloping darkness, so did someone else…

Now Fin (23)

Fin and his friends sat on a long wooden bench at the back of the makeshift theatre that had been constructed that afternoon. The lights illuminated a large patch of grass containing the bare essentials necessary for the staging of 'Much Ado About Nothing'. Fred was demonstrating the use of the spotlights with two of the lighting operators, Gary and Jez.

'Right Jez. The wedding party enter, so give me a bluey on the entrance!' he called and immediately a pale blue wash surrounded a portico to the left.

'And fade to black as Gazza gives us a white on the table.'

They had been going through this for the last ten minutes or so, when suddenly Mister Sybbilant appeared stage left.

'Enough! Enough! If it's not right now it never will be! Our audience will arrive within the hour! Avaunt thou ungainly youths.' He waved a dismissive hand at the boys and turned to Fred.

'Is everything ready?'

Fred nodded 'We're all set Mister Sybbilant, everything will be A-OK. Trust me.'

The diminutive actor sniffed and turned to the small group of musicians sitting to the right of the stage, who were quietly discussing codas and after show drinks. The actor manager clapped his hands to gain their attention and Fin saw more than one of them lift their eyes towards the skies before pasting fixed grins on their faces as they turned to the little man.

With a wave to Fred the boys jumped down from their seats and headed off towards the hostel. The show would start in less than an hour and they were all looking forward to the play. For most of the late afternoon the friends had been watching the preparations and had forgotten Fin's problems, but now Willis brought them back to the fore.

'Where's Mister Nutter then?' he asked the group in general. The other four all shrugged their shoulders and looked to Fin for their next move.

'Off with the luscious Mrs Nutter somewhere I guess.' said Fin. 'Let's get ready for the show, I'm sure he'll find us if he has any news. I'm gonna wear my combats.'

'What? Shakespeare in combat trousers?' wailed Simeon. 'Where's your sense of occasion? This is one of the works of the greatest playwright in the English language, show some respect young Finbar. We shall dress as befits the event, thou callow youths.'

Sim ended his declaration in a pose copied from the little actor they had seen earlier that afternoon – one hand on his heart, the other raised dramatically to the sky. He grinned and looked around at each of his friends, all of whom were beginning to crease up at his not-so-serious outburst.

'Just what do you have in mind Sim? Asked Willis.

Simeon winked. 'I know where the costumes are kept, and I know the wardrobe mistress. We had chat earlier, just for a couple of minutes. Want to try your hands at looking the part of a Shakespearian audience?'

No-one else looked terribly convinced.

'No chance Sim. We'd look right plonkers, wouldn't we?'

'Everyone'd have fits.'

'Total pillocks.'

'So what? Most of the lads think we're a bit odd anyway. And it'd give everyone a good laugh, including Mrs Nutter. It's not as though we'd be trying to be serious actors or anything. Go on. We've had such a weird day, let's end it on a high note. A sort of off-key high C.'

The others still looked unconvinced, until Tam jumped over to Sim, put his hand firmly on his shoulder and cried out.

'I'm with you Sim, as long as we all do it.' He looked over to Fin and Willis and puffing his chest out raised hand in the same way as Sim and decried

'He was indeed the glass

Wherein the noble youth did dress themselves.'

'I'm impressed.' said Sim nodding and pointing at Tam. 'A touch of Henry IV...'

'Part 2' interrupted Tam.

'...Part 2.' continued Simeon. 'There is yet hope for you philistines.'

Willis sank to his haunches and held his head in his hands 'Oh, God. We're doomed, doomed!'

Mike and Bev had spent a pleasant early evening at a pub just down the road in Eskdale. Mike knew he needed to get back to the hostel to help Bert with their charges soon, it was unfair to leave it all to his older colleague, but he felt so much more at ease having been able to talk to his wife alone, even if it was only for half an hour or so.

They'd chatted about Fin and his friends for a while before moving on to Professor Tome and his interest in Fin and his problems.

Mike was sure that Fin was just having vivid dreams that were occurring so frequently that the boy had built up a whole story, which he believed in absolutely, but which was founded on dreams nonetheless. His wife seemed less sure.

Bev had explained quite a bit more about Professor Tome's ideas and, once again, Mike had the distinct impression that he wasn't inhabiting the same world as some other people.

It seemed that the professor, who was still well regarded by many of his peers, and had written several well received papers on child psychology over the years - though nothing ground-breaking, had spent a considerable amount of time in the last couple of years trying to get to the bottom of the strange case of the boy who had vanished after coming to him for help. The boy's parents had blamed him to some extent for the disappearance of their son. Indeed the police had been involved and Artie had been under suspicion of abduction at one point. He had stopped attending professional conferences and rarely entertained visitors. Some friends had expressed disquiet at the direction his theories had begun to take and he had only opened up to Bev after she had gone to see him that afternoon. In a hurried discussion that had lasted only half an hour or so, he had urged her to find Fin and bring him back to see him as soon as possible.

'He seems to think he knows what's going on, but I have to admit it does all sound a bit far-fetched.' said Bev.

'Well, I knew you'd been worried about him for a while, but you never really went into any detail.' said Mike.

'I know. But I hadn't realised just how far off-centre he was heading' she replied, sounding concerned.

'According to his thinking, these boys really can travel back in time. You know, it's like those people who are convinced they've been reincarnated from historical characters. They undergo regression therapy and while hypnotised they can talk about things from history that they supposedly couldn't have picked up from books and things. You've read about the man who thinks he was a naval captain who lost a leg at Trafalgar. I remember we listened to a thing on the radio where they played a tape of him whilst under hypnosis and it certainly sounded like he was having his leg sawn off.'

'Yes, I remember' said Mike. 'and it was all very vivid, but even the chap on the radio said it all sounded rather fanciful.'

'But no-one could account for it. He knew old nautical terms that even the naval people at the Greenwich museum had to look up, they were so archaic.'

'It just sounds so fantastic, and that's only if you try to believe in reincarnation. What we're talking about with Fin takes the whole thing a huge step beyond that. How can the Prof really believe that children can time travel?' asked Mike.

Bev looked a little uncomfortable and sat looking at her G & T for several seconds before raising her eyes to Mike.

'He's been looking into the latest astro-physics papers and things.' she said. 'And he thinks he can account for a lot of it using the theories coming out of their research.'

Mike held his hands up to stop her.

'Hang on. Now we're into astro-physics? This is all getting beyond me love. You're going to have to take this slowly and we probably haven't got the time now, so just give me the gist of it. After we've managed to get the boys to bed tonight, we'll sit down and try to go through it all in more detail, because at some point we've got to come to some sort of decision – apart from anything else I've got to work out how I'm going to tell Fin's parents about what's been going on.'

Bev was concerned for the other boys as well. How were they going to react to what was happening to Fin? It seemed that they'd been taking his story at face value, but they also appeared to be treating the whole thing as a bit of fun. Soon they'd have to take it more seriously. Then their attitudes might change radically.

'Okay Mike. I'm going to try to explain the way Artie's mind is working on this, but it does all seem a little – shall we say "out there". But listen first then tell me what you think.'

Mike nodded, and took another gulp of the local brew. He'd chosen to give it a try solely because of its charming name - "Foul Fell". Anything with a name like that deserved a chance. And it wasn't half bad, if you ignored the malodorous pong it was giving off.

Bev continued.

'Artie's spent ages looking into anything that might have a bearing on the disappearance of Tony Athelston – that's the boy who disappeared. For reasons that only he knows he believed the lad totally. Not at first mind you, but after running a barrage of tests he couldn't find anything wrong with him, apart from the fact that the boy was convinced he time-travelled in his dreams. After all the fuss when he vanished – especially when it even made a few minor headlines in the national papers and he had to try to defend his actions, which were almost universally rubbished...'

'I don't recall any of this. I had no idea.' interrupted Mike.

'Well it was over and done with fairly quickly, but his professional reputation was shot to bits by then, even if very few outside of the profession realised it, or even cared - child psychology isn't *that* much of a headline grabber really.' She smiled and took a sip of her drink.

'Artie believed Tony because of something he told him, or showed him. Artie wouldn't say what it was, but it convinced him beyond all doubt.'

'But then he disappeared?'

'Exactly. So Artie began to research it really closely. He went through all sorts of other cases and found one or two that bared comparison. Cases of other children who had extremely vivid nightmares and then disappeared. He began by investigating all the normal routes. He went through their case notes, police files - where they existed - and any other avenues he could go down.'

'But I thought those sort of things were all confidential?'

'Yes, but you have to remember when he started he was still a big gun in the field, and it's amazing what you can get into when you're researching in a professional capacity. Besides, almost everyone involved wanted answers, and if Artie could cast some light onto the reasons for the disappearances doctors, police and parents were happy to go along with it.'

'But then it all went pear shaped?'

'In a very big way. Artie drew such outlandish conclusions that he was virtually ostracised by all the professions he'd been involved in up until that point. Parents threatened to have him locked up and everyone else withdrew their cooperation for fear of being tarred with the same brush. No, actually that's unfair. They stopped helping because they thought he was a nut, and who could blame them. We're talking about the very outer fringes of the outer fringes of psychology and science, rapidly approaching Sci-Fi, B-movie Grand Central here. I guess Artie was so involved he just didn't see how ridiculous and outlandish it all was.'

Mike raised his hand to stop the flow.

'So why on earth did you ever get involved with him? It all sounds a bit sad really. An eminent man in his chosen field goes off the rails, for whatever reason - and you chose to work with him. Why?'

'Well I'd known him for several years anyway, he'd helped me with my doctorate and I really liked the old boot. He was into his fifties when he lectured me and well past sixty when it all went wrong. I'd kept in touch over the intervening years and I suppose I thought I might be able to help him. You know, bring him back from the outskirts of Loonyville - give him some peace in his declining years...'

'I had no idea about any of this. Gives me a whole new picture of the old duffer. Are you sure he hasn't just gone of his head?' Mike asked.

'Well I have to admit it did all sound a bit like Alzheimers or something, but that's where the physics comes in.'

Mike looked sceptical.

Bev smiled indulgently as she smoothed back her dazzlingly blonde hair and leaned forward.

'Astrophysicists have known for a while that if all their theories are correct then the universe is too big.'

Mike raised an eyebrow.

'According to all their calculations and God-Knows-What-Else, the universe is missing about ninety-five percent of its mass.'

'Explain.'

'Apparently, for the galaxies and everything else up there to move around in the way they do, there isn't enough that isn't space.'

Mike looked confused and she hurried on.

'Speculation has grown that if celestial bodies move around under the influence of gravity, and at the moment that's not just their best guess – it's the only one, there should be far more mass in the universe. There just isn't enough stuff out there to cause the universe to behave the way it does. So some scientists have postulated the existence of "dark matter", which is there - it's just that we can't see it. Others have settled on the existence of parallel universes...'

Mike interrupted again.

'But that's just science fiction. No-one really believes in it all, do they?'

'Oh no? You try telling the leaders in their fields who reckon that, in order for Einstein to be even close in his General Theory, these things have to exist. It's the only way to explain what they keep finding out there.' She gestured up at the ceiling, but Mike understood she was really indicating the infinity of space. 'Or rather what they can't find. Artie pointed me at the research and, if you believe even half the stuff these guys keep pumping out, they really do believe in some or all of this, and who are we to argue? These are supposed to be the people with the inside track on how the universe - how everything – operates, on a scale so massive we can't even begin to imagine. They're off in space and time dimensions – and there are evidently far more than three spatial and one time, by the way - that most of us know little about and care even less.'

Bev sat back as Mike leaned forward.

'Okay. So even if you take all this mumbo-jumbo on trust, and I assume we have to since there's no way of proving, or disproving any of it – what does it have to do with our Fin and his very much hear-and-now problem?'

Bev smiled and finished her drink, waving aside Mike's offer of a second one. She looked at her watch

'Time you were on your way back to your charges, Bert will be crawling the walls if we're too late. Drink up and I'll finish my tale on the drive back.'

Mike gulped the final mouthful of "Foul Fell" and began to realise that maybe it did deserve its name. He was feeling decidedly bilious after just one pint. Stifling a belch he offered his hand to help Bev from her seat.

'Such a gentleman.' she quipped, 'Chivalry is not dead.'

'No, but it's feeling a bit under the weather just at the moment.' Mike replied.

In the car Bev picked up the discussion.

'Artie thinks that maybe all these astrophysics whiz kids have got it right. What if there are parallel universes, which can't be seen, but can influence our universe? What if dark matter is simply the unseen parallel universes? What if we live in what the scientists call a multiverse, but just don't know it? It would certainly be a big help to all those who are trying to work out the mechanics, on a massive scale, of the world, in its largest, most immense sense.'

Mike nodded as he drove.

'So okay. If I take all this as fact rather than merely speculation, where does it get us?'

Bev looked across at him.

'Well, then the final step on Artie's little odyssey seems fairly trivial by comparison.' She smiled encouragingly, willing Mike to go along with the general weirdness that seemed to be accepted by so many eminent scientists - all the men who wrote dumbed-down versions of those papers for general consumption which, if encountered by ordinary mortals, would look like great rafts of gibberish. In Mike's opinion most made far too much money from mere speculation. They guessed at what could be the answers to life, the universe and everything.

To his mind 42 was probably more accurate than any of their ideas.

'Go on then, hit me with it.'

Bev laughed.

'Isn't it obvious? She asked.

'Well obviously *not.*' he murmured, feeling a little put out by her hectoring tone.

'Artie thinks that these kids along with certain adults have a way of accessing the multiverse from our universe. In dreams, particularly in the young, doorways open to other worlds that seem to be almost identical to our own – maybe they are identical, who knows?' She shrugged in her seat. 'And somehow they can travel to them. He thinks that for most people it just results in very vivid dreams, but for a select few there's a lot more to it than that. Maybe Fin really can travel in time via his dreams.'

She glanced across and saw Mike's look of frank disbelief as he shook his head whilst keeping his eyes fixed on the road ahead in the fading light.

'You aren't convinced are you?'

'Not even slightly I'm afraid. On the other hand I can't think of a rational explanation for Fin's behaviour, or for the coat and boots we found this afternoon. Sure the boys could have planted them, or maybe just Fin did, without the others knowing, but it seems so unlikely. He's a level headed young lad, certainly not the type you'd expect to pull a stunt like this. So I'm prepared to be persuaded into almost anything, but I'm finding it hard to take any of it on faith. I mean before you came this afternoon I didn't know any of this stuff concerning The Prof.'

'And it all sounds just too implausible? Said Bev.

'Fraid so, love. We're just going to have to play this by ear and see what happens.'

Bev nodded.

'Maybe tomorrow we'll be able to sort something out if we go back to the mill with Fin, but I'm not holding my breath.'

'Fair enough Mike. I've got to admit I'm not sure about any of it, but I'd like to think that neither Artie nor your boy Fin have gone so completely doo-lally that they'd invent all this.'

'Me too.' said Mike as he stopped the car in the hostel car park, which was beginning to fill with others arriving for the play, now only half an hour away.

'Right' said Mike as they climbed out of the car. 'Let's see what we can do about organising this rabble into an audience fit for the bard, eh?'

But though nothing more was said on the matter, they both still found themselves puzzling over the strange theories of their old friend Professor Tome and a young boy called Finbar, who was somehow linked to a lad who had mysteriously vanished years before.

When Dick (24)

Dick stared as his friend turned his gaze on a point somewhere over his right shoulder.

'That wasn't you, was it?' he breathed slowly with an almost comical wide-eyed gape.

Leon paused for a moment.

'Nope. We have unexpected company Dick. Take a look.'

Leon nodded into the blackness behind Dick.

Dick swung himself around to look at the figure suspended behind him. He didn't know what he'd expected to see, but it wasn't a robed figure with a well-trimmed goatee and a clipboard.

'Ahem. Hello gentlemen.' said the man. 'I would essay a 'Good Morning' but that seems a little out-moded given our current circumstances, wouldn't you say?'

Dick and Leon said nothing. Both were too shocked at being addressed by someone who gave every appearance of being a schoolmaster. The clipped upper class accent merely added to the overall impression of a classics professor out for a leisurely stroll. Except that this was not the place to take a stroll.

'Please stop staring gentlemen. I realize my sudden appearance must be a trifle unexpected, but simple good manners dictates that you at least offer me the simple courtesy of your names, wouldn't you say?'

Leon, surprisingly seemed lost for words, and it was Dick who posed the obvious first question, ignoring the man's request.

'Well excuse me! I would have thought that good manners would have dictated that *you* announce yourself rather than creep up on us like that. May I first ask who you are sir?'

The somewhat stilted form of address seemed to fit the situation.

The man smiled and raised his hand to cover his mouth, and coughed to stifle the mirth he obviously felt.

'Of course, you are correct.' The man now took on the stern countenance of the schoolmaster again. 'I am Abel Fermion - the Watcher for the streams in this cluster, and *you* are not on my list, although I fancy it is your dark friend who has brought me here.' He nodded towards Leon.

At this point Leon had regained his composure - but immediately lost it again, moving to hover beside Dick.

'*Dark friend*? Did you just call me dark, old man? Did I hear you right?'

Dick could sense from his tone of voice that Leon was getting hot under the collar. His question had ended with a snarl that couldn't be mistaken, and the old man flinched at the venom it held.

After a lifetime of living with prejudice, every so often, but very rarely, something lit the blue touch paper of Leon's anger, and now was such a time. Dick realised it was probably due to the fact that Leon's bit of fun had taken an unexpected turn and put out a restraining hand to prevent his companion's forward momentum carrying him any closer to Abel Fermion.

'Hold your horses Leon. Give the man a chance. I fancy that political correctness isn't something this chap has come across before.'

Mister Fermion looked puzzled.

'Political correctness? Forgive me gentlemen, but I have no idea as to what you are eluding? The term means nothing to me. If I have inadvertently offended you sir, I ask your forgiveness - that was not my intention. As a Watcher I rarely have to intercede in this way. Very rarely.'

He was now beginning to look uncomfortable and covered his mouth as he gave a short muffled cough again, in what was obviously a nervous response. From his point of view this was not going very well, not very well at all.

Leon's large frame visibly shook as he forced himself to calm down.

'Sorry Fermion' he gave a wry smile, 'I do sometimes get a little upset by things that I should have learned to ignore long ago.' He offered his hand to the man. 'I'm Leon Messenger and this is my friend Dick – Richard, rather – Hedd.'

Mister Fermion accepted the proffered hand and then did likewise to Dick.

'With the introductions finished with, may I ask what you gentlemen are doing here?' he asked with a raised eyebrow. He thumbed through the papers attached to his clipboard, inspecting each one in turn.

'Neither of you are on my list and I'm sure I would have remembered such an imposing figure as yourself Mister Messenger. Incidentally, would you not consider your black apparel somewhat overstated for travelling through the streams?'

Dick and Leon looked each other up and down.

Leon nodded as he replied.

'True enough Mister Fermion, but I hadn't planned on meeting anyone where we've been – and I certainly didn't expect to bump into anyone out here. So long as we went unnoticed I decided that dark and workmanlike was as good as anything else.'

'Yes I'm sure. But we do have some rules regarding garb. Unfortunately by the time your unexpected presence was signalled to me you had already re-entered the ribbon and I had no wish to have to track you down. As a result, I have been waiting for you to re-emerge from *the moment* you had entered. I was regrettably detained and therefore missed you prior to your foray into... ah' he paused and looked at his clipboard, 'ah... yes... er... into fifteenth century Europe.' He eyed them over his reading glasses. 'In order to maintain some semblance of stability we have to log all movement between the streams. Moving back and forth as you have done is not quite so important, but if you decide to move further afield I'm afraid you will have to submit to our more stringent formalities. For the moment, a simple registration will suffice.'

He edged closer to the pair and held out a second, smaller clipboard to Leon and passed a similar one to Dick.

'If you would both be so kind as to hold these.'

Then with a cheerful 'Thanking you, gentlemen.' he retrieved the boards - and vanished.

Both men called out in alarm and surprise, but Abel Fermion did not reappear. His disappearance left both men feeling cheated.

'What the devil was that about?' whispered Leon.

'You're asking me Leon? I thought you had all this off pat. I don't know what's going on, but I do know that I'd like to go home now - my leg's beginning to ache.' Dick grimaced. 'Please.'

Leon nodded and reached across to take Dick's arm.

The transition back to the kitchen was as fast as their exit from Portugal, and left Dick swaying slightly as Leon moved away to put the kettle on.

'Tea all right Dick, or would you like something stronger?' he asked.

'Tea's fine Leon thanks.'

Dick sank onto a chair at the table and put his chin on his hands, which were flat on the table, interlaced and palms down.

'So what just happened Leon?' he asked softly.

Leon glanced over his shoulder as he finished filling the kettle.

'I think we may have been visited by some sort of policeman Dick.' He smiled. 'So you should have felt right at home.'

Dick gave a lopsided grin.

'Yeah, sure.'

Leon dropped teabags into mugs and added sugar as he tried to explain.

'Portugal was picked at random.' he said. 'There was nothing planned about that at all, especially not our run-in with the locals. So how did he know where we were?'

Dick was suddenly on his feet and hopping around the table, pulling off his boot and making gasping comically.

'God, my leg itches like the very devil, Leon!' he said, puffing and blowing as he tried to wrench his boot off. 'I doesn't hurt, it just bloody itches.' He finally succeeded in freeing his foot and began scratching manically at his shin. 'And it wasn't such a glancing blow either – it bloody well hurt when that blade went in!'

Leon bent down and put his nose only inches from Dick's hairy shin and made a great pantomime of looking for the injury.

'Ooooh. Where's da ickle scwatch gone Dickie Dear?' He laughed as Dick stopped scratching and did an almost comical double-take upon realising that the fifteenth century sword wound was nowhere to be seen. Only the dried blood around the neat cut in his trousers gave any indication that there had ever been an injury. 'Sorry mate, I should have mentioned it, but I didn't think it would matter on our first outing.' Leon was suddenly more serious, but not much. 'Don't worry, as long as you don't do something really stupid, you can't come to any great harm.'

He looked again at the leg that Dick was now resting on the table. His friend seemed mesmerised by the short faint scar showing just above his sock.

'I've got no idea how it works, but I have a feeling that time itself plays a part in this. There are other things that I can't explain, that have always happened, though it's only recently that I've really started to think about it.'

'Like how that translation thing works?' said Dick.

'Exactly. It's always happened and I never thought to question it much before.'

'Does it work where-ever you go?' asked Dick.

'And whenever as well. You can understand old Norse just as easily as Portuguese, or Spanish, or Dark Ages Saxon. Somehow the energy we use to travel allows us to communicate with everyone too. If you don't think about it too hard, it's actually quite cool. If you do start to think about it, all you end up with is a headache.'

'So what's to stop you going to back and giving everyone helpful hints. You know: *"Hmm. I'm not sure what you ever saw in that young Mister Hitler, Klara, he'll only get you into trouble. And I'm not sure about calling your son Adolf"* or *"Excuse me soldier, but the King says watch what you're doing with that arrow. You'll have someone's eye out."*

'Oh, very droll Dick. But that is actually quite a serious point...'

'I know Leon. I'm only half joking. But would young Adolf have become such a monster if Alois Schicklgruber had been dissuaded from changing his name to Hitler and beating his sons in drunken rages? Little changes could have a huge impact. Surely we could do all sorts of things to make the world a better place for everyone. It sounds a bit -' he smiled coquettishly across the table and he put on his best bimbo voice, *"Hello I'm Miss South Buttockwobble and I want peace on earth and to feed all the hungry children."* - but just think of the possibilities. All sorts of conflicts prevented. Medical breakthroughs made in time to save millions, dictators prevented from ever gaining control. All sorts of things, all sorts.'

Dick's eyes burned with a zeal that made Leon smile again, but he held up his hands to stem the torrent of ideas that was bursting from his friend.

'Sorry Dick, it doesn't work like that, or not for me anyway.'

Leon finished making the drinks and sat with Dick at the kitchen table.

'I've been to so many places and met so many people that it's getting hard to remember them all, but the one thing that they all have in common is that I haven't been able to pass on a single piece of useful information to any of them. Or not useful in the sense of preventing a war, or an assassination, or drought and famine. Every time I tried to give someone a warning, or do something concrete to improve someone's lot, it always went wrong. Well not wrong exactly, but no matter what I did, it never had the desired effect.'

Leon sat back and sipped his tea. Dick leaned forward, hanging on every word.

'Go on. How were you stopped from helping?'

'Well at first I was only trying to make small changes, just to help a friend I'd made, or prevent some minor accident - that sort of thing. But if I was talking to someone I'd find them starting to walk away, as though they'd just lost interest. They simply seemed to have forgotten that we'd been talking and I'd have to start over... and over... and over. It happened so many times I knew it wasn't coincidence. Whatever power allows us to travel the way we just did, also prevents us from interfering with the past.'

'Bugger.' interjected Dick.

'Precisely.' said Leon. 'It doesn't matter what we know with regard to past events, we can't let anyone who was, or will be, affected by them know anything. It used to drive me mad, but I couldn't find a way around it, so eventually I stopped trying.'

'Bloody infuriating though, I would imagine.'

'Oh yes. Just think, with a bit of forward planning I could have been on The Titanic and able to tell them where and when the iceberg was lurking. Just a few words in the right ear and all those people would have cruised serenely on. But try as I might, there was no way to tell anyone, so they all had a little more ice than expected in their after dinner drinks.'

'Hang on. Are you saying you were on The Titanic?'

'Oh yes. Not at the end though. Once I knew there was no hope for them and that I couldn't make even a halfpenny's worth of difference to their fate, it seemed a little voyeuristic to stay there and watch. I mean, I knew what was going to happen – I've seen the film, read the book, though thankfully never bought the T-shirt – so watching it all unfold around me, in the flesh as it were, would have been a bit of a sickener. In fact it was that that finally persuaded me to give up on trying to be a guardian angel. It simply doesn't work you see.'

Dick looked as though he was about to argue the point, and Leon became stern.

'Consider this before you try to get me to attempt something daft. Think of what would have happened if I could have travelled back a couple of thousand years and bumped off Christ, or Joseph and Mary? Think about it. Christianity would never have existed. How many lives would have been spared in the Inquisition, the Crusades? But what would we have lost as well? The great men and women who were driven to achieve so much because of their beliefs would have had totally different lives. Many of the discoveries we rely on in modern life would never have been made. Who are we to make those sort of decisions? For my part I'm quite happy not to have to make them, or take action to change history.'

'Yes, but surely we could make sure we only acted for the good of the world. Think of the wonderful things we could do if we could find a way through this.'

'No Dick. I don't want to think about it. What would happen would be that we'd end up making the changes that we consider would be best for mankind. I say again, who are we to make those sorts of decisions? Why should we be any better than the people who were there at the time? Hindsight is a wonderful thing, but in many cases the results of changing history would probably be even more catastrophic than just leaving well alone.'

'But Leon, you can't believe that! Think of what could happen if Hitler was never born, or Attila the Hun, or Nero, or if the awful effects of colonialism could be foreseen and avoided, think of what could be done if we could steer clear of the bad and enable only the best to flourish!'

Dick was speaking with an almost maniacal fervour. He'd stood up from the table and was striding about the kitchen waving his arms to emphasize each point, spinning on his feet to broadcast his desires to all four walls.

'No anti-semitism, no religious bigotry from any side. Prevention of wars, eradication of disease. Even things as simple as accidents that kill so many. To be able to have a plane grounded because we know it's going to crash….'

'Dick stop it!' shouted Leon. 'Look, I've already told you, we can't prevent anything from happening. Just think clearly for a minute.' Dick opened his mouth to speak again, but Leon raised his voice and continued. 'You absolutely cannot save the lives of people back in history. Apart from the fact that, as I've already told you, Time won't allow it, think logically about what you're saying. If we went back to say… Pompeii, and warned everyone of the approaching disaster. There would be many we couldn't convince, I'm sure, but even if we were able to save just a few, think of the impact that could have on the future. Maybe there'd be a young couple who later married and had children...'

'A good thing surely, makes the whole exercise worthwhile, just that one new life…' interrupted Dick.

'…No Dick, no.' Leon looked infinitely sad, but stood his ground against the rising fervour which was again beginning to well up in his friend. 'What we would have done is introduce an entirely different stream of ancestry into the world. Vast numbers of people would be affected by that one intervention - lives changed irrevocably, and not always for the better. So what would the effect be of saving The Titanic, The Lusitania, the Twin Towers? We'd end up spending the rest of time simply trying to put right all the things we'd upset by meddling. Save someone in the Dark Ages and maybe Shakespeare would never be born, or Darwin or Einstein. The effects could be catastrophic for everyone.'

He looked over at Dick, who was now standing with his back to Leon.

'And besides, the whole thing is academic. I've stopped counting of the number of people who've lost interest in mid-sentence and wandered of just because I mentioned something that could have altered history. It really is as though I've ceased to register in their reality. Even if you try to write something down, what you end up with is a meaningless scrawl. It seems to make sense while you're writing it, but it's just gibberish when you try to read it back, or get someone else to read it. Maybe it's the same mechanism that allows us to understand whatever's said to us, even in languages we've never heard before, – only in reverse – say something out of place and you're blanked by the whole universe. Bit of an ego shredder that, wouldn't you say?'

He stood and reached over to Dick tugging on his sleeve to turn him around. He was trying to lift the mood, but could tell that Dick wasn't about to be cheered.

'So what do we do instead, eh Dick?'

No answer.

'I'll tell you what we do – we look after those around us in the here and now, who have been, or will be, affected by things we've seen and heard – and we try not to cause problems for the future. And yes, we have a bloody good time while we're at it.'

Dick looked up at him. A faint smile twitched at the corners of his mouth but he stubbornly refused to give it full rein. Leon was so damned infuriating when he was in this sort of a mood. He obviously had answers to questions that Dick hadn't even thought of yet.

'And how exactly do we do that Leon, without incurring the wrath of time, the universe, and presumably our new acquaintance, Mister Abel Fermion - the Watcher.'

'By being sneaky and underhand, man.' laughed Leon. 'By being sneaky and underhand.'

Leon's smile broadened.

'You're a copper. You should know all about that.'

Now Fin (25)

The play began on time and amazingly all the boys were seated and ready - to be bored rigid. Fin and his friends sat together along a row. They'd all thought better of dressing up. Some things were a bit *too* dodgy even for them and they'd decided that the taunting they would receive from certain other boys just didn't make it worth the effort and denim and T shirts were the *outfits du jour*. It was a shame, but for once common sense had overridden their innate sense of fun. Fin looked at the young faces around him. Apart from Tam, Sim and himself, most seemed resigned to a couple of hours of purgatory. For most it was a price worth paying for the chance to have a holiday with their mates, away from the strictures of home and school. He began to think about something his mind had dwelt on quite a lot recently. He wasn't sure from whence it came but the train of his thoughts started heading down the same branch line that it had hauled itself down several times in the last couple of weeks. Fin was a bright lad, like his close friends, and they all felt a little bit separate from the others. They didn't quite fit in with everyone else and Fin fitted least of all, especially now. With all that was going on he seemed about as distant from normal life as it was possible to be.

Fin eyes roamed the cluster of boys around him.

For most of them, Shakespeare was still just the name of an old duffer who wrote some dead boring stuff in the dead boring past that sounded as though it should rhyme, but didn't, and looked OK on the page but couldn't be read. When there was no telly, DVDs or computer games people had no option but to watch this rubbish, but now anyone with any sense could find something far more worthwhile to do – like turning themselves into a zombie playing a game where you played someone trying not to turn into a zombie. The boys from Appleton were no different to the bulk of their contemporaries. They didn't phone - they texted, and consequently took twice as long to say half as much as they would have done by using a telephone the old fashioned way. They didn't write - they typed, and therefore forgot how to hold a pen so that they could write legibly. They didn't talk *to* each other, but rather *at* everyone. They either held opinions that would never be altered by reasoned argument, usually on inconsequential - but to them highly important – subjects, or they had no opinion at all on those things that they could - and should - have wanted to change. Entire generations across the so-called First World were learning to live their lives based on the gossip and opinions of barely literate celebrities and their obsequious hangers on. All that said, to many this did not seem a bad thing. It left the running of the world to those who were suited to the task. The nerds and geeks who actually took an interest in the wider world around them.

People like Fin.

The problem was that, almost to a man, the nerds and geeks were controlled by faceless others who had their own agendas. The primary aim of the controllers was money, and through money they garnered power. The world could go to hell in a handcart as long as they could become just that little more powerful than the next man. A lot more powerful was better, but even a microgram more was good.

Fin switched off the Private Eye in his head and returned to Bill the bard.

The play was in full spate and Fin could hear Simeon following the lines verbatim under his breath. Some of the other lads, unseen by Sim, were giggling behind their hands and pulling faces as he continued his sotto voce accompaniment. Fin began to feel irrationally irritated by boys who found more enjoyment in taking the piss out of Sim, than in watching the play. Just as he was about to make some comment, which would no doubt be treated with derision, Mister Lightfoot approached from the back of the tiered seating. In a voice quiet enough to be heard only by those at whom it was directed, he said 'Boys, any more buffoonery and you'll be sitting with me at the back. Keep the noise down, and stop messing about. We're here to watch Shakespeare and by God you'll do so without embarrassing me or the school. So, still and quiet.' His hand slashed the air in front of the boys once, and he turned to leave. Simeon had his startled rabbit-in-the-headlight expression as he looked around him.

'What was all that about?' he asked.

'Oh, nothing Sim'. Let's just get back to Billy Shakespeare, eh?

Sim settled forward on the bench again, and resumed his silent mouthing in time with the dialogue. Fin was again amazed that his friend, who was well known to be not the brightest tool in the box, was able to recite such works practically word perfect. But it wasn't just the fact that he could do it. It was that he took such obvious joy in doing so. Fin wasn't watching someone who had been forced to learn the works he now recited. Sim, the bottom set maths dunce, who couldn't remember the most basic French and German vocab, and had no idea how to use a paintbrush, had found his niche in ancient literature. Not just Shakespeare, he'd told Fin and the others earlier, but Marlow amongst others, and even Chaucer. Fin smiled at the fact that Sim showed no promise in anything at school, except possibly rugby, and woodwork and metalwork in DT, but could somehow hold entire historical works in his head, and bring them forth at will. Fin was sure that his teachers knew nothing about this. According to most of them, Sim was a good-hearted lad, who would never amount to anything. Many of them couldn't understand how the boy had ever managed to pass the entrance exam for the school, since he showed no aptitude for any of the other subjects he was taught.

Fin suspected Simeon would surprise them all one day.

He shivered slightly and looked up. The sky was heavy with stars. It seemed the Milky Way was lighting the stage tonight, so many stars, so far away. Not a cloud in the sky, no wonder it was growing cooler. With his mind so full of other things, Fin found he just couldn't concentrate on the play and looked around again.

Pauly Wright and Alan Bishop had begun pulling faces and whispering to those around them again. This time Simeon was aware of what was happening and scowled at the boys who were disturbing him. This just made them more determined to upset him. Half a dozen boys were now whispering, nudging and giggling. Pauly Wright reached forward and flicked Sim's ear hard with his finger. The boys surrounding him, at the back of Sim and his friends, smothered their laughter as best they could, but for Fin it was too much. As Sim held a hand to his ear, Fin began to get to his feet as he turned to face his friend's tormentors. Sim reached up and dragged him back down to his seat.

'Ignore them Fin.' he whispered.

'Yeah, ignore them Finny Winny.' whispered Wright.

'Don't want to get upset, do you girlies? Cos' the big lads might decide to teach you a lesson.' said Bishop, and he leaned forward to flick Fin's ear this time.

Fin clapped a hand to his ear and looked around at Sim, Tam and Willis. They all studiously ignored him. This was ridiculous. They were here to enjoy a play. They shouldn't have to put up with this! He turned again to face the boys behind him, swivelling around on the bench.

'Just stop it. Morons!' he hissed under his breathe.

'Oooh, mummy. I'm so-o-o-o-o frightened.' Bishop hissed back, and his arm shot out to push Fin on the shoulder and make him face front.

However, maybe because of the darkness, maybe because Fin was in such an awkward position in his seat, or maybe because he just didn't care, Bishop missed his aim. Instead of the shoulder, he caught Fin a heavy glancing blow on the chin – not hard but solid – more a push than a punch. Fin was completely unbalanced and went down like a felled tree, sliding off his bench and slumping onto the row in front, none of whom were boys from the school. The strike was so unexpected he didn't even know where he was for several seconds. His senses reeled, and his body joined them, knocking at least two others from their seats as he fell. The commotion spread out from Fin like ripples in a pool and the obvious disturbance in the audience conveyed itself to the thespians in full flow on the stage.

There was an impressive silence that fell across the whole makeshift theatre, as everyone strained and struggled to get a clear view of the hullabaloo.

Mister Nutter appeared, with Mister Lightfoot hard on his heels.

Neither was prepared to listen to any excuses.

'On your feet LeMott!' hissed Mister Lightfoot, hauling Fin upright and dragging him almost bodily away from his seat. 'To the back, now!'

Simeon got up to follow, trying to placate Bert Lightfoot as he marched Fin away from the performance.

Mister Nutter scowled at the boys who had been tormenting Fin and Simeon, who sat stifling their laughter as Fin was made to leave.

'I don't know what was going on here, but I want to see you two' Mike indicated Bishop and Wright, 'immediately after the play. Now just shut up and watch the play, or there'll be The Devil to pay when I see you. Understand?'

The two boys at least had the decency to look a little abashed as Mister Nutter left, following his fellow teacher and the two boys back up the steps to their seats in the darkness beyond the penumbra cast by the stage lighting.

But even as he left he could sense the boys beginning to titter again behind him. He almost turned, but realised that the whole auditorium was still watching the little performance that had been put on by the boys. Blushing, he decided that this would be better settled after the play, when the crowds had left.

Willis and Tam stayed where they were in an attempt to distance themselves from the whole debacle.

Down on the stage the players made to resume their places and the diminutive actor/manager Mister Sybbilant stepped forward to address the audience, many of whom were still following the progress of the four into the darkness of the rear seats.

'Ladies and gentlemen,' he intoned in a sonorous voice. 'May I apologise for the interruption. We shall continue as best we may with our performance and can only hope that the young men causing the disturbance will be removed from our vicinity and suitably chastised.' This raised more then a few giggles from Wright, Bishop and their friends. 'And so, we return to our narrative.'

And so the matter was forgotten by the majority of those attending, as, at least for now, the play picked up from where it had been so unceremoniously suspended.

As they reached the seats at the very back of the audience Mister Lightfoot turned to Fin and Sim with a face like thunder.

'How dare you,' he said with unconcealed rage, 'how dare you embarrass both Mister Nutter and I, and indeed the whole school, with your ridiculous antics.'

Simeon tried to interrupt, but Mister Lightfoot was in full flow.

'Never in all my years, have I had to take such action. Finbar LeMott, I am so disappointed in you that I cannot find the words to express my feelings. Not content with your ludicrous charade earlier today, you now feel the need to ruin the evening's entertainment for everyone as well. Well it's not good enough, do you hear, not good enough at all.'

He scowled over at Sim.

'And you boy, can stop hopping around like that. I will not hear one more word from either of you. Sit and watch. When the play is over I will have a damn sight more to say, and you will listen. I have absolutely no wish to hear your feeble excuses now.'

As Sim made a final attempt to speak, but got no further than opening his mouth, Mister Lightfoot raised his hand in a threatening gesture.

'I said no, Mister Carver! I have no inkling as to your part in this evening's events, but I will deal with you both later. Now is not the time.'

He pointed at the empty row of seats at the very back of the stand.

'Sit. Watch, Be silent!'

With that he settled several seats away and studiously ignored them.

Sim made to speak but Fin shook his head sharply. He wanted no more trouble tonight. Let them just sit and try to enjoy the play. Hopefully all would be sorted out later.

As the play went on in to the evening Sim returned to following the dialogue, but Fin found himself simmering with indignation. He couldn't try to explain now, not with Mister Lightfoot in this mood, but it was so unfair! He hadn't done anything wrong! And the teacher appeared to be saying that everything that had happened in the last twenty four hours was simply down to Fin wanting to be the centre of attention. That was the last thing he wanted. He just hoped that Mister Nutter and Bev could help him tomorrow, otherwise he had the feeling there would be real trouble from Mister Lightfoot.

Strange that Mister Lightfoot should act like this too. Fin had always been on such good terms with him. Why he should have such an attitude, when Mister Nutter was at least prepared to listen despite his scepticism, he couldn't fathom.

It was so feckin' unfair!

He hadn't asked for any of this, and this evening he was just trying to help a friend. Was that something to be punished?

No it bloody wasn't.

Fin was in a mood as foul as the dark clouds gathering overhead. He looked up as he felt a chill breeze blow. He could see the clouds quite clearly against the sky, even though it was now past ten o'clock. That was because of light pollution from the cities around, though they were fifteen to twenty miles away. He remembered his Dad getting onto his soap box at home about that; not content with polluting the seas and the air with poisons, now we even polluted with light.

Remembering his father's outrage did little to settle Fin's mood.

Right at this moment he'd rather be anywhere but here. He could do without the nasty kids and stupid teachers.

The wind blew colder and a he felt a single raindrop on the back of his hand and looked up at the sky again. Maybe rain would cancel the rest of the proceedings and they could get everything over with.

He hadn't asked to be a loony – if he was one. He hadn't asked to be able to see the loutishness of some of his fellow pupils, when everyone else seemed oblivious to it. He hadn't asked to be an outsider, who always stood apart from the rest. If it wasn't for his few friends and his family, life would be a living hell, that he would be better rid of.

God, he was sooooooo angry.

He could feel himself beginning to flush with the heat his rage was generating and his breathing was becoming ragged.

A cool hand reached across and touched his hand, making him shudder at the unexpected contact.

'Okay Fin?' asked Bev, who had moved over from the other side of the two masters to Fin's left. 'You look a bit wound up.'

Fin looked up into the blue eyes and felt a pang of guilt, and became very conscious of her hand on his.

Maybe all was not right with the world, but things certainly seemed a lot better with Bev on your side.

'Don't worry. I'm hoping we'll be able to make some headway with your problem tomorrow. Try not to dwell on it all. We'll be fine, you'll see.'

She patted his hand and sat on the seat next to him, almost as though she intended to act as a buffer between the teachers and the boys. Her use of *we* was a help.

'It'll be okay, Fin.' she repeated.

Now he was also very conscious of her thigh touching his and tried to surreptitiously edge away. Bev was totally unaware of the effect she was having on the boy and held his hand in both of hers, patting it gently.

'Just watch the play and forget about it all.' She looked up and gave a little shiver. 'As long as the rain keeps off. It would be a bit unlucky after such a lovely day.'

She released Fins hand and returned her gaze to the stage.

Fin couldn't take his eyes off the clouds above, becoming heavier and more doom-laden by the minute and with them grew his own feeling of foreboding. Simeon looked up too.

'Rapid clouds have drank the last pale beam of even' he muttered.

'You what?'

'Getting cloudy innit?'

'Oh yeah. As long as that's all' said Fin morosely.

Sim looked across sharply.

'You feeling okay Fin?'

But before Fin could let Sim know of his increasing feeling of dread, Mister Lightfoot looked across with a scowl and a word of admonishment.

'Quiet!' he grated at the boys.

Sim was now looking concerned as Fin began to shiver.

Although no-one else seemed to be bothered by it, Fin was growing warmer as the storm above approached. Several members of the audience were now gazing upward and pulling jackets and cardigans closer. It really was beginning to look as though they might all be in for a soaking.

Fin turned to Bev with a pleading look.

'Sorry Mrs Nutter, but can you tell Mister Lightfoot and Mister Nutter that I don't feel well. In fact I think I'm going to faint.'

She reached out to touch his forehead and felt the cold clamminess along with a slick of sweat.

'Oh Fin! Come on, let's get you inside.' And she took his arm and began to rise.

Simeon on the other side of Fin leaned across.

'Don't worry Miss, I'll take him in.' He gestured towards the stage. 'I know all this anyway, and they're not really that good.' He sighed his disappointment. 'I was going to make the best of it, but I'll look after Fin instead.'

As Bev began to argue he stood up, dragging Fin with him.

'No, no, you stay here with Mister Nutter. We'll be okay.' Sim smiled as he began to help Fin to edge sideways to the stairs that led down the side of the stand of benches. Bev looked around to see her husband and his colleague looking across, one with barely concealed fury, the other with mounting concern. She slid across the bench to sit beside Bert.

'Calm down Bert. Fin's just not too chipper that's all.'

At Bert Lightfoot's look of consternation she made another effort to calm him.

'He looks as though he's going to throw up, so his friend – Sim isn't it – has taken him off for a walk around. They'll be alright.'

This last was to Mike who was leaning across to hear.

'Maybe it was something he ate?' she said.

But Mike was now staring up at the clouds. The sky was now appreciably darker than it had been five minutes earlier and he had the strange feeling that in some weird way the sky was reflecting Fin's mood. He looked behind the stand in an effort to see the boys, who had been out of sight as they walked down the side of the stand. Behind him the makeshift auditorium spread a darkness far too dense for him to penetrate it. He leaned over further as he searched the gloom

'They'll be okay Mike. Just leave them to it. Sim will look after him.' said Bev.

'Yes, yes I know.' But he still couldn't help glancing back towards the hostel every few minutes to check.

Eventually he did catch sight of two small figures walking back in the now gathering gloom. They were across to the left of the lawn, almost at the trees, Sim with his arm around Fin's waist and Fin leaning heavily against him. He saw another, smaller figure running to join them and realised that Tam had somehow managed to slip away without Bert noticing. Leaning forward Mike scanned the seats below. Willis still sat amongst the other boys, concentrating on the stage, but no doubt thinking of his friends. Mike wondered why he hadn't tried to sneak off too.

The wind was picking up, and Bev moved in front of the two teachers to sit on Mike's left.

'Getting cold.' she muttered as she snuggled closer to her husband, gripping his arm in both hands.

Suddenly the night was lit by a brilliant light, so bright it made all those watching the night entertainment wince. It was immediately joined by a tremendous blast of noise so loud many of those in the audience clapped their hands over their ears.

'Bloody Hell!' swore Mike above the thunderous tumult as Bev tightened her grip on his arm. His ears felt as though they were full of water. After the blast of sound everything was muffled and he had trouble distinguishing any sound other than his rapid breathing and racing heart. Bev had lifted her feet and sat with her legs folded under her trying to make herself small before the onslaught of that sound, with her head buried into Mikes chest. Bert was hunched forward in his seat his hand tightly clasped over his ears, his eyes staring wildly.

In front of them a woman had apparently fainted, her husband ineffectually patting her hand and quietly saying her name, a look of complete bafflement on his face. Off to one side a little girl was crying softly whilst clinging to her mother. All around people sat looking stunned. Whatever had caused the sound had expended a colossal amount of energy somewhere in the immediate vicinity. Yet there was no sign of damage as far as Mike could see. The problem he had was that the light had appeared so unexpectedly and so brightly that he suspected that no-one had actually seen what had happened.

The actors now stood in stunned silence, one or two of them working their jaws in circles and thumping their ears with the heel of their hands as though to clear some blockage. Mike recognised the movement and realised that they felt the same as him. It was as though the air pressure had suddenly changed drastically, like going up a steep hill in the car. They all needed to swallow, or blow, to even out the pressure.

As his hearing returned he looked back to check on Fin, Simeon and Tam, but they were gone. Presumably they had run the last few yards after the initial shock and were now safely ensconced within the hostels comforting walls. He turned his attention back to the rest of his wards sitting a few rows in front. To his relief they all looked none the worse for the shock they had all received and several were now shouting and laughing at the discomfort of those around them

'What was that?' gasped Bert as he sat upright and shook his head.

'Sounded like a lightening strike.' answered Mike. 'And a close one too.'

Bert shook himself.

'No rain though. Bloody funny storm if you ask me.' he said.

Mike turned to Bev, who had released his arm and sat looking up at the sky open-mouthed, tapping him on the chest.

He followed he gaze and saw with astonishment that the clouds had virtually dispersed and the sky was lightening by the second. The threatened storm had evaporated following that one, seemingly cataclysmic, burst of energy.

'Come on Bert, let's go check on the lads.' he urged, as he got to his feet.

It took a full ten minutes for everything to settle down and the performance to continue. Many of the Appleton boys, but also others in the audience, had become so animated and noisy that for several minutes the whole scene had been one of mild hysteria and it was noticeable that several members of the cast were still paying more attention to the sky than it would normally warrant. Once the initial frenzy had died down everyone had become more subdued, except for some of the lads, who couldn't be silenced even by Mister Lightfoot. They could be heard whispering and giggling throughout the rest of the act.

The play eventually finished late, but not as late as might have been expected. Certain actors had managed to gallop through the Bard's prose far faster than he would have wished, and few watching seemed to mind. The evening had been successfully ruined by the strange lightening-that-wasn't-lightening. Mike realised that almost everyone at the play really wanted to be home rather than here.

Or maybe the pub.

As appealing as that was he knew that, once they'd recovered from the shock of what had happened, the boys would probably be even more boisterous than usual, and no doubt many would want to phone their parents to let them know about the night's events.

As everyone rose from their seats at the end of the play, the volume coming from the schoolboys in their care rose and the two teachers hurried down to make sure there were no more mishaps. They, and the school's reputation, would have suffered enough this evening and both Mike and Bert wanted to get the lads back into the hostel before any disgruntled punters or actors sought them out.

As they began the short stroll across the lawns, Bert leading and Mike and Bev cajoling any stragglers at the back, Willis approached them, looking distinctly ill at ease.

'Sir, can I have a quick word?' he asked, one finger raised slightly, as though asking a question in class.

'Go on then Willis,' said Mike, 'what have you got to say to try to assuage our anger with Fin?'

'Speak for yourself.' murmured Bev.

'Please sir, it wasn't Fin who caused all the bother, really.' pleaded Willis.

'Oh no? Well just who was it falling around all over those kids in front, eh? Looked mighty like Fin to me. And Mister Lightfoot was closer than I and he seems sure of what happened.'

'But sir! It was Bishop and Wrighty who were teasing Sim, that's what started it and it was Bish who knocked Fin over onto the others, just because Fin was trying to make them stop.' It came out as a whining little voice and Willis reddened slightly and gave a small cough before adopting a more adult timbre.

'It wasn't Fin who caused the fuss sir, Honestly it wasn't.'

Mike smiled just a little.

'Okay son. To be honest I didn't think Fin would have been making a fuss in public like that. Not off his own bat.'

The boy smiled hopefully.

'So you'll sort it out with Mister Lightfoot then sir?' he asked.

'Well I'll certainly have a word with him and we *will* get to the bottom of it. But we'll have to have a word with anyone else who saw what was going on. I'm afraid Fin isn't in Mister Lightfoot's best books just at the moment and it'll take more than you to convince him. I don't think Bert has enjoyed this trip as much as he expected to, not with all the other stuff going on with Fin.'

The boy looked a little crestfallen and made to speak again. This time it was Bev who cut him off.

'Don't worry Willis,' she said softly, 'we'll sort it out, never fear.' And she patted him on the head. 'Off you go and let Fin know that all is not lost.'

'Go on, you young sprog, bugger off and leave us in peace.' joked Mike, and Willis turned to run off in search of the other three members of the little gang.

Mike watched him leaving.

'They're all good lads eh? And I'm sure what he said is true, but Bert's taking this whole thing with Fin very badly.'

'Hmm. I wonder why?' mused Bev. 'It's not like him, is it?'

'No.' Mike sighed. 'Maybe there's more to all this than meets the eye,' He glanced across at Bev. 'Don't you think?'

As they entered the hostel, ushering in the last of the boys, they both saw Willis looking puzzled as he came down the stairs and went into the lounge. As they watched, the boy emerged and made for the sportsroom with several others. Probably to play table football with the other three, thought Mike.

But he was beginning to have a nagging suspicion that something was wrong. It was something to do with the slightly hurried movements and harried expression that Willis wore as he scurried about. He noticed Bishop and Wright make some remark or other that seemed to spur the youngster on into the room ahead of him. Mike tried to shrug the feeling off as he and Bev joined Bert at the foot of the stairs.

Bert greeted them with a no more than a glance and then switched his attention to the throng of noisy schoolboys navigating the straits from lounge to sportsroom to reception.

'May I have your attention please?' he boomed in his best schoolmaster's voice.

'I realise that we're all a little energized by that odd little storm earlier, but can you all please be quiet?'

The boys ceased their Brownian motion and turned to give him their full concentration.

'As some of you are no doubt aware, I am not best pleased at the actions of one or two of your number this evening.'

There were a few muffled comments and laughs from those gathered before him. Mister Lightfoot scanned the group with his 'I'm being serious here, and heaven help anyone who plays the fool' look.

Silence fell again.

'As a result I would like you all in your rooms before ten thirty.'

All eyes turned to the clock, which gave the current time as ten fifteen. A collective groan rose from the boys.

Mister Lightfoot raised his head, stuck out his chin and adopted his most pugilistic stance, daring anyone to voice a disagreement.

'I can only hope that tomorrow we will all wake in a better mood, prepared to spend a day involved in outdoor pursuits which will hopefully burn off the excessive high spirits which have so tarnished this evening.'

Several boys smiled at this, all those who enjoyed sports and those who just enjoyed proving that they were better than their peers.

'Therefore, those of you without a mobile phone can phone home, if you wish. All of you can grab a warming beverage and retire to your dorms where I am sure I am right in assuming, there will be no high jinks tonight. If you behave as young men, you will be treated as such. If not, you will be treated as the children which some of you undoubtedly are.

Some of the lads had the good grace to blush slightly at this.

'So. You have fifteen minutes. I would advise you not to waste it.'

And with that he dismissed the ranks with an airy wave of his hand.

As the boys began to mill around afresh, in search of phones and drinks and table football, Bert turned to Mike. With a stern nod in the direction of the lounge he indicated that both he and Bev should join him.

They made their way to the large picture window, now just a large black panel in the wall reflecting the room behind them as though through a dark fog.

They sat and Mike again felt his earlier sombre mood return as Bert spoke.

'This is all getting out of hand Micheal.'

The use of his formal name made Mike realise that even Bert was now succumbing to the melancholia that had already settled on him.

'What on earth's got into Fin? Of all the lads we brought along I thought he was going to be the one who just got on with things. What's possessed him? I'm at a loss to know what to do.'

For the first time since he'd know Bert, Mike could see that their current situation really was leaving him totally nonplussed. He glanced across at Bev, who studiously ignored them both, lost in her own thoughts. Mike moved a couple of plastic cups to one side and crossed his feet on the low table in front of them.

'Yes, it is a bit of a stumper isn't it?' He rubbed his jaw as he considered their options.

'The way I see it, we have several options where Fin is concerned.' He counted them off on his fingers as he spoke.

'First, we can ignore the whole thing and put it down to hormones or something...' Both Bert and Bev looked up sharply, the idea obviously being a none-starter with them both. 'Yes, I know. It's not really an option is it? Not as things stand at the moment - too much has happened recently. Fin has problems from whatever cause and we've got to do something to stop them getting worse.'

He moved on to the next finger.

'We can abandon the whole damn trip, pack up and go home just as fast as we can and deal with the consequences later.' Again he noted their negative responses and hurried on. 'Yes, we'd have to find some explanation for doing it, but at least we could get Fin back to his family and give ourselves a bit a breathing space. For all the good it may do us.'

He ticked off another finger.

'Three. We can try to snap him out of it somehow. Maybe just taking Fin back and leaving the other boys to finish the trip as planned. It could be that a quiet talk away from everyone else would be enough to find out what's prompted all this. Is it a problem at school, with the boys, or at home for some reason we don't know anything about or something else entirely?'

'*That's* our problem.' said Bert 'We don't have the foggiest notion of what's caused this. Maybe we're simply not qualified to have any sort of opinion on it. So should we just let it go, pass it on to someone with more idea of how to handle the matter?'

Bev leaned forward and looked over to Bert.

'No Bert. I think *we* have to help him. If we wait for someone else, someone more qualified, we may lose whatever chance we have to save him from whatever demons are tormenting him.'

Mike wasn't sure he liked the language, but understood the underlying worry.

Next finger.

'Four. We humour him and hope that by going along with his story we find some way of overcoming his belief in what he's saying. The story is too preposterous to make that idea much of an option, but maybe one of you can sway me on it.'

He paused.

'And five...' His fingers stopped. 'Well I don't think there is a five. That's as much as I can manage. I really don't know what to do.'

He looked back and forth between his fellow teacher and his wife, hoping that either one of them had something better to contribute to the conversation.

Bert looked worried.

'I can't see how we can ignore it. Not after this evening's events. The boy seems determined to cause trouble, but I'm not sure I like the idea of sending him home before the other lads either. Firstly, because I'd feel that we were obviating our responsibilities to the boy. We're his teachers for goodness sake. We can't attempt to wash our hands of him. Secondly, because I failed a boy once before and I'm damned if I'll let it happen again. The problem being that I don't think I'm the best man to deal with this. I have baggage,' Mike raised an eyebrow, 'that I have no intention of opening up to the world at the moment. Not even you two.'

'So, we either cut the trip short for everyone, or just humour him and try to think of how to deal with this later.' said Bev.

She looked at Mike.

'And I know which one I'd prefer.' she said emphatically, eyeing the other two.

'Yes, but how do we know we're not going to make it worse whichever we do?' asked Mike. 'If we cut the trip short, the boys will eventually work out why, and I would imagine some of them could make life pretty horrendous for Fin when we return to school. Whatever we do, we've got to try to keep it fairly low key.

Bev stood up and moved around to face both men, who raised unhappy faces to look up at her.

'I suggest that we leave well alone for now. Tomorrow I'll take Fin back to the mill; that seems to be where this all started last night. We can make a decision when we've had a chance to discuss whatever happens while we're there. Okay?'

Mike nodded.

'I know I haven't got anything better to suggest and we'll just keep going in circles if we keep on worrying about it.'

Bert nodded too, but looked unhappy. He waved his hand at them in a dismissive gesture.

'Do what you think best. I'm at a loss as to how we should proceed. Thirty years of teaching never prepares you for things like this. Let Bev try and we'll see how we go.'

He stood.

'Come on Mike, let's get these kids to bed. Then I'm going to have a bloody good drink and turn in.'

As he walked away they both heard him mumbling.

'As if life isn't difficult enough…'

Bev held Mike's arm.

'We will sort this out Mike, I promise. But I think we may have to do as Artie suggests and take Fin over to see him.'

'But only as a last resort love.' replied Mike. 'I'm not sure I like the idea of taking a boy in his fragile mental state to see someone who could make it even worse. And we'll definitely have to discuss it with his parents first. But at least we've decided on what we're doing tomorrow - that's a start. Come on, let's give Bert a hand.'

He freed his arm from his wife, gave her a quick hug and then led her towards the door.

An anxious looking Willis entered and hurried over.

'I can't find them, sir' he said in a frightened little voice. 'Unless you sent them on an errand or something, sir?'

Mike put his hand to his head and looked harassed once again.

'Oh Lord, what now?' he sighed as they joined the few boys still in reception.

'Don't mention this to anyone else Willis.' he whispered. 'If you're asked just say you don't know where they are. Leave it with me. Now off to your room. And try not to worry too much. I'll sort this out.' He smiled as he spoke, but even Willis could see that his heart wasn't really in it.

'Yes, don't worry. It hasn't been the fun evening we'd all hoped for, but things have a way of sorting themselves out, especially with Super Teach on the job. Don't lose sleep over it.' said Bev with a grin, nodding towards Mike, but her soft words of encouragement did little to calm Willis's agitation. It was a very subdued young man who slowly climbed the stairs as she turned back to Mike with a rare worried expression on her face.

'No. I'll be doing enough of that for all of us.' he muttered under his breath.

Now Dick (26)

Dick read through, or at least tried to read through, the great raft of documents that Leon had provided him with. There were books, magazine articles, pieces from the internet and short notes written in Leon's own hand. Several reports ripped from tabloid newspapers and broadsheets, some from abroad, were also included. Leon had suggested that Dick take a few hours to become better acquainted with the new world he'd been shown. The pile of newspaper from the dining room now lay scattered around him.

Dick surveyed his progress with dismay. In the last four hours he'd managed to create several smaller piles from the original folders Leon had provided.

'It's not exhaustive, but it'll do for now, I think.' Leon had said. 'In here is the sum total of my trawling for anything that sounded like it had something to do with my ability. Much of it still unread, unfortunately. Funnily enough I just never seem to get the time.' He gave a wry smile.

'See what you can make of it.'

Dick had been kneeling on the floor, but stood now and gave an exaggerated stretch. In all the reading he'd come to the conclusion that ninety percent of the stuff was just rubbish and not worth his time, but just occasionally he came across a little nugget and it was with a bunch of these in his hand, that he went in search of Leon. He went via the kitchen and made two cups of tea.

'Leon!'

The house was very quiet in the gathering gloom of the late afternoon. Fading sunlight still streamed through the windows, illuminating the panelled corridor as he carried the mugs outside.

'Leon! Tea's up mate!'

His voice echoed across the lawns and lost itself in the trees.

Dick could hear music from around a corner. Electronic, but ethereal. The sound smoothed its way around the garden and seemed to gather in the pools of light created by the beams of sunshine radiating through the trees.

Tangerine Dream.

Dick followed the music.

The drifting melody of Logos (Part One) suited his current mood. Life seemed a little more golden, warm and comforting. Almost unnoticed in the last forty-eight hours, Dick had begun to appreciate life for what it was; the chance to enjoy the world as it was meant to be. Without the driving need to fill every minute with the effort to earn a living, to perform every action at top speed, to fill every second with something, he had begun to understand that maybe there was more to life than to fill the unforgiving minute with sixty second's worth of distance run. Men, and women, were made for more than this. The office or the factory were not the sum of a person's life. He had a whole new world to explore at his leisure, but a small guilty voice reminded him that he was still a working copper, and tomorrow he had to rejoin the real world - for a while. He'd long since made up his mind to quit the force. He had a definite feeling that he could do more good outside the constraints imposed by his uniform.

With a spring in his step, that had not been there for many a long year, he rounded the corner and found Leon.

His friend was busy constructing an arch using huge wooden beams and wooden pegs instead of nails.

'It's a Lyche gate.' Leon said in answer to his enquiring gaze.

'Built in the traditional way with traditional tools. I was shown by a master builder back in the sixteen hundreds.' He smiled wistfully and had a momentary far-away look in his eye.

'A wonderful twelve months, Dick. Even though a Moor wasn't treated particularly well by the general populace, the men I worked with took such pride in their building, even out here in the countryside. I stuck out like a sore thumb, but they didn't seem to care. They were men of talent, who loved their lives, and their lives were damned tough at times believe me.' he sighed. 'A lost breed.'

He stood back to survey his handiwork.

'Well, maybe not completely lost - but bloody thin on the ground these days.'

He wiped his brow on the back of his sleeve and accepted the offered mug of tea and took a tentative sip.

'So Dick. How far have you got?'

Dick held out the cutting from the local paper.

'I think some answers may be closer than you think Leon. Take a look.'

Dick sat on a pile of oak beams against the high wall of the manor house.

Leon gave him a puzzled glance.

'Tell me while I read Dick. Tell me what I'm looking for.'

'Well, there're a couple of things. Daft as it sounds – unseasonal weather, and sometimes just the noise of it, without the actual weather. Vale Royal seems to have had more than its fair share of noisy summer thunder storms that are extremely localised, sometimes covering a corridor of land only a few yards across, but very long, and often at night when the rest of the area has had cloudless skies. At other times it just sounds like a storm, but there's no rain – seem familiar? Someone at the paper is getting curious about it, there're several short pieces, but no-one else seems to be taking much notice. I suppose that a small paper like that just needs to fill a few column inches between the adverts and the sports, along with the WI news. Presumably you tore it out because the weather bit caught your eye.'

Leon nodded as he continued to read.

'Then there's some stuff about a missing child from a couple of years back. His parents have put an appeal in the paper every year since he vanished, always on the anniversary of his disappearance six years ago. You've got every appeal in there and, though I'm not really sure why you kept them, I assume you think it may have something to do with you and your *magic*.'

He gave the last word an edge of mystery and excitement that made Leon smile across at him.

'Then there's a few odd bits about them blaming some trick cyclist for driving him away somehow. They think he had some weird ideas about the boy being special for some reason that they either didn't understand, or didn't want to understand. There are several pieces about bullying at local schools – no idea what that has to do with anything.' He shrugged and sipped his tea before leaning back again to keep out of the glare of the setting sun.

'And finally a short piece about a lad winning some writing competition with an essay about ley lines.'

He stood and walked over to Leon.

'The only real link between them is that they all have something to do with this area and may relate to you in some very limited way. Most of the other stuff is from all over the country and all in a similar vein, but there's also stuff about UFOs, the discovery of lost cities in various jungles, all sorts. But these...' he waved the papers in his hand, 'are all from South Manchester and Cheshire. It's as though you were searching for anything, no matter how trivial, that tied into the Vale. You're searching for clues to an answer, when you don't seem to know the question.'

Leon nodded.

'I don't even read most of them, but I can't help myself. When I scan through the mountains of crap that's in the papers I tear out odd bits that make me stop and look. It's probably time I threw most of it out.'

'Now he tells me.' huffed Dick with a grin.

Leon took the bits of paper from him and began to look at them more closely.

'I'm going to have to go soon, Leon. I've got work tomorrow.'

Leon looked crestfallen and looked up from his reading.

'Don't worry me old mucka. I'll be back tomorrow night, if that's okay?

'Sure man. Your room will be ready and waiting'

'Thanks Leon. And in the meantime try to think of what we're going to do with the rest of the life we have ahead of us.'

'And before you leave we have to try one last jaunt, but this time with you in charge.' said Leon, who stood and turned Dick towards the lawn.

'But Leon, I still don't know how to.'

'It's not a case of knowing, it's just a feeling. You have to get your head into the right place Dick, and you've got to give it a go. Now's as good a time as any. So let's try.'

He sat Dick down on a stone bench amongst the roses. The air was heavy with the scent of Zepharin in the early afternoon warmth. In the silence they could hear the drone of the bees amongst the flowers.

Leon sat opposite and settled himself into a comfortable sprawl.

'Close your eyes and relax. If it doesn't happen, it doesn't happen. We'll get past it and eventually you'll be able to do everything you want to.'

He waved a hand airily and closed his eyes, his head rolling back.

Dick did the same.

'Relax man. Lets try to give that Fermion guy a shock eh?' murmured Leon.

He continued speaking quietly, his voice mingling with the bees, and Dick felt his concentration begin to wander. His body seemed to float and in his mind's eye he pictured the ribbons of light drifting around the vale. The petals of the roses formed a cloud of palest cerise around the two figures as the rainbows pulsed to some unseen beat and an otherworldly tingling began in his forebrain. Slowly he opened his eyes and the lights danced in stately procession across the sunlit clearing. A slow smile spread across his face and he studied Leon, in his relaxed lounge. Leon languidly looked over, his eyes bright beads of delight.

'You see it don't you? You really do see it? And it's all you this time Dick. I'm just along for the ride. Let's go with the flow.'

The tingling increased and, with a sublime tranquillity and an almost imperceptible roll of thunder, they left *Now* behind.

The darkness that slowly swallowed them seemed even blacker in contrast to the scene they'd left behind.

They floated in the inkiness and Leon's voice drifted over to him.

'So where's your window on time Dick? Show me.'

Off to the right of Dick a miniscule square of light appeared and grew rapidly larger. The book that approached them was probably a dozen feet across, but it was hard to be sure - there was nothing to measure it against. Bound in tooled leather, the book was worked with extraordinary designs that seemed to writhe across the surface in the faint light that issued from the volume. Leon watched in amazement as the book drew nearer.

It was enormous.

Leon had to check himself as he realised he was edging away as its immensity towered over the pair of them..

The book opened, oh so slowly, and each page held a date.

'Oh God Leon.' whispered Dick, almost too quietly for his friend to hear, and there were tears in his eyes.

They hung before the book, their faces illuminated by the light of bygone days, as the pages turned languidly, each more brilliant than the last. Eventually the brightness ceased its increase and the pictures being revealed before them had the appearance of the illustrations from a medieval manuscript.

Leon smiled.

'Let's go back Dick. I think you've done as much as either of us could possibly have hoped for. I suspect you could do with a stiff drink and I know I could.'

He spoke softly as he reached over to take Dick's sleeve and paused.

The face before him was lit not just by the book, but by some inner glow as well.

'Come on mate, let's go home.'

As they turned away from the book it began to close and the brilliant light faded, contained within the marvellous binding.

They retreated into the darkness, or the book receded from them. It was difficult to know.

'Take us home Dick.' breathed Leon.

Dick nodded and began to search for the way back in his mind. The darkness began to brighten and *Now* began to fade into being around them.

As the roses and the lawns came back into view and the buzz of busy insects returned, Leon was suddenly aware of a strange feeling that they were not alone. He turned to look over, or rather through, the roses materialising behind him and saw, just for a moment, not Abel Fermion as he had suspected, but the face of a young girl, no older than ten. The image began to dissipate almost as soon as he had focussed on it, but it was definitely a girl, dressed in a modern school uniform and she gave a small frightened squeal, her eyes huge and round, as she vanished. Leon tried to hold onto the vision but it was gone with the rest of *When*.

Dick gave a gasp as the world solidified around him and he pointed behind him, coming to his feet and turning, as though pulled around by his outstretched finger.

'Leon!' He could see his friend had also stood to stare past him at the same - now empty - space beyond the roses. 'Did you see her! Did you?' He looked at his friend in amazement. 'There was a little girl - right there behind me!' He could hardly contain his excitement, as his hand reached out as though to caress the small head he had seen. He was still sitting atop cloud nine following his exploits and the whole world had a wondrous hue about it that had nothing to do with the rainbows streaming across the lawns.

'Yes, I saw.' said Leon.

'But she wasn't something I conjured up Leon. I'm sure she came from somewhere else.' Dick's voice sounded awed as he stepped up to Leon, staring as though mesmerised at the space where the ethereal little girl had stood.

'Don't look to me to explain it Dick, I've never seen her, or anyone else, in the region out of time when I've travelled. I always thought I was alone, but suddenly there seems to be a hell of a lot of other people out there. It's what I suspected. There is something going on Dick. What I used to consider my private little world is pulling in others. Either that or they're managing to find their way in somehow. First that guy Fermion. Now a little girl.' He sounded deeply disturbed.

'We've got to find out what's going on Dick. Ditch your goddamned job and move in here. We've got to spend time trying to figure this out.'

For the first time that Dick could remember, Leon was looking uncertain.

'Dick, you have to help me. I have a feeling this is building up to something, but I don't have a bloody clue what it is.'

Dick was still trying to shake off the euphoria of having made his first trip into the space between times. The puzzle of the little girl was a very secondary consideration.

Leon shook Dick's shoulders.

'Dick, I'm being deadly serious man. Throw in the policing. Whatever's happening, it's getting worse.'

Dick stared out unseeingly across the garden. His forehead still tingled with the last remnants of that odd feeling that, when properly focussed could let him time travel.

Suddenly he was prancing about, capering around Leon like a loon.

'Leon, we bloody did it! I've really managed to do it. After all the talk, I can actually do it. Hell's Teeth, Leon. I'm Doctor Who in person. We can go anywhere, any*when!*'

His shouts echoed around the garden as Leon reached out to stop his mad cries.

'Dick, stop it! Calm down. We have to think about this first. Come inside and let's have that drink.'

As Leon walked towards the house Dick was still skipping about, bending to savour the perfume from the roses, a smile fixed on his face.

'Oh, God life is suddenly *sooooooo* great, Leon.'

And even Leon, eventually, had to smile at his friend strutting through the rose garden.

'I'm going to chuck it in tomorrow.' Dick said with a wave of his hand. 'How can I go back to normal life after this? I truly believe we can make a difference in a way I've never been able to before. Without the restrictions of the uniform I reckon I can really start to do the things I've always wanted to. The Bad Guys had better look out – Batman and Robin are back in business!'

Leon chuckled at the reference to their childhood games, when they'd managed to save the world every afternoon as they walked home from school. He also grimaced at the memory of the teenage party they'd attended as the caped crusader and his sidekick. It had taken Leon months to live it down and taught him a valuable lesson - never wear lycra without adequate support, especially when there are attractive young women about.

He stood before the house, looking up to admire the workmanship, spanning centuries and carried out by good men now long dead, whose company he'd enjoyed.

'Better get you packed. Tomorrow is going to be a tough day at the station – trying to pretend none of this has happened, but after that... well who knows?'

'But it's gonna be fun finding out eh?' laughed Dick.

The happy sound fled away from the men as they re-entered the house.

It soared and echoed, filling the forest enclosed garden with a sound that was to be long absent in the coming days.

But such is life.

Now Bert (27)

Having spent the best part of the hours before midnight looking for the three missing schoolboys, the two teachers had finally come to the inevitable conclusion that they would have to call in the police. This was no longer just a small problem to be handled within the school. Three absent pupils on a school trip was a major incident. Both Mike and Bert knew that, as soon as the police were involved, the whole thing would be taken out of their hands. In all probability they would be under suspicion, at least for a while. After that it was anyone's guess as to what would happen.

Bev pushed all considerations of the future out of her mind. The boys were what mattered now. Where could they have gone? It was a cold night after the warmth of the day and she and the two men had searched everywhere for Fin, Simeon and Tam. Mike was convinced that they would never have run away, even given Fin's precarious state of mind. Apart from anything else, Simeon would be a steadying influence – which made their disappearance even more of a conundrum. Tam, though, would be game for most things, but even he would baulk at running away over something as small as the incident earlier in the evening. It was just so unlikely that that's what they would even consider doing. Unfortunately, it was because of their usual good sense that their disappearance was even more worrying than if it had been some of the other lads.

As she stood in the middle of the large lawn in front of the hostel Bev saw Bert coming towards her from the lakeside. He walked alone and with slumped shoulders he looked older than his years. Of Mike there was, as yet, no sign.

'Nothing?' she asked.

'Not hide nor hair, Beverley. Where have they got to?' he sighed.

'Bert?' she began, wondering how best to phrase the question she was about to ask.

'Yes luv.'

He sounded older too.

'Earlier you mentioned having "baggage".' She paused. 'What was that about?'

Bert looked over. An expression of deep foreboding cross his face briefly and he looked out towards the surrounding gloom, away from the pale light cast by the large lounge window thirty yards away.

'Wait for Mike. Then I'll tell you both.'

'But Bert, it can't be that bad. Can it?' His usual jolly face was now wreathed in fear. Yes, it was unquestionably fear. But why? Standing out here in the dark, she too was overcome by a tide of dread. Surely it was too soon to be this stricken by the boys absence? Yes, several hours had now passed, but they were out in the middle of nowhere. Abduction had seemed out of the question only a short time ago, so why did they both feel so ill at ease?

It was the unvoiced fear that something dreadful really had happened, she realised. They were both avoiding the obvious conclusion that foul play was involved. Why else would three otherwise sensible lads disappear? The only other explanation would have meant a visit to The Outer Limits and even now she found that hard to bring under serious consideration. But Bert seemed to have other reasons for his depression.

Where was Mike?

Almost as though conjured by the thought, Mike appeared at the edge of the frame of light and quickly strode over to join them.

'No luck?' he breathed and received two shakes of the head in reply. 'Damn them. Where are they?' he rasped through gritted teeth, hugging his arms to his chest against the cold air. Bev moved across and put he arms around his waist, resting her head on his chest.

'So what do we do now?' she asked.

She felt, and heard, Mike take a deep breath.

'I don't think we have an alternative. We have to call in the police.'

Bev looked up sharply, and then nodded.

'Yes, you're right of course. We've done all we can alone.' Her voice sounded resigned and she pulled him tighter. 'But it's going to cause you both an awful lot of grief isn't it? I mean once the police are involved you'll both be in all sorts of trouble won't you?'

She looked across at Bert and was surprised to see him shake his head.

'No.' he said in a harsh whisper.

'But Bert...' began Mike pulling Bev's arms from around him and moving across to the older man.

Bert shot him a look that stopped him in mid stride.

'Not the police. Not yet. *Please!*' he pleaded, looking as though he was almost ready to fall to his knees.

'Bert? What is it?' asked Mike.

'I think there's something Bert hasn't told us yet. Isn't there Bert?' Bev prompted.

'Yes.' he mumbled and beckoned them over to one of the wooden benches under an oak tree at the edge of the lawn.

'Please, sit.' He indicated the seat. 'I have something to tell you and all I ask is that you hear me out before asking any questions. Please.'

Again there was a pleading note in his voice.

Mike was about to say something, but a warning 'Sshhh!' hissed by Bev gave him pause.

'I haven't talked about this for a long time, but I think you need to know everything before you make that call to the police.'

Mike and Bev shared a concerned look as he continued.

'Several years ago there was a boy at the school. Anthony Athelston was his name. A bright lad, but deeply troubled. He was bullied, but not as much as some.' He waved a hand as if to dismiss the comment.

'But any bullying's too much.' he said. 'Especially for lads like Anthony. He had a very highly developed sense of fair play and honesty. He couldn't stand to see other lads being pushed around, even those who showed no great camaraderie with him. He was forever getting into scrapes helping other boys, when they treated him with almost as much disdain as those who bullied him. Life was deeply unfair for boys like Anthony. And Fin.'

He looked up at the pair beside him.

'Through absolutely no fault of their own, boys like these find themselves virtual outcasts, when all they want is to be accepted for what they are – very bright and very friendly lads with a lust for life that is often driven under by the petty-minded nastiness of others. Their tormentors are usually not as bright or socially adept and feel the need to prove themselves by grinding down those who they think show more talent. You know the sort Mike, there are one or two in every year.'

Mike nodded.

'They're not necessarily bad lads, but the effect they have on those who get on their wrong side can be enormous. Anthony was targeted by half a dozen boys, led by one who was known to be a bad apple. I pointed him out on several occasions to the headmaster – not Mister Greenwood, this was a couple of years before he arrived. The old Head was one of those who wanted to the school to be inclusive. He wanted to take the bad influences and turn them around. To make them model pupils - a credit to the school. And give him his due, he did it for the best possible reasons, but I had a problem with his methods. I remember having to hand out credits for good behaviour because one of the ringleaders and an acolyte hadn't given Anthony a slapping for a week.' He raised his hands in exasperation. 'He didn't seem to realise that the reason Anthony hadn't been bullied was that he'd been off school with flu.'

Anger was obvious in his voice.

'Anthony suffered in virtual silence for a long time. I learned later that the same boys had been at primary school with him, so it had to be at least six or seven years. He never complained. He was one of life's battlers. As far as I know he only ever struck another boy once, after his new schoolbag had been thrown around and jumped on. The inside ended up coated with his lunch. Several of his books, which he always took such pride in, were ruined.'

Bert had a faraway look in his eyes as he stared into the darkness around him.

'The headmaster played hell with him about it. He was banned from taking part in any sports for a month. Had to sit out games lessons and stay in the changing rooms during P.E. The Head said when a boy like Anthony misbehaved he need a sharp lesson to stop it happening again.'

His voice broke and he wiped at his eyes before continuing.

'That was about the only time I came close to handing in my notice. It was unforgivable to treat a boy like Anthony in that way. All it did was single him out again, but he learned his lesson alright. He never defended himself again. The following term he was so badly beaten as he left school that he was at home getting over it for almost three weeks. Apparently he'd been set upon by five of the idiots who always taunted him, while walking out of the gate with the few friends he had. But his friends were terrified of retribution and left him to it. One of them told me later that he'd never forgive himself for not helping, but he was only a little tyke. Although Anthony was quite big for his age his friends tended to be the smaller lads, ones he'd helped out of scrapes with the bigger boys. I doubt whether the lad could have helped even if he'd been able to overcome his fear.'

Bert's voice suddenly became louder and his hand balled into a fist and thumped his knee as he sat.

'But the point was - he should never have been put in the position where he had to make that sort of decision. They were only fifteen for goodness sake.'

He looked over at Mike.

'We abandoned them to their fate. It was the headmaster who had all the grand plans for eliminating bullying, but it became rife under his management and he seemed oblivious to it. He was so keen to help the kids - who admittedly needed some sort of guidance - who were causing the trouble, that he seemed to be blind to the boys who where being destroyed by the constant pressure at school. When he finally left, the new head sorted out a lot of the chaos he left in his wake, but it took a couple of years, and by then Anthony was gone.'

His voice had softened and he looked down at his feet, his forearms on his thighs and his hands hanging down between his legs. He seemed to have finished.

Mike was puzzled.

'And you're point is what, Bert?' he asked quietly. 'What has this to do with Fin?'

Bert looked up, with brows knit and an oddly resigned look on his face.

'A couple of weeks before he left...' he began, then shook his head. 'No, not left... *disappeared...* he confided in me. He was fifteen going on sixteen then and a fine figure of a boy, with a wonderful nature, considering all he'd been through.'

He gazed out into the darkness again.

'He confided in me that he had been having nightmares since he'd been bullied at primary school.'

Mike drew a sharp breath.

'He had nightmares that involved him flying away in storms and travelling, both in distance and time, to all sorts of places.'

Bert stood, looking like the forlorn old man he had suddenly become.

'His parents had become so worried they'd taken him to see a psychiatrist to try to sort him out. I knew they had, and I'm afraid I rather dismissed his tales as adolescent fantasy, though admittedly a little different than the usual ones we have to deal with.'

He turned, and his voice gained in strength a little, as though this confession had lifted a weight from his shoulders.

'About two weeks later he simply vanished. No-one knows where or why. His parents blamed the psychiatrist. Said he'd indulged the boy and made him run off in search of his dreamlands.'

He looked over at Bev.

'It was Professor Tome, a man at the height of his powers, supposedly, who saw young Anthony. As Bev says, to this day *he* remains convinced that Anthony really could do what he said and who knows, eh? Maybe he could. I like to think that Anthony found a better place to live. Perhaps where people appreciate his particular brand of humanity. I certainly hope he's found some sort of peace, because God knows no-one, apart from Doctor Tome, ever believed even the slightest word of what he swore was the truth. Yes, with all my heart I hope Anthony is enjoying his life now. I would like to think he's found peace. Oh, please God yes!'

His voice was low but powerful now.

'That is if he's still alive, because, of course, nobody knows what happened to him. But if Anthony was telling the truth, then why not Fin too.' He looked at Mike again. 'And if Fin has vanished just like Anthony, then we're damn well going to find a way to get him back. I'm not going to lose another boy in my care – certainly not under these circumstances. I tried to tell myself that Fin was just acting some elaborate joke at my expense, but I'm sure he can't have known about Anthony Athelston. So I'm not going to call the police until we've explored every other avenue' He pointed his finger vehemently at Mike, 'and our time is in very short supply. So let's put our heads together and come up with some other solution. I refuse to go down in the annals of the school as the teacher who lost two pupils.'

He swung around angrily and barked out his final words.

'So use your bloody brains you two. Where the Devil are those boys?'

Both Bev and Mike looked stunned as they stared back at him and Mike spoke first.

'But Bert, shouldn't we be more concerned for the boys' welfare? While I can understand your fears, it's the boys, Fin and Simeon and Tam, we should be thinking about and I don't see what more we can do!'

'But there must be something!' Bert was practically wringing his hands. 'I don't know what, but there must be! I just don't know what it is! I don't know! Oh, God!' his anguish was palpable and he began to pace back and forth in front of the others, his body hunched forward and his hands covering his face, muffling his voice. 'But we must be missing something. There must be some way to track them down – we just have to find it.'

'Or' mused Bev, 'we just wait.'

'Darling I really don't think that's one of our, very limited, options. Time is short, as Bert says. If we can't think of something constructive, I really don't see that we have any option. We're going to have to call the police. I, for one, am not about to jeopardise my career because of two lads here and now, and another who went walkies years back. I'm sorry Bert, but we both know that we should have called in help long before this.'

Bev interrupted the discussion and stepped between the two men.

'Being realistic, just how much time do we have?' she asked.

They both answered together.

'None!' declared Mike.

'Another hour or two! Please Mike.' begged Bert. He reached out to put his hand on his friend's shoulder.

'Please.' he said again.

Mike stood, irresolute.

Bev shivered and hugged her arms to herself.

'Getting colder.' she commented.

'Yet another reason to do something constructive.' said Mike, 'Standing here is accomplishing nothing, except to lose what may be valuable time when trained men could be searching. Those lads will be very exposed, out there on their own'

'If they are alone.' said Bev heavily. 'I still say we should just wait.'

'Oh for goodness sake, woman. Give me one good reason why we should. Just one!' argued Mike, growing impatient with the lack of action.

Bert was looking encouragingly towards her as she turned and sat again on the bench her gaze moving between the men who faced her.

'Because if what Fin - and Anthony Athelston – said, is actually true, then presumably Fin will return soon. Along with Simeon and Tam. Both boys claimed to time-travel, but they were never lost.' She smiled, almost absent-mindedly and her blue eyes ranged across the lawn behind her audience for a few seconds, before coming back to rest on her husbands face.

'Oh, I know Fin says he was almost stranded at the mill last night, but when it came to the crunch he was returned to his bed, albeit in some smelly old clothes. The thing is, *if* – and I know it's a very big *if*, but *if* the boys are telling the truth, and lets face it we've seen and heard nothing to disprove what they said - they always came back. Not only that, they always came back before anyone knew they were missing!' She leaned forward with an earnest expression.

'Don't you see? It's as though they have no alternative but to come back. Some force whisks them home as soon as it's - oh, I don't know – as soon as it's triggered... somehow.'

Mike, despite himself, was suddenly looking more interested.

'Yes. Fin said he'd fallen out of the mill, down some steep hill at the back and then the next thing he knew he was back in bed!'

'But where... ' Bert interrupted, 'did Anthony go, then? He never returned.'

Mike shook his head decisively.

'Oh God, I can't believe we're even discussing this.' He almost groaned.

'I've been thinking about that.' said Bev. 'Maybe Anthony didn't come back because he found somewhere better to stay. Maybe, as you said earlier, he's found peace somewhere else. Maybe even in another time! He never came back because he simply didn't want to.'

Mike flung up his hands in disgust.

'Bev! You're advocating our doing absolutely nothing. Don't you realise how insane this discussion is? Somehow these boys, all of whom are our responsibility, are suddenly just going to reappear and by midnight we'll all be tucked up safe and sound in bed? Bev, love, it ain't gonna happen.' He sat next to his wife and took one of her hands in his. 'Trust me. If we leave it much longer our heads will be on the block when people find out how long we've delayed contacting the authorities.'

Mike looked up at Bert.

'Sorry Bert, we have to make that call.' And he rose again to his feet and began to walk slowly towards the hostel.

Bev looked up, with eyes full of sadness, at Bert.

'Sorry, Bert.' she said with a resigned sigh. 'But he is probably right. I was just hoping that this wasn't all going to end badly. Now I think there's little alternative. The next few hours, and days, could be a nightmare for us all.'

Bert allowed her to link arms with him and begin to usher him after Mike. As far as he could see, there was no light at the end of this tunnel for him. The whole nightmare that he'd so carefully concealed, even from himself, these last few years, was beginning to start all over again.

Different boy, same problem.

Probably with the same awful, unfinished, unresolved outcome.

Despair settled onto his shoulders like an ill-fitting coat and his body felt its weight adding to his burden of guilt over the three missing boys.

Make that four, he told himself. He knew he would never be able to forgive himself for not listening more closely to Anthony Athelston. And now Fin, Tam and Simeon too. Bright eyed, intelligent, gentleman Fin, and his happy-go-lucky muckers, Simeon and Tamburlaine.

Gone.

He held out absolutely no hope for their safe return.

Now Lillibet (28)

Back in Daneham the sound of a mid-Summer shower faded away and Lillibet LeMott awoke from a troubled sleep. She lay in semi-darkness and wondered about the dream that the thunder had broken with its loud rumbling and the similar odd dream she'd had during an afternoon nap the previous day, with unrecognised faces and voices.

School holidays always tired her out and a quick power nap, as she liked to think of them, helped to recharge her batteries. She'd read that high flying executives liked to power nap through the day and decided that if it was good enough for them it would be good enough for her. And amazingly her mum had agreed. So much to do, so little time, as her mother would have said. Lidine had a firm belief that watching TV was simply a waste of time.

'Why watch someone else living the kind of life you may - or may not - want, when the whole world is out there for you to live your life in.' she'd said more than once.

As a result Lillibet filled her waking hours with all the things she really wanted to do, rarely having time to pause between flute practice, singing with the junior operatics, riding lessons and reading anything she could find about wildlife and in-between snatching quick ten minute snoozes when she felt the need. Her aim in life was to be a female Bill Oddie or David Attenborough and to inform the world on the wonders all around them if they only took the time to look. In this she had always been supported by her parents because, who knew, maybe one day she would attain her goals. A bright and cheerful ten year old, tall for her age, with her long dark hair framing a pretty oval face with dark hazel eyes and a ready smile, they saw no reason why she shouldn't have everything she desired, given a little luck and hard work.

Lilli was aware of the problems her older brother was having. At her school bullying seemed to be endemic, as it was all over the country. To a large extent she had managed to avoid its worst excesses, but even so suffered occasionally at the hands of Antoinette Lesser, who always seemed to have *carte blanche* from the teachers to do as she liked. There were always one or two at every school who appeared to be able to avoid the attention of the teaching staff, no matter how loutish their behaviour. She read the local and national papers and knew enough about the problem to have some fairly well-informed opinions on the matter.

Fin was fairing worse than many, but better than some she had read about.

It was the additional pressure brought on by his sleepless nights that bothered Lilli more. Several times she had been rudely awakened by Fin's calls in the night and although she was three years younger and still considered by many to be a little girl who wouldn't understand what it was that was happening, she understood far more than they gave her credit for. Though she wasn't as bright as Fin, she wasn't stupid either and was probably even brighter than either of her parent realised.

For instance, she felt sure that Fin was having greater problems than he was letting on to his parents. Having a bedroom that adjoined her brother's she heard far more than Jarmon or Lidine and knew that Fin was awake when their parents thought him sleeping soundly. Through the wall that separated them she often heard Vangelis, Rick Wakeman, Mike Oldfield et al playing quietly through the night and since he liked to play vinyl, she knew that he was changing LPs into the early hours. She also realised that if he went through the record changing routine on the few nights where she stayed up late reading, then in all probability he was doing so on other nights as well.

And now she was having similar visions where before she'd always slept like one in a coma. No dreams or nightmares had ever troubled her before.

'So why now?' she wondered aloud in a soft breath. She laced her fingers behind her head a looked up towards the dimly seen ceiling. She lay for what seemed like hours, but was probably only a few minutes, then turning onto her side, she settled down under the duvet hugging a huge fluffy teddy to her and drifted back into sleep to the faint strains of Vangelis's Beaubourg.

She was only ten after all, she mused.

Some things were better left to adults.

Probably.

Lilli awoke again to bright sunshine lighting up her gaily coloured curtains, but it was the sounds from beyond her door that interrupted her slumber rather than the early morning glare.

Lidine was shouting to her husband from the landing outside, her voice shrill with distress.

'Jarmon! Jarmon! What's he doing home?'

Her father's answer came from below in the kitchen, echoing the worry of his wife.

'What Lidine? What's wrong?'

Lilli heard his light footsteps on the stairs as he came up them, no doubt two steps at a time. It still surprised Lilli, that for such a big man he could climb steps so quietly, as though he moved everywhere on his toes. She threw back her duvet and grabbed her dressing gown as she headed for the door, which stood slightly ajar. Even though she was almost at the age for senior school, she still liked the comfort of having her door opened a little, to allow in a thin sliver of light to combat the pitch darkness of the night out here at the top of the village.

She reached the landing at the same time as Daddy to see Fin's door open, but he was on holiday in the Lakes with school.

What was Mum making such a fuss about.

She followed her father into the small bedroom belonging to her brother and was surprised to see the large double bed occupied.

'And what the devil's *he* doing here?' Jarmon said in shocked surprise pointing down at the bed.

Now Mike (29)

The police had arrived without sirens and flashing lights at the request of Bobby Owens who managed the hostel. A jovial Liverpudlian, he had immediately grasped the seriousness of the situation and without demur had run through to the local station before passing the phone to Mike, asking only that they try not to disturb the tranquil atmosphere. Best not to cause too much fuss just yet he'd said. After a brief discussion, two constables were dispatched to interview the teachers.

On their arrival, Owens greeted them with first names and showed them into the lounge where Bert, Mike and Bev were waiting. The three stood as the men entered and he left for the kitchens to rustle up some coffee.

The fire had burned down to embers in the large stone grate, and the room had a chill about it that seemed to deepen at the entry of the police.

Bev shivered.

'So Mister Lightfoot, Mister Owens says you're the senior teacher here?' asked Constable Rider, making quick notes and sounding more stern than the circumstances required, thought Bev.

'Well yes, I suppose so, but …' began Bert.

'We're both equally responsible for what's happened. Whatever it is.' put in Mike.

The man looked over.

'And you would be Mister Nutter. You reported the disappearance? He asked.

'Yes, Mister Lightfoot was a little overwrought at the time. I think we've all calmed down a bit now.'

PC Rider looked at Bev.

'And this is …?

'Beverley Nutter. Michael's wife.' she answered, indicated Mike with a half-hearted wave of her hand.

'Right, and this is PC Neal.' said Rider, turning to look at the second policemen who stood off to one side, watching the small group.

Both officers looked more like traffic cops than beat bobbies, thought Mike. The bright reflective clothing and chequered caps jarring in the pale surroundings. They had the air of authority that only came with experience of all the follies and foibles that the public engaged in on a daily basis.

'Let's all take a seat then, shall we?' said Neal moving forwards, one arm outstretched to guide them back to the sofa.

Mike felt the same sense of uncertainty he always had when faced by a policemen. There was something about the uniform and the no-nonsense way of talking that always made him ill at ease. There was no real reason for it, but it always happened, even in social situations. Probably something to do with having it drilled into him by his parents to always be respectful to the police. For some silly reason it still happened, even when the officers were several years his junior. He felt himself acting like a naughty boy who'd been caught pinching a blackjack from the penny tray at the newsagents - and that had been thirty years before.

Neither policeman felt the need to volunteer their first names, which gave the proceedings an altogether more formal air than any of the three non-policeman wanted.

'So what exactly has happened?' asked Neal as he sat with his back to the large picture window. He had an altogether softer manner than his oppo, and smiled at Bert as he leaned forward, his hands clasped before him, elbows on knees. Clearly it would be PC Rider who took any notes required.

'All we know is that three lads appear to have gone missing.' He stood and walked to the fire, throwing a couple of short logs on and giving it a stir with a large cast iron poker, in an attempt to rekindle its interest in life.

Bert cleared his throat nervously.

'Umm. Yes. Three of our more sensible boys, if truth be known.' he began.

'Names first please, Mister Lightfoot.' said Rider in the same stern voice that was becoming his trademark for the night.

'Oh yes, er ... of course.' Bert appeared flustered. 'Ah ... Finbar LeMott, Tamburlaine Riggleby and Simeon Carver. All second year boys.'

'So they'll be thirteen, or thereabouts?' guessed Neal.

'Yes ... yes.' Bert gave every appearance of drifting in and out of the conversation, such as it was.

Bev nudged Mike, a gesture caught by Rider, who continued scribbling on his pad.

'Sim and Fin are tall for their age, more young men than children.' said Mike. 'And it's totally out of character for any of them, even Tam, to wander off like this.'

Rider raised an eyebrow.

'Are you suggesting that they may not have left of their own accord?' he enquired quietly.

Mike looked aghast and raised his hands palm out as he leaned back in his seat.

'Good God no. It's just that this is so unlike them. I can't understand it. That's all.'

'None of us can.' said Bev earnestly.

Neal nodded.

'Right. Well before we go any further I'd like complete descriptions; hair colour, eyes, build, clothes and anything else you can think of. Then we'll get straight on to the station and get some more men out here. There's a hell of a lot of ground to cover and it'll take more than this to do a proper search. I'll have to have a word with someone more senior. This sort of thing won't be left to us to handle.' He gave a self-deprecating smile. 'Probably an Inspector, I should think.'

'Eddie, will you get the details from Mrs Nutter, while I give them a bell. Then we'll have a drink and try to make sense of all this. Who knows, maybe it will be sorted before the big guns arrive.'

But he sounded doubtful.

'Ah Bob, perfect timing.'

A tray with mugs and a huge percolator had arrived, with milk, sugar and various biscuits.

Neal waved the hostel manager to a vacant chair.

'Join us. Maybe you can help.'

'Yeah, sure Eddie.' Owens answered and joined them.

'Bit odd, those two doing a runner. They didn't seem the scally type, either of 'em. Now some of them other kids. Well I wouldn't trust them as far as I could spit.' he said.

'Yeah, okay Bob. But that don't help us much does it?' admonished Rider. 'Anyway, I'll just make that call first.'

Rider stood and headed for the door.

'Get the drinks sorted Bob, eh. There's a good lad.' he said over his shoulder as he left the room.

'E's a good 'un.' said Bob as he concentrated on pouring the drinks. 'An' so's 'e.' He nodded towards Rider. 'Proper street bobbies, both of 'em. Would have done well in my neck of the woods. Only they don't seem to let them out of those bloody cars these days, and it's all paperwork from what I 'ear.'

'Tell me about it.' huffed Rider, from where he sat with Bev, their heads bowed together.

A van arrived about twenty minutes later, as the big old clock on the mantle was striking two, and another half dozen policemen joined them in the lounge. At the same time a portly, non-uniformed man arrived, introduced himself as DCI Lacy, and took control.

He dispatched men to various known empty and tumbledown cottages to look for the boys and by two thirty the search was in full swing. Rider and Neal left after handing over all the information they had gleaned earlier and the car park was now empty apart from Lacy's car.

Amazingly, the coming and going didn't appear to have woken any of the hostel's sleeping occupants. A small mercy, thought Mike.

The two teachers and Bev had wanted to join the search, but Mister Lacy would have none of it.

'We've got three missing boys. No need to add you to the list as well. It's dark and the ground around here can be treacherous. We'd have twisted ankles and broken legs all over the show if I let you three troll about too, don't you think?' he'd said.

Bob Owens was off on the coffee run again and Lacy sat with the worried threesome. He lit a long cigarette and blew the smoke towards the fire whenever he inhaled.

'I have to say I am a little puzzled by the fact that it took you over three hours to report the boys missing. They could very well be the most important hours we had. They could have gone several miles in that time, even over the difficult country we have around here.' He gave them all an exasperated look. 'We're a rural force and don't really have the manpower for something like this. Neal and Rider have to cover a huge area every day. The other men I've sent out have come from miles away. The overtime will be horrendous.' He shrugged the thought away. 'Not my problem though, thankfully. But if we could have started earlier, I'd be much more confident of finding the boys.'

When it became obvious that no-one was going to give him an answer he asked again.

'So why?'

He deftly fired his exhausted cigarette into the fire, which against all expectations was now burning happily and turned back to the three sitting opposite.

Mike realised that silence would begin to look like an admission of some sort of guilt and he spoke up.

'We thought they were just playing silly beggars at first and expected them to just turn up. We'd have given them a bollocking and sent them to bed with a flea in their ear and that would be that. We just never thought they would actually be gone like this. We'd wasted hours by the time we came to the realisation that we needed to call you in.'

He stared into the fire.

'It was stupid, but we didn't expect it to go this far.'

He glanced at Bert and Bev and then looked over to Lacy. He was determined to look the man in the eye. It was basically the truth anyway. How could they possibly make this man see that they had suspicions that one of the missing boys had somehow transported them away by means unknown. Lacy would certainly want them straight down to the nick for further questioning then.

Lacy was the first to look away, but there was misgiving in his look as he again focussed on the fire.

'Well there's not a lot we can do now anyway apart from wait to see what happens next.'

And they all had to be content with that for now.

But Mike had no doubt that unless the boys were found, and found soon, they were going to have to face a great deal of further questioning from Lacy.

Now Tam (30)

Tam woke with a start, with the commotion in the bedroom. Looking disoriented he smiled wanly at Lidine, Jarmon and Lillibet. His hair was unkempt and dirty and he looked as though he hadn't washed for a week.

'Surprise!' He tried his best gameshow host voice as he sat up and faced Fin's family. He gave the sleeping form next to him a shake.

'Wotcha Fin. We're home. Well, you are anyway'

He saw the shock in the faces before him and took a deep breath.

'Hello good people… Mrs LeMott… Mister LeMott… Lilli.' He looked from one to the other along the line of faces. 'Bet you didn't expect to see me – uhhh… us – today, eh?' Again he smiled, but this time a little more brightly. 'And I'll guarantee you can't guess where we've been.'

Fin sat up behind him. He looked haggard and very much the worse for wear, but still managed the tiniest of smiles.

'Oh, bloody hell Tam. What are we doing here! We aren't supposed to be here! We should be at the hostel.' Fin was looking confused.

'Well I don't give a tinkers cuss mate. I'm just glad to be back.' said Tam excitedly. 'Wait til' I tell Mum and Dad.'

'Umm. Yeah.' mumbled Fin.

He looked out through ancient spectacles at the confused faces above him… and couldn't help smiling.

They were finally back.

Though his stomach gave a lurch at the thought of what was ahead of them, he was *sooooooo* glad to be home.

'Hello Mum. Hello Dad.' He glanced at Lilli and she gave a quick flash of a smile in return before resuming her "concerned" expression. She'd been around adults enough to recognise when she should look suitably worried and when to smile and this was not a smiling time.

But it certainly appeared to be for Fin and Tam. Their grins were widening by the second and they kept exchanging mysterious little looks. It seemed for all the world as though they were about to burst into laughter at some unheard joke.

'They promised us we'd get back Fin, didn't they? Good old Tony.'

'What's going on? You two are supposed to be in the Lake District. What are you doing home today? Why didn't you wake us when you got back?' Jarmon was in full flow and Lidine knew that bluster and noise were his way of hiding his confusion. She put a hand on his arm and when he looked around she smiled gently up at him.

'Sshh.' she urged. 'Let them wake up first. Then we'll have an explanation.' She wanted to know what was going on as much as her husband, but looking at her son and his friend, wearing clothes that appeared to have seen more than a couple of days wear, she'd decided that a good wash was first order of the day.

Ever practical. Good ol' Mum.

She found their inane grins unnerving and switched to Mum-mode to cover her concern.

'Both of you - into the bathroom. Hot showers – and don't come out until you're clean. And fresh clothes - stick that lot in a bin bag and then tie a knot in it. If there's anything alive in there with you, it's not going to be let loose in this house!' her mock horror was only partly an act. 'Then downstairs. Okay?'

She ushered her husband and daughter out of the room and as she turned to follow she gave the boys a stern look.

'Mum, what day is it?' asked Fin.

Lidine looked puzzled.

'Thursday Fin. Good Lord you've only been away two days. How can you have lost track of time so quickly.' She shook her head. 'I sometimes despair of you lads.'

Fin's smile didn't budge.

'Hurry up the pair of you and tell us what on earth you've been up to. And where you got those dreadful clothes'

She turned to the door.

'And it had better be good.' she admonished, shaking a finger at them. The lads looked abashed for a second until they caught her smile as she closed the door.

From the landing they could hear her herding the other two downstairs.

'Come on. They'll be down in a minute. Then we'll all know what's going on, but it is all a bit confusing. Why haven't the school contacted us?'

'And why on earth didn't they wake us when they got back?' asked Jarmon.

'Mum, how did they get home? And why isn't Tam at his house?' asked Lilli as their voices receded.

Lilli's voice was the last one they heard.

'And why are they talking in those funny voices and doesn't Fin's hair look horrible?'

The two boys looked at each other in silence for a moment.

'Oh boy. Now we're for it. Your Mum and Dad are never going to believe what's going on, are they?' asked Tam, looking over at Fin solemnly.

Fin looked blankly out of the window, at the blue sky that augured another warm summer's day.

'Nor are yours. No-one's going to Tam. I'm sorry mate.' He leaned over to touch Tam lightly on the shoulder. 'I never meant for you both to end up in trouble too, but at least we're home.'

months for anything that the world has to offer me. And didn't we keep saying that you'd get us back safe. So now we're back, but we'll never forget what we've been through. Never in a zillion years. The things we've seen, the people we've met, the things we know.' He shifted his position and his face became lit with an irresistible excitement.

'Anyway, we always knew this was going to be the most difficult part – convincing people. We've discussed it often enough, haven't we?'

Fin nodded as he stood and tried to be a little less gloomy. Tam was right, they'd always known that this was going to be hard, if not downright impossible. Still, some of Simeon and Tam's eternal optimism had brushed off on him during the time they'd been away and, he had to admit – come what may, it had been worth it.

'Come on then. Bathroom first.' And he turned Tam towards the door. 'And where are my lenses? My nose could do with a rest from these.' He pulled a very odd looking pair of glasses from his pocket and placed them on a shelf next to his bed. 'So I'm batlike again until I get my lenses from the bathroom. Mum and Dad are going to love the fact that I've managed to ruin two pairs of specs in one school trip.'

Tam grinned 'Ah Fin, if only they knew the truth.' Then he laughed. 'In a few minutes your specs will be the least of their worries.'

Fin smiled, but looked very uncertain, despite his friend's excitement.

'Thanks for reminding me Tam.' he muttered, but Tam was still grinning like a Cheshire Cat.

'Yeah, but this is going to be the good bit now, innit?' Tam was honestly looking forward to this. 'Trying to convince everyone. We know things that no-one else can know for sure! Oh yes, they can guess and they can infer, but they can't be sure. And we can! We met John Fletcher. We even saw William. Oh lawks Fin! We met them!' He was almost laughing in his excitement and, as ever, his enjoyment of the moment was infectious, but Fin was still not entirely convinced.

'Yes, but Tam, who's going to believe us? I'm still not convinced we're going to manage this. We'll get locked up.' But he was still smiling despite himself.

'Bollocks. Fin, we've been over and over this. There's no point in trying to lie or cover it up. So we'll just have to convince 'em. You know you can't hide this anymore – not after what we've just seen and done. Apart from anything, we haven't been able to think of any other way of explaining what we're doing back at your place when the rest of the school trip is obviously still Up North. And don't worry, you're going to be a star Fin. A twenty four carat diamond.'

'So why do I still have a feeling we're going to end up a one-week wonder, and lifetime laughing stocks?'

'Cos you're a miserable sod. Come on, lets get cracking.'

Tam went to the bathroom, but returned almost immediately, looking frantic.

'Bugger, bugger, bugger.' he whispered as he re-entered the bedroom and searched around.

'What Tam? What's the problem?' asked Fin, becoming concerned.

Tam looked across and in a very quiet voice asked the obvious question.

They both undressed and showered one after the other in a heavy silence. They had to admit though, that the shower was a long forgotten luxury that momentarily drove all their concerns to the back of their minds. They combed their hair before heading towards the stairs, with Fin carrying a plastic bag containing their malodorous garb.

Tam was looking expectantly at Fin and Fin was looking just a little wary as they paused on the landing. He straightened his shoulders and threw out his chest, taking a deep breath.

'Oh God. Come on then, lets get it over with.'

Tam grinned.

'Dat's my boy.'

As they made their way downstairs into the expectant atmosphere of the kitchen, Tam was definitely the more excited.

'O excellent! I love long life better than figs.'

And Fin couldn't help smiling to himself. If he'd learned nothing else during their trip, he at least knew that Tam could always be relied upon to lift his spirits and not let a little thing like impending doom get in the way of a good quote.

The rest of the family were sitting at the kitchen table when they heard the anguished shout from Fin upstairs. Jarmon made to rise from the table, but Lidine shook her head with pursed lips.

'Leave them Jarmon. They'll be down soon enough and then maybe we'll get some sense out of them.'

With a sigh, Jarmon nodded and then gave Lilli a half-hearted smile.

They waited a further quarter of an hour listening to the movements above them and the quite conversations, tantalisingly indecipherable.

Jarmon had to admit that even Lilli showed commendable restraint, simply waiting along with her parents for the appearance of the boys.

As the boys finally entered, Lidine rose and moved over to the kettle, stirring the expectant air in the room.

'Tea, boys?' she asked with a smile.

Jarmon and Lilli already had drinks, untouched by the look of it.

Fin sat beside his sister who gave him a small smile of encouragement, and Tam took the seat at the head of the table, opposite Jarmon.

'Oh yes, Mrs L. We haven't had a good cuppa for a long time, have we Fin?' laughed Tam.

Fin blushed.

'Where we've been it's all ale, and watery ale at that.'

Jarmon looked up sharply.

'Enough Tam. When are we going to find out what you two have been up to, because just at the moment we're all a bit concerned that all's not well - and you're not making a huge amount of sense son. So stop jabbering like an idiot and tell us what on earth's going on?'

Jarmon laid his hands on the table and pushed himself up to stand beside Lidine, who was also looking nonplussed as the kettle boiled

'Oh indeed Mister LeMott.' Tam held his hands wide and looked over to Fin. 'Here comes a pair of very strange beasts, which in all tongues are called fools.'

Fin looked pleadingly at Tam, who stopped his theatrics and sat back.

'Sorry chummy boy. Shall we start at the start then Fin?'

Fin nodded silently and so did everyone else.

'Well it all starts with Fin and his weird dreams, while we - '

'But I thought the dreams had stopped Fin.' said Jarmon accusingly. 'You said things were alright now.'

Fin looked guilty and clasped his hands in front of him on the table.

'No sir. Fin's just got very good at hiding his problems. But we'll explain it all.' said Tam with a smile. 'It's all so strange and I'm not sure you're going to believe it all, but I promise that every word is true.'

Jarmon made to speak again, but Lidine put a hand on his arm.

'Let them tell it, Jarmon. We can try to make sense of it all later. But let's hear it first. okay love?' Lidine passed over two china mugs, full to brim with tea. No-one failed to notice that her hands were shaking slightly as she put the cups down.

'Fin, don't you have anything to say?'

'Yes Mum, but it's probably better if you hear it from Tam. Not because it's any different than you'd get from me, but because you both know that he doesn't lie. He may act like a complete puddin' at times, but he's as truthful as the day is long. Probably because he hasn't the intelligence to be convincing, he's too thick'

'Oi!' said Tam indignantly.

'But Fin, we know you are too!' interrupted Jarmon. 'I mean, uh... erm... Look, I know that didn't come out right but you know what I mean.'

Lidine squeezed his arm. 'Stop digging love. I get the feeling that Fin thinks we might decide he's made it up though, to hide some other problem that we don't know about. Is that right Fin?'

'Yes Mum. But once you've heard this I think you'll realise that almost anything else would pale into insignificance compared to what we've been doing.'

'Surely it can't be as bad as that!' said Jarmon, a look of concern crossing his face. He sat down again staring at his son and reaching across to give his hands a squeeze.

Fin looked over at his father and gave a half-hearted smile.

'Listen to Tam for a couple of minutes, and then say that again Dad.'

The two adults gave each other grim looks, but said nothing.

Tam began again.

'When we all went to bed on the first night away, Fin had another dream. From what he's told me since it seems he has The Nightmare almost every night.' He looked across to Fin who nodded.

'Every night.' he said quietly.

Jarmon sat thin lipped, but said nothing.

But this one was even worse than usual. None of us knew anything about it until the following morning, when Fin was so nack... err... exhausted, sorry.' Tam gave a small *oops* shrug. 'So tired that he didn't wake up with the rest of us. Willis went to wake him later and found him wearing the most God awful coat and boots.'

Everyone gave Fin a questioning look and he cringed at the memory. In some ways it was even worse hearing the tale told than living through it at the time.

'Now here's the first big jump in faith you've got to make, okay?' Tam paused for dramatic effect.

'Oh get on with it.' said Lidine, this time with no sign of a smile.

Tam sipped his tea, seemingly enjoying having the limelight all to himself for a change.

'Fin was wearing stuff he'd... er... acquired; while he was dreaming.'

Fin wasn't sure what Tam had been expecting as a result of this statement, but he was sure it wasn't the patient silence that presented itself.

Tam looked at the adults enquiringly, just a trifle disappointed.

'I said... '

'Yes we heard what you said.' said Jarmon. 'We're reserving judgement.'

'Oh, righto!'

Lilli put her chin on her hands and leaned forward.

'Go on Tam.' she said.

'Well, Fin eventually told us what had happened. Mister Nutter and his wife and Mister Lightfoot also know.'

'Oh God.' moaned Jarmon and slumped back into his seat. 'And what did they say?'

'Well at first, I think they all felt the same as you must be, but after the last few weeks, I don't think they'll have any alternative but to believe us.'

'Weeks! But Tam, you've only been away for two days.' said Lidine.

'That's what you think Mrs LeMott.'

'Is there something else that you haven't told us? What's been happening, and why haven't we been told anything?' asked Lidine.

'Mum just let him get on with it, otherwise he'll never get to the end of it all.' said Fin.

'But I can't help feeling he's trying to make this more mysterious than it is, Fin' she said, with a look of impatience.

'Well then, he'll just have to get it all out ASAP won't he? Tam, stop pissing about and tell them.'

Tam looked crestfallen and annoyed at the same time.

'I'm not sure I deserved that Fin. I'm trying to do you a favour here. Do you want to tell it?'

'No, not really, but don't lay it on so thick.'

'Would you have me false to my nature? Rather say I play the man I am.' quipped Tam.

'Get on with it!' shouted Jarmon, whose reservoir of patience had obviously sprung a major leak by this point.

Tam sat up straighter in his seat and glared at them all.

'Look, I've had a very weird experience just recently and your son is the cause.' He pointed and accusing finger at Fin. 'So if I am 'laying it on a bit', it's because I think I have a right to. Okay? So just listen, all of you. Stop bloody interrupting all the time. Listen and then interrogate us, but let me at least enjoy the telling.'

He adopted a more upright pose, like a bard preparing a recitation and smiled again at them all. This was a story he was determined to tell his way, since Fin didn't feel confident enough. He was in charge here. For the moment at least.

'A good plot, good friends, and full of expectation; an excellent plot, very good friends.' he pronounced.

Just as he was about to begin, Lilli spoke.

'Sorry Tam, but what did you just mean? Why do you keep saying those daft things?'

Tam looked at her for a second before bursting into laughter. Fin was next and then his parents, until finally everyone at the table was laughing hysterically.

Fin looked at his sister. Good for Lilli. She had managed to shatter the ever more intense atmosphere that Tam had caused. He realised that his friend was trying to help, but speed was probably more important than anything else at this point.

As the antagonistic air fled the kitchen, everyone settled down and Fin was relieved to see that they all looked less overwrought. He noticed though that his parents still had a worried look. Not surprising really.

Tam spoke again, this time with a slight quaver in his voice that hadn't been present before.

'Lilli, I got all the 'daft things' from Sim. He's the one who knows Shakespeare and all that stuff like he was born to it.'

He paused and cast a guilty look at Fin before taking a steadying breath and continuing.

'Fin did something really amazing last night. Well last night as far as you're concerned, for us it was – '

'Tam. Please get on with it.' urged Fin.

'Sorry. Okay. Hmm.' Tam collected his thoughts. 'Okay, all in one go. Okay.'

Fin nodded and Tam took a deep breath and shook his arms in an expansive shudder, as though to wake himself.

'There was a storm last night, while we were watching the play at the hostel. Everyone was there and we were all enjoying it.' He glanced over at Fin. 'Well, I was anyway. Then a couple of the morons started taking the pis – er… Micky… and Fin got into a bit of bother with Mister Lightfoot.' Tam noticed the look shot over by Jarmon at Fin.

'Oh no!' he shook his head vigorously. 'It wasn't Fin's fault. He was trying to help Sim. It was Sim they were messing about with.'

Jarmon looked abashed and gave Fin a quick smile of apology. Fin, relieved, smiled back and then turned his attention back to Tam. Finally the story was being told.

'Fin ended up going back to the hostel early – before the play ended, so Sim and I went with him.' He shrugged. 'Suddenly the play wasn't that appealing anymore.'

'You could hear the storm approaching while we were walking back and the thunder was rolling overhead.' His theatrical side came to the fore again. He raised his arms and looked upwards as he continued dramatically. 'The wind began to howl. Well, a bit. And the thunder roared… a bit. Then, we heard a soddin' great crash like the whole world was exploding around us and…' he paused, and everyone except Fin leaned forward, hanging on his every word.

Then Fin, Tam and Simeon (31)

The sound was so enormous the three friends were stunned as they walked across the lawn. The ground vibrated and the bass–notes of the thunder surged upwards through their bodies. All three boys were momentarily stunned and Fin stumbled heavily into Simeon, pulling Tam with him, as they stopped for a second to gather their wits.

'Bloody Hell!' Simeon shouted as the rumbling died down and the two stared at each other. He felt totally disorientated his eyes seeming to vibrate strangely in their sockets and his ears ringing so that they stopped him from hearing whatever it was that Fin called in reply.

'Sounded like the stage has exploded.' gasped Fin in shock and they turned to look, from their half crouching positions, back at the stage.

'Er … Fin. What's going on?' asked Tam

'Oh, no!' Fin was practically screaming as he followed his friend's gaze

The anguished wail made Simeon looked over to the other two in shock.

'You mean… '

'Sorry Sim. Oh God. I'm so sorry Tam.' Fin looked close to tears. 'I didn't mean it to happen… honest!'

'Don't sweat it Fin!' said a grinning Sim as he looked around them.

'How very curious.' whispered Tam.

They were standing in an open field under an almost moonless sky. Of the hostel there was no sign. The brightly lit stage with its audience were gone, so too was the lake. Through the encircling darkness they could just make out the dense forest surrounding them.

'You little tinker. You've gone and done it again, haven't you?' Tam gave a little laugh and capered about like a loon. 'So where are we?'

There were no lights to be seen anywhere. Now that the sounds of the storm had passed, with almost indecent haste, there was nothing but silence.

Mind you, thought Fin, that might also be due to their ear drums having been perforated. He shook his head, just to be sure nothing had been shaken loose.

The stillness was broken by Sim, who was still laughing.

'Err, Sim. Why are you so flaming happy?' asked Fin. 'You do realise that we don't have the faintest idea where we are, don't you?'

'Yeah, but just imagine what the others will think. Maybe we got vaporised by lightening. Or blown away. Or… or… well, who cares what they think. This is just amazing.' He held his arms wide to encompass their surroundings, his excitement obvious. Fin didn't feel the same excitement as his friend.

'But Sim, we're lost. We could be anywhere and maybe even another time - remember what I told you about the mill. I'm really sorry, I've got us *sooooo* not on a school trip.'

The oft-felt, but never comfortable, hollow feeling was once again in his stomach and he felt sick. It was just like the previous night. No, actually, it was far worse, because this time he'd dragged along someone else. He'd pulled his best friends into who knew what kind of danger.

'Yeah, we're stone gone man, as the bear said. I suspect we're more lost than anyone has ever been before. Bloody marvellous mate.' Tam grinned again.

'What? Are you off your flaming head? We're lost, you sodding morons. As in Totally Not Where We Should Be.' Fin's voice was rising with both fear at what he'd done and the ridiculous attitude of his friends. He looked ready to take a swing at Tam.

'God, but what an adventure!' cried Sim and he slapped Fin on the back. 'So which way, do you think?'

'What?' Fin was incredulous and beginning to tremble a little as he realised the enormity of the problem facing them. His stomach felt empty, but at the same time ready to retch. He didn't know where they should turn and fruitcake Sim wasn't helping.

'Look Sim. I don't know how to get us back.'

'Yeah, but on the other hand... you have different fingers.' laughed Tam staring at his hand and flexing his fingers. Seeing Fin's face he continued. 'Oh lighten up Fin. You do know how to get us back - you just don't know you do.'

'Come on, buck up Fin. This is great!' shouted Sim spreading his arms wide. 'You've only bloody transported us somewhere. Imagine that. All on your ownsome, you've carried all three of us from there to... err... ahem... where are we do you think, Fin?

His two friends were obviously refusing to accept their predicament. They were treating the whole thing as a bit of a joke. Fin began to feel faint.

He knew that it was anything but a laughing matter. He shrugged at his friends, indicating his total lack of any idea about their next step.

Sim grinned.

'Well then, let's go...' He paused, with his finger to his chin as though deep in thought, then pointed extravagantly over his own left shoulder and swivelling around to look behind Fin. 'This way.'

'Oh good show' laughed Tam. 'Lead on MacDuff.'

They walked through the forest for several hours, with Sim and Tam chattering as though this was just another stroll in the Lake District and Fin lost in his own thoughts for much of the time. Finally the three boys stopped to rest for a while in a small clearing. They hadn't really paid any attention to the lack of sound, but now the silence around them was unnerving. They heard no traffic on roads and neither heard nor saw any aircraft overhead. Wherever they were, it seemed unlikely they were anywhere near the hostel and Fin noticed that both his friends finally seemed to appreciate the mess they were in. With a silent agreement they all rose to continue their journey.

Incredibly, within a few minutes Sim and Tam were bantering again.

The sky was beginning to lighten above the trees ahead of them. They were walking east, not that it really made any difference, but at least they knew. Just at the moment they didn't know anything else about their current whereabouts. They were all beginning to get a bit jumpy at the lack of any sign of civilisation when they suddenly stepped out of the trees and onto a wide path cutting a swathe through the trees. They had no way of knowing where they were headed, but at least they weren't walking in circles.

All three were beginning to feel tired, yet none of them considered trying to sleep. It seemed more urgent to them that they try to find some indication of where they were. Finally after another quick stop and a grin to each other as much as to say *Well isn't this just too weird?*, Simeon decided to try to find out exactly what had happened to them. Two hours with his own thoughts, and only the odd quick exchange with his walking companions, had not helped him to come to any firm conclusions.

'Come on then Fin, what do you think you've done with us?' he asked.

Fin glanced across.

'Dunno Sim.'

Still neither of his friends looked as worried as Fin thought the circumstances warranted. Fin grew more exasperated. He'd expected them to grow as anxious as him with each passing hour, yet neither Sim nor Tam seemed too bothered. How was he going to make them see the trouble they were in? Both of them knew that he couldn't control what was happening to them, but seemed unwilling, or unable to appreciate it. He'd spent the time they'd been walking in a sort of waking dream, hardly daring to consider what had happened. Luckily the other two had kept their ridiculous repartee going for most of the time, with only a few cursory exchanges with him as they pushed through the undergrowth. Now the going was easier, they tried to draw him out of his self inflicted silence.

'Sometimes I dream that I'm travelling around the world in the present, but more often things seem different and I'm sure I'm going back in time. I never seem to go into the future.' Fin shrugged. 'I can't do anything to stop it. I just go where I'm taken and I don't know where or when I'll end up.'

Sim gave him a quizzical look.

'Why d you think you're going back in time?'

'Well, sometimes I can see motorways and things, but then they fade away and there's only fields and cart tracks and all the towns get smaller and look older. You know, thatched roofs an' things.' He smiled to himself, 'Once I saw Stonehenge, but guess what? It was all there. None of that tumble down ruin that's there now. It was all looking new. Full of people too. With a little village about a quarter of a mile away. I just sort of gave it a fly-by, so I don't know who was living there or what they were doing, but there was some sort of ritual going on, with lots of camp fires and people dressed in white.' He gave a sigh, 'Fancied going back to it, but I couldn't control where I went, back then - it was a couple of years ago.'

'But I thought you said you couldn't... '

'No, I mean I couldn't steer myself around when I was flying – I can usually do that now. What I meant was that I've never found out how to affect the time and place where I'm taken.'

'Oh, right.' Finally Sim seemed to be starting to understand.

Fin looked down at his feet as they continued walking, kicking at a small stick in his path.

'I saw a battle once too... '

Tam immediately brightened.

'Wow, good stuff! Who was it? Romans? Vikings? Roundheads and Cavaliers? Us giving the Frenchies a good kickin' or what?'

'Dunno, but I do know it wasn't like in the films. Believe me there's a lot more blood and body parts when soldiers are using swords and lances.'

'Ugh!'

'Yeah, exactly. Which is why this isn't a fun little trip. Tam, we really are up the proverbial without a canoe, never mind a bloody paddle!"

They walked on in silence for a few seconds.

'So this is worse than usual, you mean?' asked Tam

Fin nodded.

'Last night I got dumped next to the mill we were at today, and that was the first time I hadn't ended up back where I started. The mill was different from when we all visited too. I *know* that when I was left there it was years ago. Maybe a hundred, maybe more - I don't know, but they did still have the steam engine. I'd like be able to get back there again. Apart from anything else I need to find my proper glasses – I can't think of where else they could be, so I must have lost them at the mill. These aren't much cop anymore.'

'Uh? Why not?' asked Sim.

'Old prescription. Nothing's quite as sharp as it should be. I have to squint to see things properly. Gets a bit annoying after a while and your eyes start to hurt.'

'Oh, right. Obvious really, but I don't need them m'self , so I never considered it.'

'Lucky you.'

Sim had crossed the track so that they were now walking side by side.

'Must be a bit of a sod – wearing specs.'

'No, not really. You get used to it.' Fin shrugged, 'Anyway, I can see okay with these, so don't worry about it.'

'But I can remember when Bishop and that lot used to tease you,' said Sim quietly, 'and we were all too frightened to say anything.'

Fin looked up in surprise. He hadn't realised that anyone else had been aware of the rubbish he'd had to endure from some of the other kids.

'Sorry.' mumbled Sim, putting an arm around his friend's shoulders. 'We were all a bit weedy back then.'

Fin gave a small smile as he looked at his friend, seeing the shame on his face.

'Don't worry. It's character building, that's what they say isn't it?'

'Yeah, I bet.'

Tam joined them and they walked on in companionable silence for a little longer. Then Sim dropped his arm and stepped in front of Fin, turning to walk backwards with his hands shoved deep into his jeans pockets, facing Fin as he spoke.

'So, what do you think happened tonight? Strikes me, that you don't normally do this sort of thing while you're awake. So this is something new for you as well.'

'Too true. I keep hoping this is just *The Nightmare*, but it's gone on too long and, as you say, I'm not asleep. And you're with me. I've never had company. I'm not sure whether it's a good thing or not. I'd hate to strand you here – wherever here is.'

'Chill mate, do you see me complaining? Anyway, maybe this is my dream and I've dropped you in it.' said Tam.

'Dead likely, shorty.' said Fin, pushing Tam playfully out into the middle of the path.

Tam shrugged and smiled.

'This is okay by me mate. Dad always says that you have to just get on with it when life drops you in the do-do and you have to admit, with three of us at least we might be able to work something out together.'

'Yeah, sure!' Fin looked unconvinced.

'No honestly. Look, at least you've got some company - and anyway, I'm not going to get worked up yet and I don't think Sim will either. You told us you always get back to where you started don't you? You may not know how it all works, but you always end up safe and sound, don't you.'

Fin gave a reluctant nod.

'So don't sweat it. Sooner or later we'll end up back at the hostel.'

'Yes, but this has lasted a lot longer than last night and – I'll say it again – this is *not* the usual stuff. Maybe you should worry just a bit more than you are.'

'Nah,' Sim shrugged, 'what's the point. We can't do much about it, can we? So let's make the best of a bad job. Until we know we're in real trouble, let's assume I'm right. We'll be okay, don't fret Doctor.'

Fin and Tam both gave him a quizzical look.

'Well you're the nearest thing to Doctor Who that I've ever seen.' laughed Sim.

'Pillock.' said Fin, but, despite himself, he grinned too.

And, strangely, despite his nervousness for the safety of all three of them, Fin did feel better for having his friends along. He'd never really realised before that Sim was definitely a glass-half-full kind of lad. Fin seemed to remember he had been once, but with all that had happened to him, he was more of a half-empty type now. And Tam was the sort who just went with the flow and always made the best of things. Yes, if he had to be stranded somewhere, or, he hated to even consider it, some*when*, he could do far worse than to be with these two miscreants. Fin found himself smiling and his feeling of foreboding began to lift.

Sim had turned again to walk alongside Fin and Tam, when he suddenly put an arm out to block their progress and stopped them both with a finger raised to his lips.

'Shhh! Listen.'

Fin strained to hear and above the rustling of the trees all around he caught a snatch of sound from around the bend in the path ahead. Tam turned his head to try to catch whatever it was that Sim had heard.

Sim crouched low and crept forward. The others followed.

It was still early morning twilight, but they could now clearly see through the woods. They stepped as quietly as they could as they left the path and cut across the corner of undergrowth at the apex of the right hand bend in the road.

The grassy path opened out into a small clearing, bisected by the track. On the right hand side of the clearing was a small cart, covered over with a large tarpaulin-like sheet to which was harnessed a pair of small dark horses.

A short, stocky, middle-aged man stood at the back of the cart beside a pile of beams, talking heatedly with someone obscured by the huge baulks of wood protruding from under a canvas-like sheet.

'Do'st thou seek to cozen me daughter? For too long have I forborne to entermeddle in thine affairs. Nay more. I say'st enough! In this thou shalt mark my words! And in this I will be obeyed! 'Swounds! Now by my faith, my counsel is yet just and in this shall not be flouted. Or must I cut myself a switch from one of these boughs and teach thee a hard lesson in respect!'

The man looked ready to strike the unseen daughter. His stance was rigid and his hands bunched into fists. Both the boys were straining to make sense of the heavily accented language. It was surely English, but sounded like it came from the very deepest Wiltshire, where words like "enough" and "bough" could be made to rhyme, each ending with an "ow" sound as in "cow".

'But Father… '

'Nay! I say I will hear no more on the matter! Thou shalt abide by my word! Am I some blatherskite that thou should force 'tween us such dispute? Nay, I am thy sire. Get thee to thy place girl and in this matter remain silent.'

The man's whole figure shook with indignation and the boys heard a girlish sob and the sound of someone clambering up onto the cart and saw a flash of sunlight as it blazed off golden hair.

The man turned to present his full visage to the boys and they were surprised to see the face crumple into a look of heartbroken anguish. Sim felt his own heart sink in concern. Dark eyes looked out from a face framed by a mass of black hair as the man gripped the side of the cart, his whole body trembling.

'What was that all…' he whispered, when he was gripped by a sudden violent nausea. As he swooned at the sensation he stumbled into Fin, who appeared to be having the same problem. Tam was crouched behind the nearest tree retching uncontrollably, while the other two both reached out into the surrounding foliage in an attempt to steady themselves as they stumbled in the undergrowth.

Fin dry-heaved painfully and he felt his whole body tense with the precursor to a violent chunder. Then, just as suddenly, the feeling passed and he was left with a vague disorientation. Looking over to Sim in alarm he could see that his friend was obviously recovering in the same way.

'Augh! What was that!' gasped Tam, as the boys all fought to regain their composure.

Fin had a flashback to the night at the mill, where the same feeling had assaulted him when he first met Bill. How many hours, or years, ago was that? he wondered.

'Shhh!' he hissed at Tam, but it was too late.

'Ho! Who is't skulking in yonder bracken? Blackguards shall receive short shrift from me and mine. So begone!' There was a long pause while the man waited for a reply and, receiving none, he reached under the cover of the cart and hefted a thick piece of timber in his large hands, as though balancing it ready for action. 'Do'st thou attend my words? Begone foul caitiff!'

Thus armed, the man stood, feet firmly planted, staring out towards Fin and Sim, though it was unlikely he could see them.

'Oh, well. Nothing ventured and all that.' muttered Sim as he rose unsteadily to his feet.

'Hold, goodman!' called Sim. 'We are merely three young travellers, lost whilst on our journey! We mean no offence to thee and thine!'

Both the other boys were vaguely aware that what was being heard was not exactly what was being said. It seemed as though some strange half-heard, simultaneous translation was taking place. They exchanged shocked looks.

'Then stand to and show yourselves!' shouted the man, still holding his stout timber before him. The boys began to push through the bushes around them and approached the cart.

The noise they created made the man glance worriedly towards the front of the cart before quickly returning his gaze to the trees and adjusting his grip on the club.

'Keep thine eyes about thee, Kate. There may be more!' he shouted.

Sim was first out into the open, brushing leaves and grass from his trousers and sleeves, followed almost immediately by Fin, with Tam bringing up the rear, having suffered worse than the other two from their recent stomach churning.

The man's eyes widened as he surveyed the three.

'And what hast we here then. Three less likely dastards I have yet to see. Methinks thou may relax a little Kate, yet remain attentive to our care.'

The man glanced again towards the front of the cart with rapidly diminishing apprehension, where its occupant could now be seen looking back. Tam had finally straightened up and, seeing the face looking back at him, gasped.

The face he saw was framed with long blond hair, the early-morning sunlight catching coppery highlights and turning it to burnished gold. Eyes, so blue as to be almost turquoise, stared steadily back at him with evident curiosity. Her face had a flawless symmetry with nose straight and upturned a little, and a perfect mouth, the lips slightly parted in a coy smile. The girl looked to be about the same age at the three boys and a vague smattering of freckles did nothing to mar the glow that suffused her skin. Tam was smitten. He felt his breath catch in his throat and his stomach give a lurch that had little to do with the nausea of a few minutes ago, as he gazed upon the most beautiful girl he'd ever seen. He fancied he could see the soft focus closing in on her and hear the music welling up in the background.

Fin couldn't help but notice his friend's reaction to the girl and it wasn't wasted on her father either.

'Hold sirrah! 'Tis I to whom thou should'st turn thy eyes. Daughter, look thee to the trees for sign of others.' He let his arms drop to his sides, but still gripped the wood in his right hand, and the movement caused Tam to start as he switched his gaze back.

'Come closer, thou callow youths, and explain thyselves.'

The boys stepped closer, but warily eyed both the man and his somewhat basic weapon.

Fin spoke first, before Sim had a chance to put his foot in it and giving Tam a chance to gather his wits.

'Sir, we meant no offence and were cautious in our approach only because we knew not who we would meet.'

He smiled slowly to try to assuage the man's obvious suspicion.

'We have wondered all night through these woods and have no knowledge of where we are. As you can see, we are not here in arms and seek only directions to the nearest village or town.'

The man nodded brusquely. 'Indeed. Thou have, most certainly, none of the appearance of knaves, but in these woods and of so early an hour, any man would do well to remain circumspect.' He looked each of them up and down, appraising the young men before him and appeared to come to a favourable conclusion. He visibly relaxed.

'It must not be doubted good sir,' Fin continued, 'but we mean no ill to any man, and would continue on our way if thou could'st but name this road and these woods.'

The man frowned deeply, obviously bemused by Fin's manner of speech. The odd shadow translation persisted to the ears of all three boys, but the man showed no signs of being aware of it.

'Methinks I may have too soon have hailed thee as sirrah, but am not yet made certain of your intent. How came you to be so unsure of your surroundings that you know not that this is the Forest of Arden, close by the village of Rowington?'

In the distance a bell rang solemnly and the forest came to life with the sounds of birds.

'See. E'en now the bell of the Hospice of Saint Wilfrid, close by the village, do'st call that small house of monks to Prime.'

'Prime, that's about six o'clock isn't it Fin?' asked Sim, looking at his watch.

'Yeah. There'll be no more bells until Terce, at nine.' answered Fin looking at the man, who was glaring suspiciously at Sim, who was now adjusting his watch.

'Sim,' he whispered urgently, 'forget your watch for now. I think trying to explain it could get us into trouble with the locals.'

Sim looked up and seeing the mistrustful look being directed at him, pulled his sleeve over his wrist.

'Methinks we're not in the twenty first century, Sim.' Tam said quietly.

'What is this talk of sixes and nines? And who are you that you should be abroad and lost in the forest and dressed in such a manner? Tell me now, for my patience wears thin.'

Their questioner shook his club, though not in a very threatening way.

Sim took a step forward and bowed.

I am Simeon Carver sir, and these are my companions Finbar LeMott and Tamburlaine Riggleby. We are merely travellers who know not the lands through which we walk.'

Fin and Tam gave a bow too, they'd seen enough Shakespeare the previous night to know how it was done.

'Most elegantly done *sir*.' mocked the man. 'Though I medoubt we are either of us knights. I would have said you travel far from home, by the most strange aspect of your clothing and your manner of speech'

He smiled, but did not bow in turn.

'I am Edmund Turner, a woodsman of these parts and this' he indicated the girl atop the cart, 'is my daughter Kate. We are for Rowington, to deliver this load. And you three, ha'st still not said where you go. Are thee for Stratford mayhap, it being the largest market hereabouts? Or do'st thou know not?'

At their blank looks, he laughed and turned to look at the girl.

'Most assuredly Kate, we have here three of the most unfortunate vagabonds to bestride the lands of Warwick. They profess to know nothing of the ground on which they stand. A sorry little band indeed.'

Fin stepped forward to address the man more forcefully.

'Sir. We do not offer thee harm by any means and yet thou do'st mock us in a most ungentlemanly manner. We are but weary travellers who art lost. Is this the way folk in these lands treat such as we? Come Sim, Tam, let us begone and leave this joker to his merry jests, we have no need of such dissembling. Let us find our way to those who may aid us despite our appearance. Surely not all men in these parts will be so discourteous.'

He made to catch hold of Sim and turn to leave.

'Hold hard, young sirs!' called the girl. 'Father! Is this any way to treat wayfarers come into our company in such odd circumstance? May we not at least offer some help to them?'

'And why Kate? Give me more reason than your sharp tongue and it may be that I should offer aid.'

Sim stepped forward again.

'For help in loading your wood, friend? Would'st that not incur some stipend? If we could but beg that thou take us, along with thy load, to Rowington, from where we may be offered further help in our journey.'

Fin eyed the wood pile. It was certain that the four of them would be able to load it far faster than the man alone, and surely it wouldn't be much help for his daughter to lend a hand. Whilst she was a capable looking girl, the beams looked impressively heavy. Even with the three of them to help, it would be quite a task. Surely by himself, Edmund would struggle.

The man glanced towards the pile of timber and then back at the boys, taking obvious note of the fact that two, at least, were well-formed for their apparent age.

Tam was significantly smaller in comparison. Finally, with an audible sigh, he came to his decision.

'Very well lads, thee may help me and, in payment, I would'st offer thee transport to Rowington. From there mayhap thou wilt find another who may be persuaded to offer thee help.'

With almost unseemly haste Simeon made for the pile of wood and waved the others to join him.

As he hurried over Fin smiled to the man and his daughter.

'Gramercy Goodman. You need but instruct us in the loading. The hard work is ours.'

The man dropped his baulk of wood and set about manoeuvring the cart and horses back towards the lumber.

It took almost half an hour to load the wood and make all secure, during which time they learned that master Edmund and his daughter lived several miles away and had travelled from before dawn to deliver their load. Fin noticed that Tam was sparing no effort in trying to impress the girl, lifting along with Sim. He realised that both of his companions were vying for Kate's attention and they laughed and joked as they worked, though several times the humour was wasted on both their new-found friends. Fin found himself amused at their antics, but they had the desired effect and Edmund, initially unsure, had settled in to a happy banter with all three of the boys. From their clothes and a few throwaway comments made by Kate, Fin decided that although not rich by any means, the two did live reasonably comfortable lives even though Edmund's wife Mary - Kate's mother - had died several years previously. Fin had the impression that even without her steadying hand, the two had settled into a happy, if humdrum, existence. They both wore cotes of rough but warm cloth, made by Mary for the most part, with Edmund wearing pattens to protect his boots from the mud along the road. These were something new to all the boys, wooden soled overshoes didn't appear in any of their history books. He wore no undershirt, but Fin noticed he sat on a thick cote-hardie that would no doubt keep him warm when worn during cold days out in the woods. Kate wore a chemise of fine linen under her cote, which must have cost Edmund a goodly amount. Her bounteous hair was held back with a simple fillet made of expensive looking thread. Both wore hose, which Fin thought unusual for a girl, but perhaps it was just that she helped her father and it was easier in what he always thought was a male fashion in days gone by. Only minutes before the arrival of the boys, they had argued - the subject of the argument they kept to themselves, but both scowled as the tale was recounted by Edmund – and during the course of it Kate had succeeded in spooking the horse which had shied, tipping the cart and spilling half their load. The sudden appearance of the boys had, in fact, been a godsend to the pair, since, as Sim had surmised, there was no way that they could have continued on their way so swiftly without help.

Sim and Tam climbed atop the cargo and lay down with their eager faces turned towards Kate, and Edmund climbed up beside his daughter and took the reins. Fin jumped up too, but sprawled out further towards the back of the cart, staring up at the increasingly blue sky.

As they moved slowly through the trees, travelling north, the girl turned to talk to them.

'And how is it that you three came to be travelling through Arden without even knowing where thou wast?' she asked in her quiet melodious voice.

There was an awkward silence as the friends desperately sought some excuse for their predicament. It was Tam who came up trumps.

'A group of us were being taken to work on an estate further south. We'd been caught up in an argument in Nottingham and rounded up with a bunch of others. The Sheriff had sentenced us to work off our misdeeds elsewhere, but we escaped and wandered through the night to avoid the clutches of the guards who were taking us to Lincoln.'

Sim looked up sharply from where he lay, head propped up on his hand atop the rough-sawn wood, at this amazing piece of tale-telling and gave a lopsided grin towards Tam, in salute to his friend's imagination. Fin didn't see the look that passed between them; he now had his eyes closed and looked completely relaxed despite the sharp edges and splinters surrounding him.

At Edmund's look his friends tried to rearrange their grins into a less suspicious expression. Fin took up the fairytale from where Tam had left off.

'We are far from home and alone, but I promise you good woodsman, we are innocent of any wrong doing and seek only to make our way in the world unhindered by the unfair chains with which others seek to shackle us.'

He opened his eyes and smiled over at Kate as he finished the short but, he hoped, convincing lie. To himself he though *Keep it short guys. Keep it simple*, for he knew that the more involved the lie, the more likely they were to be found out.

Kate, at least, was totally certain that the boys had been the victims of a callous injustice.

'Oh Father. To think that we almost left them! Surely we are in the right to help such as they. Anyone can see that they are but three honest lads mistreated by the law in this.?'

Edmund looked less convinced, and cast them a look that said *By the rood, what have I landed myself with here.* Fin could tell that the tall tale had failed to satisfy him of their reasons for being abroad without any knowledge of their surroundings.

'Oh aye lads. Such a sorry tale.' he said with exaggerated pity, but then he winked and looked back to the horses. 'Lucky for you we took you under our wing before the Sheriff's knaves could catch up with thee.' He gave a little chuckle and shook his head, knowing that he was unlikely to ever know the story behind these three ne'er do wells. But they had helped him with his load and for that they deserved a little aid on their own journey.

'Where do'st thou mean to go from Rowington?' asked Kate, her eyes shining with curiosity.

The boys looked at each other. Now there was a question. Where were they going? If this was England in the Middle Ages there was nowhere they could go that might offer help in getting home. It was a case of making the best of things until Fin took them back to their own time, and no-one knew when that might happen. They were adrift on a sea of uncertainty and, as Tam had said the night before, they just had to go with the flow and see where the fates took them.

'London.' said Sim with a smile, 'That's the place for us. They do say the streets are paved with gold, so who knows what we might find there.'

Fin gave a sigh of resignation and lay on his back again, returning his gaze to the clear blue sky above, as Sim continued the chatter with Kate. Now it was he, rather than Tam, who was making the running with the damsel. Fin closed his eyes and staring at the bright red-orange glare of his eyelids, tried not to think about what might be happening at home. The buzz of early-rising insects and the slight wind in the trees soothed his racing mind. Along with the steady rocking of the cart beneath him and the smell of the woods all around, he slipped towards slumber, safe in the knowledge that, although strangers in a strange land, this was Merrie England and, as long as they were circumspect, all would, in all probability, be right with the world for the uncertain length of their stay.

Now Mike (32)

The day was going from bad to worse.

The police had taken statements and suggested that the parents of all three boys would have to be told. Lacy had asked if Mike or Bert wanted to make the calls rather than have the families contacted by the local police. Mike had realised that it would be far better to have one of them give the bad news, but wasn't looking forward to it. Bert was in no state to talk to anyone, he seemed to have retreated into his own private world of agony over the disappearances and Mike had undertaken to make the calls.

'Sooner, rather than later.' Lacy had suggested, 'Before the press get hold of it.'

That had shaken Mike. It was only then that the full enormity of their predicament had struck him. If the boys were lost, what had happened to them? They had been their responsibility. It was he and Bert who would have to take the full brunt of any media coverage. Speculation as to how three young boys had vanished while in their care would be rife. Many a teacher's career had been smashed on the rocks of malicious gossip and tabloid headlines and effectively brought to a premature end by far less than this.

And what of the boys themselves? Fin was obviously going through some sort of breakdown. Surely they should have paid more attention to what had happened during the previous twenty four hours? It would look like they'd just left an unstable schoolboy to fend for himself and drag his friends off to God knew where. And the other two. What was their role in all this? Why had they left with Fin?

Add to that the history of Bert, and Mike knew they were in deep trouble.

Now three more boys who had been at the same school as Bert had disappeared in unexplained circumstances, and although Bert had never been under suspicion in the disappearance of Tony Athelston, this new one could reopen old wounds. Who knew where that might lead?

And then there was Bev. Her boss had evidently been involved in the previous disappearance and was thought, by Tony Athelston's parents at least, to have more to do with it than had been uncovered by the police.

They were all facing ruin.

Where in God's name were Fin and his two friends?

As he picked up the phone Mike checked the time. Seven thirty might be a little early to be making this call, but he dared not delay in case it just added to their problems. A delay in informing the parents might take on all sorts of unwanted connotations. He straightened up, standing almost to attention and read the contact numbers off the sheet in front of him, but which to call first? He decided on the LeMotts, then Tam's parents, leaving poor old Silas Carver, who had already had a wife walk out on him, until last. Mike wanted to delay, however shortly, having to break the news of Sim's disappearance.

He'd expected to have to wait for someone to answer the phone, bur surprisingly, it was picked up on the second ring.

'Hello, Jarmon LeMott.'

As ever the voice at the other end sounded friendly and Mike remembered that the few times he'd met Jarmon he'd always seemed a nice guy, perhaps a little shy, but always with a ready smile. That just made things worse.

'Hello?' came his puzzled voice down the miles from Cheshire.

Oh, Good Lord! Mike realised he was standing there with the phone and hadn't said anything yet.

'Uh, Mister LeMott, it's Mike Nutter. I'm one of the teachers up in The Lakes with the group from school.'

Now what? How did he break this to them?

'It's, erm..., it's about Fin, Mister LeMott.'

But before he could continue the voice at the other end broke in.

'Ah yes. Not unexpected Mister Nutter. Before you go any further – Fin's here.'

Mike's heart skipped and his stomach seemed to clench.

'And Tam as well.' Fin's father finished.

There was a pause.

'Mister Nutter? Are you still there?'

'Oh, errrr... yes. Just a bit surprised Mister LeMott that's all.'

A chuckle came down the line.

'Glad to hear it Mister Nutter. Glad to hear it – I'd be disappointed if you weren't.'

'What are they doing home?' Mike's mind was racing. How had they made the trip in the time, and why?

'Good question. We're just finding out know. But I'm afraid I can't tell you yet, since the stuff we're getting at this end sounds just a bit far-fetched.'

Mike groaned quietly and could think of nothing to say.

'Yes, Mister Nutter. From what Tam tells us, you know something of what they claim has been going on.'

'Yes, yes. Fin has been having some problems while we've been here. We still haven't got to the bottom of it, but rest assured we will try to.'

'Oh I'm sure you will Mister Nutter, I'm sure you will.' Again there was a hint of amusement coming down the line. 'In the meantime I'm afraid I've got a tale to hear and you're delaying the telling. So if there's nothing else...?'

Mike almost shouted down the phone.

'Please! Mister LeMott, don't hang up! How are the boys? I mean, they are alright, aren't they? We've been at our wits ends up here. The police have been out searching and everything. Those kids have put us through hell over the last few hours! Can I at least speak to one of them?'

'Errr... no, I don't think so. There are a few things we need to sort out at our end first, before either of them will be speaking to anyone and especially if the police might be – will be - involved. So, if that's all, I'm going to have to... '

'No, no! Just one thing before you hang up! Can you get them to ring their parents and let them know that everything's okay. I think it would probably be better coming from them.'

Again the chuckle from Cheshire.

'Oh I doubt that Mister Nutter. I doubt that very much. But I'll give Tam's parents a call. They'll probably want to come around and see him anyway. Maybe then we'll get a bit more sense out of both of them.'

Mike could hear cries of protest in the background.

'So don't worry Mister Nutter. I'll phone him. Things are well in hand - I think.'

There was a pause.

'Tell Mister Lightfoot and your wife that the boys are quite well, just disorientated I think. Yes, that's probably the best way to describe it. A bit disorientated. So please don't worry. You can call off the dogs, though you may have some trouble explaining how they got here from there in only about six hours, with no money and no transport.'

Mike couldn't think of anything to say to that. It was quite easy to make the trip in less time, but not when it was at least an hour on foot to the nearest decent road out of The Lakes. Add to that the fact that they had to find a driver going in the right direction, possibly several drivers, and it seemed unlikely that they could do it. Especially in the dead of night.

Another obvious question was why would they do it?

'So anyway. You have a think about how you'll sort it out at your end and I'll speak to you later. Could I have a number I can contact you on? I assume you'd rather not discuss this in the hostel with all the boys around if you can avoid it?'

'No, no, of course Mister LeMott.'

He gave Fin's father his mobile number and with only the briefest of goodbyes Jarmon LeMott was obviously about to ring off.

'Mister LeMott!' Mike hurried on. 'One last thing.'

'Yes?' came the exasperated answer. Fin's father wanted to get back to his son, understandably.

'You mentioned Fin and Tam.'

'Yes.' This time the word had a hint of suspicion behind it. 'They're both here and they're both fine, as I said.'

'Yes.' said Mike in turn, but with more than a little concern. 'But where's Sim?'

The silence at the end of the line was eloquent.

Then came one very quiet word.

'Bugger.'

'Are you still their Mister LeMott?' asked Mike.

'Umm... yes. And I'm afraid neither of them has explained that. I'm going to have to go now and try to get to the bottom of what's been going on. I'll call you back as soon as I know anything.'

'No please! Mister LeMott, can you ask them now? Just to put our minds at rest? We've had a bloody awful night and would feel much happier about things if we knew they were all safe.'

'Hang on a sec.'

The line went quiet as Jarmon pressed 'Hold'.

Mike stood holding the silent receiver to his ear, straining to hear anything from the other end. Cheshire stayed silent for what seemed like several minutes, but was probably only a few seconds. When Jarmon came back on the line he was sounding far less sure of himself.

'They say he should have come back with them. They're going to try to explain things but they both reckon it will take a bit of time. I'll let you know as soon as I know anything more. I'm afraid you're going to have to settle for that.' The voice from home was sounding distinctly unsettled. 'Sorry Mister Nutter, but I must go now. I *will* call back as soon as possible.'

And with that the line went dead.

'No! Mister LeMott!' called Mike, but the only noise that greeted his frantic cry was white.

Well that could have gone better...

Mike stared unseeing at the wall as he replaced the phone and turned, to find both Bev and Bert standing behind him. Bert was puce with barely suppressed rage.

'So the little buggers went off home, did they? My God. When I see them they'll get what for. The little bastards. I'll have them expelled, that's what I'll do. You'll back me up on this won't you Mike? The little swines.'

Bert was almost ranting and Mike put a hand on his shoulder.

'Actually, no Bert. I won't. And it's just swine by the way, it's plural as well as singular.'

Bert looked ready to explode and Mike smiled at the two of them. Bev just looked relieved, but Bert was incandescent.

'After the night they've put us through. And the police. Thank God the other boys don't know what's happened.'

He shook off Mike's hand.

'And you give me one good reason why we shouldn't go straight to the Headmaster when we get back. Or call him today for that matter, why wait 'til we get back?'

'Because there's something going on here that we don't understand yet, Bert.' Mike was, he thought to himself, being very patient and clear-headed now. Bev would be proud of him, but later, after she'd had a chance to think about it. Probably.

'Come and sit down and I'll tell you what the problem is.'

They returned to the lounge and settled once more onto the seats they'd occupied when Lacy had been questioning them. The fire a distant memory, the room was again chill and gloomy, not yet warmed by the sun which would not enter the room for several hours.

'Well?' asked Bert truculently.

Mike gave a short, small smile.

'Look Bert, are any of them the sort of lads who would run off for no reason?'

Bert nodded his head defiantly.

'Yes! I caught Fin acting the goat and gave him a good bollocking and he decided that life wasn't fair and he was going to take his ball home.'

'The ball being Sim and Tam, eh Bert.' put in Bev unhelpfully.

'Yes, if you like. The little twerp ran off home to Mummy and Daddy, like the spoilt little brat he is.'

'But Bert, they're not like that. Any of them, are they?'

There was no answer to that that would satisfy Bert, and Mike knew it.

It was easier for him to just ignore it.

'So what did happen last night then? Answer me that!' asked Bert through gritted teeth.

'I don't know Bert. That's the point. And until I do I'm not going to try to second guess anymore. And we also have a new problem, well sort of.' The others looked at him as though already prepared for the worst.'

'Go on.' rumbled Bert.

Mike looked up towards the window, now awash with early morning sun.

'We don't know where Sim is. Apparently only Fin and Tam arrived home. Fin's dad is trying to find out where he is.'

'Oh my God.' moaned Bert and Bev gave a strangled gasp.

'So I want to see both of them before I do anything rash.' finished Mike.

He glanced over to his wife.

'Don't you agree, Bev.'

Bert also looked across and she blushed slightly.

'Well I don't think it's really up to me, is it love? I mean, you're the teachers here, not me and I can understand why Bert is so mad.'

Bert looked triumphant.

'Ah hah. See Mike? Even Bev agrees with me, she just doesn't want to say so because she'd have to side with me against you.'

Mike shook his head sadly and Bev interrupted whatever he was about to say.

'Bert! That's not it at all, I simply meant... '

Only for Bert to cut across her.

'Alright, come on, give us your opinion. You're a professional at this Bev, what do you think we should do given that those two little sods ran off home without Sim? They've dumped him somewhere...' the phrase made him pause because of all it might imply and with a calculating expression he continued, 'and buggered off home. What can they have done? You deal in child psychology. Do you think we should forgive the little dears whatever they've done, or give 'em a bloody good kick up the arse?'

Bert's voice was rising and Bev made urgent shushing motions.

'For goodness sake Bert. What's got into you? Keep your voice down or you'll have an audience if the boys are up and about.'

She sat back in her chair.

'Let's all calm down and at least try to discuss this rationally, shall we? It certainly doesn't help that none of us had had more than a cat nap all night.'

Bert subsided slowly, but still looked aggrieved and Mike sat forward looking intently at his wife.

'Okay then Bev, what *do* you think we should do?

'Well for a start I don't think we should rush at this. We need to talk to the police first before they take things any further. For all we know they're organising a full scale search - helicopters and all the rest. We have to think of what we'll tell the other boys, particularly Willis. He'll be the first to want to know why his friends are at home instead of here. So what do we tell them? And we need to know what's happened to Sim. That's my biggest worry.' She shook her head. 'But I can't imagine that Fin and Tam would do anything to endanger him.' Her voice sounded plaintive in the silence of the room. 'I just can't.'

'Oh, don't worry about telling Willis.' said Bert with a growl. 'I'll let him know how his mates ran off home. I don't see why we should make up stories to protect them.'

'But what about Sim?' asked Mike. 'Should I ring his dad?'

Neither of the others had an answer.

'What if he's not home? What do we do then?' asked Bev. 'Maybe Fin's dad will come back to us with some good news. Just for once in this debacle there has to be some of that, surely.' But even to her that sounded a bit feeble.

'We'll sort that out when we know more, I suppose, but we can at least try to keep a lid on things here. I'll let Willis know, but not with anyone else around. No point in starting gossip.' said Bert. 'But we can't keep trying to hide what's happened.'

Mike shook his head as if unsure, but after considering it for a couple of seconds, he realised Bert was probably right. If they tried to make excuses or cover it up it they might just be storing up trouble for later on, and maybe if Bert could get it off his chest while he spoke to Willis, he'd be a bit more conciliatory when it came to making other decisions.

'Okay Bert, you do that.'

Bert nodded, satisfied with this small victory for now and crossed his arms as he sat back.

'And could you talk to the police too?' asked Mike, much to Bev's surprise. Mike shook his head slightly at her raised eyebrow. 'It's probably better coming from the more senior teacher here. Plus they'll get the same story as Willis. But we must try to stop the other lads inventing things. Let's just tell them the three of them were sent home in the night for some infraction of the rules. Tell them you took them, Bert. That would also explain why we all look like death warmed up.' He cringed at the inappropriate sounding phrase.

He nodded towards Bert.

'Okay Bert?'

Bert nodded sharply, then pushed himself to his feet using his hands on the arms of his chair.

'Better sooner rather than later then.' he quipped as he strode from the room to make the call.

Bev looked concerned.

'Are you sure we should let Bert do it? After all he's hardly sympathetic towards Fin and Sim, or Tam. He may make things worse for the three of them when the time comes for them to explain what's going on to a wider audience?'

Mike shrugged.

'It's possible, but I think it's probably better to give him something to do rather than dwelling on last night and the way he reacted when the boys went missing. I've never seen him so morose. I mean, you saw him - he looked like a man heading for a breakdown and I don't think it really matters what we say, it's going to take a long time for him to forgive Fin and the others for putting him through that.'

He heaved a huge sigh.

'What made them do it, Bev? I know you hardly know them, but they always seemed well adjusted and level headed. I'm still finding it hard to believe that they just ran off, but what else are we supposed to make of it? Bert gives Fin a bit of a telling off and he ups and runs home, taking Tam and Sim with him. It all seems so implausible.' He looked unsettled. 'And what's happened to Sim?'

Bev sat forward and reached over to take Mike's hand in hers.

'It's all rather pointless even trying to work it out until we know what they've told the LeMotts. We have to wait for them to call back, then maybe we'll have more idea about what they were thinking when they left. I think the best we can do is carry on as though nothing out of the ordinary has happened, for their sake as well as ours. I agree with you, it does seem so out of character from what you've told me about them.' She paused. 'On the other hand, you can't argue with the fact that Fin does seem to have a problem and it seems to be getting worse.'

The two of them gazed into each others eyes.

'And of course, if Fin is to be believed, maybe something happened that none of them could control.'

The sentence was left to hang in the air like a feather awaiting a nudge from a summer's breeze.

'Well, as you say, maybe we're better off not thinking about it too much just at the moment.' said Mike quietly.

Bert re-entered the room, rubbing his hands, with a beatific smile.

'Hah! Let's see them talk their way out of this.'

Mike looked alarmed.

'What? What did the police say, Bert?

Bert sat himself down again with an 'Oomph' and a self satisfied smile.

'They're sending one of their men around to see Fin sometime this morning. And Tam too, at some point. They'll want to know what's happened to Sim. But I let them know it would have been Fin who started it all. Soft lad Tam will have just followed along.'

He looked almost smug.

'Wasting police time - as well as ours – at the very least, they said. Going to give them a good talking to. Maybe that will teach the little beggars. Goodness knows what they'll want to do with them when it comes to Sim'

'Oh God, Bert.' Mike seemed to deflate into his chair. 'I hoped you'd just tell the police we'd sort it out. Now who knows what the boys will say. You may have just made things worse instead of better! For God's sake man, what's got into you?'

Bert looked taken aback at the vehemence of his friend's outburst.

'What do you think their parents are going to do? Just sit back while some copper harangues their sons - on your say so!' Mike looked ready to erupt. 'And what are they going to say to the Silas Carver? You've dug a damn great hole for us as well as them, Bert!'

Bev reached out to calm her husband, whose voice was rising dangerously.

Bert took the opportunity to launch a counter attack.

'Now just you hang on a minute. You're the one who said 'Go and deal with it'. I've just made sure they know who's in the wrong here and it's not us!'

Going red in the face, Bert thrust himself to his feet and aimed a finger shaking with anger at Mike.

'So don't you start getting on your bloody high horse with me Michael Nutter. You're too damn soft, that's your trouble. So you can just bugger off!'

And with that Bert was gone. Leaving a chill in his wake that made Bev shiver and wrap her arms across herself.

'Oh Lord, what has he done?' breathed Mike. 'There's more to this than he's letting on. Why has he got it in for Fin and Tam? Yes, I know that we could have all done without last night's problems, but I'm sure that this isn't the way to cope with it, and until yesterday I would have said Bert would have agreed with me. We needed to keep this quiet, now we've got the local coppers involved too and sooner or later it's all going to come back and bite us. We've still got a missing schoolboy, in all probability. Doesn't the stupid berk realise that. They were our responsibility and now he's bringing in the police again.'

Mike slumped in his chair and gave another heartfelt sigh. He still looked ready to cry and Bev was at a loss as to how to make things any better.

'Let's face it love, the police were never going to just let this drop, were they?'

Mike shook his head slowly as he whispered. 'Lord help us all.'

Bev couldn't think of anything to say to that.

They both sat in gloomy silence.

Then Fin, Tam and Simeon (33)

Amazingly Sim found himself forgetting the strangeness of their situation as he bumped along on the cart. Tam had dozed off next to him and Fin had been asleep for a fair while, but Sim was feeling more excited than he could ever remember. He reckoned they were probably somewhere around sixteen hundred. Certainly Elizabeth was on the throne, that much he'd gleaned from references to Her Majesty and a couple of other names he half remembered from his history lessons. Edmund and Kate made pleasant travelling companions and so far Sim had managed to steer clear of anything that might show him to be almost completely ignorant of the day to day workings of the old world of which he was now a part.

Edmund was delivering wood to a carpenter in Rowington, who was working on a large Hall being built on the edge of the village. It seemed that the woodsman would provide the timber and possibly some labour for the building, whilst Kate would visit with the family of the builder, whom her father obviously considered a possible match for his daughter. Kate, it seemed, did not altogether agree with her father. Adam Woods was the son of a builder, well known in these parts, and, on the death of his father, he had taken on the role of head of the household. He lived with his sister and mother in the centre of Rowington and had made plain his liking for the woodsman's daughter. Kate agreed that Adam was a comely young man with a good head on his shoulders, but she intimated that there was still too much of the lad about him. Too much at least, for her. She had no desire to be wedded to a well formed young man with still too much of a roving eye and a head far too hot.

For some strange reason Sim felt rather pleased by that.

As midday approached they reached the village of Rowington and, when the cart drew to a halt at the edge of the green, Tam roused himself and Sim shook Fin awake. The three surveyed their new surroundings. Although the village looked to be quite large, there was only one single, well-defined road. It came in from the south and ran straight past the green. They had stopped outside a tavern which stood detached from its neighbouring shops – two, it seemed, for the entire village. Between the surrounding houses were worn grass tracks, all of which led to the green. Opposite the tavern, some fifty yards away, stood a small stone-built church, fronted by a huge oak tree. The entire community occupied little more than a clearing in the surrounding woods, but some of the houses, particularly those alongside the church, had the look of money. A small population, but not a poor one Fin guessed.

As they climbed down they said their 'fare-thee-wells' and bowed again to both Edmund and Kate, with Sim lingering longer in the pose than the others, smiling up at the girl. Kate giggled and blushed. Edmund looked less pleased, Fin noticed and gave Sim's arm a tug. Tam waved happily as they turned to leave.

'Come on, time we were off.' urged Fin, and Tam nodded.

'Oh yeah, off where?' Sim was still watching Kate as she walked around the back of the cart. Even Fin couldn't help laughing quietly when he realised she was mincing away from Sim, twirling a long golden lock between her fingers and making cow-eyes over at him as she joined her father, who was deep in conversation with a tall, handsome young man in his late teens, whose hair was almost a match for Kate's.

'Watch it Sim, she's got her eye on you and Edmund doesn't like it.' laughed Tam, who'd apparently given up the hunt, but still enjoyed watching Kate teasing Sim. And that's all it was to her - a bit of fun with three lads she probably wouldn't ever see again. A chance for her to try out her womanly wiles, to hone her skills.

'Yup, I know. He's a nice enough chap, but suspicious as The Devil.'

'Who can blame him with a daughter like that to watch over. I don't think she cares much for being treated as a child though. At her age, around here and now, she's probably ripe for marriage.'

'Ummm... and I think that *that*' Sim nodded over towards the tall blonde-haired young man. 'must be lucky ol' Adam Woods.'

Indeed the man could hardly take his eyes from Kate as she stared over at Sim. Whilst he greeted Edmund, Woods noticing her preoccupation and, looking over, his face darkened.

'Ooops! Careful Sim. The last thing we need is trouble with the locals.' Fin nodded towards the frowning man. 'And he looks as though he'll be a bit useful with his hands.' He slapped Sim on the back and gave a short mocking laugh. Both he and Tam knew that although Sim was used to manual work, often helping his dad shifting engine blocks and suchlike at weekends, he would be no match for the older boy - more a man - who looked for all the world like a throwback to the Vikings. As though to confirm the impression, Woods flexed his considerable muscles and gave a slight sneer as he stared across.

'Looks like you made a favourable first impression on her, but I don't think Adam is going to want to be best buddies. Come on.'

He tugged at his friend's sleeve again.

Sim still watched the scene intently.

Edmund put his arm around Kate to turn here attention back to the man he hoped to make his son-in-law, and Kate smiled once more at Sim and said something to her father. Whatever it was, it didn't go down well with Woods, who voiced an angry retort as he glared again at Sim.

The object of his ire sighed and, giving a final wave, turned away.

'True enough, Fin me old mucka! So, where to now?'

'Which way be London, ahah!' cackled Tam doing his best pirate captain impersonation, with one eye closed and a great grimace on his face. 'Come me young rapscallions, 'tis time to get us gone from here!'

Sim grinned too.

'Great, I'm stranded four hundred years from home with a half blind nerd and a halfwit.'

'Oi. I'm not a nerd.' said Fin in a hurt voice and for a moment Sim thought he really had offended his friend.

'Come hither, foul prattler.' laughed Fin giving the lie to the impression he'd created, and with their arms around each others shoulders the three danced like Artful Dodgers as they made their way up the track towards a large barn-like building at the northern edge of the green. Fin fancied he could hear Kate laughing behind them and laughed himself at the thought of the beautiful young maid enjoying their antics.

Edmund had suggested that they may find another waggoner at the livery stable in the barn, who might be willing to help them on there way.

As they made their rowdy progress towards some hoped for further transport, Sim gasped between guffaws.

'So what's brought on this sudden change in demeanour Fin? You were like a wet weekend earlier.'

'A quick kip makes all the difference. That, and the fact that you and Tam are right. There's nothing we can do about going home, so we might as well make the most of it until I manage to whisk us back somehow. I've never been gone this long before, but worrying ain't gonna help. So with a hey-nonny-nonny, let's get on with it!'

'Yeah, bring on the Stick and Bucket dance!' cried Tam as he danced a quick and very inexpert jig. All three laughed again.

At a cry from Kate and a shouted warning from Edmund they turned to find Woods bearing down on them and all three involuntarily flinched at his aggressive growl. He was looking positively murderous - and was aiming for Sim. He grabbed the front of the younger man's shirt and pulled him forwards, until their faces were mere inches apart and Sim's feet, for all his newly acquired and fast growing man-boy size, were barely touching the ground.

'Thou cozener! Mayhap thou has sought to impress my leman Kathryn betimes, yet now shall I catechise thee in the art of choler. The maiden is mine! Long have I courted her and now thou would seek to steal her away. Thou art an atomy, hardly worthy of mine attention, and I shall spare me little time on thee! Thou art but a malapert rudesby.'

As he raised his fist, Fin jumped forward to try to free the struggling Sim. He grabbed for Wood's hands only to find the older man's wrists were like banded steel. Although making no impression, Fin was an annoyance Woods could do without and he struck out with almost impudent nonchalance at the boy. He caught Fin a glancing blow on the side of the head and Fin stumbled backwards, his spectacles falling beneath him as he fell to the ground.

Sim was making ineffectual attempts to ward off the blows that Woods was aiming at him while Tam flapped around them, making high pitched squawks of fright and indignation.

Panic had Sim in its grasp and wasn't about to let him go. His hands flailed at his attacker but tears were blinding him – not so much because of the pain, although his head felt at though it was being pummelled by a gorilla, but more because of the shame of being totally unable to defend himself, and his two mates were neither use nor ornament. He'd never been in a position like this and stood no chance of beating off the bigger man. Behind the tears his vision was clouding and there was a buzzing in his head.

Again there came an angry shout from Edmund and Fin could hear running feet. From his position at ground level he had a very blurred view of a very small slice of the world. The smell of the damp ground was in his nostrils, the muddy earth on his face and hands. There was also a trace of something else too, a slight reminder of bodily functions. His hands scrabbled around for his glasses and, when he finally got them back on nose, he realised they were going to be next to useless. Both lenses were scratched and one was cracked pretty well straight across.

This was too bloody much!

Fin leapt to his feet and jumped back to help Edmund in his struggle with Woods. His anger was rising now. What the flaming hell did this prat think he was doing? Sim hadn't been doing anyone any harm. He and Kate obviously liked each other and had got on well during their short trip. They'd enjoyed a friendly chat, nothing more, and besides Edmund had been sitting beside his daughter throughout, but Adam obviously saw things differently. It was bloody typical of Sim to end up in this sort of a situation, but it was up to his friends to try to restrain the moron who was shaking him like a rag doll whilst bellowing abuse.

The trouble was, the moron had lived a life of hard graft, and Sim and his companions were a trio of softy-Walters by comparison.

Fin grabbed at for Wood's wrists again.

Good Lord, but he was strong! His hands had all the softness of the oak he worked with every day. Work-hardened, they were like tanned leather wrapped around anvils. It took both Fin and Edmund to pull Sim's attacker away, with much cursing from the older man. Finally they freed Sim, who had turned a curious shade of puce and was retching as he fell to the ground on hands and knees.

Edmund pulled the golden haired youth to face him – incandescent with rage.

'Thou art a fool Adam Woods! God's Blood! A simpleton would'st have more sense than thou. What! Do you mean murder to a stranger who hast done thee no injury? Thou art an unmuzzled dog to act so. Marry, I would not have my daughter e'en in the same house as such as thee! Certes thou shalt not have my Kate to be thine. Thou art a hasty-witted puttock! Aroint!'

He thrust the man away and bent down to haul Sim to his feet, then turned again to face Woods, who stood shaking with barely suppressed rage.

'Begone, thou blackguard!' shouted Edmund again, and turned with ill-concealed disgust back to Sim.

Fin and Tam had been trying to comfort theirs friend, who was still gagging and holding his neck with both hands and breathing hard. Not being used to open aggression of this sort he was at a loss as to what to do. This was so far beyond the day-to-day bullying that he'd had to endure at school. He'd never been so close to such animal violence and was feeling very shaken himself. He was thankful for Edmund in more ways than one; for his strength, righteous anger and help.

'Sim, are you alright?' asked Fin holding his friend by the shoulders and trying to help him straighten him up.

'The bugger was trying to kill me! He's a flamin' nutter Fin.' gasped Sim.

'Don't I know it Sim. You're only standing there because of Edmund. We weren't much use... sorry.' Fin smiled wanly through cracked glazing and a bruised face and Tam stood back a little, looking shame-faced at how ineffectual he had been during the fracas. Fin wiped his hands on his jeans and sniffed. 'And to make things worse, I can't really see much now.'

He squinted at his mate and looked set to cry.

Sim gave a final hacking cough and gave his neck a rub as Kate stepped up to him, having given her erstwhile boyfriend a wide berth.

'Master Simeon, prithee make no further ado!' Even Sim would have admitted that he wasn't in any position to take matters further with Woods, even if he had been inclined to, but was pleased that Kate appeared to think he was capable of taking the fight to the now retreating builder. 'By my troth, I did'st not think to cause such fuss from such a small comment. I did but say that thou were amiable company. No more than that.'

'Mayhap you were right in thinking Adam too hot-headed.' said Edmund eyeing the retreating man dolefully. 'Though, in truth, I had never seen sight of this side of him. Fie! What a fool he be. For ne'er would'st I deem him fit to be relative to me and mine. How are my simple plans flown, like leaves in the wind. How fair thee Simeon?'

'Bloody sore!' croaked Sim.

Edmund couldn't help grinning, though unsure of the exact meaning of Sim's phrase the import was obvious .

'Aye, even such a bawcock as thee would not overcome Adam Woods when he has set his hands upon thee. Thy neck dost bear witness e'en now to thy trials at the hands of that knave. Come, we shall go thither to the tavern, where thou mayest sooth thy throat with an ale.'

As they made their way across the green Kate fell in beside Sim and made soothing noises. Fin couldn't help feeling that his friend was laying it on a bit thick, even though a dark bruising was beginning to colour his neck.

As they followed Edmund, Tam was aware of the curious stares from the few villagers around the green and the outright animosity being aimed at them from Woods and his cronies, as the man pleaded his case to all who would listen. Angry sounds of agreement and the sharply nodding heads of those around him made it obvious whose side they would take in any future dispute between him and his three adversaries.

Edmund indicated the building that rejoiced in the name of 'The Travellers Rest' and the five shaken companions made their way in, to sit at a long table; Fin, Sim and Tam on one side, father and daughter on the other.

Edmund ordered five blackjacks of ale and turned his attention to Fin.

He was looking at the broken spectacles as Fin turned them over in his hands.

'And pray, master LeMott, what would it be that you inspect with such crestfallen mien?'

'Oh, these? These are my eyeglasses Goodman Turner. I do not see well without the aid of these.'

Edmund leaned over and took the glasses from Fin, turning them over in his big rough hands as though he hadn't noticed them before, although Fin had been wearing them all day. He held them up to his eyes and jumped as the world went very blurred.

'Never have I seen the like! And tell me young fellow-me-lad, how can'st these help anyone to see the world more clearly? They do but cast a fog upon mine eyes? Finbar LeMott, thou art truly a most strange boy.'

He eyed Fin with something akin to fear as Edmund continued.

'I have never seen glass worked in such a way, indeed rarely have I seen glass, even in such small amounts. How can lads such as thee afford such a thing?' he asked, looking askance at the trio in front of him. 'From whence have you come lads? Come, let us have no more dissemblance. We are, I hope, good enough friends now - certes after our brouhaha with that shandy Woods - to be trusted with knowing thy full circumstances.'

He looked down at the spectacles again and held them out to Kate while he waited for the boys' response.

'See Kate, the fine working on the metal, and the cleverness of the hinge here.' he said as he looked across at each of the boys in turn.

Kate looked up from the glasses to Fin, looking crestfallen.

'Methinks it is but little use now Fin and I doubt me that there are any in this shire who could repair such a strange article.'

'Aye, my thoughts exactly.' said Fin sadly. 'I'm going to be pretty much blind for the rest of the journey lads. This has really messed us up I'm afraid.'

Sim looked thoughtful.

'Edmund, this will sound a bit daft, but could you tell me the year please?'

Edmund looked nonplussed.

'What? I mistake your import Simeon Carver. Art though so lost that you know not even the year?' He stared in disbelief at the boys and his voice rose slightly. 'Gods Teeth, I will offer no more aid until you tell us whither thou hast come. I fear me that we have fallen in with three lads who suffer from some strange malady.' He snatched a quick glance at Kate. 'Mayhap, they are bewitched?' He took Kate's hands and edged her back into her chair, sitting back from the table.

The first reaction of all three boys was to laugh at the comment, but they immediately saw that both father and daughter were in deadly earnest. At this time, for all people like to think that under Elizabeth's reign things were moving away from the dark ages, now centuries behind them, in fact some things had changed very little. The two good, kind people sitting opposite were really prepared to believe that the three friends could be under the spell of a wizard or suchlike. The thought was quite stunning. They really did believe in magic!

Kate said in hushed tones 'Thou mean thou knowest not e'en the year in which we live?'

Sim blushed and looked from one to the other across the table.

'Look, it's a bit difficult to explain exactly what's been going on, but if you'll just trust us on this, I promise we'll try to let you know why we're having such a difficult time.'

Tam shook his head as though to clear his mind.

'It's just that everything's a bit weird at the moment.'

Edmund still looked puzzled and totally unconvinced.

In an angry whisper he said 'I have offered thee friendship and given thee aid in thy time of need and still I know not who thou art, whither thou hast come and why thou art in such seeming ill straits. And thee offer us "wyrd". Explain wyrd young ragamuffins, for I say we will do naught else until thou offer us some explanation. And do not repeat thy prattling of a heroic escape from unjust punishment, for methinks thou hast but woven a spider's web of deceit from the moment we met. I'll have no more of it!'

Sim looked across at Fin and Tam. Bit of a poser, this, he thought to himself. Both Edmund and Kate had shown them friendship, with little cause, and it did seem unfair that they should do nothing but lie. Then again, how on earth did they explain themselves to the man and his daughter seated opposite.

Kate made to speak, but Edmund gave her hand a hard squeeze.

'No Kate. We shall say naught 'til we have more than mean words from these three.'

Kate nodded.

'Yea father. In this we are in agreement. There is much here that requires more truth than we have yet been offered, for we have received little enough of that in the last few hours. Let me say only this: tis nearing the fortieth year of the reign of her gracious majesty Queen Elizabeth, the year of Our Lord fifteen hundred and ninety three.'

Sim's eyes lit up.

'Great!' he turned to Fin, 'This may sound a bit daft Fin, but I reckon we might be able to get your specs fixed.'

'What?' Fin was surprised, to say the least.

'Doctor Dee lives in Mortlake, near London.' said Sim. 'At least I think so. He's probably the only man in Britain who might be able to help us. Certainly he's the only one I can think of. And since we haven't anything specific to do while we're here, we might as well give him a try.' He was almost bouncing in his seat with excitement and grabbed the proffered tankard as the ale arrived. The blackjack appeared to be made of leather coated with tar – an ugly but serviceable tankard. He took a gulp and almost dropped his cup, 'Ugh! Flaming 'ell. Our beer's bad enough, but this is like dishwater!'

Fin sipped his drink but had the good grace to keep a straight face. Sim was right, it was like watered down slops. Tam was busy taking extravagant gulps.

'Doctor Dee... ummm... yes, but wasn't he a bit of a mystic? A bit frowned upon by all and sundry?' Fin remembered having read a book about the Queen's Conjuror the previous year that seemed to be about as in-depth as you could get about the mysterious man. 'Wasn't Walsingham after him?'

'Can't remember to be honest, but I read a book that mentioned he was one of the first men in the country to have a telescope. How big a step is it from telescope to glasses, eh?'

'Probably easy peasy!' gurgled Tam.

'Yeah, probably glasses are simpler. So, other than just sitting about, I can't think of anything else we should be doing. At least it gives us a reason for making for London, eh?'

Fin had to agree. At least there was a chance that he might be able to see better if they visited Mortlake. As it was he'd be bumbling about for the entirety of their 'visit' if they did nothing.

Sim was infecting them all with his enthusiasm.

'I'm sure we'll find it okay. Everyone around there will know where the infamous Doctor lives. I think even the Queen herself visits him.'

Fin's grin was a little lopsided, he'd just thought of a problem.

'Yeah, great Sim. How are we going to get to London? It'll take forever to walk, and we've go no other form of transport. We've been lucky so far,' He nodded over to Edmund and Kate. 'but if Adam Woods is anything to go by, we might not be so lucky in the future.'

'Ahhh, Fin. You're slipping back into your old ways. Let's just rely on serendipity. Something will turn up. Trust me.'

And blow me, thought Fin, something probably will. Things work out when Sim's around. Not always the way you might plan it – but it was surprising how good luck seemed to follow him about.

But possibly not today.

Edmund slammed his tankard down on the table and thrust himself to his feet. He shouted over to the tavern-keeper as he threw a small coin onto the table.

'Ho Tippler! Here's thy shot!'

With a withering glance at the three boys, he grasped his daughter's hand and bade her stand.

'Come Kate, we'll suffer no more of this stupidity. These buffoons do flout our friendship and we have better ways to spend our time! Come hither daughter, I am sorely disappointed in these milksops.'

He certainly sounded let down by the boys and without further word he turned on his heel and stamped out of the tavern without a backwards glance, a solemn looking Kate following in his wake, her eyes full of reproach.

Fin sat with head bowed and sipped his ale. Good Lord! It tasted even worse at the second attempt.

'Do you think there's any chance of a glass of water, Sim?'

'Shouldn't think so. Everyone drinks alcohol in the Elizabethan era; the water will probably have you trotting into the shrubbery all the time.' said Simeon with a laugh, but his expression was serious.

'I think we've just made another enemy lads.'

'Well probably not an enemy, but we've certainly lost a friend' said Fin.

'And they deserved better, I think.' said Tam. 'You two babbling on about Dr Doom, or whoever he is, didn't help either. They wanted an answer and they weren't being too unreasonable expecting one, were they?'

'No.' agreed Fin. 'Let's go and find them again and try to explain.'

Sim barked another quick laugh.

'And how do you propose to explain anything about what's going on, Fin?' he said.

The silence that ensued was eloquence itself.

Tam reached past Fin and swapped tankards.

'It's not half bad after the first couple of sips, not quite Boddies, but acceptable to the more educated palate.' he quipped. Then he saw the amazed faces of the others and Sim slid his tankard across to him without a word.

Sim was aware that Fin was no longer paying either of them much attention. He followed his friend's gaze around the room. Several of the patrons were clearly intrigued by the three strange young men in their midst and more than a few were passing whispered remarks as they studied the boys.

'Time we were off chaps.' whispered Fin as he and Sim rose from the table. He had to reach down and haul Tam to his feet by the shoulder as his friend struggled to down the last of the beer. Tam almost fell over the bench as he tried to negotiate his first step whilst taking a final pull on the blackjack.

'Waste not, want not lads.' he said, putting the cup back on the table.

'Come on Tam, leave it!' hissed Sim. 'There are more important things right now. We're going to have to find a way to earn our way for one. Any ideas Fin? I think we're well and truly stuffed so far as Edmund is concerned.'

'I have a feeling you could be right there.' admitted Fin. 'But it's hard to see how we can explain ourselves to anyone. Everything's so alien here – we just don't fit in.

Simeon looked puzzled as he nodded.

'But don't you think it's a bit odd that Edmund and Kate, and everyone else for that matter, haven't noticed that we're dressed all wrong and speak in a distinctly non-Elizabethan way?'

Fin nodded.

'Yeah., but have you noticed that when we talk to anyone they're not hearing what we say? There's an odd echo at the back of my mind whenever we talk to anyone. It's as though we've got a Babel Fish stuck in our ears. Edmund heard Old English and we hear modern English even though we were just chatting.'

'Oh, I'm glad you got that too. Hmmm… All a bit odd innit?' agreed Sim. 'And it's the same with the clothes. It's as though they see them, but only as they expect to see them. Let's face it, there should have been at least some curiosity about denim and cotton, but they seem to see what they expect to see and hear what they expect to hear. It must all be part of 'That Old Black Magic' that you weave so well.' He grinned again and pushed Tam towards the door. 'Anyway, this isn't getting the baby bathed. Let's be up and at it or we'll starve to death before you find out how to get us home, and skeletal doesn't suit me.'

Fin decided he was happy to abandon the tavern in search of... well none of them were sure about that, but Sim seemed confident that something would turn up. For the moment Tam was just along for the ride. He was happy to go where he was pointed, with a decidedly unsteady gait. The ale might have been watered down, but it was still more than enough to inebriate a thirteen year old whose only previous foray into alcohol was a sip of his mum's gin and tonic at Christmas.

As they re-entered the morning sunshine they looked about them, with Tam performing the feat of doing so with his eyes screwed shut.

'Lovely day!' he called out as he stumbled into Fin. 'Super weather for the time of year, doncha know!'

'Brilliant! Now we're down to two brains trying to sort this mess out.' said Fin.

'Well, let's be honest it was never more than two and a half, with Tam along, was it?' grinned Sim. 'Don't worry Fin – we'll be fine.'

The village wasn't exactly bustling. The sun was warming the air and the smell of the surrounding woods was filling the air with an earthy perfume. Sim noticed that the smells of nature seemed stronger than back at home; as though the air was more receptive to it. Maybe the lack of modern pollutants made you more aware of the odours of the world around you. Certainly the sky seemed a deeper blue than he could remember seeing before, the birdsong more startling. The whole world was more alive somehow. He took a deep, satisfying breath, filling his lungs with air of a purity that must be unknown in the modern day. He had an odd feeling of fitting in, of being home, despite the fact that at this time Daneham was probably no bigger than this little village at the moment, and unrecognisable as his boyhood stamping ground. True - it would have the nearby salt trade, but given that in four hundred years time it would still be little more than a hamlet, if they went there now it wouldn't look like home, anymore than this place. Nonetheless, this felt right. Like putting on an old jumper you find at the back of the wardrobe. Old and out of fashion, but somehow *right.* He shrugged as he and Fin took in their surroundings again in an attempt to decide what to do next.

Across the green they could see Edmund and Kate leaving for home, with Woods angrily muttering to a small group of evil-looking and drably dressed men and casting dark glances at the retreating pair.

'Can't help thinking we've ruined his day.' whispered Tam with a giggle as he eyed the bad-tempered builder.

'Aye.' answered Sim, 'And I'd rather not be seen by him just now. I reckon he'd like to take up where he left off and I don't fancy our chances, even if his mates don't join in, and frankly they don't look the types to just watch if there's a chance of knocking a couple of heads together. I'm not sure we should try to find a lift from anyone who might know Mister Woods.'

Fin nodded and, by mutual consent, the two headed into the trees beyond the church alternating between pushing and pulling their puddled friend between them. Once they'd entered the woods they sat Tam down and looked back.

'So, should we give the livery stable a try, Fin?' Sim asked uncertainly, with a worried glance back towards the hamlet.

'Maybe not, eh?' answered Fin, much to Sim's relief. 'Let's trust to good fortune again and just head off.' He looked off into the woods. 'Only we don't really know which way, do we?'

'Good point.' smiled Sim, 'But I'd feel a hell of a lot safer if we go it alone. I don't think the natives are going to be very friendly just now.'

'Phat! Wobbly bum! Molly whoppit.' blurted a giggling Tam, now lying at their feet as he studied the grass with alarming intensity, his nose thrust into the greenery.

'Thankyou Oscar.' replied Fin.

'We can always trust you to have a witty Wildean repost ready, can't we Tamburlaine?' said Sim, resisting the temptation to give Tam a good kicking. This was all they needed now he thought. Then he grinned, *ah, so what,* Tam was at least happy.

'Futtock!' giggled Tam rolling onto his back and staring unseeing into the treetops and then suddenly drumming his heels into the grass as though running in his drunken daydream.

'Plobby!' he called at the top of his voice.

To a background of nonsensical gibberish Fin and Sim contemplated their options and eventually concluded that they should try to make the journey on their own for now.

'So it's south, then?' offered Sim pointing into the trees.

'Okay, but we'd be better off on a track at least.' replied Fin.

With a nod of agreement and a sigh of resignation the two bent to help a now quietly sniggering Tam to his feet and bore him away, each taking an arm over their shoulders, in a generally southerly direction.

'Jeez! For such a little pillock he dunt 'alf weigh a lot.' grumbled Sim and then laughed along with Fin.

The going through the woods was quite easy, the trees being fairly sparsely scattered and the ground mainly short grass.

'Deer and other wildlife that's probably long gone in the twenty first century - I bet there's loads of it around now – maybe we should keep an eye out for wild boar and suchlike.'

At Fin's startled myopic stare into the distance Sim stifled a laugh.

'Don't worry mate, *I'll* keep a sharp eye out for bears and wolves.'

Fin didn't look that reassured.

'Daft bugger. You'll give me a feckin' heart attack!'

'Nah, trust me, we'll be fine.'

As they followed their slightly meandering path, Fin mused on their predicament, as he dodged the branches that suddenly emerged from the mist of his dreadful eyesight.

'How's your neck?' asked Fin as he stumbled along.

'Not bad at all. I know it sounds stupid, but I really can't feel it any more.' said Sim, with an air of surprise. 'I'd forgotten all about it.'

'And I can't see any bruising now.' said Fin.

'Weird. I would have expected traffic lights where Woods had me. I know it bloody hurt at the time.' Sim raised a hand and touched his neck gingerly, at the risk of dumping Tam. 'No. Not even a bit of an ache.'

'Odd.' said Fin. 'But if you recovered so quickly... if this time travel thing *helps* you recover quicker – and I can't see what else it could be...'

'No, I was never a particularly quick healer.'

'Right. So if time helps you stop bruising... and whatever... how come I still can't see?' asked Fin.

Sim mused over the question and saw the answer dawn on Fin at the same time as he came up with a reason.

'Maybe we stay the same as we were back home, do you think?' said Fin.

'Yeah, so injuries here may not last as long.' said Sim. 'A Tudor bruise can't exist on a body that hasn't been born yet.'

'But I'm not suddenly going to be able to see better.' said Fin, his disappointment evident.

'Well, you never know.' said Sim, trying to jolly him along.

'Yeah. So maybe we're immortal instead.' suggested Fin in an excited whisper. 'Maybe we can't die outside of our own time either.'

'Oh yeah? Well are you going to test that out Fin? 'Cos I know I'm not.'said Sim seriously. 'Let's not mess around with what we don't know okay?'

'But Sim, just think...'

'No Fin! Let's not *just think*. I like to be as optimistic as the next guy, probably more so, but I'm not going to take a gamble on being immortal. There are enough ways to die nastily here! We'll probably have plenty of opportunities to try to avoid being dead without looking for them.'

Fin looked crestfallen.

Sim couldn't understand why.

'You weren't really going to jump off a cliff or something to prove a point, were you?' he said.

'Course not.' said Fin emphatically, but Sim wasn't altogether convinced.

They stumbled along and Sim purposely let Fin crack his head on a low branch.

'See? Not much fun testing your theory is it?' he laughed.

'Buggroff.' Fin laughed back. 'I didn't say it wouldn't hurt did I?'

Even on the animal trails their progress was slow, hampered as they were by Tam.

'Pootle!'

Who was showing little sign of emerging from his self-induced trance.

'Where's Mumsy?'

Hic.

'He's not going to throw up is he? I always hiccup before I throw up.' said Sim.

Hic.

The two bearers tried to carry Tam at arms length, but that was so awkward as to be virtually impossible.

Hic.

They gave up and regrouped into their previous tight huddle, pressing on through the undergrowth.

'Sim. You know you mentioned Doctor Dee?'

'Yeah.' Sim replied. 'Whoa - watch the tree Fin'. Sim nudged Tam, and like a Newton's Cradle, steered Fin to one side, to avoid a particularly sturdy limb.

'Cheers.' said Fin. 'Well, do you really think it's worth trying to get to see him?'

Fin stumbled over a root and caught his balance using Tam, almost spilling the three of them into undergrowth.

Sim laughed again.

'Well, given that you can see about as well as a stone, and that we have nothing else to do, we might as well give it a try.' He guided Fin onto a more open stretch of path and made a great show of carefully aiming him down the centre of the channel between the foliage. 'Fire one!'

Fin grinned.

'Thanks. Yeah I *am* sure I read that he was one of the first Englishmen to have a telescope, and he made a pair of glasses, though I've no idea if they were any good.' He sounded as though he were trying to convince himself as he pulled his smashed spectacles out of his pocket and waved them in the general direction of Sim, 'but they can't be any worse than these.'

'True… true...' Sim chuckled. 'So let's see where we get to. In any event you'll probably whisk us back before we can get into any more trouble.' He let go of the comatose figure beside him and spread his arms wide to encompass the world around them, 'The sun's shining, the sky is blue. Things could be an awful lot worse, so, I say again, what have we got to lose? Eh?'

Tam had silently subsided to the horizontal like a ship hitting the ocean depths, pulling Fin down into an untidy heap beside him, and it took them a little while to hoist him up to a vertical position again.

'So stick your broken specs on and see if they're better than no specs at all, and lets be off to London. The bright lights, the towers, the open sewers in the streets…'

'Heads on spikes...' joined in Fin as they adjusted Tam between them.

They laughed together as they set off again.

'Oink!'

Since neither of the boys had been in the scouts, they had only a very sketchy idea of their direction and were basically trusting to the luck of the Carvers to bring them out somewhere worth the effort.

Then out of the trees ahead there came the strident cry of a man in distress and a second, female scream, that sliced the warm, still, midday air like a knife and stopped the two friends and their oblivious baggage in their tracks.

Now Tam (34)

Jarmon put the phone down and looked at each face around the table.

The silence in the kitchen hung around the boys as the two adults and Lilli sat and stared at Tam. Fin looked distinctly uncomfortable, Tam had now lost his air of gleeful excitement. It was obvious to both of them where the discussion had led and even Tam's cheerful mood had evaporated.

Well, how on earth do you respond to something like this? thought Jarmon. In his mind's eye he could see the lads comfortably ensconced in a nice warm and reassuringly padded room – all brilliant white and minimalist. A life sentence no doubt unless they could come up with a far better explanation than had so far been forthcoming. They hadn't mentioned what had happened to Sim and Jarmon had just assumed that he was back at home with Silas, but then why was Tam here instead of back with Sue and Ian, his parents? Something had happened that they weren't in a hurry to reveal, but time was running out if Mister Nutter was to be believed. It was time that Tam's story reached its end.

'Super tale Tam. More tea anyone?' asked Lidine brightly, apparently unaware of the lunacy only recently released and now prowling threateningly around the table.

'But Mummy, shouldn't we call the men in white coats?' giggled Lilli. 'I think Tamburlaine's gone to La-La land.'

'Lilli!' scolded Lidine. 'Tam is a guest in our house.' But then she spoiled the stern effect she was trying for, by smirking as he finished, 'Even if he has been holidaying with my son in Xanth. Or maybe Ankh Morpork.'

Now she was laughing openly with her daughter and with almost hysterical ease everyone ended up joining in – until they noticed that Jarmon was still standing stern-faced by the phone.

'Jarmon! For goodness sake. If we don't keep our sense of humour over this I think I may end up hysterical.' gasped Lidine, through tears of merriment that were rapidly drying up. 'I'm sure we should be more serious about this, but I'm not sure how.'

The merriment was now gone from the room and Fin and Tam were looking worried again. They knew the subject of Sim couldn't be put off any longer.

Jarmon returned to his seat alongside his son.

'Fin, where's Simeon?'

The import of his words were lost on Lilli.

'I bet Sim's still back in Ye Olde Days, Dad. Isn't he Fin?'

But Fin looked as though he were about to cry, and Tam looked little better.

'Well Fin?' asked Jarmon again. 'He's not here, is he, so where is he son?'

'I don't know Dad, and nor does Tam. Maybe he's at home.' But even as he said it he knew it wasn't true. Silas would surely have rung to find out if his son's friends were okay. It's what Fin should have asked his father to do straight away, but now he was afraid of the answer to the question his father has just posed. What had happened to Sim? While they were upstairs Tam had managed to convince him that all would be well – of all of them Sim was the one who always seemed to come out of things alright. But now they had to face up to the possibility that something was horribly wrong.

Memories of their departure from the past hung over him like a large, damp chilling cloak.

In truth, both he and Tam didn't know where Sim was.

Maybe he was home – but he doubted it - and from the look on Tam's face, his friend had the same doubts.

'Fin, you've got to tell us, and quickly. Mister Nutter tells me that the police were involved in an overnight search, so we have to assume that they may be round here soon to find out what's been going on, especially since we appear to have lost Sim and I'm not one hundred percent sure that what Tam's said so far is going to convince them?' The heavy sarcasm wasn't wasted on any of them.

'We don't know Dad. You could call Sim's Dad and see if he got home okay.' But even Fin could hear the lack of conviction in his voice.

Jarmon rose heavily from his seat and went, once again, to the phone.

'This is serious now lads. We've got to face the fact that no-one's ever going to believe your tale. While we've been laughing at Tam's retelling and maybe even keeping a vaguely open mind about it, sure as eggs is eggs no-one else is going to do.'

Both the boys looked dumbstruck.

'But Dad, we *are* telling the truth. Sim will be able to confirm it - then there'd be three of us. People would have to believe us then. What would they do if we all told the same story? Lock us all up in an asylum? They'd have to take notice, wouldn't they?

'I think I better had ring Silas. Let's not jump to any conclusions before we know about Sim.

He checked his watch and knew that a quarter to eight wouldn't be too early to catch Simeon's dad. Jarmon knew Silas well enough to know that he'd be about to head off to the garage where he worked, if he thought Simeon was still on the school trip. The same garage Jarmon and Lidine always used for servicing and any other work on their cars. Silas was not just a friend, he was a damn good mechanic, although his heart wasn't in it these days. He, like Jarmon, had begun to yearn after something else, something... better. '*It*' as Tom Good would have said. Though neither wanted to get back to the land, like in the sit-com, both were unsettled. Jarmon had turned to local politics, Silas had bought himself a wood-turning lathe and a seemingly endless collection of chisels and suchlike. Jarmon had been surprised to discover that Silas loved designing little puzzle boxes, with hidden hinges and secret locks. The children each had one, designed by the little mechanic with his love of wood. Though he wasn't averse to stair spindles and coffee tables, it was the little boxes that took most of his time.

Each to his own Jarmon had thought, and at least Silas could share his new interest with his son; Sim had already created several beautifully finished chests that doubled as fair-sized seats, with intricate turnings on the corners and superb carvings on the sides and lids. They'd agreed it was probably just a mid-life crisis, but it made everything uncertain when they looked to the future, and secretly both hoped it would be a short-lived episode in their lives. What on earth am I going to say if Sim isn't there? He thought to himself.

God help us.

He dialled the number and waited only two rings before Silas answered.

Those around the table heard only this side of the short conversation.

'Wotcha Silas. Sorry to ring when you're probably about to leave but I just thought I should let you know Tam is here with Fin.'

Pause… with a barely audible reply from the other end.

'Yes, gave us a bit of a shock too, mate.'

Again the pause, but shorter this time.

'Well, we were wondering if Sim was home too.'

Short pause during muffled response.

'No,no. I understand Silas. It's just that something happened last night and Fin seemed to think that Sim might be back with you.'

Tam looked over at Fin. It was now obvious that Sim wasn't home. Suddenly what had been a very awkward situation had nose-dived into an impossibly complicated one. Jarmon was right. Now it was going to be very difficult to persuade anyone that their story was true. It had gone from being a fantastic escapade with three friends to something far more sinister.

'Right Silas. I think maybe you should hear what they've got to say for themselves…' This time an obviously anxious interruption. 'No, no, nothing like that - it's just a bit unusual that's all and we're not clear on exactly where Sim is. Look it would be better if you could spare some time to pop over and listen in on it.' Jarmon ran his hand through his hair as he listened to Silas at the other end.

'So that's okay?' Jarmon bit his lip. 'Yeah, but once you've heard this you might decide to take the rest of the day off. At least one day.'

Final pause.

'Yeah, see what you think first then we'll decide what we should do. Okay Silas. See you in a couple of minutes.'

He replaced the phone and turned back to those sitting at the table, his face now seamed with anxiety.

'He's coming straight over, so we'll forgo the next episode until he arrives. We'd better give your mum and dad a ring too Tam.'

Tam nodded back looking very subdued now. Fin looked crestfallen.

'Dad, did you mean what you said about no-one believing us?'

Jarmon looked so sad it made Lidine want to take him in her arms and tell him everything was going to be fine, not to worry. The problem was this was beyond anything they had ever expected from Fin. It was, unfortunately, total madness, and even though they had treated it as a light-hearted prank until now, real life was about to come knocking at the door.

Jarmon looked at both the boys with a stricken expression.

'Well come on! Do you honestly expect people to just accept the story you've told us; that you and me laddo here have been back to sixteenth century Warwickshire. You have to admit' and here he looked both of them in the eye, 'that it does all sound more than a little far-fetched.'

Tam sat up straighter and looked his friend's father with an unwavering stare.

'We know Mister Lemott, but all three of us decided while we were 'away', that there wasn't anything better to do than just tell the truth. We both know it sounds ridiculous, but we do have some evidence of what we did. Though it's probably not going to convince many people.'

'Yeah, well let's save that 'til everyone else is here, okay?' It was a statement more than a question. 'I'll give Ian a call.'

With a heavy heart he lifted the phone again.

The knock at the door came after about ten minutes – Terry Wogan had, as usual, just crashed the eight o'clock pips on Radio Two and the kitchen had an air of expectation only lightly disguised by the silence that hung over breakfast. Lidine noticed that the unspeaking boys ate ravenously, as though they hadn't had a decent meal for a long time.

Fin nudged Tam as he spoke around another mouthful of bacon and egg.

'Here's where things start to get serious. It's going be tough from now on, so let's just do exactly as we agreed when –'

'Sshhh! Fin. We said we'd wait until Silas and Ian and Sue had heard a recap before Tam carries on.' said Lidine raising a finger to her lips as Jarmon went to answer the door. 'That's unless Silas wants to know about Sim straight away.' she sighed. 'And who could blame him, eh?'

'Sure Mum, but –'

Lidine shook the finger at Fin, with arched eyebrows.

'Tell you what Tam, I'll put on one of our favourite songs. I'm sure I've got it on a CD. Just wait 'til you here this.'

He ran off to the living room and returned with a CD that he placed on the kitchen hi-fi hanging on the wall. Jarmon was still at the door, the sound of muffled conversation reaching them in the kitchen and the voices became raised

Lidine looked up in surprise as the sound of a lute filled the kitchen. Fin hastily adjusted the volume as a clear female voice sang out a hauntingly beautiful song. This certainly wasn't the boy's usual fair of rock which, if not heavy, was leaning towards overweight. Jim Steinman it wasn't.

'Ah, Awake sweet love, though art returned.' said Tam with a sigh. 'Mister Dowland picks a mean orpharion, eh Fin?

Both boys had a twinkle in their eyes.

'No, this one's with a lute Sim. Not as silvery upon the ear, don't you think?'

'Most certainly Master LeMott.' grinned back Tam.

Lidine and Lilli rolled their eyes at each other.

'La - La Land.' muttered Lilli.

'Boys, for goodness sake, try to remember the dreadful situation we're all in.' said Lidine with exasperation.

Any further quips were forestalled by the arrival of Jarmon back in the room, closely followed by Silas. Dark unkempt hair and unshaven face detracted from what would have otherwise been an attractive if not exactly handsome face. Silas was looking harassed as he strode over to Lidine and gave her a quick peck on the cheek she raised.

'What's been going on Liddy?'

'Oh if only I could explain it Silas, but, as I'm sure Jarmon has told you, we can't make much sense of it either'.

The two boys looked crestfallen and the same thoughts went through both their heads at once.

'Oh no! Even she doesn't believe us.'

'We're sunk!'

'We're damned if we lie and really damned if we don't.'

'Simeon, where in the name of God are you?'

Jarmon stood behind Fin and stroked his son's hair, putting the other hand on Tam's shoulder.

'We're just waiting for Tam's parents, then we'll try to get to the bottom of this.'

'But where's Simeon, Fin?' Silas looked alarmed and transferred his gaze to Jarmon. 'Jarmon, what's happened to my son?'

'I don't know yet, but when everyone's here, we will sort it all out, won't we boys.'

Jarmon felt his stomach give a lurch when he felt the boys beneath his hands slump. It was probably then, for the first time that he realised just what sort of trouble they were in. He could almost feel the strength leeching out of the two young men before him. *They didn't think it was going to be sorted out! Just what had been going on? What had they done with Sim?*

As several ghoulish thoughts tried to muscle into his mind he shut the door on them as firmly as he could. He couldn't bring himself to believe either of them were capable of doing their friend any harm. It just wasn't in them. The three of them were .like the Musketeers, nothing could cause them to be anything other than ever the best of friends.

But like it or not, Silas needed an answer and nothing they'd heard from the boys thus far, was going to provide it.

'Don't worry boys, everything's going to be fine.' He patted their heads and gave their hair a quick ruffle.

There was another knock at the door and with relief he went to let Ian and Sue in.

Again there was a muffled conversation and then the kitchen door reopened.

The uniform shocked the whole room into a stunned silence.

'Good Morning.' said the policeman, who gave every appearance of thinking that the morning was anything but.

'Jarmon, what's going on? Where are Ian and Sue and why did you let *him* in? Can't we hear what's been happening before we have to bring in the police?'

'It's not down to us love. It appears that one of the teachers up at The Lakes has prompted his visit. Ian and Sue haven't arrived yet.'

The policeman held out a hand to Lidine.

'PC Flint.' he announced shortly, nodding towards the others in the room. 'Sorry Missus LeMott, but it sounds like yer lads here 'ave caused major problems. They've 'ad search teams out for most of the night up there an' there's a lot o' people wantin' an explanation.' The officer paused and his dark little eyes surveyed the room. 'Has the third child turned up yet or is 'e still missin?'

He spoke to Jarmon, but it was Silas who shook his head and replied.

'No, Sim is missing, but I'm sure Fin and Tam can explain.'

The policeman turned to the boys.

'Oh, I'm sure they can.' he said, with more than a hint of sarcasm.

Lidine was about to offer a retort, when the sound of a knock came again from the further end of the hall.

'I'd better get that - it will be Tam's parents.' said Jarmon as he left the kitchen.

Flint eyed the two boys as he spoke.

'The finger is bein' pointed at Finbar LeMott. Which of you two is he?'

Fin paled as he raised his hand slowly into the air.

'Oh, but this is ridiculous!' scolded Lidine. 'They've done nothing wrong have they? Not mugged anyone or stolen a car have they?'

The constable looked taken aback at the aggression in her voice.

'That, Missus LeMott has yet to be established.'

'It wasn't Fin's fault though. Well not really.' put in Tam loudly.

Lidine patted his arm, 'Quiet Tam. Best not make a fuss yet.'

Then, seeing the look on Flint's face, she quickly added, 'That's not to say we won't kick up a hell of a brouhaha if things get out of hand. Don't worry Tam. We'll all make sure Fin's okay.'

'Damn right.' chimed in Silas, which made Flint give him a stony glare.

'And you are the father of the missing child?' he asked coldly.

'Yes Simeon Carver is my son, and a friend of both of these lads. I'm sure he's okay. I'm also sure Fin and Tam can explain last night.' Even so Silas looked far from happy and Fin couldn't blame him. Although Silas knew them all, his son was missing and Fin didn't think they were going to be able to give him any sort of satisfactory explanation.

The policeman raised both hands, as though to deflect any criticism of his attitude. He was beginning to look flustered. The situation was heading in altogether the wrong direction. This was supposed to be a soft little job, just a some of kids who'd run off from a school trip, but everyone seemed to be very defensive, and even the missing boy's father was defending the two who were here, without apparently knowing where his son was!

The door opened and Jarmon entered followed by a small, jolly looking couple. Tam jumped up and hurried over to give his mum a hug.

'There, there luv.' she cooed, patting his head as she and her husband surveyed the room, both looking flustered at the sight of the uniform at the head of the table

'Silas, what's to do?' said Ian puzzled. Silas just gave a small shake of the head.

'Jarmon?'

'Best sit down Ian. I think PC Flint will have plenty of questions for us.' answered Jarmon.

The silence in the room as Lidine went to brew more tea was like a dark foreboding cloud.

Silas rolled a cigarette and Jarmon lit up, '*just to keep him company*'. Lilli frowned in disgust.

'Dad!' she said in disapproval, with a frown.

Flint spoke quietly into the uncomfortable atmosphere.

'I came here to find out wot 'appened last night. We 'ave a missin' person to find an' only two witnesses. I'm not 'ere to arrest yer son, or 'is friend - yet.' That sounded ominous to everyone. 'I've bin sent 'round ter find out wot 'appened last night. Now can ev'ryone just settle down, so that I can ge' some details? Everyfin' seems very confused from the little I've been told.'

The atmosphere calmed slightly and Lidine and Lilli sat down at the table with the boys. Silas and Jarmon remained standing, not taking their eyes off the policeman. Ian and Sue sat alongside Tam, she patting his hand lightly and giving him a small encouraging smile, he looking far more worried.

Flint took out a notebook which he laid before him on the table.

Within a couple of minutes Flint knew he was out of his depth. The kids were spinning some yarn about nightmares and thunderstorms – utter bloody rubbish. Added to that was stuff about time travel! He'd laughed at that and ordered them to stop telling such stupid tales and remember that he was a policeman. His position demanded that they tell the truth and he'd had enough. Unbelievably *all* the parents had leapt to their defence! Flint had the distinct feeling that he'd stepped into a madhouse. Maybe they were all in one of those bizarre religious cults or something – all brainwashing and group sex.

He prided himself on being able to dominate small groups with his glaring aggression, but even that seemed to have little effect here. The missing boy's father was obviously unhappy and wanted a realistic explanation of where his son was, but seemed unwilling to believe that he had come to any harm. The two kids were obviously hiding something and using this ludicrous story to cover it up. He had a feeling that they thought they were clever enough to cover up whatever they'd done, but they'd not counted on Magnull Flint! He let the others in the room allow the kids to spout on for a few more minutes, but finally he'd had enough.

'So yer stickin' ter this story are yer?' he asked with obvious disdain.

The room fell silent at his interjection.

'I'm sorry?' replied Lidine. 'What are you implying?'

'Oh, I'm not implyin' anyfin' Missus LeMott. But I fink I should point out tha' no-one in 'is right mind is gonna believe a cock and bull story like that.'

'Now just a minute ...' started Jarmon, but the PC interrupted.

'Mister LeMott. I 'ave never, in all my years, 'eard so much rubbish.' He continued despite raised voices around the table. 'These two,' he waved his notebook in a nonchalant gesture, ' ave so far said nothin' ter indicate ter anybody that they are prepared ter give any indication of wot 'appened to their friend - of wot maybe they did ter 'im.'

Jarmon was on his feet.

'How dare ...'

'Mister LeMott! I am a police officer. I am not collectin' stories fer a fairy tale book.' He kept on despite the rising tide of sound from Jarmon and Lidine. 'Do not raise yer voice to me! Eever of yer.' he thundered. 'I 'ave finished 'ere for now, but I can promise yer that these two will 'ave a lot more explaining ter do.'

He stood up and put his notebook back in his pocket. As he turned to leave he played with the button on his biro.

'Please do not leave the area. In fact I'd stay in yer 'omes, cos someone from the station will be ringin' as soon as I make my initial report.' he snorted to the room in general. 'And I only 'ope for your sakes that yer decide to tell the truth.'

He opened the door and strode down the hall without a backward glance.

At the sound of the front door closing the room erupted with talk again, everyone with an opinion of the policeman who had so enraged the parents present.

Quietly Silas sat down between Fin and Tam, seemingly un-noticed by the others and, putting a hand on Fin's arm, asked gently 'Fin, where's Simeon?'

The room fell silent and Fin looked across Silas, to Tam. All eyes were on him and he knew he had no answer to give this gentle man, who wanted so desperately to know about his son.

'Mister Carver, you know that Sim and Tam are my best friends. They stuck with me through all the crap I had to take at school, when we were all bullied by idiots who thought we were fair game, just because we didn't fit into their idea of what we should be. We always looked out for each other.'

He realised that he was using the past tense.

'We will always look out for each other. Like the three musketeers – All For One and all that. You have to believe me when I tell you that we would never do anything to hurt Sim. He's like a brother to us.' Tears were in his eyes and he did nothing to try to stop them. Silas could see that this was hard for the boy, but he had to know.

'Sim feels the same, I know Fin. But what happened last night? And why are the police involved?' Silas looked around at Tam, including him in the query. 'Where is my son?'

Jarmon put a hand on Silas's shoulder.

'Silas, I'm afraid you, and Ian and Sue, are going to have to suspend your disbelief for a while. Tam has been telling us the weirdest story you're ever likely to hear.' He saw both the boys stiffen as he said it, but there was no other way to try to help them here.

'They're both adamant that what they're saying is true and until we know for sure, we've got to take it at face value.' At Silas's questioning look he hurried on. 'If they continue with their story, we're going to have major problem with everyone who hears it, but I, for one, have no alternative but to believe them. Fin is my son. He wouldn't lie about something like this and nor would Tam. If they did they'd certainly make more of an effort to come up with something better than this.'

'Yes, but what is *this*?' asked Silas, more urgently now.

'Jarmon, what on earth have they told you?' asked Sue, with more than a hint of anxiety in her voice.

Ian looked across at his son. 'Tam, what's going on?' he asked gently.

The whole atmosphere in the little kitchen had become tense – expectant.

Neither Fin nor Tam seemed able to say anything. Silas was losing patience now.

'Look, I know you were very close. I know you wouldn't intentionally hurt him.' Fin looked stung by the qualifier and leaned back in his seat, his shoulders dropping. 'But all this is beginning to sound as though there's something very nasty you're not telling me.' He stood and moved around the table to sit opposite the two families. He gave each boy a searching, slightly haunted look. 'Tell me everything. Now.'

He hadn't raised his voice, but the finality in the command was hanging there for all to hear. Ian and Sue moved closer to their son and Lidine moved behind Fin and put both hands on his shoulders as though to reassure him with her presence, her unqualified trust.

Jarmon moved over to the kettle.

'Okay Tam. You'll need to recap what you've already told us, but be brief, alright. Silas and you're mum and dad, need to know it all.'

He switched on the kettle and looked over to the other parents. 'But I meant what I said. This is going to be hard to swallow. All we can do is let them tell it. Then we can decide what to do about it.'

Silas nodded, and with a sigh, Tam began again …

Now and Then Dick (35)

The news that old Miss Binster had been burgled was, sadly, not treated as anything unusual down at the station. Dick heard about it over lunch in the canteen, overhearing a couple of other PCs who had been round to the little house on Church Street earlier in the morning to find a scene of total devastation.

A neighbour had called 999 to report screams from the house and a man running away. Miss Binster had not appeared and the neighbour, a Mister Reilly, had gone to investigate. To his credit he'd rushed in without a thought for his own safety. That was becoming a rare occurrence these days, even in Daneham where people still tended to look out for each other. He'd found his elderly neighbour lying face down in her living room, with the contents of drawers scattered around her. It was obvious from even the most cursory inspection that life had just changed irrevocably for the lady who'd been known to everyone since the year dot, with a fondly indulgent smile, as Spinster Binster.

She had no enemies. She was well known as owning apple trees that were always heavily laden with juicy Jupiters every year. She'd often giggled to herself in that jingling schoolgirl way she had, as she watched the local lads daring each other to climb through the hedge and pinch a couple before racing back to safety on the other side of the privet. Generations of schoolboys knew that she never begrudged them their prize. The game was not to be seen by Spinster Binster. Not because she'd scold or call the local Bobby, but because that was *the game.* At every village fayre, her apple pies and tart were always the first to be sold, they fairly flew off the trestle tables - and always for more than she was asking. She gave things away to the local children at school fetes. They knew they didn't need to scrump her apples, but it was *the game.* It always would be, as fathers passed the secret down to their sons. 'Impress your mates, son, the game is fun.' But it was harmless. Everyone knew that Spinster Binster was a stalwart of village life.

She was a well loved village character for longer than anyone cared to remember – and now some bastard had robbed her. They'd forced her to give up the pitiful amount of cash she held back from her pension. In all probability it would have gone on cat food for the local strays, who seemed to know that they'd get a welcome at her little back door.

Any copper who had walked or cycled the Daneham beat knew Miss Binster, several from their early youth, and they were in a better position than most to know the effect that such a robbery could have on an elderly woman, living alone, who'd never felt the need to lock her doors. She expected to be treated in the same way that she treated the rest of the world, but the world didn't work on the same wavelength as people like her. Not anymore.

Dick could have wept when he saw the report of the incident. It made grim reading. The old lady he so fondly remembered would probably never return home. Her assailant had broken her right arm above the elbow, broken her jaw and left cheek bone and caused her to fall and break a hip. At her age, Dick knew, she would never recover. Someone who had always been there for the local kids, who would be an affectionate memory to hundreds of apple-loving fathers and their sons, was gone forever now. Spinster Binster was just another statistic to the station. The village would mourn the loss of a local character for a while, but, as is so often the case, life would move on without her. She would end up in a care home, visited occasionally by a few concerned friends, if she was lucky. The handful of policemen who knew Miss Binster as more than just another blip on the force's charts, would try to bring her attacker to justice, but it would be scant consolation for the loss of the smiling little lady who loved children, but had none to help her now, in her hour of darkest distress.

Dick wasn't prepared to let her go through this...

PC Magnull Flint arrived back at the station in the sort of mood that suited his natural disposition.

Foul.

He shouldered past his fellow officers at the reception desk and through the security door into the passageway beyond. He'd received the call to go straight back to the station almost as soon as he left the LeMott house. His sergeant was under some pressure to find out what had happened to the Carver kid and Flint knew he would be far from happy at the explanation, or rather the lack of it, that this morning's visit had thrown up.

As he stood alongside the Sarge's desk, the older man busy with a heated phone conversation, he saw Hedd go into Interview Room One with a look of grim determination on his face. Flint was puzzled by that. He'd always considered Dick 'ead a complete waste of everyone's time. As a copper he was a dead loss; always trying to understand motives and sympathising with victims. Flint had a different outlook. Some people were just born wrong, they'd always be villains, and some were born victims, bullied at school, overlooked at work. Then there were people like him. He was born for greater things. His superiors had not noticed his talents for too long now, but his time was coming. What he needed was a big case, something to bring his abilities to the fore. He wasn't so conceited as to believe he was the perfect copper, but he knew he was better than anyone else in the Vale Royal force. He understood the criminal mind and he understood the law and he *knew* he was bloody good. His bosses may like men like Hedd, but they would recognise his superior ability eventually and sooner rather than later, he reckoned.

As he stood there waiting for the Sarge to finish his phone call he'd been thinking about the Carver kid. It was obvious that the two little buggers had done something to their mate. Three had left the school group in the middle of the night and only two had arrived home, with no believable explanation. They must have argued, or maybe the two had planned to commit some sort of crime involving the third. In his mind's eye he pictured a broken body on a railway track, or lying at the bottom of a quarry somewhere. Maybe this was the one. Maybe this was his chance to make a name for himself, move up to CID and out of his uniform. That would be a shame in some ways. He liked the uniform – it showed everyone that he was a man. A man you didn't want to mess with. On several occasions he'd used his position to put pressure on those who were weaker than himself. His aggressive approach had broken lesser men and particularly younger women. He could force confessions out of them to prove his suspicions without a hint of his tactics reaching the ears of those who would shy away from his methods. He knew how to prove the case when only he could see the truth. While men like Hedd pussy-footed about, he, Magnull Flint, could cut to the chase and get to the truth. So far it had been in small-time muggings and drug related offences, but maybe this missing kid would be his key to higher things. He'd break the LeMott brat and show his genius at criminal investigation. Pity he wasn't a black kid, he particularly enjoyed proving that they were the biggest problem in today's multiracial society. It was the Blacks and Asians who caused most of the crime in his opinion – they were born villains and he loved to show the rest of his namby-pampy hoity-toity colleagues that he wasn't going to let them pull the wool over his eyes. If that meant he sometimes had to resort to putting a few E's in a pocket, to be found later in a search, or threaten some co-conspirator with a good slappin' if needed, well that was his way of making sure that justice was done. He prided himself on always getting his man and the threat of his anvil-like hands made sure there were rarely complaints. He smiled as he remembered the couple of times he'd had to carry out his promises to visit retribution on those who'd had the temerity to try to face him down. The mud might fly, but it never stuck, he was too good for that. Yeah, the LeMotts and their ilk didn't stand a chance. Their son was a villain of the worst sort and it was up to him to show the world the truth.

His smile widened. In the space of less than a minute he'd managed to sort the whole thing out. As long as he could hang onto the case, it would be the start of his meteoric rise. He knew he was the best copper here and now he'd prove it. He became conscious that his fists were tight balls of muscle. He forced himself to relax as the Sarge put the phone down. The smile slipped away, to be replaced by his usual stony expression. Best not to let them see his confidence just yet. His final victory would be so much sweeter if no-one suspected that he'd virtually solved the case before anyone else even knew that there *was* one.

He turned his attention to the older man seated in front of him.

'So Flint, what's to do with those kids?' asked the sergeant, without any great interest.

'Well sarge, I reck'n the two of 'em 'ave done for th' other one. They got 'ome last night, apparently, and can't account for the whereabouts of the third kid.'

'What? But they must have some explanation as to what happened to him. According to the information we got from the Cumbrian lads, there were three of 'em left the place, so the two that are back here must know what happened. What do you mean, they can't account for him? What exactly did they say.'

Flint grinned.

'You won't believe it sir. They've cooked up some cock an' bull story 'bout time travel an' all sorts of other crap.'

'Oh for God's sake man! Did you get any solid information about what they were doing last night. Where did they go - and when? How did they make that trip in a night? Three kids alone. Come on, you must have got more than that.'

He sighed heavily and rubbed a hand across his face.

'Sometimes Flint I bloody despair of you. I really do.'

Flint realised that this wasn't going quite as he'd planned and his voice took on that slightly whining edge that set the sergeant's teeth on edge. Though Flint never seemed to notice the tightening of his superiors jaw in these situations.

'Sir. You wasn't there. The parents of the kids, even the missin' one, made such a bloody fuss. You'd 'ave thought they believed every flamin' word. But it were bollocks! Even when I said that no-one would go along wiv it - they still persisted wiv their story. If y'ask me sir ...'

'But I'm not Flint.' grated out the Sarge. 'For Pete's sake. This should have been straightforward. Three kids run off from a school trip. One of them goes missing on the way home, and all you had to do was ask a few quick questions and find out what happened!'

The Sarge was clearly not happy.

'Go and find Rich Hedd, Flint. I should have sent him out there in the first place, but I thought that even you couldn't get this one wrong. Guess I was mistaken.'

As Flint flushed with anger at the not-so-subtle recrimination the sergeant waved him away and looked around.

'Where is Hedd anyway? He should have finished his lunch by now. Go find him Flint.'

Well stuff me! What did he have to do? Flint was stunned. What had he done that was so dreadful?

Right, he'd nobble soddin' Dick 'ead and show them the right way to handle this sort of thing.

'E just wen' into IR1, Sarge.' said Flint, as he crossed over to the door. He gripped the handle and the sound of a distant rumble of thunder whispered through the office as the door opened.

'Oi, Dick 'ead! The Sarge wants yer.' he called as he entered.

But answer, came there none...

Dick waited as Church Street materialised around him and grinned; Leon would be proud! The coloured ribbons of light faded away and he stepped up to number twenty-eight and gave a smart rat-a-tat knock at the faded red front door.

He waited patiently for Miss Binster to open the door. According to this morning's report he was about ten minutes early. He smiled at the happy little face that presented itself when the door opened.

'It's Richard isn't it?' asked Spinster Binster with a twinkle in her eye. 'I haven't seen you for quite a while young man. My, aren't you a handsome young devil these days? Come in, come in.' she ushered Dick into her front room, there being no hall in her small cottage.. 'And what pray, do the police want with an elderly ex-school teacher?'

As she spoke she indicated a chair.

'Please sit down officer.' She turned to the door through to her kitchen. 'Cup of tea?'

'Thanks, yes. Milk, one sugar.'

Dick was looking around the cosy room. He always felt as though he'd stepped back fifty years in here. A large wireless stood on a mirror-backed sideboard, alongside some rose-coloured glasswear. Sepia photos stood on almost every surface, interspersed with more up-to-date pictures of old friends and young children. The hollow ticking of a mantle clock was the only sound as the old lady busied herself with the Assam.

'So how's things then Miss B?' he called.

'Oh, much the same as usual Richard. Each day tends to be much like the last - and the next - when you reach my age.' Dick heard a giggle through the doorway. 'Basically I just drift along nowadays. Gone is the excitement of my youth. There is little opportunity for drives out with young gentlemen in their shiny new automobiles. The roads are too crowded, the motorists too aggressive and the cars too fast for my liking. There's the Chapel of course, but there are fewer and fewer of us with each passing year, despite the best efforts of our worthy vicar.'

She bustled in with a tray holding a cosy-covered tea pot, china cups and saucers, sugar bowl and jug and, of course, the obligatory rich tea biscuits.

Dick realised that Miss Binster would pour the tea, through a strainer, into the milk and he could then add his own sugar. He remembered that tea in a mug was not part of Miss Binster's vocabulary. 'Milk and one sugar' made no difference to her tea-making routine.

As she poured, Dick waited for the knock that would announce the arrival of her life-changing visitor. He assumed that her attacker had come to the door and then forced his way in. The report had said nothing about forced entry.

'Good Oh, Miss B. Just thought I'd pop in and check that everything was ticketty-boo.' He knew that she was too sharp to accept his reason for calling, but at short notice he hadn't been able to come up with anything else and, to be honest, it didn't really matter.

Miss Binster eyed him suspiciously. She could see he was obviously pre-occupied with something and was puzzled. Happy to see him, of course, but puzzled. Why did he keep checking the window, as though he was expecting company?

'Richard Hedd, I've known you for too long for you to try to fox me! What is going on?'

She was sounding impatient now and Dick was actually relieved when the knock at the door came. It was a powerful, no-nonsense rap, that spoke of authority, perhaps the gas man or postal delivery. Miss Binster would naturally answer without a qualm.

And her life would be changed forever.

'I'll get that for you!' Dick shot out of his seat, spilling tea on his shoes and splashing the bottom of his trousers. He banged his cup and saucer down on the small table beside his chair and launched himself for the door, giving Miss Binster no time to act. She sat immobile, clearly shocked by his actions and more than a little annoyed at the tea spilt on her somewhat threadbare, though otherwise spotless, carpet.

Dick reached the door in three strides and opened it to find himself faced by a stocky, dark-haired man. The sight of the uniform brought the man up short. Expecting an elderly woman, the man took a step backwards and off the doorstep. Dark and unshaven, he didn't have the appearance of anyone who had business with Spinster Binster. Furtive, dark eyes tried to look past the policeman filling the doorway.

'Yes? Can I help you?' asked Dick.

'Wot? Yeah… Noh... I… erm… is th' old lady in?' asked the man.

'And who shall I say is calling?' asked Dick, with a winning smile.

'Er…' the man was now very flustered and gave the impression that the last thing he'd expected was questions. Dick was sure that he was now looking at the man seen running from the scene of Miss Binster's attack. 'No-one... Nuffin'... Nevah mind. I'll see 'er later.' From his accent he clearly wasn't a local. The Mancunian overtones were coming through loud and clear.

'I don't think so mate.' said Dick in his most ingratiating voice, with a shake of his head. 'I'm afraid the lady in question is unavailable for a mugging at the moment. Perhaps you'd like to try your luck with me instead?' Dick thrust out his chin invitingly.

'Yuh wot? Yuh a bleedin' nutter, you!' The man took another step back. 'What you goin' on 'bout! I wuz only gonna ask if she needed any odd jobs doin'.'

Dick stepped forward and prodded him forcefully in the chest.

'Look chummy, I know you now, right? I could pick you out anywhere. So don't let me see you around here again, okay?' He gave the man a shove. 'So push off, before I find an excuse to arrest you!'

Amazingly the man stood his ground and leaned closer, seemingly without any alarm, a slight sneer appearing.

'Don' yoh push me, yoh soddin' prick! Yoh got no right, yoh…'

Dick grabbed him by the front of his jacket before he could finish.

'Shut it, right now, and listen very carefully.' He tightened his grip as the man tried to pull away and brought his face to within inches of the other man's. 'I know why you came here. She's an easy target, eh? Well she isn't. What you've got to ask yourself is: how did *I* know *you* were going to be here? How did I know to wait for you?'

The man looked far less certain of himself now and struggled to free himself from Dick's iron grip.

'This is police soddin' 'arrassment this is!' the struggling man cried and finally pulled away as Dick released him.

'Just push off' said Dick in a low menacing voice, 'and remember, I'll be keeping an eye on you chummy, if you ever show up around here again.'

'Arse 'ole!' shouted the would be mugger, with a none too friendly hand gesture, as he took to his heels.

Dick watched the man disappear towards the village centre at a rate of knots and fervently hoped that his surprise appearance would be an effective deterrent. He knew that with the best will in the world he wouldn't be able to correct every wrong performed on his patch. Miss Binster was a special case though. Look upon it as my final good deed as a copper, he thought to himself. With stored-up holiday entitlement, he would be able to leave the force almost immediately and be free of the restrictions of a steady job. Free to join Leon in his strange new world.

He was about to close the door when the disappearing scally stopped and shouted something about Dick not being able to be everywhere and coming back later.

Dear God! What did it take to discourage casual muggers?

Dick relaxed and let his mind slip into that other place that he was coming to know better each day.

The world slipped away for a second and came back into focus with Dick standing around the corner from Miss Binster's house.

Dick braced himself and the strolling villain walked straight into him because he was too busy checking that Dick wasn't following him.

'Boo.' said Dick.

The shocked expression would have been comical in other circumstances.

'I think you'll find I can be everywhere at once, chummy boy.'

With a strangled curse, the man shot passed Dick and raced off casting occasional frightened glances at the mysterious copper.

Dick did the time thing again and waited for the mugger to arrive at the next corner, a smile playing on his lips.

The man appeared again – now out of breath and looking harassed, constantly glancing over his shoulder.

'So don't forget it.' whispered Dick in his ear as the man paused to catch his breath, leaning heavily on the Accrington brickwork of the first terrace of the street.

This time Dick thought he might have gone too far.

The man's eyes rolled back in his head and he gave a small whimper, trying hard to merge with the wall, pressing his back into the bricks and avoiding Dick's stare. Shockingly, he appeared to have lost his bladder control.

With a final dismissive wave and a smile, Dick sent the man stumbling away.

'On your way... and remember – I'll be watching.' said Dick, in an overly jolly voice, as though reminding a child to be careful.

A damp trail marked the departure of the now thoroughly chastened would - be mugger.

Dick grinned before relaxing himself and returning to his position at the front door.

As he turned back into the homely room – a room no longer destined to be ransacked by an opportunist thief – he was confronted by an angry old lady with fire in her eyes.

'Richard Hedd! What do you mean by interrogating my visitors? Am I such a sad old biddy that I have to be protected by every Tom, Dick and Harry by the strong arm of the law? Do you think me incapable of looking after myself?' She gave him a hefty whack on the arm with an antimacassar. 'Just what do you think you're playing at?'

She stood, all four foot ten of her, glaring up at Dick in high dudgeon.

'Miss Binster! Stop! This is assault and battery madam!' laughed Dick at the comical figure before him. The sight of the elderly lady ready to thrash him with a piece of household linen was so unexpected, he couldn't help it. He held up his hands in surrender. 'That visitor, as you call him, was up to no good, I promise.'

'And just how would you know that, Mister Plod?' she said in a quieter voice. 'Are the Vale Royal constabulary now monitoring all visitors to old ladies?'

Now it was her turn to smile at his discomfiture. Hmm, that was a poser for him.

'Ah, now that would be telling wouldn't it?' he countered. 'Let's just say, we have our methods. And you, young lady, will have to be more careful before you answer the door.' He turned and pointed to the chain hanging from the doorframe. 'You see this? It's there for a reason. Always make sure you use it. It's there to stop ne'er do wells gaining access without your permission and trust me, he was as big a ne'er do well as ever I saw.'

He gestured to the armchairs.

'Shall we resume our seats Miss B and try to forget that nasty little incident?' he asked in his best 'I'm a policeman and I know what I'm doing' voice.

Miss Binster sat, but wasn't about to let the subject drop. In a quieter voice she said.

'Richard, I may be moving along in years, but I'm not yet so soft in the head as to believe that what just happened was coincidence. You came here with the express intention of intercepting that young man.'

'Oh dear, was it that obvious?' he smiled.

'Just a little, Richard.' Miss B. sipped her tea and looked over at Dick with a knowing look. 'I think it was the momentary disappearance that gave you away.'

Something about her smile made Dick suddenly realise that Miss Binster might be elderly, but she certainly wasn't beyond putting two and two together and arriving at exactly four.

And she seemed perfectly capable of taking in all that was happening around her without any disturbance of her elegant equilibrium.

With a twinkle in her eye she asked. 'So tell me Richard, how is young Leon?'

Oops!

Leon was clearly shocked when Dick explained the day's escapades. They were seated at his kitchen table, the large house silent but for their voices and the faint Einaudi drifting in from the distant media room.

'But Dick, I've tried intervening in things before and it's never worked! Hell, who wouldn't try to stop Hitler or Hussein, but whenever I made the attempt I was whisked back to the present. Whether I tried to take direct action or used some round about means, it was as though History itself, or Time, wouldn't allow me to interfere.'

Dick nodded as he sipped yet another cup of tea.

'Well I've been thinking about that.' He leaned back and looked up at the beamed ceiling. 'So how about this. You can't alter anything that's had too many knock-on effects'. He rocked forward as he brought his gaze back to Leon. 'You know. Lots of people have tried to explain how Time, with a capital T, works. Not the stuff from Hawking, about black holes, or Einstein and relativity, but the paradoxes that time travel would cause. You know, things like meeting yourself or killing your great granddad. How does Time prevent them happening? So I've come up with my own theory.'

Leon smiled. 'Okay Dick. I'll humour you. What's the big solution to it all, Oh Mighty Oz?'

'No Leon, listen. I'm being serious here. We know we can't go forward, I reckon simply because the future depends on decisions we've yet to make, so for us the future doesn't exist and if it doesn't exist we can't go there.'

'Sounds reasonable.' said Leon, resting his head on his hands, elbows on the table.

'So that's the future dealt with.' said Dick. 'But the past is a different story. As you've already said, we can't alter things that have had a big effect on the future. You can't kill someone hundreds of years ago, or prevent a couple from meeting and having children, because there are already too many knock-on effects prior to the present day. If Hitler was stopped at the first rally he went to, the second world war could have been prevented and there would potentially be millions of people still alive today. So we can't alter what he did, because the present day would be so different that we might not be here. If we're not here then we couldn't go back to make adjustments in the past. That's got nothing to do with paradox, it just makes common sense.' Dick took a sip of tea again, looking earnest. 'If science has taught us anything it's that the more simple and obvious the answer, the more likely it is to be true. Nature likes things to be simple. So small adjustments in the not-too-distant past are possible because their effects aren't so pronounced, they don't affect the balance of nature too much. If the power we're tapping into is due to the energy surrounding all living things and we upset that balance in the present by messing with the past, then Time and the Earth – Gaia if you like – prevents us doing it.' Dick shook his head as though to clear it to make room for what was to follow. 'Does that make any sort of sense?'

'All sounds reasonable to me.' said Leon, then raised a finger and gave a knowing look. 'But I get the feeling there's more.'

'Oh yes indeedy. Having said that we can't upset the past because of the ripples that eventually reach our present and could cause untold problems, what about tweaking the very recent past? I think that if we'd been around in, say, the early thirties and been able to go back just a few years, we could have stopped the Nazi ball rolling before it had even started. The problem is knowing what's going on in the world now that we can change. Me popping back to early this morning didn't shake things up too much, so I was allowed to help Spinster Binster. If I'd left it a few more hours or days then maybe I wouldn't have been able to help. There would have been all sorts of additional incidents that couldn't be wiped out without affecting the 'balance' of power.'

Dick sat back and gave Leon a speculating look.

Leon for his part didn't look particularly surprised by Dick's conclusions. The Einaudi had come to an end and he picked up his cup and nodded towards the rest of the house.

'Let's find some more music, while we think about this.'

Dick followed him through the main hall into the large room beyond which held his cinema setup and computers. The projector Leon used in place of a TV was splashing random patterns onto the huge blank wall of the media room. He ejected the CD and began to search through his collection for another. Dick had come to expect this; Leon liked to have appropriate music to accompany his activities. He selected one and inserted it into the nearest PC and moved the track count forward to seven.

Dick was surprised to hear not more classical music, but an odd Morris Dance type of melody. When he gave Leon an enquiring glance his friend grinned.

'Well, given the subject of the conversation, I thought something a little bit other worldly was called for. We're into somewhere that's a bit odd, but still not totally alien. The Stick and Bucket song seemed appropriate – olde worlde, but modern at the same time, and just a bit daft.'

The two men laughed and Dick sat in one of the twenty odd armchairs scattered around the room. They sat in silence until the short dance stopped and Leon swapped it for The Hilliard Ensemble and their English Madrigals. The beautiful harmonies filled the room and the swirling colours danced to the voices from across the centuries.

'So, Time itself controls what we can, and cannot, do?' said Leon returning to the interrupted conversation.

'Yeah. It's basically what you'd said before. Time even gives us a helping hand with the simultaneous translation.'

Leon chuckled.

'That was a shock for me the first couple of times it happened. I think it's just that our brains are capable of doing all sorts of things, they just need a little nudge in the right direction. The power we tap into – the power that originates in all living thing – makes us capable of almost anything.'

'Hmmm… sobering thought that.' said Dick, staring into his now empty tea cup. 'Time for something a little stronger?'

'I think so, Dick.'

And to the centuries old music, the two friends became comprehensively plastered.

The following morning, Dick left Leon to his construction work, using ancient timbers cut by his own hands with the help of Elizabethan master craftsmen and then hidden away in the surrounding woods until he recovered them four hundred years later.

The station was quiet when Dick arrived and changed into his uniform. He double checked the reports from the previous day, smiling at the complete absence of any mention of Miss Binster. He'd searched through them on his return the previous day, but looked again, just in case it had all been some sort of glorious dream. He'd also noticed Flint giving him a wide-eyed stare when he'd walked passed after coming back out of the interview room where he'd conjured up the *then*. Dick had used the empty room to settle back into the state of mind that allowed him to tickle his forebrain into taking him back several hours, and several miles, to Church Street.

He thought no more of it until he caught Flint giving him a look of such unadulterated hatred that he gave the Sarge a nudge.

'What's up with Flint this morning, Brian? He looks like the cat that got the cream, only to find it's turned to cheese.'

Brian Cope, the sergeant behind the desk, gave a short barking laugh.

'Yeah, he is a bit cheesed off. I asked him to pass the missing child case to you, only it got passed upstairs. It's non-uniform's case now. They're out picking up the other two now.'

From Dick's face it was obvious that he didn't have the faintest idea what the Sarge was talking about. The older man harrumphed in disgust.

'Night before last. Three boys ran off from a school trip, but only two arrived home. Like a fool I sent Flint around to the house of one of the kids to see what was going on.'

'And?'

'And he came back with nothing of any worth. Both the lads who came home said they'd just lost the third. Then there was allsorts of rubbish about time travel and God knows what else. Load of bollocks, but our man Flint came back without having found out anything about what had actually happened. Succeeded in winding up the parents though. So now CID are involved, for obvious reasons. The kid's been missing for over twenty four hours and we still don't know what happened.'

Dick was dumbstruck and must have looked it.

'Don't worry Dick, it's out of our hands - and was never in yours.'

'But what do they mean – time travelling?'

Brian shrugged. 'Don't ask me, but it sounds like foul play and no mistake.' He passed a couple of sheets over to Dick. 'Be a good lad and take these to Doris will you? And then out and about to protect the good citizens of Vale Royal from ne'er do wells.'

With a friendly grin Dick made for the stairs, but he was thinking about the missing boy and the tale his friends were telling. He'd have to look into this a bit further. Whether it was out of his hands or not, he could still keep an ear out for any gossip and an eye out for any reports. It sounded like too much of a coincidence for him to just let it slip by.

'Oi, Dick 'ead!' called Flint as Dick was about to head up. 'What wuz yer up teh yesto'day?'

Several heads turned at the sound of the raised voice. Dick stopped and turned, his mind racing. What could Flint know about yesterday? Flashing an ingratiating smile to those looking over in curiosity, Dick replied in as light hearted a manner as he could muster.

'Sorry Magnull? To what would you be referring, in your usual subtle manner?'

Flint flicked a glare around the room at the muffled laughter.

'I wuz lookin' fer yer an yud vanished.'

Dick managed a nonchalant air when he replied. 'Well, maybe I'd decided to nip back home using my super time travelling powers and have a quick kip.'

The sarcasm wasn't wasted on those listening. Again the muffled laughter told Dick that news of Flint's abortive interview with the kids yesterday had done the rounds of the station. Flint couldn't think of an answer to that one and turned his attention back to his paperwork, an embarrassed blush showing on the back of his neck, but his mind was filled with an almost blinding rage. 'I'll bloody 'ave you, Dick 'ead. Sometime soon I'll show y'all that I'm the best man 'ere, an' you got sumfin' to 'ide. I'll 'ave yer.'

Dick had been out on foot patrol when the two boys were brought into the station. The foot patrol was almost an oxymoron these days, a throwback to quieter times when the village bobby was an everyday sight. They still occasionally carried them out in Vale Royal, though most people considered them a mere public relations exercise. But Dick enjoyed them, even if the weather was a bit dodgy. Whether their political masters thought them a waste of time and played with the crime statistics in an attempt to make them a thing of the past, they were a comfort to many, particularly the most elderly citizens. They, at least, could still remember when a policeman on foot was a common sight, back when they could safely leave their door open all day and crime was mostly a metropolitan problem. It also helped to discourage the local kids from being antisocial. If a copper might turn up at any moment, it tended to curtail your most boisterous activities. For most kids anyway.

Apart from a couple of stops, one to chat to the Daneham barber about the prospects of the local soccer team and another with a group of lads playing football in one of the quieter backstreets, where a sublimely taken free kick had wrung applause from the attacking team and muted respect from the defenders, the morning had passed without any sort of incident.

On his return he'd asked the Sarge about the lads involved in the missing schoolboy case.

'Upstairs being questioned, Dick. Sounds like they're not getting very far though. The parents are in as well. By all accounts they're backing the boys, but soon something's got to give. It won't be long before the local rag gets hold of the story and then the fans going to get very messy. As far as I can see, there's no chance of finding the lad unless the two upstairs start to come clean. Right now, they still insist that they don't know where he is.'

Dick looked thoughtful as he went in search of a phone where he could talk to Leon without being overheard.

Jarmon was feeling sick with worry. He'd been left in a small unused office for almost an hour now, with Lidine, Tam's parents and Silas. Conversation was stilted to say the least, with Silas having withdrawn into himself over the last twenty-four hours and Ian and Sue at a complete loss as to what to do to help their son. They'd all tried to talk Fin and Tam into changing their story, but the boys were adamant that to say anything else would be a lie and still not help in the search for Sim.

Jarmon looked over to Silas, who looked like a man in mourning. Like it or not, Sim's father was drawing away from the other four. His son had disappeared while out alone at night with his, supposedly, best friends. What was he supposed to think? That the three of them had actually managed to conjure themselves back into the Middle Ages and then somehow mislaid Simeon? That was so improbable as to be laughable – except that the loss of his son would break Silas, just as the departure of his wife, Angela, had done. It had taken him months to come to terms with her leaving, if he had ever really recovered. Sim was his life now and the thought that Fin and Tam might have done something to deprive him of his son's love was unbearable. Jarmon had tried to talk to him, but, understandably, Silas was not in the mood to hear his pleadings on behalf of the two who had returned without Sim.

Sim had been gone for over a day now and everyone was expecting the worst. Whilst he was by no means a child, Sim was not equipped to be alone in the world. He would have contacted his father if he were able. The fact that there had been no news from him spelled disaster for his father.

Even when Tam had completed his story, with Fin providing corroboration, Silas had had nothing to provide any comfort. Basically they offered no believable reason for anything that had happened since they'd run away from the hostel in The Lakes. The school party returned later today and the teachers would be brought to the station the minute that their remaining wards were safely in the loving arms of their families. Willis Masseer was also needed by the officers investigating. Unfortunately, both Fin and Tam had said that while he would be able to confirm their statements about the hours before their disappearance, he could tell them nothing about occurrences after it.

Lillibet was, thankfully, at school, but would be returning to an empty house in a few hours unless either Jarmon or Lidine left the station soon. Neither was in the mood to abandon their son to the comforts of the police, but one of them would have to go. All they could hope was that something would happen to cast some light on the happening of the night before last before the decision as to who would leave had to be made.

No legal representation had been called in by either set of parents, there had seemed no point. Even the best legal mind would have been hard pressed to help. The officer in charge had already said that the boys wouldn't be kept in overnight, since there was, as yet, no evidence of foul play, but there was every chance that this little magnolia office would become very familiar over the coming days.

Jarmon sat, head in hands, desperately trying to see a light at the end of the tunnel, but all he could see was pitch black ahead. The trouble was that there was nothing to offer up any hope. All the talk of time travel was, frankly, ridiculous, but nothing could persuade the lads to come clean. Much as he wanted to believe his son, the story was just so far-fetched as to beggar any chance of belief. The only answer was that they had done something unthinkable to Sim having slipped into some sort of psychotic episode. All the shouting, pleading and tears had done nothing to shift the boy's conviction that everything they were saying was true.

Ian and Sue sat opposite him, on the uncomfortable plastic chairs, holding hands and staring unseeing at the floor. Lidine had been silent for longer than Jarmon could ever remember, managing only the smallest smile of thanks when a female officer came to hand out tea. Muttered '*Thankyous*' were all that had been heard in the room for several hours.

Eventually the door opened and the officer in charge entered. DCI Old was in his mid-fifties and had thought that he'd seen it all in his thirty years in the force. Now he realised he'd been massively wrong.

Those seated around the room sprang to their feet, all except Silas.

'Where are the boys?'

'How's Tam doing?'

'When can we take them home?'

The rush of questions didn't appear to disturb the policeman. He raised a hand and waited for silence.

'Please sit' he waved towards the uncomfortable chairs, 'and we'll try to sort things out, so that everyone can go home.'

At the looks of relief that flooded four of the five faces, he hurried on.

'Though I'm afraid that both the boys will have to come back again, unless something unexpected happens soon.' He sat heavily and leaned forwards, his elbows on his knees and his hands clasped in front of him. He looked down for a second and then looked up, searching each pair of eyes as he spoke.

'You must realise that this situation is now very serious. Simeon has been missing for almost two days now, a young lad on his own. Your sons' he looked at the four parents in turn, 'still insist on their story. A story which, even you must admit, beggars belief.' He paused, waiting for the expected interruptions, which surprisingly didn't materialise. Turning his gaze to Silas he continued. 'Mister Carver, I know this must be very difficult for you, but we are doing all we can to trace your son. However, I have to say that the longer this goes on, the less optimistic we are. Without any clue as to where the boys went after leaving the hostel all we can do is continue the search around the hostel and along what, we believe, may have been their route home.'

He leaned back, stretching his back as though relieving the fatigue brought on by long hours of sitting.

'Does that mean we can take our boys home now?' asked Ian hopefully.

Again Old paused.

'Yes, as soon as we've taken their prints.'

'What? You're taking fingerprints? But they haven't been charged. They haven't done anything wrong.' pleaded Lidine.

'Possibly not Mrs LeMott, but we can hardly just let them go as though nothing has happened. We need their fingerprints, along with their clothing and shoes, so that we can at least attempt to track their movements during the night in question. I'm not best pleased with how this is going, but given the attitude of the boys we've no alternative.'

He stood and repeated his long look at each parent.

'I must emphasise that whatever happened that night, the boys aren't doing anyone any good by persisting with this ridiculous tale. They're only making things worse by not telling us what really happened.' He gave a deep sigh, 'If this continues and we can't locate Simeon,' Silas looked up sharply at this, 'then you had best prepare yourselves for the worst. One, or both, of the boys will be going to receive a custodial sentence.'

He reached for the door handle, but paused with the door unopened.

'You must try to get them to see sense. Maybe the shadow of a young offenders institution hanging over them will make a difference. I can only hope, for all your sakes, that they do come to their senses and sooner rather than later. The teachers involved will be coming in tomorrow, along with young Willis Masseer – it sounds as though he may be able to cast some light on young Fin's state of mind prior to the disappearance.'

He finally opened the door.

'Right then. Let's go and let you all get away.'

He held out his arm to usher them through the door.

As Silas rose to leave, looking totally bereft, the policeman put his arm around his shoulders.

'Don't give up hope yet Mister Carver. I'm still optimistic that something will turn up.'

He patted Silas on the back.

'It may help if you try to have a word with them about -' but Silas shrugged the arm off. 'Don't you think I've tried. They were Sim's best friends. I still can't believe – I won't let myself believe – that they would have done anything to him. I know he wasn't ever going to be a superstar, but he'd never hurt a fly, and he loved those two like they were his brothers.'

Tears began to roll down his unshaven cheeks and he made no attempt to wipe them away. He slumped back against the wall, knocking several sheets off the noticeboard behind him. Drawing pins rattled to the floor. He looked down, but the older man stopped him bending down to pick them up with a gentle hand on the shoulder.

'Leave them Mister Carver, I'll get them.'

'Sim will be back. I'm sure.' Silas sniffed deeply and shook himself as he wiped his face with a tired looking handkerchief pulled from his jeans. He managed to conjure up the ghost of a smile.

'He'll be back.' he repeated quietly, and then turned to leave the station, while his oldest friends reclaimed their sons from the long arm of the law.

DCI Old watched him leave as he bent to retrieve the papers and, despite his years in the job, couldn't help feeling guilty about the fact that he could offer so little comfort to a man so clearly in pain.

Dick was checking through some paperwork at the front desk when the forlorn little group walked by. Despite having been reunited with their families, the boys looked apprehensive, as they made their way to the door through to the reception. Several officers stopped to look in curiosity at the little group. Word had spread of the missing boy and his two friends, who refused to reveal their part in his disappearance.

The strange tale they'd woven had swept like wildfire through the station and no-one believed a word of it – except maybe Dick.

He'd seen and heard enough in the last few days to believe almost anything and Leon had said that things – whatever *things* were – were building to a head. Just as the taller of the two - that would be Finbar - was passing he glanced across and Dick was gripped by the urge to give the lad some sort of sign that he wasn't alone in this, that at least one person may have an inkling as to what he was going through.

Fin started, and almost bumped into Tam ahead of him, as the capable-looking young policeman gave him an extravagant wink and quickly turned back to the desk beside him. No words passed between them. To Fin it was as though the PC was sharing some secret with him, a secret that he didn't want anyone else to know about.

'Bloody moron,' thought Fin spitefully, 'He's got no idea what's going on. No-one has.' He felt close to tears again. It was all very well trying to be adult about this, but they were only thirteen and there was every possibility that he'd killed one of his closest friends just because he could do something that should have been a wonderful gift, but was still *The Nightmare.* Only now he wasn't asleep. He wouldn't be waking up from this. Last night had been the first for months, if not years, that he hadn't travelled. Maybe he couldn't do it anymore. In that case their doom was sealed and Sim would never return. And poor old Tam was going down with him. He cursed vehemently inside. 'And all *that* idiot can do is act like he can help. Sod off!

His depression became deeper. He was drowning and it was getting colder in the dark recesses of his mind where a dark fear was hiding... a fear that was going to pull him down into the icy depths if he didn't do something about it. The trouble was – he had no idea how to help himself... or Tam... or poor Simeon, who was God knows where - *or when* - facing who-knew what perils... on his own.

The warm afternoon sun did nothing to disperse the chill that seemed to engulf him

Now Tam (36)

As they drove home in uncomfortable silence – *what was there to say?* Fin thought back to the previous day. Following the departure of the unpleasant PC Flint, Tam had tried to continue his retelling of their travels, but somehow all the wind had been taken out of his sails. He'd repeated his initial story to his parents and Silas Carver, but the fun had evaporated following the realisation that telling the truth isn't always necessarily the best option. He could tell, even as he was talking, that he'd lost his audience. What everyone had wanted to know was *where was Sim?*.

And, unfortunately, he couldn't tell them.

Nor could Fin.

The Rigglebys followed Jarmon's car back to the LeMott home. Silas was conspicuous by his absence. In all honesty no-one could really blame him. At the back of his mind must surely have been the suspicion that Fin and Tam had done something to Simeon. Their inability to give any sort of credible explanation only served to heighten his fears. The last thing Silas needed or wanted to hear was more of the same from Simeon's erstwhile friends.

Having waited for Fin and Lidine to exit the car, Jarmon immediately reversed off the drive to make the short journey to collect Lilli from school.

The Rigglebys joined Fin and his mother in the kitchen.

Over a fresh cup of tea the five resumed their seats around the table. Tam noticed that they all occupied the same seats as the previous day and thought it strange how quickly people form habits over even the most inconsequential things.

Ian finally broke the silence.

'Boys, I know this has been a very difficult day - for all of us – and I know we went over things yesterday,' he looked at Tam, 'but your mother and I would like to hear again what happened before you lost Sim.'

'Yes love,' said Sue, 'maybe we've missed something.' She shook her head despondently. 'The problem is that the whole thing is so unbelievable it's difficult to know where to start trying to understand what could have happened to him.'

Fin looked up, ashen faced.

'But that's the problem isn't it? We decided that we'd tell the truth – we all decided it together. We just never expected to lose Sim and now we've gone down this road, we can't turn back.' He flicked a quick sidelong glance at Tam. 'It's too late to try to make something up.'

Tam nodded, looking shell-shocked. 'I never thought it would be like this. We all thought it was going to be an amazing story to baffle everyone, not the start of a murder hunt.'

'Oh Tam, I'm sure it's not as bad as that' said Lidine, bending to put her arms around the two boys, trying to comfort them, but at a loss as to how to go about it.

'Oh Mum!' burst out Fin. 'It's about as bad as it could be. The police think we killed Sim and so does his dad.'

Everyone looked shocked.

'Oh I know he puts a brave face on things, but even while he's saying *Everything will be okay*, I can tell he thinks we did something ...' he sobbed as he spoke, 'They all reckon we've killed him ...' He waved his arms extravagantly, 'and who can blame them.'

Tam's head was so low it was almost resting on the table.

'But we're not going to lie to make people feel better.' he muttered. 'Whatever happens we're not going to make things up. You have to believe us! No-one else is going to – we realise that now,' his voice had a pleading edge to it, 'but you must! If it's just the two of us and we can't find Sim again, then we're all lost.'

'Oh Tam. We *do* believe you. We know that neither of you are capable of harming Sim,' said Lidine, 'but you're right. No-one else will ever believe you unless you can bring Sim back and have some evidence to support your story.'

The door opened and Jarmon entered, followed by a nervous looking Lilli. When she saw her brother and his friend her smile suddenly lit the room up and she ran around the table to hug Fin fiercely. His silent fears withdrew, fleetingly, at her touch, but only for a moment.

'I knew you'd be alright Fin, but I'm ever so glad to see you and Tam. I've been worried all day.' She sat beside Fin and looked solemn, for the briefest of moments. 'But I was really good at school; I didn't say a word to anyone about what's happened.'

Jarmon walked behind his daughter and ruffled her hair.

'Good girl.' He was amazed at how well she was handling all this.

Lidine motioned for him to sit and poured another cup. 'We're about to go through it all again, in detail, to see if we can come up with some way of finding Sim.' she said.

Tam sat straighter in his seat and looked across at his parents, whose obvious love and unwavering belief shone through their earnest looks, and seemed to gain strength.

He looked over at Fin.

'Well, you're going to have to go through the start again,' he looked a little shame-faced. 'I… err… I don't remember it very clearly…' his voice trailed off.

So Fin, with a little self-conscious cough and a sip of tea, began the retelling of how they misplaced Sim.

Then Fin, Tam and Simeon (37)

The cry from the woods was so heart rending that for a second Fin and Sim stood stock still, their hearts pounding. Tam, held unconscious between them, dribbled silently down his shirt.

Sim let go of his friend's arm, causing Fin to release his grip and once more Tam fell unceremoniously into a senseless heap at their feet.

'Come on!' called Fin as he set off in the direction of the call. Sim was hard on his heels. Much to their own surprise, neither boy considered waiting to see what would happen. In this strange old world they'd learned the hard way to act first and think about it later. They wouldn't be caught napping by Woods and his ilk again.

They crashed through the bushes ahead of them without a thought for their own safety. Fin was having to steer his way through slitted eyes, trying to see through his smashed glasses. Mercifully there were no large branches lying in wait for his headlong rush. Sim had moved ahead, unencumbered by myopia, and Fin followed.

They burst onto another woodland track and off to their left they could here the sounds of a struggle. Again came the high-pitched scream – definitely female and the startled whinnying of a horse.

Sim side-swiped through a ninety degree turn and Fin stumbled across the path into the undergrowth on the other side of the track, before righting himself and taking off after his friend. Adrenalin coursed through them as they finally found the origin of the clamour. They recognised the cart immediately, the flash of golden hair confirming Fin's worst fears.

Edmund lay on the ground, being assailed by three thugs. The sturdy woodsman could have handled any one of them, possibly two, but being so outnumbered, he was at the mercy of their kicks. Atop the cart stood Adam Woods, Kate held tightly against him and an unholy light seeming to illuminate his animal features, his lips drawn back in a snarl.

Before he could shout a warning to his gang the two friends were upon them. Unseen by the three blackguards the boys made no attempt at a fight. They simply ran full-pelt into the nearest two men. Though both were larger than either Fin or Sim the advantage of surprise paid off. Unused to the aggression that had gripped them both, all the pent-up anger of young lives spent under the yoke of bullying burst forth. Sim hit the first man full in the back, literally bouncing him into the back of the heavy cart. The solid head proved no match for the heavy oak rail along the base of the cart bed. With an audible crack the man went down as though pole-axed.

Fin was so close behind his friend that Sim's arrival was insufficient warning to help his targets take evasive action. Fin leapt at the two remaining men, hitting them while flying horizontally through the air. Both men were felled by his ballistic onslaught. Even in his rage, Fin had time to think – *Oh yeah, move over Jackie Chan!*

Both boys were so infuriated that they gave no thought to their own safety – maybe time travel does something for your testosterone levels. Either way Fin was five foot two of blindly windmilling menace.

The men fell in a heap of flailing arms and legs. Only one rose to his feet, the second crying out in pain and then lying in a whimpering bundle. As he scrambled back to his feet, Fin had a fleeting glimpse of the man's ashen face, but had no time to see what had happened. Joined by Sim he faced the third man who was surprisingly quick to get back on his feet. The two boys slowly converged on the now wary-looking villain. At a shout from Kate on the farther side of the cart, Fin glanced up to see a red-faced Woods coming across the cart-bed at a run.

There was no sign of Kate.

The last of the three original assailants smiled a wicked gap-toothed grin and the boys realised that the tables had been turned and the odds had moved very much in favour of Woods and Co.

Even though they'd managed to leave one man out cold and a second nursing a recognisably dislocated elbow – Fin gulped as he saw the wickedly angled lower arm – they were no match for two large and undeniably belligerent thugs.

'Tis time to learn these younglings a lesson, eh cuz?' said Woods, his stance belying his soft, silky words. He waved a hand to indicate that his companion should move further round to force the boys to split their defence. Both men smiled - tight vicious smiles - and crouched into what the boys took to be the precursor to an attack.

'Methinks we are undone, Master Fin.' whispered Sim, with no sign of a smile.

'Aye, we've shot our bolt. All that's left is for us to make sure we leave good big stains when we bleed viciously all over them.' replied Fin, warily eyeing the opposition as it circled with belligerent swaggers. 'You realise they've probably done this before?'

Sim nodded breathlessly. The adrenalin high was leaving both the boys and each now carried his own knot of fear. Suddenly their wild bravado seemed a little overplayed.

'Forget blood. The way I'm feeling right now they're going to have more trouble with the smell. Can you cack yer breeks in self-defence?'

'I'd say it's a definite possibility.' said Fin grimly.

The banter appeared to give their two opponents pause for thought. Hopelessly outclassed, the boys should have been begging for mercy, but strangely it didn't occur to either of them. The years of being the butt of everyone else's jokes had somehow conjured up a sort of reckless abandon in the face of a soon to be vicious slapping.

'Come on ya feckers.' said Simeon in a quiet voice, that must have carried to Woods and his man. 'Let's get this over with.'

With grunts and snorts the two men began to close in.

'We're dead.' stated Fin flatly, raising his hands to ward off what would undoubtedly be serious violence that he was ill-equipped to deflect. *What have we gotten ourselves into?* His stomach was a churning cauldron of bile. Sweat stood out on his brow and dampened his back, where his shirt began to stick. He saw that Sim had paled. Both boys prepared for the biggest hidings of their lives.

The men appeared confident - and who could blame them.

Fin became aware of the silence in the forest, as though the trees themselves were braced for the injuries about to be inflicted. The birds were hushed and a strange calmness settled over the scene.

Woods lunged towards Sim as the man facing Fin suddenly burst into angry motion.

Fin gave an almost comical leap backward, colliding with a retreating Sim.

And the scene around them became a frozen tableau.

The boys, breathing hard, stared in amazement, Sim hanging on to Fin's hand for support.

'Err... Fin?'

'Yes Sim?'

'Is this usual?'

'Not really no, Sim.'

'Ahh... right.'

Sim released his friend's hand and the two moved apart as Fin went to inspect his opponent more closely. The air around him seemed thicker and he broke out into a fresh flood of perspiration as he slowly moved forward. Even breathing was more difficult. Standing still he was fine, but as soon as he moved it seemed that the very molecules around him were becoming sluggish.

'Sim, are you having trouble moving?' asked Fin breathlessly without looking behind him. His full attention was focussed on the statue-like man before him.

Sim was oddly quiet and when Fin turned it was immediately apparent why. His friend had joined the others in the land of *not-with-Fin*.

Fin was now alone in this strange time out of time. From the corner of his eye he could see bands of colour emerging from the trees, swirling in an unfelt breeze. He turned to check on Edmund, forgotten until this point, who was still lying on the ground at the back of the cart. Despite being motionless, the man had colour in his cheeks and no apparent injuries. Probably just winded, thought Fin, leaning closer to make sure his assessment was correct. Edmund's eyes were clear and bright, reflecting the strange bands of coloured air that were now all around. Fin straightened and inspected the twisting ribbons again. He'd never seen anything like it. He recalled seeing the Northern Lights in a documentary and decided that this was far more intense. The kaleidoscopic performance seemed to emanate out of the trees and undergrowth, even the very ground itself. He was aware of a tingling in his forehead and the warmth of the air around him, a heat generated by more than the sun beating down through the trees. The boughs overhead cast sharply defined shadows and twinkling motes were visible in the beams of light that had an unnatural stillness about them. He passed a large pollen-laden bumble bee, trapped in this moment, hanging in the heavy air as though in amber.

He moved slowly and uncomfortably through the humid air to the front of the cart. The horse captured by an unseen artist in the act of stamping a heavy foot, obscured his view of Kate. As he rounded the animal she came into full view. Woods had roughly thrust her off the bench seat and she lay, half raised on an elbow on the dusty ground. From her expression Fin guessed that no harm had come to her apart from the affront to her dignity at being so rudely manhandled. Satisfied that she and her father were unharmed Fin worked his way back to his original position. His heart was pounding against his chest and his breathing was becoming laboured. He stood in front of Sim, with the growing feeling of alarm that he might somehow be stranded alone in this limbo. His hands were shaking as he mopped his brow. Had he done this? He'd certainly never experienced anything like it. Maybe he was going to spend the rest of his life – and it would probably be a very short and unpleasant one – stuck all alone, surrounded by mesmerising dancing rainbows. He shook his head. No chance! He'd spent enough time with Sim for some of his unquenchable optimism to rub off. He'd be damned if he was going to just lie down and give in. Somehow he was going to get them all back, even dipso Tam. He glanced over to the trees behind him. He hoped Tam was drunkenly oblivious of all this. Even Tam might baulk at Fin's current situation. His whole life had been turned on its head in the last few days. Suddenly *The Nightmare* had moved on to new and extreme heights. Bad dreams that reduced sleep to a few snatched hours each night had developed into an ever present daymare of unimaginable complexity. He'd managed to strand them all years from their everyday lives and now he'd slipped away from even that, to leave them behind while he wandered in yet another solitary cell of time. His head ached and his stomach roiled as he placed the flat of his hand against Sim's shirt, fingertips resting on the skin of his chest..

Sim recoiled in horror and opened his mouth to call out as soon as he felt Fin's touch and, as the contact was broken, he once again entered his seemingly catatonic state. Fin stood shocked and shaken, his whole body trembling, as he slowly brought his hand up and examined his fingers as though expecting to see something. With wonder he turned his hand. There was nothing to indicate why Sim should have been so shaken – unless there was more to his inanimate condition then Fin could imagine. Still, it appeared that his mere touch could bring Sim into the same strange realm as he occupied. This time he positioned himself to the left side of Sim and, with both hands, reached out to hold Sim tightly by the arm.

Nothing happened.

Oh no! He had assumed that his touch was enough to bring Sim back into *Now*, but apparently not.

For want of anything else to do, he reached down to his friend's hand.

This time Sim jumped so much that Fin almost lost his grip. Sim tried to pull his arm free, but his Fin clung on.

'What the flaming hell's going on Fin?' Sim cried out, the same look of fear on his face, eyes wide and face pale, but he stayed with Fin.

Fin sobbed with relief and almost let go of his friend.

'Oh Sim. Thank heavens. I though for a while I'd lost you.'

'What? You're the one leaping around.' said Sim. Then he noticed the stillness again. 'Err… Fin, what's happening?' Now it was Sim's turn to panic as he desperately turned this way and that. 'Do you know how you're doing *this*?'

Fin could forgive the accusation in his friends' question. This was going to be difficult for them both.

'Listen Sim.' He jerked Sim's arm in an effort to get his attention. 'If I let go of you, if we aren't touching, you'll end up like them.' He jerked his head towards the statues around them. 'Don't break the contact, please!'

Sim looked at him aghast and immediately tightened his grip.

'And it has to be skin to skin. Just touching doesn't seem to work.'

With a face filled with wonder and more than a little fear, Sim held on to Fin. The two would have looked like drowning men clinging to the wreckage – if there had been anyone to see them. Sim watched the colours as they streamed across the sky and between the trees.

'Wow. This has gone beyond odd, my strange little friend.' he breathed.

'Sim, I don't know what it is I've done, but we seem to have stepped out of time.'

'Truly, deeply, madly weird.' said Sim in awe, then hurried on. 'You looked like something out of a video game or something. You suddenly flashed up in front of me – out of thin air - and then you were standing next to me. It was like you were just bouncing in and out of here. Really creepy! Like, bowel quaking stuff mate'

Fin nodded with a lopsided grin.

'Tell me about it Sim. I've just spent the last couple of minutes walking around by myself while you lot did your Elgin imitation. Thank God you're back with me. I was beginning to think I'd really lost it this time.'

'Hang on. You're saying that while we're here, time is standing still there?' He waved his free arm around him, whilst making sure he didn't move away from Fin.

'Yeah. That's why I seemed to flash on and off. We can move around and they can't see it – it would be instantaneous for them. The problem is, I don't know how to switch it off.'

Despite their situation, Sim smiled. 'Eh Fin, we could sort these two out with this. If we can pop in and out of their time, they're going to have a hell of time trying to duff up someone who's only there for an instant.'

Fin smiled too. They might be caught up in yet another of his odd time slips, but Sim was going to make the best of it whatever was happening.

'And maybe get back into Edmund's good book?' he said.

'Can't do any harm.' agreed Sim, with a shrug.

'Right, but just remember that if I let go of you, you're back with them.' reiterated Fin.

'Okey doke mate.'

Hand-in-hand they walked the few short steps to the man about to help Woods give them both a good hiding – or maybe something worse. The boys had begun to realise that life in these times were governed by different laws. It seemed that some men were prepared to take whatever they could by whatever means necessary and that if the taking entailed bodily harm to others, that didn't discourage them. Indeed to some - and here Woods and his companions were a prime example – the possibility of doing physical damage was a positive plus.

As they stood before their first target neither of them had any idea of what they were going to do. They looked around, feeling a trifle foolish as they held hands.

'No good Fin, I can't see how we're going to manage this.' said Sim eventually.

Fin looked just as stumped, until he looked back at the cart.

'Got it Sim. Come on,' he said pulling Sim back towards the horse where it stood beside the supine form of Kate. Sim stopped when he saw Kate lying there.

'Don't worry, she looks to be alright. Just a bit dischuffed at being chucked away by Woods when he came back to see what was going on.' said Fin as he moved to the horse.

'Hang on Fin' gasped Sim, as he pushed his way through the treacle-like air, 'this is hard work!'

They finally stood beside the horse.

'Now what?' asked Sim.

'We need these things.' said Fin 'The traces.' He indicated the long reins running down the side of the horse. 'Problem is, I think ol' Dobbin here is going to get a bit of a fright when we touch them and suddenly appear in front of him. If he decides to bolt I'm not sure we'd never catch him.'

'So lets walk up to him from behind. If we talk to him he'll be calm enough. He knows us – a bit anyway – and we'll take them off quietly. We'll be fine Fin.'

So they retreated to the horse's massive hind quarters and Fin laid his hand on the silent beast. The horse - incidentally called Morris, not Dobbin – hardly even flinched as the boys released the leather straps. During the whole procedure they kept up a constant stream of low-voiced words of encouragement, always ensuring that one or other of them was in contact with the horse. Although obviously puzzled by the stillness all around, and possibly the thickness of the air, Morris seemed perfectly happy for the two boys to unharness him. Job done, they again stepped back out of the animal's line of sight and Fin removed his hand.

They went back to the man, patiently awaiting their ministrations and Fin went about carefully arranging the tack around him. The straps ran twice around the man's feet and then around his neck. All the time the boys had to be careful not to make contact with the skin of their erstwhile attacker, but finally they were finished and stood back, hands clenched, to admire their work. Satisfied, Fin nodded.

'Great. So, that should take care of him. Now for Woods.'

This time it was Sim who had a plan.

'Lets just make sure we're behind him with Edmund when we switch back to the *here and now*.'

'What?' Fin was shocked. 'But that means waking Edmund too.' He shook his head. 'I'm not sure I can bring him along too.'

Sim simply smiled.

'We won't know until we try, eh?' and this time it was Sim's turn to pull Fin along, but Fin resisted.

'Hang on Sim. What's he going to do when we let him see this? Isn't it just as likely that he'll go mental if we touch him? This is bad enough for us. For a peasant from the

Middle Ages it could be catastrophic. What if the shock gives him a heart attack or something? I'm not convinced about this.'

Sim stopped trying to move him and thought for a second.

He nodded. 'Yeah, you could be right. It could be a bit difficult to explain, couldn't it? Okay, let's go to plan B.'

'Which is?'

'Dunno, let me have a think.' Sim sank to the grass to think. Fin sat too, it was easier than holding hands while he stood.

Ye Gods, he thought, this is insane. We don't even know if I can get out of this. I could be stuck here for the duration. And we still don't know if we'll ever get home. He thought of the terrible effect their disappearance would have on three families back in the present. They'd been gone for almost a day now. Someone, probably a lot of people, would have missed them by now and no-one would ever believe where they'd been.

'Sim,' he said in a timid voice, 'what are we going to do if I can't get us home?'

Sim gave his hand a squeeze. 'Don't know Fin, but let's sort that out later.' Again he gave his infuriating smile. 'For now let's just try to solve one problem at a time. No point in worrying about it now. Anyway I still think we'll get back without a problem. I trust in your abilities, even if I don't understand them. We aren't stuck here forever, even if you think we are.'

'But Sim –'

'Oh for heaven's sake Fin! Stop it.' Sim's angry interruption brought Fin up short. 'Look. You got us all into this and I *know* you'll get us out. If we don't believe that we might as well give up now. But if we make the best of it we'll be fine. Treat people as you want to be treated and most of them will let you just get on with your life. We'll get by here and sometime we'll wake up and find ourselves home. Just like Dorothy. So forget about what might happen and help Edmund and Kate here and now, cos we can't do anything about anything else.'

Sim's voice had risen as he spoke and Fin realised he was trying to convince himself as much as Fin.

And he's right, of course, thought Fin. Why worry about things you can't do anything about? Better to just get on with things.

He smiled sheepishly.

'Sorry Sim.' he said. 'You're right… sorry.'

Sim gave his hand another squeeze.

'Come on mucker, we'll be alright.' he said in his best Lancashire accent. 'Ah cun feel it in me water.'

They both gave a small smile and then Fin's eyes lit up.

'Right Sim, I've got it. Let's keep it simple – and let's get Tam while we're at it. I don't like the thought of him being comatose in the woods by himself.'

And he quickly outlined his simple plan while they collected the still unconscious Tam.

Sim settled into position.

'See you in sec.' he said with a wink, and they released their hands.

Fin was, once again, more alone than he could ever remember. Only he could find his way back to the real world, even if it was four hundred years away from the real real world - a*nd now would be a good time.*

Hmm... easier said than done.

Adam Woods couldn't understand what had happened. He and Bill had been about to exact their revenge on the two strange boys that had been causing him so much aggravation, when it had all gone horribly wrong.

Bill had found himself hobbled by long leather straps that had become wrapped about his feet and neck. He'd almost strangled himself with his first rushing steps towards the lanky youth and now lay gagging in a heap, bulging eyes staring in disbelief at the taller of the boys, whose head was currently at a level with his own.

And that youth had somehow appeared at the feet of Woods, so suddenly that he'd been sent sprawling onto the dusty forest floor. Before he'd been able to get back to his feet the other ragamuffin had leaped onto him, throwing all his weight onto Wood's shoulders and causing his face to smash into the earth. Fin heard a sickening crack followed by a rush of air and with a hastily snatched glance saw a blast of dust that caught the sunlight and sparkled like a halo around Wood's head. A muffled growl, that was half groan, rose rapidly to a roar as Woods felt his arms bound tightly to his sides and attempted to push himself upright, only to discover that his legs were also hobbled. The boys quickly jumped away from the struggling man and lay panting a few feet away.

They looked at the men prostrate before them and neither could suppress a laugh. In the end it had all been so easy. Sim had lain at Wood's feet, his leather belt set like a snare ready to be tightened as soon as the man sprang back into life. Meanwhile Fin had been behind Woods, ready to lash his arms together with his belt. By using his weight to keep the man down and force him to gasp for air through a helpfully broken nose, Fin had given himself just enough time to pull the leather loop around his victim's lower arms and tie it in a viciously tight knot. In effect, Woods had his arms folded painfully behind his back, unable to loosen either the bonds around his arms or feet.

'I knew we'd be able to give 'em a good belting, Fin.' said Sim, studying Woods, just to be sure that he was completely shackled. The second man was struggling to breath, every twist of his body wrapping the thick leather strapping ever tighter around his neck.

Fin tapped Sim on the shoulder and nodded over to the man.

'If he'd just stop struggling he'd feel a lot better.' he said, with feigned concern. 'He'll do himself an injury if he's not careful.'

'Yeah, what a bonehead.' Sim pushed himself to his feet and turned towards Edmund.

He wasn't sure what he'd expected to see, but the look of sheer horror plastered across the woodsman's face wasn't it.

Fin joined him, looking past the cart towards Kate. She came running towards them, obviously expecting the worst and skidded to a halt at the sight of the two boys looking quietly pleased with a job well done, rather than bloody wrecks beneath the feet of the two older and stronger men. Taking in the scene with a single glance she turned to her father, and blanched at the expression she saw.

Concern filled her face and she knelt beside him.

'Father, art thou injured?' she asked anxiously. When he didn't reply, but just kept staring at Fin and Sim, she gave him a gently shake. 'Father? What is amiss?'

Edmund raised a hand to point at the boys.

'Kate, they are bewitched! It is as I supposed when I heard mention of the foul Dr Dee.' he gasped in an anguished tone. 'These are not mere children, lost and alone.' His voice grew stronger. 'Begone foul theurgist! Begone I say!' Now his voice shook with rage and Kate looked up in bewilderment.

'Master Simeon, what's to do?'

'Nay Kate, do not commune with such as these. I doubt me not that they seek to deceive us in some fashion.'

Fin stepped forward aiming to placate the distraught man.

'Hold hard, thou fiend! Come not closer to me and mine, for I have seen thee as thou truly art.' He came unsteadily to his feet, pushing Kate behind him. 'Against such as thee, how could'st even Master Woods prevail. Thou art diabolic in thy nature and shall not come closer.'

'But father, what hast happ'd. Why dost thou rail so against these two lads, who have done us good service twice this day?' Kate's voice had a pleading edge to it.

'Nay Daughter, they art evil turned to flesh, come to bring down God's wrath upon our heads. Move back daughter. They shall come no closer!'

'But, Goodman Turner, we bear you no ill will.' said Fin. 'We have offered thee service again, as thy daughter hast said. We thought only to protect you from such men as these.' He indicated the four men; one unconscious, one with a wicked looking injury, moaning quietly, and the final two still struggling violently against their bonds.

Edmund's eyes blazed.

'Aye, but 'tis the manner of thy help that I mistrust.' He pointed at Woods and his still hostile looking companion and adopted a defensive stance, the knife held out before him. 'I saw witch, *I saw*! And no man could act in combat as thou didst. I will have no further converse unless thou canst explain what I have seen with mine own eyes.'

Fin and Sim were both dumbstruck. This was the last thing either had expected, but Fin realised that if Edmund had actually seen what they'd done, he could be excused his attitude. Even Sim had been shocked, and he knew about the sort of thing that could happen when Fin was around.

Taking their silence for some sort of admission, Edmund stepped back, shielding Kate from the boys.

'Hah. So thee hast no words of explanation? Begone, foul rakehells. We would have no more to do with thee.'

And with this last departing shout he pushed Kate up onto the cart and leapt up after her, ready to abandon his erstwhile attackers to the satanic caresses of the devils who now stood, looking somewhat perplexed, behind the cart.

'Goodman Turner!' called Sim. 'Methinks thou shall have little fortune in trying to drive thine horse without full harness!'

Edmund searched around for the reins with growing panic. He knew that unless he could escape now, taking his beloved daughter with him, there was every possibility that they would end up in that place that the priest warned them of each Sabbath. In his mind's eye he had a fast running film of the tortures that lay ahead. He almost wept at his inability to save beautiful Kate, for it would surely be her who would suffer the greater torment.

The Church, in many ways, had a lot to answer for at the time of Good Queen Bess.

Edmund began to rummage around in the cloth bag behind the bench seat.

'Fear not sweet Kate, they shall not take thee!' Edmund breathed and with a shout of triumph he dropped his small kife and pulled out a long, wicked-looking dagger. He reached for his daughter.

'No Father!' she screamed and jumped down from the cart, racing back towards Fin and Sim.

'No Kate, they art demons!' cried Edmund, almost hysterical with fright now and leaping down to chase his daughter.

She ran into Fin's arms, tears streaming down her face and Sim stepped in front of her to protect her from her father.

Edmund stopped a few feet away.

'Kate, come to me my daughter.' He too was crying. Hot, bitter tears that seemed to scour his cheeks as he faced these two demons who would condemn her to an eternity of debase slavery in the halls of Satan. He stood, his face flushed with the urgent desire to save his daughter from the legions of Hell but frightened beyond belief to be so lightly armed against such as hellspawn as these.

Sim raised his hands in an attempt to calm the almost hysterical man who faced him.

'I pray thee – ' he began, but before he could say anything more Edmund lunged at him with the knife and thrust deeply into Sim's upper arm.

With a shriek of pain Sim staggered backwards into Kate who fell against Fin, who tripped over the bound body of Adam Woods, who had been watching the entire encounter thus far, with an almost gleeful expression. He roared anew as the three children tumbled onto him, driving elbows, knees and outstretched hands into his back and once again driving his smashed nose into the ground.

Edmund stood aghast, staring at the tangled, struggling heap before him and then down at the bloodied knife held loosely in his hand, now slick with body fluids that Sim, for one, would have preferred never to have seen the light of day.

Fin had paused in his narrative. He looked at the faces around the kitchen table.

'Sorry, pee break.' he said as he stood and made for the door.

Tam sat hunched beside the empty seat. He wanted to say something to lighten the atmosphere, but couldn't think of anything that wouldn't have sounded crass. This was not the time for jokes or whimsical comments.

'More tea anyone?' asked Lidine, as much to break the silence as anything else, 'Or is it time for something a little stronger?' she pointedly stared at Jarmon.

'Oh… yes… a beer Ian? White wine with soda Sue?' Jarmon asked rising.

'Thanks Jar – yes - a beer might be beneficial just at the moment.' Ian nodded.

Sue nodded too, but never shifted her gaze from Tam.

'Son' she said quietly, 'you've been very quiet while Fin's been talking. Is there anything you want to tell us while he's out of the room?'

Lilli looked up sharply. She was well aware of the implication of Sue's question.

Tam silently shook his head.

'Look Tam, no-one would hold it against you if you changed your story' said Ian softly, 'but do it now, before things get even more out of hand. Come clean and maybe the police would be prepared to forget what's happened today. You don't have to protect Fin you know. Whatever happened, it's got to be better to get it off your chest.'

'This can't go on.' said Sue gently reaching across for her son's hand.

Tam looked up suddenly, tears in his eyes.

'You still don't believe, do you?' he shouted. 'You think the same as all the others. You think we did something to Sim and invented this story to cover it up. Well we'd have come up with something a sight more convincing than this, if that was the case'

He looked up at Jarmon who'd just re-entered the room carrying two drinks, which he put down quietly on the table.

'You believe us don't you Mister LeMott?' he asked.

Jarmon looked solemnly at the boy, who appeared even smaller than usual as he sat, distraught, at the table.

'Tam, what I believe is academic at the moment – it's your mum and dad that you have to convince, not me or Lidine… or Lilli.'

Tam looked as though the tears were going to get the better of him.

'But for what it's worth, I don't care how ludicrous your story is, I do believe you, with all my heart. Because if I don't, I have to accept that you and Fin have committed some sort of crime and a particularly nasty crime at that, against Sim.' Jarmon gave a small smile of encouragement. 'And none of us going to allow ourselves to think that.'

He nodded across at Ian and Sue, who both looked close to tears too.

'And what's more, they don't want to either.' he said. 'It's just that we're constantly trying to shore up our conviction. Even you have to admit that it doesn't matter how often we hear the story, it does sound so far-fetched that we're going to have the devil's own time trying to make anyone else believe you both.'

Fin came back in and it was obvious to everyone that he'd been listening at the door.

'It's not that we don't want to believe you love' said Sue plaintively, staring intently at the table, 'it's just that it's so difficult.'

'I'm sure they understand that, Dear.' said Ian, trying to sooth his distressed wife with a protective arm around her shoulders.

'If we can't convince even you – *especially* you – we're sunk.' Fin said. He pressed play on the hi-fi hanging on the wall and the music of John Dowland once more laid its soft, healing harmonies upon those around the table. 'Anyway Tam has no option but to let me tell this bit.' he said, referring to Sue's initial comment. 'He can't tell you much about what was happening – he was a bit the worse for wear.'

'Not so much compos mentis, more mental compost at this point.' quipped Tam. He just couldn't help himself, and despite the worry and confusion surrounding them all, the gloom in the kitchen magically lifted... fractionally.

Jarmon brought two more drinks in, duplicates of those for Ian and Sue, and sat once more next to Fin.

'So tell us the rest.' said Lidine and Lilli nodded enthusiastically.

The three children struggled to their feet, warily eying Edmund. Kate and Fin wore expressions of shock and disbelief.

Sim just stood there and bled.

A lot.

The sight of the blood emerging from the wound on the boy's arm seemed to shake Edmund out of his stupor.

'By the Rood, what have I done?' he cried.

'Aye Father, well might you ask.' replied Kate harshly. She raised the hem of her cote and tugged at her undershirt, tearing off a strip and attempting to bind the wound that was pouring blood down Sim's arm. She could see that the boy was too shocked at what had happened to do anything more than hold his arm, as though frightened that it was going to drop off altogether. Unable to stem the flow of blood, Kate withdrew the cloth and ripped Sim's sleeve open using the tear made by the knife. With the arm exposed, she quickly bent to pick up a short length of branch that lay at her feet and used it to twist the cloth into a tourniquet higher up the damaged limb.

Fin was standing on the other side of his friend unable to think of anything to say or do to help his friend and trying not to look too closely at the damage wrought by the frantic woodsman. All he could do was hop frantically from one foot to the other and dither about in the way that one does when feeling totally useless in such a situation.

'Master Finbar!' shouted Kate. 'Look to the cart and bring my pouch. Tis amongst the gear beneath the seat.'

With commendable speed Fin ran off to the cart, but struggled to find the small leather bag. He had to turn his head this way and that to be able to look through the few undamaged areas of his glasses. The cracked glazing made close-up work well nigh impossible.

'Hurry lad!' called Kate as he rummaged under the seat.

With an exhalation of relief he found the object of his mission and rushed back to Kate with a small leather bag held closed by a drawstring. Sim was swaying where he stood

'Now, hold Simeon's arm whilst I find that which is needful.' she said, as she turned Sim to allow Fin to grip the, now sodden, makeshift bandage, which was wound so tightly around Sim's upper arm that it was biting into his skin.

She rummaged for several seconds before emerging with a long bodkin with a wickedly sharp looking point and a length of silk thread.

'Master Simeon, you must lie down now so that I might repair the injury done by he who is pleased to call himself my protector.' said Kate in a soft voice, accompanied by a withering glance in the direction of her father. 'Wilt thou not help now Father, or hast thou done enough?'

Edmund sprang to life, dropping the knife and stepping quickly over to help Fin lower the injured boy to the ground and Kate settled cross-legged beside him This time Fin forced himself to inspect his friend's injury. Sim's skin had a grey pallor and his entire left side was coated with a bright scarlet stain. The cut in his arm was only about two inches long, but was wickedly ragged where the notched blade of the old knife had literally ripped it apart. When Kate released the tourniquet they could all see that blood was literally pumping from the wound, creating a slick that made it difficult to manoeuvre the limb. Finally setting the arm in a more comfortable position across her lap, she began the task of sewing it up.

Again she gave her father another venomous look.

'Dost this look to be a devil to you now father.' she said, through gritted teeth. 'I think me that for such offence as this, a true devil wouldst surely have dragged thee down into the very bowels of Hell. What did'st thou see to cause thee to act so? Thou, who art so gentle, wouldst not inflict such grievance if thou were in thy full senses. For the love of God what *possessed* thee?'

Edmund, visibly shaken by his daughter's turn of phrase, looked at Fin squatting beside him, with something akin to awe. Fin, head held only inches away, blinked owl-like behind his broken spectacles.

'Master Finbar, I knowest not, for certain, what I saw. But you two did'st seem to me to flitter hither and yon, like the flame of a wind-blown fire. No God-made child, or adult, could do what I *did* see you two do. What *are* you? For I know that I did see something that should not be possible. By my eyes I am certain of what I saw! It is for you to explain, not I.'

As Kate bent to her task again, gradually closing the ugly wound on Sim's bicep together, Fin sat back on his haunches and looked directly at Edmund. This couldn't be avoided. Edmund deserved to know the truth now, but how could Fin explain in any way that the man would understand. Hell, even Fin didn't really understand!

Sim groaned loudly as the stitches were administered with as much care and gentleness as Kate could command. It was just as well that shock and lack of blood were numbing his senses to the pain emanating from the sliced flesh. The wound was deep and Kate was having to try to squeeze the sharply defined edges of the cut together as she worked.

'I promise I will explain all, Goodman Turner, once Sim has been seen to.' He suddenly looked up at the trees behind them. 'And I'd forgotten about Tam, he's over there in the trees. I'll need your help to load him into the cart. He's in no fit state to do anything for himself.' To Edmund it appeared that the self-control the boy had been exercising over these last few minutes was beginning to crack; Fin was almost hopping in his agitation.

Fin put his hands to his head and whispered.

'Oh! What I have I done? What more harm can I bring to them?'

The urgency of the low voice made Kate look up.

'What? Is there more? Is Master Tamburlaine hurt too?'

Her obvious concern made Fin shake his head in an attempt to reassure her, as he stood to look down at the pale face of Sim. Even though he knew things would probably turn out fine in the end, getting there was proving a hell of a trial.

'Nay, Kate. Tam did partake of too much ale at the tavern. He's sleeping it off in the bushes.' he said, almost absent mindedly.

Kate managed a smile at that.

'So he's a drunkard eh? Well there's naught I may do to offer aid there. A thick head and a little pain will be all that may prevent further rub for a lad such as he. And if that is all that ails him why art thou in such distress?'

She bent her head to bite through the thread binding Sim's ichor covered wound, her gaze leaving Fin for only a fraction of a second and her mouth coming away bloody. She reminded Fin of an image from an old Hammer horror film, the beguiling vampiress rising from her latest victim. Here, nothing could be further from the truth. Fin shook his head, partly in wonder at her efficiency and partly in despair at the problems he had visited on his best friends.

Kate ignored the lack of answer from Fin and gently smoothed back the hair from Sim's brow. She stared down into the ashen face.

'Now we must hope that the balance of his humours is not too long upset, else we must search for an apothecary, and there are none in these parts that are known to me.'

Fin must have looked as confused as he felt.

'Fear not young Finbar' said Edmund gruffly, putting a heavy hand on Fin's knee, 'for I doubt me not that we will find one amongst the monks of Saint Wilfrid, for theirs is a place of succour for all those in pain.'

'But what has Sim's sense of humour got to do with anything? He needs a doctor not a laugh!'

Now it was the turn of Edmund and Kate to look puzzled.

'Master Finbar,' said Kate, 'at the hospice they can care for Simeon using knowledge that is far beyond my understanding. I have sewn up cuts and used poultices on bruises since before mother went to heaven and I know that the humours of the body must be kept in balance and that bleeding can be used, either by leech or by hand letting, but as to how it is done, I know not.'

'Aye, tis best left to the hospice herbalist or - at worst - a friar.' agreed Edmund with a nod. 'My Kate can cope with most hurts, but now is the time to call upon the knowledge gained by those who spend their lives in the service of God.' He dropped his eyes with shame and clenched his fists against his sides, in an oddly childish gesture. 'Pray that they may undo what I have done in my most ungodly rage.'

'Aye, and pray that Master Simeon will forgive thee thy unwarranted fury.' said his daughter, this time with some compassion.

'No Kate, be not so hard with your father, for what he did, he did out of love for thee. The greater fault here is mine, far more than his.' said Fin. And he really did believe that there was no-one else on whom to hang this horror. His friends would never have been in such a terrible position if he hadn't brought them here. As he looked down at Simeon, looking so helpless, covered in blood, depression rested its skeletal hand on his shoulder. This really did seem to be about as bad as things could get. If Sim were to die through some God-awful infection in this medical wilderness there would be no-one else to blame. Even recent experience hadn't prepared him for their current situation, though he did feel better after being able to discuss it with someone who had been through similar ordeals.

Someone who hadn't had any help in the same situation.

Someone who'd told him that it would all turn out right in the end.

Someone who seemed to have the same sunny-side-up outlook as Simeon, whatever the circumstances.

He needed to speak to Tony again.

Even though hearing this for the second time, the others around the table felt just as stunned at the turn the tale had taken as they had the first time... and they knew what was coming.

Fin paused to take a sip of tea.

'Come on Fin, get on with it.' urged Tam. He was due to re-enter the story in the next few minutes and was eager to join in telling the next act.

'Sshhh!' hissed Lilli, with a disapproving look at him, then glared at Fin. 'Come on Fin, get on with it!'

Edmund joined Fin in collecting Tam from the undergrowth at the side of the road; the tough woodsman making somewhat lighter work of carrying the boy than had Fin and Sim only minutes earlier. That is, minutes to everyone else, somewhat longer to Fin.

They laid Tam in the back of the cart among the shards of wood remaining from the morning delivery.

'How came Master Tamburlaine to be so close by?' asked Edmund. 'I saw him not when you and Master Simeon didst make thine approach.'

'Err. He must have come over when we were otherwise occupied.' said Fin lamely.

Edmund gave him a sidelong glance, but said no more.

Sim was laid gently alongside him. They made an odd couple; one boy quietly sleeping off one too many draughts of ale, the other lying looking close to death, in a shirt stiffened with his own blood.

Fin looked down at them with grim determination. Somehow he was going to make this right – he just wasn't sure how yet, but he knew that Sim at least should recover, though it seemed hard to believe at the moment.

While Fin held the still bloodied knife to Woods' throat Edmund trussed him up and the two of them rolled the indignant mugger into the weeds beside the path. They repeated the procedure on the second hobbled man. Bill allowed Edmund to bind him tightly without the threat of the knife, but he never took his wide eyes off Fin. He'd seen exactly the same thing as Edmund, but had reacted in a totally different way. In the presence of this magical being, almost certainly from another earthly sphere, he wasn't going to cause any sort of trouble. He'd overheard the occasional mention of such things from those more educated than himself and knew enough not to antagonise such things. Fin was disconcerted by the incessant trembling of the man, who in ordinary circumstance would have swatted him out of his path, in much the same way that Fin might have reacted to a fly. Bill wasn't going to risk the wrath of this unnatural being clothed in the guise of a young boy, not when lying still seemed a far more favourable course of action.

They left the third ruffian cradling his broken arm – he wasn't in a position to cause any further nuisance. Indeed Fin would have offered to help him, but he shuffled away whenever Fin stepped closer, and his constant whimpering was enough to make Edmund override any more humane considerations voiced by Kate.

'He meant to do us harm, Kate. Let him make his own way to the ministrations of the brothers at the hospice. We have another who requires more urgent help, if we are to save him from the wound I gave him.' He let his eyes wander over the neatly closed cut on Sim's arm.

'Worry not Father. Master Simeon will survive, never doubt it. Though it will be weeks, maybe months, before he can make good use of that arm again.' Kate sounded less certain than the words implied.

Edmund nodded.

'Aye, but maybe to such as he, it is a mortal wound. How can we know?' He gave Fin a searching look. 'These two – nay three – are not ordinary boys, daughter.'

Fin knew that the time was fast approaching when he would have to try to explain things to them. He just wasn't sure how to, but now was not the time.

'Nay Edmund - he will be well. Do not fret over Simeon - or Tam.' he chuckled, slapping Tam's foot which protruded from the cart before him. 'It will be he, not Sim, who will have to bear the jests regarding this day's actions. Whereas Sim will be the battle-scarred hero.'

They had worked around and over the fourth man as they loaded the two bodies onto the cart. Now Edmund made cursory checks of the still form, before, satisfied that the man wasn't in danger of his life, rolling him after the two bound figures at the side of the path. Woods seemed to be working his way through an admirable store of invective at an ever growing volume, much of which Fin couldn't understand. Edmund on the other hand seemed to know exactly what was being spat out at them from the poisonous mouth of his now never-to-be, son-in-law. As he made a final inspection of the area and checked his knots in the stout ropes that tied their former attackers, he gave the voluble Woods a hefty kick in the kidney region.

'Be silent, thou foul-speaking adder. Be thankful that we have tasks of greater import than returning thee and thy playmates to the village, tethered like the beasts thou art!'

Kate, witnessing her father's brief loss of temper, raised her gaze to the skies and gave a heartfelt sigh as she shook her head.

Fin failed to hide his grin of appreciation and both father and daughter saw.

'Fin! Shame on thee!' Kate scolded.

Unfortunately, Edmund seemed uncertain of how to behave around Fin now. He was obviously ill at ease to be in the presence of the someone who could perform such rare and inexplicable feats and, to be honest, Fin couldn't blame him. He'd feel much the same himself if he'd seen what Edmund had.

Kate on the other hand, seemed even more friendly. She had witnessed only the bravery of the lads as they had waded into the fray to help her father, and doubtless realised that she had been saved from a far worse fate.

Once they had all climbed into the cart - father and daughter together on the seat in front, Fin sitting in the back with his friends - Edmund made to turn back to the village, no more than a mile or so behind them.

'No Edmund.' said Fin softly, making the older man start when he placed a hand on his arm. 'We three are still for London and Doctor Dee.'

He saw Edmund stiffen at the name and continued quickly.

'I know that you may have heard things about him Edmund, but I think me that only he can help me - and then probably only a little.' He removed his ruined glasses and held them up to the other two for inspection. 'Apart from anything, I need to try to have these repaired or replaced. Without good eye glasses I can't see well enough be of any use to my friends and I don't want to go on being unable to see clearly. ' He indicated the two recumbent figures beside him. 'I'd just be a burden to these two and they don't need that, especially when all this is my fault. They will both recover before too long and I have no desire to remain in these environs any longer than absolutely necessary. I must protect them from further ill, else it will all fall on my shoulders. I have to try to keep them safe until I may undo the wrongs I have caused them' He looked down at the two bodies. Tam snored noisily. 'Well, Simeon anyway. Tam is his own worst enemy in this instance.'

Kate smiled at that, then tilted her head to one side, raising a hand to shield her eyes as she squinted against the sun, now well over the treetops.

'How so, Master Fin?' she asked.

Fin could tell that he had their full attention and realised the time had come to tell all.

'Please Edmund, take us as far as you are able and I shall tell you the reason for our seeming strangeness while we journey.'

Edmund hesitated.

'I promise no harm will come to either of you, Edmund, and you'll find my tale well worth the listening.'

The woodsman made up his mind and urged Morris into a slow walk away from Rowington.

'I can promise only to take you as far as the turning for our home at Wilmcote. That will take some hours, but from there, you three must make your own way south for my work is not finished providing timber for the hall and we must needs return to Rowington.'

There was a tone in Edmunds voice that clearly said he couldn't see how the boys could possibly continue south without his aid and the prospect of another visit to the village obviously didn't fill him with joy. His next meeting with Woods was not one that Fin envied him, especially if his business necessitated his being civil to a man who had attempted to steal away his daughter using violence. That gave Fin pause for thought; if Woods had been going to have his evil way with Kate, his intention would have been to leave no witnesses. In all probability, he and Sim had just saved the lives of both father and daughter.

Now there was a sobering thought!

Fin doubted that Edmund would allow Kate out of his sight whenever a visit to Rowington was unavoidable. Nor could the father take the chance of leaving his daughter at home. Who knew when Woods might take it upon himself to pay a visit, particularly if he knew that Edmund would be away, hauling beams to the village?

Fin gained what little comfort he could from the knowledge that, while he and his friends may have precipitated Woods' actions, in all likelihood they had just brought forward the timing of an inevitable event, once Kate had made it known to the man that she would never willingly be his wife. Fin doubted that Edmund would have forced a union on her, he thought too much of her to have treated her so badly. No, here was a father who would never knowingly cause his daughter pain or suffer any harm to come to her while there was breath in his solid little frame.

These were good people and he felt he owed them the truth, whether they chose to believe it or not.

The journey back towards Wilmcote lasted long enough for Fin to tell them everything. Strangely he felt more able to unburden himself with these two than with either his friends or family. They showed an unexpected capacity to believe the whole thing, not even questioning the fact that the three friends had somehow travelled back in time. While obviously over-awed by it all, they seemed to accept the whole thing. At one point Kate had looked over at her father, who had given a quick shake of his head to some unasked question that Fin failed to grasp.

Eventually he finished the story and settled back, awaiting their reaction; they had said little while they had listened.

'Tis truly a most awful tale that you tell, young Master Finbar.' said Edmund finally and Fin, misinterpreting the comment flushed with indignation.

So they hadn't really believed it after all! They just thought it was some dreadful concocted fairytale! Well, sod them!

His thoughts must have shown clearly on his face, for Kate looked puzzled at his reaction.

'Fin, father means only that thy tale is of most grievous events. He meant no ill. Whyfore dost thou take such offense?'

Fin did a double take, confused by the ever-present simultaneous translation going on in his head. He'd obviously taken Edmund's words in the wrong way and the Babel Fish had failed to give him the correct meaning. Edmund had used exactly the right phrase, it was Fin, using a modern interpretation, that had misunderstood.

'Apologies, Edmund. I mistook thy meaning.'

Edmund nodded his head briskly, glad to have the matter cleared up, though in truth he had little idea of what had caused the problem.

Fin sat up straighter and looked around. The trees were beginning to thin around them and the heat of the early afternoon sun was hot through his shirt. Tam stirred in the bed of the cart beside the sleeping form of Simeon.

Tam groaned loudly as he eased himself up onto one elbow.

'Where we goin' Fin?'

'Off to London care of Edmund and Kate. Well part of the way anyway; then we're on our own.'

Tam tipped his head back to see an amused looking Kate staring back at him.

'Uhh, hullo.' he said, suddenly feeling and looking considerably brighter. 'Fancy bumping into you again.'

Edmund turned to give Tam the quick once-over.

'It would seem that an overmuch intake of ale does not agree with thy fine young body, master Tam.' He shook his head. 'Never have I seen a strutting cockerel laid so low with so little brew.'

'Well, it wasn't my fault.' mumbled Tam, gazing at his feet with the air of a petulant child. 'I haven't eaten anything for hours and I've got a delicate stomach.' He began rooting through his pockets with exaggerated care.

'I bet I've got a note from me Mum somewhere...'

Eventually he had to join in the raucous laughter around him even though he was trying hard to look forlorn and misunderstood.

'Tis not thy stomach that is weak, Master Tamburlaine. Methinks 'tis thy pate that is addled.' said Edmund grinning.

Fin marvelled. Within seconds of waking, presumably with a very thick head, Tam had lifted the somewhat morose air that had been following them during Fin's tale.

Tam held his head and groaned even louder, laying it on thick.

With a mischievous twinkle in her eyes, Kate reached under the seat and brought out a large kerchief wrapped around a parcel.

'Why Master Tam, mayhap thy stomach is in need of some sustenance – and I have just the thing.'

With a flourish she swept away the cloth to reveal a pie of alarming proportions.

'Aye, young sir, time for a little humble pie?' laughed Edmund over his shoulder.

Tam's eyes seemed to glaze over as his stomach rejected the idea of anything being parachuted into its ale-filled interior.

'Mmmmm.. humble pie Tam. Great!' enthused Fin, with a wicked grin. He settled forward to inspect her handiwork with unexpected culinary interest. 'So tell me Kate, what exactly goes into humble pie?' But it was obvious from his air of forced innocence that he already knew. He was just enjoying the effect the home-baked monster was having on his friend.

'Why, tis only the best that is good enough for my dearest Father.' she replied.

'And that is?' asked Tam with trepidation gripping the side of the cart like a drowning man clinging to jetsam.

'Deer humbles and good mutton suet of course. Cooked to my mothers own recipe.'

After a brief pause, Fin burst out laughing.

'Tis very good eating Master Finbar, be not so unkind to my Kate. She knows that tis my favourite!' cried Edmund in defence of his daughter, and dearly loved - but now sadly departed - wife.

'No Edmund, you misunderstand *me* this time.' said Fin, almost crying with laughter. Looking over at Tam he couldn't help adding. 'That's entrails isn't it? Guts and intestines and that?'

Edmund snatched a quick glance behind him as he heard the retching from the back of the cart and grinned in sudden understanding.

Tam could stand no more and unceremoniously dumped three jacks worth of ale onto the roadside. The noisy expulsion made Kate wrinkle her nose. Fin thought she looked even more girlishly attractive. Her face had a quality that made even the smallest expression magnify her beauty. Fin shook his head to clear it of such thoughts; he couldn't afford to develop a crush on a girl who was over four hundred years older than he. He knew about toy boys, but there were limits!

Tam slumped back beside Simeon with a heartfelt groan.

'Ahhh, verily,' said the woodsman, shaking his head. 'methinks Sir Tamburlaine has a stronger stomach than he credits. It has certes strains to its very utmost to be rid of that troublesome ale.'

The riotous laughter at Tam's expense drifted away from the little group to dissipate into the surrounding trees, setting startled bird into flight and causing several small animals to seek shelter.

Fin heaved a sigh of relief. Though he may not have realised it, Tam had managed to thaw the unhappy chill that had fallen over the small group.

Now only Sim's unmoving form remained to remind them of the unfortunate events of the last few hours.

Now Mike (38)

It must have been obvious to everyone on the school trip that something was wrong. Three boys had been sent home, in the middle of the night no less, and both of the accompanying teachers looked as though they'd had very little sleep.

Whispered gossip was rife among the boys.

In addition, as Pauly Wright was eager to point out, "That tasty bird of ol' Nutter's has left. More's the pity, eh?"

Try as he might Mike was finding it increasingly difficult to deal with Bert, never mind the curious stares of the boys. He could see that they all knew something was amiss. Willis was never going to accept the story, cooked up hastily just before Bev had left, that the three missing lads had done something so grievous that the teachers had had no option but to despatch them home immediately. Most of the others were too busy taking advantage of the preoccupation of both Bert and Mike, to care much about the cause.

The next two days passed in a whirl of accusation and counter-accusation regarding the disappearance. The Head had phoned during the first day to leave the men in no doubt that the school would disown them if necessary. A stain on the reputation of a fine Grammar school… possible implications for the funding of the new language block… unwanted publicity, both locally and – horror of horrors – even in the tabloids. This last reference was said with almost palpable disgust; The Head viewed the tabloid press in much the same way that Mike might view something nasty on the bottom of his shoe.

Yes, it seemed that they were going to be on their own in this. The school had washed its hands of them when it became apparent that one of the boys was now missing, when he should have been in the care of two of the most senior staff. They had been entrusted with the well-being of some of the finest young men in Cheshire and they had failed in their duty. As a result The Head had, in effect, thrown them to the dogs. As soon as the trip was over they would be on suspension, pending further police and LEA inquiries.

Bert had taken it far worse than Mike had expected. Even knowing about the older man's brush with the authorities over Tony Athelston, it was as though Bert was heading for some sort of breakdown, a situation made worse by not knowing what would happen to their careers at the end of it all. Bert was expecting the worst and, unfortunately, Mike couldn't think of a way to avoid what was seeming inevitable.

When they eventually returned home, Bev was waiting along with the parents, most of whom now knew that Simeon was missing. Though the story had appeared in the local papers, it hadn't yet made it to the dailies, but no-one was in much doubt where the whole thing was heading.

Mike and Bert had both been advised by a local education official to say nothing to anyone. Apparently it was now fairly common knowledge that one boy had vanished without trace and the two who had accompanied him had failed to account for their part in his disappearance.

On the way home, following an uncomfortable few minutes as the luggage was unloaded and the curious stares from the adults had to be borne, Bev had let Mike know what had been decided by the powers that be.

'Bert was being very standoffish with everyone Mike. What's he said to you?'

'Not much I'm afraid love. I think that there's a lot he hasn't told us about the last lad who disappeared. He's no better than when you last saw him and I just don't know how to help him.'

'Mike, you've got enough to think about without worrying about Bert. They still don't know what happened to Sim, and Fin and Tam are sticking to their story about going back to the sixteenth century.' Mike shook his head as she continued. 'Artie seems to know far more than the rest of us. It sounds like the police have been asking him about it all, because of his involvement with Bert and Tony Athelston The police still seem to think that Fin and Tam have done something that they're trying to hide and they were hoping for some sort of insight from Artie. Unless they come up with something concrete – and soon – there's no way it can be kept from the papers – it's already been in the Chronicle. It's only a question of time until we have reporters camped outside the house.'

She looked ashen faced at the prospect.

'I've spoken to Artie about it a lot and he was quite excited by the whole thing.'

'Excited! Why? Doesn't he realise the problems we've got – well not you personally, but certainly me and Bert and the lads. For God's sake Bev, what does he think's going on?'

'Mike, calm down. Artie thinks that Fin might have a clue to what happened to Tony Athelston.'

'Oh Lord, Bev. Not Artie too. Does he honestly think that Fin's story could hold even a nugget of truth?'

Bev looked shocked.

'Why Mike, don't you?' she asked quietly.

'Oh come on, Bev. Do you really think that any of it can be true? I've had two days to think it all over and, tough as it is to believe it of them, I can't help thinking that maybe the police are right. Those two must have done something, but God knows what. I'm bloody terrified that this is going to end horribly.' He stared at the road ahead, his expression bleak. 'For all concerned.' he added.

'But the local police called in Artie partly because of all that happened with Tony Athelston. I have a suspicion that more than one or two of them think he's a little off the beaten track these days, but he has a reason to find out the truth. The Athelston affair almost ruined him and he's out to prove that these boys have a problem – or whatever you chose to call it - that couldn't have been foreseen.' She sighed heavily. 'I think it's to prove to the Athelstons as much as himself that he couldn't help the boy all those years ago because no-one could understand what was going on.'

'Meanwhile me and Bert are on indefinite suspension and we've been told that we mustn't talk to anyone. This is all so out of hand!'

Bev reached across and lightly laid her hand on his, where it grasped the steering wheel.

'Let's just try not to think about it now love. I've arranged for us to see Artie tomorrow. Maybe he can tell us something that might help.'

'Yeah.' Mike grinned crookedly. 'There's no point in dwelling on things we can't do anything about. I just wish I could think of a reason for Fin and Tam to have done such a thing.'

'Shhh, Mike. Let's just wait until we've seen Artie.'

And for the rest of the night Mike allowed himself to be comforted by Bev and forget, sometimes for whole minutes at a time, the agony of not knowing what the future held.

Then Fin, Tam and Simeon (39)

It was only when Fin awoke and realised that the sun was beginning its descent in its arc across the blue sky that he thought to ask about the length of time that they had been heading for the home that Edmund had said was only a few hours distant at the start of their journey.

Edmund blushed at his enquiry and it was Kate who answered.

'Fin, long hast thou slept. We have been to our home and gathered what few belongings we need, along with our monies, held in a chest beneath our seat.' Edmund gave her a quick look of reproof at revealing this to the strange lad lying behind him. "He's still not certain of us." thought Fin. "And who can blame him really".

'You three slept whilst we loaded. See the blankets and vessels beside thee? These are all we shall require until we reach our destination.' At Fin's look of incomprehension she giggled and gave him a dig in the chest with her foot. 'My father is a freeman, owing allegiance to no-one but The Queen. E'en the lord of this manor holds no sway over us. He is his own man and methinks thou hast caused him to consider a change in our circumstances.'

'Aye, they do say, Master Finbar, that the city dost cry out for men with a talent for working wood – and that I have. Though I may, of late, have been more used to hauling timber for others, I am a fair carpenter. Therefore shall I kill two birds with but a single stone.'

Kate clapped her hand with delight.

'We are for London, Fin! Father didst not remain in Wilmcote when he couldst – and maybe shouldst..'

At Fin's continuing look of bewilderment she continued.

'Zounds! Truly thou art a barnpot young sir; Wilmcote lies behind us Master Fin.' She clapped her hands in delight. 'We have forsaken our home, such as it was, and are now to find employ among the builders along the banks of the Thames.'

'But Edmund,' Fin spluttered, 'what of your life in Warwick? You can't just abandon your home.'

'And why can I not?' asked Edmund. 'May I not choose to make my life where I will?' he said with mock severity. 'Would you now seek to prevent us?' He shook his head as he coaxed their horse to a faster stride, as though to confirm his decision. 'Nay lad, we are for the capital - and a new life amongst its populous!'

Fin found himself grinning too. This was better than he could have hoped. At least now he wouldn't have to worry about how they would get to Mortlake. Suddenly the future brightened. Not only would they be able to make the journey in the fastest time possible, but they would also be making it in fine company.

Simeon shifted position with a moan and Fin squatted down to check on his friend. Fearing the worst, he was surprised to see that the colour had returned to Sim's face. He was breathing easier too.

'Ist aught amiss?' asked Edmund sharply, his concern obvious, as Kate shifted around to look more closely

'Nay Edmund. It would seem that Simeon does prosper. See,' He gestured to Kate, 'he is on the mend, though how, I do not know.'

Fin gingerly inspected the bloodied wound and was stunned to see that the stitches, though still in place, bordered a thin pink scar – the raw jagged wound from Edmund's knife was all but gone.

He looked up to see the wonder in Kate's eyes mirroring his own.

She crossed herself hurriedly, as though to ward off some unknown spirit that shadowed them through the forest, but said nothing to her father.

That night they made camp just off the beaten track through the trees, amongst the oak and alder that grew so thickly all around them. Kate prepared a light meal over a small fire laid by her father. As the night closed in around them their conversation turned to practical matters; where they would find food and drink during the long trip to London and what they would do once they arrived.

Tam had recovered sufficiently from his hangover to join them, while Sim still rested in the cart, not yet able to rise from his wooden bed, but nonetheless improving far more rapidly than anyone expected. As Sim lay sleeping, Edmund regarded the three children around the fire across a thick slab of humble pie.

'The Lord knows we have left little enough behind.' he said. 'Our old dwelling will be no great loss and we carry all we need with us - apart from victuals. After tonight we shall have to trap our meals as we travel, for I have no wish to spend what small amount of coin we have when the Good Lord can provide for us. There is game aplenty in these woods, and roots and mushrooms as well as fowl should we happen upon water. We shall, more's the pity, have to buy our drink and that will put a hole in our pocket before London.'

'Aye, Father, but we will arrive with still some small amount of money and once you have work we shall survive. And who knows what may happen in London. They do say that a good man may make his fortune there, so long as he may find the right employ.' said Kate, her eyes asparkle from the firelight and the excitement of their adventure.

Fin sipped from a small earthenware tankard of ale.

'Maybe Doctor Dee will have some advice for us all.' he said. 'He has the ear of the Queen, they say, and he is sure to know more about the goings on in London than we.'

'True, true.' breathed Edmund. 'But I would rather rely on men other than he. They do say also that he dabbles in witchcraft and that the paths to worlds other than ours are open to him .'

'Yes, but alchemy may lead on to many wonders in later years. We would do well to work our way into his good books.' said Fin. 'He has travelled far and knows more than almost any other man in the country.'

Edmund still looked dubious.

'Never mind.' said Kate, hugging her knees as she stared into the fire. 'I fancy me, that although decided in a moment, we shall come to be grateful for our rash decision. As master Simeon is wont to say "keep thy mind open to the possibilities and who knows what may hap." '

Tam laughed quietly as he finished the small piece of bread that was all he felt he could eat in his current delicate state.

'That's true. And blow me, things usually turn out for the best for Sim.'

'Let's hope I haven't brought his charmed life to a sudden halt, eh?' said Fin.

Edmund smiled across at the bespectacled boy squinting at the fire.

'Master Fin, at some point you will have to try to trust in the fates to guide thee. Even though I have heard thy strange tale, I cannot understand why thy view of the world is so tainted with the expectation of sorrow. Surely we five can look forward to some reward for our vexations.'

Tam glanced over to his friend and replied for him.

'Bullying does that, where we come from. If it goes on long enough you start to feel as though you'll go through your whole life as the butt of everyone's jokes. It's difficult to be optimistic when people are so bloody obnoxious, for no good reason.'

'Howso?' asked Kate, puzzled.

'Well, it's different where we come from Kate. Here you tend to reap what you sow. If you're a nice chap, people like you. If you're a bright fella, people respect you. It's not the same back home. Being good and kind, being intelligent, doesn't necessarily get you anywhere. It should, and sometimes is does, but for a lot of children like Fin, who only want to be liked and who are a lot brighter than most of us, life can be more difficult than you'd think. Take me and Sim; I'm bright, but I'm not as clever as Fin. I don't stand out in a crowd. And Sim... well with the best will in the world, he's never going to win any prizes for his intellect, but he is good with his hands, he's intelligent in a different way. So we get by largely unnoticed by most of the other lads. Fin though, he stands out. He's dead clever, but he's not cocky, he doesn't make a fuss about it, but they notice. He can't help it. He's a big lad too, as big as Simeon, and when he takes his specs off he scrubs up well. So, apart from being blind as a bat he seems to have it all an' all he wants is for people to like him. I remember when we were little, he used to just hang around the other kids, waiting to be invited into their games, but he never was. He was too clever - too smart for them. So instead of just accepting him, they turned on him. He's had a pretty miserable time at school.'

Tam looked at Fin, who was sitting very still and said nothing. The fire blazed off the cracked lenses of his glasses but Tam could see nothing of his expression, except maybe just a hint of the sorrow that his friend always seemed to carry with him, lying just beneath the surface. Like the suffocating algae on a pond.

'You see, in the future, if you're good at sport, they treat you like a king. If you're clever, most other boys treat you like a leper – they keep you at arms length. And a lot of others just treat you as an object of ridicule. Whenever they have problems, for whatever reason, the clever kids are an easy target. It's as though lots of children can only make themselves feel better, feel worthwhile, if they grind down others that they see as more fortunate.' Tam shook his head. 'If only they knew the truth. In so many ways, you're better off being like Sim, - a bit thick, than being gifted like Fin. You know he can read Latin and Greek? Give him a page and if he reads it a couple of times, he can practically read it back to you a month later. His brain just sucks up knowledge. He's amazing.'

Tam looked over to Fin again.

'And he's the best friend I've ever had, bar none – and Sim would say the same.'

Kate and Edmund looked over at Fin and both could see in the gathering gloom, the firelight sparkling off the tears that were rolling freely down the boy's cheeks.

'He's admired more than he knows.' said Tam quietly. 'And he needs to forget about the morons back home. He brought us here, by whatever means, and we seem to be stuck here.' There was no malice in the words that floated across the small fire, just a heartfelt belief. 'But neither me nor Sim would change things, 'cos we're with the person we want to be with in a situation like this.'

Edmund was surprised to see Tam brush away his own tears as he paused.

'Except maybe Mum and Dad.' he said, a little wistfully. Then visibly pulling himself together he finished with. 'And he'll get us home sometime. We don't know how... or when... but he will - even if *he* doesn't know how. Because he's Finbar and that's what he does.' Tam gave a short chuckle. 'He figures things out. Oh sure, sometimes serendipity lends a hand through Sim, but usually Fin sorts stuff out for me and Sim - that's why he's the best friend either of us could have.'

Fin was no longer trying to ignore his tears and took off his glasses to wipe his eyes on his sleeve. Edmund moved around to put a comforting hand on the boy's shuddering shoulder and offered it a gentle pat. Kate looked ready to join Fin in floods.

'Hear, hear. You sentimental little fart.'

Edmund's head snapped up in shock as he stared over to the cart, but quickly recovered himself. He was beginning to realise that there was much about these three that he would find hard to understand or believe. But, for the nonce, they gave the appearance of, if not lost souls, at least lost boys in need of a friend.

'Welcome back, Master Simeon.' he said with a grin, as everyone leapt up to see how their invalid was recovering. 'Thy mouth has returned to the land of the living e'en if thy head is still away with the Pixies.'

Now Tam (40)

Fin and Tam spent several hours going over it all again. At the end, with darkness gathering at the kitchen windows, the atmosphere was as gloomy as it had been after the first run through.

'Well, top marks for consistency.' said Ian, coldly.

'Consistent, presumably because it's true.' replied Lidine, taking the temperature to sub-zero.

Jarmon looked up from holding his head in his hands.

'Okay, you two. Let's try to think this through without jumping down each others throats.' He sighed heavily.

The two boys looked from one adult to another, seeing doubt and mistrust in all their faces.

'The problem is' said Fin, 'that we've got no way to prove anything.'

'Apart from your glasses.' said Lilli, trying to lift the obviously flagging spirits. Lidine smiled over at her, but it was a weak attempt and Lilli went back to studying her father's face. There was an implicit belief there that Daddy would think up some way of helping her brother and his friend.

'Well I'm sorry Jarmon… Lidine, but this has gone on long enough.' Ian rose from the table and Sue followed.

'We're taking Tamburlaine home now' he said, 'and until someone can make sense of what happened…' he raised his voice to continue over the attempted interruption from both the boys. 'we shall not be allowing Tam to see Fin. Neither of us…' he looked to Sue for confirmation and was given a firm nod in return, 'can see how Tam was persuaded into going along with such a cock and bull story, but it ends here and now.'

He turned to the door, reaching for the knob.

'Tamburlaine! Come!'

Tam left the table with a look of helplessness aimed a Fin.

'Sorry Fin. Don't worry we'll…'

'Now Tamburlaine!' ordered his father, as he swept him out of the room, closely followed by Sue.

The door closed with finality behind her and the LeMott family sat dumbfounded as they heard the front door closed heavily. The silence that followed was weighed down with deepening misery.

'Dad, I…' began Fin, but Jarmon held up a hand.

'Shhh, Fin.' he said quietly. 'There's no need for you to try to defend either yourself or Tam. Or Ian and Sue for that matter. Tam's parents have made up their minds and so have we.' He gave Lidine a questioning look and was greeted with a nod every bit as definite as that given by Sue only moments earlier.

'Yes Fin, we believe you both. It's either that or believe the unthinkable. We may not be able to convince those two, but we're with you son.'

'And me.' piped up Lilli. 'I *know* you're telling the truth, Fin.'

Fin shot her an enquiring look.

'It's got something to do with a man I saw when I was in bed a couple of nights ago.'

At Lidine's shocked look, Lilli hurried on.

'Not really *saw* Mummy. He wasn't in my room or anything!' She had a far-away look as she finished.

'I saw him in a beautiful garden, but sort of floating in the air in my bedroom. It was dark, but the sunshine in the garden was in my room.'

Her parents stared aghast.

'And he saw me too! Really he did.'

'Lilli, there's no need to try to help Fin by making up stories...' began Jarmon.

'Thanks anyway Lilli,' Said Fin with a wry smile, 'but one nutcase is probably enough for Mum and Dad to have to cope with.'

Lilli sat back with a scowl, obviously wanting to say more, but keeping quiet. Her tense body indicating that she was not happy with the reaction she'd received.

Jarmon patted her head.

'Let's think about Fin first, eh love?' he said quietly.

They were all surprised to see large tears rolling down her cheeks as she pushed herself to her feet and ran out of the kitchen, slamming the door behind and stamping up the stairs.

Lidine was about to follow when Jarmon held her arm.

'Leave her for a few minutes, love. Maybe she just needs a bit of time to try to make sense of all that's happened. I know I do.'

'Yes, but are any of us going to get anywhere, no matter how long we think about it all?'

And with that, Lilli's input was brushed to one side and pretty much abandoned.

Even loving parents can be bloody stupid sometimes.

Now Flint (41)

Knowing you're right but having no one to listen to you was a feeling not unknown to Magnull Flint. While Dick'ead was pussy footin around with them kids, Flint knew that they was getting away with murder – literally. An he was goin to see that justice was done. If the high an mighty Chief Constable was prepared to hand it all over to the non-uniform pratts upstairs, Flint would just have to give em a push in the right direction.

And he knew just how to do it.

Stanley Jones, better known as Baccy Stan, was a man renowned for his malodorous environs. Sixty a day, unfiltered, had left him with an atmosphere all his own and a hacking cough.

He watched the nondescript car pull onto the pavement outside, which served as a car park, and waited.

The cough was making its cacophonous presence known when Flint pulled up a chair in the smoke filled corner of the back-street pub. The nicotine stained walls reflected the dismal glow from a bare forty watt light bulb overhead. Even Flint was loath to lean his elbows on a table that testified to decades of too much smoke and not enough cleaning.

Baccy looked perfectly at home in the gloom as he wiped his mouth on his sleeve and regained what little breath he could muster. As a reporter on some of the seedier tabloids, more recently those that reported only the less favourable antics of the rich and famous, he was used to life in the less salubrious haunts of those with a story to sell. It was customary for his kiss-and-tell customers to choose establishments that were unlikely to attract those they wish to expose – and there were plenty of those around Manchester.

'Wot yer got then, Flint?' asked the writer peering through the haze created by the cigarette hanging limply from his mouth.

'That's *Mister* Flint to you, Baccy.' said Flint sitting upright in his chair. There was no need for a conspiratorial heads-down chat; the pub was empty apart from the barman watching the small TV in the corner of the public bar and Flint had no desire to join the man opposite in his self-imposed fog.

'Yeah right.' replied Stanley Jones with an air of disinterest. 'And mine's a pint of the piss that passes for beer in 'ere.

'Get it yerself, Baccy, I'm not 'ere for a likkle social gaverin' yer know.' shot back Flint, wondering – and not for the first time – whether Baccy Stan was the man for the job. He watched his tame hack shuffle over to the bar and shook his head. Had the man got no dignity? Fancy lettin' yerself get into such a state. Flint prided himself on giving the outward appearance of a no-nonsense copper, an upright pillar of society. Very few people knew of his preference for dark alleys and lower-rung hoods. Several of the up and coming local lads had seen the error of their ways after a "quiet chat" with Magnull Flint and he hadn't restricted himself to Cheshire. Here in this pub he was as anonymous as the grey little man he'd come to meet, but out on the streets those who lived outside of the normal rules of law and order knew to avoid the squat little PC with the nasty little eyes. For a beat copper from Vale Royal he'd managed to cast his influence over a wide area without attracting undue attention from those who might disagree with his methods. Oh sure, Dick'ead might suspect sometimes, but Flint was good at covering his tracks - and he did get results, so maybe the odd transgression was overlooked even if his brothers in uniform did occasionally try to do something about him. Flint smiled an evil little smile at the thought. The victims of his brand of justice never tried to pin anything on him. They were too clever. Or, more probably, too terrified. Besides, Flint knew that most people, if they were honest, would agree with his form of policing. A short sharp lesson was all that was needed - and his were certainly sharp. Over time he had cultivated a collection of snitches that criss-crossed the entire North West and Baccy Stan, for all he looked like a dead loss, was one of his best – always with the face in the trough of high living low lifes that passed for minor celebrities and not so minor hoodlums.

Tonight however, Flint was going to give something back.

His informer-in-chief rejoined him at the table, with a pint of some unidentified liquid that made Flint feel like getting up and vacating the premises forthwith. But no; there was work to be done.

'Wot's this about then *Mister* Flint?' asked Stan, his question laden with sarcasm.

Flint was surprised at the tone of voice. Baccy wasn't usually so sure of himself around the policeman. He'd been left in no doubt as to who was top dog in this relationship and he well knew it wasn't him.

'Listen you old git,' said Flint in his best interrogators voice, 'I've got a bit 'o news that might make you a few bob.' Baccy's watery little eyes glistened at the thought of earning something – he wasn't at the pinnacle of his career anymore. Not that his pinnacle had ever been that high anyway. Somewhere along the way he'd taken a wrong turn, but for the life of him he couldn't see where, when he looked back over his miserable adult years.

Flint smiled when he saw Baccy visibly wilt under his gaze and the heavy menace of his tone. Just like a flamin' mongrel, glad for any scraps that came his way, thought Flint. His smile grew, causing Baccy to shrink back even further into his seat.

'I don't know who you're workin' for at the moment, but I've got a story that should keep you in ciggies for a good few weeks.' said Flint.

Baccy leaned forward. 'An' why would you be letting me have it, Mister Flint?' he asked.

Flint's smile vanished and now he did bring his head down into the hot smoke-and-sweat-filled air that was Baccy's world.

'Cos I want in on a case that's been moved upstairs.' he said, trying to keep the disgust out of his voice. 'And if it became known that they weren't tryin' to solve it, that the trail was growin' colder by the hour, maybe I could get in on it. Get the papers to pay some attention and start askin' questions and maybe some good old fashioned policing would be called for – and we all know who's the best at that round 'ere – don't we Baccy?' He stared hard at the smaller man, who nodded his head so vigorously, Flint was surprised his dentures didn't rattle.

'I know who done it and I want to break it. It could mean my ticket out of this backwoods hole. Maybe Manchester, or even London. Who knows?'

Baccy thought this a bit of a long shot knowing that Flint had a reputation throughout the local police forces, but if there was a chance of a few quid in it for him, who was he to try to dissuade the gorilla sitting opposite? He hunched forward over the grimy table as he listened with increasing astonishment to the tale Flint had to tell.

Now Jarmon and Lidine (42)

Fin went to bed knowing that things were going to get worse before there was any chance of them getting better. Strangely, since his return with Tam but sans Sim, he hadn't had *The Nightmare* at all. It was as though the malevolent forces that had tried so successfully to screw up his life now felt that their work here was done. Maybe their job *was* done. Maybe this was as good as it was going to get now – with everyone but his family, and hopefully Tam – thinking him at best a liar and at worst a murderer.

He considered what had happened earlier; would Tam's parents find some way to convince him that the last few weeks he'd spent with Fin and Simeon were all some sort of dream? Would they turn Tam against him as well, by simply brow-beating him into submission? Certainly their reaction was understandable, if a trifle extreme. He'd trusted that they would come around to believing their son, just as his parents believed him; a belief based on their love and understanding of how basically decent he was, but with Tam's mum and dad that now seemed a forlorn hope.

The evidence they had to back-up his story was pretty weak - even he had to admit that. As he lay on his back staring at the unseen ceiling above, he could feel depression and hopelessness settling around him like an old friend. Before he'd lost Sim, there was always the hope that things would sort themselves out. Now it was difficult to see how that was possible. Over the last six months, in London with his two friends, he'd begun to grow into the man he was always supposed to be. Back here, at home with a loving family, that man seemed a distant dream. It was as though recent experiences were just another nasty facet of *The Nightmare.* The euphoria of their return had been short-lived. Now there was just the horror of the unknown.

He wondered how Simeon was getting on and in a strange way, half wished he could get back to him. Back there life was much simpler, even if it was a lot harder. The people they'd met were, for the most part, trustworthy and kind, with the obvious exception of Adam Woods and his ilk. Sure they were a bit rough, but it was their lives that made them that way. On his return, he'd realised that just because we have all the modern amenities these day; running water, electricity, cars and so on, life wasn't necessarily more fulfilling on an individual basis. People were so mean because they couldn't find what they wanted out of life; whatever it was, money and fame weren't the answer

Fin tossed and turned, but failed to find a restful position. Sleep would not come, but a morose blanket settled more comfortably over him, wrapping him in its gloom.

Yet again he had the nagging suspicion that maybe Simeon wasn't where they'd left him. That maybe their return had triggered some other occurrence that had transported Sim somewhere else - maybe in time as well as space. He gave a mental shrug in an attempt to clear his head of the thoughts that were fighting for prominence and rolled onto his side to find a more comfortable position and try, yet again, to let the arms of Morpheus enfold him.

Sim could look after himself, that's his talent, was the last thought that strolled through the empty shopping mall of his mind before his overspent brain finally gave in and shut up shop for the night.

The following morning everyone was subdued over a breakfast of bacon, sausage and eggs and the first phone call of the day gave an idea of how things were going to progress.

Jarmon had a short, but loud discussion, terminated by his slamming the phone down. Given that it was a cordless model with a push-button cut off, the slamming seemed overly dramatic to Fin, but when Jarmon explained what had happened they could all understand his need to demonstrate his anger.

'The local rag wants to do a piece on "the missing schoolboy mystery" and the friends who are "under investigation" about his disappearance.' Jarmon scowled as he returned to the table and with exaggerated care, put the phone down in front of him. 'Sounded like a nice enough chap, but there was an underlying tone there. Someone has leaked this to the press and I don't think they had Fin's best interests at heart.'

Lidine looked shocked as she tidied the greasy plates into the dishwaster.

'But apart from the teachers from the trip and the school – and I can't see any of them them wanting more people to know than absolutely necessary – the only ones who know anything about this are the police.'

Jarmon nodded with a grim expression.

'Yeah. But why would they want it broadcast to the world? At the moment they have no more idea than the rest of us what's happened to Simeon.'

He saw Fin settle lower in his seat – silent, but scowling.

'Oh, come on Fin! You know what I meant. I'm not saying we don't believe you – it's just that none of us can explain what happened, can we?' he asked, trying to retain his patience with Fin. 'So stop moping about. I know you didn't ask for this, but neither did we. So lets not fall out over it, eh?'

'Not this early in the morning anyway.' said Lidine, trying to inject a little levity into the doom-laden air in the kitchen. 'The day is young. We've got plenty of time to get stroppy later.' She looked from Fin to Jarmon. 'So what are we going to do, Jar?'

'Get out of the house for a start. Lilli – no school today I'm afraid.' He smiled at her annoyance and allowed himself a fleeting feeling of happiness. How many of her class mates would get upset about *not* having to go to school? 'Sorry Lilli, but I'd like to keep everyone together until we know what's going to happen today. Alright?'

Lilli nodded grudging acceptance.

Jarmon looked over to his wife as he sipped his, now tepid, cup of tea. Lidine was well into her second cup already and, as so often, he marvelled at her ability to drink liquids capable of steam-cleaning his internal piping.

'As to what we actually do today...' he shrugged and gave Lidine that look that she knew so well. Whenever he was out of his depth he relied on his wife to be the ideas man... woman... person.

She gave him one of her *Okay. I'll come to the rescue again* looks and considered their alternatives.

There weren't many.

'Well, since we can't leave the area until the police are satisfied with Fin's story...' she paused, with a look that said *And that's not going to happen any time soon*, and came to the only decision she could see making any sense. 'we've got to go back to the police.' She eyed Jarmon, expecting an interruption, but getting none. 'They must have had to deal with things like this before and since it's very likely that it's someone at the station who's let the story out, they can help to get us out of this mess.'

Fin and Lilli looked puzzled.

'But what's the problem?' asked Fin.

'The problem' said Jarmon with exaggerated care, 'is that we'll probably end up with photographers and reporters camping out in the garden, once word spreads. While your story may not rank with international terrorism or celebrity gossip, it *will* attract attention. Especially if your explanation of how it all happened gets out.' He threw his cold tea in the sink. 'And from the tone of that call, I get the feeling it's already been hinted at, at the very least.'

'Oh, no.' sighed Lidine.

'Oh, yes.' said Jarmon.

'Sorry Dad.' said Fin quietly staring at the table top in front of him.

Lilli said nothing, but was looking close to tears. Lidine moved her chair around and gave her daughter a hug.

'Don't worry love, we'll sort things out.'

Jarmon gave her a sideways glance and forced a smile.

'Okay. Come on. Let's not waste any time. Go and brush your teeth – Tam can borrow a toothbrush and then grab your coats.' He checked his watch. 'We might as well get this over with.'

Lidine was watching him, aware that her husband was trying to keep himself from worrying about what the day was going to bring. He lit his first cigarette of the day and switched on the radio. Terry Wogan was busy mocking the world with Deadly and Boggy Two-sheds. Jarmon pressed the button for Classic FM and Mozart made the world seem a less frightening place for a while.

As they sat in companionable silence Lidine reached out to hold Jarmon's hand.

'You know, if Fin really is telling the truth, I think we're in for some interesting times.'

'Hmm.' he replied. 'You know in China that's a curse, do you love?'

She rolled her eyes.

'You're definitely a glass half empty man, aren't you Jar?'

He laughed, and for the first time that day, it sounded as though he meant it.

'Only 'cos I've drunk half of it.'

'Well there's nothing wrong with being drunk occasionally.' said Lidine.

'Try telling that to a glass of water.' he replied, and had to be quick to dodge her half-hearted swipe at his head. Then he reached over to embrace her and the two clung together unsure whether they should be laughing or crying at the situation.

Laughter won.

Upstairs their children looked at each other as they cleaned their teeth, wondering what could have caused so much hilarity in the kitchen.

When they arrived at the station the desk sergeant called up to CID and they were finally taken upstairs to one of the small interview rooms. The sterile box did little to make any of them feel at ease. Maybe that was the whole point.

When Jarmon told the young plain-clothed officer about the phone call, he quickly excused himself and was gone for several minutes. On his return he was accompanied by an older man, who seemed bemused by their unexpected arrival.

'Mister LeMott, DCI Beswick.' He held out a hand. 'We have a problem, it seems. Baron here tells me that you've had a call from the press. Is that right?'

He gestured towards the vacant chairs and they all sat around the cheap little table set against the back wall of the room. Fin looked at him closely. This was a new man, who looked more understanding than the others who had interviewed him and Tam the previous day.

'First thing this morning.' said Jarmon, nodding. 'He seemed to know quite a lot about what's been going on. I don't know how *The Herald* got hold of it though. I know we haven't discussed this with anyone, other than Silas Carver and the Rigglebys.'

'So are you saying that you suspect it may have been one of them?' said Beswick quickly.

'What? Oh no, no!' The thought had never occurred to him, but then he considered it. Was it so unlikely? He shook his head. 'No, I'm sure they wouldn't. I think they're just as stunned as us about everything that's happened.'

Beswick settled back in his seat.

'So that leaves either one of you…' he began.

'Or one of you!' interrupted Lidine. 'And I'm sure that neither I nor Jarmon, or Fin or Lilli have spoken to anyone outside of those immediately concerned. The papers have been told about this by someone inside this building.' Her voice had risen as her anger burst forth to sweep over the policemen sitting opposite.

'We appear to be in an impossible position here. As yet we don't know where Simeon is, but if the papers get hold of this what are we supposed to do?'

Beswick had no answer and the younger man beside him looked uncomfortable.

Jarmon decide to put in his oar.

'Someone here has hung us out to dry. In all probability we're going to have to go into hiding…'

This time Beswick did react.

'No, no Mister LeMott. I can't see that that will be necessary. We can try to prevent *The Herald* taking this any further…'

At Lidine's sceptical look, he hurried on. 'And we will Mrs LeMott. You can be sure that we will find out who went to them with this. And we will put a stop to it.' He paused to take a deep breathe and raised a hand to forestall another interruption by Jarmon. 'In the mean time, we want Fin to meet with a doctor who has some experience and interest in such cases. We're hopeful that he may be able to cast some light on it all.'

'What?' shouted Jarmon. 'Who is this doctor? Do we have any say in this?'

He looked at Lidine, who nodded emphatically.

'I don't think Fin will be talking to anyone without us meeting him first.'

'Yes of course, Mister LeMott – that goes without saying., but we really do think that Professor Tome could be of help. We're hopeful, as I said, that he'll be able to help Fin – Fin more than anyone else involved in this. We all need to know what happened during that night and the professor is our best bet.'

'Are we talking about hypnotism or something here?' asked Jarmon.

'I don't know Mister LeMott.' said the policeman patiently. 'I don't know what he wants, or needs, to do.'

'No, I'm sorry, we'll need to meet this man first, before we would even consider letting him talk to Fin.' said Lidine. She noticed that Fin relaxed visibly on hearing his parents defending him, but he was obviously very scared at the prospect of being investigated by a psychiatrist.

'I assume he is a qualified psychiatrist, this Professor Tome?' she said.

'Oh yes. We could probably get him in this morning if you wish to meet him.' said Beswick. 'And then, if you're agreeable he could talk to Fin as soon as possible.' He gave Fin a searching look, trying to see whether the boy's discomfort was due to a fear of being caught out in the most monstrous lie in this DCI's experience, or simply the fear of a child when confronted with an unknown adult, of indeterminate power over him, in such strange circumstances.

Fin was upset when his parents both capitulated to the policeman's request without any further argument. Jarmon didn't look happy about the situation, but it was obvious that he and Lidine could see little more that they could do. Everyone needed to find out about the claims Fin – and Tam – were making.

'But that still leaves us with the problem of the press.' said Jarmon stubbornly, defeated on one question, but not on the other serious problem, which was, after all, the reason for them coming to the station in then first place.

'Yes, well... umm... leave that with me for now. Baron here will find out just what's been going on with regard to that.' He looked over at the younger man. 'Okay Baron?'

The other man rose from his seat with a small nod.

'Good man.' said Beswick. 'Make it sooner rather than later, eh? Then we'll know where we stand and can come to some sort of decision about how to proceed.'

The LeMott parents looked a little happier with the conciliatory tone of the officer across the table. Both were, for the moment, prepared to wait a few hours before trying to make any firm decisions about where things were going to go later in the day.

Beswick clapped his hands together and rubbed them in a vigorous workmanlike way.

'So, can I ask Professor Tome to come in?' he asked.

Lidine looked at her son.

'Is it alright with you Fin?'

Fin nodded slowly. 'I suppose so. Will Tam be coming in too?'

Beswick nodded.

'Oh certainly, I would have thought, though we've not yet contacted the Rigglebys. I was hoping to have both boys here for a first meeting with the professor, but I'm afraid they won't be allowed to talk alone before they see him.'

Fin looked crestfallen at that.

'Don't worry son, it's just the way things have to be done. Professor Tome is going to want to hear everything you have to say without the possibility that you've been helping each other to *remember* things.'

At the inference that the boys had concocted the whole story and would be comparing notes, as it were, Lidine looked outraged, and was obviously gearing up for another argument when the look on Beswick's face stopped her. He'd blushed almost crimson and, for the first time since he'd entered the room, looked uncertain.

'Mrs LeMott, please. You must understand that what we have here, from our point of view, is a missing child with no acceptable explanation as to his disappearance. We must be seen to be investigating this as carefully and as thoroughly as any other case, especially if the press are onto it. We'll do all we can to keep them at bay, but if you are correct we may not be able to keep a lid on it.'

Beswick looked decidedly uncomfortable. He was after all facing the parents of a boy, and the boy himself, with every possibility that this would develop into a murder investigation. The lad didn't look the type, but he'd met many older villains who hadn't looked like the monsters they were. He was steering a very difficult course. On the one hand, he needed the boy to trust him and the professor whom he was depending on to dig around in the adolescent mind. On the other, he couldn't trust either the boy or his parents until he knew at least some of the facts – and they were in very short supply just at the moment.

'But what do we do then?' asked Jarmon.

Beswick settled back in his chair with a faint smile, trying to give the appearance of being able to handle whatever may come their way. Though in truth he was unsure of that himself, until he knew just what it was he was going to have to handle.

'Don't worry, we'll find a way of keeping them at arms length.' he replied.

No-one on the other side of the table looked convinced, and Beswick couldn't blame them really.

'How about a cup of tea? Or coffee?' he asked. He turned to give Baron instructions, then realised he'd already sent him out. It wasn't usual for an officer to be in an interview room without a second man to offer corroboration, but then again he wasn't actually interviewing and he could leave the LeMotts alone while he went out for the drinks. Then again maybe this family needed handling differently to their usual clients.

'Tell you what, let's find you somewhere a bit more comfortable, shall we? 'He smiled again and this time the parents smiled, uncertainly, in return.

He eventually found a small lounge unoccupied due to the early hour. He was aware of the curious glances that his small group attracted as they made there way through the station, but there was nothing he could do about that. Almost everyone had now heard about the young lad with the ludicrous story about time travel and they were all desperate to find out more. The looks weren't lost on the entire LeMott family either, who walked in a tight little group, carefully avoiding eye contact with those around them. Beswick had asked a young woman about that possibility of an empty office, but she'd directed him to the lounge without ever taking her eyes off Fin. Fin stared at his feet.

'This is the room used by the night shift. Feel free to watch the tele if you want. Make yourself comfortable and I'll sort out the tea.'

After he'd left, Lidine sat next to Fin while Jarmon organised Lilli in front of early morning children's TV. As he returned to his wife and son, he marvelled at the fact that Lilli was taking this so well. With no warning at all she'd been dropped into an episode of *The Bill* and apparently was coping with it with inspiring equanimity.

As he sat, Fin was talking quietly.

'... can't see Tam, Mum. Is it because they think we did something to Sim?'

Lidine tried to smile brightly.

'No Fin. They just need to know what happened in your own words. They want to make sure you don't just copy each other when you speak to this professor. That's all. Don't worry love.'

Jarmon nodded in agreement and was about to try to help to cheer Fin up, when Beswick arrived with a tray holding tea for the LeMotts and coke for the children. When he put the drinks down on a small coffee table he cleared his throat hesitantly.

'I'm afraid I've got some bad news.' His tone of voice told them that this was serious. 'The front desk has had a couple of calls from the nationals. Your story has reached the broadsheets as well as the tabloids.'

'Oh no.' gasped Lidine, looking stricken.

'It seems unlikely that we're going to be able to keep this quiet.' he said sadly. 'And believe me it's the last thing we wanted. It makes it much more difficult for us to carry out our investigations if every step we take is going to be relayed to the public at lightening speed. Soon it'll be picked up by the television people and then the whole circus will descend on us.'

'So we can't go home again unless we want to risk being jumped on by reporters and photographers?' asked Jarmon.

'I'm afraid not.' confirmed Beswick. 'We're going to get a couple of men, or rather a male and a female officer to pop round and pick up some things for you. If there's no-one watching your house, they'll let us know, and you can go and do it yourself.' He shrugged apologetically. 'But better to send our people first.'

'Oh, God. What are we going to do? This is a nightmare.' gasped Lidine.

At the mention of that word, Fin went pale.

'I'm so sorry Mum. I never meant any of this to happen, you must believe me! I can't stop these things from happening! It's the bloody, sodding Nightmare!'

Without warning Lilli burst into tears and Lidine rushed to her side to hug and try to comfort her. Jarmon looked to be in shock.

'Fin... don't worry. We don't blame you for what's going on.' he said trying to give his son a look of encouragement. Then Lilli spoiled the attempt.

'Well I do!' she shouted. 'It is because of Fin that all this is happening.'

She threw her arms wide and glared around, while Lidine tried to sooth her.

'We're in a police station because of Fin!'

Lidine's *Shush*ing seemed only to upset Lilli more.

Beswick,along with everyone else, looked shocked.

'But it's true. I know it's not Fin's fault that he has nightmares, but what's happening now is his fault. He left Simeon behind when he came back with Tam... and now we're all in trouble because no-one believes him!'

Her small frame shook with anger. Fin looked across to his sister and when she returned his look he realised from her expression that she wasn't really angry with him. She was shouting her defiance at the world in general – a world that didn't help children who were different.

'I want to go home!'

Her despairing wail shook Jarmon out of his immobility. He really hadn't realised the effect all this was having on his daughter. She always seemed so confident that he'd forgotten just how young and in many ways fragile she was. Just a little girl caught up in police investigations and strange stories about missing boys.

'Look Inspector, is there somewhere else we can go. You can see how this is affecting the children.'

'Yes, almost anywhere would be better than this.' said Lidine quietly.

Beswick looked thoughtful for a moment and then appeared to come to some sort of decision.

'Give me a couple of minutes and I'll see what I can do.' he said and then left the four LeMotts to sit disconsolately in the cold little lounge. Lilli was sobbing quietly into her mother's shoulder. Fin sat staring out of the window overlooking the memorial hall and gardens with the magistrates court beside it, probably wondering how long it would be before he had to pay a visit to the forbidding concrete block outside beyond the glass.

Jarmon studied his son. Despite all that had happened, Fin was standing up to all this better than he might have expected. He was getting an inner strength from somewhere and Jarmon couldn't help feeling a pride in the way he was handling it. They were, to all intents and purposes, completely on their own and he realised that his family's future lay in their own hands. Tam's parents hadn't been in touch since the ill-tempered meeting the previous day and Beswick hadn't mentioned them. Silas seemed to have dropped off the face of the earth, traumatised by the loss off his son - goodness knew what he was thinking, or how he must be suffering.

Somehow they had to get to the bottom of this whole mess and maybe this psychiatrist could help.

Jarmon hoped he wasn't straw-grasping too much.

The door re-opened and Beswick entered with a younger uniformed officer. Both were looking slightly flustered.

'I'm afraid things are getting ahead of us Mister LeMott.' he said. 'The front desk has had several calls from the papers and we may have to make some sort of statement at some time today. I'm going to have to talk to the Rigglebys and Mister Carver as soon as.

He cleared his throat and addressed himself to Lidine and Jarmon.

'If you'll agree, we'll do what I talked about earlier. Cloney here will go along with one of the WPCs, in plain clothes, and pick up anything you might need for the next few days. We're going to put you in a house attached to Manchester University where you can meet with Professor Tome and move to and from his office without being harassed by anyone, if that's okay.'

Jarmon moved over to stand by his wife and took her hand. It was as much to comfort himself as her. She looked up and reluctantly nodded agreement to his unasked question.

'I don't see that we have much of an alternative, do you?' he asked Beswick.

'Fraid not, no.' replied the DCI.

He turned to the younger man.

'Cloney, get one of the girls and head off to Daneham. Mrs LeMott ccould you make a list of what you think you'll need and let them know where they'll find everything.'

Lidine didn't look happy about it.

'I'd prefer to be able to do it ourselves.' she said.

'But what do we do if we get doorstepped by some journalist or other? What would we say?' he asked.

Beswick nodded.

'I'm afraid that's what I think, Mrs LeMott. Let our people handle it for you - I'm sure it will be less upsetting.'

Jarmon looked down at his children with a worried expression.

'But how long are we going to have to do this? What about school? What about my job?

'Well, that's up to you of course Mister LeMott, but I wouldn't want to put times on anything that we're going to be doing. I'd prefer to leave things open-ended until we know what Professor Tome has to say.' He shrugged apologetically. 'I know it's not ideal, but it's the best I can offer.'

Jarmon looked crestfallen, having hoped for something more definite from the policeman, but also realising that the other man had had far more experience of situations than this than he had.

'Okay, let's go with your plan for now.'

'But we're not saying we'll keep going along with you if we don't like the way things are heading.' said Lidine firmly.

'Fair enough Mrs LeMott. Let's just hope that things don't come to that.' said Beswick. 'Come on then Cloney, get that notebook out. Mrs LeMott, if you could give him your instructions we'll get started on this straight away.'

The Constable moved over to a table in the corner of the lounge where Lidine joined him.

Beswick moved over to stand beside Jarmon, digging his hands deep into his pocket and hunching his shoulders, then relaxing as he spoke again.

'Mister LeMott...'

'Call me Jarmon, please. It seems that we might be talking a lot in the next few days, so we might as well drop the formality.'

'Okay, Jarmon, and I'm Alan.' Beswick smiled. 'I'm sorry about this. Let me reassure you again that we will get to the bottom of this. Some daft bugger leaked this and I can't see why any of you would.'

He was eyeing Jarmon closely.

'But what about the Rigglebys.? And Mister Carver?'

Jarmon shook his head.

'No. I really can't see what they'd think they had to gain. Silas is a very private chap, he would want to avoid drawing attention to himself, I'm sure.'

He paused and Beswick filled the gap.

'But what about the other boy's parents?' he asked, not taking his eyes off Jarmon.

'Again no.' said Jarmon, but this time there was more of a hesitation. 'I wouldn't have thought so.'

Beswick could see that Jarmon was trying to convince himself as much as anyone else.

Fin had obviously been listening in.

'Mister Beswick, I'm sure Tam wouldn't do anything to cause problems.' He appeared ready to laugh, a small smile playing upon his lips. 'Well no more than we already have.'

'Young Master Finbar, let's not forget that the Riggleby's may have other aims. Could it be that they would try to protect their son - and themselves - by pointing the finger for whatever might have happened squarely at you?'

He aimed a finger at Fin to emphasize his point and Fin had no answer.

'I still think it's unlikely.' said Jarmon, stubbornly. 'Check your people first.'

Beswick nodded, but looked unconvinced, but before he could carry on the conversation Lidine rejoined them along with Cloney.

'Everything alright Cloney?' asked Beswick trying to sound more upbeat than he felt. All this messing about to avoid the press was just one more thing he didn't need in this investigation. Knowing that every decision you made would end up being discussed in minute detail by people with only the most superficial of interests in it was an added pressure he could do without. Most punters who professed concern for the missing were usually just waiting for the next juicy, exploitative episode to emerge, courtesy of the tabloids and, Beswick had noted with despair, a growing number of the so-called up-market papers.

He dismissed Cloney with a wave and turned back to the LeMotts.

'So, shall we head off to see Professor Tome?' he asked with a small smile.

Then Fin, Tam and Simeon (43)

Simeon, after a couple of days rest and the constant attentions of Kate, was back to his old self in every way and was revelling in the consideration being displayed for him by the girl. Fin marvelled at the fact that following the attack by Edmund he had looked to be at death's door. He shivered at the memory. Even though he'd known, or been assured by someone who seemed to know far more about what was going on than he did, that Simeon would be okay and that there was little anyone could do for him, other than look after his basic medical needs, he'd been more worried than he cared to admit – even to himself.

But his trust in Tony had been justified. Things had worked out just as he had said they would. As yet Fin hadn't told anyone else about the visit of the strange man during his period "elsewhen" as Sim liked to put it. They'd tried to explain it to the others and Tam found the whole thing fascinating, but Edmund and Kate had struggled to understand the concept of "being outside of time" and in a very short time had simply moved the conversation on to other things, exhibiting what was, to the three boys, a mystifying lack of interest. By an odd sort of mutual agreement the matter was not discussed again.

Time passed slowly, but very happily for Fin, apart from a constant nagging doubt about getting back home. Even with the assurances from his new-found mentor Tony, Fin was still at a loss as to how to get everyone back into their present day. And that was another thing – Tony had promised to come back, but that had been three days ago and there was still no sign of him. Fin hoped he wouldn't have to wait to long. He'd noticed that Sim didn't seem to be particularly bothered about home apart from worrying occasionally about his father. Tam was desperate to get back, more to see his parents and tell them about their adventure than anything else, but at least he wanted to be home - Sim didn't seem to. With each passing day Sim wanted to discuss his future *here*, with Edmund and Kate, eager to learn about the possibilities in store in London, anxious to know what the woodsman and his daughter would do, having abandoned their previous lives to help the three mysterious boys. Neither Fin nor Tam had really tried to discuss their return home with Sim since the fight with Woods, more frightened by his possible reply than by the unknown.

For their part Edmund and Kate seemed perfectly happy to be facing the unknown.

With Kate it was more understandable. The bright lights, if that was the right phrase to use in Tudor England, were beckoning, with who knew what possibilities in store. Certainly something more than rural Warwickshire and the probability of marriage to the likes of Adam Woods. Things were ever thus, thought Fin.

Edmund was more of an enigma. Though not rich by any standards he made a reasonable living as a woodsman. He coppiced and hauled timber for local folk, supplying builders and farmers with wattle and fencing material. Life, if not good was at least bearable for the solid, dependable yeomen. His small amount of land would survive in his absence and its worth – a mere forty shillings - would increase as his trees grew. Fin suspected that he was thinking more of Kate than himself when he took the shock decision to travel south – and into the unknown.

The five made agreeable travelling companions. Edmund had fashioned a bow for the boys from a yew tree they had passed and a few arrows from some other source and it was Sim who had finally managed to shoot a pigeon. The man kept his own bow and a handful of much more professional looking arrows along with an old sword under the seat at the front of the cart, along with the few personal items they carried. As for Simeon's companions; Fin couldn't see enough to hit a barn door and Tam couldn't face killing anything, showing a side to his character that neither of his friends had ever suspected. Edmund showed off his skills with bow and snare and they had rabbit or small boar-like pig most evenings, along with various nuts and berries, whose names Edmund knew and the boys instantly forgot. Occasionally they purchased vegetables from small farms and bread from village bakers, but Fin noticed that most people seemed to eat meat of almost any sort and fish seemed to be preferred even to meat, to good healthy greens. At noon one day Edmund had even presented the children with larks. Apparently almost anything that moved was edible as far as the Tudors were concerned.

It took them almost two weeks to gain their first sight of London, looking surprisingly small in the distance with the sun setting beyond. The Great Tower of London could be seen above the general maze of lower buildings, with only two or three large halls and Lambeth Palace and Westminster Abbey distinguishable by their size. A third large and obviously religious pile soared above the general buildings and the boys were surprised when told by Kate that it was the great cathedral of Saint Paul. The huge dome-topped, post-fire construction instantly recognisable to all Englishmen was absent, instead a majestic stone and wood Gothic edifice stood in its place and beyond it the spires of dozens of churches pointed towards the heavens. Fin found himself wondering if the churches still existed, merely dwarfed by more modern constructions. Here they ruled the skyline, indicating a piety lost over the intervening years and they gave the city a romantic air, though Fin knew that life in the crowded metropolis could be anything but.

By common consent they camped on a hillside overlooking the city that night, preferring to enter the walls the following morning when they were rested and more able to face whatever the nation's capital had to offer.

Kate slept inside the cart with a thick woollen blanket to ward off any chills, though the sultry nights didn't warrant any sort of cover. Edmund lay under the cart, as he did every night, the better to protect his daughter should the need arise. The horse was hobbled nearby with plenty of grass and possibly an apple or carrot as a thank you for his efforts. The boys lay together without blankets, happy in the warmth afforded by the unexpected weather. Kate had told them on their first evening that during the summer it was unlikely that rain or wind would make their sleeping uncomfortable and she had been proven right. Clouds were rare and only the lightest of summer breezes danced across the turf where they slept.

Fin and Tam had had trouble sleeping on a couple of nights, not because of bad dreams, but simply because they couldn't switch off their brains, which kept turning to the problem of how to get home. Thankfully neither of his companions had ever uttered a word of reproach to Fin, but he felt certain that they must hold him responsible for their predicament.

Still, as Sim always reminded him if he broached the subject, blaming Fin wasn't going to help them.

Good old Sim.

The following morning when Fin awoke their small camp was already bustling with barely suppressed excitement. Kate had prepared a sort of thick porridge. Fin had always quite liked porridge, but this was virtually tasteless and - with no sugar to hand – not as sweet as he would have liked. However all three boys were beginning to realise that in their current situation they needed to take sustenance where they could.

To make any sort of disparaging comment would have been unforgivable. After all Edmund and Kate were helping them out of the kindness of their own hearts, they had no other reason for what they were doing. Except that Fin still had the suspicion that Edmund was hoping to find a better match for his daughter than rural Warwickshire could provide.

Breakfast over, they packed everything under the cart seat and jumped aboard as Morris set off on the final leg of their journey, warmed by the early morning sun that blazed down over the metropolis.

Fin was stunned by just how small London looked through the crazy paving before his eyes. There was no recognisable Saint Paul's, no Tower of Westminster, indeed until the Great Fire over sixty years in the future, London would lack the grandeur of its later life. From this distance the Thames could be seen winding through the city with surprisingly large cranes along its banks, visible even at this distance. As Morris continued on, the boys realised that there was a city wall, though there were many buildings and gardens outside of its protective barrier.

As they came closer Sim described the walls to Fin, none of the boys had realised London had ever had city walls, until they were on level ground and much of the view was obscured by the outer suburbs. All the occupants of the cart were then busy pointing out odd little houses and the pretty gardens dotted around the open areas they moved through.

Rather than join the long lines passing through the gate ahead, through which they could see tall wooden buildings on either side of the entrance, Edmund turned east and drove along the walls as though inspecting them. He was, in fact, simply looking around in much the same way that tourists do now. Indeed Kate pointed out several outrageously bright figures passing through the gates, some on horseback, some afoot and some in small coaches, all of them looking oddly foreign amongst the duller garb of the locals. Many of the more drably clothed figures carried baskets or pulled handcarts, filled with foodstuffs or cloth. There were larger carts hauling wood or barrels, driven by large, hard looking men. Edmund nodded as though confirming some idea he'd been mulling over as they passed a second gate. By now the four younger occupants of the cart were almost weeping with frustration, eager to enter the great walls and find out what lay beyond.

And everywhere there was shouting and cries of recognition.

Fin, hardly able to see anything through his broken glasses, was more frustrated than his companions, being able to hear their exclamations of excitement, but not identify the reasons for them.

The cart skirted a sharply defined corner of the walls and on their right they passed a much another large gate, around which beggars were clustered with only a handful of people strolling through, while in the distance they could see a third, much smaller postern gate. As they made their way passed this entrance to the city, they could see fields beyond a large vehicle-accommodating gate. Before they reached this entrance though, thy turned their inquisitive eyes to the left as they passed a church of middling stature.

'Bethlehem.' breathed Edmund quietly, reading the wooden sign from a distance, the single word sounding almost like a prayer. Fin had the feeling that simple words and names carried much more meaning to the people of this time. Sure, it was the name of the birthplace of Christ, but in modern times it had lost an awful lot of the power it obviously held for Edmund and Kate.

Beside the church stood a second building, looking somehow ominous when viewed along with the pretty little place of worship. It had a brooding presence that offended the eye as if acting as a cruel counterpoint to the Church Of Bethlehem, and it had a sobering effect on the companions aboard the cart. A small group of women and children were coming into view through a large door as they passed, though the distance made it difficult to make out anything more – except that an air of melancholy seemed to hang over them.

'The Hospital of Saint Mary of Bethlehem.' read Kate, squinting into the distance.

'Oh Lord.' muttered Fin from behind her. Everyone looked at him with varying degrees of puzzlement.

'Whyfore dost thou call upon The Almighty at sight of a hospital Master Fin?' asked Edmund curiously, looking at the boy over his shoulder.

'Tis Bedlam, Edmund.' said Fin.

Seeing that Edmund and Kate were still confused, he explained. 'The mad house beyond the city walls, a place for those with minds no longer of this world.'

There was a pause as the cart trundled on its way – a pause heavy laden with unspoken meaning.

'Er... you mean a bit like us then Fin?' asked Tam with a mixture of humour edged with fear. Trust Tam to give the silence an explanation. He was staring fixedly at those making their way across the turf towards them. Several of the children appeared to be crying, their mothers offering varying degrees of comfort.

'No more of this!' said Edmund roughly. 'E'en now the gates of London do beckon us. Let us throw off such mean thoughts and enter into that which is our destination.'

Fin was surprised when Tam pointed out two men involved in archery practice on one of the fields to their left.

'Oh Aye.' put in Edmund. 'Everyone between seven and eighty must be proficient with the bow, even freemen.' His brow knitted in puzzlement – it was becoming a habit in the presence of the three strange boys. 'But surely thou did'st know that it is the duty of all to be prepared for war?'

Fin shrugged a non-commital reply, but Sim entered into a discussion on why Yew trees grew in all the church yards, bows were made of yew and why Sunday, although a day of rest observed by all, was used for archery practice by all the lower levels of society. The two men spotted by Tam were obviously just putting in a bit of extra work.

Fin's attention was caught by brightly coloured patches of colour beyond the bowmen and when Kate turned to check for him, she was amazed to see women laying out large sheets of fabric on the grass, weighed down at the corners. In the light breeze drifting across the suburbs that morning it was Kate who realised that they were drying dyed cloth – laying it out in this large public space seemingly without any fear that it could be stolen.

Tam was of the opinion that if it was a common practice to do this, then everyone would know the women involved and therefore theft would be unlikely with so many witnesses around.

And indeed the fields were filling up with a surprising number of folk; some out for a morning walk, some drying cloth or leather, others involved in bow or sword practice, several selling food and drink and some – here even Sim was mildly surprised – playing football.

'But surely soccer wasn't around now?' asked Fin, struggling to see the group of boys kicking around the solid-looking ball and aware that his grammar wasn't all it might have been.

'Apparently it is.' said Tam, with a grin. 'Up the Rovers!' he called loudly, waving his arms at the boys in the distance, one or two of whom stopped to look at the lunatic in the cart shouting nonsense at them.

'Master Tamburlaine,' scolded Edmund, reaching over to pull Tam down into the bed of the cart, 'Kindly restrain thyself from showing that thou art a nigit before the entire population of London. We shall have business here and needs must be sober in our language and appearance if we are to find employ.'

Tam blushed slightly.

'Sorry Edmund, I got carried away in the excitement.'

'Okay Tam, but Edmund's right. Now we're here let's try to spy out the lay of the land before making ourselves known.'

'Especially if you're set on making us known as complete plonkers.' said Fin with a laugh.

'Oh bog off, Fin. Why don't you concentrate on getting us home, eh matey?' As soon as the words had left his mouth Tam regretted them. He saw Fin's face fall back into its old look of fear and misery. For the last few days, none of them had even thought much of home. It was as though the longer they spent here the more real this Now became, and the less their old lives had any relevance. Now with one thoughtless remark he'd brought their predicament hurtling back to Fin – and it was with a nasty shock that Fin realised he'd virtually forgotten that it was he who had brought them to their present situation.

'Oh put a sock in it Tam, for Christ's sake.' said Simeon. He looked at Fin with pity. 'Come on Fin, remember, we're all in this together and *we will get home*. We just don't know when.' He gave Fin a nudge with his foot, but he could see that his friend had retreated into his own little morose world where he blamed himself for the ills of the world and more specifically, their current ills. 'Tam you really are an ass sometimes. Fin! Don't worry, it will all work out for the best. Remember, the glass is half full!'

Tam sat silently looking shame-faced at the effect his words had wrought.

Edmund and Kate looked at each other and shrugged. Not for the first time they were wondering about the wisdom of travelling with three young men with such strange manners.

They joined the line entering the gate and processed through the huge oaken doors and passed two stout guards leaning on their solid-looking morglags (so named by Edmund seeing the boys eyeing the large-bladed halberds), without incident. Beyond they entered a world of narrow alleys and wider thoroughfares. Traffic jams, thought by the boys to be a modern phenomenon, were common. There were no road signs, so carts, horses, coaches, herds of animals of all sorts, and pedestrians uncountable, simply milled through the streets. Their progress was slowed further by their constant pointing out of unexpected sights, even Edmund, who wanted to appear respectable and worldly wise, couldn't help staring at the men carrying water butts on their backs and selling a cup of liquid refreshment for a farthing.

'Bit pricey for a drink of water, isn't it?' wondered Tam aloud.

'Not if its going be cleaner than the norm.' said Sim.

'Aye.' said Kate. 'Tis known even at home that the water of London causes all manner of ills.' She shivered slightly. 'There are those that believe the plague, that hast cursed the city so oft and at times spreads out well to the north of our locality, is brought on by the foul water of the Thames and the unclean practices of some of those poor souls within the city.'

'Steady on old girl.' said Tam. 'You make it sound like Lucifer himself was stalking the streets.'

'You may mock sirrah, but have no doubts, there are those within this place that would harm each and every one of us, for no more than Morris and the cart in which we sit.' said Edmund with a touch of heat.

Maybe the mention of other worldly personalities was reminding him of what he'd seen during their encounter with Adam Woods, thought Fin, *He's still not absolutely sure about us, and who can blame him?*

Fin looked at the older man again, wondering what was going through his mind. Here they were in the largest city in the kingdom; they had nowhere to stay, no work, no food and, as far as Fin could tell, very little money. Yet Edmund and his daughter seemed quite content to simply trundle around the place as though just taking in the tourist sites.

In some ways the five of them were now all in the same position. Sure, the boys had unintentionally been transported four hundred years from home, into an environment that was largely alien to them, and the woodsman and his daughter had made a conscious decision to journey along with their erstwhile rescuers, but now they were all in a strange place. In many ways just as extraordinary to their companions as to the boys. Edmund and Kate had never been to London before, to encounter such crowds and noises – and smells.

'But I still wouldn't drink the water.' said Sim, trying to lighten the atmosphere aboard the cart. 'It's probably straight out of the river anyway.'

'So Edmund, what's our plan of action?' asked Fin, still sounding withdrawn, but trying hard to come out of his melancholia. Sim could see him almost visibly shake himself off his inner demons.

'Well, my young moon-men, Kate and I are for the river and passage over to Southwark, where an old friend may be able to offer help. But for the nonce I should'st like to find this Mortlake and the mysterious Doctor Dee, for the easement of Master Fin's travails.'

Fin couldn't help smiling at the fact that Edmund at least hadn't forgotten that he was in dire need of aid in the ocular region. It would be nice if there was some way to enable him to see a little clearer and it was obviously at the forefront of Edmund's mind.

'Grammercy Edmund, but should you not first seek out your friend so that you might find somewhere to stay the night. It is to Kate that you should be looking.'

'Fiddlesticks Fin.' said Kate hotly. 'We shall first find this magician, that you might see the world plain again, rather than through they cracked eyes.'

Edmund nodded.

'Aye, but where might we find this Doctor. I know not where Mortlake may be, but like not the name. Are we to search out a 'dead lake' by smell? Or shall we ask for aid in our quest?'

'Methinks the help of another would be our best course goodman Turner.' answered Fin.

'Maybe if we go to Southwark we can find your friend and he could point us in the right direction.' offered Tam.

'Mayhap.' said Edmund. 'Better to ask someone we know can be trusted than assay an answer from these folk.' He had been mulling the problem over in his mind and judged that the boys were probably in the right as he indicated the throng that milled around the cart. He had hoped to offload the boys before searching out a friendly face on the South bank, but didn't want to abandon them to another's care. The quickest way to end this leg of their trip would be to find his friend James and seek his advice on the Mortlake problem. James had come south some years before and although Edmund had heard little from him since then, he had no doubt that their long friendship would stand them all in good stead.

Then, there was also the fact that as they looked around they realised that they would have trouble recognising an honest reply from an attempt to set up an ambush and remove Morris and their belongings from them. The sea of faces pressing in on all sides seethed like a human river and few friendly faces looked in their direction. For the first time Edmund appreciated the magnitude of the decision he had taken back in Warwickshire. Here was a world to which he was ill-suited. Even in the Midlands they had heard stories about the thieves and deceivers in the capital. This was not the place for a country dwelling honest man to let his guard down, no matter how straightforward the guidance offered might seem.

'So, we are all for Southwark?' he suggested.

A chorus of agreement went up and he urged Morris forward through the throng.

As they made their slow progress down Bishopsgate Street, the magnificent sight of London Bridge hove into view and Fin and Simeon mocked Tam for expecting Tower Bridge.

'You donkey!' laughed Sim 'Tower Bridge is centuries away. Make do with London Bridge.' He said waving an arm to encompass the bridge and its amazing array of houses, some four stories high. As they crept over the river they gawped at the shops lining the roadway, for almost every dwelling consisted of a ground floor offering various goods for sale while the upper floors were obviously domestic abodes. Grandest of all was the great Nonsuch House, its name proudly proclaimed by a sign above its lower storey. Made entirely of wood, the building was a Renaissance extravaganza that overhung the river on both sides. Everyone in the cart was stunned into silence by the opulence of the structure, with gilded pillars and brightly painted carvings.

As they reached the south bank and continued along the road to Southwark, they had to pause for several minutes while a man drove a dozen or more bullocks passed them, causing chaos before and behind him. The travellers laughed at the spectacle of the muddy animals moving down the overcrowded street. The three boys began to comment on how bright everything seemed in the afternoon sun. Used to a diet of Pythonesque images of muddy downtrodden peasants they had not been prepared for the garish colours displayed everywhere – and not just the clothes. Many of the houses they had passed were decorated with vibrantly painted carvings of men and women, not all religious by any means, and mosaics of country scenes, many of them of hunter and quarry running past the onlooker. Both shops and houses appeared to use signs rather than numbers, often seeming strangely incongruous. The Swan seemed very popular, as well as a lot of variations on the theme of Arms. Edmund gave them a long talk on the connection between the signs and the many Livery Companies who sounded as though they ran the city. No man could hope to amount to anything in London unless he was a member of a City Livery Company.

'I thought livery was to do with stables and things.' said Fin.

'Sounds more like a Trade Union to me.' said Tam.

'Aye, with a closed shop too.' agreed Sim.

Edmund and Kate chose to ignore the comments as though such strange phrases simply never made it through to their brains, being filtered out by their ears somehow. Fin was still puzzled at the way their travelling companions viewed and heard them. It seemed that if it couldn't be translated easily into something that the Elizabethan mind could understand, it just failed to make any impression. This was reflected in the fact that neither Kate or her father seemed to be capable of noticing zips, watches, Velcro, even denim jeans went unnoticed by the many folk who had seen and talked to the boys. Time was keeping a close eye on their progress and wasn't about to let them cause problems with oxymorons, when the easiest way to maintain the status quo was to prevent people perceiving those things that were out of place. Fin tried to make sense of the way people were reacting, but unless he imbued Time with some sort of intelligence he couldn't see how the things that were happening were possible. He let his mind dwell on all this for several… seconds… before calling it a day.

He had enough things to worry about.

At the moment, the most pressing of these was not how he was going to get everyone home, but whether he was going to be able to persuade Simeon to return at all. With every passing day his friend slipped further away from his *Now* and fitted more comfortably into this *Then.*

'So are you planning to join a City Company, Edmund?' asked Sim.

Edmund shook his head.

'Nay, Simeon. I should first have to be apprenticed' he grinned at the thought, 'and I have no wish to spend the next seven years or more at the beck and call of another. Nay, I wouldst be a journey man, methinks.'

'A journeyman?' said Tam puzzled. 'Is that some sort of travelling worker?'

'By no means Master Riggleby. A journeyman is a freeman who is paid a fair days pay for a fair days work. I would settle in London now and work alongside James Brooks, whom I have not seen these past ten years. James and I were as close as two men may be until he thought to take himself off to London in search of his fortune. I doubt me that he ever made a fortune - or managed to keep it if he did – but he was as fast a friend as ever I have had.'

As he spoke his eyes took on a faraway look as if he was recalling happier days when he was youth, as these three boys were now. He shook his head as though to clear it of his memories and smiled down at his daughter.

'And you Kate, you will be a surprise for him. He last laid eyes on you when you were no more than three years old.'

Edmund laughed heartily.

'James will be surprised that my daughter has become such a beauty and I doubt me not that he shall have something to say regarding mine own rough countennace.'

He turned back to guiding Morris through the throng that still filled the streets in all directions.

Fin was surprised at the number of beggars abroad at this time of day and several times Edmund had to push questing hands away from the cart and its meagre contents. The three boys quickly learned to turn a blind eye and shut their ears to the calls from the palliards. It was Sim who asked Kate what she meant when she used the term.

'Beggars and sons of beggars.' she replied. 'Pay them no heed young masters, we shall be away from them soon enough, but look to your coin and possessions for there'll be boungnippers among them, no doubt taking us for know-nothing boobies and easy pickings, but we'll have none of it.'

All five felt relieved when they eventually cleared the jostling crowds. At this point Edmund finally chose to halt their progress and climbed down with a word of caution.

'Simeon, come sit by Kate and take the reins. Lads, do not suffer any person to lay hands upon the cart or your persons. We are in unknown environs and must needs be careful.'

He made his way into a tavern bearing the incongruous name "The Mermaid". Fin smiled; they were neither on the banks of the Thames or near the sea, so he wondered how the inn had acquired its sign. They were on a narrow side street, there being just enough room for pedestrians to walk past the cart and the inn was the only one they could see. The buildings all around were small, none more than two stories and mostly domestic; just one or two shops displaying there signs over the roadway. There were few people around and the city seemed oddly quiet after the crowds of Bishopsgate Street. The mid-morning sun poured down the street, lighting the puddles that ran along it. A central rill overflowed with a smelly stream of water and... other things. The smell, whilst not overpowering, was not particularly pleasant, yet strangely the sunshine reflecting off the water draining down lit the street with a golden glow.

'Hey, would you believe it? The streets are paved with gold!' said Tam with a grin as he jumped down with Fin onto the damp ground. 'But watch were you put your feet.' He held his nose with an over dramatic gesture 'Phwoar!'

'Don't be so bloody noisy Tam!' said Fin. 'We don't want to upset anyone.'

'Yeah, Tam. You don't have to let them know what an idiot you are straight away.' said Sim with irritation.

Tam, far from being stung by the comment, shielded his eyes from the glare of the sun and replied, 'You know light travels faster than sound. It's why some people look clever until you hear them speak.'

'Yeah, well you'd know, wouldn't you?' chided Sim.

'Aaagghhh! Shot through the heart with the barbs of your wit.' laughed Tam, clasping his hands over his chest.

'Just stop mucking about you two.' said Fin.

Kate had withdrawn into the shade offered by the upper floor of the inn, as the boys basked in the warm air, standing astride the drain and gazing around, leaving Sim alone aboard the cart. All three were strangely affected by their surroundings. Here they were - four hundred years and two hundred miles from home, yet they had an oddly comforting feeling. It was as though this spartan little back lane in bustling London was welcoming them into their new life. They all looked at each other, Fin and Tam with a look of longing to be home, Simeon with a smile that seemed contented to be here.

'God Fin, I'd like to get home.' whispered Tam. 'This reminds me a bit of the High Street in Northwich. You know - the half timbered buildings with the carvings.'

'Yeah, I know what you mean.' answered Fin in a low voice. 'I wonder how things are going. We need to get back and try to sort it all out.' He shook his head. 'One thing's for sure, they're never going to believe this.'

Sim turned to him.

'But I don't see that we can try to cover this up. With the length of time we've been away I don't think you have any option but to try to convince them that this really has happened. Do you?'

Tam shook his head. 'Nah. If we make something up we're bound to be found out and then if we do tell the truth no-one'll ever believe us.'

Fin nodded.

'Daft as it sounds, we've got to tell the truth, even if they think we're all nutters.'

'And of course, we're all assuming you get home.' said Sim, looking down at his two friends.

The other two looked stricken as the import of his words hit home.

'Of course we will!' said Tam emphatically. 'We all will! We've got to.'

'But what if this is it?' said Sim. 'Would it really be that bad? I'd miss Dad, of course, but I can't honestly say that life back home was better than this.'

'What!' Tam almost shouted. 'No TV. No videos or DVDs. No cars or trains or planes...'

'Or radio.' added Fin, looking at Sim with dread. 'Or chips.'

'And anyway, you could always bring Dad back here. I think he'd prefer it too.' said Sim.

Kate, standing several yards away, was watching curiously, unable to catch the words or their meaning clearly, but conscious of the urgency of the conversation, evidenced by the attitudes the boys had adopted in their stances.

'Yeah, me and Dad don't have that much anyway. We like each other's company and doing woodwork and stuff. We don't actually need all those other things.' He sounded oddly subdued. 'If Dad was here, I'd be happy to stay, even if we could get back.'

His friends were dumbstruck. They were prepared to make the best of things, but the thought had never occurred to them that they really would be stranded here for the rest of their lives. And it had certainly never occurred to either Fin or Tam that Sim didn't feel the same way. All the horrors of their first night, the terror at having done this to his friends, the shock of having dragged them through time with him, came flooding back and he sank into a squat in the roadway.

Kate hurried across to them, immediately bending to speak to Fin.

'Master Finbar, art thou ill?' she asked looking at his shocked face. He turned unseeing eyes towards her, staring blankly ahead.

'Oh God, what have I done.' he moaned.

Kate looked at the other two with anger and stood to address them both.

'What has passed here? What hast thou done?' she demanded, squaring up to Tam as though to cuff him around the ear, her arms held rigidly at her sides and fists clenched and then staring angrily up at Sim.

The target of her vehemence seemed oddly unconcerned. 'I just said that I liked it here and wanted to stay, that's all. It's those two who keep on whingeing about going home – I don't care that much.' He turned away with a worrying lack of interest in his friends.

Tam was crouched with Fin, coaxing him to his feet. Fin looked ready to pass out. His brain was buzzing and he felt nauseous. Thankfully his stomach held itself in check, but his head felt empty. Clouds appeared overhead and a distant roll of thunder was the only sound out in the narrow lane. Tam was holding tightly onto his friend, taking almost his full weight. Bloody Sim! All the effort they'd put into the last days in making Fin feel better about the whole situation had been torn away with just a few careless words. Tam was surprised to realise that it was Sim who had done most to keep Fin on an even keel and suddenly he didn't seem to care. What had happened in the last few hours to cause such a change in his attitude?

Despite his anger and foreboding in relation to Sim, Tam's gaze was drawn to the threatening clouds that had appeared out of the clear blue summer sky and felt Fin tense and begin to tremble beside him as he also stared upward, with something akin to fear in his eyes. It was as though Fin suspected that the evil weather that had gathered overhead was related to his foul mood – but that was impossible, wasn't it?

Best thing would be to get Fin inside at least and try to sort things out with Sim when Fin was feeling better.

At that moment a young lad stepped out of the tavern and looked uncertainly at the scene that greeted him.

'You are to join those inside.' he said. 'Master Robert says I am to stable the horse.'

He took Morris's halter and waited for Sim to climb down.

'Well give me a hand you arse!' Tam shouted to Sim, who was about to follow Edmund's steps into the tavern.

Sim didn't even pause at the threshold.

Tam was at a loss as to how to sort this out and wasn't being helped by the almost deadweight of Fin. They began to make their staggering way to the door and Kate grabbed Fin's other arm to help. Together the three made their way into the gloom after Sim.

Inside, the room was quiet, with only one man besides the travellers. The floor was covered in rushes, acting as a sort of carpet. The air was heavy with the heat of the day and a redolent with sweet smell of herbs. Edmund was deep in conversation with the other man and looked up with curiosity when the children entered and broke off to hurry over and help Fin to a bench beside a long oak table. He gave Kate an enquiring look and she simply nodded over towards Sim, who seemed totally unconcerned as he approached the innkeeper.

'Master Simeon, what's to do here?' Edmund asked.

'Oh naught of any concern Goodman Turner. We were but discussing our next course of action and Master Finbar didst take my words ill. There is no problem and I doubt me not that Master Finbar shall return to his former self anon. Wilt though have a draught with me Goodman?' Without waiting for a reply he turned to the innkeeper. 'A jug of ale, tippler, if you please, for we are all chapt.'

Even Edmund could sense the change in Simeon. It was as though he were no longer the staunch ally of the two smaller boys, the three of them as close as friends could be. Edmund walked slowly over to the counter and was intercepted by the innkeeper.

'Edmund, we serve no ale here. We have only beer and that only for those who can pay, and those that I wish to serve.' He eyed Sim suspiciously. 'Is this greenhead good for his credit or is he likely to pike?' he asked.

Edmund shook his head. 'Nay, Robert, he hath no coin, but I will stand his shot.'

If he'd expected effusive thanks from the boy, he was disappointed - Sim nodded his thanks, but continued to ignore the others as he surveyed the room, seemingly content with the world.

Edmund was none too pleased with the inexplicable change in attitude of the lad and tapped the hand of the keeper where it lay on the counter top.

'Mayhap we may teach this lad a lesson in good manners Robert. We shall have a jug of hum cap, if you please.'

Robert smiled from behind his bar.

'Aye, a stomachful of Stingo will perchance, take the wind from his sails and allow him a few moments to rethink his strategy, eh Edmund?'

The woodsman nodded with his own smile in return.

'To the table if you please.' he said with a nod towards the others gathered around Fin and Robert nodded in reply.

'Come master Simeon, let us see what may be done with your friend.' said Edmund, grasping Sim by the elbow and leading him back to the table.

Outside, rain had started to fall in sheets against the window. Edmund glanced up, silently wondering if the women out on Moor Fields had managed to gather up their brightly dyed sheets before the deluge.

The sound of the rain drumming against the windows and on the earth outside seemed to bring Fin out of his dark reverie. Or maybe it was just the chill that entered the room as the downpour washed away the heat of the morning that brought him back.

In the yard, Morris lowered his head in an attempt to escape the worst of the rain and edged under the cover of the first storey overhang as the stable lad, who had been dawdling up until now, the better to avoid any further chores, hurriedly unhitched him from the cart. Through the window Morris could see his erstwhile passengers. In the dry. If a horse could shrug, Morris did so, as he watched his master draw closer to the children at the table.

'Master Fin, what's to be done? You seemed happy enough but a short time ago.' said Edmund.

'He doth but ache for his return home Edmund, as does Tamburlaine.' said Sim. 'For me, I am happy enough here and would know more of your plans. For we are in thy tender mercies for the nonce. It is these two who pine for home and wouldst take themselves hence if they could. But for the presence of my father I would be content here - and maybe even without him.'

Fin looked up, grief stricken for what had happened to his friend. The thought of Simeon abandoning his father, after they had both been deserted by Sim's mother, was almost unbearable. It would destroy Silas. It was obvious, even to Fin and Tam that Silas lived for his son. They were inseparable when not at work and school. How was it possible that Sim could be talking this way?

'Sim we have to get home.' said Tam.

'We all came here together and we'll go back together!' said Fin, now red in the face with his fear and anger. 'We will not let you stay here. Think of your dad, Sim. What is he supposed to do? What will you do without him? How do you propose to live?' Fin's voice rose. 'Damn it you selfish git. What are we supposed to do if we go back and have to tell everyone you're four hundred years in the past?'

The question hung in the air. Edmund and Kate both looked between the two boys, puzzled at the twist the exchange had taken and obviously not understanding the import of the last question. Time travel was so inconceivable to them, unless magic was involved, that their brains just bypassed the whole idea. The question then became a nonsense and their minds subtly bodyswerved the entire thing, a deft Welsh fly half avoiding a thunderous attack from the English forwards. They were waiting to see how Sim would react to the idea of leaving his father, not the time travel thing. Yet Edmund still had a nagging suspicion that he was missing something here; he vaguely recollected Fin and Sim performing some physically impossible actions, which could only be explained by witchcraft, but the memory was more a tingle in his mind than a clear vision of what happened. His scalp prickled, but he didn't know why and that just made it worse. Fin was just a lost and frightened boy, the thought of sorcery was so ridiculous that as soon as it entered his head it evaporated.

'Ahah. There it is. Laid in the open at last. Thou art a mere cozener! Thou dost not care for me or mine. Thou art only afeared for thyself. I think me that I should look to mine own welfare, for thou and thy damber are concerned only with thyself. Fool am I that I thought thee friend. I shall look to mine own care from now on!'

He turned angrily to Edmund.

'And you Goodman. Wilt thou aid me now, in mine hour of need, for I wouldst remain in they care, as thy lacky if needs be, while these pettifoggers do steer their own course.'

Edmund was taken aback at this turn of events and in trying to maintain some sort of equilibrium almost unconsciously gave the reply that Sim welcomed , but that his two friends dreaded.

'Aye Sim, I will offer the friendship and aid if I may.' He looked immeasurably sad, aware that this might be a simple spat, as soon forgotten as created, but that such arguments could sometimes lead to a lifetime's estrangement. He would do his best to help all three, in the hope that whatever had caused this situation would be soon forgot. 'But is there noways in which this discord may be brought to an easy peace. For in my heart I believe these hot word, that cause such pain, may not be thy true wishes. Surely these two are friends the like of which a man might search a lifetime. Think on it, am I not in the right here, Master Simeon?'

Robert arrived with the beer while the four awaited Sim's reply. His arrival with the drinks gave Sim a breathing space and it was not until the inn keeper withdrew that he answered.

'Nay sir. I am not such as these two. I am my own man and would travail with thee, if thou wouldst have me.' he said.

'But Sim. Think of what you're saying. Never to see home again. Never to see your Dad? Surely that's not what you want. Is it?' asked Tam, his voice breaking in his anguish. 'It can't be.'

'Ah but ist so! I would I could see my father again and would do my best to make it so, but as for the world we left behind and as for thee,' He looked from Fin to Tam. 'I have no great care for any of it, or you. I am for Master Turner. Here. My mind is set.'

And with that, he reached for the first tankard he could see and took a great draught of beer.

'Oh Sim. Please no.' begged Fin, tears in his eyes.

Kate too was looking concerned. Over the time they'd spent travelling with the three boys, she had become aware of the strong bond that held them. Though she failed to understand much of what they said, she knew that they were outsiders. It seemed that they had few other friends and comforted each other in their times of need. Yet here was one who had changed, almost beyond recognition in such a very short time.

Strangely, she found that her concern was less than she would have expected.

Edmund was happy enough to offer to help Sim, but his heart was heavy as he saw the effect the boy's words had had on the other two. He couldn't abandon Sim, having brought him this far, but it had not been his intention to create such a dreadful rift in their friendship. He decided to do his best for all three and perhaps repair the wound that had been done to their relations, though he wasn't sure how he would do so.

'Very well.' he said and held up a quieting hand when Fin made to speak. 'We shall talk no more of this now, but I shall not let things remain as they are. We shall seek to build bridges where we may. Do not fret on it too much lads.' he said to Fin and Tam. 'Rest assured things will be made well again.'

Sim disregarded his words with a huff into his tankard as he downed the last of his beer and took up another. No one stopped him and Edmund reached across for one before addressing his daughter and the other two.

'Would thou have beer, or something less heady.' he asked.

Robert who had been standing nearby, studiously trying to look as though he wasn't eavesdropping. Gossip was the lifeblood of an establishment such as his after all.

'I have cool water for the girl' he said. 'and these two.' He indicated Fin and Tam. 'They do not look to have the belly for beer the nonce.'

'Uhh. No thanks. I don't think water's a good idea.' said Tam.

Robert looked puzzled and Tam continued.

'If it comes from the river, it won't be fit to drink.'

Robert laughed, doing his bit to lighten the atmosphere.

'Oh nay master. The water is drawn from the conduit down the lane. The spring is only half a mile yonder and the pumps have filters, so the water is as pure as it may be.'

'Oh. I've never heard of there being mains water at this time.' said Tam.

'Never occurred to me.' said Fin numbly. His head was still filled with the awful words spoken by Sim. He felt numb, and very, very guilty.

'Mayhap we shall even have a conduit and quill here sometime.' said Robert. 'But not for a while methinks.'

At their blank looks he explained.

'If the cost can be met, I could have water actually inside, supplied by a quill to a tap. Then there would be no need to go down to the conduit. But the expense is great, and tis easier to send one of the lads to collect it. He it is who is licensed to sell water in this parish. And I'll warrant that sales are good on a day like today.' Then he glanced outside. 'Well up until a small while ago.'

The water was still barrelling out of the dark clouds overhead. Customers would be few until the downpour ceased, so Robert joined them after bringing three water filled blackjacks. Simeon had moved away, still at the table, but sending out the unequivocal signal that he wished to be excluded from all talk of returning home.

'Robert here, who is I might add, as good an ale-draper as ever I met, certes on the evidence of our very short acquaintance, knows of James.' Edmund raised his tankard in a quick salute, acknowledged with a smile by the inn keeper. 'This was to be expected - James resides hereabouts and was ever one for his ale, being such a two-handed fellow. I would hazard that he is known to many such establishments in the parish. Rather than venture into the veritable river outside to find him, Robert believes he will partake of some drink before returning home to his wife. So we shall remain here and wait.'

Everyone nodded silently.

While they waited, Edmund went out into the yard to check on Morris, who was now out of the rain and stabled behind the tavern as the young lad saw to his needs. It was while Edmund stood brushing the coat of the bedraggled horse that James entered through the archway into the stable yard. Morris glanced up from his oats and gave a snuffling whinny as he saw the large man emerge from the rain. Edmund looked up at the noise and saw his old friend for the first time in many years.

'James! James Brooks! Is it thee?' called Edmund.

The tall man came to a halt and stared into the gloom of the small stable.

'And who is it that shouts my name in such fashion? Come out that I may see thee.' The voice was deep and full of mirth. A man sure of his own powers and at ease with the world. A good friend to have.

Edmund hurried forward, relieved at having finally found his quarry. Even with the assurances of the inn-keeper he had been uncertain of finding his man so easily.

'James. Tis I, Edmund!' he called.

James Brooks did an almost comical double-take and held his arms wide a load roll of laughter booming forth.

'By my life, Edmund Turner! Is that you, you old ragamuffin!'

The two men embraced in a heartfelt hug that threatened to crush the breath from the smaller man. James looked down, a huge grin splitting his visage.

'It is thee Edmund. For so long a mere memory, now here in the flesh.' he laughed again. 'What in God's breath are you doing in London? I thought thee a Warwick man for life.'

Edmund looked up into the guileless face above him – a good eight inches above his own – and couldn't help grinning himself. There is a feeling like no other when old friends meet and realise that things remain just as they were on parting. There were no awkward silences or uncertainty about these two. The intervening years simply melted away.

'Ahh. Now there's a tale to be told and no mistake. But come inside man out of this rain, before we both drown!'

'Aye Edmund, for I still cannot swim!'

The two men entered the main room, slicking the heavy drops from their cotes, and laughing at the waterlogged state of themselves, to be met by Robert.

He too seemed happy at the reunion and had warm mulled wine ready.

'Ho! So the friends are well met methinks. Forgive the lack of a fire, but this cloudburst will not last and the afternoon sun will soon dispel the chill that hast crept in.'

He beckoned the men over to the table occupied by the still silent children. Sim still held himself apart, looking more than a little drunk, but not in the least cowed by the anxious looks being cast towards him by Kate and Tam. Fin still looked ready to faint, his head held in his hands, his broken glasses lying on the table before him.

'Come children.' chided Edmund. 'See, here is James! Can you not summon up some greeting for an old friend?'

Oddly, it was Fin who stirred, even before Kate. His hand sought out his glasses and he stood so quickly that Tam reached over for fear he would fall, but Fin was standing tall and straight, a look of defiance on his face as he turned, very deliberately, from Sim. Stuff him, he thought, I will not give in to this! I will get *all* of us home! And it's Sim who always says to look on the bright side! Fin thrust out his hand to the big man.

'Sir, I am most happy to see thee. Please forgive my demeanour for I am besieged by ill thoughts. It is a pleasure to make the acquaintance of any friend of Goodman Edmund.'

'Gods Arse, Edmund! This surely is not one of yours?' bellowed James. Then he caught a proper look at the pretty young woman who stood just after Fin. 'No indeed! For here is surely young Kathryn, whom I last saw as a babe barely weaned. Edmund, here we have a damsel of rare beauty.'

He hurried forward to envelope a now blushing Kate in a bear hug that was as heartfelt as it was tender before holding the girl at arms length, the better to scrutinise her face.

'Truly she has the look of Mary, Edmund. And sorry I was, to hear of her death my friend. Such a fair maid.' he said, shaking his head to emphasize his feelings.

Edmund nodded his thanks for the comment and took his daughter's hand as James released her.

'Aye, she is the light of my life, James. A daughter of which any man would be proud. Robert! Another jug of beer, and water for the children.' ordered Edmund beaming.

'Not children surely Edmund, for these lads are all of an age to be apprenticed and earn good money for their work, if I'm any judge. Though that one is a little smaller,' he pointed to Tam, 'he's still a well built lad. And, if trustworthy, there's more than enough work for us all and he' here he indicated Sim, 'looks to be man enough e'en now.'

Sim didn't even look up, just stared into his rapidly disappearing beer.

'So tell me Edmund, how thou dost come to be in London, in such strange company?'

'An odd tale to tell.' said Edmund with a small smile.

'Well, I have the time to listen old friend. Whilst the rain does persist there will be no more work done this day, so we shall abide awhile with Master Robert and partake of his most excellent beer.' He nodded over towards the man along the table. 'And the fayre here is of the best. Is that not so Robert?'

'Tis most kind of thee to say so, Master Brooks.' replied Robert with a grin and leaning forward to listen in. He too was curious to find out what Edmund and his daughter were doing with these strange lads. There was something about the boys that wasn't quite right, but no-one could quite put their fingers on it, not even Kate and her father. Having travelled for such a time with the lads they still had little understanding of the predicament that the youths were facing.

The following hour passed with yet another retelling of the story, though Edmund carefully dodged the whole magic/witchcraft episode, along with his attack on Sim - and no-one considered it sensible to correct him.

By the end of it all the children, even Sim had recovered somewhat from the gloom of the early afternoon.

The sun had reappeared and the lane outside was steaming quietly as the inn warmed up.

'So Edmund, you have three strangers in tow and come to the sudden decision to traverse the country in search of fame and fortune. Is that it? All my tall talk of years ago hast finally borne fruit.' James chuckled and playfully punched Edmund on the shoulder.

'In no way Master Brooks.' replied his friend. 'It was simply that the rural way of life no longer held me in its thrall. Kate was meant for better than Warwickshire could offer. The lads gave me the chance to take my life back unto myself. Twas too simple to drift along on the ebbing tide of life without any real thought to the future, but I owe Kate more than the likes of that vile hoggish bellswagger Woods.'

'Here, here, Master Edmund.' said Tam, looking more like his old self. 'But you need have no fear, for whilst I am here Mistress Kate need have no worries from the blackguards of this or any other place.'

'Well said young Tamburlaine. Tis a pity thou wast incapacitated so sorely during our last encounter with ruffians. As I recall,' Edmund adopted a mocking thoughtful air, one finger held delicately to his chin, 'thou hadst enjoyed rather too much of the ale of Warwick.'

Everyone laughed this time.

'Yes, what was the battle cry of our small hero?' asked Fin.

'Plobby. As I recall.' said Sim, grinning.

'Ah yes. That ancient call of the wild northern tribes.' said Tam, with a faraway look in his eyes. 'How well I remember the heat of battle as we issued the call of our forefathers.'

'Wibble!' said Fin, po-faced.

'Bloppsy!' added Sim.

'Furtle!' returned Tam.

Then all three burst into uncontrollable laughter, much to the amusement of everyone else. Fin was relieved. The edginess of the day was now completely gone, but, he wondered, how long would it be before Sim was drawn further into this *Now* and began to forget once again about home and his father

'Thou see'st.' said Edmund to James and Robert. 'Truly we have here three of the strangest young men abroad today. How could I in all faith leave them to the good graces of the cutpurses and ner'do wells.'

'Indeed sir. Twould seem that thou hast fallen in with a strange lot!' said Robert, rising to bring more drinks and the seven settled into a far more convivial afternoon's drinking.

By the time the roadway beyond the doorway had dried out to a damp earthenware, the inn had begun to fill and, having paid the bill, the small group made their way outside.

'Not bad for tuppence.' said Tam.

'Aye, but it's tuppence we don't have.' said Sim, soberly. He seemed to hold his beer far better than Tam could handle ale. 'We've been living off Edmund for more than a fortnight now. We need to start paying our way, since we have no idea when we'll get home.'

Tam cast a quick look of relief to Fin; maybe Sim was coming back to them, but a dark cloud was still lingering just over the horizon.

They left Morris in the care of Robert's lad and retrieved the few possessions that had lain under an oiled sheet in the cart. James led them down New Common Street to Snowfields and on via Jamaica Road to, eventually, Southwark Park. He lived in a pleasant three storey building along with several other families – all headed by journeymen.

It was, to all intents, a block of flats owned by a private landlord and with an introduction from James, who was held in high regard by all, a set of four rooms was soon secured for two shillings a week – four weeks paid in advance. Edmund had worried about the cost, but James was confident that Edmund would earn well above a shilling a day if he chose to join him in building houses in the southern environs of the city.

That night Fin found it difficult to let sleep take him. He no longer suffered from nightmares, indeed since they had made the leap back he had slept well most nights, but now he was kept awake by daymares. He had a growing fear that he was going to lose Sim somehow.

His head buzzed and his stomach ached, though not through want of food. He had a feeling of growing unease that had begun earlier in the day and seemed to be building.

To some unimaginable climax...

Now Dick (44)

The following day, Dick came to the realisation that he was being targeted for all the menial, boring little jobs that no-one else wanted.

He resigned himself (he punned) to the fact, since it was perfectly understandable. If the Sarge had to give someone a necessary, but stultifying dull job, it made sense to give it to someone who wouldn't really care. And that was Dick to a "T".

Since handing in his resignation he'd been acting as a glorified clerk, seldom making it out of the door during his working day. He'd also noticed that Flint seemed to be keeping an eye on him, as though suspecting that he was up to no good.

Today Dick had had to print several dozen copies of a sheet promising retribution for anyone found to have been talking to the press regarding any of the cases currently open. Upon checking it had become evident that the missing schoolboy investigation had been compromised almost as soon as it had been passed on to CID and the suspicion was that someone on the second floor had decided to make a few bob by selling the story, such as it was, to the gutter press.

Flint had let it be known that he would have handled the whole thing differently and - Flint being Flint – believed that he would have solved the whole thing by now. As it was, they were three days into what might prove to be a lengthy job, with only two prime candidates for culprit. The two young boys had been interviewed already and given their unbelievable stories to incredulous CID men. No-one would ever give them any credence.

Except Dick.

Flint had identified the taller of the two, Finbar LeMott, as the ringleader in the murder, even though there was no body. That, he predicted, would lie somewhere in a lake, probably weighed down with rubble from a drystone wall.

Dick had had to grin at that and told his fellow officer that his fantasy land was almost as rich as that of the LeMott boy, but Flint had merely smiled a knowing smile and stated that soon the case would be handed back to uniform and he would be on it. CID were incompetent and it would take a keen policeman's mind, such as his, to solve the case.

Anyone with half a brain could see that it was Flint who had leaked the story, but there was no proof – yet. If the trail did lead back to Magnull, Dick didn't fancy his chances of keeping his job. He was known to be over zealous in his treatment of suspects and Dick had the impression that it wouldn't take too much evidence to have Flint removed from the service altogether.

But that would be after Dick had left to begin his new life as a time travelling copper – righting wrongs on a scale beyond the comprehension of the likes of Magnull Flint. If the episode with Miss Binster was anything to go by, there was a good chance that *very* early intervention could prevent all sorts of minor, and possibly not-so-minor, crimes.

Dick shook his head to eradicate thoughts of both time travel policing and bad policing as The Sarge appeared.

'Ere you are Dick. A quick job escorting a family off-site.' He handed Dick a preprinted sheet, hastily filled in by hand. 'I needed someone we could be absolutely sure of – this is the family that's been causing us upset with the press and it seems to be getting worse by the minute. So get them out of here with a minimum of fuss – CID have probably got that all in hand – and look after them. CID can be a mite heavy-handed in cases with kids, so you're there to make sure they don't overstep the mark. Okay?'

Dick nodded and read the sheet. The details were sketchy to say the least, but CID wanted a uniform to travel with the LeMott family to a safe house at the university and then onwards to see a Professor A. Tome at the Human Sciences faculty.

Dick's heart almost missed a beat. What appeared to everyone else to be a brainless drive of ten miles or so, should prove to be most enlightening for him, and possibly young Finbar LeMott as well.

'Well go on man!' urged The Sarge. 'Hop to it. And remember I picked you 'cos you're the most reliable man I ever had for handling things with a bit of discretion and common sense. So don't let me down in front of those buggers from upstairs!'

Dick leapt to his feet, grabbed his jacket and made off in search of the room in which the family were currently awaiting transfer, leaving The Sarge shaking and scratching his head and looking a trifle surprised at the things that seemed to excite younger officers.

Dick knocked on the door to the breakout lounge and entered immediately. In the little room were the LeMott family as he'd seen them before - two adults - two children - DCI Beswick and a couple of other CID juniors he didn't recognise.

'PC Hedd?' asked Beswick.

'Yessir.' said Dick buttoning the last of the buttons on his jacket.

'Good man. Let's be off then shall we? I'll finish the introductions in the van and fill you in on what's required on the way.'

The journey through Manchester took less than half an hour but the van with the "privacy" glass had the effect of making the family feel imprisoned already. Dick watched the pinched and worried faces around him and tried to take their minds off their predicament. The photographers outside the police station did nothing to calm them and the little girl in particular looked close to tears. Dick smiled at her in an attempt to coax one in return, but she turned away and buried herself in her mother's arms. He could hardly blame her.

Jarmon, the father, made a couple of abortive tries to jolly them all along, but it was so obviously forced that the attempt died almost before he'd finished whatever small comment he made.

They arrived at a large white tiled building behind one of the imposing Victorian edifices that formed this part of the university and all trooped out into a white, aseptic reception where they were greeted by a strikingly attractive blonde woman, who obviously knew the boy. She smiled a welcome and Fin managed to force one in return. The atmosphere was so brittle Dick feared that at any moment the parents would refuse to go on. Goodness only knew what the CID men would do then.

The blonde introduced herself as Beverley Nutter and the significance of the name wasn't missed by anyone. The CID men exchanged looks and any further discussion was cut short when Beswick interposed himself and began to ask the woman what she proposed to do with the rest of the morning.

'Oh. I'm taking you to see professor Tome, who will want to speak to Fin alone.' Dick noticed the use of the boy's shortened name and made a mental note to talk to Mrs Nutter at the earliest convenient moment, to find out what she knew about what had passed between her husband, for he was obviously one of the teachers who had reported the boys missing, and Fin. No doubt Beswick had the same intention and he held sway here, Dick was little more than a bystander.

'Alone?' said Lidine, with obvious disquiet.

'Don't worry Mrs LeMott. I'll stay too, if that's okay with Fin… and you?' Bev was trying hard not to appear too personally involved, but she wanted Fin's family to know that he would be looked after while he was away.

'No problem Mum. I'm sure Mrs Nutter will take care of me.' Said Fin.

Bev smiled at him and Lidine was at least partially mollified, though still not happy.

'Are you sure Fin? They can't make you do this you know.'

'No, honest Mum I'll be fine.'

When they arrived at the office of the professor, Beswick positioned Dick in a chair in the outer office, whilst all the others proceeded into the professor's inner sanctum. Frustrated, Dick found himself almost holding his breath in an attempt to eavesdrop on the discussions going on beyond the opaque glass of the inner door. His job, it seemed, was to act as blocker if anyone sought to enter whilst the LeMotts were in there.

After about ten minutes the three CID men left, Beswick leaving instructions that Dick should not allow anyone in or out without his express permission. A few minutes later the little girl and her mother emerged with Mrs Nutter and stated their intention to proceed to the accommodation that was to be provided as their "safe house" away from the prying eyes of the press.

Dick put a quick call through to Beswick who, after a brief exchange with Mrs Nutter, agreed that the three could leave, but Dick must remain to keep an eye on the boy and his father.

Dick looked over at the desk clock.

11:15.

At 1:30 the professor, Bev and Fin emerged and Dick was shaken from a semi-doze.

Dinner was called for and the professor, a small man running slightly to fat, ordered food for all, to be delivered to their accommodation. The four of them then walked out of the main building and over to a small annexe which housed several small flats used by visiting staff.

Once reunited the LeMott family showed their obvious relief. Little had been said during their walk and Dick was as eager as the rest of the family to hear what had happened during the interview.

After a few perfunctory words from the professor, he left to organise himself for the afternoon ahead and everyone sat awaiting the arrival of lunch. Beverley Nutter explained that the professor had listened attentively, recording everything that had been said during his discussion with Fin, but had offered no opinions regarding anything revealed by the boy. Finbar himself had asked after Mister Nutter and seemed genuinely relieved that aside from being suspended, his teacher was as well as could be expected. He also seemed genuinely saddened by the fact that another teacher, a Mister Lightfoot was taking the whole thing very badly. It seemed that both had been interviewed extensively, with more than a hint that they may have had something to do with the child's disappearance. However, since there was absolutely nothing to tie them in with what occurred that night, no further action was being taken – at the moment. It was the "at the moment" that was weighing heavily with the older teacher apparently.

Whilst the discussion went on, the little girl, Lilli, smelled and rearranged the little posie of pink roses that was on the coffee table, though never straying far from her mother.

Dick answered the knock at the door and took the trolley from an apparently disinterested woman, who didn't even seem to register the uniform that would normally have evoked some curiosity surely.

He mentioned this to Mrs Nutter.

'Call me Bev, please. No point in standing on ceremony here, is there?' she said. 'The staff here are used to uniforms. Professor Tome has worked with the police many times and this won't appear to be anything out of the ordinary.'

She followed Dick over to the table where he laid out the plates of sandwiches and poured tea for all but the little girl, who had a glass of water.

Then Dick almost dropped his cup and was completely convinced that something unusual was going on here.

And it wasn't because of the boy, Fin.

There was a tug on his sleeve.

'Is Leon a policeman too?'

The whole room stood frozen - all but one of them in puzzlement.

'Who's Leon, Lilli?' asked Lidine quietly, wondering why her daughter should ask such an odd question to a policeman they had never even seen before.

Lilli stood patiently waiting for an answer.

Dick was aware that everyone was now looking at him also awaiting an explanation. He put his cup down slowly and bent to bring his face onto a level with that of the little girl.

'No, Lilli. Leon isn't a policeman, but he is a very good friend of mine.' he said softly. 'How do you know him?'

But already Dick had realised what the answer would be.

'I saw you in a garden filled with roses. I wasn't sure it was you until just now. I think it was the smell from them,' here she pointed to the little vase, 'that made me remember. It was you wasn't it, with a big black man, in the roses?'

Dick gave a throaty chuckle.

'I'm not sure he'd like the description, but yes it was me... and Leon.'

'Mummy and Daddy didn't believe me when I told them. They thought I was making you up to join in with Fin's story,' Lilli smiled triumphantly, 'but I wasn't was I?'

Dick straightened up and looked directly at Lilli's parents, seeing the shock registering as yet another inexplicable episode was piled onto those they already had in abundance.

'No, you weren't Lilli. Leon saw you too, in amongst the roses late on Tuesday night. Too late for a little girl to still be awake.' he said, with mock severity.

'Oh, I was in bed.' she said with equal seriousness. 'It was just as I was going to sleep, you know, when you feel all warm and cosy.' Her whole face lit up. 'But then I woke up and I could hear you calling his name... and the smell from the roses was in my room.'

She looked up at Dick.

'And I wasn't afraid, even though I knew it wasn't a dream, because the garden was so nice and you were smiling, so I knew you weren't a bogeyman or anything, and even Leon wasn't scary, because he looked nice when he looked at me.'

Fin was smiling too now, but Jarmon and Lidine looked as though they'd been pole axed. They both sat down, their hands desperately intertwined.

'What on earth is going on?' asked Lidine.

'And who *are* you?' asked Jarmon.

Both of them sounded resigned to the fact that events were well beyond their control and they were just going to have to cope with them as best they could.

'I am Police Constable Richard Hedd.' Then he waited while Fin explained to Lilli why he had laughed out loud. 'Thank you Fin, I hadn't heard that one before.'

He rolled his eyes with mock exasperation and continued.

'Up until a few days ago I was just a jobbing bobby. I was good at my job, but not someone who was ever going to set the world alight.' He looked at every face in the room. Slowly - one by one. 'But my friend Leon, whom I've known for more years than I care to remember, suddenly changed all that. And I think Fin here can do the same things as Leon.' His gaze rested on Lilli. 'And I think his sister can probably do the same, or something very similar.'

Lilli giggled and blushed and even Fin looked surprised, but his surprise soon turned to anger.

'But she never had the nightmares! How can she do it too?' Fin made it sound almost as though he had been betrayed by his younger sister. His annoyance sounded more like an accusation.

Lilli stopped laughing, realising that Fin was genuinely upset and having enough sense to realise why.

'But I don't do what Fin does.' she spoke quickly, looking up at both her parents as she did, but Dick had the feeling she was trying to placate her brother. 'Really I don't. I just saw him and the other man once. That's all... I don't know how it happened.'

Lidine's hand sought her daughter's shoulder protectively.

'But how can this be happening?' It was almost a sob. 'The whole world is going mad.'

'Shhh. Alright, love. Don't worry. We'll get this all sorted out... somehow.' said Jarmon quietly, trying to comfort his wife and staring at Dick as if for a solution.

Dick was now in a quandary. He didn't feel he could reveal what Leon had kept secret for so long, but he desperately wanted to offer something to this family. He had to give them something to explain the fact that he knew Lilli and understood more about Fin than he should.

'And who on earth is this Leon?' asked Jarmon.

'Oh, Leon's a good guy. Honest. And so am I.' Dick was trying hard to see how he could come out of this looking like a friend without giving too much away. 'And I promise that we will get you out of this – I'm just not sure how at the moment.'

'Great!' said Fin. 'That professor said he'd help as well, but I don't think he believed a word I said.'

'Well can you blame him Fin?' asked Dick. 'I didn't believe any of this at first either. Leon had to show me.'

'Yeah, well it's not something I can just switch on and off you know! It happens without me doing anything and I certainly don't know how to give you a quick demo. I'm *sooooo* pleased for your mate Leon, but it doesn't help me much does it?'

Even though the comment was made without heat, it was obvious that Fin wasn't expecting help from any quarter and his parents looked anguished at their lack of ability to aid or protect their son from what was going on around him.

Dick was thinking, his mind whirring with the possibilities here. Leon had said that something was going on – building up. Maybe Fin's ability was just one manifestation of that increasing tension. Given that Lilli also seemed to be able to use whatever the power was, maybe others could too. So maybe he should share a little more with this family, who were suffering from the fallout of whatever was going on, far more than anyone else seemed to be.

Apart from the other boy who had "returned" with Fin – Dick guessed that he wouldn't be having the best of times either.

Dick decided he needed to confirm his thoughts with Leon.

There was a sudden warmth in the room and the young police officer appeared to flicker, like a film with a couple of missing frames.

Everyone took a step back and a low rumble of thunder sent small vibrations through the building, moving upwards through their bodies from the floor.

Dick smiled, but offered no explanation.

The decision had been made; it was time for him to lend a hand, merely offering comfort would no longer suffice.

Action was required.

Both Lidine and Jarmon could see that the officer had come to some sort of decision and, although he had already been acting unlike any policeman they had ever met, they were surprised when he unbuttoned his jacket and tossed it onto a chair in the corner and came back to sit opposite Fin. He beckoned Bev over to sit beside him and looked conspiratorially at the small group he now had gathered around him.

'I'm going to tell you all about my friend Leon and the things he's told me, and taught me, over the last few days. I don't think Fin and Lilli will have any problem believing this, but you Mrs Nutter, and both of you,' he waved a hand at Lidine and Jarmon, 'may have a little more trouble coming to terms with what I'm going to tell you.'

'Nothing would surprise us anymore, Officer.' said Lidine with a sigh of resignation.

'Call me Dick, please'

'But… Dick… are you saying that you believe Fin? Absolutely?' asked Bev, with obvious concern. The whole situation had taken an unexpected turn for her and she still didn't know how to take the attitude of the policeman beside her.

'Absolutely, yes – and don't look so sceptical Fin. Don't you want to believe you?' asked Dick with a smile.

'Yeah, of course, but how do I convince everyone else – not least the other policemen and that mad professor?'

'Fin!' gasped Bev. 'Professor Tome is renowned for his work with children. Although I have to say, I'm a bit surprised at the attitude he's adopted with you.' She shrugged. 'I've worked with him for a long time now and I'm sure he only wants what's best for you.'

Fin didn't look convinced.

'And let's not forget the others involved Fin. There's Tam and his family and my husband and Bert Lightfoot, who I might add is taking this very badly, and Sim and his father of course. This isn't just about you.'

The tone was friendly, but the admonishment was there, for all to hear.

'I'm sorry Bev, but at the moment our chief concern is for Fin.' said Lidine angrily.

She was about to continue, but Dick raised a hand.

'If I could explain what I know at this point, then I'm sure we'll come up with a way to convince the professor and everyone else.' Dick looked Fin directly in the eye. The boy could see a twinkle there too. 'If needs be, I know I can convince him.'

This last sentence was so emphatic and his listeners were all finally silent. Even Fin began to look a little more hopeful.

'How?' he said.

Dick smiled, and everyone leaned forward, eager to hear his story now.

Fifteen minutes later Dick finished and was surprised to realise that no-one had interrupted him at any point during his recounting of the last few days.

Fin was very still, but Lilli was grinning.

'I told them, but they didn't believe me.' she reiterated and Lidine put a hand gently on her arm and gave her a lopsided smile of apology.

All the same, the adults were giving him a look that spoke volumes – filled with phrases like "Yeah, and I'm a monkey's uncle" and "You're a looney" through to "Prove it, Oh please God let it be true. Don't let us down, because then my dear son – not to mention you, Officer Dick Hedd – are complete lunatics". (This last one was from Jarmon – ever the optimist.)

Time to put your money where your mouth is, thought Dick.

He stood up and all but Lilli leaned away from him as though afraid of what would happen next. Still looking at Fin, he smiled, and it was difficult to believe he couldn't be telling the absolute truth.

'Come Fin,' he said, holding out his hand to the boy, 'let's find Sim.'

'Now hold on just a minute...' began Jarmon.

But he was too late.

Now Mike (45)

It was now two days since their return from The Lakes and Mike couldn't see how things could get much worse. He'd been to see Artimus Tome with Bev earlier in the day, to be told that the police were expected within the hour bringing Finbar LeMott and his family for a first interview. Professor Tome had come pretty close to frog-marching them off the premises, determined that nothing should colour his first impressions of the boy and refused point-blank to discuss anything regarding the case. He did at least have the good grace to look a little shame faced when Bev reminded him that it was she who had stood by him in his hour of need, so why was he acting this way now.

They did manage to extract the small concession that he would speak to them as soon as his meeting with Fin was over.

That still left Mike none the wiser as to how Fin was at this moment and surprisingly he found himself worried more about his erstwhile ward than about himself. Considering his future as a teacher was on the line here, his attitude actually cheered him up in some strange way.

Bev had led him into an annex where her own small office lay, and together they had consumed an inordinate amount of tea before the phone rang and Professor Tome invited them back in.

The interview had a profound effect on Artimus Tome. For the second time in his life he was faced with the choice of believing the unbelievable or following the accepted line and trying to overcome a patient's neurosis. The first time he'd got it wrong – he wasn't about to make the same mistake again.

Finbar LeMott exhibited all the same classical signs as Tony Athelston had all those years ago. For over a decade his failure to help the Athelston boy had haunted him and come very close to ruining him professionally. Now the police had once again asked for his help in a case. *They* had called him, even knowing what had happened the last time, or maybe because of it. Perhaps they thought he would have more of an idea of how to get to the truth than their normal criminal profilers and psychologists.

Professor Tome was still worried though. Having been so sure of his methods with Athelston, he was going to be far more careful this time.

'You're going to what?!' Bev shouted in disbelief after the professor had outlined his plans. 'What possible good will that do?'

The small man held his hand up as though to ward of a blow. When he spoke, a vague accent came through – German, Swiss, East European? Mike wasn't sure, but he wasn't sure he liked this man either. Bev had always spoken of him in terms of a slightly dotty uncle, as though he were a bit befuddled all the time. He was showing none of that here. Drawing himself up to his full height, about a foot shorter than Mike, he addressed his remarks to Bev, to the total exclusion of her companion.

His dark eyes glittered with an almost manic glee as he repeated his last statement.

'I have permission to perform brain scans on the boy, although it took some time to persuade his parents. I plan to prove to him that what he is insisting upon, that he somehow travels in time through the power of his mind, is not possible, because the human brain does not function in that way. We shall scan his brain and show him the images. We shall prove to him that his is no different to mine or yours.' He waved a finger to emphasise his point. 'By taking simple logical steps, we shall prove to him that he is *not* out of the ordinary - *not* some sort of super being. When he is persuaded that the entire time travel idea is impossible, merely a product of an overactive imagination or something maybe of a more serious nature, then we shall be able to start to work on finding out what is causing him to invent these time-travel stories. Step by step we shall unravel the mysteries of his psyche and so begin his journey back to safety. And along the way we shall hopefully discover what really happened to his friend.'

He lowered his hand and perched on the edge of his desk, with a faraway look in his eyes.

'For he is a troubled young man. That is obvious.'

Bev looked stunned.

'But professor, I thought you believed in Fin. I thought you were going to try to finally uncover the truth about what happened to Tony Athelston – not prove that both boys are just deranged. What happened?'

When the small white coated figure failed to answer, she repeated the question louder, and Mike stepped forward to hold her gently by the shoulders from behind. It felt almost as though he were restraining her, her body felt so tense, ready to spring at the little figure before her.

For the first time since being introduced and uttering a brief "Hello", Mike addressed the professor.

'Doctor Tome, what do you honestly think is going on? How is it that two previously sober and sensible lads suddenly start acting like this – years apart? And more importantly what do you think happened to Sim?'

The smaller man looked troubled for the first time.

'I'm not prepared to go into this further at the moment. We shall see what we shall see.' He stood and moved around to his chair behind the desk. 'I, and you too Beverley if you wish, will meet the LeMotts at the teaching hospital tomorrow for the first of our tests. Then we'll see where we go from here.' His voice became stern and his small dark eyes seemed to drill into them from behind his pebble spectacles. 'I would ask that you speak to no-one about this, from what the police have told me it's possible that the press may be trying to find out what we're doing and that would not be in anyone's interest.'

He picked up a sheaf of notes and began to study the top page. Their discussion was, for now, terminated.

Bev stood rooted to the spot and Mike took her by the elbow and steered her towards the door.

'Come on love. It seems the professor is too busy to take this any further at the moment. Let's go.'

'But professor...' began Bev, resisting Mike's tug, and as they reached the door, the professor raised his head to tell her he would text to let her know when the family arrived and not to stray too far.

Outside in the brightly lit corridor Bev looked stunned.

'Well that wasn't very nice was it boys and girls?' she said.

Mike grinned. At least she hadn't lost her sense of humour.

They turned towards the lifts and the car park, where sanity might return to their world.

'Come on love.' Mike said encouragingly. 'We're no use to anyone here and at least you're invited to the interview with Fin. Let's grab a coffee somewhere and consider our next move. Okay?'

Bev nodded and with barely a backwards glance they left the squat, ugly building with its maze of nondescript corridors to the rats that inhabit such places, she thought.

In a coffee shop just around the corner they sat over their cappuccinos and pondered the next few hours.

'So, are you going to join the prof when he speaks to Fin?' asked Mike.

Bev looked shocked at the question.

'You don't really think I'd miss the opportunity do you?' she said. 'Apart from anything, I should think Fin would like to see a friendly face among the enemy.'

Mike suspected she was only half joking. The attitude of the professor had clearly upset her. She'd been of the opinion that he would try to help Fin prove his story. Now it seemed he was going to tear it down and prove to Fin that he was mentally ill in some way. Bev thought his whole strategy a betrayal of the boy, but then she also had to admit that there was no earthly reason why anyone should actually believe him.

Which begged the question *Why did she?*

Bev didn't know why she was so convinced that Fin's extraordinary story was true. There was just something about the boy that made her feel it *was* possible and certainly more likely than that he had murdered Sim and dumped his body and persuaded his friend to go along with a ridiculous tale to cover it up.

Then again, maybe she just wanted to believe it.

'Hey love. I think I lost you there for a minute.' Mike's voice interrupted her thoughts. 'Where have you just been off to without me, eh?'

'Sorry Mike. I was just thinking about Fin. Do you think it might be worth trying to talk to his parents. See if they have any clues that could help us?'

'Well I can try, but we may be *persona non grata* as far as they're concerned. Remember all this happened on my watch. And maybe I won't be allowed to speak to them anyway. I don't know if the police will be keeping us apart whilst they investigate. I fancy you'll have more chance to talk to them.' He paused. 'If you do, give Fin my best and let him know we're on his side.'

Bev gave him a sidelong look.

'Are we Mike?' she said. 'Are we on his side, or is that only as long as he can help us?'

Mike looked astonished.

'Bev! How can you even ask? I know we have different opinions on what probably happened that night, but whether Fin is a time traveller or... something far worse... one thing's for certain - he's in a lot of bother and I can't believe it's all down to him. He is very definitely a troubled young man and I want to help him as far as I can. I don't know if I'll still feel the same if it means throwing away my career – we'll just have to see, but for the moment he's still the boy in a million that I've been teaching for two years. I think I know him better than most of the teachers and he's always been a delight in school; conscientious, well mannered, always prepared to give anyone a helping hand, even those kids who give him grief.' Mike shook his head slowly. 'He really isn't like the other kids Bev. There's something that sets him apart. So I won't give up on him – not yet anyway.'

Bev smiled.

'I always knew you were a knight in shining armour.'

'Yeah, well find me a dragon to tilt against and let's see how I get on.'

'How about the mill?'

'What? You mean the mill up in Eskdale?' Mike was puzzled.

'Yes, exactly.'

'Yes, exactly... what?' said Mike with mild annoyance.

Sometimes Bev had an irritating way of saying something that gave no hint as to what she was actually thinking, whilst at the same time saying "Come on, isn't it obvious? Keep up." Making him feel like he was doggy-paddling in the shallow end of the gene pool with under-inflated armbands, whilst she was gliding elegantly along with the dolphins in the higher ability group.

'Yes, exactly – the mill in Eskdale.' Bev sounded excited, as though she'd just realised something very important. 'That's where this all started isn't it? As far as we're concerned anyway. We know that Fin has had nightmares for years, so what happened up there to suddenly cause everything to go off the weirdness scale and into the Outer Limits?'

'Good question.'

'I know.' She was almost clapping her hands in her enthusiasm, her eyes shining as she looked at her husband..

'So you're suggesting I go back up to The Lakes and snoop around the mill?' asked Mike.

'Well not snoop, no. But you could play at being Eddie Shoestring. You've always fancied playing at being a private dick, haven't you?'

'Should that have a capital D?' he asked.

'Dunno. Don't care.' Her whole face was alight with fervour for her plan. 'I reckon the key may be up at that mill.'

'What key? There's a key involved?' Mike grinned, acting the idiot he felt.

Bev reached across and gave the top of his head a quick rap with her knuckles.

'Hello! Is there anyone in?' she said, as she sat back to eye him with more than a hint of exasperation. 'No. The lights are on, but no-one's at home.'

'It's a hell of a way to go for what's probably a wild goose chase.' he argued.

'Oh, and you've got so many other things to occupy your time, have you? she asked.

'Good point.' he murmured, pointing a finger to emphasise his concession. 'Good point.'

They both chuckled.

'Okay. But you keep me posted with regards to anything that happens this afternoon. I'd like to know that Fin and Tam are alright.' His smile faded. 'If I go as soon as we leave here, maybe I should call in on Bert too. You know we haven't spoken since we got back?'

Bev nodded sadly.

'It's as though he blames us as well as Fin for what happened.' she said.

'Yeah, but I think it all ties back to that other lad who disappeared.' said Mike. 'I suppose it's just that they both left. But Fin was back within a few hours – it's hardly the same thing. Is it?'

'No, I suppose not.' Bev sighed. 'I don't suppose it can do any harm for you to try to speak to him and just check that he's alright. I *am* worried about him, Mike. This seems to have been so much worse for him than for you.'

'Ah, but that's because I have you, love of my life.'

They gazed lovingly into each other's eyes, hands clasped above their empty coffee cups.

Then neither of them could hold the moment and they both burst out laughing, much to the amusement of the coffee shop owner and the two small elderly ladies eating far too much cream and butter than was good for them, with their scones and jam.

And Fred the cocker spaniel of course, though the crumbs dropped by the ladies tended to hold his interest more.

One has to have priorities.

His meeting with Bert proved to be so short as to be virtually non-existent. The older man refused to open the door and a muffled "Bugger off!" was the total extent of the conversation. Bert was certainly suffering some sort of crisis, but Mike had other things to worry about at the moment - not least his own career, which could be seen swirling down the lavatory pan of life following a prolonged flush. After a couple of further attempts to talk through the front door of Bert's neat end-terrace house, Mike abandoned all possibility of having any sort of meaningful exchange and left Bert to his own private purgatory.

His only hope now might well lie with the mill in Eskdale and whatever was going on in the consulting rooms of professor Tome.

The drive to the Lakes took less than two hours. At that time of day the M6 was quiet and Mike soon found his mind drifting as the car ate up the miles on autopilot.

Mike had often been amazed at how often he had found that he could have driven miles with no clear recollection of the journey. It was as though sitting in the car on a motorway threw a switch in his brain that allowed him to drive safely without actually paying any conscious attention to what he was doing. He wasn't asleep at the wheel. His mind was alert and responsive to other road users and traffic signs and signals, but his brain was free to puzzle over whatever it felt required attention.

And today the subject under discussion was Time.

He had never really thought that much about the nature of time. He knew that great minds, even before Einstein, had been intensely interested in the nature of time and its measurement, and its properties – if that was the right word.

The Great Minds had decided that Time wasn't the linear stream that most "normal" people accepted as an everyday, ongoing event. In effect, every living thing was a time-traveller of sorts, since time measured the difference between observable events and every living thing experienced events at a minutely different time to everything else. An event acted as a source of time, sending out a cone of perception observed by everything else.

Now where had *that* come from?

The miles swept by and Mike's brain kept juggling.

Depending on where you were in that cone of time, you made your observations at a sort of offset from all other entities making their observations. Mike grinned. *Hawking eat your heart out.* He grinned a little more. *Maybe not. Don't worry too much yet Steve.*

The Great Minds also said that space and time were interwoven, creating a universe with no start and no end. He seemed to recall a diagram showing a doughnut shape. Now what was that about?

And The Multiverse. There was another thing. Lots of universes stacked one on top of the other, any one moment cutting across them all. Separated by causes and events being minutely different in each universe, cutting across the whole.

And did Time flow? Many of The Great Minds were of the opinion that just because we only experience time as passing moments in the here and now (and how long is a moment before it ceases to be now and moves from the future into the past?), doesn't mean that time moves as a smooth flow from the unknowable future into the knowable past. The past is only known because it *is* the past. The future is only unknown from our present position in our *now*. From further into the future, the future we might be contemplating will already be known. So does that mean all things are predetermined and that Free Will is just our way of dealing with the slightly disturbing possibility that our entire future is already mapped out for us?

Or does every decision we ever make move us between universes, which are so unimaginably numerous that all possible futures are already predetermined across the multiverse? So every universe is set in stone, from the distant past and Big Bang, to the distant future and the Big Crunch and we move ourselves unknowingly between them to steer towards a future we fashion for ourselves from the infinite choices available.

Now there's a thought.

And if that is so, do we all have our own separate universes within the multiverse? If every decision shifts us to another universe, does everyone and everything we know come with us? Or are we constantly meeting old friends for the first time?

What happens if our old friends make their choices and they move to another universe? Are we already there? Or are we about to arrive from our own leg of the trousers of time?

Having arrived at Terry Pratchett, Mike shifted himself into another universe by deciding to pull into the next services and have a nice cup of tea. Or probably not. One thing that seemed to be an inarguable fact throughout the multiverse, was that tea from wherever and whenever, was always naff at a motorway services.

Then Fin, Tam and Simeon (46)

Their plans for Mortlake had been put in abeyance for the day and Fin was becoming fidgety. James had been more helpful than any of them could have wished; Edmund had almost certainly found gainful employment, Kate had rooms in which to impose her authority and the boys had been given some more information regarding the strange Doctor Dee.

Of the group, Kate seemed the most content. She'd been uprooted from the life she knew, but was busy ensuring that their new home would be every bit as comfortable as the only other home she had ever known. The rooms they had were sparcely furnished, but James had assured her that she could find everything she would want at the Cheap that was held every day along the road which overlooked Southwark Fields. Apparently even tables and chairs, cupboards and beds were to be found either at the market or in nearby workshops. For now she had to be content with the mattresses they bought for a few shillings at Master Buttery's joinery establishment on Abbeyfield Road, with a promise of beds to follow. Serendipity had brought them to the shop just as an order for the beds and mattresses had been cancelled, so the mattresses could be taken immediately. Master Buttery had been quite insistent, needing the space they occupied for storage and had parted with them for only a few groats. The beds were half made and would be delivered by cart the following Wednesday. What few chairs they had, along with an old table, would suffice until Edmund had the time to find items to replace them of a quality that suited his daughter. It was agreed that the following day Edmund would accompany James to the building site on the south bank of the Thames a few hundred yards from London Bridge. At the end of the day they would collect Morris and the cart from Robert and move them to a livery barn close by where Edmund had organised stabling and fodder for their trusty steed.

Meanwhile Kate would help the boys organise their journey to Mortlake, about twelve miles to the west, for the following day. Although Sim seemed to care little for the idea, Edmund had insisted that he go with the others. They would take Morris and the cart and hopefully make the round trip within the hours of daylight. If not, Edmund - and possibly James - would come to meet them along the road. Edmund was unsure as to the wisdom of their plan, but again James had assured him that the route was well populated and that naught ill would befall them, so long as they kept to the most direct route.

The idea of Sim wanting to be separated from himself and Tam worried Fin a great deal. Even the possibility of spending more time with Kate seemed to appeal to him less than that of accompanying the men to their work. With every passing hour Sim was becoming more and more immersed in Tudor life. It was as though his life were missing a piece that he had finally found within an alien jigsaw. Sim was settling into the rhythm of living with Edmund and Kate.

Fin could tell that Tam had the same misgivings regarding Sim, but neither wanted a repeat of the disagreement that had erupted in the morning, so both held their tongues when Sim had pressed James and Edmund into letting him join them in their job-seeking expedition. James was confident that Simeon would find work as a labourer until he could prove his worth and Sim seemed overjoyed at possibility.

'That I might repay Goodman Turner's great help in these last few weeks.' he'd said. He sounded as though he was only too happy to become, in time, a journeyman carpenter. Fin could have wept with frustration. Didn't the barnpot realise that within a few days they might all be heading home, with all this nothing more than memories?

Apparently not.

Sim was becoming a member of this society in ways that his friends could not understand. His speech was almost indistinguishable from those around him and Fin had begun to detect the odd "echo" that followed the speech of everyone but Tam. That was surely not a good sign – Sim was using words and phrases that were so old and out of use back in his own time that his friends were having to use the phantom simultaneous translator almost continuously.

Fin lay awake that night desperately trying to think how he would be able to escape this world and return to his present, taking his friends with him.

No great insight managed to muscle its way into his chaotic thoughts before sleep took him, wrapping her comforting arms around him and cradling him safe 'til the following dawn.

A little more poetic than usual maybe, but that's what the sixteenth century does to a young mind…

The sunlight illuminated the room the three boys were sharing, glinting off the motes that floated in the still air. Fin rubbed his eyes and reached for his wrecked glasses. The world settled into a disjointed kaleidoscope of colours and shapes as he swept aside the woollen blanket that was threatening to boil him where he lay.

Fin checked his watch.

6:45.

Sim was already up and dressed; Fin could hear him talking from the next room and went over to shake Tam awake.

'Come on Tam. Up and at 'em.' he said as Tam slowly dragged himself from the arms of Morpheus.

They both quickly dressed and joined the others for a breakfast of weak beer, bread and butter. James had rejoined them earlier and he and Edmund were ready to head off to the site, both still with high hopes that Edmund would find gainful employment when they arrived. Sim was still arguing that he should go with them rather than making the trek to Mortlake, but Edmund would not hear of it.

'Four travelling together will be safer than three. For all James has said that the way is not dangerous I would deem it a great favour if you would accompany Kate and the others. You are the most stalwart of your company and even though you are all still young I doubt me that there would be many who would seek to detain you should you not desire it.'

He cast a jaundiced eye at Fin.

'And should the necessity arise, I would that you might prevent Master Finbar from calling upon his... abilities... to ward off blackguards.'

James gave Fin a quizzical look, obviously wondering what aid the boy with the broken eye glasses could possibly offer. Of the four, surely only Simeon was capable of offering resistance to ne'er-do-wells?

Still Edmund seemed adamant regarding the matter and James could see no great cause to argue.

So by seven fifteen James and Edmund had taken their leave, with stern warnings regarding the safe-keeping of Kate, and the younger members of the group were preparing for their journey to Mortlake.

The morning was still barely born when the four, along with the ever-faithful Morris, headed off towards London Bridge, retracing their route of the previous day to follow the map drawn by James, towards Lambeth; and onwards to Wandsworth and then Putney and beyond to their destination.

The journey, of a little over ten miles passed without incident and well before eleven in the morning the little group of travellers found themselves in the hamlet of Mortlake. A modest church was their first sight of the village, its cluster of houses mostly nestled alongside the Thames. A steady flow of river and road traffic fed through the narrow streets and along the waterway. Sim explained, as they made their entrance, that even this far from the centre of London there was a fair amount of traffic due to Mortlake lying on the route to palaces and towns upstream.

Neither Fin nor Tam wished to find out how Sim had come by his knowledge. Maybe James had told him, but maybe there were other forces at work here, that they had no desire to know about. Sim was, for the most part, an agreeable travelling companion, keeping them all fascinated with the knowledge of the areas they passed through. Mortlake, for example, had little agriculture associated with it apart from the asparagus fields - that were situated exactly where he had said they would be.

Kate, possibly sensing the unease of Fin and Tam, also showed a distinct lack of interest in how Sim had acquired his local knowledge.

On alighting outside the pretty church on the village green they sought directions to the house of Doctor Dee. Sim was about to head to the inn on the opposite side of the green when Kate stayed him with a hand on his arm.

'Simeon, might it be better to eschew the tavern and ask instead someone who will not have friends with whom to discuss our request? This Doctor is accounted a conjuror by many and we do not wish to stir the curiosity of any who might hear.'

Sim nodded.

'Aye, mayhap thou hast the right of it Kate. Let us stop someone less likely to chitter chatter with others about our destination.'

He turned and moved instead to a young woman with a little girl of maybe six or seven who emerged from the bakery a few yards from the church.

As Sim approached she looked up, a plain, homely woman in her early twenties, who gave him a cautious smile.

Sim gave a short bow and received a bobbed curtsy in return.

'Beg pardon Mistress, but wouldst thou know the way to the house of Doctor Dee? We know he lives hereabouts but are uncertain of the way.'

The woman smiled again.

'Why certes lad. His house lies there, do'st see?' She pointed at a large, but somewhat rundown edifice alongside the tavern across the green.

Sim tugged his forelock.

'Thankyou Goodwife...?'

'Faldo, sir.' replied the woman and she bobbed the curtsy again, causing her daughter to giggle and hide her face in her mother's skirts.

Sim smiled and turned to go as Mistress Faldo said. 'Pray young sir, wouldst thou wish the doctor a good morning from me and mine.'

Sim nodded and then returned to the others.

'Well it seems that not all folk are afraid of his reputation. Certainly she seemed to know him and wanted us to let him know it was she who gave us directions.'

'Probably wants to be in his good books. Better to be friends with a wizard than an enemy.' said Tam. 'You know - princes into frogs and all that.'

At the shocked look from Kate, Tam hurriedly made to set her mind at rest.

'Jesting Kate, Just jesting.'

She looked unconvinced.

'Aye. Well from the little I know of this man, you would do well to keep any jesting to thyself.'

She gave him a look of disgust, obviously worried now that the object of their search was so close at hand. Her hands were clasped tightly in the folds of her skirt and the look of discomfit could not be disguised.

'Worry not Kate.' said Sim. 'Mistress Faldo was not afeared of the man, so nor should you be.'

Kate still looked unconvinced.

'But if he be sorcerer as they do say, who knowest what may befall us this day'

The four friends stood beside Morris and looked over to the house of Doctor Dee. It looked innocuous enough. A larger building than those around it by virtue of having had several obvious extensions added in the fairly recent past. Indeed even without the help of Mistress Faldo, they would have recognised this as the home of the famous – or infamous - Doctor Dee. The building stood on a plot several times bigger than any other and was set back further from the road, as though shunning its neighbours. The whole was comprised of many separate parts, each seemingly added on at slightly differing angles and heights. The house had a not unpleasant, but distinctly odd, appearance. It was as though each addition had been made in haste; the builders happy to just get the damn thing up and then retire from its vicinity as soon as possible. It certainly had an air of mystery; an other-worldliness.

The uncertainty spread out from Kate as an almost palpable thing and none of them seemed willing to take the next step.

It was Sim who dispersed the air of foreboding that threatened to halt them so late in their search.

'Look. This was the whole point of us coming to London wasn't it.' he said. 'We can't turn away now that we have found our quarry.'

Kate gave a little start, as though unnerved by the word.

And though it was Sim who talked bravely, it was Fin who actually stepped forward to cross the green.

'Look. You lot stay with Morris here.' he said. 'I'll go and see if he's in and whether he'll even see us.' He shrugged. 'After all, he has no reason to want to speak to us, does he? For all we know he may be out, even in Europe somewhere. Didn't you say he travelled all over the place Sim? So I'll make a first move and see what happens. Is that alright with everyone?'

'I'm pretty certain he'll be here.' said Sim. 'I'm sure he was back from Europe by now but …'

Before he could finish, the question about whether the house was occupied was answered, when two young girls emerged from the large oaken front door. The younger one who looked to be three or four years old, was racing as fast as her small legs could carry her, whilst the older girl - of about ten or eleven - kept a watchful eye on her progress. Waving gaily back to an unseen figure, they ran laughing and calling across the green and up a lane to the left of the four travellers.

'Well. No point in standing here, is there?' said Fin, and he started across the green with a determined stride.

'Hang on Fin!' called Tam. 'Wait for us!'

The other three climbed back onto the cart. Kate took the reins and walked Morris along the road to meet Fin outside the house of Doctor Dee.

Fin waited for them to jump down and was surprised that even Sim seemed reluctant to stand beside him at the big wooden door. Kate, Tam and Sim sat atop the cart as though poised to flee, Kate's eyes imploring Fin to abandon this meeting and hurry back to London. Even with his crazed glazing Fin could see the tension in all of them, yet oddly he felt far more at ease than he'd expected to.

He turned to the door.

Here, inside this Hollywood style mansion, lived the legendary Doctor Dee; a great man of sixteenth century science, but also strangely given to a belief in scrying; an alchemist of renown, distant ancestor of modern chemists, who also believed in daemons and angels. A very complex character all round, thought Fin.

Then he stepped forward and knocked solidly on the very solid door. The sound of the door reverberated back through the space behind and for several seconds elicited no response.

Behind Fin, atop the cart, Kate was willing him to just turn away so that they could all return to Southwark without further ado. All this talk of conjurors and wizards had unnerved her more than she was willing to show.

Beside her Tam and Sim were eager to see who opened the door, though neither was prepared to stand beside Fin.

It suddenly occurred to Fin that he was actually braver than either of his two male companions and the realisation was really quite shocking to him. Not being the sporty one, or the one with the quick repartee, he had always seen himself as something less than they. Being the constant butt of the bullies in their year had never helped his self-esteem, even if the teachers always seemed to like him. At thirteen, boys want the respect of their peers, not their teachers and parents. Such peer recognition had never been Fin's and as a result he had rarely given himself the approbation he deserved.

Suddenly, standing before the abode of one Doctor John Dee in sixteenth century London, he did.

As the door before him slowly opened, Fin no longer felt fear. He was exhilarated.

He had travelled through time to arrive at this spot. He was about to meet a man born four hundred years ago. A man who had knowledge greater than almost anyone else alive at this time – a time when it was possible for a man to know almost all there was to know. When written scientific knowledge still harked back to ancient Greece and Rome. When a true polymath could honestly be said to know almost everything. How often could that be said of anyone in the modern world? Not often, Fin thought.

And now here was that extraordinary man.

Behind this door.

Or not, he thought as the door opened to reveal a short, rotund lady, somewhat older than middle age. Fin could feel an almost physical wave of anticlimax wash over him as he looked at the woman.

'Yes, may I be of help young man?' said the woman quietly, looking Fin up and down with distrust evident in her dark eyes.

'Oh. Err… ' Fin shot a quick glance back at the others on the cart, at a loss for words now that the moment had come.

'Err…'

'Come young sir, out with it.' said the woman with just a hint of impatience. 'I have no time to be wasting in conversation with children this day. I am busy, even if thou art not.'

'Please madam, I would beg audience with Doctor Dee, if he is within.' asked Fin in a somewhat strained voice. 'Mistress Faldo hast said this is his house and I would have discussion with him if I may.'

Perhaps it was his open and earnest countenance that persuaded the woman of his good intent, or his strange manner, but suddenly her features softened. He must seem like a flustered child, standing at her door and begging entrance. Maybe they had few callers so young and timid, being used to scholars and royalty. Or maybe it was the fact that there was something of the otherworldly about him. Fin didn't know, but something put her at her ease.

She smiled and looked over to the occupants of the cart.

'And is it only thee who would seek my husband, or these others too?' she asked quietly.

'Oh, it's all of us mistress. If possible. I have travelled far to seek his wisdom, in the hope that he may aid me in my plight.'

'Indeed.' she replied, looking a little more cautious now. 'And with what purpose is your visit?'

Fin was aware that he must look a little pathetic standing there, his hands anxiously clasping and unclasping at his sides.

'If I could but talk to the good Doctor, I am sure he would wish to hear what I have to tell him.'

'Hmm.' The lady eyed him up and down, a look of merriment in her eyes, which now held a much kinder expression. She seemed to be looking at him out of the corner of her eye, but not in a sneaky way. Almost as though she were trying to see something that she couldn't quite catch if she viewed it straight on. She eyed him up and down again and came to a decision.

'Then you had best call your friends down and we shall see if the Doctor is busy. Come young sir, let us waste no more time dilly dallying upon the threshold. Come in.'

Fin beamed at her and waved his friends in.

Kate called.

'I will stay with Morris without. The day is pleasant enough and we shall come no ill whilst we wait.'

Fin realised she was still afraid of the reputation of the owner of this strange place, but could see no great need to force her to enter against her will.

'Very well Kate. But be not afraid to call out if needs be.' shouted Fin and he turned to enter, followed by Tam and finally Sim, who cast one last look at Kate over his shoulder, as though to convince himself that she would be alright on her own. But the village was quiet and the sun not too hot; there was little enough to cause her anxiety, apart from the proximity of the man they had come to see.

As she closed the door behind them the lady of the house introduced herself.

'I am Jane, wife of he whom you seek. My husband is within his study at the moment, but he may be persuaded out to meet such as thee.' she said inspecting each of the boys closely. 'Is the maiden to remain with your animal?' she asked.

Fin looked her in the eye and decided that honesty would probably be the right course with such a lady.

'Beg pardon Mistress Dee, but Kate has heard much to make her nervous of entering the house of the renowned Doctor Dee. I think me that she would feel safer without.'

To his surprise the woman smiled.

'Aye. There are many such who come here. They listen to gossip and heresay and believe all they do hear. But not all that are so young are so gullible it seems.'

She smiled a secretive little smile again and led them to a table in the small room to the left of the hallway, the while casting odd sidelong glances at all three of them. At one point Fin was sure he caught her squinting at them.

Very peculiar.

Then again, maybe she had bad eyesight.

Fin shrugged inwardly.

'Please remain here while I find my husband. There is wine on the table.' She indicated a flagon with six goblets as she left the room.

The three boys looked about them. The room was small and bare of furniture apart from the table and chairs and one small sideboard displaying some plates. The walls, rather than the usual bare plaster they were used to in the few houses and inns they had visited, was painted with landscapes in blue and red, of deer and foxes and stylised flora, on a pale yellow background. Across one wall hung something that seemed to be halfway between a tapestry and a large square of wallpaper. It was suspended from a rod just below ceiling height and filled the entire wall with depictions of dragons and various other mythical beasts. Taken in its entirety Fin could see that the room was not meant to convey an air of hospitality, but more a feeling of otherworldly power residing within the house. It was as though the Doctor sought not to make friends by the statement made by the room, but more to warn his enemies that here lived no ordinary man, whom you would cross at your peril.

The boys stood as they waited. None of them felt comfortable enough to take a seat in that strangely powerful room and no-one felt compelled to break the silence that filled it.

They heard Mistress Dee returning down the wooden panelled hallway and waited with baited breath to hear her husband's response.

'Please come through gentlemen. My husband is occupied, but will see you whilst Arthur makes preparations for the afternoon.'

Without further explanation she led them into another, larger room. This one was darker than the first, being oak panelled throughout and with a curtain drawn across the large window. The gloom was illuminated by several large candles which filled the room with an acrid smell and a not inconsiderable amount of smoke. Fin felt tears spring to his eyes as he entered and heard both Tam and Sim give small but uncontrolled coughs.

Two men stood at the far end of the room, bending to gaze into what appeared to be a large crystal ball. Upon hearing the boys enter, the taller of the two straightened up and threw a cloth over the glass. The younger man withdrew into another room via a small doorway to one side. Closing the door behind him it merged into what was a solid wall of books. Of the doorway there was no sign.

Facing the window, the man threw back the curtain allowing the late morning sunshine to assault the murk within the room and opened the window with a flourish to allow the smoke an egress.

'Extinguish the candles if you will. I have lucifers aplenty to relight them when they are needed.' said the man in a deep sonorous voice waving to the guttering lights around the room.

'Ian McKellern.' Fin heard Tam whisper behind him.

'Nah. Christopher Lee.' argued Sim.

'What? I caught not the import of thy comments young sirs.' said the man in a schoolmasterly voice. 'Perhaps you would favour me with thy names and thy purpose in coming here. I have not so many young visitors that I am prepared to give up my time for naught, but my wife seemed to deem you worthy of inspection.'

With that the man turned finally to look upon them in the full light of day and all the boys noticed his small double-take. None of them could think why he should react like that to the sight of the three of them.

Using a snuffer, he began to extinguish the candles burning about the room as he studied the boys, who in turn studied him as they licked fingers to snuff out the nearest flames. He was tall for men of this time, with a finely chiselled, stern face and intelligent, searching eyes. His hair and beard were white and his dark clothing collared with a brilliantly white ruff with dozens of sets, or figures-of-eights as the boys had learned to call them. He carried himself with an upright, almost regal air and his gown swept around him as he moved.

'Ahh. I see me why Jane shouldst have believed you to be other than ordinary travellers.' He stepped closer and reached out to touch the sleeve of Fin's denim jacket. Fin edged away but the man leaned closer to inspect the cloth, a look of puzzlement on his face.

He straightened suddenly as though keen to get on with things.

'Come now young sirs, you know who I am or you would not have come here. I would know who it is that I have invited into my home.' His voice was not unkind, but definitely brooked no argument.

Which was fine with Fin.

'Doctor, I am Finbar LeMott of The Vale Royal in Cheshire. These are my friends - Tamburlaine Riggleby and Simeon Carver' Fin waved an arm towards the others. '- also from Cheshire.'

'Indeed.' was all Doctor Dee replied as he seated himself in a large upholstered chair near the extinct fire and indicated with an airy wave that Fin should continue.

'We have a strange tale to tell, but would ask a boon of thee before the telling.' said Fin.

Doctor Dee, who had begun slowly stroking his white goatee as he settled to listen, stopped and studied Fin hard.

'And what pray, would thy request be, Master Finbar?' he asked quietly in that voice that filled the room even unto its dustiest corner.

Fin gulped and reached up to his spectacles.

'Mine eye glasses were damaged several days ago and I have no means to repair them. I was wondering whether you could help me with them?'

The question hung in the air as Fin held his spectacles out to the doctor.

For his part Doctor Dee inspected the glasses carefully, from every angle before carefully taking hold of them and replying.

'And where did such a child as thee come across work such as this?' he asked, emphasising his question by pointing with the glasses. 'And before you think to beguile me with thy tales I would ask you to remember to whom you are speaking. Thou hast come to seek mine aid have you not - and before it is given I would know how thou came to be here, from whence thou came and how it is that they speech and dress are so passing strange?

As Fin opened his mouth to reply the Doctor repeated.

'The truth now, for I shall recognise lies and my wrath will be great.'

This was said without heat, but with complete conviction and Fin had no doubt that this silver haired man of some sixty odd years was not someone you wanted to cross. The Doctor put the glasses down on top of a small trunk beside his chair.

'Give me the bare bones, then shall I attempt a repair.' He half closed his eyes as though preparing for a nap, a self-satisfied smile playing on his lips. 'Then we shall settle to and have discussions regarding any further help you may desire.

Does that mean he could help us get home? Thought Fin. *But how could he even suspect our problems?*

'Sit and begin.' ordered the Doctor, nodding towards three wooden chairs in one corner.

Fin was obviously having trouble finding a seat and the doctor hastily returned his glasses with a pitying smile. Fin nodded his thanks as he settled them back into place.

The boys grabbed a chair each and sat ranged before their host and sparingly told their story. There were no embellishments and very few details, but Doctor Dee seemed to take it all in, making only a couple of minor interjections.

'So thou sayest thou art from the future?' he asked quietly when they had finished.

'Aye sir, but we art marooned here and cannot see a way to go home.'

'Indeed that is a conundrum that will take some unknotting.' said Doctor Dee with a short barked laugh.

He said nothing for several seconds, merely watched the boys who shifted uncomfortably.

'You do believe us then, sir?' asked Sim.

'Oh aye lad. I have the evidence of mine own eyes and ears that thou art not of this world – unless thou art wizards of passing skill and I would know of such long before now. Especially if thou art from mine own country.'

'What evidence is that?' asked Tam, puzzled.

'Why this!' said Dee, pointing at the boys. 'Thy clothes are of a cloth and design that I have never seen – and I have travelled far in my life. Yet even that would not have convinced me were it not for the glimmer thou hast cast over thyselves.'

'Glimmer?' echoed Tam.

'Aye glimmer. Thy proper garb may only be discerned by looking askance and even then only if thy hast the ability to question thine own senses.' Dee smiled.

'It is the same with thy speech. There is some small echo about it. I have the impression that I am not hearing what it is that you utter. It is as though the angels are telling me the import of thy words so that we may have discourse.

'The *angels*?' asked Tam with more than a hint of sarcasm.

Doctor Dee's face darkened.

'You would mock me child?' His voice boomed out and he thrust himself to his feet to stand over the boys.

Fin quickly replied, his response speeded by fear.

'Please sir, he did not mean to mock!' He made a deprecating gesture towards Tam. 'It is more that he is a little simple and dost not understand thee.'

From the corner of his mouth Sim hissed 'Apologise you pillock! Apologise now, before you really piss him off!'

Tam was at least quick on the uptake.

'Doctor Dee! Sir! Prithee forgive me my oafish tongue. I meant no disrespect and do not need the ungentle coaxing of mine companions to crave your amnesty upon my foolish utterances.'

Fin thought that Tam might be going a little bit over the top here, but there was no hint of his usual joking. Then Tam fell to his knees in front of the conjuror, his hands clasped in supplication as though begging forgiveness from a priest. If they hadn't all been so worried about Doctor Dee throwing them out, it may have been slightly comic. As it was, neither Fin nor Sim could have raised a smile even if they had wanted to.

'I wouldst not give thee offence. On my life I would not! For it is through thee that we hope to return home, if thou canst help us. Without thine aid we must rely upon Fin and he knows not how our return may be brought to pass. Thou art our only hope sir.' Tam looked close to tears, and Fin wasn't sure whether they were crocodile or not. 'Please do not abandon us through the knavish babblings of my foolish mouth.'

He remained on the floor with head bowed, his hands before him.

All three of the room's other occupants were stunned into silence. Even the Doctor seemed to be at a loss for words.

The plea had been heartfelt, of that there could be no doubt. Given that Tam had shown so little interest in the visit prior to their arrival and appeared to have little knowledge of Doctor Dee, both Fin and Sim were surprised that he should believe so absolutely in the mystic's ability to return them home.

Then it came to Fin in a flash.

Tam believed that only through the actions of others would they be released from this time. He did not have faith in Fin being capable of the feat and was prepared to enlist the help of anyone who might have any inkling as to how to get them home, by whatever means he had to employ.

Fin was almost angry, until he realised that Tam was probably right and his anger cooled almost before it had begun to rise. They'd been here now for almost three weeks. Three weeks in which Sim had seemed to drift away from them and during which Fin had been unable to return them home. Aside from the altercation with Woods early on – which Tam had missed thanks to topping up his ale intake beyond the overfull mark - Fin had shown no evidence of his ability. Even the vague assurances of those who claimed to know about such things, did little to assuage his fears that he had trapped them all here. So maybe Tam had the right idea.

Maybe the tall, silver-haired man before them was their only hope.

Doctor Dee stood looking down upon the crown of Tam's head. He slowly reached forward to place his hand there as though offering a benediction and Tam flinched slightly at the touch. Fin was struck once more by the religious overtones that were evoked by the scene.

'Come boys, we shall have no further upset this day. You shall have to trust in my words as I must trust in thine, if we are to have any further dialogue. There are things afoot here that intrigue me greatly, but I have been deceived before by those who, on first sight, had the look of honest men.'

'Like Kelley.' said Sim.

The searchlight stare from the Doctor cut short any further comment by Sim, who had the distinct feeling that he should have kept that observation to himself.

'And what, *sirrah*, wouldst thou know of Mister Kelley?' said Dee, in a low voice filled with menace, staring fixedly at Sim.

Great! They seemed to be stumbling from one cock-up to the next with breathtaking dexterity. No sooner had Tam scrambled out of his hole, than Sim was busy digging his.

Tam regained his seat with alacrity, eager to be further away from this strange commanding figure and happy for the man's attention to be settled on another.

All three boys edged back into their seats, insofar as you can edge back into a wooden chair, away from that voice edged like a razor. Fin was rigid with worry. This man changed his mood faster even than Sim and who knew what might happen to them whilst "guests" in his house. They could not afford to annoy Doctor Dee – he was the only person he could think of who might be able to help and goodness only knew what he might be capable of if they offended him. Fin's mind began racing away into worse-case-scenario land. Would anyone even know if they disappeared? Or care?

Then Fin remembered Kate sitting patiently outside and Edmund and James, hard at work in The City and realised that yes, they would be missed, but only by those who could have little influence on a man such as Doctor Dee. In many ways the man before them stood outside the law. He had the patronage of the Queen, Lord Walsingham, William Cecil and many others who would surely protect him from any charges that might be laid against him.

'Well boy? Out with it.' urged the Doctor in sugared tones. 'What dost thou know of Mister Kelley?'

'Only that thou and Mister Kelley didst have common interest in certain other-worldly things, sir,' Sim had avoided the word supernatural – he had no way of knowing how the man would react to references to witchcraft. This was after all a time of strange conjunctions between science, religion, magic and superstition and Sim couldn't remember just how far this man had progressed down any of the available paths. 'but parted company some three years ago, following a disagreement regarding your... errr... family life.'

As far as Sim could recall it was one of those News of the World "Three In A Bed Alchemists Romp" stories, but he doubted that either Dee or Kelley had made that public. He only hoped he was remembering the story correctly – and that it wasn't just a story.

Dee looked shocked.

'But how couldst thou know?' he gasped taking a step back. 'Hast thou spoken to Kelley?'

'Who *is* Kelley?' demanded Tam loudly, feeling somewhat left out of this scene and wanting to be able to take a more active role.

Sim maintained his eye contact with the Doctor and answered.

'Up until a couple of years ago Doctor Dee here would converse with "angels" with the help of an assistant. That assistant had worked here previously under the name of Talbot, but something happened -' Sim shook his head slightly, 'I can't remember the exact circumstances – and Talbot became known as Kelley for some reason. Together with the good doctor he carried out what they called "activities", where Kelley would commune with angels and then relate any messages to Doctor Dee. As I recall even Kelley sometimes doubted the veracity of his angels and believed that sometimes he conversed with demons during the "activities". And indeed there are many - very many - who doubt the whole story. But Doctor Dee believed him and that was vindication enough for many people. After all Doctor Dee is pre-eminent in his field. And his field is... well... everything. Isn't it Doctor?'

Sim gave a quick little smile, totally lacking in mirth.

'Sim, are you remembering all this from that book I gave you last Christmas?' asked Fin quietly. Though why he bothered was hard to say. The silence in the room made even the slightest breath as loud as a shout.

Sim nodded.

'Hmmm. Must give that a read.'

'Right so far Doctor?' asked Sim.

Dee nodded soundlessly, his firmly shut mouth no more than a thin line.

'But Mister Kelley – Edward, I think his name was – got too big for his boots and started hiring himself out to other rich patrons. Indeed he'll be knighted within the next few years.'

Dee looked taken aback.

'Oh, don't worry Doc. He'll be dead within a couple more years' said Sim carelessly, 'so it's unlikely that he'll cause you too much anguish.'

Sim paused and looked fearlessly at the Doctor.

'Do you wish me to continue sir?' he asked quietly.

'No, young sir, I believe you have said quite enough.' replied Dee. 'However, I must correct you slightly on one point. Kelley and I parted company for several reasons, his odd demands – prompted by the angels - regarding our living arrangements being the least of them.'

Still looking slightly bewildered Dee sank once more into his seat.

'Amazing. You say that all this is known from a book?' asked Dee.

'Yeah. I bought it for him last Christmas. Sim always reads stuff like that.' said Fin.

'So do you!' accused Sim. 'Remember that one all about London under Elizabeth the First? I seem to remember you devouring that one for your last birthday.'

'True. True' nodded Fin, with a grin.

Dee looked upset, switching his eyes between the two boys.

'Thou dost devour books?'

It was Tam who explained that one, and they all breathed a sigh of relief when the Doctor appeared to be completely convinced regarding their story.

'But just one thing puzzles me.' said Tam to Doctor Dee. 'How is it that you understand what you've just heard, when no-one else we've talked to seemed to be able to? They just sort of lose interest half way through whenever we talk about any of it.' He tugged at his T shirt. 'And you can see our clothes and hear the Babel Fish, when no-one else can.'

After a further explanation from Tam regarding the fish, Doctor Dee understood the concept enough to be able to clarify how he believed his ability to absorb information lost on the vast majority of his countrymen (if not all of them) operated.

'Tis simply put. I have long experience of looking beyond the obvious outer vestments that adorn articles and persons. I can see past that which would beguile most of the common men of this island. With the aid of first Kelly and now my son Arthur, I have seen and had discourse with angels – and mayhap others who live outside of the basic fabric of our world. I have familiarity with other realms and may be better placed to recognise those things that are concealed from the eyes of most men.'

'So, it's more to do with a state of mind?' prompted Fin. 'It's knowing how to look at things in the right way, rather than just looking at them harder?'

'Just so.' said Dee. 'The glamour that dost surround you three is but a haze to me, but is a solid body to others. And so it is with thy speech. This strange double-talk that I hear clearly must go unperceived by most, since you have travelled untroubled for so long. If others had heard or sensed it, I doubt me not that you would have been apprehended long before you reached London and held, if not burned.'

Fin looked alarmed and the Doctor shook his head slowly as if in sorrow – or pity – for his fellow man.

'The peasantry have little understanding of the worlds that exist beyond our own, and likewise many of those of higher estate who should possess the faculties to see and comprehend. I have merely glimpsed them, but it is enough for me to have a greater grasp of that which is, as yet, unknown to the generality of the populous. They, on the other hand, would have no truck with such matters and see such things as unwholesome and ungodly. Therefore they seek to destroy such as we, who seek knowledge beyond the restrictive boundaries of their feeble reasoning.'

He smiled at the three boys.

'Worry not.' he said, his manner brisk. 'Thy secrets are safe within these walls and I would hear more of such things as ye have seen.'

'But first Doctor, I would ask thy help with the matter of my spectacles.' said Fin, pointing across at the man with his glasses. 'I have languished too long in this misted haze that bedevils my sight.'

'Certes, Master Finbar. Though I doubt me that I can repair them. Let us settle instead for fresh eye glasses.'

Fin looked crestfallen, so the Doctor hurried on.

'Nay lad, look not so glum. For I will furnish you with a pair which, though not so pretty, will put they vision to rights. At least then thou wilt no longer squint like a babe in the sun.'

He smiled and leaned his head back to call. 'Theodore! Come by me child, for I have an errand!'

A dark haired child, only slightly younger than Fin, entered and looked curiously at the others.

'Yes father?' he said, without taking his eyes from them.

'Take bread, and butter and a cup of mead to the maiden who waits outside.' He gave Fin a knowing look. 'She will not come in - even if invited, but at least she shall not starve or thirst while she waits. Also inform her of the location of the privy, for she may well feel the call to do the needful before we are finished withal.'

'Aye father.' The boy turned to hurry from the room.

'And have Arthur come and join us!' called Dee after his vanishing son.

'Aye father!'

A few minutes later an older boy joined them. Almost an adult, indeed considered so by the folk of this era for several years no doubt, Arthur was every inch his father's son. The hair was darker and though he lacked a beard, he still had the aquiline nose and firm jaw of the older man and was, if anything, even more solemn of mien. Fin realised that this was the figure who had so quickly vacated the room upon their arrival.

Not a man for a fun night out in the tavern, thought Sim, a little unkindly. For Sim knew from his reading, of the trials that had been faced by the family of the great Doctor Dee and Arthur, as the eldest son, would certainly have been more aware of circumstances than his siblings; of being trailed around Europe whilst his father searched for benefactors and sponsors; of the rapid departures when he upset the said benefactors and sponsors; of the arguments with fellow scholars; the vaguely heretical practices and suspicious conversations heard from behind closed doors; and of the constant surveillance by a suspicious populous wherever they went. Only in Mortlake was there some peace to be found, but even that had been rudely torn apart when the house had been ransacked during their last visit to Poland and the Low Countries.

Yes, thinking about it, Sim could not blame the young man for his dark demeanour.

'Arthur, could you find the eye-glasses that arrived last week?'

The young man nodded and made to leave, but his father stayed him with a hand on his wrist and an upwards glance as his son passed his chair.

'Bring all four pairs, Arthur - and the extra lenses.' Dee added.

Once again Fin's gaze followed the blurred image of a son of Doctor Dee as he left the room. The Doctor returned his own gaze to Fin, his expression softening.

'We shall see what may be done for your eyes when Arthur returns, though the items are somewhat spread about through the house and he may be some time. So whilst we wait, why dost thou not make your second request, for I am sure that there is something else thou wouldst have me help thee with. Am I correct?'

Doctor Dee looked at the boys and paid particular attention to Tam, who had been subdued since his beseeching request earlier.

'Master Tamburlaine would wish to return home methinks.' said the Doctor, not unkindly.

Tam nodded.

'Yes please sir.'

'I own I am uncertain as to our course in this.' said the doctor. 'Though I doubt me that we shall find some method to send thee back from whence thou came. But I would have further discourse on thy mode of travel from thine own lands to this.'

Fin thought that was an odd way to put it. Maybe Doctor Dee had not quite grasped their situation, but nevertheless he was at least prepared to try to help them. He obviously saw them as travellers from a different place, though not necessarily a different time. Sim's knowledge of what had passed between Kelly and the doctor evidently intrigued the man, but he seemed to see it more as a matter of scrying rather than the boys having a broad knowledge of history. Still, if an Elizabethan alchemist and mystic was their best bet, Fin was prepared to go along with him.

Anything that had even the most remote chance of getting them home was worth a try, given that Tony didn't appear to be in a hurry to help them. Fin couldn't help feeling a trifle miffed at that; he'd promised to come back to lend moral support if nothing else, but he hadn't and it had been quite long enough now.

'Come lads, tell me more of what has befallen thee.' said Doctor Dee, settling himself back as though preparing for a long session.

Now it was Fin's turn to essay an attempt at describing what he had done. He told the older man of his nightmares ('Surely visions sent from the Nether Worlds.'), his ability to travel in space ('Truly a gift from Above.') and finally his barrelling around in time, friends in tow ('A most singular occurrence, mayhap a joke played by a mage upon unknowing children, for his own sport.').

When Fin mentioned the bullying and particularly the incident that lead to this latest leap across time, the doctor nodded his head vigorously, his face stern.

'Twas ever thus. Those who can see no further than their own noses, who aspire to nothing more than that which is most simply achieved, will always seek to bring low those of us who would seek a higher understanding. I have had to suffer the barbed wit and ill-aimed slingshots of many others who would be well pleased if I were brought low, both in England and abroad. You have my sympathies lads. All of you.'

All the boys had a feeling that the doctor was trying hard to fit their circumstances into practices he could understand, rather than stepping outside of his own broad - but still Medieval - world view and into the unknown. Thinking outside the envelope was probably more difficult in the sixteenth century, particularly for a man who believed he knew almost all there was to know. Doctor Dee gave a definite impression that he knew he was pre-eminent in the field of science and that he was the sole repository for knowledge regarding alchemy and such like, including what many would call *the spirit world.*

They were interrupted by the re-entry of Arthur carrying a small wooden chest crammed with glass baubles and an odd assortment of wires and string.

'Ah, Arthur. On the chest please.' said the doctor, tapping on the trunk where he'd previously placed the spectacles.

Wordlessly Arthur placed the box down and then lifted the whole, to place them before his father. Then he pulled up a chair and settled himself beside the doctor awaiting further instructions.

Fin smiled at Arthur and received the briefest of flicking smiles in return, before turning his attention to the doctor who was busy rummaging in the wooden chest. From it he produced several lenses - all much thicker than those in the broken glasses, and several very rough frames made of what appeared to be copper wire.

'This may take some little time.' said the doctor. 'Perhaps now would be an opportune moment for you two others to return to your companion outside and see that all is well.'

Sim gave Fin a look of alarm, returned with interest by Fin.

'Come sir! I wouldst hope that we can trust each other. Certain it is that we shall not steal away your friend whilst you are outside and he would appear to have few lurries about him that would cause us to suddenly become footpads! Indeed there is still much to discuss and I would do so with all three of you in good humour.' He waved towards the door. 'Be off, young cakes, whilst we restore what little sight Master Finbar still retains.'

Fin nodded to the others to go ahead and check on Kate, who had been sitting alone for almost an hour, and must be getting worried.

'Go on Tam. I'll be fine Sim. Go and see if you can persuade Kate to come in.'

With that, they left Fin to the ministrations of Doctor Dee and his son.

The two friends emerged into the bright sunshine, blinking and shielding their eyes.

'Is aught amiss.' called Kate, still sitting atop the cart.

'Nay lass. The good doctor is attempting to restore Fin's sight and suggested we join you for a few moments.'

'And is it safe to leave Fin inside?' asked Kate looking up at the sprawling house.

'Oh aye. Methinks Doctor Dee will do all he can. In us he sees a mystery that he would have explained and he can't have that if any ill befalls Fin.' said Sim.

Kate noticed that Tam didn't look so convinced.

'And what say you master Tamburlaine?'

'The whole place gives me the collywobbles.' he said quietly, as though worried that he might be overheard.

Whether he intended it or not - and he almost certainly didn't – he did at least bring a smile to Kate's lips.

She shook her head as she laughed.

'What strange lads you are indeed!' Then her face straightened.

'But I shall miss you, should Doctor Dee find some way of sending you on your way. Indeed I will.'

Tam caught the sudden firm set of Sim's jaw and realised that there was still some question about whether all three of them would return should the opportunity arise.

'The doctor wondered whether you would care to join us inside, rather than sitting out here all alone. Mistress Dee would enjoy some company, I shouldn't doubt.'

Kate looked startled at the very idea and Tam was sure she was searching for a reason to remain outside, when the two small girls who had earlier run across the green returned. They raced gaily towards the house, but slowed when still twenty yards from the cart and shyly looked out from under their dark hairs. Eventually the older one mustered the courage to speak.

'Hast thou come to speak with father?' she asked quietly, one hand guiding the tot against her skirts. For her part, the toddler peered out from the cover of her sister.

'Aye miss.' said Sim. 'I am Simeon and this is Kate and Tam. Our friend Fin is within.'

'Aye. I thought there was another.' said the girl, her eyes lighting up and her words suddenly coming in a rush. 'I am Katherine and this is my sister Madinia. We have come to help mamma with dinner.' Her face dropped. 'Though today is fish and we don't like it overmuch. Is that not so Maddy?' she said crouching to look at her little sister.

The little one shook her head, but smiled nonetheless as she looked up, seemingly mesmerised by Kate's golden hair.

Kate for her part was completely disarmed by the two girls. Hardly surprising given that she had had nothing but the company of boys and men for what seemed like an eternity. Making a sudden decision, she jumped down and tied the reins to the gatepost and reached up for the feed bag for Morris.

'Come then ladies, let us not keep your mother waiting.' she said, reaching out to the smaller girl with one hand, whilst giving the horse a solid slap on his neck.

'Methinks Morris will be happy the nonce.'

Little Madinia gave a small twisting motion, swirling her kirtle, as she grasped the offered hand and the three girls strode to the door.

Tam looked over at Sim with raised eyebrows.

Girls! Invite them in and they don't want to know. Give them a poppet to cling to and they'd walk through fire.

The boys followed Kate and the sisters into the house, where Madinia immediately shouted for her mother to come and see her new friend.

Jane Dee seemed genuinely unfazed by having four extra mouths to feed at dinner time. Tam had the impression that this happened on a regular basis and with far more important personages than she had to entertain today.

Everyone but Fin and Doctor Dee congregated in the kitchen, where Kate and the boys were introduced to all the Dee children - and there were several that they hadn't met. Arthur joined them and took a back seat as his sisters busied themselves arranging the seating plan around the large table and running out to distant corners of the house to find extra chairs.

By the time dinner was ready, Fin and the doctor had joined in the general hullabaloo in the kitchen and the boys were surprised to see the way that Doctor Dee behaved with his younger children. Though he smiled often, he was still rather stiff and formal with them, not deigning to take the smaller girls in his arms, even when they called for his attention and tugged on his gown. He was a patriarch who gave his love to his family, but had difficulty in showing his affection. It was a shame; to be so clever and yet be unable to really enjoy his family life. Fin could see that the doctor needed advice on his work/life balance. He'd heard Jarmon talking about the difficulty of getting that right and determined to give this genius of the Elizabethan age the benefit of his experience before they parted company. Then, remembering how quick the Doctor was to anger, he had a rethink.

Dinner, or lunch if you were of the higher classes, consisted of a salad the like of which none of the boys had ever experienced.

Forget the lettuce and cress. Here was arrayed a cornucopia of edibles that none had ever even considered eating before; strawberries and blackcurrants (*in a salad*?), the petals of violets and several roots, shoots and fruits that they couldn't identify, but found to be delicious.

Following the meal the menfolk withdrew to Doctor Dee's study to complete the fitting of Fin's new eyewear. While the others watched in admiration, Arthur fashioned a tidy frame to hold the lenses selected earlier, with nimble fingers and rudimentary tools and Fin soon found himself with a much improved vision of the world. It had to be said that the lenses were heavy and not altogether uniform but at least the kaleidoscopic effects were reduced to almost nil. There was a certain amount of distortion, but Fin could at least see without having to squint through his crazy paving any more.

During the fitting, Doctor Dee questioned the boys regarding their time with Edmund and Kate and tried to understand more about their own time, far into his future. Although all three boys tried as best they could, it was impossible for even this great mind to understand the workings of the internal combustion engine, CDs or television. Without some knowledge of modern day chemistry and electronics it was ultimately impossible to describe many of the household items they used on a day-to-day basis. This was frustrating for everyone, since it was clocks, radios and phones that seemed to hold the greatest fascination for Doctor Dee.

It was only when the fitting was complete that they realised that Fin's original spectacles were gone. He'd been wearing them at lunch, but had removed them once Arthur had begun shaping his new pair to fit his face.

They had been lying on the large trunk next to the small chest holding all the lens related articles. When Fin came to put them back in his pocket, they were simply gone. Certainly Arthur had had no time to hide them. Nor did Fin believe him capable of theft. The eldest child of the Dee family was a man of solid morals and ethics. Even the short time they had spent in his company had convinced the boys that Arthur could be trusted almost as one of them. Though of sombre nature, he was also pleasant company who was clearly enthralled by the discussions between his father and the three strange boys. He also appeared to be genuinely pleased that his handiwork was greeted so appreciatively by Fin.

So if Arthur hadn't taken the glasses and certainly Doctor Dee would not have pilfered them - he would have asked outright if he could have them, that was his nature, and no-one else had entered or left the room – where had the glasses gone?

Once Fin was back in the land of the seeing and had given effusive thanks to Arthur and the doctor for his new glasses, the question of payment arose.

'Nay, lad. It is enough that we have had such merry meetings and I would hazard that you have little enough money between thee.' said the doctor. The boys looked shame-faced at their lack of finances and the doctor smiled. 'Be of good cheer, for I ask for naught from you other than your company and that you have given in good heart. Though I have much to think on, I must confess that I am perplexed by a great deal of what we have discussed.'

He looked sombrely at the three of them

'And as to giving my aid in thy return from whence you came: I must own that I cannot see how I may be of assistance. The things of which thou hast spoken, Finbar, are beyond my knowledge to repair.' He shook his head. 'And if I cannot be of help, I know of no-one who may be.'

He could see the crestfallen expression on the faces of Fin and Tam. He also noticed that Sim looked little bothered by his statement.

'I am most disquieted by my lack of ability in this, but can see no point in dissembling further.' He paused and gave a small smile of resignation. 'I fear me that your salvation rests in your own hands.'

Fin nodded. He had been foolish to expect anything more. His final straw had slipped from his grasp and his stomach felt hollow.

'But be not so down hearted young sirs, for surely what has happed is for a reason and when you have discovered the wherefore, then surely thou find the end of thy perplexities.'

Doctor Dee gave Fin a hearty clap on the shoulder.

'I wouldst have called Arthur to prepare for an activity this afternoon had I any thought that *The Angels*,' he emphasized the term and looked at Tam and Sim as though daring them to make light of his choice of words. 'might offer any fortuitous tidings. But I doubt me that they would be of assistance in our quest for answers - and the interpretation of their words can take overlong. However, if we should learn anything that may be of help, fear not, for I shall with all despatch send Arthur to seek thee out with whatever information we may glean from our investigations.' The stately man paused and sought the eyes of the boy before him and, with a small smile, continued. 'Worry not Finbar, for all things have a purpose. You have but to perceive the substance of this puzzle and you will be safe returned to home. Of this I misdoubt me not'

Fin nodded.

'And I thank thee, good Doctor, for your aid, and you too Arthur - e'en though this is not how I foresaw our meeting ending.'

The group were a trifle solemn as they returned to the kitchen and Kate too looked crestfallen on hearing their news, but also pleased that they would not be stolen away from her so soon. She reached out to take Sim's hand and squeezed it tightly, with a small sad smile playing on her lips.

The mystery of the spectacles remained even after the boys and Kate had bid their final farewells to the Dee family. But to be fair, no-one was really that bothered by the loss of some broken glasses, which were of little use to anyone.

The sun was well down in the clear blue sky and the hedges bounding the fields alongside the western road through Southwark were casting ever deeper shadows, when the foursome in the cart were met by Edmund and James. Both the men looked as though they had been running and the sweat stood out on each brow as they came closer.

'Well met, Kate!' called Edmund as he hurried along the road and leapt up to his daughter. Fin, who was sitting alongside Kate, moved across to make space as Kate embraced her father. James heaved himself up onto the back of the cart where he joined Tam and Sim, giving them both hearty slaps on the shoulder and calling to Edmund.

'See Edmund, did I not say all would be well? I pity the prig who would take on these fine lads.'

Laughing, James lay down with the hands locked behind his head and gazed up into the cloudless sky.

'I told him he should not worry overmuch, but Edmund would not be lifted from his fear of vagabonds seeking to rob thee on thy journey.' He gave another short barking laugh and closed his eyes. 'Not even in these squalid environs would any seek to harm such a merry band of younglings. Ah, children, could there be a finer place and a finer time to live than here and now?' he asked, as much to the open air above his head as to his companions. 'Truly we are men blessed. Eh, Edmund?'

'Aye, James. With my Kate beside me and youthful friends such as we have here, who would argue.' Edmund laughed along with his old friend, ruffled the hair of Fin and turned to do the same with Sim and Tam, when suddenly Morris shied and Edmund, caught off-balance, almost fell from the cart.

And the sound of thunder rolled overhead.

Now Mike (47)

It had taken almost three hours to complete the drive to Eskdale and Mike was ready to stretch his legs in the warm summer air. His intake of coffee at two different service stops on the way had also ensured the urgent need for a pee.

Feeling strangely pleased with himself for having navigated the entire journey without the need to refer to his "AA Road Atlas 1967", he made his way slowly through the almost deserted car park. He ruminated on the wisdom of using a decades-old road map, given the amount of road building that was going on. Still, it had served him faithfully ever since he had inherited it from his father. In some strange way its age made him feel more secure when he did have to use it, even though even he had to admit that it was now more ornamental than useful.

The mill looked exactly as it had on the previous Tuesday. The air was warm and damp, even though there was no evidence of rain. The surrounding trees seemed filled with a summer torpor, as though the hazy afternoon had driven even the birds back into their nests. It was very quiet and almost unimaginably peaceful, strangely so, since the old mill had, in an earlier incarnation, been a hive of activity practically 24/7. Mike shoved his hands in his pockets, resisting the urge to soft-shoe shuffle across the yard.

Well everyone gets the urge to be Fred Astaire sometimes. Don't they? Certainly Bev had been sanguine about it, that time in London, when an unexpected downpour had caused him to burst into "Singin' in the rain" on a deserted Saville Row.

Mike gave a quick chuckle and made his way around the left side of the mill to the shade behind the main workshop. The short-cropped grass looked much the same as when Fin had been so sure they would find a massive pile of wood shavings against the high wall of the mill.

Searching about in the gloom, Mike could see no trace of sawdust and looked up at the edifice before him. Several windows let light into the ground floor within and a couple of smaller windows marked the offices above.

Mike scanned the wall and there, high up and flush with the ancient brickwork, unseen unless you were right below it, was the door.

He pictured the size of the pile of sawdust that would be needed to make that door of any earthly use.

How the bloody Hell had Fin known about it?

Then Fin, Tam and Simeon (48)

The booming drumroll of sound died away as Edmund looked up, alarmed, into the pristine blue sky overhead and scanned their surroundings to try to identify the source of the unexpected noise; the dying echoes dissipating away through the surrounding streets and over the fields beyond.

Ahead of him, some twenty yards beyond Morris's huffing nose stood two men. One younger than the other, the older man in the black gowns of a mage and carrying a small board with papers and a quill, the younger man in nonedescript garb of the Parish Clerks Company. They had appeared suddenly on the long, straight and otherwise deserted road. Fields lay all around and Edmund was certain they had not been there moments before.

'It's Tony.' said Fin in a whisper, turning to Tam and Sim. 'He's come back.'

Fin jumped down from the cart and ran over to the younger of the two men who shook hands enthusiastically with him grasping his upper arm with his free hand as they greeted each other. The older man appeared to place a tick on his board with a quick nod of his head.

'Who's Tony?' asked Tam.

Sim shrugged, making no comment.

Fin was obviously very excited at the sudden appearance of the pair, who walked towards the cart with him.

'How's things then, Fin?' asked Tony, brightly, looking over at everyone else in the cart.

'Great!' beamed Fin, looking up to those still aboard.

'This is Tony, everyone. We met a couple of weeks ago during our "argument" with Adam Woods.'

Sim looked askance at his friend.

'Well I don't remember seeing him there.' he said, puzzled, looking the man up and down. Tony looked to be about twenty, though his sunny disposition, obvious to all, made him seem younger

'No, it was while I was… er… some*when* else.' said Fin excitedly, before looking over at Edmund, realising that he'd have to be careful to avoid mentioning the aftermath of his last time-altering jaunt. He had a feeling that Edmund would prefer to forget the whole event - especially his reaction to the sight of Fin and Sim flashing in and out of the scene.

Tony raised a hand to Edmund.

'I am Anthony Athelston, sir. Short-term companion to Master LeMott here, and this,' he motioned towards the older man, 'is Mister Abel Fermion, Piece Keeper to –'

'Thank you Anthony. I think that is quite enough!' said the Fermion sharply. 'We are not here to bandy words, but to reconcile this matter with all speed. Expediency is, after all, our watchword in affairs such as this.'

Tony's smile vanished at once, though his grin remained and he bowed his head to hide it.

'Of course, sir. Please forgive my over-enthusiasm.'

He took a short step back, placing Abel Fermion firmly in the lead in whatever was about to occur.

'Sir,' said Edmund, 'an explanation is forthcoming I believe.'

'Indeed sir. But not here.' The man spoke with authority, with the air of one who would brook no argument. 'Let us accompany you to the nearest hostelry, where we shall make clear our aim in having had to make this unfortunate imposition upon your good self.'

Edmund and James both looked far from pleased at the manner in which this stranger was addressing them. The jollity of mere seconds earlier had evaporated.

All the children were acutely aware that this was not going well, yet Fermion appeared not to notice.

'Please Edmund, might we allow them to join us?' asked Fin.

Edmund switched his gaze to Fin, and could see the entreaty in his face.

'Aye Fin. If thou wouldst have it, then so we shall, for I think me that you seek their aid. Is't not so?' he said, not unkindly and Fin nodded his thanks before climbing into the cart with Tam and Sim.

James moved forward to join Edmund and Kate on the bench seat, where the three remained, only Kate glancing back in curiosity.

Everyone in the cart had visibly relaxed, but an air of mistrust remained – and who could blame them? Despite Fin's obvious joy at meeting the young man again, the older gentleman had done nothing to endear himself to any them.

It was Tony who came to the rescue as he helped his older companion into the cart.

'So, how goes it with you all?' he asked, with a twinkle in his eye. 'Eager to be home yet?'

There was something about the way he said it that made Tam look even more closely at the two new arrivals.

'You know don't you!' he cried, managing to look both amazed and angry at the same time. 'You know what's going on.'

'Yes of course. Fin told me all about it when I found him last time, but you as I recall young fellow-me-lad, were in no fit state to remember very much of anything at the time.' Tony chuckled to himself. 'A skinful of ale was sloshing about in you I seem to remember.'

Tam blushed furiously and all the children laughed and even Edmund and James raised a smile at that.

Fermion stared stonily ahead.

'So why didn't you mention this to any of us?' asked Simeon irritably. 'Did you not think it worth the time – to let us know that there was someone else out there who knew what was happening... someone who might be able to help?'

But it was Tony who answered.

'I asked him not to tell anyone. I had to talk to Piece Keeper Fermion first, to know if I would be allowed to return.'

'What do you mean "allowed to" - ' began Fin, but Fermion interrupted.

'All in good time, boy. Be patient and we shall try our utmost to undo what has been done.'

His demeanour was sufficient to make it plain that there would be no further discourse on this subject until he allowed it. Tony sat silently, but seemed otherwise unperturbed by the attitude of his companion. He gave Fin a quick wink and a smile.

Edmund cast a quick look over his shoulder to Fin, as a thought occurred to him.

'How is't Fin, that I saw not this young man during our last meeting with that wastrel Woods?'

Fin looked stricken, not wanting to get into all this at this moment. He wasn't sure how Edmund would react if he knew too much about Tony.

It was Abel Fermion who replied for him.

'Master Edmund, it was Anthony here who helped Fin to retrieve this young pup' He indicated Tam, 'from the woods whilst, I believe, everyone else was otherwise occupied.' and then looking Edmund straight in the eye as though daring him to argue he said, 'All will be made clear – in good time. First food and refreshment I think. Then explanations.'

Edmund was obviously less than satisfied by the reply, but held his piece. There seemed little to be gained by antagonising this odd fellow, but when they came, the explanations had best be fulsome or both Edmund and James would have more to say on the subject of good manners and respect for your peers. Though their new companion might dress like a mage, he had more the air of a schoolmaster and in their book that made them social equals as far as James and Edmund were concerned.

Edmund reined Morris into an inn about a mile further down the road as the byway began to fill with people heading east towards London Bridge and over the Thames to the city, or onwards on the south bank to Deptford.

'Wherefore dost so many head towards the bridge James?' asked Kate, gazing out over the suddenly crowded street.

'Tis the bear pits over yonder.' said James pointing towards the river. 'and bulls too. I did hear that Sackerson was to be tested today and that is a spectacle that many would pay to see. Even with the plague taking its toll of the local populace, the bear pits stay open, though the theatres have been closed these twelve months.'

'Who's Sackerson?' asked Fin, turning to look at James, who opened his eyes to look at the boy as he replied. Tam meanwhile was craning his neck in an attempt to see the pits from which the crowds were streaming.

'Plague!' he squeaked. 'No-one's mentioned plague before! You mean we're in the middle of the plague?'

'Worry not lad. So long as you remain fastidious in matters of cleanliness, there is little to fear.' said James seriously. 'Though forsaking the less wholesome taverns and neighbourhoods is advisable, there is little to fear. The blight lurks only where the air is dank and fetid. So long as you keep to clean air and shun the darker alleys, particularly those that follow some of the smaller streams and rivers, all will be well. Even without the danger of plague, you would do well to shun the darker sides of city life where the punks and cutpurses do dwell.'

James chuckled and ruffled Tam's hair as the boy sank back in his seat, with yet more reason to long for home and family.

'Sackerson is the last of the great bears.' said James, returning to Fin's question, with no more thought of expanding on the evils of the metropolis. 'George Stone and Harry Hunks were finished a few years ago – and none have arrived to take up their mantels, but Sackerson remains to entertain those who have a taste for such entertainment. I earn my money through the sweat of my brow and am loath to fritter it away at the pits. Nor do I frequent the cock pit at Smithfield. I would'st most earnestly advise against all forms of gambling, especially when a payment is required just to watch and even more must be handed over if you wish to wager. Money is too easily spent in the normal course of life, without throwing it away on gaming.'

He shook his head sadly.

'But many are they who would disagree, doubt me not.'

The cart came to a standstill and all disembarked without further comment, all with their own thoughts on the matter of death for entertainment. Fin and his time-travelling friends were only just beginning to realise how different life was here, but then again, so-called sports like hare-coursing were still classed as a fun pastime for a minority in Britain and bull-fighting was still practised in Spain and Mexico.

Maybe we're not so different, Fin thought.

Edmund gave instructions for the care of the horse to a stable-man and they all entered the inn together.

They settled in a corner and ale and water were ordered, with the older man, Fermion, settling for wine. Fin was surprised when it was Fermion who paid for the drinks with a small gold coin, at sight of which, the inn-keeper became much more amenable.

After shooing away the tippler with a request that they be left undisturbed all eyes were on Fermion as he took a first tentative sip of wine. He looked up and realised he was the centre of attention and sat back with a lop-sided grin.

'First let me say that I have been persuaded to intercede here against my better judgement.' he said with a scowl.

'It was only when Anthony informed me of his initial visit to you,' He nodded towards Fin, 'that I became aware of the situation.'

He glanced down at the small clipboard on his lap.

'I did have the three of you marked down, but normally I would not interfere in any way. Those few who make such journeys are usually quite happy to be left to their own devices. It was only when Anthony described the strange way in which you had become one of our small, but usually self-contained, group that I decided that intervention may be justified.'

'You mean there are others who can time travel Mister Fermion.' asked Tam in surprise.

'Why of course, er... Tamburlaine, isn't it?' replied Fermion, consulting his board. 'Did you think that only young Finbar here could perform such a feat?' He shook his head in mocking disbelief. 'The innocence of youth.'

James gave a chuckle into his blackjack at this and even Edmund smiled. Kate looked puzzled and Fin realised that although the odd phrase probably made sense to them, as this conversation continued the inhabitants of this time would soon find themselves taking less interest in what would seem like a foreign language.

'So I told The Piece Keeper that in this instance our help would probably not be cited as interference in this time loop.' put in Tony with a smile at all around the table.

But Edmund and James were already settling into a discussion about building methods, all sectional oak frames and wattle, whilst Kate was still trying hard to follow the conversation, but looking annoyed at the fact that it was beginning to slip away from her.

So it was to the three schoolboys that Fermion addressed himself.

As official Piece Keeper for this Timespace Moment, I have virtual carte blanche to do as I see fit, provided that I do not unbalance the Ribbon to any great degree.'

He gave the appearance of a man who was of the opinion that he was teaching his grandmother to suck eggs.

This, of course, was not the case.

'I'm sorry Mister Fermion, I didn't understand any of that; Piece Keeper, Timespace Moment and Ribbons. It's all meaningless.' Fin said as he gave the man an enquiring squint and went on. 'Can you pretend that we are just three lads, lost in the Middle Ages, who know nothing about time travel?'

Fermion looked slightly nonplussed and looked at Tony with raised eyebrows, as if to say: *How on earth did such a know-nothing come to travel some four hundred years?*

'I did tell you Mister Fermion, that Fin was like me, just a little younger. The big difference is that I met you because I used the void between. Fin appears to jump straight from when to when, without passing through the void at all.'

Fermion nodded.

'Yes of course, you did tell me.' He tapped his temple with a long forefinger. 'My memory is not what it used to be.' He smiled, for the first time since they had met and gave a small shake of his head. The smile transformed his face and the schoolmaster's aura was replaced by that of a kindly absent-minded professor. 'There is so much going on just at the moment. So much to-ing and fro-ing, don't you know. I do however remember that Tudor England was not the Middle Ages, which was the period of

European history from the fall of the Roman Empire in the West in the fifth century, to the fall of Constantinople in fourteen fifty-three. Or often more narrowly, from the years one thousand to fourteen fifty-three.'

For a couple of seconds the school master had returned, but just as swiftly he made his departure.

He put aside his clipboard and placed a hand against his chest and began to explain things as though to a class of schoolchildren, because even Abel Fermion had not forgotten his training early in the nineteen thirties. He slipped again into the teaching style that had made him a favourite amongst his pupils all those years ago.

"Age shall not weary them, nor the years condemn." he thought.

Now where had that come from? Something to do with The Great War surely.

No matter. He may have lived beyond his expected lifespan, but he had the nagging suspicion that he had forgotten far more than he would ever learn in the future. Age may not be wearying him, but he could feel the weight of the condemning years, heavy on his shoulders, like a burden he could no longer support alone.

'I shall try to explain that which is more complex than you can imagine, in the same way that I explained to Anthony here, when first I made his acquaintance.'

Fermion laid a hand lightly on the shoulder of the young man next to him.

'And Anthony has been an able pupil, as will you, I have no doubt.'

As he began, Fin saw the veil descend upon Kate, Edmund and James. These three would not be party to the explanation. Something happened that excluded them from the discourse. Without them even noticing, they took up their own conversation and this time Kate was part of *their* world, not that of the three boys, young man and old teacher.

'The universe is more vast than any man, or woman, has ever postulated.' said Abel Fermion. 'Indeed, The Universe is a misnomer, in that we – and I mean even the most learned of mankind – use it to put a name to the cosmos; of all that is seen and unseen. Even they do not envisage that which lies beyond their comprehension.'

The boys leaned forward as though to hear more clearly.

'The universe as envisaged by man, is but a small part of the whole. Even the greatest minds do not realise that time and space are infinite in a way not even speculated on in human science. Men of immense knowledge theorise that if only they had a telescope large enough to see the most distant galaxies, if it were possible to see those heavenly bodies that are travelling away from the origin of All, the "Big Bang" they call it, at faster than the speed of light, they could measure the size of the universe. Beyond that lies nothing, in that space and time are curved back on themselves and if you travel at immense speed in a straight line, you would come up on your own shoulder. There are no boundaries since you would come back to where you started, but always travel in a straight line. These great men theorise on doughnut shapes and dumbbell shapes to use mathematics to explain all, but they are missing the most obvious problem. Space and time are linked as spacetime – they know this already and some have discussed a multiverse, pictured as layers of spacetime lying one upon the other. Thus time can be imagined as a dimension much as any other. The problem is, it is impossible to picture spacetime. It is too vast.'

Fermion looked up and realised that he was making this too complicated.

'Suffice to say that every decision causes a fork in the road of time.' He gave a nod to Tony. 'Anthony once described a film called "Sliding Doors" to me. In many ways that film encompasses the effect I am trying to describe.'

'Yes, I saw that once.' said Tam and Fin nodded. He knew of it to, seen once late at night when Mum was away for a couple of days in London.

'Good.' said Fermion. 'So, if every single decision, made by every single living thing causes a bifurcation in the... let's call it the ribbon of time, then every single second of every single day, time is multiplied a million fold... a billion fold. Any decision causes time to take one of two paths and we move gaily down the road we chose.'

Fermion took a sip of wine.

'But what of the one less travelled by? In what dimension does that now exist? And on it are there not others, large as a whale, small as the smallest sentient agent, who will also make their own decisions? Thus time splits and resplits until time and space are indeed infinite. Many ribbons are identical in all but the smallest detail, many are so different that they become unrecognisable as related to their antecedents.'

Fermion looked deep into Fin's eyes, for Fin was the traveller here; Tam and Sim mere passengers.

'What you have found Finbar, is a way between the ribbons of spacetime. Across what we call The Void, which separates each from its neighbour. All the travellers I have ever met - and there have not been so many, I must confess – have travelled via the void and it is there that I - and now Anthony here – keep watch. Eons ago we were given the title Piece Keepers, when the first so called "time travellers" realised that some sort of check should be kept on who was going where – and *when*. They thought it very droll to make reference to Time Pieces and Peace Keepers, given that they were uncertain as to whether it would be possible to create dangerous paradoxes if someone of ill intent travelled. There are others who have different names for those who do as we do. You must remember not to fall into the trap of many men, in believing that only humanity is capable of performing such feats, there are many others. Others whose origins are lost in the mists of spacetime, who do not even know themselves from whence they came. We are not alone in the infinity of spacetime gentlemen.'

'So there are aliens out there?' asked Tam, mind filled with War of the Worlds imagery of alien conquest and Star Wars.

'Aye Tamburlaine, there are. Yet strangely, there has never been conflict between the different aspects of spacetime. Those who are able to traverse The Void are few and seem restricted, or possibly chosen, to allow only those minds that quest, but ask for no reward. There has never been a despot or commander able to travel through spacetime. It is as though some degree of childlike innocence and imagination must remain, but constrained by a maturity of mind that will show restraint where necessary. You will find you are unable to have any but the lightest impact on the worlds you visit.'

At the look of astonishment of Fin's face Tony almost laughed out loud, but restrained himself for fear of breaking the spell that hung over the five of them, cast by his mentor Abel Fermion.

'Oh yes, Finbar. Make no mistake, it is possible to travel to other worlds in exactly the same way that you travel through spacetime, for what *is* that sort of journey, other than another aspect of the dimension in which you show such ability to move around at will. Remember Finbar, it is spacetime, not space *or* time, or space *and* time. It is spacetime. '

'Well not exactly at will.' muttered Fin.

Fermion looked perplexed.

'Finbar, seek not to make light of what you have done. If you travelled here without passage through The Void, where you would have most certainly have come to my notice – it is my… talent... shall we say - to be able to track those who travel through the void - Anthony here possesses the same ability, but not everyone who travels does, not by any means. You are the first being I have met who has managed to avoid The Void.' He grinned. 'Excuse the pun.'

Everyone had a quick drink in the ensuing pause.

'And that brings us to your current situation. You travelled, along with your two young friends, from your Timespace Moment to this. The passage of time is measured in moments, each so small as to be impossible to capture, but all present nonetheless. The fact that you did not enter The Void means that you travelled along your Ribbon of Timespace Moments to arrive here. I have never known someone to travel backwards down a Ribbon; everyone I have encountered has stepped outside into The Void in order to find their target. You are something of an enigma at this moment.'

'Was that another pun?' asked Tam.

Fermion gave him a mock glare and then addressed himself to Tam in particular, as though aware of his homesickness.

'So, Anthony tells me you wish to return home.' he asked quietly. 'Is that right?'

'You bet, sir. As soon as possible please.' said Tam breathlessly. 'A change is as good as a rest they say. Well I'm well rested and want to go home. Now. If not sooner.' He paused before repeating. 'Yes, as soon as possible please.'

Sim said nothing, but there was a rigid quality to the way he sat, that boded ill. Tam seemed not to notice, but Fin was immediately aware that there was at least one of them that wasn't quite so keen to be gone.

What he couldn't understand was why.

Exactly what was it that was making Sim so adamant that he wanted to stay here, leaving behind (or was it ahead) all that he had in the future?

True Sim had settled in faster than either he or Tam, but there was more to it than that, Fin was sure.

Sim was staring over at Kate and Fin, catching his gaze, followed it and was surprised to see that she too gave the impression of being less than euphoric about a possible departure. Oh-oh, Fin realised he'd been missing something obvious.

Everyone else around the table caught the odd shift in mood and even Edmund and James were brought back to the main discussion group.

'Is aught amiss Kate?' asked Edmund anxiously, seeing her expression.

Her face crumpled.

'Oh father. Close comes the time of their departure and with them...' She blushed bright scarlet and couldn't finish he sentence. Her breath came in short gasps and her face was twisted with anguish.

Her father was shocked at the tears that suddenly coursed down her cheeks.

'I will truly be sorry to see Fin and Tamburlaine leave, but...' With a stifled sob she broke off and rushed out through the door to the yard.

Edmund sat dumbfounded for a second and then with a scowl at the boys he shot to his feet and hurried off in his daughter's wake.

Now it was the turn of James to turn a searchlight glare on Simeon.

'Now then Master Simeon, what's to do?' he demanded.

As Sim, now also crimson and looking decidedly discomforted, struggled to answer, James held up a hand to stay him.

'I would that you remember this before you seek to explain; Edmund is a friend of long standing and the health and happiness of his daughter are of great matter to me lad. If you have done aught to cause her pain it will go ill with thee.' hissed James. 'Now tell me what should have brought about such distress. And be honest with me *sirrah*, for thy lies will find thee out in short time and great will be my wrath, but it will be as nought compared to that of Edmund. Now out with it!'

The anger that accompanied his low-voiced outburst made all those seated opposite shrink back, as did his furious visage.

'Sir, I have done nothing to cause her such dismay.' said Simeon. He sat straighter and his voice was even.

'These past few weeks have been the happiest that I can recall. I do not long to be home as do Fin and Tam. I would stay here if I could and labour under the tutelage of Master Edmund, for I can work wood and am as able-bodied as any boy my age. ' He looked over at his friends as though daring them to argue. 'If it were not for the absence of my father I would indeed stay and seek to remain in the affections of Kate.' James's eyes narrowed at this and his lips compressed, and Sim hurried on to forestall any comment the man would make. 'For I believe that Kate feels as I do, sir. With the consent of Goodman Edmund I would seek to become more than journeyman companion to the Turners.' He paused and James did not seek to interject. 'It is for this reason that Kate is upset with this discussion of our leaving. At least that is my hope.'

'And what have you done to warrant such affection, lad? asked James shortly. 'Heaven knows there must have been opportunity a plenty whilst Edmund has had his back turned.'

He almost spat out the accusation and Sim blushed anew.

'Sir! I would that you had not said such a thing! For not only do you accuse me of impropriety, but thou dost cast aspersions upon fair Kate – a maid of most sweet nature - who hast captured my heart. I would never do anything to sully her reputation and it is you who should be ashamed to have made such a suggestion.' Now it was Sim's turn to bring his simmering temper to the boil. 'Thou art a lout indeed and if needs be thou mayest cast aside thy mish topper and we shall have at each other in yonder yard!

In his anger Sim made to rise and both Fin and Tam made to pull him back into his seat. The sudden grim laughter from the doorway did little to calm him. At the sound, Sim shot to his feet and whirled around, looking for all the world as though he would take on all-comers in his righteous fury. He almost struck James, who was fastest to his feet and gripped the younger man's arm in a vice-like hand that would not be shaken off.

'Hold thyself, Master Simeon.' said Edmund smiling, with a subdued Kate at his back. 'Methinks that fisticuffs in the yard will not be called for here.'

He smiled over to James and gave a quick nod. His friend released Sim, who took two long strides to stand beside the father and daughter.

Edmund stopped smiling, appraising Sim with serious mien.

'I have it in my mind to stay here with you and Kate, if you are agreeable, sir.'

Sim looked Edmund straight in the eye as he made the request and Edmund clapped him on the shoulder.

'Ah lad, I think we are long past "sir", are we not?' said Edmund gently. 'And it would give me pleasure to have you stay, but methinks you have a life to live elsewhere.' Edmund shook his head. 'And a father who will be missing you, I doubt not.'

Sim came rigidly to attention.

'Aye, sir, but...'

'Nay lad, there is no "but". I cannot steal another man's son. I know I could not live without Kate here at my side and from what we have heard these last few weeks, we know that your father loves you as much. I could not, in all conscience, deprive thy father - and Kate dost understand my thoughts in this. We cannot pretend that we understand all that has passed between us regarding your situation, but we know that such a bold decision may not be made on such a short acquaintance.

It didn't occur to Simeon to use the argument that Edmund had made almost as great a life-changing decision when their acquaintance was barely a day old, when he had packed his life into his cart and come south.

It did occur to Fin.

But he wasn't going to mention it.

For some reason Kate was having difficulty looking at any of them. Whether through embarrassment or something more, Fin could not decide. His mind was in turmoil. He simply hadn't noticed that Sim had grown so close to Kate since their arrival. The signs had been there, he recalled, but he'd always assumed that home would have a stronger pull. What would they tell Silas if his son failed to return?

'But Sim, what about your dad?' asked Tam, as though reading Fin's mind.

'Oh Dad will be alright.' said Sim with almost callous disregard. 'Edmund, I wouldst stay, even so.'

It was then that his two friends realised that there was a very real chance that he would not be coming home with them. The possibility had been hanging in the air for several days, but they had refused to acknowledge it. Now it was out in the open and had to be dealt with.

Abel Fermion was considering the same possibility and was obviously not best pleased.

'Am I to understand young man, that it is your intention to remain in the sixteenth century when your friends return home?' he asked quietly and with obvious concern.

'Aye, sir. Thou hast the right of it.' said Sim. 'So long as those whom I would seek to stay with will agree.'

Edmund shook his head, but said no more and Kate, hidden behind the bulk of her father, gave a muffled sniff.

Simeon turned to Fermion.

'You cannot make me go back!' he shouted and bolted passed Edmund and Kate and into the yard.

Fin moved to step past Tony and Fermion to follow Sim, but Edmund restrained him before he reached the door.

'Leave him be, for now Fin. I doubt not that he needs time to gather his wits. He will see that this is the only course.'

Fin could see that strong conflicting emotions were competing for supremacy in this good man's mind. He had come to regard these strange, other-worldly boys as more than just travelling companions and would happily have had them with him for as long as they cared to stay.

But Edmund also knew that it would be wrong to take advantage of them when their minds were in such turmoil. It seemed that the tide of fate had washed them up on the beach of the Turners' lives, but even the most happy of castaways would, at some time, long to return home. He knew that in the future Sim would want to return to his father, though the boy may not realise it for many months or even years. After such a time, it would be much harder on all of them if he was to leave.

No. Better to make him yield to the inevitable now and join his friends when they returned to their own lives. He was grieved at the thought of the pain that it would cause Kate, but better now than after she had grown more used to his presence.

'Once he has had time to think on this, he will see the truth of what I say. Though you are all fines lads and I have... we... ' He gently tugged forward Kate to stand beside him. 'have much to thank you for, this is not your place. I understand but little of what is happening here, but I know that you are not happy as you should be, even Simeon is not truly happy, though he knows it not.'

Edmund put his arm around Kate, hugging her close and patted Fin on the arm.

'Tis better that you leave now that Master Fermion has the means to aid thee.' He smiled weakly. 'Few are those who have been able to offer thee hope of return from whence you came. Even the great Doctor Dee could do little to speed thee homeward and these two' He waved a hand towards Tony and Fermion. 'can do so, it would seem.'

He looked over to Fermion.

'But be minded sir, that in these three you have a rare cargo, that must be treated with care, for I doubt me not that they have bold futures ahead of them.'

Fermion nodded sagely.

'Have no qualms, Master Turner, that I stall treat them as a most precious consignment, for there are few who are able to do what these three have done.'

Tony gave Tam a nudge.

'I can do it.'

Fermion gave him a megawatt glare.

'Well, not quite the same thing, but not far off.' said Tony petulantly

Once Fermion had returned his attention to the others, Tony whispered. 'It's all to do with ley lines believe it or not.'

Tam gave no reaction. To be honest he didn't care how it was done, just as long as he could go home.

'We could probably get you to do it to, if you want. Once you know what to do, it's foolproof.'

Tam's eyes lit up.

'Just remember Tone, nothing is foolproof to a sufficiently talented fool.' And he jerked a thumb towards his chest with a knowing look and a wink.

Tony chuckled quietly.

This one was going to be alright anyway. They just had to get him back into the arms of his family.

'But seriously Tam, it's all about finding the right mindset… and the ley lines of course.' said Tony.

Tam gave him a look that spoke eloquently.

It said "Oh yeah, pull the other one, chummy boy. You've said it twice and the chiming's getting on my nerves.'

'Go on then,' said Tam with only a pretence at boredom. 'explain.'

It would be interesting to have some sort of explanation after all, regarding this mysterious ability that Fin had used to land them in this predicament.

'It sounds a bit hippy-ish – all sort of…' Tony waved his hands in an attempt to look stoned and mystical, both at the same time. 'hey man, pass the pot and the crystals.' he said in a zoned-out sort of voice, like some rock star after a heavy night. 'but actually it makes sense if you have time to think about it.'

Tony gave Fermion a sideways glance, but the others around the table were discussing what they could do about Sim. Fermion was obviously worried about the possibility of his not returning with all three boys.

Tam leaned closer as Tony lowered his voice.

'All living things – and I mean everything – generates an aura, a sort of power that surrounds it. Bacteria and viruses, amoebas, plankton, microscopic tiddlers right up to the big buggers like whales and giant redwoods – they all generate this power, that most other living things can't detect.' Tony was in full flood and for once Tam could understand, if not quite believe, what he was hearing. Up until now, all the talk of moments and multiverses had sounded like science fiction gobbledegook. This wasn't much better, but least it made sense.

In a weird sort of way.

'So there's all this... this... energy, being shunted out by everything and it has to go somewhere. So it flows like water all over the earth.'

He paused to think and Tam for once managed to keep his mouth shut until Tony continued.

'Well maybe not everywhere. Presumably at the top of mountains and out in deserts there isn't so much, cos there aren't as many living things. But almost everywhere on the earth there's something living. So where does all this energy go? It may only be tiny amounts coming from each thing, but there's a lot of things on the earth and it mounts up. Go on then – guess.'

'Well I don't know do I? I can't even take a wild stab at it. No idea. You tell me.' said Tam with mock exasperation.

'It lies around all over the place. It doesn't drift away into the sky, although there is some up there, from the organisms that drift around in the air currents – even miles up. But most of it lies close to the ground, like a net lying over the grass and the trees and the sea.'

Tony took a sip of water and, again, Tam sat patiently waiting for him to continue.

'So there's all this energy slopping about with not a lot to do. And it's primeval, this stuff. It doesn't think or do anything. It just lies around making the place look untidy – if you can see it. No, that's wrong. It's not untidy. In fact it looks rather wonderful; all sorts of colours. In long ribbons of light, but only visible to a few people.' Tony's brow furrowed in thought. 'Maybe it's what guides pigeons and eels and salmon and things.' He shook his head as though to clear it. 'I don't know. Anyway that's beside the point. What matters is that some of us can see it - and Fin should be able to. The last time I spoke with him he said he'd seen it for the first time during that mess with the morons around Edmund's cart in the woods. The energy lies in "rivers" or "ribbons" of light – and it's everywhere. Anyone with the right sort of mind can see and use it. Fin has been using it for years without even being aware of it and it's reached a point where Mister Fermion thinks we need to lend a hand before Fin really does some damage to himself or others.'

'Like me and Sim?'

'Yeah, just like you and Sim, but maybe we've left it a bit late.' Tony looked grim for the first time since meeting Tam and that caused the younger boy to start worrying all over again. Just when he was beginning to feel better, this new friend started him thinking that maybe all was not as hunky-dory as he'd thought.

'Trouble is; I didn't know where Fin was – or you and Sim. So we had to try to track him down by following a trail through all the moments between your home spacetime and here. And it took us a bit longer than we expected because we can usually spot the holes left by someone stepping in and out of The Void. It leaves a sort of gap in some of the moments. But Fin didn't use The Void. Crafty beggar went back down a ribbon and Mister Fermion didn't expect that. So it took us a while – but we got here in the end.'

Another pause for a sip of water.

'But having found the right year *in time*, we had to find you *in space*. Now that's usually a piece of cake, cos the hole in the moment leads you straight to the entry point in space *and* time, but you lot kept moving around. In the end I told Mister Fermion that you *had* to be in London - Fin had mentioned it to me, but we hadn't thought you'd get here this fast. Once we decided that Edmund must have given you a lift, it was just a case of asking all and sundry until we found you. We actually arrived here yesterday afternoon, after going back to check whether you'd managed to get home by yourselves, and it's taken us until now to find you. Mind you, it would have helped if you'd stayed with Edmund instead of gallivanting off into the suburbs.'

Tony scowled.

'I hadn't been back home for a long time. Really I should have gone to see a few people – let them know I was okay.'

Tam looked puzzled and Tony went on.

'I left a bit unexpectedly. Once I found that I could control my travelling, there didn't seem much point in going back. There weren't many people who were going to miss me.'

'But what about your mum and dad?'

'Nah. I think they were probably glad to be rid of me. I messed up their party plans, what with having to visit the doctor and explain to the school why I was always absent and things. They'll have had a whale of a time without having to consider me – and I'm better off without their constant sniping about me being awkward and troublesome.'

'Sounds pretty awful.' said Tam glumly. 'Makes me realise how lucky I am. I just want to get back to tell mum and dad about what's been happening.'

Tony gave a derisive laugh.

'Yeah – like anyone's going to believe you. The best thing is for us to take you back and for you to pretend nothing ever happened. We can put you back just about when and where you left, so there shouldn't be any difficult explanations.'

'Cool Tony.' Tam beamed. 'So let's get on with it!'

Tony grinned too and looked over at Abel Fermion, who was still deep in conversation with the others.

'But Tam, we agreed that we weren't going to lie about this! Remember what Sim said, right form the start, we're going to be honest with everyone. What we've been doing is fantastic and we're not going to pretend that it didn't happen.'

Tam's smile faded.

'Well... I suppose so.' he mumbled. 'But maybe Tony's right. Maybe it would be better to forget about it all and just get back to real life.'

'Tam, this is real life! We aren't dreaming this.' said Fin emphatically. 'So promise that we'll do what we said. We will tell people exactly what happened. Please Tam... you were the one who thought it would be great to tell everyone.'

Tam's smile brightened again and he gave a small laugh.

'Yeah. Okay Fin. We'll do what we said.'

He turned to Tony.

'Sorry Tone. Come hell or high water, we're all in this together and we've got to stick together when we get back. If we don't tell the truth, sooner or later we'll get caught out and then if we do tell the truth no-one will believe us.'

'They won't anyway.' said Tony quietly, with infinite sadness.

'Well maybe not, but at least we'll know that we haven't tried to pull the wool over anyone's eyes, won't we.' Tam seemed to sit taller and looked Fin straight in the eye. 'You're right Fin. Sorry about that, nearly gave way to common sense for a second there and let's face it, common sense isn't really part of this, is it?'

Fin smiled back. Great, at least they were agreed; honesty really would be the best policy. Fin suspected that Tam had known that all along, it was just that hiding the truth was sometimes easier, especially when it was bound to prove unpalatable to those listening.

Now all they had to do was get back.

All three of them.

But, of Sim, there was no sign.

Now Mike (49)

Mike made his way into the mill. Dust motes floated in the still air, caught in the light that streamed in through the grimy windows. The smell of freshly cut timber was strong enough to make him take a quick gasp as he walked slowly towards the stairs.

An almost unearthly calm overlay the silent machines and the sawdust coated floor. The mill looked much as it must have been for the last several hundred years. Mike found himself surrounded by the ghosts of the many men who had spent their years working in the wood-laden atmosphere. There is something melancholic about old factories, he thought; places that in the past were so alive with the blood and sweat of men, and women, and now only exist because of the curiosity of present day tourists. Life moves on, but we still have a lot we can learn from those who toiled in the past.

A heavy tread behind him brought him back to the present with a jolt and he turned to find the storyteller from his previous visit standing behind him.

'Hello there...' Mike tried to dredge up the name from the shallow end of his short-term memory. Bev was forever taking the mickey out of the fact that for names Mike's brain had the retention span of a goldfish, but on this occasion she would have been proud. 'Mister Iveson, isn't it?'

'Aye, it is. And what can ah do for you?' said Mister Iveson in a friendly tone.

'Hmm...'

There's a good question thought Mike. He hadn't really considered how he was going to try to find out about the mill and its possible connection with Fin. He'd come up here with a vague idea that something might help to explain Fin's aberrant behaviour, but now he was actually here, he wasn't sure how to go about it.

Mister Iveson was waiting patiently, watching Mike carefully.

'Err... I was here last week with a group of schoolboys and one of them mentioned that there used to be a huge mound of sawdust outside... around the back of the mill.'

Iveson looked surprised.

'Oh aye, but how would your young lad know? It was created by all the machinery blowing the stuff out of the windows 'ere.' He gestured at the large windows all along the wall. 'They decided it were easier to leave it be rather than cartin' it away all the time. After a while they put the door in as a back way into the office upstairs, 'cos the dust set hard as rock. It were a bugger to shift it when they decided to spruce the place up. That were back... oh ten... twelve years ago. Ah s'pose he might 'ave seen an old photo of it.'

'Yes, I suppose so,' said Mike, 'but you told them a tale about a boy who fell through that door upstairs,' he nodded towards it, 'and disappeared.'

'Oh aye – an old tale me grandfather used t' tell. Keeps the kids entertained on their visits.' Iveson looked puzzled as he leaned back against an ancient workbench. 'What about it?'

'Look, this going to sound very strange, but…' Mike was unsure about this, but realised that there was only one way to proceed. 'the boy who described the pile of sawdust had already told me the same story, and he was adamant that he'd never been here on holiday before.'

Iveson shrugged.

'Maybe he'd just heard it from someone else.'

Mike nodded.

'Possible yes, but he was also adamant that he knew the story *because he said he was the boy who fell out of the door.*' he said, with emphasis on the unbelievable bit.

Iveson shook his head with a smile.

'Don't be a berk man.' He shook his head. 'You've been watchin' too much telly, you 'ave. Nah. Can't be true. Granddad was just a lad when it happened – that is, if '*e* were tellin' the truth. 'E was a bit of a one for makin' up tall tales was Granddad and 'e loved to play up to 'is grandkids.' He gave a small smile and shook his head again. 'To tell truth, ah always got the impression he was a bit soft in the 'ed. You know, one chip short of a plank.' he laughed. 'Nah. This lad o' yours is jus' tellin' tales - like my ol' Granddad. I'm surprised you bothered to come back to talk about it.'

Iveson shook his head in disbelief and Mike was beginning to feel like a bit of an idiot, but this was too important for him to fall at the first obstacle.

'I know it sounds ridiculous, but the boy involved has never been like that before. He's got a bit of an imagination, that true, but he's sticking to his story and I'm tying to find out if there's any possibility that, by some incredible means, it's possible.'

'Don't be such a barnpot mate.' said Iveson shortly. 'That lad o' yours would have to be like bloody Doctor Who and that's hardly likely is it? Eh?'

The older man stood up from the bench and was about to leave.

'No. Please Mister Iveson.' said Mike stepping closer. 'I know I sound as daft as a brush, but I promised myself I'd at least try to get to the bottom of this. You see, the boy involved is in trouble... a great deal of trouble. They think he may have done something so out of character… so unthinkable… for me… that I've just got to find out what has been happening to him.'

Iveson was looking uneasy, understandably given the strange circumstances.

'Is there anything else you can tell me about that story… anything that might help?' pleaded Mike.

Iveson shook his head.

'I dunno any more than ah've already said.' Iveson replied, ',but Ah'll tell you what, why don't we ask Dad?'

Mike was taken aback.

'You mean you father is still alive?'

'Ahm not that old, lad.' retorted the older man. 'An' me father is still alive and kickin' thank you very much.' said Iveson indignantly. 'E's ninety-four, but e's still got all 'is marbles. Unlike 'is Dad.' And he winked to show there had been no offence taken.

Iveson headed for the door, beckoning Mike.

'Cum on lad, let's ask Dad.'

Mike let himself be led across the mill yard and on towards the cottages that lay on the other side of the car park.

'So your father may know something more?' he asked.

'If there is any more to know.' said Iveson. 'Remember, it might just be another of Granddad's stories, but if anyone knows, it'll be Dad.'

They entered the first house, at the end of the little terrace and Iveson called out.

'Oi Dad! Visitor for you!'

There was no answer.

Mike looked around as he followed Iveson through the cottage. He suddenly felt as though he had himself travelled back in time. The two-up two-down gave every appearance of not having changed for at least a century.

Ancient faces stared down from faded sepia photographs lining the walls and the furniture wouldn't have been out of place in a museum; threadbare armchairs with greying antimacassars; an old wireless tuned to Radio Three by the sound of it; an old sideboard displaying china dogs and assorted tablewear. The atmosphere held an all-pervading whiff of dust and mustiness.

'Dad doesn't like change much.' said Iveson, by way of explanation. 'Never got to grips with television and such like.' It sounded almost like an excuse for the conditions his father lived in. 'We tried t'get 'im to have central 'eating put in, but he damn near bit me 'ead off when we suggested it. Me an' Jessie, me wife, live nex' door. That's to say, I live nex' door now Jessie has passed away. Couple o' years ago now, god rest 'er soul.'

They moved through to the small room beyond.

The range in the kitchen looked as though it had been black-leaded that morning and the pots from breakfast were neatly racked on the draining board of the Belfast sink. Overhead, an intimidating array of underclothes were draped haphazardly over a bamboo drying rack, secured by string from the high ceiling.

'Dad!' shouted Iveson again. 'Ah've got a visitor for you!'

Still no answer – and now they were emerging onto the green sward that led up to the trees that surrounded the mill and the attached dwellings.

Twenty yards away, sitting in an old folding chair was a man dressed in faded clothes, looking for all the world like a mannequin in a museum display. As they approached he looked up and the ancient face split into a huge grin.

'Bobby!' cried the occupant of the chair, then his rheumy eyes focussed on Mike. 'And you've brung a guest! Eh?'

The old man shaded his eyes from the sunlight slanting over the top of the house and began to struggle out of the seat.

'No Dad, you stay there.' said Iveson quickly, putting out a restraining hand. 'This 'ere chap just wants a quick word. Then yuh can git back to 'avin' a kip, eh?'

'Yuh young bugger! Ah were jus' restin' me eyes.' shot back the old man. 'Avin' a kip, indeed.' But the ever-widening smile belied the rough tone. 'Ah reckon ah deserve a sit down at my age. Eh?' This was directed at Mike.

'Yes indeed sir.' answered Mike.

'Sir! Did you 'ear that Bobby. 'E called me sir! Nice to know there's some of the younger generation know how to treat their elders and betters. Lissen to 'im Bobby, an' maybe you'll learn some manners. Eh?'

Bobby Iveson looked down at his father with fierce pride and looked over at Mike

'Told you 'e 'ad all 'is marbles, dint ah?'

Mike couldn't help smiling. These two men represented a bygone age, where sons did as their fathers told them and respected the fact that age was an indication of wisdom and experience. Somewhere over the years we've lost it, thought Mike.

Shame.

'Dad, this is...' Iveson paused, realising he hadn't asked for a name and looking slightly shame-faced.

'Mike Nutter.' filled in Mike. 'I'm a teacher. I was here with a school group a few days ago.'

'Oh aye?' said Iveson Senior, curious, but not overly so, but a smile played on his lips. 'Nutter, you say?'

'Aye Dad. An' ah told 'im that you knew all o' Granddad's old stories – 'bout ghosts and such.'

'Oh aye.' confirmed the older Iveson. 'Dad could tell a good tale, when 'e 'ad a mind to.'

There was a pause.

'Aye Dad. Well Mister Nutter 'ere would like t'know if one of 'em is more'n a story. 'E thinks one of 'is kids knows summat abaht it.'

'Oh aye.' said Iveson Senior nodding, with a secretive smile and a shake of his head, not taking his eyes off Mike.

'Nutter? Well ah'll be blowed.'

The old mans attitude was perplexing. He seemed to want to be asked a direct question before he would be willing to give further details.

Mike and Iveson settled into two rickety-looking garden chairs that had seen better days.

Mike leaned forwards, his elbows resting on his knees and decided that a full-frontal assault would bring enlightenment far quicker than beating about the bush.

'Mr Iveson, Fin is adamant that he is the boy who disappeared in one of your father's old tales... but that's obviously complete twaddle, since Fin's only thirteen years old. I'm trying to get to the bottom of things and I'm hoping that you might be able to help.'

The older Iveson smiled even more broadly.

'It seems t' me, that you're more than a bit uncertain about it though. Am ah right?'

'No... no... I can't believe that Fin could know about any of this unless he heard the story from someone, but he told his story in such detail...'

'Like 'e was really 'ere you mean?' asked Old Iveson, leaning forward.

''Well... yes, but that's just not possible.' said Mike.

'Are you askin' me or telling me?' asked Old Iveson.

Mike was stopped in his tracks by that. It wasn't so much that the old man could sense his uncertainty about Fin, but more that he gave off the air of a man who knew more than he was telling.

'Excuse me? Do you mean that you believe Fin's telling the truth?'

Now it was the younger Iveson who intervened.

'Now then son. No-ones saying anythin' of the sort, are they Dad?' he said flatly. 'Dad's just pullin' your leg, aren't you Dad? Just like Granddad used to'

'Maybe ah am.' said his father. ', but then again, mebbe ahm not. Ah know you think yuh Granddad was a bit daft, lad. Well maybe he was... but then again mebbe 'e wasn't.'

'Dad!' exclaimed Iveson. 'Stop messin' im about. 'E just wants to know about Granddad, so stop playin' silly buggers.' He gave Mike an appealing look. 'E's just playin' another of 'is games. 'E's done this is whole life. Aven't you Dad?'

'Well mebbe I 'ave, and then again mebbe I 'aven't.' said Old Iveson, in what was becoming an infuriatingly amused tone.

'Tell you wot Bill, go upstairs an get that little beechwood box o' mine, there's a good lad. Then we'll see whose playin' at silly buggers.'

Iveson looked confused.

'Go on son. Go an' get the box. It's sittin' by the bed.' The older Iveson waved towards the little house.

As his son set off in search of his father's box, the older man leaned closer to Mike.

'Bill there is named after my father.' he said proudly. 'And a fine bloke he's turned out to be.'

Mike nodded, humouring this strange little man, who whiled away his days staring out at the trees as he sat in the sun. Where on earth was this leading?

'An' 'e thinks 'e knows all about 'is Granddad.'

The man paused and then his leathered old face split into a huge grin, showing ancient, uneven teeth.

'But 'e don't know Dad's secret.' he said conspiratorially, with a wink.

'Secret?' asked Mike, wondering what on earth this queer old man was leading up to.

'Oh, aye. There's something that only ah know, 'cos Dad never told no-one about it.' said Old Iveson. 'But 'e told me just a coupla days before 'e died an' ah never told anyone either... maybe 'cos it sounded so daft, but ah think maybe it's time to tell Bill – an' it might help you too. Dad said that someday someone would come.'

The old man lifted his head and smiled as Bill Iveson emerged from the house, a small box held in carefully in his big gnarled hands. Mike noticed that they both had big, hard hands for such small men, probably a result of a lifetime working with timber.

'Just wait a few more minutes and you'll know as much as ah do about Granddad's *stories.*' said Old Iveson with a smile so wide that Mike thought he was in danger of splitting his face.

'An' ah promise you, it's a relief to know that 'e was tellin' the truth, cos, much as ah loved 'im, ah was never too sure meself.'

Bill Iveson arrived back at his rusting chair and sat as he handed the box to his father, who took it from him almost reverentially and chuckled.

'Eee, ah could do with a mint son.' he said to the younger Iveson, who reached into his pocket and retrieved a half eaten packet of the ones with a hole. Then by way of explanation he said, 'The only sort o' toffee ah ever bovver with these days. Don't mess abaht wiv me teef, yuh see.'

Then he grinned his wide, uneven grin as he watched Mike open the box.

'You'll love this next bit lad...'

Then Fin, Tam and Simeon (50)

They couldn't find Sim.

That was the long and the short of it. In this city, under the lowering cloud - only recently disclosed - of plague, where most public gatherings were frowned upon, Fin had managed to misplace his friend.

Here they were, all ready to finally go home… and Sim had vanished.

Everyone had joined in the search. They had been back to their lodgings, but no-one had seen Sim and nothing seemed disturbed, so Sim had run off without bothering to take anything with him. Luckily the weather was warm enough that Sim would be fine without any other clothing, but where could he have run to?

Abel Fermion was adamant that there was no way that Sim could have returned back to his present day without leaving some sort of trail. Fin didn't fully understand how Fermion knew, but took Tony's assertion that his mentor was never wrong about things like this - Fermion could follow a trail through time like a hound after a fox.

So Sim had simply run away to avoid returning to their time and Fermion was anxious to return Fin and Tam, whether or not they found Sim. Eventually all those involved in the search returned to their lodgings and ate a subdued meal of bread, butter and vegetables with water for the children and a little wine for the adults. No-one had had time to buy anything that day and their collective mood precluded heading out to purchase victuals.

Kate was tearful and spoke little as Tony explained that he and Fermion would come back to find Sim once they had ensured that Fin and Tam were back where they belonged, but there were no guarantees that they would find Sim. Apparently they could follow a trail through time, but once they had reached the right moment, it was a case of foot slogging around to try to find their target.

If Sim decided he didn't want to be found, they probably wouldn't be able to track him down. After an initial arrival it was still possible to "sniff out" a time traveller, but after a few days the trail would go cold as they became immersed in the time period they were visiting.

'Luckily I found you fairly quickly after you arrived.' said Tony to Fin as they sat quietly in the boy's bedroom. 'A day or two more and who knows whether we'd have found you at all.'

He said it in a jokey, off-handed sort of way, but Fin felt a chill at the possibilities that came to mind when he thought of what might have happened if Tony hadn't tracked them down.

'Don't worry Fin, we'll find Sim.' He put a comforting hand around Fin's shoulders and have him a quick squeeze.

'But first we'll get you and Tam home, then at least we know you two are safe.'

'Yeah, but for how long?' asked Fin glumly. 'Remember, I can't control what's going on. I never meant to come here. And I certainly didn't mean to drag Tam and Sim along too.'

'I know, I know Fin.' said Tony. 'But don't worry. I asked Mister Fermion if I could come back once we've got Sim and try to teach you a bit more about how to control your abilities, otherwise I might have to come chasing after you again.'

Tony laughed but Fin didn't.

'Yeah, won't that be fun.'

'Ahh. Don't worry Fin, you'll be fine.'

Fin didn't look convinced.

'Honest.' said Tam, giving the younger boy another squeeze. 'And tomorrow we'll get you home. Okay?'

Fin nodded.

'Maybe we'll even have Sim too. Then this whole mess will be sorted out.'

Hmmm.

Maybe Tony was being just a mite optimistic, thought Fin.

The following day, James and Edmund set off to the building site after an emotional farewell to Fin and Tam. The boys had been taken by surprise at the depth of feeling displayed by Edmund. Though they had only known each other for a matter of weeks, the woodsman had begun to look upon them, if not as sons, then at least as favourite nephews. Knowing that they would probably never meet again - even Fermion didn't have the heart to tell him they would *never* meet again – Edmund had shaken them both firmly by the hand and wished them a happy life, his eyes filled with tears. Then abruptly he had clasped each of them fiercely to his barrel-like chest, before turning to walk briskly away without a backwards glance. Kate had remained in the house, unwilling to expose her emotions to the world at large. After a peck on the cheek and a lingering hug for each boy, she had tearfully closed the door to her humble abode and, out of sight of the four outside, she had subsided onto her lumpy mattress and muffled her sobs in the depths of its woollen blankets.

By common agreement Fin, Tam and Tony had decided that searching for Sim would merely waste time. If he didn't wish to be found, there were hundred of places where he could hide in the maze of city streets. Though both Fin and Tam felt like traitors, they could see no point in prolonging the agony. They had to rely on the Piece Keeper and his apprentice to find their friend and return him home safely.

They walked south through the small suburbs and out into the fields beyond. Fin had an empty feeling in the pit of his stomach. How could he leave without Sim?

Easy - just let Fermion work his magic and they could be home almost before they knew it, leaving Sim in a stew of his own making, as Fermion put it.

Fin felt light-headed at the thought of finally leaving, but apprehensive as to the reception they would receive when they got back, but Fermion had decided that it would probably be better to take them back to the instant, or more properly *the moment* they had left. Then, when they located Sim, they could do the same with him and as far as anyone at home was concerned the last few weeks would never have happened. If they really wanted to, the three friends could just go back to their normal lives and pretend that they had never been away.

Yeah, like that was a realistic approach to the whole fantastic experience.

The knowledge that it was possible to do what they had done, was something that couldn't - probably shouldn't - be kept secret.

But how on earth could they convince people?

Fermion and Tony had advised that it would be better to keep quiet.

But the three schoolfriends had discussed this so often during their time here, their minds were made up. They were going to tell everyone what had happened - there didn't really seem to be any alternative.

Maybe they were wrong, as Fermion had earnestly advised.

Who knows in a situation like theirs?

But surely honesty was the best course of action.

Fermion disagreed strongly, but the boys had made a pact from the moment they had arrived; the truth was always better. Lies were always a bad idea, they always caused trouble in the end.

Didn't they?

From over to their left there came an excited shout and suddenly Sim was racing across the field.

The group of four waited for him to reach them; Fermion looking stern and more than a little annoyed; Fin and Tam with ear-to-ear grins and Tony with an enquiringly raised eyebrow.

'Sorry everyone, got a bit delayed.' gasped Sim, as he turned and waved to two figures several hundred yards away. Dressed all in black, one of the two was tall, the other shorter by a head, they were otherwise indistinct. Hands were raised in silent leave-taking.

'Who's that Sim?' asked Fin.

'Oh… doesn't matter.' Sim said in a matter-of-fact voice. He took Tony's arm.

'Can I have a quick word.?'

He led Tony a few yards away from the other three and spoke in an undertone. Tony nodded a couple of times and looked over to the place where the figures in black stood. He shook his head vigorously, but Sim spoke again. Eventually Tony gave a shrug and said something as he looked over at Mister Fermion, having come to some sort of decision.

The two rejoined the other and Fin thought they both looked a bit shifty. Fermion raised a quizzical eyebrow to Tony, which the younger man studiously ignored.

'Righty-ho. Everyone join hands and we'll have you back home *in a moment* eh?' said Tony with a half hearted smile.

Without another word they stood together in the bright sunshine. Fin on one end, Fermion, Tam, Tony and Sim on the other, all holding hands to make a human daisy chain. The boys becoming excited and unable to keep from smiling, closed their eyes, as instructed by Fermion.

Tony and Sim, had anyone cared to look, weren't quite as buoyant as the other two boys.

At the very last moment, too late for anyone to notice, or do anything even if they had, Tony released Sim's hand and the younger boy stepped away, his face sad, yet strangely content and gave Tony a nod of thanks.

When it came, the transition from *then* to *now* was almost instantaneous for them all. Mister Fermion made them all hold hands, close their eyes and...

The air grew warmer.

The birdsong of early morning sixteenth century London suddenly stopped.

The air grew colder.

The boys were swept away under a tide of sudden exhaustion (where had that come from, they had only been awake for a couple of hours?.)

Fin awoke as though from a deep sleep to find Mum, Dad and Lilli staring down at him.

Oops.

Now Tome (51)

The phone rang as professor Tome sat alone in his office, surrounded by memories that had been fading for more than a decade. The pain of failure, the recriminations of a family following the disappearance of their son, the endless police and press speculation. For so many years he had been trying to forget about Anthony Athelston and now suddenly, out of a clear blue sky on a beautiful summers day, it had all come back to haunt him.

With Anthony Athelston he had tried all the usual techniques to make sense of what the boy was going through. Hours of interviews and gentle probing had uncovered nothing. Family life for the Athelstons had certainly been unsettled, but probably no worse than for thouands of other young boys. School bullying had been prolonged, deeply upsetting and occasionally violent, with the school seemingly powerless to stop it. The boy was a social misfit, bright, outgoing and virtually friendless. The school had classed him as bright, the educational psychologist as "in the top nought point one percent" for his age-group and his exam results bore this out, but in the end intelligence had not led to happiness.

Not for Anthony Athelston.

So the boy had retreated into his own world of make believe, where he could travel into worlds where intelligence and friendship were valued. A world peopled by bards and knights, fair maidens and evil villains. He was adamant that time travel was possible and that in his sleep he would transport himself back to byegone ages.

And no matter what he did, Professor Tome could not dissuade Anthony from his certainty that it was all true.

In the end, the boy had simply vanished.

The obvious conclusion was that he had run away, or been abducted by persons unknown. When professor Tome had refused to state categorically that Anthony was somehow unbalanced, for he had found no evidence of this, other than the boy's implacable belief that he could time travel, the full weight of public and professional opinion had fallen upon the academic's head. The affair had virtually ruined him, but by diligent application he had slowly begun to rebuild his reputation.

And now, for reasons he was having trouble identifying, he had agreed to see young Finbar LeMott, who was apparently suffering from the same psychosis.

He lifted the receiver and took part in the strangest conversation of his professional career - and there had been some very strange conversations across the years.

He was still musing over the repercussions that might result from what he had just been told when the door opened and Beverly entered, followed by the LeMott family and the police officer who had been assigned to them.

There was a levity to their expressions and a lightness of step that should have warned him that something was amiss, but he was still preoccupied by the odd telephone call.

The group left Professor Tome's office and made their way through the Human Sciences faculty and over the road to the hospital buildings that faced the university precinct. The afternoon sun warmed them as they crossed under the trees and entered the unremarkable double doors that led into the medical research block. At the reception desk a young man with a friendly smile waved the professor and his companions through to the brightly lit corridors beyond and they followed the signs to the MRI scanner suite.

The room housing the scanner was divided into two by a large glass wall; on this side lay the computers and monitors that controlled and displayed the scanner's processing, on the other lay the scanner itself: a large tunnel of metal into which a gurney could slide under the control of an operator on the opposite side of the glass divider.

A young man of oriental descent, dressed in the regulation white coat of the medical staff, turned to greet them as they entered and, rising, shook the professor by the hand and nodded a greeting to Bev.

'Righty-ho. So this is young Finbar, is it?' he said without a trace of accent, looking at Fin and extending a hand.

'I'm Ken.' he said with a grin. 'Ken Li. I'm the guy who's going to have a look inside your head.'

To his surprise the LeMott boy looked excited rather than daunted by the prospect. Indeed, the entire group, apart from the professor, looked at ease as they found chairs and settled themselves down while Ken went through the procedure. He paid particular attention to the claustrophobia caused by the narrow tunnel, but Fin said he was fine with that and the banging of the huge magnets would be okay now that Ken had explained it all. The policeman, who gave the impression that he was more of a family friend, had to leave the room to locate another chair, but returned and sat, unprompted, next to the boy.

Looks more like a bodyguard. thought Ken.

The room quickly acquired the atmosphere of a jolly family get-together, rather than a serious scientific investigation and Ken found himself warming to this odd band of scientists, policeman and ordinary-looking nuclear family.

Finbar was immediately led away, to return minutes later in a hospital gown that fastened – very loosely – far too loosely in Fin's opinion - up the back, much to his embarrassment and everyone else's glee. Lilli in particular couldn't resist the opportunity to comment on the lack on draft exclusion in the pants area and the presence of a young nurse called Linda, who studiously ignored Lilli's giggles.

The picnic atmosphere continued as Fin was positioned on the gurney by Nurse Linda, his head and shoulders restrained by belts attached to body-moulding foam and slowly inserted into the scanner under the watchful eyes of everyone, at which point PC Hedd excused himself and withdrew to make a call to the station to keep The Sarge informed of progress so far. As he stood up to leave he gave Fin a thumbs-up, just as the boy's head entered the confines of the metal doughnut, but in time for Fin to see and mouth *Okay* in answer. PC Hedd nodded and left. The eyes of all but Professor Tome and Ken Li followed the exchange of looks and Lilli gave a quick giggle, which she stifled with her hand, while Jarmon hugged Lidine and Bev stood staring at the soles of Fin's feet with eyes like saucers.

'Remember, Fin.' came Ken's voice over the intercom. 'You need to keep still for the entire proceedings. Okay?'

'Fine.' called out Fin from his horizontal position, with his head held in place by a heavy metal hood-cum-mask which fixed him to the gurney. He relaxed, ready to remain immobile for the duration. In a strange way it was quite comforting to be held so securely inside the metal tunnel. Like being in one of those sensory deprivation thingies he'd once read about in one of the Sunday supplements; the sort that rich people pay a fortune to use so they can go off their heads in private for an hour or so and no doubt indulge in all manner of hallucinatory, technicolour, probably X-rated experiences, without the need to resort to their usual expensive mind-expanding chemical cocktails. At least from Fin's thirteen year-old perspective, that was the only possible reason for banging yourself up in a water-filled casket for hours on end.

Ken inserted a CD of Gregorian chant. When Fin had selected it Ken had been surprised.

'Not pop, or rock? I've got American or British; old and new, 70s, 80s, 90s, thrash, metal, boy bands, girl bands… all sorts Fin.'

But Fin had been sure.

'If I've got to lie still for an hour I'd prefer this, or Mozart maybe?'

But Ken's collection didn't stretch to many classical pieces, indeed the Russian monks intoning the scriptures was only there because a previous scanee had left them behind patiently awaiting another airing. Usually subjects for scans were allowed to bring in their own music, but from what Ken could gather, this had all been a bit of a rush job. In fact Ken was sure the scanner hadn't been booked for use today. It normally operated on the first Monday and Wednesday of the month, there being a shortage of staff and money to use it any more than that. The Prof was lucky to have caught Ken on his day off from travelling around the area running different scanners, at different hospitals, each day.

Ken was happy to earn a few extra pounds… and, he thought, doing a favour for the boys in blue couldn't do any harm either.

As Fin lay there, he relaxed and hoped that the outputs in the control room were being watched by everyone and that Ken was recording it all, as well as storing away the supremely accurate images of his brain.

The moment of truth was finally upon them…

Now Leon (52)

The house felt a little chilly compared to the warmth outside and Leon had opened the windows to allow the summer to enter.

In the large dining hall he carefully positioned the two wooden chests so that they would be to hand when called for. He couldn't help placing them in such a way that the sunlight slanting in from the large leaded windows came down upon the boxes, as though holding them captive within their beams. The dust motes twinkled like tiny fairy lights as they flitted in and out of the shafts of golden sunshine.

Having an overly developed sense of the dramatic sometimes has its place, he thought.

Outside the comforting sound of wood pigeons drifted across the rose garden, otherwise the house was silent, apart from the sounds of Leon's activity.

He laid out a leather runner on the dining table. Atop this he placed a flask of two-hundred year old Malmsey along with cut lead crystal glasses and two large thermos jugs; one of orange juice, the other of water. Shuttling back and forth from the kitchen, Leon continued to load the table with sandwiches, salads made up of various flower petals as well as the usual fare; cold poultry and other cooked meats and potato crisps for the girl.

Eventually he stood back to admire his handiwork and try to estimate the volumes he'd provided. Satisfied that there was sufficient, he checked his watch before going upstairs to change.

He guessed he had about half an hour before his guests began to arrive.

Now Mike (53)

Mike felt the urgent vibration of his mobile phone in his shirt pocket as he received an unexpected text message as he negotiated the slip road from the M6 at Knutsford. He reached inside his jacket and was surprised to see that Bev was sending him directions to a meeting.

He pulled over and scanned the instructions before taking the left turn into the shaded lane through the woods that lined the dual-carriageway.

He desperately wanted to share his news with his wife, but the tone of her message suggested that she also had information that needed to be passed on in person. Puzzled, he slowed as the dappled sunlight played tricks with his vision through the windscreen.

He had the feeling that things were coming to a head.

Now Bert (54)

Euphoria was too small a word for the emotion that was washing over Herbert Lightfoot as he made his way to the gathering to which he had been so recently invited. He was having trouble concentrating as he sped along. The unexpected lifting of his heavy depression had left him light-headed and riding a motorbike whilst feeling so intoxicated probably wasn't the brightest thing he'd ever done.

But the journey was short and the years of biking experience served him well, though he couldn't restrain his whoops of joy. He felt like a teenager again and knew that the ridiculous grin that he couldn't wipe from his stupid great mug would be instant cause for a breathalyser and almost certain arrest – if anyone could see it through his visor. It was all he could do to stop himself pulling wheelies down the by-pass.

Not a good idea, what with speed cameras and eighteen-wheelers all around.

Finally he reached the turning into the trees and calmed his racing heart as he manoeuvred onto the shady track.

So many questions to ask…

And the answers were all here.

Now Tam (55)

The phone call was short and to the point and suddenly Tam could see the light at the end of the tunnel. Not a bright light, mind, but at least the inky blackness that had been facing him only a few short minutes ago had begun to recede. The arguments he'd tried not to listen to as he lay in bed over the previous nights, would hopefully now be forgotten.

His parents had virtually refused to discuss the events being investigated by the police with him. Mealtimes were filled with silent accusations and Tam had spent most of his time alone in his bedroom. His father had retreated back to work and his mother seemed afraid to speak to him, only doing so when absolutely necessary, even though they had spent the whole day at home together.

At no point had Tam been left alone in the house and he couldn't help thinking that neither of his parents trusted him any more. At least Fin appeared to have the support of his family, which must be of some comfort.

Bloody Fin! This was all his fault.

As he sat silently, trying to read one of his many books, he fumed over the way his friend had managed screw everything up.

Having said that – *what an adventure!*

The problem was that they had no proof of what had happened.

Tam knew that it wasn't really Fin's fault, but he felt the need to blame someone and Fin was the easy target. Sure, that bloody Fermion and his oppo Tony-bloody-Athelston, had cocked up the return flight, but it was Fin that had whisked them away in the first place.

Strangely his semi-anger at Fin gave him no solace in the silence of his room where he lay sprawled on his bed. And he couldn't concentrate on reading, or anything else for that matter.

Tam shook his head ruefully and smiled, they were up a small tributary with no means of propulsion – but lord what an experience!

He was surprised when his mother came in and silently handed him the phone, ignoring his questioning look as he laid aside his book and sat up on the edge of the bed. She stood over him as he talked, listening out for any hint of anything untoward.

'Hello Tamburlaine, this is PC Hedd from the Vale Royal police station. We haven't met, but I'm at the university with Fin and his family. Can you talk?' The officer's tone was friendly, but Tam was still nervous.

'Yes, sort of.'

'Ah. You mother is there, is she?'

'Yeah.'

'Okay. Well when I've finished, can you pass the phone back to her, so that I can have a quick word?'

'Sure, yeah.' Tam was apprehensive now. He had heard nothing from Fin, or anyone else, since the angry exchange the other night and was worried about how things were going, but he couldn't ask about the LeMotts, not with Mum earwigging.

'I'm calling to put your mind at rest about everything that's been happening... to let you know that Sim's fine and we're planning to give everyone proof of Fin's abilities. Well... when I say everyone, I mean only those that are involved.' The voice paused. 'However, I suspect that pretty soon everyone's going to have heard something about it.'

Tam's heart was pounding.

'So we're in the clear, the police know what's been going on?' he asked, making sure that he spoke loudly enough for his mother to hear. She straightened slightly, tensing with the effort to try to hear what news was coming down the line.

'Well... not exactly, but things are moving on apace and it's all going to out in the open very soon.' said the policeman.

'And you believe us?' Tam asked breathlessly.

'Oh yes! Absolutely... no doubt in my mind, Tam. I've seen Sim with my own eyes and he's happy as a sandboy. All we have to do now is offer some proof to people like your mum and dad... and that's why I'm calling. I just thought I'd let you know before I talk to your mum.' The policeman sounded positively jubilant as he spoke, trying to encourage and comfort in the same sentence. 'So don't worry Tam, it's all going to be fine. I promise.'

'You've seen Sim! You mean he's back? Tam felt almost faint with relief and he could see his mother cast a quick shocked look his way. 'But how?'

'All will be explained very soon Tam, I promise. Okay?'

Yeah. Okay.' But Tam still wasn't convinced. This copper wasn't being very forthcoming.

'Pass me over now, will you?' said the policeman. 'And *don't worry!*'

Tam held the phone out. 'He wants to talk to you now Mum.'

Sue gingerly accepted the phone from her son, as though frightened of what might be about to happen.

'Yes?' she said tentatively.

'Mrs Riggleby? Good news. As I've just explained to young Tam, we're in a position to drop the case regarding the disappearance of the Carver boy.'

'What? I... I heard Tam say something about Sim being back. Is it true? Have you found him?' Sue was visibly shaken. What else had been happening that they hadn't been aware of?

'Yes we've found him... and he's safe and sound, so we would like to see you and Tam, and your husband of course, as soon as convenient.' The officer sounded very pleased with himself. 'Just to go through everything and let you know what we've found out. I'm sure it will be a great weight off your minds.'

'Oh yes!' cried Sue. 'Oh, yes! We've been so worried.'

Tam noticed his mother's hand was shaking and tears were beginning to roll down her face.

'We've been at our wit's end.' she snuffled. 'Tamburlaine is still refusing to tell us anything about that night… and it's so unlike him… he's such a good boy.' She turned her tearful gaze on her son. 'We've been so worried.'

Sue pulled a handkerchief out of her sleeve and dabbed at her eyes. She shook her head as she looked down at her son, but the smile she gave him was radiant. Tam realised that he'd almost forgotten what his mum looked like when she smiled. Even the dark rings under her eyes seemed less pronounced.

'It's all been so awful… oh, Ian will be so happy… is it alright if I call him? I mean, it's not still some sort of secret, is it?'

'No, no Mrs Riggleby, of course you *must* let him know. We feel it would only be fair to let everyone know at the same time – so the LeMotts will be there, along with the staff from the school.'

Sue was doing her best not to skip around the room in her relief. To Tam it seemed that she was almost vibrating with excitement and she kept on looking down at him as though ready to smother him with long overdue kisses and hugs.

'So we should bring Tam down to the station with us?' she asked.

'No Mrs Riggleby!' The policeman's voice sharply down the line, causing the smile to slip momentarily and the ebullient hopping stopped.

Sue missed the next couple of words as she asked 'What? Why ever not?'

Tam tensed at the puzzlement in his mother's voice.

'… wise to try to avoid the press, who have been gathering at the station over the last hour or so. We've arranged for everyone to meet at a house close by, but away from prying eyes. Will that be okay with you and your husband?' The voice was back to its friendly coaxing.

'Oh yes. I'm sure Ian will be as happy as me just to get this whole thing settled. Oh, it's such a relief.' The smile was back and Tam relaxed.

His mother left the room in search of pencil and paper and wrote the directions down before explaining what was going on to Tam. Then she went quickly downstairs to make a cup of tea and ring her husband. The gloomy atmosphere was gone as though it had never held the house in its icy grip.

Tam spent the hour prior to his father's elated arrival trying to think of what Fin had managed to do. How had he managed to get Sim home?

By five o'clock he was almost bursting in anticipation of finally discovering what had happened to Sim, and what had changed his mind about returning home. Maybe he'd come to his senses after his friends had come back and become as homesick as Tam had been. Though he had tried not to show it, he'd been missing his parents so much during their Tudor sojourn that it was all he could do to stop from crying himself to sleep. He'd forced himself to maintain his happy façade for Fin's sake as much as anything, knowing that his friend was wracked by guilt of his own making and didn't need an extra helping from Tam.

He could only imagine how excited Sim must be to be back.

Then, when the waiting was becoming unbearable, his father – now returned to his usual happy demeanour – gave the call for Tam to hop in the car so that he could be reunited with his friends.

Now Fin (56)

The scanner hummed gently around Fin and he felt an odd vibration thrumming through his entire body. It wasn't uncomfortable exactly, just a little disconcerting, as though something was inspecting each individual cell of his body in turn. The machine began a rapid banging noise as it started probing his head, the earplugs supplied by Ken muffling the sound to an bearable volume.

Then he felt the nudge of another mind and the vibration stopped. His mind, which he had thought was calm to the point of being comatose, suddenly reached a whole new plain of tranquility. He had never felt such an odd sensation before, but knew it could only be the presence of PC Hedd. Fin knew that Dick was nearby, helping him to reach that plateau of stillness, which would allow him to control his mind so that he could begin to use the power swirling invisibly around him.

Dick had told Fin as much as he understood about the abilities they had; of how the very earth itself radiated a power that could be used to bend space and time. Tony had mentioned it in passing, but hadn't explained it half as well as Dick.

Ribbons of light suffused the manmade cave in which he lay and slowly the gurney began to slide out from the scanner.

Fin felt hands on his legs as he cleared the lip of the machine and then Dick was there smiling down.

'You okay Fin?' he asked, with little attempt to conceal his total lack of concern. They had discussed this process during their first trip away to find Sim, and both knew exactly what they were doing.

'You bet Dick.' said Fin with a familiarity that made him smile. Dick had insisted that Fin treat him as a friend and in turn he would treat Fin as an adult; no silly cover-ups if things were going wrong, no lies to protect him from the evils in the world, no attempts to treat him as a child. Dick was sure that Fin had a grown-up part to play in what was ahead and saw no reason to treat him as anything but an equal. A shorter and weaker equal to be sure, but Fin had shown that he was capable of at least as much as Dick, and that was without understanding what he was doing. With a clearer idea of how everything operated in the new world of which he was a part, who knew what this young lad was capable of.

Fin had been flattered that Dick had shown such faith in him. Certainly neither Fermion nor Tony Athelston had told him so much. Oh, sure, they had tried to explain spacetime and all that, but they had acted as though they just needed to get him home. They hadn't tried to help him come to terms with what was happening to him in any meaningful way.

But Dick had.

And did he but know it, the young policeman had gained a lifelong friend who, though not yet in his fully developed manhood, would one-day be his protector in return.

For now though, the two of them were playing a game with those who disbelieved and Fin was pleased that Ken had turned out to be such a nice guy. They were giving him something to pass down to his children and grandchildren. No-one, as far as Fin and Dick were aware, had ever seen this before – apart from Spinster Binster, and she was quite happy to keep the secret with nothing more than a twinkle in her eye and a girlish giggle whenever she saw Dick. Dick smiled at the recollection of the old lady who seemed so contented with life, a life which she suspected she might owe to Dick... and knew she owed to Leon.

Ken, on the other hand, was going to be able to live off this for a long time. Fame and fortune awaited the little Oriental, Fin was certain – just as long as he was capturing it all on tape, or whatever it was the scanner used.

Dick helped Fin out of the mask and off the trolley and together they concentrated as the ribbons grew brighter and the room grew warmer. This was something new to Fin. – to jump in space and time from an already frozen moment. No doubt Fermion would disapprove, but Dick seemed to pay scant attention to the instructions issued to Fin by the odd little schoolmaster with the clipboard.

'Oh, he's okay in his own way, but me and Leon tend to do our own thing, you know?' Dick had said.

Although he'd told Fin about Leon, the boy had yet to meet the mysterious friend who had only recently introduced Dick to the wondrous possibilities that now lay before him, and Fin. Dick had explained that Leon had a feeling that something was going to happen soon, and that it was people like Fin who would hold the key to the future. As to exactly what that future held, Leon was uncertain, but he felt that trying to hide children like Fin was not what it was all about. Maybe it was time the world was introduced to the endless possibilities that Fin and any others like him – and surely there were others - represented.

Fin had the feeling that this guy Leon had been living alone with his secret for long enough and now he wanted to let the world know that something new and exciting was happening.

Fin wondered just how many other children there were like him; living in misery, trying to shake off the nightmares that might so easily be turned to something incredible.

Certainly Leon and Dick were eager to see what would happen if the earth-power they manipulated was revealed to the world at large and with Fin's help they were going to do just that.

Jarmon and Lidine had been unsure and Bev had counselled caution, but they were all so happy to see the effect the young policeman had had on Fin that they could not, in all honesty, refuse to let Fin go his own way, with the help of Dick. The news that Sim was alive and well had helped too, though Jarmon had gone ballistic when Dick had first whisked Fin off to see Sim.

And Fin could understand that.

To see you first-born melt into thin air, before your eyes, must have been a severe shock. At least his family were prepared for this disappearance; Dick and Fin had explained their plan several times before the others had agreed to go along with it.

Lilli was just excited at the thought of finally meeting Leon.

Now Everyone (57)

The first guests arrived at five-thirty.

Leon had known they were the LeMotts before he even answered the door. He instantly recognised the family group (minus their son/brother), along with the pretty young schoolmaster's wife. The adults had stood hesitantly on the threshold, until Leon had given them his brilliant white smile full-beam and bent to say hello to Lilli.

Her parents were surprised to see Lilli reach out to shake the proffered hand with a solid grip. The handshake, performed in silence, had an almost ritualistic air to it as Lilli solemnly met the man from her dream.

'Come in, come in Mrs LeMott, Mister LeMott, Mrs Nutter. And welcome Lilli… we meet at last, eh?' The large black man waved them past him into the large, oak panelled entrance hall.

Though her parents were a trifle over-awed at the place, Lilli immediately settled herself into one of the large armchairs that Leon had arranged around the large fireplace. This, he hoped, would allow them all to sit it a semi-circle and therefore enable them to have a conversation that would include all-comers. No-one would feel as though they were peripheral to the discussions.

'We were expecting Fin to be here.' said Jarmon. There was no accusation in his tone, it was just a statement of fact. He had realised several hours ago that he had absolutely no control over what was happening now. In fact, he had the distinct feeling that he and Lidine had been invited out of simple courtesy because they were Fin's parents and not because they had any intrinsic value in what was to happen. Lilli, on the other hand, had the same abilities as Fin, or so it seemed, and Jarmon had the growing suspicion that there was every possibility that he and Lidine could lose both their children today. Not that they would be stolen away. No nothing so straightforward as that. He felt, somewhere deep in his being, that his son and his daughter would discover that they no longer needed their parents, that they had the power to provide for themselves. That didn't necessarily mean that they would leave… but one of the most basic links between a parent and their child would have been severed. Never to be rejoined. His children would not depend on him for anything. His heart gave a lurch, and he wanted to gather Lilli into his arms and run away with her. Out of this house. Away from these men who had invaded their lives. Back to the security of their normal family existence, which, for all its ups and downs, was as good as it gets for most people.

But even as he considered taking some sort of action, he realised it would be futile. His children were facing problems immensely greater than any he had faced at their age. They had strange abilities that would have to be controlled and used to fulfil some kind of… was destiny the right word? – Jarmon wasn't sure - otherwise who knew what might happen to their fragile egos?

On the other hand, Jarmon realised in admiration, they both seemed to be coping with all this every bit as well as he and Lidine.

So maybe he should just go with the flow, after all he'd managed to drift through life up to this point on the assumption that he could cope with whatever fate decided to throw at him.

There didn't really seem to be much alternative.

'Yes, he should be here any moment, with Dick.' said Leon. He led them to the food-laden table. 'Tea, coffee, maybe something a little stronger? Help yourselves.'

He turned to where Lilli sat.

'Water or orange, Lilli? Or would you prefer some sort of cordial?'

'Do you have any dandelion and burdock, please?' the little girl asked, smiling shyly.

Leon beamed.

'Oh yes! Never without some dandelion and burdock. It reminds me and Dick of when we were kids. You know you used to get thruppence back on the bottles?'

'What's thruppence?' asked Lilli, looking puzzled.

Leon laughed and shook his head as he went out to the kitchen.

The remaining adults took their drinks (tea for Jarmon and Lidine, coffee for Bev) and joined Lilli in front of the empty fireplace. The heat had gone out of the day, leaving a pleasant warmth that removed the need for a fire.

'What's thruppence?' asked Lilli again.

Lidine looked at her daughter and smiled.

'It's three pennies Lilli. From before decimalisation, when we still had pounds, shillings and pence.'

'And thruppenny bits.' said Jarmon. 'Funny little brass coins, like a short, fat fifty pence piece that was the colour of a pound coin.'

Lilli nodded her understanding and looked over her shoulder to see where Leon had gone.

'So you saw Leon at the same time as you saw Mr Hedd, Lilli? Is that right?' asked Lidine.

'Yeah.' Lilli nodded. 'Mr Hedd was looking over his shoulder and was closer to me, but I saw this tall black man looking at me from further away. And there was a smell of roses too. I know they were roses because I could see some before it all faded away.'

'And you thought it was a dream? Like Fin and his nightmare?' asked Lidine.

'Well, sort of.' said Lilli. 'I was just waking up and it was like a picture hanging in the air by my bed, but it looked so real, like I could just reach through and touch them. And then Mr Hedd said something and called to the other man, so I knew his name was Leon. That's what made me think it wasn't a dream, because I'd never heard of Leon as a name, so something made me think it was real and when I squealed… a bit… they jumped like they could hear me… and dreams don't usual do that do they?'

'Hmm… no, I suppose not.' said Lidine smiling and running her hand over Lilli's hair.

'So you weren't afraid?'

'No not really, but I thought maybe the big black man was going to step into my room or reach out to me somehow when he stood up. But no, I wasn't really afraid.' She shrugged. 'I don't know why, but I wasn't.'

Leon re-entered and gave Lilli a glass of fizzing brown liquid.

'Dandelion and burdock, as requested.' he said with a smile.

'Thankyou.' said Lilli smiling in return.

'So, what shall we talk about whilst we await the arrival of the others?' asked Leon, settling himself into a chair beside Bev.

'Well Lilli was just saying how she saw you and Dick a few days ago. She saw you over PC Hedd's shoulder.' said Jarmon.

'Oh yes?' said Leon, with a grin. 'That was a bit of a shock to both of us.' He leaned back in his chair. 'And call him "Dick", Mister LeMott. I know he'd be more comfortable with that.'

'Sure.' Jarmon nodded, 'and I'm Jarmon and this is Lidine.' He indicated his wife, who smiled across, before pointing to the others. 'And Bev, who's married to Fin's English teacher, Mister Nutter, and also works with Professor Tome, who's had a bit of a shock today.'

They all smiled at that.

'Yes, I bet he did.' said Leon.

Before they could continue there was a knock at the door and Leon jumped to his feet, eager to have everyone here so that they could get down to the real reason for their invitation.

Everyone looked around to see who had arrived as Leon opened the door and waved Mike Nutter in.

Bev leapt to her feet and hurried over.

'Had a good day, love?' she asked.

'Well, it's been right up there with listening to Stockhausen, for weirdness.' He gave her a peck on the cheek and then looked over to the other occupants of the room. 'And what exactly are we all doing here?' he asked.

It was Leon who answered.

'Once everyone has arrived, we're going to explain what's going on.' he said.

'Well that should be interesting.' said Mike with mock brevity. 'And I suppose then you'll be ready to here my Weird Tale, as well.'

'Wouldn't miss it for the world.' said Leon, leading him over to the drinks.

When Leon turned back to the door, there was another figure standing in the rectangle of light, framed by the view out to the courtyard and lawn beyond

'And you would be...?' asked Leon.

'Bert! So you're here too!' called Mike.

'Ahh... Mister Lightfoot, isn't it?' asked Leon, extending a hand. 'Welcome. Come in. Come in.'

Bert was looking confused, but so excited that Mike found himself almost in tears at his transformation. Something had happened to put a new spring in his step and a smile on his face and Mike didn't know what the cause was, but was thankful for its effect on his old friend. He had begun to despair of ever seeing Bert looking so happy again. He hurried over to greet his old friend.

By the time Bert had been introduced, another car had drawn up outside, and the Riggleby's duly arrived at the door.

Jarmon was relieved that Ian and Sue looked genuinely pleased to see them and Tam and Lilli were relegated to the floor so that all the adults could have seats.

Leon was determined that there would be no discussions that revealed any part of their stories until everyone had arrived - and there were still two obvious absentees.

He aimed a remote control at the small hi-fi hanging on the wall, behind a wooden grill set into the panelling. Speakers all around the room came to life and *Carmina Burana* started up quietly in the background. Jarmon looked over and nodded his appreciation.

'Multi disc.' said Leon by way of explanation. 'It'll run for hours playing stuff that's been compressed on the computer.'

Lilli, who was laughing with Tam, ever the joker, paused to listen to a deep rumbling that was vibrating the floor. It was clearly also getting through to Tam, who also stopped to listen and try to determine where the sound was coming from. Not loud, but resonant, Lilli thought at first that it was thunder, but then realised that the sound was coming from one of the doorways that led off the main hall where they were sitting.

As it grew louder, the general hubbub of conversation died down and all heads turned expectantly to the doorway.

Fin and Dick strolled nonchalantly into the room, chatting together as though they hadn't a care in the world and studiously ignoring all its occupants, but Fin couldn't maintain the façade and with a broad grin he ran over to his parents and sister, where hugs and kisses were exchanged in excited confusion.

Dick shook hands with Leon, again amid much back slapping and laughter and the others stood to join in. Ian and Sue were noticeable by their lack of cordiality, but introductions were repeated and everyone refreshed their drinks in what was rapidly becoming a party atmosphere.

As the sun began to set, Leon lit candles and lit the fire to take off the slight chill that was entering the room. The heavy velvet curtains were left drawn back – who was there to peer in? – and a cosy aura surrounded the group of old – and new – friends, chilled only slightly by the adult Riggleby's.

Tea and coffee gave way to ancient Malmsey and fine single malt as the night closed in - and even Fin and Tam were allowed a nip. The food laden table became noticeably lighter as all partook of the fayre provided by their host.

Lilli snuggled up against her mother on one of the deep armchairs, whilst the others enjoyed a companionship they hadn't expected whilst sitting contentedly in the grand house in the middle of the woods off the main Chester by-pass.

Leon acted as a master of ceremonies, allowing each speaker to talk without too much interruption, until eventually the entire story was told.

They started their voyage of discovery with Mike – who had missed much of the day's excitement, but who had a present for Fin.

'I see you've got your lenses in Fin.' he said, closely inspecting his student's eyes. 'Fancy having at least one pair of decent specs?'

Fin looked surprised and Mike reached into his inner jacket pocket.

'Courtesy of Bill Iveson, now long gone, but not forgotten.'

He handed Fin the glasses he'd lost all those years ago, earlier in the month.

'They've been handed down through three generations of bobbin makers, all because the boy you met that night found them after you vanished - and hid them away.'

Even Leon looked surprised at this.

'But I've had things vanish when I've taken them back with me! I'd assumed that unless they were kept somewhere swimming in Ley energy, they disintegrated.'

Ian and Sue were looking more and more uneasy. This was not what either of them had been expecting.

'Now hang on a second, just hang on a bloody second!' Ian turned accusingly to Dick. 'We were under the distinct impression that all this talk of time travel was over. You said that Sim was okay now and the police were closing the case.'

Dick nodded his affirmation, but a trifle hesitantly.

'Well not exac...'

'Too damn true "Not exactly!"' shouted Ian. He reached down to Sue, who looked pale and close to tears. 'Come on Tam, we're going.'

He clapped a hand to his head and his voice rose along with the rest of him. He stood staring look aghast at everyone sitting around the fire

'You're all bloody lunatics!' he shouted as Leon made to get up. 'And don't even think about trying to stop us!' He raised his hand before him as though to ward off a blow and extended his other arm across the front of his wife in a protective gesture.

'You just stay there, Mister Leon bloody Messenger!'

He turned to Mike.

'Are you telling me that you *believe* all this claptrap. Even *you* Mister Nutter? Mr Lightfoot?'

Unfortunately both teachers nodded solemnly, which did nothing to cool the heat of his rage.

Sue was also on here feet now and the fear was obvious in her eyes. Suddenly the happy gathering had become far more sinister. She looked shocked and overwhelmed as she glared down at Tam.

'Please Tam! Come now, before something awful happens.' She took a step towards the door while imploring her son to hurry. 'I don't think we're safe here.'

But Tam stayed right where he was, a defiant expression on his face.

'No Mum. You're wrong! You're both wron...'

But before he could finish the sentence, silence fell over the room.

Ian found himself looking into the cool blue eyes of Leon, while everyone else in the room – no not just everyone, but everything - even the flames in the grate – froze.

To his horror there was a glass of sherry motionless in the act of falling from Dick's hand. It's contents spilling out towards the oak-planked floor.

It was as though the whole world had stopped, leaving only him and the ominous bulk of Leon able to move as though somehow trapped in some sort of unbelievable polaroid.

He flinched, releasing himself from the grip of the taller man… and the world sprang back into life. Sue screamed and the glass smashed on the floor as Leon reached out to him again. This time he took a stronger grip of Ian's shirt, folding it around so that the back of his hand touched the skin of Ian's chest, preventing him from pulling lose a second time.

And once again the world became a photograph.

Like insects petrified in amber.

'Mister Riggleby.' Leon's voice was cold and authoritative. 'Please calm yourself. This is doing no-one any good.' He resisted Ian's attempts to struggle free and brought his face to within inches of the other man's.

'If it's all claptrap, then what's happening now?' he said calmly. 'Look around you. We are standing… talking… in the time between time. A moment can last forever here. This is less than the blink of an eye for them.' He nodded back towards those behind him.

'You have to believe. This is not some parlour trick.' He could see the sheer terror in Ian's eyes and kept his grip tight on the shirt. 'Believe Tam. Really believe him. He hasn't told you anything that isn't perfectly true. He *did* go back in time with Fin and Sim. They *did* meet with people who have been dead for over four hundred years. This is not a joke. It's not hypnotism or drugs. It's true.'

He could feel Ian relaxing very slowly as he spoke.

'And I think Fin is capable of doing exactly what we're doing here. He just can't control it. That's why Tam and Sim got dragged along with him. They were just unlucky to be touching him when he made the leap, but you can't force him to deny what he experienced. He knows what happened. Just give him… us… a chance to prove it. If you need any more proof.'

He stopped holding onto Ian, but kept his hand resting on the bare skin below Ian's rolled up shirt sleeve.

'Just let us convince you.'

'No. No. It's okay. This has to be happening. Unless I'm as mental as the rest of you.'

'Right then. Now I'm going to take my hand away and we're going to drop back into the same time as everyone else and I need you to stop Sue losing it altogether. I could do this to her as well, but I think Tam would like to know that she believes him because he, and you, tell her so.'

'Take it on faith, you mean?' said Ian with a wry grin.

'Yes, I suppose so. Though don't try to make this out to be some sort of religious thing. It isn't.'

Leon relinquished his contact with Ian.

And pandemonium erupted around him.

Sue was still finishing off her scream and was ready to bolt for the door. She had just seen Leon leap across the space between his chair and her husband so fast that her eye had been unable to follow the movement. If she'd been inclined towards church going, she'd be off in search of a priest and bell, book and candle.

Incredibly Ian had calmed. In less time than it takes to gulp down a breath for another hysterical scream, he had switched off his anger and was now holding her tightly and whispering in her ear.

'Sue. It's alright. Really it is.'

Now she was looking at him as though he were insane and she began to struggle for release from his embrace.

'No Sue. Calm down. Let's listen.' He pulled his arms tighter. 'I promise you it'll be okay. Honest love. Please believe me. Believe Tam.' He turned to look at the others.

'Believe them.' he said quietly.

He guided her back to her chair, where she sat shivering. Looking for all the world like a rabbit in the headlights, waiting for that final, exquisitely painful impact. Her eyes were like saucers and she was switching her gaze rapidly between each face.

In this room full of strangers, she had to cling to something. And the something was Ian. And Tam.

She wiped away her tears with the back of her hand and, although still breathing hard, she remained in her seat.

Leon turned and crouched down to gather the shattered glass that he'd knocked from Dick's hand in the instant before he entered the narrow crack between the seconds.

'Dick, go grab a tea towel will you? And yourself another drink. And get Sue a sherry. I think she needs one.' He smiled at the still trembling woman over his shoulder.

Everyone else, though shocked themselves by the last few seconds of excitement, was trying to give Sue looks of encouragement. Lidine wanted to go over to her, but recongnised that for the moment her friend was happier clinging to the lifeboat that was her husband.

The charged atmosphere began to slip away as Leon and Dick mopped up and Sue was given a drink, via Ian. He coaxed her to take a few sips and serenity made a manful attempt to re-enter the house as dusk descended outside.

'Right, where were we?' asked Leon, as Tam slid himself across the floor to set at his mother's feet. She slowly stroked his hair and he looked up and gave her one of his big, wide open smiles.

'Mike was explaining about the specs.' said Jarmon.

'And you mentioned *Ley energy?*' said Lidine in a puzzled tone.

Leon looked over at Mike, checking that it was alright for him to take this diversionary route. Mike looked as interested as everyone else, so Leon explained.

'The reason I've been able to do what I have, for virtually my whole life, is something to do with the energy that courses around the entire planet.' he said. 'But I don't think it just washes around. It seems to flow along what they call Ley lines.' He looked up to check that everyone understood. Lidine didn't but refused to display her ignorance, hoping that these lay lines would be explained at some point.

'Ley lines have been around for ever. They have various names depending on where you are, but most ancient peoples believed in them. When I use their energy, it becomes visible as ribbons of light, that swirl and flow like rivers and just like rivers they have routes.'

He paused to sip his Malmsey, and gave a contented sigh, before smiling around his attentive audience.

'This place,' He looked up at his ceiling above, 'has been built in a special place where numerous Ley lines meet. It's a sort of pool of Ley energy. The power I can use is particularly strong here. I demonstrated it to Dick a couple of weeks ago. Remember Dick with your bike?'

Dick nodded, though everyone else looked confused.

'I took Dick's bike back several hundred years and put it over a little oak sapling. Then I showed it to Dick. It's out in the woods here.' He stopped short. 'Well actually it isn't any more, because I went back and got it for him. It's good as new now. In fact, it is pretty new still, but for four hundred years it was out in the woods. It didn't disintegrate the way things usually do, because the power of this place kept it here. For centuries, while the tree grew through it, it was bound together by Ley power. I'll bet that mill up in The Lakes is also sitting in a pool of energy, or at the very least on a Ley line. So the glasses stayed right *when* Fin dropped them. Until Mike picked them up.'

Mike nodded.

'Sounds reasonable to me… if that's the right word for what we're discussing.' He gave a lop-sided grin.

'Anyway, Bill Iveson kept Fin's glasses in a little wooden box under his bed and passed them on to his son, who's now in his nineties by the way, and he gave them to me. So now a third generation, the guy who took the boys around the mill,' He looked at Bert who nodded and smiled, remembering the older man at the mill, 'knows about the mysterious other-wordly boy who vanished but left behind some spectacles, the like of which a young mill worker had never seen, before or since. So that young boy kept them locked up in his box and waited for the lad to reappear to reclaim them Of course he never did, but he told his son that they would be needed one day and had to be kept safe.' Mike turned to Leon. 'Actually I don't understand that. How could young Bill have known that, so many years ago?'

Leon shrugged.

'Maybe, he was just living in hope.'

'Or maybe he had a visitor who let him keep them as a memento of the kindness he'd shown a complete stranger?' said Dick with a sideways look at Fin, who was studying the floor.

'Ah.' said Mike. 'That explains the almost empty and very ancient packet of Polo mints that were in the box with the glasses.'

It sounded so daft that the whole room sat open mouthed and Fin couldn't suppress a giggle, and Tam was relieved to see that even his mum managed a smile as the rest of the room erupted into laughter.

'But hang on.' said Ian over the general mirth. 'When you say, ancient, how ancient do you mean? Are you saying Fin dropped a packet of mints as well as his glasses when he time travelled?'

There was still a mocking, cynical edge to his voice as he tried to deny everything that seemed to be happening, but Fin simply grinned when Ian looked at him with disbelief written all over his face.

'No, not that ancient really, but then again they had been in the Iveson family for over a hundred years.' said Mike, straight-faced.

'And how's that?' asked Ian equally deadpan.

'There was a till receipt to go along with the mints. It had the price and the date, you see. They'd been bought from the local shop in Daneham.'

'So?' asked Ian irritably.

'Ahem... the receipt was dated next Friday,' Mike checked his watch, '... and some wag had written "Have a polo Mister Nutter and close your mouth before you catch a fly." on the back.' Mike smiled at Fin, who was sharing a not-so-secret smile with Dick. 'But most importantly, not only did it look old, but the older Mister Iveson, who's in his nineties, swears blind that his father gave him the box and its entire contents over sixty years ago.'

There was silence in the room, apart from a barely concealed chuckle from Fin and the Anonymous 4, singing medieval polyphony softly in the background, the voices emanating from the walls.

Ian still looked unconvinced, despite all that he'd heard.

'So either everything we're saying here is the absolute truth, or three generations of a mill-working family living in the Lake District, who I met fleetingly on a school trip, decided to play an elaborate practical joke on me. Both seem ridiculous, but I'm afraid I'm leaning towards the time travel explanation, much as it grieves me to admit it.' said Mike looking over to Bev, who nodded her agreement with his slowly dawning conviction.

'There is, of course a third option.' said Ian and when all eyes turned to him he continued. 'You - for reasons best known to yourself and possibly the rest of this oddball group - are lying.'

Mike silently shrugged. There was no more for him to say. It was up to someone else to try to make Ian understand that something extraordinary was going on. Mike was now certain that there were events unfolding here that had no rational explanation.

He awaited developments.

At this point Bert decided to intervene.

'Mister Messenger... if I may?' he said rising to his feet as Mike sat next to Bev and took her hand in his.

'Of course Mister Lightfoot. Feel free.'

As Bert spoke he paced back and forth in the space between the fire and the enclosing semi-circle of chairs and settees, making dancing shadows sweep across the panelled walls.

'I have to admit that up until today, I too felt just as Mister and Mrs Riggleby here. He looked down at Fin. 'Sorry Fin… and Tam of course.' He smiled at Tam as he came to the rightmost limit of his pacing and turned.

'But then I had a visitor today. Michael had come around this morning, but I was in no mood for guests, as I'm sure he will confirm. However, about an hour later I had the most astonishing visit, from someone I had thought dead. It was quite a shock I have to say, when a young man I hadn't seen or heard from for twelve years suddenly showed up in my living room. All the doors and windows were locked you understand - I had locked the world out, dreading the coming days and weeks, convinced in my own mind that my career was over and that the future was as bleak as a Sartre novel.'

He looked at Mike.

'Anthony Athelston came to see me.' Bert smiled at the astonishment on Mike's face and heard a gasp from both Fin and Tam and a sharp intake of breath from Bev, who sat straighter in her seat as she listened even more attentively – if that were possible.

'Seemingly appearing out of thin air.' He swept his hands out in a gesture of incredulity. 'He was older certainly, but gave every indication that life was treating him well and… he… he explained a lot of things to me that had been gnawing away at the back of my mind for years. He said I wasn't to worry. That everything had turned out fine.' Bert gave a sniff and Mike could see his eyes becoming glassy as he struggled to hold back the tears. 'All these years I've been thinking that I should have done more to help him, that it was somehow my fault that he ran off the way he did, but it wasn't like that at all. He'd simply found a better life for himself. Out there, between time. "Living in the moment" was how he described it. Apparently he found another teacher who was better able to guide him through the strange world he now inhabited. But then he'd met another young boy,' Bert looked over to Fin, 'who happened to mention the name of his school and that of one of his teachers… and Anthony Athelston decided to come back, just for an hour or so, to share a cup of tea and some old memories and to try to explain things to a silly old fart who was feeling sorry for himself.'

Bert stood in front of Fin and looked down with a face that showed a mixture of relief and sadness.

'Thank you, my boy, for helping to chase away the phantoms from an old man's heart. Anthony said he wasn't sure exactly what was going to happen, but he was pretty sure we were going to have *a hell* of a lot of fun finding out.'

Bert stood and returned to his chair, sitting forward and facing the fire as though searching for something, or maybe just gazing into nothing at all. He spoke again to the room in general.

'He also said that some chap called Fermion was a little annoyed that things seemed to be getting out of hand, but had agreed to leave you all to it. Apparently he said it's down to us to do as we see fit with the knowledge we now have. He also said something about the time being right.' Bert smiled as his eyes refocused on his surroundings. 'Probably.'

Bev leaned forward.

'Did he mention Professor Tome, Bert?'

Bert shook his head.

'No. Sorry Bev. After his initial revelations we ended up just reminiscing, but I'm sure he didn't mention anyone called Tome.' Bert sighed heavily. 'And then he went out to the hall... and disappeared. I went to see where he'd got to and he'd just gone. And the front door was still locked. From the inside, of course.' He sat back in his chair, closing his eyes and smiling. 'Maybe not as exciting as Mike's experience, but infinitely more satisfying. For me at least. Anthony has grown into a happy, thoughtful and considerate young man. Everything that an old teacher could have wished for him.'

The room was disturbed only by the quiet plainsong.

'I am content.' said Bert, almost too quietly for those around him to hear and indeed his smile said it all for him. 'The world can go hang for now. I really don't care just at the moment.'

His eyes remained closed and he settled back to enjoy the peace of mind that had seemed so distant only a few short hours ago.

This time Ian said nothing, but everyone could see that even he was struggling to disregard the testimony of both the schoolteachers. Sue was also looking a lot calmer and Tam had settled back, leaning against her legs and no longer looking torn between his parents and all those around him. The only people in the room still struggling to believe him and Fin were the only two he really wanted to.

But things seemed to be heading in the right direction now at least.

'My turn now?' asked Bev, looking at the LeMotts for permission.

'Sure.' said Jarmon and Lidine nodded too.

'I've been with Jarmon and Lidine throughout the day, so I can speak for all of us...'

'And me too.' said Lilli in a sleepy voice as she snuggled closer to he mother, her face pushed into Lidine's shoulder.

'And Lilli too.' said Bev smiling. She stayed where she was, rather than pacing around like Bert. The settee was comfortable, sitting alongside Mike and holding hands, the fire warming her.

'I started the day hoping, rather than believing, that Fin and Tam were telling at least an approximation of the truth. There was no proof. Nothing aside from some inordinate overnight hair growth, antique-looking glasses... and their story. Of course there were coincidences up at the mill about Fin's tale of overnight travel and Professor Tome's story about Anthony Athelston, which tied in with what Bert had said. But nothing really solid to get a hold of. Nothing that is, until a certain PC Hedd put in an appearance.'

She paused and took a sip of sherry.

'I have to say Officer Hedd, I've never met a constable quite like you.'

Dick gave a lopsided grin to the room in general.

'While we were waiting to go to the teaching hospital to see Fin have his scan, Dick here, let us in on his own little secret… but still I found it hard to believe that a boy, even a boy like Fin, could do the things he'd said. Dick however, decided to give us a practical demonstration that took our breath away.'

Jarmon and Lidine nodded. Lilli was now asleep.

'He and Fin vanished into thin air before our eyes! Not even a by-your-leave. They just popped out of existence, leaving us staggered by what we'd seen, or rather what we weren't able to see any more. And then we all began to suspect that you'd nipped off for a second just before you left with Fin. Is that right?'

Dick smiled and nodded. 'I'll let you know about that when you've finished. Don't want to spoil the surprise.'

'Okay… so… here we have a policeman who steals young Fin away right in front of us and then pops back again, calm as you please. Gobsmacked isn't the word for what we were feeling, I can tell you.'

She looked over at Fin and smiled.

'They were only gone for a few seconds and I'd love to know where they went. I suppose we'll find out pretty soon?'

Dick nodded.

'So, there we were, suddenly all believers, but still with the problem of how to convince everyone else. Then Dick came up with the obvious answer; instead of trying to hide what was going on, we had to prove it to everyone… do something that they couldn't ignore. Something that could not be dismissed at smoke and mirrors. So Fin arranged to get his disappearance down on tape. And disc. And whatever else a hospital scanner uses.'

Bev took another sip.

'About half an hour later he took himself off – to wherever he goes to – *right in the middle of his scan.*'

Again she smiled over at Fin, almost laughing now.

'You should have seen the look on the Professor's face when you went. All the screens looked as though they were taking pictures of a supernova. They burst into brilliant light as they monitored your brain and then, when we looked out at the scanner, they all went blank – because you weren't there any more. It's just as well you let us know what you were going to do, because it looked for all the world as though the scanner had vapourised you. I know I had trouble keeping a straight face when that operator started yelling and tapping all his keyboards. It was as though he thought he'd disintegrated you.'

Fin grinned, pleased that his little show had caused such pandemonium.

'We were all ushered into another room with bars on the window - and they locked the door! Can you believe it. The police locked us in, as though we were some sort of criminals! But we could hear all sorts of commotion going on out in the corridor.'

Her voice had started to rise and her eyes flashed with indignation, or mirth, or possibly a mixture of both.

'I'd have loved to see their faces when they went back into that room, because of course we left with Dick. Without using the door.'

'Yes, and pretty bowel quivering that was too.' put in Jarmon.

'Yes., but then we were at Dick's house, and after a quick cup of tea, we came here.'

Ian was looking flabbergasted.

'So you're telling me that you've all been doing this... this... travelling?' he asked.

'You betcha!' said Lidine with glee.

Dick stepped towards Ian and reached out a hand. Without thinking Ian reached out too, as though to shake hands and Sue shrieked as the pair appeared to quiver before her eyes.

Ian was still in his seat, but now his face had a look of consternation, rather than fear.

'Good God!' was all he said as he leaned back in his chair, gazing at Dick in wonder.

'What? What?' cried Sue, having left panic in her wake and sprinting up to hysteria. 'Tell me Ian!'

'Sue' said her husband quietly.

'What?'

'It's true. Bugger me, but it's all true. Can you believe it?'

And suddenly he was grinning from ear to ear and ruffling his son's hair.

'It is all bloody true!'

His shout echoed around the oak panelling and he rocked back, his feet rising and his hands shooting up into the air in exultation.

'Sue it's all true. Fin and Tam did exactly what they said they did. I've just seen England win the world cup back in sixty-six.'

Ian looked at Jarmon in amazement.

'And that Hurst goal did cross the line!'

'Yes!' shouted Jarmon punching the air. 'Always knew it of course, but nice to have it confirmed all the same.'

Even Sue was beginning to laugh, without the previous hysterical edge, as she hugged Tam's head.

Lilli managed the ghost of a smile as the contagious merriment burrowed its way into the depths of her sleep.

Ian stood up and looked at the others, now utterly convinced. He'd now had two totally inexplicable experiences in the space of a few minutes. He could no longer argue against what was going on, unless he was prepared to declare himself insane.

And he wasn't going to do that.

Life had just become far too interesting.

'So now what's going to happen?' he asked.

The laughter slowly subsided as they all looked at each other and thought about that.

What would happen now?

Dick looked over at Leon, with a slightly sheepish expression on his face.

'Well, first I think I have to apologise to Leon.' Everyone looked puzzled, so he went on quickly. 'This has been his secret for over thirty years. It was Leon who told me all about the power we use, about the ley lines and everything. And now everyone's going to know.' He gave an expansive shrug. 'Sorry mate.'

'Ah, never mind.' Leon waved aside the apology. 'It had to come out sometime, I suppose. It's like I told you Dick; there's something building – even old man Fermion can sense it and now's as good a time as any to let people know that there's a power around them that they know nothing about. Let's worry about the consequences later. For now we just need to convince the police that Simeon Carver is alright and get these two off the hook.' He nodded towards Fin and Tam.

'Oh Heavens, of course. I'd forgotten about Sim.' gasped Lidine.

'And that's where I come in.' said Dick.

'And me.' said Leon. ' In half an hour or so.'

Fin giggled and ignored the scowl from Ian.

Leon gave Fin a hard stare and gave a wry smile.

'Apparently.' he said.

Everyone looked puzzled and Ian tensed, obviously about to say something.

'Don't worry Dad.' said Tam, looking up at his father and patting his knee. 'I'm sure Sim's okay – otherwise they'd have told us by now.' He gave his friend a mock glare. 'And Fin wouldn't be looking so flippin' smug.'

Leon turned to poke the dying fire back into life and added another log.

'More drinks anyone?' he asked.

Ian raised his empty glass wordlessly and, despite Sue's disapproving look, Leon poured more sherry.

Everyone else seemed to have finished their various drinks, so Leon took a minute or so to refresh them. Dick smiled to himself; Leon's stock of fine old Malmsey and single malt were taking a battering tonight, but he suspected that restocking would be more a pleasure than a chore, involving a visit to eighteenth century Spain and nineteenth century Scotland.

Leon always bought his alcohol direct from the most reliable sources.

'My turn.' said Dick sitting back in his chair.

All eyes turned to him and he smiled back.

'When I took Fin to look for Sim, we managed to track him down without too much difficulty. He's alive and well… still with Edmund and Kate...'

Before he could continue Leon interrupted.

'If I'm not much mistaken, I spy another car pulling up outside.' he said, looking up at the windows either side of the massive front door, which were briefly illuminated by headlights sweeping across them as a car turned in the courtyard.

Everyone sat adding to the air of expectation as Leon strode across the room and opened the door just as the bell jangled loudly in answer to the tug on the chain hanging in the porch outside.

As the final arrival stepped through the archway and into the room the music of Ed Alleyne-Johnson burst into the silence.

Silas Carver entered, looking more than a little flushed, as the violin-sourced electronics of *Sweet Child O'Mine* sought to fill the astonished void.

Jarmon rose to greet his old friend, but halted at the furious look directed towards first him and then Leon, by Silas.

'What's going on?' Sim's father asked angrily. 'And what are this lot doing here?'

Silas looked ready to explode.

'I'm not in the mood to deal with these people!' His face was livid and his voice was raised high in indignation. '*Where is my son!?*' he thundered angrily at the room in general and Leon in particular, since he had the disadvantage of being closest.

'PC Hedd told me he'd sorted everything out and I could see Sim if I came here at nine-thirty.'

He looked about, taking in the room, its occupants and the obvious lack of Sim.

Leon made to guide him to a seat but he furiously brushed the hand aside and stepped forward.

'*Where is my son!?*' he shouted again.

Despite the volume of his bellow, he had the look of a man defeated by recent events. Lack of sleep and food had taken its toll in the last few days. His eyes were sunken and his skin looked grey.

His fists bunched as Dick spoke.

'Please, Mister Carver, I promised you that Sim was okay and I told you that you'd be able to see him – and he is and you will.'

'Please join us Mister Carver.' said Leon gently.

This time Silas did not shake off the guiding hand, but his frame quivered with barely suppressed rage as he stepped closer to the group gathered around the fire. Lidine reached up to pull Jarmon back into his seat. He glanced down to see her give a quick shake of her head. Not yet. He's too overwrought to accept your friendship again Jar. Sit. Be patient.

Amazing how much a simple gesture can convey, but Jarmon picked up on all of it.

He sat and looked forlornly at his erstwhile best friend.

Leon pressed a glass into Silas's hand and quickly refilled it when the man downed it in one. Silas gave the impression that it was an action he'd been practising for several days.

Alone and very, very lonely.

'Before you see Sim, I need to explain something to you.' said Dick.

'Oh God, no!' cried Silas. 'Please tell me he's alright! Please tell me my boy's okay!'

Dick realised that his choice of phrase hadn't been ideal and had served only to heighten the man's fear that his son was in some sort of danger - or something very much worse.

Silas was staring around him, almost unseeing and his face crumpled as he saw the shocked faces staring back.

'Oh no! He's dead isn't he? My little boy's dead.' His glass crashed to the floor.

Leon sat on his haunches before Silas and took both the man's trembling hands in his own strong grip.

Looking into the other's eyes Leon said quietly. 'Silas, Sim is fine. He really is. Let Dick and Fin tell you what's been going on. Then we'll go and see him.'

The use of his first name by the huge black man with the mesmerising blue eyes brought Silas back from the pit that threatened to engulf him.

'I know your son will be overjoyed to see you again – and more than a little surprised.' Leon turned to watch Fin and Dick and they both smiled and nodded.

The atmosphere in the big room eased.

'Just listen for a few minutes. There are some things you have to know before we go to see Simeon,' he said. 'but then I'll take you straight away. You have my word.'

Silas spoke as though in a daze.

'But who are you? And why should I trust you - or anyone else here?' he said quietly looking at the others.

'Because we know the truth Mister Carver.' said Dick just as softly. 'And no-one else does. No-one at all.'

Silas looked confused (and who could blame him?)

Leon returned to his position alongside the now roaring fire.

Dick took centre stage.

'Mister Carver... Silas... let me start by saying that what you are about to hear may sound ridiculous... fanciful in the extreme. Ask Mister Riggleby and his wife.' He nodded towards Ian and Sue, both of whom looked uncomfortable under Silas's scrutiny.

'They took a lot of convincing believe me, but they – and indeed all of us – now know what happened on the night that Sim went missing.'

Silas had the look of a rabbit caught in the headlights of an onrushing car. The agony of hope and despair etched clearly in his face.

'Forgive us the melodramatics Silas, but both Fin and I think that you need to know what has happened before you go to see Simeon. I promise it won't take long, but you have to understand why Simeon didn't come back with the other two boys.'

'What do you mean *Come back*?' asked Silas, the fear beginning to return behind his eyes.

'Silas, you know the story that Fin and Tam told the police – and everyone else?' said Dick, answering the question with a question.

'Aye. I know.' said Silas looking at the boys. 'Bloody nonsense.'

There was a terrible silence.

'Well actually' said Dick. 'it wasn't.'

Silas looked again at the faces around him. The teachers he vaguely recognised from school, the two boys and their parents, long time family friends – when he had a family.

Silas bent his head to hold it in trembling hands. His empty stomach seemed to expand to fill his whole being. This was arrant nonsense, but he sat quietly, his eyes closed, while the world as he knew it gently unravelled.

Dick's quiet voice continued.

'The three of them really did do just what they said and they could all have returned safely, but...'

Silas raised his anguished gaze.

'But what?'

'But Sim didn't want to come back Silas. He wanted to stay with the friends he'd made four hundred years ago.'

Silas looked as though he was about to cry and his shoulders began to heave in great silent sobs and he dropped his head once again into his hands.

Dick put a hand on his shoulder.

'But he wants you there too.' said Fin's soft voice.

Silas raised his head and wiped his tears on the sleeve of his faded sports jacket.

'What?'

'Sim said he wanted you there with him. You were all he wanted to make his life perfect.'

Fin eased forward as he spoke.

'He said he wouldn't miss anything...'

'Cheers Sim.' said Tam under his breath.

'Shhh. Tam!' hissed his mother, but then wrapping a comforting arm across his chest.

'... anything but his friends' said Fin giving Tam a glare. '...and you. He stayed behind because he wanted you to go back to stay with him there and he couldn't think of any other way of making you go.'

Silas looked confused.

'He wasn't sure if he – and you – could go back there if he'd come home with us. This was his way of making you do it. For him.'

'But is that possible?' asked Silas his eyes bright with wonder. 'Could I go back in time and stay with Simeon?'

Leon straightened up beside the fireplace.

'That's where I come in Silas.' he said. 'It seems I am to be your means of rejoining your son in Tudor London. Complete with home and family... and not just Simeon. Apparently there are a few things that only he is allowed to tell you.'

Fin nodded vigorously.

'But I promise it'll be a nice surprise Mister Carver.' he said. 'I went back with Dick and we saw what he's up to, but Sim wants to tell you all about it himself. He made us swear not to let the cat out of the bag.'

'And just to make sure you believe us,' said Leon. 'he gave me something for you.'

The tall dark man walked over to the table and returned with a small wooden box, which he held out to Silas.

'Open it.' was all he said.

Silas took the box in trembling hands and slowly opened it.

Inside was a slip of ancient, but also somehow new- looking, paper.

Silas took it out and attempted to read it, his brow furrowing.

'What… what does it say?' he asked. 'It looks like Sim's writing but the spelling's all over the place. Must be Sim.' He gave a sigh and passed it to Fin who had come over to stand at his side. Silas passed the box to Dick.

Fin carefully read the note before speaking. He already had a good idea of what it said and was just making sure he hadn't forgotten any of its content. The writing was spidery, but unmistakenly in Sim's hand, complete with ink blots.

'It is from Sim, Silas. I watched him write it.'

He smiled as he translated.

'It says "*This note was written this day, 13th April 1601, by mine own hand to give eise and relef to the heart of my dearly beloved father whom I shall one day see again. Simeon Carver, aged 15 years, of the Royal Vale, England.*"'

The room was very quiet when Fin finished, except for the heavy breathing of Silas.

'Oh Simeon… Oh Sim. My son… where are you?' Silas was weeping openly now and took the note back from Fin. 'I'm sorry Fin… and Tam. I'd started to believe the worst – especially when you told me that story. Oh, Lord... Sim's okay. Thank God.' He gave a gulping breath and sighed again as he repeated. 'Oh, thank God.'

Lidine, Bev and Sue were crying now too, but smiling as they wiped their eyes and joined in with the exclamations of excitement from everyone in the room. Even Ian managed to raise a smile.

Bert Lightfoot didn't bother to open his eyes, but his Cheshire cat-like grin broadened.

'So, ready to go?' asked Leon.

Silas stood, looking at all those present and gave Fin a crushing hug before saying.

'But if I do go back to Sim, what will I do? I'm a mechanic for goodness sake! What do I do for a living? What if I want to come back?' He turned to Leon. 'Could we come back if we wanted to?'

Leon shrugged.

'I should think so, but I don't think it's likely.' He smiled a great beaming grin.

'Distinctly unlikely.' said Dick.

'No chance.' said Fin. 'But you'll have to wait for Sim to tell you why.'

'Don't worry about work though. Fin tells me you like to work with wood, so I can see your hobby becoming your life's work.' said Dick.

'Lots of wood back then.' said Fin. 'Lots and lots.'

Everyone could see there was something they weren't telling, but they'd made a promise to Sim, so no-one was going to try to make them reveal anything more.

Not until they'd sorted out Silas anyway.

'I think it's time to say your goodbyes now.' said Dick, placing a comforting hand on Silas' shoulder. 'Then Leon will take you to Simeon, he's been given directions. Okay?'

The finality of his situation suddenly came home to Silas – and everyone else in the room. If he wanted to see his son again he was going to leave everything that he had worked so hard for in his life.

Then again, as he thought about it, he realised that all he really wanted was waiting for him four centuries in the past. With his wife gone and no longer showing any interest in either him or their son, there was little he would actually miss. True, he had a few good friends, Jarmon and Lidine in particular, but everything else was just froth. None of it really counted for anything when compared to being with Sim. His son was his world and if it meant living in Elizabethan London, well – things could be a lot worse.

What's the point of life without the ones you love?

And for Silas that meant Sim.

He turned to Jarmon and saw in his friend's eyes complete understanding. This was probably the last time they would ever see each other and Silas was sad, but at the same time elated at the possibilities that were opening up before him.

The two men hugged, as only true friends do. Then Silas quietly took his leave of the others.

Lidine and Sue were crying, but they were tears of happiness for their friend, who had lived through so much heartache. Now maybe he would find the happiness and comfort he so richly deserved, but which had always seemed so elusive.

Finally Silas turned to Fin and held him in a crushing embrace for almost a full minute. Fin felt no desire to release the man and Silas for his part seemed content to say his thankyou without any further words.

Then he let go of the boy and stepped over to Leon.

'Take my hand Mister Carver - and prepare for the ride of a lifetime.' Leon said, with a sad little smile. He knew that Silas was giving up everything for the love of his son and stepping into the unknown with a courage that was ill-suited to the unshaven, tired-looking little figure beside him.

'Goodbye.' whispered Silas with a last glance back at Fin and the others as he reached for the proffered hand.

'Godspeed, Goodman Carver.' said Fin in a soft voice.

But Silas was gone.

In his place, the sound of thunder filled the room, booming and reverberating around those left behind.

Mozart started to play quietly in the background, his *Requiem* seeming to fit the atmosphere; sad yet uplifting, soaring above the emptiness that roared in Silas' wake.

Dick stood still holding the little wooden box.

'Where did it come from?' asked Sue timidly, taking it from him.

'Oh, Leon travels back to Tudor London quite a lot. It's where he learns how to build like this.' said Dick, waving a hand to encompass the manor house. An awful lot of this stuff was made up by carpenters and joiners who lived and died in Henry and Elizabeth's reigns. Leon transports it here and leaves it wrapped in oil-soaked cloths for a few centuries before recovering it and building onto this place. He likes the feeling of age that the timber has if he does it that way, rather than just lugging it back directly. Says it feels as though it holds the character of the men who cut it more if he lets it age naturally. Apparently there's rucks of it in pits all over the woods. Anyway, one day he saw this box and liked it. So he brought it back with him. Fin and I brought the note from Sim this afternoon. The two have no relation to each other.'

'But we knew that Leon would take Silas back with him one day.' said Fin. 'When we made our second trip this afternoon, before leaving the mints for Mister Nutter and saying thanks to Bill Iveson – he had a packet too, by the way - we went back to see Sim again, to try to persuade him to come home, but we saw something that made us realise we were wasting our time.'

He paused to take a sip of his drink.

'You see, when we first went to find him we though he might still come back. He was missing Silas so much, even though he was happy in his new life. I think even he was surprised at how much he wanted his Dad there. But the second time, we saw him with two other men. I recognised Silas immediately, but I had no idea who the other guy was. It was Dick who told me who he was, even though Dick had never met Silas.'

It was Lidine who caught on first.

'So you saw Silas with Sim, with Leon there too?' she exclaimed.

'Yeah – could have knocked me down with a feather.' said Dick smiling. 'So we knew that somehow Leon had to know about Sim and everything else, otherwise what was he doing there with Silas.'

'So we came back and told Leon that he would be taking some man he'd never met back to see Simeon, whom he'd also never met.' said Fin. 'It all got a bit complicated.'

'It's giving me a bloody headache just trying to keep track of who was where and when!' said Tam.

'Language Tamburlaine!' said Sue.

And everyone laughed, just in time for Leon to make his noisy reappearance.

He reassured them that Silas and Sim were now happily esconsed together in rooms in Southwark. They shared lodgings with Edmund and Kate, and even Leon felt the need to comment on the beauty of the girl to whom Sim was so attached. An affection which, he happily confirmed, was fully reciprocated.

The room became what Leon had always planned it to be; a haven of comfort and peace in his idyllic manor. All the generations of craftsmen who had helped to create his little bit of heaven, here in Vale Royal, would have been pleased to see the results of their efforts. Leon had learned well during his journeys into the past. The house held its occupants in its cosseting embrace and was filled, for the first time, with merry laughter and companionable silences, as they spoke of the future.

Like it or not, they were all along for the ride now.

And it promised to be a very diverting journey.

Because the earth was waking up and trying to tell them something.

All they had to do was listen attentively and do something about it.

Lilli had awoken and now had the little box that held Sim's note. Whilst all the others drank and talked, she quietly took the box over to Fin.

'Fin.'

She tugged at his sleeve.

'Yeah, what?' asked her brother, a bit annoyed at having to detach himself from the general conversation to talk with his little sister.

'Look.'

Lilli's eyes were shining as she poked and prodded at the box which seemed to magically spring apart. Fin watched transfixed; Lilli had always been the best at puzzling through the strange boxes they had all been given for their birthdays the previous year.

When she stopped taking the box apart, a new drawer was revealed, and inside it a small, very carefully folded, piece of velum.

Lilli held the box out to Fin, who unfolded the secret note, for that was surely what it was.

The paper contained a single line of writing.

"Mafter Fin – pardon this moft urgent appeal, onelye dost I feare our friend ChristopherM. is in need of thy excellent counfel – hasten unto me."

It was signed *"Euer your friend in all dutie, William Shakefpeare (1593)"*.

Fin was speechless and Lilli silently exultant.

'Err... Leon?' Fin said, loudly enough to cause a hiatus in the general merriment. 'Where did you say you got this box?'

Outside, night had fallen, clothing the surrounding gardens in darkness. Unseen by those inside, a figure detached itself from the blackness filling the courtyard and silently slid into the cover of the woods.

Several minutes later a small, nondescript car drove away from the lay-by on the bypass and rushed off into the Manchester-bound traffic.

Epilogue

The End…

Or is it?

For as Simeon Carver would say…

The story's begun and diverse histories remain to be revealed.

And the future is not as certain as the past.

And the past isn't all that certain, is it?

Not with an eternity to search for answers to all the questions raised by a story told

In A Moment…

About the Author

Russell K. Lewis is a nearly 50 year-old Englishman in search of a mid-life crisis.

Having discovered that database design wasn't quite as fulfilling as expected, he spent 30 years trying to decide what to do about it.

His first book is the result of having read far too much and having done not nearly enough.

Approaching middle age made him consider his options and resulted in a wade through an under-achieving imagination and finally getting some of it down on paper.

Printed in the United Kingdom
by Lightning Source UK Ltd.
121618UK00001B/196-213/A

9 781434 320148